A GIRL'S GUIDE T○

Victoria Clayton is married and lives in Northamptonshire. She is the author of many previous novels, including *Clouds Among the Stars* and *Moonshine* for HarperCollins.

Visit www.AuthorTracker.co.uk for exclusive updates on Victoria Clayton.

By the same author

Dance With Me
Out of Love
Past Mischief
Running Wild
Clouds Among the Stars
Moonshine

VICTORIA CLAYTON

A Girl's Guide to Kissing Frogs

HARPER

This novel is entirely a work of fiction.
The names, characters and incidents portrayed in it are
the work of the author's imagination. Any resemblance to
actual persons, living or dead, events or localities is
entirely coincidental.

Harper
An imprint of HarperCollins*Publishers*
77–85 Fulham Palace Road,
Hammersmith, London W6 8JB

www.harpercollins.co.uk

A Paperback Original 2007
1

The author asserts the moral right to
be identified as the author of this work

A catalogue record for this book
is available from the British Library

ISBN-13: 978 0 00 721961 2

Set in Sabon by Palimpsest Book Production Limited,
Grangemouth, Stirlingshire

Printed and bound in Great Britain by
Clays Ltd, St Ives plc

To Zachary

1

How did it happen? After my accident Alex told everyone that it was entirely his fault I had broken several bones in my foot, but then, like all dancers, Alex craved attention. Despite his perfect technique and marvellous legs, Nature had cruelly contrived to prevent the spotlight shining on him as much as he would have liked. So, to please him, when people asked me if he had been responsible for the near ruination of my career, I would reply with a lift of my eyebrows and a cryptic smile.

It may have been the studio stove that was to blame. It was sulking on that chilly February morning and though I was wearing legwarmers my muscles might have begun to stiffen. But in fact I was practically certain that I had lost concentration in that crucial second before springing into a third *sissone*, one of several in rapid succession, towards the end of Act II of *Giselle*. The lift is not difficult but it is *épaulée*, which means 'shouldered' – high, in other words. Obviously it only works properly if Giselle and Albrecht jump and lift at precisely the same moment. I thought I sprang too late, Alex that he lifted too soon. The result was that the *sissone* was clumsy and I landed heavily amid the dust and rosin on the studio floor with all my weight on the side of my foot.

Madame had an eye as sharp as a knapped flint and usually

it flew inexorably to the tiniest error, but on this occasion she was distracted by temper. Orlando Silverbridge, our chief choreographer, had insisted on reviving an *enchaînement* from the original ballet which had been scrapped – and with good reason – from later productions. It was a complicated series of steps weakening the dramatic impact of the pas de deux and demanding more than was kind from the already exhausted dancers.

'Stop!' shouted Madame. 'Zis will not do! *C'est un joli fouillis.* Orlando, listen to me, you crazy *fou!*' She struck her chest. 'Either ze *enchaînement* it goes – or I go!'

'Be reasonable, Etta!' pleaded the choreographer. Then, seeing her eyes flash, he paled with anger and he too struck his chest. 'Go, then! It might be that we can manage without you. Yes, go! It will be a breath of fresh air. A new ballet mistress is exactly what this company needs!'

'*Bête!*'

'Has-been!'

'*Oh!*'

'*Oh!*'

They both prided themselves on being aesthetes with exquisitely tender susceptibilities but at that moment they reminded me of howling monkeys squabbling over the last banana.

Madame threw back her head and hooted mockingly. 'I see it! I see it! First you will try to take all ze classes your own self and chaos will be ze result! Zen you seek anozzer *maîtresse de ballet.* Mimi Lambert, per'aps, or zat fool, Popova – *zut! tais-toi, imbécile!*'

This last was directed at the pianist, who had continued to play, her eyes fixed dreamily on the racing clouds beyond the window. The pianist stopped abruptly and picked up her knitting. She was used to these rages. Madame clapped her hands. 'One 'alf-hour for lunch, everyone,' she called before returning her attention to Orlando, who stood cupping his elbow with one hand, resting his chin on the other, looking gloomy. I saw his face brighten as his eye fell on the sinewy buttocks of Dicky

2

Weeks. Dicky, who was from New York, had only recently joined the Lenoir Ballet Company but already his elevations were creating something of a stir.

'You're limping,' said Bella in an accusing tone when I joined her at the barre. 'You came down too hard on that third *sissone*.' She looked down at my foot in its grubby pink satin shoe, then up at my face. Sweat poured down our foreheads and cheeks and dripped from our chins. Her hair, pulled back and fastened into place by a wide band, was as wet as seal's fur. A dark triangle ran from neck to waist of her scarlet leotard. We had been friends, on and off, for twelve years, since the day we had arrived with braces, plaits and flustered mothers at Brackenbury House in Manchester to begin the arduous years of training necessary to become dancers. At this moment the friendship was definitely off.

'No.' I seized the foot that was beginning to throb and stretched up the adjoining leg so that my knee was close to my ear, just to show her that everything was still in working order.

Bella hooked one heel over the barre and leaned forward to put her chin on her leg so that I could not see the hunger in her eyes. 'You'd better get some ice on it.'

'Good luck for this evening, Marigold *dar*ling.' Lizzie, who had remained a staunch friend despite a stalling of her career due to a wobbly technique and the refusal of her insteps to be sufficiently pliant, put her arms gracefully round my neck. Her fair hair, which escaped her headband to spring into tight ringlets, tickled my cheek. Unlike everyone else in the company, she was not desperately ambitious and was content to remain in the corps de ballet. 'I'll hold my thumbs for you. I know you'll be wonderful.'

'Thanks,' I said. 'I'm going to need it.'

'Bella's a bitch,' she whispered in my ear. Lizzie was as violent in her hates as in her loves. 'Don't let her jinx things for you.'

'It's only a workshop,' put in Bella, who had no doubt heard the whispering though not what had been said.

'Ah, tonight, maybe, but on Friday it's the real thing.' Lizzie executed a hasty *entrechat quatre* to express her excitement, 'and I for one can't wait to see Marigold's name in lights.'

The workshop was in the nature of a dress rehearsal before an invited audience. Had Lizzie and Bella known it, a very great deal rested on this evening's performance and now, when I thought about it, my stomach did a *jeté battu* followed by a *ballotté*.

'Marigold! *Venez ici!*' Madame was beckoning imperiously. 'Lizzie! Zat was an *entrechat quatre comme un* poor old cripple woman wiz ze 'ob-nailed boots. Alex, come 'ere also.'

Alex and I skipped across to the spot designated by her pointing finger. I was conscious of pain rippling up from my foot into my ankle.

'We 'ave decided. At last ze agreement!' Madame spread her fingers and looked heavenward. From the slam of the studio door as Orlando went out, I guessed that agreement had little to do with it. 'Ze *enchaînement* we cut!' She made a slicing movement with her hand. 'Instead for five bars we 'ave a pause – when you two act like crazy wiz your eyes. It will be *un moment* of consequence ze most dramatic. You express to ze audience all ze love, all ze regret, all ze sorrow . . .'

Alex's face obediently mirrored these emotions while Madame talked. I tried not to think about my foot and instead envisaged the apple, cheese and yoghurt that awaited me. I was absolutely starving. After Madame had decided to her own satisfaction how our limbs should be disposed during this pregnant moment of eye-acting, we were free to go.

'Fancy coming down the Pink Parrot after the performance tonight?' asked Alex as we made our way down the corridor towards the canteen. 'It's Dicky's birthday and he's promised to stand us drinks for as long as his grandmother's cheque holds out.'

'How kind of him. Yes, I'd love to if—'

A hand gripped my shoulder. 'Sorry, Alex, but I've already

made plans for Marigold.' Sebastian Lenoir slipped his arm through mine so that he was walking between us. 'And I'm in a hurry.'

Alex slid away up the stairs to the canteen.

Sebastian was the director of the Lenoir Ballet Company, or the LBC as it was generally called. What he decreed, no one even thought of contradicting. Madame was the only person who from time to time stood up to him, but she always had to admit defeat in the end. Sebastian never raised his voice, but he saw no reason to make concessions to anyone. He would wait patiently, impassive faced, while Madame argued, pleaded and occasionally raved, before lifting and dropping his shoulders – a gesture which seemed to say 'tiresomely a ballet company *must* have people in it' – and replying, 'All right. Now we do as I say.'

In many ways Sebastian was an ideal director. He had trained as a dancer, then worked for ten years as a choreographer, so he had a thorough knowledge of the business. It was largely thanks to Sebastian that we were, in the opinions of those who counted, the third most successful company in England. It was not impossible that we might one day improve our rating. His hair, black with a silver streak, was swept straight back from a high brow that looked noble until you came to know him better. Often people suspected him of dyeing it in emulation of the great Diaghilev but, having had frequent opportunities to examine it close to, I thought it was probably natural, since it never showed signs of growing out. On his handsome sardonic face was usually an expression that could scare you half to death. He certainly frightened me, even though I was beginning to know him quite well. For the last twelve months we had been lovers.

'Come into my office.' He steered me through a door into a room that was as elegantly shabby as the rest of the building. The LBC was housed in a row of unrestored Georgian houses in Blackheath. It lacked central heating, but the dancers warmed themselves by their exertions, and in Sebastian's office there was a grate where logs burned through the winter. He had hung drawings by Gainsborough, Lawrence and other eighteenth-century luminaries, lent him by an art-dealer friend, on the flaking walls. Curtains of faded green silk hung at the windows. There was about his quarters a rich beauty which was reflected in all his tastes.

Money was the end to which all Sebastian's efforts were directed. He needed it to entice gifted dancers, choreographers, designers and costumiers. He had to find money for travelling expenses for the touring part of the company, for publicity, for bribes, for paying people off. The acquisition of money was germane to all his decisions. I imagined that he thought of little else by day and probably dreamed about it at night. Yet no one could have accused him of personal extravagance. He wore his father's old Savile Row suits and ate sparingly unless someone else was paying for it. As he seated himself languidly behind his desk and picked up the mother-of-pearl penknife he used to open letters, he had the negligent air of a country gentleman with comfortable estates and an agent to see to the horrid necessities. He tapped on the mahogany surface before him with the closed knife.

'I hear Miko Lubikoff is coming to the workshop tonight.'

'Is he?' I aimed for something between mild interest and surprise in my tone to disguise the apprehension that seized my innermost parts. Miko Lubikoff was director of the English Ballet, the company whose reputation stood higher than the LBC's and lower than the Royal Ballet's. 'Goodness!'

'You didn't know? Everyone else in the company seems well acquainted with the fact. Why should you be an exception, I wonder?'

'Now I think of it, perhaps Alex did mention . . .' I sort of hummed the rest of the sentence away.

'Alex?' A slight frown appeared between dark symmetrical brows. 'Don't pretend you think Miko is interested in *him*.'

'Oh, *no!*' In my eagerness to exonerate Alex I was perhaps too emphatic. 'I-I mean, perhaps Miko just wants to see what we're doing – there hasn't been a new production of *Giselle* for ages . . . I expect he gets awfully bored with seeing the same old dancers—'

'Miko does not allow himself to be bored. Nor –' he sent me a glance that was distinctly unfriendly – 'do I.'

I folded my hands in my lap and tried to look insouciant, though I was certain that the rapid pulse in the hollow of my throat must be visible from a hundred yards.

He stroked the smooth handle of the knife with long fingers. 'I suspect he's coming,' he put his thumbnail into the slot provided for the purpose and brought out the blade, 'because of you.'

'*Me?* I don't suppose he even knows who I am. I've never actually spoken to him.'

'Oh? Yet Etta tells me that last week there was a letter from Miko in your pigeonhole.'

Damn and blast and hell! It was well-known that Madame, who would have allowed herself to be chopped to atoms for the good of the company, had extraordinary powers of divination and could detect a disloyal thought the moment it sprang newborn, damp with amniotic fluid, into a person's mind. But presumably she did not have X-ray eyes that could penetrate layers of Basildon Bond.

'Oh, no! That's impossible.'

Sebastian speared a paper polo – one those little rings for reinforcing punch holes – with the blade of his knife. 'Miko's hand is distinctive. And the green ink, regrettably jejune, is a trademark.'

'I remember now,' I blurted out. 'It was a letter from my aunt!'

I realized at once this was a mistake.

'Oh? Your aunt?' He did not bother to hide his scepticism.

I was thoroughly rattled. 'Yes . . . she's a terrific correspondent . . . she writes every week, sometimes twice . . . she lives in the Highlands of Scotland and is awfully lonely, poor old thing . . . no one to talk to but her old blind collie . . . you see, she's in a wheelchair and can't get out . . .' I was supplying too much detail, the common mistake of liars.

'In that case her letters are unlikely to be franked with an NW3 postmark.'

I felt myself grow cold. Everyone knew the English Ballet had their headquarters in Belsize Park. He smiled, much as a torturer might smile on hearing a bone crack. My entire body tensed in a silent scream, but acting is an important part of a dancer's bag of tricks, so outwardly I smiled back. He continued to watch my face. The effort required to look innocent and unconcerned was agony. I was on the point of confessing everything and throwing myself on his mercy, if he had any, when he said, 'Lock the door.'

I leaped up to do his bidding. I had been so distracted by the latent menace in the interview that I was unprepared for the pain that shot from the sole of my foot to my knee. The door fastened with an old-fashioned brass rim lock. It took a little while to persuade the key to turn, which gave me a chance to compose my face. As I walked back to the desk I was relieved to see that a lightning change had taken place. His eyes had lost their coldness, his smile was almost affectionate.

'Oh Marigold! What a little schemer you are!' He laughed softly. 'Take off your tights, my little *amuse-gueule*.'

This was his nickname for me – and no doubt countless others – a play on '*gueule*' and 'girl'. I accepted the sad fact that I was nothing more than a snack. Also that my Dutch cap was sitting on the shelf in my locker. I knew better than to suggest that he might wait while I fetched it. I scrambled out of legwarmers, tights and knickers. Luckily I was wearing the sort of leotard that fastens with hooks and eyes at the crotch so I could keep on my top half, including my cardigan. Despite the fire there was a chill in the air that was more than metaphorical.

8

'Sit on the desk,' he was unbuttoning his flies as he spoke, 'spread your legs wider . . . arch your back a bit . . . ah! yes! . . . that's better! That's good! . . . mm! what a nice little conformation you have . . . tight, virginal . . . a perfect body . . .' He began to thrust with slow strokes, in harmony with our restrainedly elegant surroundings. 'I could, if I wanted, make you the greatest dancer of the decade . . . one of the greatest names of the twentieth . . . century . . .' As he grew more excited his words came faster and with more of a hiss. 'But if you leave me . . . you little . . . baggage . . . I'll make sure you never get another good notice as long as you live . . . move that fucking thing.'

I pushed the inkstand to one side and leaned back across the desk. He took hold of my ankles and lifted my legs so that I could hook my feet behind his head. A small, hard object on the blotter pressed into my spine. Probably the emblematic penknife. Was it true that all critics were open to threat and bribery? I had no way of knowing. Surely Mr Lubikoff had as much influence? If not more? But then he might decide that an all-out war with Sebastian did not suit him. Despite the fact that competition, individually and collectively, was fierce – ruthless would be more accurate – a pretence was maintained by all parties that we were above petty rivalries, that the only thing that mattered was the great art of which we were the humble exponents. It was all art for art's sake.

Everything depended on how badly Mr Lubikoff wanted me to dance for him. It might be that he had a partner in mind for me. As with candlesticks, ornaments, occasional tables and so on, a pair was worth more than the sum of its parts. Karsavina and Nijinsky, Fonteyn and Nureyev, Sibley and Dowell, couples who struck sparks from each other's dancing as well as looking good together filled theatres faster than anything. But Mr Lubikoff would not show his hand immediately. For the time being I could not afford to do anything that would make Sebastian my enemy. In my perplexity I almost folded my hands behind my head, the position I generally adopt for serious thinking, but a loud hiss from Sebastian, like a train building up a head of steam before pulling out from the station, prompted me to sigh and look swooningly at his face, now in the grimace of imminent orgasm, the silver lock of hair falling forward across his high bony forehead.

'Be . . . good . . . and . . . you can . . . dance with . . . Freddy!' Each word was accompanied by a powerful thrust that made the boiler blow.

As he leaned, panting, over me, mission accomplished, I added Freddy to the equation. Frederick Tone, LBC's *premier danseur,* and Mariana Willoughby, both dancing at this moment with the touring part of the LBC in America, had failed to become one of those desirable partnerships. No one could say why, it was just one of those things. Freddy had a virtuosic technique with unequalled elevations. Also he had a perfect physique and was breathtakingly handsome. Poor Alex, with whom I usually danced, had no neck, narrow shoulders, a rugby-ball-shaped head and tiny pink-rimmed eyes like a French bull terrier. And although he was technically first class, he never seemed to catch fire, at least not with me. Alex was a nice boy and I was fond of him, but niceness is irrelevant in a partnership – which was lucky because Freddy was an absolute shit.

Sebastian was already adjusting his clothing. I got back into mine with a feeling of relief that had nothing to do with the act of coitus. Though dancers are usually tremendously sexy, perhaps as an extension of the intense physicality of their lives, and will couple with more or less anyone and anything, I personally could not see what the fuss was about.

I had lost my virginity at the age of seventeen to a sixty-year-old dramaturge who had been working with Orlando Silverbridge on a revival of *Frontispiece,* an eccentric ballet which combined dancing and verse. It had been my first professional engagement in the corps. The dramaturge had seemed very old to me then, almost geriatric. He was well connected, a chum of royalty, with a long and distinguished career behind him, and was feted by everyone worth knowing in the arts. He had a bald head but, as if to make up for it, furry ears and a mass of curly grey hair growing over a stomach distended by good living. I made myself go through what was a ghastly experience by reminding myself of his promise to get Orlando, with whom the dramaturge was having an affair at the time, to kick me out of the corps if I didn't cooperate. I knew he could because Orlando was tremendously ambitious and, despite the furry tum, sat up and begged whenever the dramaturge offered a titbit.

The deflowering had taken place in one of the rooms beneath the stage where props are stored. Princess Aurora's bed had been conveniently to hand. Afterwards I had wept in Lizzie's arms because in those days I had entertained silly romantic notions about love. Unfortunately, when Orlando discovered that I had slept with the dramaturge – I always suspected Bella of sneaking, he had been so annoyed about me poaching on his preserve that it had taken me nearly two years to get back into his good books.

'I'm late for lunch.' Sebastian looked at his watch and spoke with a hint of annoyance in his tone, as though I had detained him. While I was fastening the ribbons of my shoes he consulted his address book, picked up the telephone and dialled a number.

'Hello? Wilton's? Will you tell Lord Bezant I'll be fifteen minutes late. With my apologies.' He put down the receiver. 'It won't do the old skinflint any harm to realize that some of us have jobs to do. I want him to cough up for *Les Patineurs*. I'll see you this evening after the show. We'll go back to Dulwich.'

Dulwich was the location of the beautiful but dilapidated Regency house where Sebastian lived, which contained little furniture apart from essentials. The drawing room was quite empty, apart from the sofa on which he conducted his love affairs when at home, and his one luxury, a magnificent Steinway grand piano. It was sign of extraordinary favour to be invited to Sebastian's residence. I knew for a fact that Sebastian's previous lover had not once crossed the threshold.

11

'Oh, how lovely! The only thing is . . . I expect I'll be rather tired. And there's the problem of taxis.'

I had been invited to Dulwich for the first time after Sebastian's birthday supper at Les Chanterelles. That was two months ago, and when Bella had heard the gossip which had flown round the company about this signal honour, she had given up even pretending to like me. She might have been comforted had she known what a miserable evening it had been. At the restaurant Sebastian had been too busy charming the guests he had earmarked to sponsor forthcoming productions to spare even a glance for me. I had sat between an embittered choreographer who had twice been passed over in favour of Orlando and an impresario whose wife had recently run off with a scene painter. They were glassy-eyed by the main course and sobbing by the pudding. Even the excellent food had not consoled me. Dancers have to be light so they can be lifted easily. I had eaten a few oysters, a small piece of chicken, three lettuce leaves and a slice of pineapple, and looked on hungrily while everyone else made beasts of themselves.

After several gruelling hours, Sebastian had grabbed my arm, shoved me into a taxi and swept me off to Dulwich. I had had little time to admire the beauty of the house. Sebastian had removed my coat and pointed to the sofa. Sex burns up a lot of calories. Throughout the lovemaking I thought about the dish of *pommes frites* the weeping impresario had left untouched. I could have eaten the lot without putting on an ounce. When Sebastian had satisfied himself, he helped me into my coat, conducted me to the front door and closed it firmly behind me. It was two o'clock in the morning and not a cab in sight. I had spent a grim three-quarters of an hour in a telephone box which stank of pee until I found a minicab to take me home.

'You can stay the night,' said Sebastian. I must have looked amazed for he added, 'You won't disturb me. You can sleep on the sofa.'

'Thank you,' I said humbly, well aware that this was largesse almost without precedent.

12

He looked at his watch again. 'Scoot.'

I scooted. The canteen was full. I had to eat my apple and cheese – there were no yoghurts left – standing up.

'Where've you been?' Lizzie came over to join me.

'In Lenoir's office, fucking, probably,' said Bella, who was sitting at a table nearby. Her companions laughed with detectable hostility. Since I had become Sebastian's mistress, and especially since I had been given the role of Giselle, my friendships had evaporated with a speed that would have alarmed me had I not seen it happen to others in the same circumstances. Should I become tremendously successful they would come crowding back. Meanwhile I was in an unhappy limbo, no longer one of the crowd nor yet one of the gods. It was wretched but there was nothing I could do about it.

I ignored the sniggers and assumed an air of calm superiority. 'I've been breaking in a pair of shoes actually.'

'Really?' Bella spoke scornfully. 'Then why have you got paper polos stuck all over your back?'

I waited, hidden from the audience, inside the wooden construction that was painted outside to represent the cottage where Giselle lived with her mother. Behind me in the wings, the corps, dressed like me as village maidens, were stretching and flexing, preparing themselves for their next entrance. My heart beat so hard it seemed to vibrate against the boned bodice of my tutu and my bare arms broke into goose pimples. Tears of excitement filled my eyes. Now I knew that the tremendous, relentless effort to fashion my body into the perfect instrument – the aching muscles, the strains, the sprains, the bruises, the bloody toes, the starving, the rotten pay, the rivalries, jealousies and disappointments – had been worth it. From the age of six when I had been told to run round the village hall pretending to be a butterfly, my life had been directed towards this aim, to express with my body beauty, fear, love, grief, joy, hope, despair, evil, apotheosis.

13

The percussion struck the notes that mimicked the knocking of Count Albrecht on the cottage door. The stage hand who was waiting with his hand on the latch to open it for me wished me luck. I heard him as though in a dream. Already I was a peasant girl in a state of tremulous expectation, sighing for her mysterious lover whose wooing had transformed her humdrum rural existence into a life of transcendent bliss. I burned to see him, to feel his arms about my waist, to look into his eyes, to marvel at his beauty, to express my gratitude for his love, to share with him a glorious vision of future happiness as man and wife. The music slowed, anticipating Giselle's entrance. The door opened, I counted the beats, drew in my breath, rose to *demi-pointe*, and launched myself into a world of sound, light, colour and intoxication.

2

Daylight crept through the gap in the curtains that hung round my bed. Out of the confusion of sleep emerged one clear idea, a craving for a glass of water. My eyes and mouth were dry and my skin felt splittingly tight. I barely had time to register these discomforts before a flame of pain in my left foot banished all other sensations. I opened my eyes and lay still, concentrating on not tensing the muscles in my left leg, hoping to lull my foot to a tolerable ache. Siggy, the darling, stirred, stretched and rolled on to his back, snoring faintly.

After five minutes or so the searing seemed to cool a little. I stared at the canopy of gold sateen above my head. The sateen had cost less than a pound a metre and was meant for lining things, but when gathered into a sunburst of pleats with a lustrous crumpled fabric rose in the centre to hide the stitching, you really couldn't tell how cheap it was.

When I was eight my mother had taken my sister and me to Newcastle to see *The Sleeping Beauty*. The moment the lord chamberlain in his full-bottomed wig had come mincing on to the stage in high-heeled red shoes, I had been ravished from the crown of my head to the soles of my feet by the beauty of that sparkling, starry, fairytale world. I had made a secret resolution, so thrilling I had hardly dared to acknowledge it even to myself, that I was going to be a famous ballerina.

A little later in the performance I had also resolved to have a red and gold bed like Princess Aurora's. This was much easier to achieve. I had spent many enjoyable hours with a hammer, nails, scissors, glue and a needle and thread. The crimson velvet curtains that hung round my four-poster had once separated the stage of the Chancery Lane Playhouse from its audience before the theatre closed for good. The gilt cord, stitched into triple loops at each outside corner of the tester and ornamented with gold tassels, had trimmed the palanquin of King Shahryar in *Scheherazade*. However tired I was, however discouraged by a less than perfect performance, however tormented by Sebastian's demands, my beautiful bed embraced me, soothed me and cheered me. Every night, unless the weather was really sweltering, I drew the curtains all the way round so that Siggy and I were warm and safe inside our little red room with the critical, competitive world shut out.

I stroked Siggy's chin gently. He stirred and stuck out the tip of his tongue. He was incontestably my favourite bed companion. But why was I at home? Why was I not even now basking in the perquisites of director's moll, lying on the hard little sofa in the unheated drawing room at Dulwich, my already shattered frame having been probed, impaled, bounced on and generally misused? Then I remembered the extraordinary events of the day before.

At first Fortune had seemed to be on my side. I had been spared the customary two hours of *répétition* after lunch. Madame had decided to devote the afternoon to rehearsing the corps since they had, she asserted, 'ze elegance of a 'erd of cattle. You 'op about as zo you are being prodded in ze rump by ze cow'and. Togezer!'

A free afternoon was a rare luxury. I had gone back to the flat I shared with Sorel and Nancy, also dancers in the LBC, to wash my tights – frequent washing was the only way to get rid of wrinkles which were so obvious on the stage – and break in an extra pair of pointe shoes. A virgin pair clacks as loudly on the stage as the husks of coconuts imitating a trotting horse. The second act of *Giselle* calls for feather-light landings. I had already broken in three pairs for that evening's performance but, with the state my foot was in after that unlucky *sissone*, I thought it might be wise to have a fourth. Once the box – the hard section your toes fit into – becomes soft through wear your foot isn't supported properly. I was worried but not despairing about the injury sustained that morning. Dancers spend practically all their professional lives in pain. Often our feet are soaked in blood. They have to be wrapped in bandages and lashings of antibiotic ointment. The rest of our bodies are tortured by strained muscles and ligaments and the overuse of joints. Perhaps the undeniable romance of suffering for one's art helps to make the agony bearable.

Each dancer has her own method for breaking in new pointe shoes. Some people smash them on the floor, some shut them in doors, but I always used a rubber mallet. A few judicious blows weaken the brittle layers of hessian and glue that the toe box is made from. Having moulded them to the shape of your foot so they fit like a second skin, you paint them with shellac which hardens to preserve the exact shape. Then the tips have to be darned to give a good grip and the ribbons sewn on. It was a process with which I was so familiar that it always acted as a tranquillizer for mounting nerves.

When I had prepared the shoes to my own satisfaction, I examined my body for hair. Dancers have to be perfectly smooth. Everything except eyebrows and eyelashes must be plucked away. This was no problem for me as my body hair was fine and easily discouraged, but girls with dark hair spent hours each week painfully engaged with tweezers and hot wax. Then I sat by the window and contemplated a fading photograph of a woman wearing a long tutu with a garland of flowers round her skirts and more flowers in her hair, *en arabesque penchée*.

Dancers are a superstitious lot and before performances they resort to whatever sympathetic magic they've convinced themselves will help them to give of their best – invoking saints, lighting candles, hiding amulets in their underwear, or in my case attempting to commune with the spirit of Anna Pavlova. Pavlova had weak feet, poor turn-out, a scrawny physique and bad placement, yet she was one of the greatest ballerinas of the twentieth century. She was famous for the power and passion of her dancing which she combined with a delicate expressiveness. Technique alone does not make a good dancer. I always reminded myself of this before I went on stage.

Giselle was due to start at half-past seven. I arrived at the theatre at six. An enormous bouquet of dark pink lilies, pale yellow roses and green hellebores took up much of the valuable space in my dressing room. I looked at the card. *With respect and admiration, Miko Lubikoff.* I almost screamed aloud. Who else would have read it? Certainly Annie, my dresser, and Cyril, the stage-door keeper. Like everyone else they were gossips. The arrival of the flowers must be all round the theatre by now, which presumably was what Mr Lubikoff had intended. Sebastian was too lofty for mundane conversation, but Madame would lose no time in letting him know. I cut the card into tiny scraps with my nail scissors and threw them into the bin. I would have to tell a lie and it ought to be a good one.

'Hello, darling.' Lizzie was wearing a mauve quilted dressing gown full of holes. Her face was covered with Max Factor pancake. Her ringlets had been temporarily tamed by a hairnet and her round brown eyes had been extended with black lines almost to her temples. 'Just came to wish you good – my God! When Annie said it was a enormous bunch she wasn't exaggerating! Lubikoff's serious then? You sneaky thing! I *do* think you might have told me.'

'The flowers, you mean.' I tried to look unconcerned. 'They're from my godmother, actually.'

Lizzie snorted. 'You're going to have to do better than that if you don't want Sebastian to rend you limb from gorgeous limb. That bouquet can't have cost less than twenty pounds. Everyone knows that godmothers are mean as hell.'

It was certainly true that mine was. For my last birthday she had sent me a card with a 'reduced to half price' label on the back and a cookery book which was clearly second-hand as half the pages were stuck together. As I cannot afford to be wasteful, I had hollowed out the middle, carving my way through splashes of bygone soups, kedgerees and charlottes to make a cache for valuables. It would come in very useful when I had any.

'Oh, Lizzie! I've hated not telling you. But there isn't actually anything *to* tell. I got a letter from Mr Lubikoff last week saying that he was coming to the workshop and was hoping to be able to talk to me alone afterwards. That's all.'

This was not quite true. He had gone on to say that he considered me a fine classical dancer with extraordinary vitality and a magnificent line. He was anxious that because of my undoubted fitness for the ballets *blancs* – things like *Swan Lake, Giselle* and *La Bayadère* in which the girls wear white tutus – I might be denied the chance to interpret contemporary works. He thought the role of Alice in *Through the Looking Glass,* which the EB were putting on in a few months' time would be perfectly suited to developing my range of dramatic expression. I knew this paragraph by heart. Everyone is hungry for praise but I believe dancers are more famished than any other group of artists. During classes we receive a continual flow of negative criticism which, although intended to be constructive, lowers morale. Even after a good performance there is always a painstaking analysis with emphasis on improvements that could be made to the curve of a wrist here, the turn of a head there.

However, modesty forbad taking Lizzie fully into my confidence. Besides, words cost nothing, and in the theatrical world are flung about like autumn leaves.

19

'Mind you don't accept less than twice what Sebastian pays you.' Lizzie giggled. 'Oh, my! Won't he be hopping mad!'

I felt my stomach lurch at the idea of Sebastian's rage.

'Marigold! *Dar*ling!' Bruce Gamble, who was dancing the *caractère* role of Hilarion, had stuck his head round the door. 'Who's a lucky girl then? I know for a fact that when Lubikoff wooed Skrivanova he only sent horrid pink carnations.' He sucked in his cheeks and lowered his eyelids to express disgust. 'Nasty vulgar things that never die, fit only for cemeteries.'

'You mean these?' I pointed to the lilies, roses and hellebores. 'My uncle sent them. Wasn't it kind of him?'

Bruce pursed lips blood-red with rouge. 'I'm afraid you'll never get on if you can't lie better than that, my pet. Only people on the make send expensive flowers. Now the person to whom you represent money at the moment is Sebastian. But he's already got you signed up professionally and he's fucking you. We all know he's too stingy to spend as much as a ha'penny on his spunk-buckets.'

I considered, then abandoned, the idea of taking issue with this graphic description of my status in Sebastian's life. Scabrous language was Bruce's only vice. Temperate in all his appetites, he ate only nuts, fruit and sprouting things, drank nothing but tisanes, eschewed sex of any kind and devoted himself, mind and body, to dancing.

'But of course if Miko Lubikoff is thinking of you as his dear little honey-pot—'

'Aie! It is true!' Irina Yzgrouchka pushed past Bruce and went to bury her face in the flowers, breathing in their delicious scent with a moan of pleasure. She was dressed in a dark blue riding habit and a lavishly plumed hat for the non-dancing role of Bathilde, Count Albrecht's fiancée. Irina's age . . . forty-two . . . and an accumulation of injuries had put paid to her suppleness. 'How I will miss you, my own sweet Marigold!' Irina put her arm round my neck and shed a few tears. Emotions are always near the surface in any ballet company, and illusion

20

and reality are inextricably mixed, but I paid us both the compliment of believing that some of the tears were genuine. I was no threat to her now.

'They're from an unknown admirer,' I said, blushing a little beneath the gaze of Bruce and Lizzie.

Irina looked at me from beneath false lashes clotted with mascara. In accordance with the almost universal practice, she had put a red dot in the inner corner of each eye to make them appear more open, but it looked very odd close to. 'Darlink, the poor little falsehood is stillborn, no pathetic infant cry, not even a gasp. Admirers send red roses or some such *gaucherie*. Only a queer sends flowers so beautiful as these. Besides, at least ten people read the card before you arrive.'

It was some comfort to know that Sebastian never came backstage before a performance. Afterwards he made a point of doing so, to give the company his opinion of our achievements, which ranged from mediocre (which meant very good) through pretty poor (good) to atrocious (some careless *port de bras* in the corps). I put on my peasant girl dress – white blouse, green laced bodice and scarlet knee-length skirt for the first act, wondering how I could manage to have a private conversation with Mr Lubikoff afterwards. Human traffic flowed continuously in and out of my dressing room. I could hardly lock myself in with him. That would be the same as hanging a sign on the door saying 'Marigold Savage is negotiating a new contract with a rival company.'

Annie came in to plait my hair and tie it into coils with scarlet ribbons. Because my hair was such a distinctive colour, I rarely wore a wig. Dancers, particularly dressed in white with their hair fastened into chignons, look very much alike from the back of the auditorium. Though it was tiresome always to invoke the spirit of Moira Shearer in the minds of the critics, it was an advantage to have a physical characteristic that made one instantly recognizable.

'Is he coming tonight?' Annie mumbled through a mouthful of Kirby grips. She indicated the flowers with a jerk of her head.

21

There was no point in pretending not to understand. Many years ago Annie had danced in the corps herself so she knew what was at stake. I don't know why I felt so guilty. Sebastian would not have hesitated for one solitary second to replace me with a better dancer. Or a more desirable lover.

'He said he would. But you know . . .' I shrugged.

'I know all right. When my bones ache and I can't afford a packet of fags, I thank my lucky stars my next month's salary doesn't depend on the fancy of some self-obsessed old faggot.'

The first act went as well as anyone could have hoped. When we danced together I forgot about Alex's resemblance to a French bull terrier. As Loys, my mysterious suitor, he became handsome and charming. I was astonished and elated that he had chosen to love me. I responded with a passion I didn't know I was capable of feeling because my life until that point as a simple village girl had been so ordinary. When Loys admitted that he was really Count Albrecht in disguise and already betrothed to the beautiful, blue-blooded Bathilde, I could not at first understand it. Surely there had been a terrible mistake? The pitying glances of his courtiers assured me it was true. My love was a poisoned apple. I had been deceived, my dreams were dust and ashes and there was no peace for me in the world but death. And die I did, after a fit of madness that demanded tremendous technical skill.

The part of Giselle is one of the greatest tests for a ballerina. It is not only extremely difficult technically, but it requires a great range of expression. The ghost of the second act must make the strongest possible contrast with the simple red-cheeked village girl of the first. Because every gesture is minutely circumscribed, it tests one's ability to communicate to the utmost. I barely noticed the applause as I came off the stage in the interval because I immediately began to think myself into a state of ethereal otherworldliness. Pavlova always danced the dead Giselle in burial cerements, but I had been given the more usual romantic tutu. It was only as I was struggling into the basque which holds the costume together that I noticed that my foot was hurting. As soon as I thought about it the pain increased to something that approached but was not quite agony.

Annie came to hook up the bodice of white slipper-satin covering the basque that held the tutu together. A pair of delicate gauzy wings was attached to my shoulders.

'You danced well, dear. Those *ballottés* with the *jetés en avants* straight after are pigs to get on the beat and you were spot on.' Annie had seen Fonteyn, Markova and Barinova dance, so praise from her was worth having. 'Lubikoff'll be pleased.' Annie bent to smooth out the three layers of snowy tarlatan that finished at mid-calf. 'You don't want to let Lenoir bully you into doing just as he likes.' She fastened a silver girdle round my waist and brought me a new pair of shoes while I removed trickles of sweat and mascara and powdered my face, neck and arms. 'I know you've got to get on, dear, and goodness knows we've all done it, but he's such a cold stick, such a brute of a man. I hate to think of you having to let him . . . whatever's wrong with your foot?'

'It *is* a bit swollen.' I flexed it and winced. 'Be an angel and tie it up for me.'

Annie's experience with dancer's feet was second to none. She tsk-tsked volubly when I took off my tights to disclose the hot, reddened flesh of my left foot but, after she had bound my instep and ankle, it felt almost comfortable again. I pulled on my tights, fastened my shoes and kissed her gratefully before running down to the basement, known as 'hell', to take up my position on the little platform which at the appropriate moment would shoot me up to the stage as though I had risen from my grave.

I adored the thrilling moment of stepping into the blue starlight and bourréeing towards the centre as though I weighed less than a mote in a moonbeam. Annie's bandages held my foot in a secure yet flexible grip and at first all went well. Then

23

it came to the moment when Giselle hops *en pointe* on her left foot, traversing half the stage, which is difficult to do gracefully in the most favourable circumstances. I found it doubly hard when each hop sent a thousand volts from my toe to my knee. An expression of mournful tenderness was called for. The pain forced me to grit my teeth and it was all I could do not to grunt with pain. During the pas de deux with Myrtha, the Queen of the Wilis, the throbbing and stinging was nothing less than excruciating. I seemed to be dancing on white-hot knives. Perhaps something of the agonizing struggle to control my arabesques may have been interpreted by the audience as passion and pity for the distraught Albrecht. Anyway, the clapping, whistling and stamping of feet as I sank back into my grave was terrific.

'You look terrible!' said Bella, Queen of the Wilis, who was waiting with me in the wings while the corps de ballet took their curtain call. 'That foot's playing up, isn't it? Bad luck!' Bella's words were sympathetic but I saw excitement in her eyes. The first night was only five days away and Bella was my understudy.

'I'm all right.' I grabbed a towel to mop the sweat from my neck and shoulders. 'You were wonderful.'

Bruce, as Hilarion, scampered on to the stage and received measured applause. It is not much of a part.

'Thanks.' Bella ran gracefully into the spotlight and curtsied to a lively reception. She was considered an exceptional dancer with tremendous precision and serenity, but unfortunately one critic had labelled her cold and the epithet had stuck. The part of Myrtha suited her admirably, but I knew she longed for the chance to refute this and show a greater emotional breadth as Giselle. I didn't blame her one bit.

Smiling beatifically, Bella took her place among the line of soloists in front of the corps. Alex a.k.a. Albrecht came on to an enthusiastic response which he received with elegant bows. When the audience began to tire, he flung out one arm towards the wing where I was standing and I tripped across as lightly as I could, considering my foot was on fire, to take his hand.

I was startled by the roar of appreciation. Alex stepped back to let me take the call alone. I smiled and tried to look as though I was gratified without actually purring. Some dancers make a great play of kissing hands and gesturing from the heart to the audience, which I think is irritating as it smacks of spurious humility. I stepped back into the line as a bouquet of flowers – oh dear, chrysanthemums again, well, the LBC was hard up – was brought on by the conductor, darling old Henry Haskell. More clapping. The curtain came down. As I was looking directly at it and no one could see, I allowed myself to pull a face of hideous suffering. The curtain rose again. Henry led me forward for further congratulation. I gave them a serene, Buddha-like smile, though my whole leg felt as though it was being flambéed on a spit. Another curtain. I was on the point of weeping.

'One more! One more!' cried the stage manager.

'Come on! We'll take it!' said Alex, his eyes shining.

'They're still clapping like crazy!' Annie, who had been watching my terrific reception from the wings, took the chrysanthemums from me. 'Go on. Just one last curtain, dear.'

'Not if it's my last one ever,' I said, lifting my foot and only just managing not to howl like a wounded dog.

I reached my dressing room, pressed my face against my dressing gown which was hanging on the back of the door and screamed into its folds. Then I hopped over to the mirror and sank into the chair before it. I knew it would not be long before the room was crowded with a mingling of friend and foe and I had to get myself in a state to receive them. I took two painkillers with a glass of Lucozade and then, as an afterthought, swilled down two more. I examined my foot. The flesh was protruding either side of the ribbons. Hang the expense, I would order a taxi. While I was framing excuses to avoid going to Dulwich there was a tap on the door and Mr Lubikoff came in.

'Let me be the first to congratulate you.' He closed the door firmly behind him.

Miko Lubikoff had been born plain Mike Lubbock and at the age of fourteen had been selling cabbages from a barrow; he was an example to us all of how hard work and perseverance in the teeth of all odds will pay dividends. He had put the money he earned from the cabbages into ballet classes and, though it was late to begin, talent and diligence had earned him a place in the corps of a fourth-rate company. From this modest beginning he rose rapidly. Though without an extraordinary technique, his strong personality and musicality, particularly in the caractère roles, brought him to the notice of the cognoscenti. Here luck played a part for, whereas Sebastian had an appetite only for young girls, Miko's taste was for sodomy – preferably with angelic little boys, but he was not fussy. Sebastian's nymphets rarely had enough money for the bus home, whereas Miko rolled happily about in bed with any balletomane with a large bank balance. Pillow talk bought him partnerships, investments, even a theatre, and currently he was one of the biggest cheeses in English ballet.

He was now past the age of dancing and had grown corpulent with rich living at other people's expense. His face was round and his nose was fat. His head was a naked dome above two stiff triangular wedges of hair, dyed bright gold so that he looked like a cherub whose wings had mysteriously risen from his shoulder blades to above his ears.

'My dear Marigold!' He bowed as low as his stomach allowed. 'Permit me to say how awed I feel at finding myself in the presence of the outstanding artist. My fingers and toes still tingle from the stimulation of your performance. What attack! You snap from the ground in the first act and in the second you float. Superb! Exquisite!' He kissed his fingertips.

Rumour said Miko had been born in Stoke Newington, but now he spoke with an interesting mixture of dramatic inflections, trilled consonants and stilted constructions that could have passed for Slavonic. I did not despise him for this. Illusion and invention are the lifeblood of ballet.

'Thank you so much for the flowers. They're beautiful.' A wave of pain from my foot made me feel sick.

He shook his head, smiling. 'A paltry tribute to one who will go down in the history books with Pavlova, Karsavina, Kchessinskaya, Ulanova and Fonteyn.'

For a moment I wondered if it could be true. In which case 'Savage' would sound rather discordant in this catalogue of greats. Then common sense asserted itself. There were plenty of dancers as technically competent as me. Some were better. It would take a piece of extraordinary good fortune to persuade people that I had something special that merited a place in the exosphere of stardom. So far critics had been content to call my performance 'fiery', probably because of an unconscious association with the colour of my hair.

'You have received my letter?' Miko continued. 'You understand that I would like you to come to work for me? I can offer you the great classic roles and besides them the exciting new ones, which you can make your own.' He smirked a little. 'But there are some sweets that, alas, I cannot promise.' He pretended to look sorrowful while keeping his merry little eyes fixed on mine. 'I am told on the good authority of the ladies who have been favoured – and there are so, so many of them – that Sebastian is inimitable in the bedroom.' He need not have stooped to be catty. For me Miko's sexual orientation was not the least of his attractions.

'Naturally I'm terrifically honoured to be asked to join the English Ballet,' I began, 'but my contract with—'

Miko held up a stubby finger. 'Let us leave the business details for now. It has been an evening of the consummate delight. We do not want to spoil it with the . . . how you say, nitty-gritty? Come and see me in my office at six o'clock on Monday evening.'

I hesitated. If I kept that appointment it would be the end

27

of my career with the LBC. News of my visit to enemy head-quarters would fly back to Sebastian as fast as Miko could send it. My goose would not only be cooked but eaten and digested. This left me with almost no bargaining power. How could I be certain that Miko would offer me a principal and not a soloist contract? Miko smiled winningly. My thoughts flew about *en gargouillade*, that is, a *double rond de jambe en l'air, en dedans* with the first leg, *en dehors* with the second, all in the course of one leap and really tricky.

'It's a little awkward.' I pulled a face to express the delicacy of the situation, and also to relieve the emotion caused by a throbbing so bad that I wanted to clutch my foot and yell. 'You see—'

'Hello Miko.' Sebastian had entered as quietly as a cat, which was his habit. 'Come to see how *Giselle* should be done?'

They gave each other tigerish smiles.

'I congratulate you, Sebastian. A superb production. Rarely have I seen one that was superior. Not for three years that I can remember.' The last production of *Giselle* had been the English Ballet's, three years ago almost to the day. 'And Giselle herself . . . no, I have not seen a better. Certainly not Skrivanova. By the end of the second act, that one, she land with a thump, like a tired horse.' This was generous, as the rustling and whispering from just outside the door, which Sebastian had left a little ajar, testified to a larger audience than us three. Skrivanova, his prima ballerina, was bound to hear of this disparagement. The intense interest created abroad by this discussion was not just idle inquisitiveness. If I joined the English Ballet, there was a chance that someone in the LBC, probably Bella, would get a principal contract. All the coryphées – the dancers in the corps who had shown promise and who were under consideration for a soloist contract – were hanging on every word.

'Skrivanova. Yes.' Sebastian lingered in a hissing way on the last consonant. 'Naturally I don't blame you for wanting my dancers for yourself. There isn't another company in the world that has such a flair for discovering talent.'

I felt a stab of guilt, for this was true. Though I had worked insanely hard, it was Sebastian who had promoted my career

'Ah yes. The men, no, there we have the edge, but when it comes to the ballerinas, my dear Sebastian, you have an exceptional success. Almost, one might say, you are a Svengali. You take over their minds and bodies until they become an extension of your artistic vision.' I understood that Miko was making an appeal to my pride and independence.

Sebastian raised an eyebrow. 'I don't sleep with them all, if that's what you're suggesting. Only the desirable ones. Skrivanova has a face like an amiable frog and the brain to match. It never even crossed my mind to take her to bed.' Another appeal to my pride and also a stab in the traitorous Skrivanova's back.

Miko shrugged. 'With make-up she looks all right. But I agree with you, old fellow, she cannot hold a candle to Marigold.'

They looked at each other with a man-of-the world cordiality which hid honed steel, and then at me, much as two hungry tigers might contemplate a fresh kill.

'So,' Sebastian was unable to conceal another hiss, 'let's not beat about the bush. This isn't a social call. You want to lure yet another of my pretty birds into your net. And you think that Marigold will betray her old friends for money. Isn't that rather insulting to her?'

I wondered if it was. Certainly I was awfully fed up with having to scrimp and make do. I was prepared to be insulted if it meant I need not worry about the rent and could afford to wash my hair with shampoo instead of washing-up liquid.

Miko laughed and spread his hands. 'I come clean. I want Marigold to dance for me. And naturally I pay her more because I can afford to.' How much more? I longed to ask. 'But it is you who insult her if you think it is only money which will make her come to me. She will be a fool not to do so. It will be the making of her.' He hesitated, then brought it out in a rush. 'A principal's contract with the second finest company in Europe is not so easily come by.'

There was a crescendo of muttering and whispering outside and the door creaked open a fraction wider. Despite my agony I felt a surge of joy. Sebastian, intentionally or unintentionally, had forced Miko to show his hand.

'Yes. I admit she *would* be a fool, if no other consideration came into it. But you see –' Sebastian also hesitated for a moment, then walked over to the door and closed it – 'it's not just a question of her career.' He shot a glance in my direction. Never had those Atlantic grey eyes looked colder. 'You're the first to be let in on the secret, Miko. I've asked Marigold to marry me.'

Miko was clearly taken aback, in fact he practically rocked on his heels, but his astonishment was as nothing compared with mine. No word of marriage, love or even mild affection had ever crossed Sebastian's rather thin lips. I realized that my mouth was hanging unattractively open. He came over and put a proprietorial hand on my shoulder.

'I know Marigold too well to believe that she would put ambition before my – our happiness.'

The idea was preposterous. This must be a trick, invented on the spot, to put a spoke in Miko's wheel. Miko's little eyes were still twinkling but a frown puckered the cushions of fat above them.

I felt Sebastian's hand tighten on my collarbone. 'Marigold?' he said softly.

I stared up at him, trying to fathom his mind. Could it be . . . that he really wanted to marry me? If there was even the smallest possibility that he was sincere I could not decline his offer abruptly and callously in front of Miko. It would be discourteous, even cruel. Even as I thought this I chided myself for a fool. Sebastian had never given me a moment's thought except as a potential money-maker and – how had Bruce described me? – a spunk-bucket. God! What ought I to do? My whole future might depend on my present answer and my entire leg was pounding, bursting with pain. For a moment I thought I was going to be sick. Perhaps that would be the best thing. Though it would be embarrassing it would save me from having to make a decision. In the event I did something less messy and more serviceable. I fainted.

3

'This is *so* kind of you,' I said to Sebastian the following day. 'I've never had so much luxury.'

Things had taken such a dramatic turn for the better that I had to pinch myself several times for reassurance. On my way to class that morning, getting downstairs and crossing Maxwell Street had hurt so much that I had groaned aloud. I had fainted in the bus queue and been rushed by ambulance, with flashing light and wailing siren, to hospital. Once there all sense of urgency seemed to evaporate and I had sat in A&E in great pain, ignored by everyone for at least a couple of hours until it occurred to me that I ought to find a telephone and let the LBC know I probably wouldn't be coming in that day. Sebastian's sudden appearance among the bored staff and grumbling, impotent patients was as galvanizing as a lion's among grazing wildebeest. I had been taken by wheelchair to a waiting taxi and driven to the Wyngarde Private Clinic.

Now I had a room all to myself which looked like a set in a Doris Day film. The bed had a pink velvet quilted headboard, there were curtains with roses on and two pink wing chairs for visitors. An enormous television stood at the foot of the bed. I had my own pink bathroom complete with bathrobe and the end sheet of the lav paper folded into a point.

'Proudlock-Jones is the best man in the business for feet.' Sebastian wandered about the room, inspecting the view of Wimpole Street from the window, the telephone, which he unplugged, the arrangement of artificial roses – pink, of course – on the bedside table and finally my cotton nightgown which the pretty nurse had brought me. 'Unfortunately he doesn't work on the NHS.' Sebastian put one knee experimentally on the bed.

'Ow-how!' I yelled.

'All right, no need to make a fuss,' he said rather grumpily.

The pretty nurse came back just then, wreathed in smiles and bearing the ubiquitous kidney-shaped dish. It seems a peculiar fetish of the medical profession. After all, it must be comparatively rarely that they actually have a kidney to put in it. I saw to my dismay that it contained a syringe with a needle as thick as a pencil. 'Here we are, Miss Savage. I'm just going to pop in your premed. If you'll wait in the corridor, sir, for one minute . . .' The nurse dimpled in response to Sebastian's dramatic good looks as she held up the syringe and squirted out some liquid.

'I don't see why I should leave,' Sebastian protested. 'I'm not squeamish.'

'Ah, but I'm going to put it in her derrière.' She gave him an arch look. 'And you can take away that champagne. She's on nil by mouth until after her op.'

'All right, I'll come back later. Don't do anything stupid, Marigold,' he added by way of valediction.

'Your boyfriend's awfully handsome,' said the pretty nurse. 'Just a teeny prick.' I bit back the obvious retort. It was actually quite a large prick but as nothing compared with the agony of my foot. 'Well done!' The nurse patted my arm sympathetically. 'You'll start to feel woozy very soon. Nothing to worry about, dear. Mr Proudlock-Jones is a wonderful surgeon. You couldn't be in better hands.' She tapped my cheek with her finger, then went away. I felt comforted by so much kindness. My mind began to unravel as whatever had been in the syringe swirled in my bloodstream. It was a glorious feeling

'Hello, darling,' said Lizzie's voice what seemed like five minutes later.

'Oh, Lizzie,' I said sleepily. 'Thanks . . . coming . . . see me. Going . . . have operation . . . soon.'

'You've had it,' said the pretty nurse, beaming over Lizzie's shoulder. 'It's all over, dear, and it went very well. Mr Proudlock-Jones is very pleased with you.'

'Oh, good,' I said, though I couldn't think why he would be. I hadn't actually done anything, as far as I was aware.

'Would you like to sit with your friend for a while?' said the nurse to Lizzie. 'I'll pop back later. Press the bell if you want anything.'

'I say,' said Lizzie. 'This place is utter bliss, isn't it? Fancy a chocolate finger biscuit?'

'Not . . . just now.'

I must have dozed again, for when I came to Lizzie was deep in the copy of *Tatler* that came courtesy of the Wyngarde Clinic. 'How are you feeling?' Lizzie leaned forward sympathetically. She had quite a lot of chocolate at the corners of her mouth.

'Okay. No pain. Thirsty.'

'Nurse Thingummy's been back and she said to give you little sips of water if you wanted it.' The water was iced and deliciously refreshing. 'Marigold, do you think I could possibly have a bath in your wonderful bathroom? Ours is heated by the range and Granny always lets it go out during the day to save coal. I haven't had a hot bath in years.'

'Go right ahead.' I waved my hand in a lordly way.

I woke up again a little later to hear the sound of splashing and lots of oohs and aahs.

'Crikey!' said Lizzie through the open door. 'I didn't know water could be this hot.'

'You'd better not faint,' I said, 'because I'm in no state to fish you out – oh, hello!'

'I'm Anthony Proudlock-Jones.' A middle-aged man with a pinstriped suit stretched over his corpulent form strode into the

34

room and seized my hand in his plump smooth one. 'We've met before but you were unconscious.' He chuckled throatily in a way that suggested whole humidors of cigars. 'I'm sure they've done a good job of plastering you up.' He lifted the bedclothes to look at my leg. 'Yes, very nice. You had a nasty comminuted fracture of the metatarsals. I oughtn't to blow my own trumpet, but I think it's true to say that in any hands other than mine you'd be waving goodbye to your career.' He rubbed sausage-like fingers together. 'But I'm reasonably confident it'll heal all right. Take it easy for the next six weeks, then we'll take the cast off and have another dekko.'

Reasonably confident? I felt perspiration spring out on my forehead at the suggestion of a doubt.

'Remember, no gymnastics! You can wriggle your toes but that's all. Patience is a virtue, virtue is a grace and Grace was a little girl who wouldn't wash her face, ha ha!' He breezed out to dispense healing and wisdom to the next patient.

'Help!' called Lizzie as soon as he'd gone. 'I didn't dare move. I've probably given myself third-degree burns. I had to suck the flannel to suppress bloodcurdling screams. I'll just put in some cold.'

Mr Proudlock-Jones had put paid to sleepiness for the time being. While torrents of water flowed into the bath, I asked myself what I would do if his confidence proved for once to be unjustified. No course of action occurred to me. If I could not dance I could not live. Of course it would be all right. It had to be.

'This is the most sensual experience I've had in years.' Lizzie's voice, floating through the open door, had gone down several tones and was gravelly with relaxation. 'Much better than sex. And no evil consequences.'

Six months ago, Lizzie had fallen insanely in love with a Russian guest artist who, when wearing a wig and full make-up, looked slightly like Rudolf Nureyev. Certainly from behind the resemblance was remarkable. He had stayed only three weeks

35

before being recalled to Leningrad and, two months after that, the company had a whip-round to pay for Lizzie to have a termination at the handy little nursing home in Southwark where all the female dancers in the company went when self-control or rubber failed. Since then, Lizzie had been much less keen on sex.

'And generally much less worrying,' I said, sitting up and helping myself to a biscuit to begin the process of repair. It was the first thing I had eaten for thirty-six hours and it tasted extraordinarily delicious. 'No fretful evenings waiting for the bath to ring. No need to agonize over whether the bath thinks you were insufficiently enthusiastic and imaginative. One good thing about making love with Sebastian is that he's so self-absorbed one might as well be an inflatable – Hello, Sebastian,' I said loudly as he walked into the room. A violent splash came from the bathroom followed by silence.

'Well! You're looking quite a lot better already.' Sebastian picked up the bottle of champagne, untwisted the wires and popped the cork. He picked up my glass and chucked the iced water over the artificial roses. 'We'll have to share this.'

'I probably oughtn't have alcohol so soon . . .'

'Oh, rubbish! It won't hurt your foot. Drink up.' He held the beaker-full of foaming liquid under my nose. 'It'll relax you.'

Actually I was feeling quite relaxed already, but Sebastian was forking out zillions for my operation and my room so I could refuse him nothing.

'Go on,' he said, 'finish it.'

The chocolate biscuit was powerless to counteract the effect of the champagne when it hit my otherwise empty stomach. When it combined with the remainder of the anaesthetic that was still in my bloodstream, I felt as though I had been shot into outer space in a large pink rocket. The world grew distant and all the consequences thereof.

He stroked my bare arm. 'Mm. You've lost a couple of pounds.' Sebastian was as obsessed with body shapes as the rest of us.

'Don't overdo it. You'll start losing muscle.' I wanted to say that it was nice of him to care but whatever part of my brain was in control of my tongue seemed to be paralysed. 'It's not unattractive, though.'

I set off on an orbit of the earth and very colourful it was, too, just like those photographs in the *National Geographic* magazine.

'Marigold.' Sebastian was bending over me. 'You're giggling like a schoolgirl. Just be serious for a moment. Shall I tell Miko to get lost?'

I bared my teeth in a grin as in the intervals between him talking to me I found I was flying over snow-sprinkled mountains and deep dark lakes.

'Stop giggling.' Sebastian sounded annoyed but I didn't give a damn. 'Move over. I want to fuck you.'

I thought I heard another splash from the bathroom and what might have been a stifled cry.

'Now?' It sounded a strange thing to want to do when one could soar like a bird over oceans and continents. '. . . nurses? . . . Lizzie?'

'I've locked the door. Lizzie can wait outside.'

I wanted to explain that Lizzie was already inside but his hands were pulling up my gown. Too late his body was on mine, in mine.

'I don't know what's so funny,' he said afterwards in a slightly offended tone.

'Neither do I.' My voice boomed and in the distance someone cackled like a hen. Could it possibly have been me?

I spent two more enjoyable days in the clinic, warm, fed and practically killed with kindness, before Sebastian visited me again and said I must go home as it was costing a hundred pounds a day which the company could not afford.

'As much as that?' I flung back the covers and threw my good leg over the side, almost crushed by a terrible weight of guilt. 'I had no idea. Of course I'll leave at once. Oh, thank you, Sebastian, for paying for me.' I seized his hand. My gratitude was so tremendous I felt I quite loved him.

Sebastian's eye fell on several inches of naked thigh below my crumpled nightdress. 'Mm. There's no immediate hurry. I'll just lock the door.'

'Oh, yes, *do!*'

'Your enthusiasm makes an agreeable change,' he said after a while. 'Of course I'm perfectly aware that the motive is mercenary.'

An increase of guilt encouraged me to submit willingly to a predilection of Sebastian's I hated, the details of which I'd rather not go into.

'You needn't feel overburdened by indebtedness,' said Sebastian as he rolled away from me, elegantly pale with effort and, one hoped, thoroughly sated. 'I shall deduct the four hundred pounds from your salary in instalments over the next year.'

As I lay mute with indignation he laughed long and low.

4

'Marigold! It's me,' called Lizzie, coming in through the front door of the flat accompanied by the most delicious smell of vinegar. 'How are you, darling? Have you been horribly bored?'

I had been taken by ambulance back to 44 Maxwell Street that morning. The flat was up four flights of stairs and our miserly landlord had set the timer switch so that you had to run like mad, taking three steps at a time, to get from one landing to the next before the light went out. The ambulance men, manoeuvring the stretcher with difficulty round the narrow bends, had complained volubly about being plunged into absolute darkness every eight seconds while comparing the stink unfavourably with a ferret's cage. I explained that the pungent smell was due to the third-floor lodger treating the stairwell as his own private pissoir. After that they advised me to throw myself on the mercy of Social Services and plainly disbelieved my protests that I was actually quite fond of the place. Because Nancy and Sorel were in America with the touring part of the company, I could only afford to heat my bedroom, and the temperature of the rest of the flat struck cold as a tomb. The men looked at my extravagant interior decorations with expressions of wonderment not unmixed with derision, but they had been sympathetic and friendly and I was sorry to see them go.

I had spent the intervening hours between their departure and Lizzie's arrival shivering and dozing. 'A bit. What's in those parcels?'

'Fish and chips! Isn't it utter bliss?'

I agreed that it was but habitual caution could not be entirely suppressed. 'Should you be eating a zillion calories, dear girl? For that matter should I?'

'Oh, who gives a damn! You need nourishment and I need cheering up. Let's for once just forget about our waistlines. Want a plate?'

'Certainly not.' I opened the newspaper on my knee. 'Oh, the smell of ancient reheated fat! So sinful yet so delicious! Why do you need cheering up?'

Lizzie tucked her springing blond hair behind her ears and looked at me regretfully. 'Oh, you know . . . I cocked up in the rehearsal today . . . So what's the verdict on the leg, then? I asked Sebastian but he wouldn't tell me.'

'Cast off in six weeks. No dancing for two months.'

'Darling, don't worry. The six weeks will go in a flash and then after a few weeks of class you'll be dancing as well – in fact better – than ever. Does your leg hurt very much?'

'It's okay when no one's crashing it against banisters. I'm going to be pretty much marooned up here until the cast comes off.'

'Oh dear.' Lizzie looked anxious. 'Six whole weeks! It couldn't have happened at a worse time.'

'What do you mean?'

'Well . . . it's so cold . . . and Nancy and Sorel are away . . . I know! I've got something that's going to cheer you up.' She took a newspaper from her bag. 'Take a look at this!' She turned to a page on which she had outlined a paragraph in red. 'It's by Didelot!'

I screamed and grabbed the paper. 'I'd no idea he was there. I'd have been a hundred times more nervous if I'd known. Does he say terribly cutting things? I hardly dare look.'

40

Didelot was the nom de plume of a ballet critic with a formidable reputation, an unforgiving eye and a pitiless pen. Tales of careers ruined by his caustic criticisms abounded. It was enough for him to point out that a dancer had dropped an elbow or had landed one fraction of a second behind the beat or had 'spoon' hands for that dancer to feel that they might as well pack their bags. In his favour he would not allow himself to be courted, refusing all invitations to fraternize with directors, dancers and choreographers. Apparently, when approached by an interested party, he would give them a blank stare and turn on his heel, disdaining even to notice their greeting. Sebastian had once pointed Didelot out to me as he sat in the audience taking notes, an insignificant figure with a bald patch, a fringe of grey curls and a large black moustache. It was widely acknowledged that his judgement was as much to be respected as it was feared.

I read the review carefully. *Marigold Savage gave us a refreshingly different Giselle. In Act I the shyness, the sensitivity, the innocence were there as the role requires, but there was a waywardness in the extension of the arms, a suggestion of abandon in the* épaulement *which satisfactorily prefigured the descent into madness. When Albrecht's treachery was revealed, Savage's dancing expressed anger as well as pathos. When she lifted the sword it was a matter for debate whether it was intended for Albrecht or herself. She was triumphant as well as tragic. This brought into sharper contrast the ethereal, intangible spirit of Act II who is permanently either* en l'air *or* sur les pointes. *Here Savage's unusual colouring, her startlingly red hair and alabaster skin served her particularly well. Her dancing was unearthly, as transparent as a skeleton leaf. Alex Bird was an imperfect Albrecht, however. His* tours en l'air *were almost faultless but his performance was undermined by his inelegant* port de bras . . .

There was more in this vein.

Though naturally indignant on Alex's behalf, I was thrilled

41

by Didelot's praise of my own performance. When I looked up, having committed every plaudit to memory, Lizzie was smiling at me. I thought, as so often before, what a good – what an exceptional – friend she was to delight in my success. All the same, so she should not think me conceited, I tried to conceal my elation. 'One's only as good as one's last performance in this game.'

'Yes, but this might persuade Sebastian to give you an increase in salary to stop you signing up with Mr Lubikoff. Of course it's incredibly selfish of me but I *dread* you going. We'd hardly see each other.' She patted my hand. 'But naturally you must make the best decision for your career. I shall completely understand if you opt for the EB.'

For a moment I was tempted to tell her about Sebastian's offer of marriage. But since he had not mentioned it again and continued to behave with the same offhand un-loverlike impatience, without a single word of tenderness, I was beginning to think I must have hallucinated the whole thing. Or else that Sebastian had never for a moment dreamed I would take him seriously. He probably assumed that I would understand he was playing some sort of game with Miko. In which case I would look an awful fool if I mentioned it to anyone. Lizzie was a darling and absolutely my best friend but discretion was not her strong suit.

'I don't even know if he'll want me now I'm injured. It's easy to get a reputation for unreliability.'

'You've never had to pull out before. Nobody could be so mean as to hold one injury against you.'

'No.' I attempted to put on a bright face. 'I'm just feeling a little bleak. But it's unfair when you've struggled all the way over here and brought me these heavenly chips. Sorry. I promise not to be glum any more. I'm so grateful – and you've got to flog all the way back to Brockley—'

'Well, actually, no. I left my suitcase in the hall – oh God, I'm so sorry, I feel as though I'm letting you down . . . The thing

42

is –' Lizzie looked apologetic – 'I'm on my way to Heathrow. One of the corps in the touring company has pulled a ligament and Sebastian insists on me replacing her. I tried to tell him that you'll need someone to bring you food and things but he just walked off . . . you know what a beast he is. I'm catching a plane in three hours' time.'

I tried to prevent my dismay from showing on my face. 'How long will you be away?'

'The tour ends in three weeks.'

'What about your grandmother?'

'She's going into a residential home for the time I'm away. I've brought you the entire contents of our larder. I'm afraid it's mostly brawn which is Granny's favourite.'

'How delicious! Thank you.'

'Do you think so?' Lizzie looked surprised, which proved I was a better actress than I'd thought. 'I never eat it for fear of finding bristly hairs. There are some tins of frankfurters as well. Oh, Marigold, I feel awful about leaving you.'

'You can't help it. Don't worry. I'll be fine. At the dentist's the other day I read this article in a magazine – hang on, I've got it somewhere,' I opened the drawer in the table beside my bed, 'I sneakily tore it out: here it is. *The Art of Making Conversation*. "*Do you ever feel at a loss for something to say at parties?*" Well, I always feel a complete dunderhead unless I'm with someone to do with ballet. "*Ever embarrassed by an inability to make witty incisive remarks?*" I should say so! I've never made a witty incisive remark in my life. "*Do you find yourself resorting to banal topics like the weather and your children's schools?*" Well, not the latter obviously. Apparently, good conversationalists talk about ideas, the second rate talk about things and the third rate talk about people.'

'Okay, so I'm third rate,' said Lizzie. 'There's nothing I like better than gossip.'

'The article says in order to be an interesting dinner-party guest you have to have a cultivated mind. It gives a list of the hundred most essential books one ought to have read. I've bought copies of the first five books on the list and now's my opportunity to read them. I shall begin with Gibbon's *Decline and Fall of the Roman Empire.*'

Lizzie's eyes widened. 'Jolly good luck.'

'So you see I'll be as merry as a grig – whatever that is.'

We smiled bravely at each other.

5

The winter of 1982 was the coldest on record. I read in the newspaper Lizzie had brought the fish and chips in that they were restoring the hothouses at Kew and one of the rarest plants, a Chilean palm, had been wrapped in a polythene tower through which warm air was pumped to keep it alive. I envied it. Shortly after Lizzie left, the boiler that provided hot water for the bathroom and heated the tiny radiator in my bedroom broke down. In the morning there were frost patterns all over the window and my breath curled up like a whale spout into the crimson canopy.

The hours went by at the pace of an old woman crawling on arthritic hands and knees. My spirits drooped but I told myself not to be so self-indulgent, hopped over to the bookcase and found the first volume of Gibbon. I managed to read for ten minutes before sleep overwhelmed me. I awoke with a dry throat and a feeling of loneliness so acute that even Siggy in all his transcendent beauty could not console me. I read more Gibbon. Gibbon-lovers I had met always held forth in a lofty way about the elegant simplicity of his prose. Probably you have to be in a cheerful mood for it to do you any good. After three-quarters of an hour I was ready to throw myself out of the window.

I had a jolly good cry for about five minutes which made

me feel marginally better. I mopped my swollen lids with a hanky soaked in cold water and stared through the grimy window at the darkening sky bisected by pigeons and starlings. If I could not show more strength of mind than this I deserved to fail. Emotional resilience is not the least of the requirements for a dancer. From the moment training starts at the age of ten or eleven, there is a high possibility of failure. At the end of each summer term, weeping girls are driven away, never to return. If you are one of the lucky ones chosen to go up to the next level, your elation is moderated by the knowledge that the following summer it could easily be you packing your suitcase in tears because you are too tall, too fat, too heavy-footed or not strong enough. Or you might lack the right temperament, be unable to take instruction fast enough, have a muted personality, be unmusical or simply not please the eye. After six years of gruelling work, if you meet the requirements of the selection board, you graduate into the upper school and become a student. But this is not a guarantee that you will get a place in a company. Even those who attend ballet schools that feed specific companies have only a small chance of a contract. Perhaps half a dozen a year are taken into the corps.

When I showed an aptitude for ballet my parents sent me to Brackenbury House in Manchester. The teaching was excellent but we girls always felt ourselves to be provincials. At the age of sixteen, five of us, considered the best dancers in the school, were determined to come to London to audition for the Lenoir Ballet Company. We chose the LBC because it had no feeder school of its own. Bella, Lizzie and I got in. The other two, good though they were, had to face the fact that their careers in ballet were effectively over. One went into musicals and the other became a PE teacher. That's how hard it is to get anywhere.

I had to convince myself that this injury was a temporary blip on the upward trajectory of my career. The gods had been with me so far. I would earn their respect by maintaining a positive cheerfulness in the face of this minor disaster.

I put on a hat and gloves and tried to read more Gibbon with nothing but my watering eyes over the bedclothes before giving in and shivering with Siggy in the darkness beneath the blankets, popping our heads out at intervals for oxygen. I had never thought about it before because I had been too busy, but now I realized that happiness, my happiness anyway, depended on structure and order. From the age of ten almost every minute of my life had been organized. A dancer's body is like a fine instrument that needs delicate tuning. After even a few days' rest, one's muscles become stiff and uncooperative. However tired we were, however bad our headaches or colds, six days out of seven we went to at least one class a day. On Sundays, Nancy, Sorel and I exercised for several hours in our sitting room, which had a barre and a large mirror that we had fixed to the wall ourselves. Now the hours stretched ahead of me, blank, frighteningly empty.

I was roused from a state of semiconsciousness by a knock on the front door. I looked at my clock. Half-past seven in the evening of the longest day of my life. The knock came again. Pulling the eiderdown round me, I limped into the hall. I lifted the letterbox flap. A delicious and reassuring scent drifted through the draughty rectangle. I opened the door.

'Marigold! Thank . . . goodness!'

'*Bobbie!* How wonderful! But you're almost the last person in the world I expected to see! I thought you were in Ireland.'

'I am . . . usually. Can . . . come in? . . . as . . . phyxiating out here.'

'Of course!' I embraced her enthusiastically. 'Oh, sorry, I probably stink to high heaven. I haven't been able to have a bath today and you smell gorgeous.'

'Luckily . . . bottle of scent to . . . drown myself . . . might not . . . made it . . . top.' Bobbie was puffing like one of those little funicular trains that run up cliffs. '. . . going to see . . . *Giselle* . . . last night but you . . . not dancing . . . rang the company . . . at home . . . broken leg.' She hugged me again then held me at arm's length. '. . . look at you.' Her eyes took in my cap, my gloves, my cast and my shivering state. 'Marigold! . . . mauve . . . cold! Bed . . . at once!'

I was too weak to do other than obey. Bobbie brought a chair up to the bed and sat panting for a while, holding my hand and chafing my back.

'All right, I've got my breath now. Why is this place colder than a polar cap?'

I explained about the boiler. She went away and came back with the blankets from the other two beds. She piled them on my recumbent form, keeping one to wrap round herself. 'That's better. Now tell me about your poor leg.'

'Foot actually. It's a comminuted fracture but the surgeon thinks it'll mend all right. I'm starting to feel warmer already. I don't know why I didn't think about Nancy and Sorel's bedclothes.'

'I expect you've got mild hypothermia. The mind is the first thing that goes, apparently.'

'Oh, Bobbie!' I looked at her with pleasure. Even had she been as ugly as a warty old crone I would have been thrilled to see a fellow human being, but she happened to be remarkably beautiful. 'I hope you aren't a dream. I couldn't bear it if you vanished now.'

'I'm here, darling, and I'm not going to leave you until I know you're all right. Why aren't you being properly looked after?'

'Sebastian told the clinic I was going to a nursing home so they'd let me out early, but it would have been too expensive. And everyone in the company's either away or too busy.' I brought Bobbie up to date with the events of the past week, feeling warmth return to my extremities and optimism to my powers of reasoning. 'I don't need looking after, really. I can hobble about. It's just that it's so difficult to get up and down the stairs.'

'I'll find something for us to eat and then we'll think what's the best thing to do.'

'There's a tin of frankfurters.' I pulled a face. 'Otherwise it's brawn, I'm afraid.'

Bobbie picked up a pale green carrier bag with 'Fortnum and Mason' written on it. 'I stopped on my way to pick up a few bits and pieces. I won't be a minute.'

She returned with a tray piled with good things.

'Smoked salmon!' I cried. 'Oh, the luxury! A whole camembert! Tomatoes and olives! Cold chicken!' I felt my mouth fill with saliva. 'And little fruit tarts! You angel!' I winked away tears of gratitude.

She had also brought a bottle of claret that tasted deliciously of raspberries and liquorice. While we ate and drank we talked as easily as though we had met yesterday, though in fact it had been two years since we had last seen each other.

I had known Bobbie all my life. Our mothers had been at the same boarding school. As a homesick new girl, my mother, who was much given to hero-worship, had developed a crush on Bobbie's mother, who was several years her senior. She had run errands for her and written her passionate notes and spent all her pocket money on presents of chocolates and bath salts. To judge by her adult personality, Bobbie's mother, Laetitia, had been a good-looking but reserved and probably rather friendless girl. It must have suited her to have an acolyte.

Somehow the relationship had lasted beyond school and even after marriage. Laetitia was invalidish. My mother spent weeks with the Pickford-Nortons in their large, gloomy house in Sussex, surrounded by dripping trees and sodden shrubberies, cooking little delicacies, running baths, fetching books from the library, a willing slave. After she married my father the visits became much less frequent, but once a year my mother, my sister Kate and I made the long journey from Northumberland to the south coast to stay for a week or two at Cutham Hall.

Given the eight-year age gap, it would have been quite understandable had Bobbie chosen to ignore me altogether during these visits, but she had been angelically kind and looked after me like a mother – which was just as well as my real mother was too busy to have time for me. Laetitia became more demanding with age. She had to have shawls, spectacles, hats and pills fetched, and constant cups of tea and cakes made while she lay either in bed, on a sofa or in a deckchair in the garden. Her cook and her daily gave notice almost hourly and had to be cajoled into staying. During the sulking periods, my mother had to vacuum acres of carpet, polish her way through cupboards of silver and rustle up lunch and supper for Major Pickford-Norton, a small man with a peppery temper and a selfishness quite as colossal as his wife's.

Bobbie had taken us for walks and helped us make daisy chains and grass whistles or collect conkers, depending on the time of year. Sometimes we went to the beach. Bobbie would give us piggybacks down to the place where it briefly became sand and we'd make mermaids with shells and bladderwrack and skate's-egg cases and she would plait my hair so that it wasn't torture to brush afterwards. On wet days she took us in turn on her knee and read us stories and played Happy Families and Ludo. I thought her the most beautiful creature in the world, with her long fair wavy hair and eyes that were the colour of the sea. Despite my dislike of Cutham Hall and my fear of Major Pickford-Norton, it was a huge disappointment when Laetitia wrote to say that her indifferent health precluded any more visits.

'How's your mother? Is she managing without your father?'

Bobbie's father had died two years ago.

'Very well. She has a companion called Ruby who's a dear and looks after her brilliantly. She's put on two stones since my father died. The marriage wasn't a happy one, you know. How's darling Dimpsie?'

Despite being very different kinds of people, Bobbie had always been very fond of my mother. Most people were.

'All right, I think. She came backstage after a performance of *Swan Lake* when we toured the north last year. We had supper together.'

'And Kate? And your father?'

'I haven't seen either of them for ages. We only have a few days off at Christmas and it's too far to go home. Tell me about Ireland. What made you rush back there so suddenly? Are you really going to live there permanently?'

Bobbie's life had been interwoven with mysterious comings and goings. I had received several enigmatic notes from her over the last few months postmarked Eire.

'Oh, yes.' Bobbie stretched out her hand to show me a wedding ring. 'Finn and I were married six weeks ago.'

'*Married?* Bobbie, you *might* have told me! And who is Finn?'

'I know it was bad of me but truthfully we didn't tell anyone. We married in the register office in Dublin with two colleagues from Trinity College as witnesses and afterwards we went out to dinner, just the two of us, and that was it. He has three children, you see, by his first wife, and we didn't want to make a fuss. Most people in Connemara – that's where we live – wouldn't even consider that we *are* married. Divorce isn't recognized in Ireland, though Finn went to a lot of trouble to get his first marriage annulled. I wouldn't have minded living in sin for the rest of my life as long as I could be with him.'

'Tell me about Finn. It's a beautiful name.'

Bobbie smiled. 'Oh . . . he's very clever. And very good . . . though he'd laugh if he heard me say that. He's very handsome, very Irish, though that could mean any number of things. He's writing a biography about Parnell – the Irish politician – and he's an advisor to the government on education. Does that make him sound dull? He certainly isn't that. I only have to see the back of his head and I get butterflies.' She was silent for a moment, thinking. 'He's in everything I do, in everything I see, in every thought, in every hope, every dream. Yet I don't really know how to describe him.'

I laughed. 'Well, the picture so far is encouraging. Tell me about the children? How do you get on with them?'

'I love them. And I hope they love me. It would take too

long to tell you the whole story now and I want to hear about you, but Curraghcourt – that's Finn's house where his family have lived for centuries – is the most wonderful place and we've opened it to the public to help pay for repairs. And I've started an antiques business. That's why I'm here, looking up dealers, people I used to know when I worked for the auction house. Finn and I never have a minute to call our own, except sometimes after dinner we sneak off alone together and then – well – it's paradise.'

I tried, but failed, to imagine wanting to be with someone that much. This was worrying. Was I a cold heartless person, incapable of love? I had no time to answer this question because Bobbie was asking me about my leg.

'I've got an appointment in six weeks.'

'And how long till you can dance on it?'

I looked down at my glass. 'About two months. That's if . . .' Despite my best intentions my nose began to prickle and my throat became tight. Tears began to well. 'Bobbie, I'm terrified . . . if it doesn't heal properly I may never be able to dance again.'

'Oh, darling!'

'And the awful thing is, life without dancing seems . . . utterly pointless. If I try to imagine myself not dancing – I don't even know who I am!'

After this confession I broke down completely. Bobbie got up and put her arms round me and I sobbed hard on her shoulder. At last the storm of weeping blew itself out. I mopped my face on the handkerchief she offered. 'Thanks. I never seem to have one. I'll wash it and send it back.'

'Keep it. I really am sorry to have touched such a tender place.'

'I needed to say it. It's something we're all so frightened of that it's like a taboo. But it's been in my mind all the time, haunting me like something terrifying you think might be under the bed only you can't bring yourself to bend down and look in case it's staring at you with glaring red eyes . . .'

'Your problem is you've got so much imagination. Don't you

remember, when you were little, that story about a scarecrow who came alive? Kate thought it was funny but you woke screaming for several nights after. Not that imagination isn't generally a good thing, and you wouldn't be such a good dancer if you didn't have it.'

'If I can't dance again I've just got to try to face up to it. I certainly won't be the only one. It happens all the time. Mostly feet but sometimes backs and knees – then it's goodbye career, hello teaching, reviewing, whatever you can get.' I was annoyed to hear my voice wobble pathetically. 'When you think how few opportunities there are to dance the principal roles and how many good dancers there are I ought to be grateful that I've had the chance to do *Lac* and *Giselle* and *Manon* and all those brilliant parts.'

'What you need is—' Bobbie broke off with a little yell as Siggy poked out his head from beneath the eiderdown and bared his incisors at her.

'It's all right, it's only Siegfried. He's hungry, I expect.' I leaned over the side of the bed and put a morsel of chicken on his saucer. He pushed his head out further, looked at Bobbie with unfriendly eyes and hopped down to the floor. Siggy was possessive and jealous, but his marked preference for me above all other beings was good for my morale.

'A rabbit!' Bobbie laughed and bent down to stroke him.

Too late I cried, 'Look out, he bites!'

Already his head had flashed forward. For a slightly over-weight creature he could move fast when he wanted. She drew back her hand with a cry of pain. A drop of blood burst out on her finger.

'I'm *so* sorry,' I said. 'Please don't feel hurt. He bites everybody but me.'

'It's all right. I like animals – even savage ones.' Bobbie really was an exemplary guest. She sucked the wound, then examined it. 'It's all right. Just a tiny puncture. He's certainly a very good-looking rabbit.'

Most people were insulting about Siggy after he had bitten them. Though I deplored his character, I could not help feeling proud of him. He had lovely orange eyes, neat little ears and a beautiful fluffy coat of thundercloud grey.

'I've had him a year now. I found some children trying to push a sack down the culvert at the end of the street. I asked them what was in it and they said it was a rabbit which bit them all the time so they'd decided to drown it. Of course I took the sack away from them. Immediately they all ran off so I was lumbered, really. He's never once bitten me. It's as if he knows I rescued him from a horrible fate and he's grateful.'

'A very intelligent rabbit.' Bobbie looked kindly at Siggy. I felt the sort of glow parents of an infant prodigy must enjoy. 'Marigold, do listen to me a minute.' Bobbie offered her camembert crust to Siggy who chomped it down, making a mess of his whiskers. 'I don't think it's good for you to stay here. You're lonely, freezing and semi-starving. People who are recovering from operations need warmth and good food and fresh air.' She looked apologetic. 'I can smell the stairs a tiny bit in here. You mentioned someone called Sebastian. Who is he and why is it up to him whether you go into a nursing home or not?'

'He's the director of the Lenoir Ballet Company. And my lover . . . sort of.'

'Sort of?'

'Well, strictly in the physical sense. Not in the sense of loving each other. Though we might be engaged to be married. I'm not really sure.'

Bobbie took away our plates and refilled our glasses. Then she lay on the bed next to me and rearranged the blankets to cover both of us. 'That's better. I can feel the blood returning to my feet. Now, tell me all.'

I was entirely frank and did not bother to garb the relationship with spurious romance. Bobbie listened intently, putting in the occasional question which I answered truthfully.

When I had told everything there was to tell she said, 'I see.

Now I feel more strongly than ever that you ought, for a time at least, to have . . . a little holiday. If you could contemplate the journey to Ireland, Finn and I will be absolutely delighted to have you to stay. You never saw such wonderful countryside and you'd love Patience, his sister who lives with us and . . . why are you shaking your head?'

'Thank you so much, darling Bobbie, for asking me, but I should be conscious the whole time that I was yet another person requiring attention and taking up your time. You said it yourself. It's paradise when you can be alone with Finn. It's enormously kind of you to offer and perhaps when you've become used to him and are content just to rest your eyes on him across a crowded room, I'll come willingly.'

Bobbie laughed. 'I'd love to have you. Truthfully.'

'Thanks. But I'd be a martyr to guilt the whole time.'

'Well, then, the alternative is—'

'All right! I know whither this is tending. You want me to go home.'

'Just for a few weeks.' Bobbie looked at me pleadingly. 'Dimpsie's such an angel and she'd love to have you. Think of the scenery and the clean air. Proper food, relaxation, new horizons. You might even enjoy it.'

'I might,' I replied rather glumly.

Less than twenty-four hours later I was standing on the platform at King's Cross with Siggy in a travelling basket and a one-way ticket to Northumberland.

6

'Safe journey, darling.' Bobbie had been saintly, getting me and my suitcase downstairs and into a taxi, coming to the station with me, helping me on to the train and stowing my suitcase behind my seat. We kissed each other. 'Give Dimpsie my love. Goodbye Siggy.' She tapped the door at one end of the wicker cage that she had kindly bought that morning from a pet shop. We had draped it with a shawl, leaving the door uncovered so he could breathe. Siggy launched himself at the bars with snapping teeth. 'I hope they won't make you put him in the luggage van. Perhaps you'd better put the coat over him as well when the ticket inspector comes round.'

'Not your beautiful coat,' I protested. 'I'd never ever forgive myself if he chewed it.' When Bobbie had seen the state of my fur cloak which had once lapped the shoulders of the Snow Queen and in which Siggy had bitten a hole in just where my tail would have come through if I'd had one, she had insisted on lending me her own pale-honey-coloured cashmere coat to travel in. The arrangement was that I would return it when next she came to London.

'It really isn't that precious. I'm going straight to Heathrow and I'm being met by Finn the other end. I shan't miss it.'

'You've been angelic.' I hugged her again.

'Write when you get the chance and let me know how things are. There's the whistle. I must go. Goodbye, darling.'

She put a carrier bag on the seat beside me and rushed to get off. She waited on the platform until the train drew away. I saw her smiling figure recede with a sharp pang of parting. To console myself I opened the carrier bag. Bobbie was a friend in a million. Paper parcels contained slices of ham and salami, lettuce, poppy-seed rolls and a bar of hazelnut chocolate. There was also a bottle of apple juice and a copy of this month's *Vogue*. Including the change at Newcastle, the journey was going to take five hours. I burrowed in my knapsack to find *The Pilgrim's Progress* by John Bunyan, which was second on the list of required reading for the intelligent conversationalist. Gibbon and I had gone far enough together for the time being.

It was a second-hand copy from the bargain box of a local bookshop. The binding was an attractive blue but the book smelt as though it had been macerated for a hundred years in a leaky coffin in a subfluvial vault. *And Esau sold his birthright for a mess of pottage,* I read, dipping into the middle. This was the stuff all right, I thought to myself, and prepared to be enlightened. *But Little-faith was of another temper. His mind was on things divine . . .*

I woke, absolutely starving, as we were drawing into Grantham station. I blessed Bobbie's forethought. Getting to the restaurant car would have been quite as difficult as anything Christian could possibly have undergone. I ate much of the picnic and surreptitiously fed bits of ham and salami through the bars of Siggy's prison-house, then wiped my fingers and took up the magazine. I was enjoying *The Pilgrim's Progress*, of course, but *Vogue* might be a better *digestif*.

I studied the models with interest. We dancers feel acute anxiety about our bodies, not surprisingly as we spend most of our time staring into mirrors. We observe people's body shapes before faces, voices, cleverness, niceness. This probably seems terribly superficial, but how a dancer looks is extremely important. A small head, long neck, short torso and long, long slender legs are the ideal. The models were clearly giants, with large thigh bones, huge feet and big jaws, quite the wrong conformation for a dancer and the opposite of everything I had been taught to admire. They stood pigeon-toed with their hips and knees thrust forward and heads drooping and all their weight on the back of their feet.

Dancers spend a great deal of effort in perfecting 'turnout' with not just our feet but our knees and hips at a quarter to three. This is the most fundamental aspect of classical ballet technique. Some dancers have perfect turnout naturally, but I had really had to work at it. I had drilled myself to make it second nature to turn out my legs during every single second of class and in performance. On stage, with the appropriate clothes, pointe shoes and perfectly disciplined movements, what is actually a distortion looks superbly graceful. When I was walking in the street or anywhere not to do with dancing I had to remind myself all the time to turn my toes in, so as not to look like a waddling duck.

We were trained to stretch our necks, lift our chins and chests, straighten our backs and stand with just the skin of our heels on the ground so that our weight was centred on the arch of our feet. The models scowled with what Madame would have called 'dead' eyes. We were supposed to look engaged, expressive, reflective. It just shows how subjective beauty is.

After I had marvelled at the prices of the clothes and read the advertisements, I closed my eyes in a well-stuffed haze and thought long and hard about Sebastian without coming to any conclusion except that now I had at least five weeks with no possibility of seeing him he seemed much less frightening. I imagined signing a contract with Miko and receiving ovations and rave reviews from Didelot for my interpretation of Kitri in *Don Quixote*.

I must have slept again, for the next thing I knew we were drawing into York station. As we travelled further north the ridges of the ploughed fields were frosted with white and the occasional snowflake glanced against the window. By the time we left Darlington, snow was falling steadily and the sky had taken on a bluish tinge presaging dusk. While dreaming about taking the Met by storm in the jazzy, flashy Rubies section of Balanchine's *Jewels*, I finished the rest of Bobbie's picnic. Siggy deigned to eat some of the hazelnut chocolate, which could not have been good for him but the nuts kept him busy. I enjoyed looking at the white hills and dales that formed graceful parabolas like giant elbows and knees carved from marble.

A ticket inspector came aboard at Durham, so I dropped my shawl over the front of Siggy's cage. When I removed it later he had eaten half the fringe, this despite my having given him an old jersey for this very purpose, which as far as I could see remained untouched.

'You really are a *naughty* boy!' I said with some heat, because the shawl was a fine wool paisley printed in lovely colours of rose and ochre which I had been delighted to find in an Oxfam shop.

A man sitting opposite, wearing a dog collar, glanced at me with an expression of alarm and then stared sternly out of the window, slowly reddening.

It was nearly dark when we chugged into Newcastle. The rawness of the weather had stolen the colour from people's lips and cheeks and restored it to their noses. Each light had its own murky halo and every cold surface a silvery sheen of condensation. Our train was late, which left me five minutes to catch the connection to Haltwhistle. With my bag slung round my neck and Siggy's basket in one hand, I tried with the other to pull my suitcase from where Bobbie had stowed it between the seats.

'Excuse me,' I said to the clergyman. 'I'm awfully sorry, would you mind . . . ?'

He pretended not to hear me and made a bolt for the exit, coat flapping.

'Give it here, pet.' A small stout woman in a grey gabardine mackintosh took hold of the handle of my case and tugged it into the aisle, along the carriage and down on to the platform. Luckily, a cool-looking porter sauntered up with a trolley.

'I'm so grateful,' I said to the woman, whose forehead glistened with perspiration.

She glared at the other passengers who were flowing around us like a torrent round a boulder. 'It's come to something if we can't help a poor bloody cripple.'

I smiled. 'It's only temporary.'

She clicked her tongue. 'I *hope* so, I'm sure.' She trotted away on fat little legs.

My porter was waiting patiently by an open carriage door at a platform on the far side of the station when I hobbled up on my crutches, feeling feverish with anxiety and exhaustion.

The carriage was one of those old-fashioned ones with a corridor and compartments seating six. An old lady sitting by the door drew back her legs to accommodate my elephantine limb. I fell into the window seat and brushed my damp hair from my forehead with a glove beaded with moisture. The porter put Siggy's basket on the seat beside me and my suitcase into the rack. I gave him a twenty-pence piece, which I could ill afford. He looked at it as though I had handed him something phosphorescent with putrefaction. A whistle blew and the train began to crawl out of the station.

While I waited for my breathing to return to normal, I ran a cursory eye over my fellow passengers. Opposite me was a wispy blonde with magenta lipstick. She was studying a magazine with intense concentration, holding it at an angle that made it possible for me to see photographs of the princess of Wales peeping shyly from beneath the brims of various neat little hats. The marriage of Charles and Diana the summer before had provided the stuff of dreams for every woman in the land. She turned to a picture of the balcony kiss, put her head on one side and pursed her lips slightly, perhaps imagining what it was like to be kissed by a prince of the blood royal.

Next to her was a small boy, who fixed his eyes on my plastered leg. The corner seat diagonally opposite mine was taken by a dark-haired man who wore a coat with an astrakhan collar. He was reading the *New Scientist*. The old lady who had drawn back her legs to make room for me had taken out a bag of sweets and was sucking one with a slow circular motion of her jaw, while staring at the picture of a heathery mountain and lake above the man's head.

'What've you done cha leg?' asked the small boy.

'I've told you not to ask personal questions, Gary,' said the woman with the magazine, not looking up. 'It's rude.'

'Was you run over?'

'I've broken my foot.'

'Was there masses of blood?'

'No.' I stared out of the window, hoping to discourage further questions. As it was dark I could see nothing but smeary, shivering trickles, twinkling lights and my own reflection.

'How're they goin' to get it off? With a hammer?'

'A little saw, actually.'

Gary seemed to cheer up a little. 'They might saw your leg off too, by mistake. What's in that box?' He pointed to Siggy's cage. 'I thought I saw it move.'

I put my hand on the basket to hold it still, for Siggy had decided he had had enough imprisonment and was trying to tunnel his way through the wicker with his teeth. 'Nothing interesting.'

'I wanna see.'

It seemed a good moment to visit the lavatory. I stood up and took hold of the basket.

The elderly woman's eyes had closed. She sat with her knees apart and her feet rolled outwards. I tried to step over her but my cumbersome limb made manoeuvring difficult and I accidentally trod on her foot. She drew herself up with a little scream, kicking my good leg on which all my weight was resting so that I fell back on to the knees of the man with the astrakhan

61

collar. He muttered something incomprehensible beneath his breath and put me back on my feet.

'I'm so sorry,' I said to the woman. She looked furious.

I apologized to the man but he was busy smoothing out his *New Scientist* which I had accidentally crushed and did not look up. I struggled down to the lavatory at the end of the corridor; it barely had room for me, my cast and Siggy's cage all at once. Returning to the compartment I accidentally buffeted the man's knees with Siggy's cage. This time he met my profuse apology with a nod of his head and a fleeting glance in which I read exasperation.

'So I should think!' said the elderly lady waspishly, and unfairly; this time her person was unscathed.

'C'n I see what's in it now?'

Gary was a maddeningly persistent child.

'There's nothing to see . . .' As I teetered towards my seat, the shawl caught on the old woman's knees and Siggy was momentarily revealed.

'I saw it! I saw it!' shouted Gary. 'It's a rat! A huge grey rat! With a long tail like a snake's!'

'No, it isn't!' I replied above the elderly woman's screams. 'It's a rabbit. Look! You can see he has long ears. And a dear little fluffy tail.'

I whisked away the shawl to show the company my beautiful Siegfried. Gary's mother shot him a look of dislike before going back to her magazine, continuing to wrinkle her nose and pull down the corners of her mouth as though she could smell something unpleasant, though Siggy, for all his faults, was never malodorous.

'Wassis name?' demanded Gary.

It was quite as bad as being accosted by a drunk.

'Siggy.'

'Issat short for cigarette?'

I was reluctant to open channels for further conversation. 'Yes.'

'I'm allergic to animals,' said the elderly woman. 'Perhaps,' she addressed the man in the astrakhan collar, 'you'd open the window. I must have fresh air or I can't answer for my asthma.'

The man stood up and made his way over to the window. As he fought with the little sliding pane at the top, the train careened round a bend and he lurched sideways, knocking the magazine from Gary's mother's hand and treading heavily on Gary. For a boy he was a disgraceful cry-baby. It was some time before calm was restored and the readers among us allowed to return to their literature in peace. The elderly woman sat sucking and staring angrily at the heathery mountain with one hand pressed to her chest. I tried to give my whole attention to *The Pilgrim's Progress*. Snow blew in through the open window directly on to my lap, and the wind from the motion of the train parted my hair, but I did not dare to protest. Instead I concentrated on the Discourse between Mercy and Good Christiana.

During the next half-hour, as I brushed the snowflakes from my increasingly sodden page, I conceived a great dislike for Mercy, who wept for her carnal relations sinning in ignorance of a better course. Good Christiana, a prig if ever there was one, comforted her, saying – I thought obscurely – *bowels becometh pilgrims*. I looked this up in the notes at the back. It referred of course to bowels of compassion, nothing to do with digestion, but the vision conjured by this maundering, complacent couple was unattractive, and when they reached the Slough of Despond, through which I had already waded earlier that day with Good Christiana's husband, suddenly I could stand it no longer. I stood up and hurled *The Pilgrim's Progress* through the open window into the whirling darkness. Because it was an ancient copy it fell into at least three hundred separate pages, of which a third blew back in through the window and distributed themselves about the compartment.

'Tickets, please.' A uniformed man had slid back the door. His eyes took in the mess. 'What the bloomin' heck's going on in *here*?' The elderly lady was brushing off the pages that had landed on her with as much shuddering abhorrence as though they had been cockroaches. 'There's a ten-pound fine for littering of railway property.' His stare roamed round the compartment to rest on each of us in turn.

'It was the wind,' I explained. 'I'll clear it all up before I get off.'

'I hope so, young lady.' The ticket inspector's already extensive frame seemed to swell with menace. 'I'll just have a look at your ticket.'

'She's got a rabbit,' shrilled Gary, pointing at Siggy. 'In that cage.'

The little swine! I would have liked to have chucked Gary after Bunyan.

'Ho!' The ticket inspector advanced into the compartment, trampling on several feet. The elderly woman gave a screech of pain and the man with the astrakhan collar winced and closed his eyes. 'No Livestock Allowed In Passenger Accommodation,' the ticket inspector said impressively. 'You'll have to put it in the luggage van.'

I summoned all my powers to charm. 'I'm getting off in half an hour at Haltwhistle,' I pleaded. 'And,' I put extra pathos into my voice, 'I've just had an operation on my foot. It'll be difficult – almost impossible – for me to fetch him from the van as well as get my luggage off the train. Couldn't you please, just this once, out of the kindness of your heart, overlook the rules?' I gave him my ecstatically happy Giselle smile from the beginning of the first act. 'I'd be eternally grateful.'

'No,' said the inspector.

The man was an ass, a lackey in the pay of a hygiene-obsessed bureaucracy. I gave him my furious Titania scowl.

'I'm sure I've caught a flea already,' complained the old lady petulantly.

'We done the plague at school,' said Gary. 'Teacher said it was fleas that killed everyone. Proberly you're goin' to come out in black boils. It looks like a plague rabbit.' Before I could

64

stop him he had darted forward and stuck his finger into Siggy's cage. Siggy struck like a cobra. Gary screamed until my hair practically stood on end and his finger became a fountain gushing blood.

His mother lifted her eyes from her magazine long enough to say, 'Shut it, you little tyke,' and to give him a hard clout on his ear.

Gary howled and knuckled his eyes with a grubby fist. I saw the man in the astrakhan collar take out his wallet and discreetly press something into the ticket inspector's hand. It looked like a ten-pound note. All the bluster and bullying went out of the ticket inspector. He grinned sycophantically and touched his cap as the note disappeared into his pocket.

'Well, sir. Seeing as the young lady's getting off soon it might be as well to make an exception, bearing in mind as she is a disabled person.'

'That would be most sensible,' said the astrakhan collar in a lordly way. There was a trace of something foreign in his accent.

Deferentially the ticket inspector withdrew his paunch and slid the door shut with an air of respectful solicitude.

I examined my benefactor. His hair was very dark and his skin was what people misleadingly call olive, though it was neither green nor black nor in the least oily but a sort of yellow to gold colour. Though he was much better looking than Alex, there was a similarity in the colouring and the long thin nose. Alex's family were Lithuanian Jews. They lived in a poor but jolly community in Bethnal Green and a group of them always came to cheer his performances. Afterwards they got plastered and homesick together. I wondered if this man was a Lithuanian. Perhaps he was a refugee, as Alex's father had been. He might be travelling north to find work so he could send money back to his starving family in Sovetsk. Perhaps he did not know the value of a ten-pound note. I imagined him sitting in a grim bedsitter in Carlisle, tears rolling down his face as he counted his remaining change and thought of the feast his hungry children could have enjoyed if only he had known . . . this flight of fancy was checked when I remembered that astrakhan was exorbitantly expensive.

I rose from my seat and leaned forward to tap him on the knee. He looked at me with black eyes like Alex's, but unlike Alex's, his were hostile.

'I saw you give that man money. You must let me pay you back. I'm afraid I haven't got enough cash but I could give you a post-dated cheque.'

He held up his hand. 'Please. The bribe was offered in an entirely selfish spirit. I have already been interrupted in my reading more times than I could count. I have been sat on, trodden on, blown by the wind, snowed upon, had my ears tortured by screams and cryings. I would consider it a sufficient return if you could contrive not to excite any more disturbances.'

He returned his gaze to the printed page. I sat down, feeling thoroughly snubbed.

Gary was still snivelling. Though he was a repulsive child I couldn't help feeling a little sorry for him.

'Tell you what, Gary. If you help me pick up all this paper, I'll give you fifty pee.'

When Gary had collected them we put them in my picnic carrier bag with the sandwich wrappers and other rubbish. I gave him fifty pence.

'You said a pound.'

'I didn't!'

'You did, you did, you *did!* A pound!' Gary began to jump up and down with excitement.

'I said fifty pee. It only took you five minutes. Anyway I haven't got a pound.'

This was true. I only had twenty-six pence and an overdraft in the entire world.

'Listen,' said Astrakhan Collar to Gary. 'If you do not sniff, cry, speak or move until I get off the train, I will give you two pounds. He raised a finger as Gary opened his mouth to say something. 'Not one syllable more.'

Gary sat as though entranced for the remainder of the journey. When we were within five minutes of arriving at Haltwhistle, I stood up and began feebly to pluck at my case.

'Sit down,' said Astrakhan Collar. 'I will assist you when we reach the station.'

There was a hint of something almost like violence in his voice, so I did as I was told. When we drew alongside the platform, he went to the window and shouted for a porter. So peremptory was his tone that the stationmaster himself came running up.

'Take this lady and her belongings off the train,' said Astrakhan. I could not be sure but I thought another note changed hands. The stationmaster appeared in our compartment faster than a genie after a hasty rub of the lamp. My suitcase, Siggy's cage, the bag of rubbish and I were manhandled off the train. I had no time to express my gratitude.

I heard a scream of joy. 'Marigold! My angel!'

My mother was skipping towards me down the platform.

7

I put my arms round my mother and hugged her, registering the familiar maternal scent of orange blossom, joss sticks and damp from the hall where our coats hung.

'Hello, Dimpsie darling.'

She did not like to be called Mother, Mum or Ma because it made her feel old. She was forty-six, which is certainly not ancient.

Her eyes glistened with happiness. 'It's been such *ages*.'

I acknowledged to my shame that it had been. Who can put their hand on their heart and say with absolute truth that they have fulfilled the expectations of a fond parent? She examined me by the dim lights of the platform.

'You look wonderful, poppet, so beautiful and glamorous. But you're shivering. Let's run to the car. It's right outside.'

'Sorry but I can't. Run, that is. My leg.'

'Oh yes, poor sweet! Is it agony?'

'Not at all.'

She embraced me again. 'Well, let's hop then.'

She hopped all the way to the exit, laughing gaily, while the stationmaster brought my case and I followed at a more sedate pace with Siggy. The car, a Mini, painted purple and stencilled with flowers in primary colours, was, as she had said, parked at the station entrance, much to the annoyance of the taxis and the local bus. We jerked away. The car was old, the road was slippery with snow and Dimpsie was a bad driver.

'I barely slept a wink last night I was so excited you were coming! You're looking so gorgeous, sweetheart. I can hardly believe you're my daughter. You take after your father, of course.'

'Only superficially – look out!'

The car mounted a kerb and rolled off it with a suddenness that made the chassis judder on its springs.

'Sorry, I can't see where I'm going. Your case is weighing down the back so the headlights are up in the air. Head*light,* I should say. I meant to ask the garage to put in a new bulb.'

I closed my eyes, envying Siggy's ignorance of the danger he was in. We headed west to Gilsland and then turned north on the snaking road that climbed to Black Knowe and Reeker Pike.

'How lovely that you've got a little holiday, darling. Everyone will be so thrilled to see you. Evelyn rang this morning to ask you to dinner tomorrow night. I don't suppose you can drive with that leg. I'll run you across.'

'With or without the leg. I've never taken a driving test.'

'Goodness, Marigold, haven't you? Never mind, I'll take you about whenever I can. The only trouble is I'm standing in at reception for the moment. The last girl had some sort of breakdown, poor lamb. I tried to get her to do some yoga breathing, but if you're always in tears you can't control your diaphragm. Boyfriend trouble I think, but she didn't confide. Tom was furious.'

Tom was my father. I felt the car slithering on bends, imagined it plunging over the precipice, turning over and over before crashing into the river and bursting into flames.

'How is Evelyn?'

'Marvellous, as always.' My mother worshipped Evelyn Preston with the same devotion she had once given to Laetitia Pickford-Norton. 'She hasn't changed a bit. I've put on weight, my jaw line's saggy and my neck's beginning to go, but Evelyn looks marvellous, she hasn't changed a bit! *And* she's ten years older than me.'

I had noticed that my mother was a slightly more generous armful. I felt mean for noticing but I couldn't help it.

'She certainly doesn't look her age. She came to see me in *The Firebird*. Did you know?'

Several months ago, Evelyn had nobly taken a cab from Brown's Hotel where she usually stayed when in London, all the way to Hammersmith, to watch me dance in an absurd costume that shed feathers so fast that by the time Prince Ivan had destroyed the egg containing the soul of the magician Kashchei and set the princesses free I was practically naked, but for a tissue-thin flesh-coloured body suit. Evelyn and I had exchanged kisses and congratulations briefly in my dressing room afterwards before she had rushed to catch a plane back to Newcastle.

'So she did. I'd forgotten. That's so like her, she's so loyal to her friends.'

'What did she say about it?'

'She said you were brilliant, far better than anyone else.' This was both kind and untrue. But what Evelyn knew about ballet could be written on a grain of rosin.

'I suppose Shottestone looks just the same?'

'It's looking wonderful. How she does it with only a cook and a butler and two daily helps, I can't imagine!'

Dimpsie intended no irony. For one thing she was too loyal to be critical of Evelyn, and for another Shottestone Manor was large and ancient and you would have needed a fairy godmother with an inexhaustible wand to run it without staff. One of my earliest memories was of Evelyn's commanding features bending over my pram. Apparently she had been my first visitor at Gaythwaite Cottage Hospital, my father having been called away elsewhere. She had looked into my cot and said, 'That baby's hair is remarkable. You must call her Marigold.'

Dimpsie had at once agreed, though my father, who liked plain names, had intended that I should be called either Jack or Jill. My father's personality was essentially combative, but I guessed

70

he had given in because Evelyn's patronage was extremely useful. As well as being chairwoman of the hospital board and a governor of the little school to which they intended to send Kate, she had a finger in all the local pies. Besides, Evelyn was good-looking, and in those days he probably had designs on her.

In the days of my youth I had spent almost every day of the school holidays at Shottestone Manor and Evelyn had treated me like a second daughter, something she was fond of pointing out. There was no denying her generosity – not that I wished to, nor that she had been influential in the course my life had taken. Luckily Dimpsie's nature was not competitive. She had humbly accepted that Evelyn's rule was absolute.

'It will be lovely to see Shottestone again. And I'm dying to see Dumbola Lodge, too, of course.'

'I'm afraid it's looking awfully shabby. Tom says we can't afford to have it redecorated. You've got a treat in store, darling. Rafe's home. You used to admire him so much, remember?'

'Is he?' I felt a quickening of interest. Admiration was too temperate a description for the violent infatuation I had entertained for Evelyn's son. He must have been about seventeen years old and I a passionate child of eight when he had patted me on the head to thank me for fetching his jersey after a tennis match. This insignificant act had been enough to light the fire. The top of my head had tingled for months afterwards whenever I thought of it. He had gone up to Cambridge shortly after that and then into the army. I had not seen him for – I did a quick calculation – nine years. 'Just for the weekend, you mean?'

'No. He came home in September to rest his nerves. He was serving in Northern Ireland and the tank he was in was blown up.'

'How awful! Was he badly hurt?' I opened my eyes just as we were yawing towards a tree picked out in hideous detail by the single headlight. I screwed up my face and waited for the crunch of metal and the somersaulting of my stomach as we flew into the abyss.

'Only a few cracked ribs and a broken jaw.' Dimpsie wrestled with the steering wheel and changed down. The engine screamed in protest but somehow we remained in contact with the road.

'Only?'

'Almost everyone else in the tank was killed. Though it might have caught fire at any minute, Rafe waited inside until the rescue team could get to them and made a tourniquet of his socks to stop the other survivor bleeding to death. He was given a medal for conspicuous gallantry.'

I imagined Rafe as a war hero with a troubled mind. It added a piquancy to my idea of him, which until now had been too smooth, too bland, to keep the flame of memory burning.

'Evelyn's delighted to have him home, of course. Not only for his own sake – she's always adored him, as you know, but Kingsley's become something of a problem.'

Kingsley Preston was much older than his wife. I remembered him as a sort of caricature of a country squire. He had not been much interested in children, preferring horses and dogs. We had had the same conversation each holidays.

'Hello, Marigold.' He would smile and shake my hand. 'It's good to see you back. How are you?'

'I'm fine, thank you, sir.'

'Good, good.'

Then he'd walk quickly away, calling his spaniels to heel. At the end of the holidays, he'd say, 'Well, well, so you're off again.'

'Yes, sir.'

'Going to make Margot Fonteyn shake in her shoes, eh?'

Polite laughter from me. 'Not yet.'

'Jolly good.' The smile and handshake again. 'Keep it up.'

'What's the matter with Kingsley?' I asked.

'He's terribly forgetful. He was eighty last birthday, so perhaps it's not surprising. Evelyn's marvellous with him, so patient. She never complains, you know how strong she is, but it must get her down all the same.'

It seemed to me a little forgetfulness in an old man was not much to put up with. But then, in my mother's eyes, everything Evelyn did, from organizing balls to raise funds for more camels in Africa, to getting poor Mrs Stopes into an old people's home despite her wish to remain independent, were feats of the highest order. My mother kept on her desk a framed photograph of Evelyn in evening dress and tiara, which had appeared fifteen years ago in the *Tatler* above the caption *The Beautiful Mrs Kingsley Preston, Indefatigable Society Hostess of the North.* I was pretty sure the rest of Evelyn's friends had consigned the offending image to the dustbin before returning indoors to dose themselves with bile beans.

'Could we have the heater on?'

'Sorry, it's broken. I keep meaning to get the garage to fix it.'

'Will Rafe be there tomorrow, do you know?'

'Yes. *And –*' Dimpsie's voice took on a slightly anxious tone – 'so will Isobel. She's come home to be with Rafe, to help him get over it. You know how devoted to him she's always been. Darling, I do hope you'll be pleased to see her.'

Isobel. The rush of memories were a welcome distraction from being cold and frightened. From babyhood to the age of ten she had been my best friend. She was a year and a half older than me, a significant age gap then. Probably she would have preferred an older companion but there were no other girls nearby whom Evelyn considered *convenable*. My family was not well off but my father was a doctor and my mother had been privately educated, which made me acceptable.

Naturally Isobel had been the dominant one. She had taught me how to ride a bicycle and how to swim, how to serve overarm, how to make a camp, how to waltz, tie knots and mix invisible inks. Sometimes she had been friendly, sometimes patronizing and sometimes beastly. There had been spats, naturally but most of the time we accepted that we were yoked together, an ill-matched team, seemingly in perpetuity.

We had started dancing lessons together at Evelyn's instigation: 'So good for their deportment, Dimpsie, and the car's taking Isobel anyway so Marigold may as well go, too.'

We had attended Miss Fisher's ballet classes in Haltwhistle. I had adored it from the moment my fingers made contact with the barre and my pink leather pumps with the splintery floor. After three terms we took our first ballet exam. When I had been awarded a distinction and Isobel a pass, there had been indignation and tears. Evelyn had been cross with her.

'You can't expect to excel in *ev*erything, darling. Marigold is so tiny that she can hop about easily. You should be glad for her that she has done so well, even if it is only in dancing.'

When Miss Fisher sent letters home with us to say she thought Isobel was ready for grade two but I was to move up several classes and try for my intermediate certificate, Isobel had wanted to give up ballet altogether. Evelyn had told her not to be silly.

'You must learn not to make a fuss about trivial things. It's very nice for Marigold that she has a little accomplishment. It may come in useful later for balls and dances.'

After I had passed my intermediate certificate with the highest possible mark, Miss Fisher asked to see my mother and told her she should think seriously about sending me to ballet school. Dimpsie went to Evelyn for advice. I remember Evelyn's face became rather long as she read the letter the examiner had sent privately to Miss Fisher, commending my physical attributes and technical promise. She was silent for a while as Dimpsie and I stared anxiously at her pinched nostrils and compressed lips, waiting for the oracle to pronounce. Young and unsophisticated though I was, I dimly understood that, because of the Preston supremacy in birth and upbringing, for a child of Evelyn's to be surpassed in anything was something of a facer. An inward struggle was evidently taking place as she folded the letter into small sections.

Then her better self got the upper hand. Talent must never be wasted. She had heard of a ballet school in Manchester that had an excellent reputation. She would ring at once and ask them to send a prospectus. She congratulated me very kindly and asked us both to stay to tea. There was no more talk about 'little accomplishments' and 'hopping about'.

When Isobel heard about the letter she went down to the beck that races through the valley of Gaythwaite and threw in her ballet pumps. Then she put a note through our letterbox. Unless I dropped the whole idea of ballet school she would never speak to me again. Furthermore she would put a curse on me so that my nose would be permanently covered with blackheads.

After a terrifying audition at Brackenbury House Ballet School, I was awarded a place for the following term. This meant I had only a few weeks mooning about Dumbola Lodge in a state of excommunication, shut out from the paradisial delights of Shottestone Manor – the pony, the swimming pool, the tennis court, the garden, the dogs and Mrs Capstick's celebrated orange cake, which, being a greedy child, I regretted perhaps most of all.

The curse had been lifted by Christmas, much to my relief. I had spent anxious moments, in my precious free time at Brackenbury, examining my face for blackheads. Isobel had been sent to a smart boarding school in Berkshire, and she needed an audience during the holidays for tales of her new life and her new friends. It was about then that Isobel began a campaign of pubescent rebellion against her mother and I was drawn in as her sympathizer and support. Fortunately Evelyn was too busy reorganizing Northumberland to take much notice.

Superficially our relationship had survived the storm. But I had learnt to be guarded. I said almost nothing about my life in Manchester. I played the part of Isobel's admiring friend, conscious that it behoved me to be generous. Together we celebrated her triumphs, when she was made a school monitor and captain of tennis, when she came top in English, when she was given the role of Jo in *Little Women*. We went shopping for clothes suitable for visiting school friends' houses, mansions, chateaux, palazzos, once even a yacht. I listened and marvelled and praised without resentment, for I was going to be a dancer and nothing in the world could compare with the glory of that. First Isobel and then I became old enough to go to proper parties and dances. The best bit about these were the post mortems held in her bedroom when we discussed in minute detail and with tremendous scorn the boys we met there.

When Isobel was sixteen she was sent to school in Switzerland. Eighteen months later I moved to London to join the LBC and the friendship lapsed. I had not seen her for six years. 'What was Isobel doing before she came home?' I asked.

'She finished her course in Fine Arts. Did I tell you that? Then she got a job at Sotheby's. She sent a message to say how much she was looking forward to seeing you.'

'That was kind of her.'

'You were good friends once. I know she could be difficult, but you're both grownup now . . . sometimes I think the friendship between women is the most sublime that's possible between two human beings. Oh, I know the Greeks thought the same about men,' she dismissed Homer and Plato with a wave and the back wheels skewed as they hit the mound of snow in the middle of the road, 'but men never really *talk* to each other, do they?'

I felt sure a sweat of terror must be breaking out on my benumbed brow. 'Being women, can we know that?'

'What? Oh, I see what you mean. Well, if Tom's anything to go by, they never admit to anything more self-revealing than their golf handicap or the size of their socks.'

I realized she was being merely illustrative. My father despised golf and had never given a second's thought to his socks, which my mother always bought for him. 'The men I know are usually only too ready to invite you into their psyches. But I don't suppose they're typical. But neither is Tom, would you say? I've often wondered why he chose to do something that requires being nice to people. He'd be much happier locked in a laboratory on his own.'

76

I was making idle conversation to take my mind off the narrowness of the road and the steepness of the drop as we reached the head of the valley, but I heard a defensiveness in Dimpsie's reply.

'That would have been a great loss to the community though, wouldn't it? I mean, he's the cleverest doctor for miles around . . .'

While my mother rambled on in praise of my father's diagnostic acuity, I indulged in a brief moment of pleasurable nostalgia. This first view of the valley into which we were now descending always moved me by its beauty. At this time of day only the lights of Gaythwaite were visible. Eagleston Crag, the highest point in the circle of hills, was only a darker mass in a sky swollen with inky clouds, but it was so familiar to me that I could have drawn its shape – like a bent old man with a sack on his back – with complete accuracy.

I closed my eyes tightly and tried to think about other things while we whooshed downwards and bounced over the bridge. 'Nearly there,' cried Dimpsie, braking hard to negotiate the sharp turn into our drive. What made it dangerous was a sheer drop of twenty feet into the river below the house. I opened my eyes to see the bright lights of another vehicle approaching. We had lost most of our speed by now and just managed to trickle across the path of a large lorry, with inches to spare. Dimpsie accelerated up the steep drive and ran gently into the mattress placed on its side at the back of the garage to act as a buffer.

'There we are, darling. Home at last!'

Dumbola Lodge was a solid stone house built in the last century. Going into the hall, I was surprised by the vivid familiarity of things not seen or called to mind for several years. The wallpaper with its pattern of ivy leaves had been put up before I was born. The flagstones undulated at thresholds where generations of footsteps, including my own, had worn them away. Opposite the door was a serpentine chest of drawers to which Dimpsie had applied something caustic in the days when stripped pine was all the rage. Evelyn had been cross with her for ruining

77

a good piece of eighteenth-century mahogany. To the right of it was the longcase clock that had belonged to my maternal grandmother.

Throughout my childhood I had held this clock in special affection. Above the dial were painted billowing clouds and gilded stars surrounding a cut-out semicircle in which the moon, the size of an orange, appeared according to its phases. It had small, kite-shaped eyes above fat cheeks, with lips curved up into a smile, but as a child I had discovered that when I was sad the moon's smile became a grimace of sorrow. On the day the letter came offering me a place at Brackenbury Lodge, his bright little eyes had flashed with triumph. I was too old now to believe in the existence of a secret ally. It was my guilty conscience that made me imagine a hint of reproof in the moon's expression. I sniffed the instantly recognizable smell of wet plaster, rubber mackintoshes and the fainter scent of medicated soap from the downstairs cloakroom.

'Let me look at you.' Dimpsie pulled off her red tam-o'-shanter and slung it in the direction of the hat stand. '*Fab*ulous coat, darling. Evelyn's always said that you had all the beauty in the family.'

'How unkind of her. Also untrue. You have remarkable eyes.'

They were large, light brown and transparent with good nature.

'Unkind? Evelyn? Darling, how can you say that when she's been so good to you?' My mother looked hurt.

'Oh well . . . all I meant was that you're still attractive.' I released one of her dangling silver earrings, which had become hooked on a ringlet that had once been brown and was now greyish.

Dimpsie peered into the mirror above the chest of drawers and pulled a face. 'Evelyn ticked me off the other day for letting myself go. She said she'd pay for me to go to her hairdresser but I don't know that I ought . . . she says I should use make-up but mascara always makes my eyes puff up . . . and who's going to notice anyway?'

78

Dimpsie had been my age, twenty-two, when she married my father. He had been in his final year at medical school. Kate's imminent arrival had been responsible for this catastrophic mistake. The immediate need for money put paid to his plan of specializing in epidemiology. Instead they moved to Northumberland where he went into general practice. My mother suddenly found herself with a hardworking husband, a house and a baby to look after and no idea how to do any of it. In a spirit of noblesse oblige, Evelyn had invited the new GP and his wife to dinner and my mother had wasted no time in pouring out her feelings of loneliness and helplessness.

This much I had been told by Dimpsie. I guessed that Evelyn might also have been lonely. She liked to rule and the women who stood high enough in the world to be Evelyn's friends for that reason declined to be bossed. Dimpsie's unbounded admiration for Evelyn's beauty, style, strength of character and knowledge of the world must have been flattering. She was thrilled to be asked to fill out invitations, lick stamps and make telephone calls. But I knew that Dimpsie was more than an unpaid secretary. That mysterious chemistry which dictates true friendship operated in their case. Dimpsie was incapable of deceit, she always said exactly what she thought, and I guessed that Evelyn enjoyed being able to do the same without fear of competition or criticism.

'Never mind.' Dimpsie did some alternate nostril breathing to dispel negative thinking. 'There are lots of things more important than one's appearance . . . being true to one's inner being . . . expanding one's consciousness . . .'

When Dimpsie was in her early thirties, some hippies had formed a commune in the ruined farm on the hill behind our house. The local people had complained of drugs, loud music, uncontrolled livestock and neglected children. Dimpsie alone had been enchanted by them. While Evelyn was busy sacking headmasters, reprimanding matrons for dusty windowsills and sending wife-beaters to jail, Dimpsie used to go up to the commune and sit on mattresses covered with Indian bedspreads, smoke joints, eat beans, and have long conversations about the significance of the *Tibetan Book of the Dead*. It was a sort of kindergarten, with nothing to do but be self-indulgent, and Dimpsie loved it. For the first time in her life she had found people who accepted her without wanting to change her. The hashish made everyone affectionate and giggly, which must have been in strong contrast to home.

It was a cause of great sadness when the hippies tired of emptying bucket lavatories and collecting firewood to burn under the pots of beans. One by one they drifted away into advertising and accountancy. The ruined farm was untenanted now but for feral kittens, descendants of the original cats brought by the flower children.

'Oh, blast!' Dimpsie had picked up the notepad from beside the telephone. 'Your father's had to go out on a call. Vanessa Trumball a*gain*.'

'Who's Vanessa Trumball?'

'She moved here about a year ago. She lives up at Roughsike Fell. She must be terribly lonely there on her own – her husband's left her; such a shame. I thought he was a nice man. Your father has to go up there at least twice a week. It's lucky for her he's so dedicated to his profession.'

I wanted to ask if she was young and pretty but I was afraid of causing pain.

'Never mind.' Dimpsie hung up our coats, then twirled on the spot with her knee bent and her foot stuck out behind her, a characteristic movement which I had forgotten. 'We won't wait for him. Let's have supper.'

'I must feed Siggy first and let him have a run. He's been cooped up all day.'

'Siggy?' My mother looked vaguely about the hall.

'My rabbit.' I indicated the cage on the flagstones.

'A rabbit? Oh, how sweet!'

'Don't do that!' I cried just in time to prevent bloodshed, as she bent down, finger poised to stroke him through the bars. 'He has the meanest temper. I'll take him upstairs and shut him in my room so he can run about.'

'But what will your father say?'

Tom hated animals.

'Need he know?'

'I suppose not. Not telling isn't the same as lying, is it? Shall I get him some lettuce?'

I understood that she meant Siggy.

'He'd rather have meat. Preferably raw.'

It took a while to set Siggy up with a bowl of water, some scraps of chicken breast and a litter tray. Because of being incarcerated all day, he refused to have anything to do with me and sulked among my old shoes in the bottom of my wardrobe. By the time I hobbled downstairs to the kitchen my mother had supper on the table.

'Lentil soup, darling. And homemade bread.'

I remembered the bread. Dimpsie made it herself from wholemeal flour ground by the watermill in the next valley. It required strong teeth and a stalwart colon. It was, in its own way, delicious. I had a second helping of the soup to gratify Dimpsie. My father considered food a boring necessity, which must have been discouraging for an anxious cook.

'Lovely,' I said. 'Just what I needed after such a long journey.'

'Poor darling.' She opened the Aga door and brought out a large pie. 'This'll set you up. Cabbage and Jerusalem artichokes with a layer of cheesy mashed potato on top.'

'Oh goodness! I hadn't realized there'd be anything else. I don't think I can . . .' I saw her face fall. 'All right, because it looks so tempting, I'd love just a little.'

While my mother spooned the explosive mixture on to my plate, I looked fondly at the kitchen. The walls had been stencilled with vegetables. I knew they were vegetables because I had helped Dimpsie cut them out years ago. We had had much trouble with the bulb of garlic. However we trimmed it and shaped it, it had continued to remind us of the horribly swollen scrotum my father kept in formaldehyde in his study.

'Now, darling,' said Dimpsie when I had eaten as much of the vegetable hotpot as I possibly could, 'I'll make some coffee and we can have a lovely cosy chat before Tom comes in.'

I answered her questions about my leg with vague reassurances, then I told her about my flat and *Giselle* and Lizzie and Bella and the other members of the company. Dimpsie rested her cheek on her hand and looked at me with dreaming eyes.

'It all sounds such *heaven*. Now tell me about the *men* in your life.' A note of wistfulness crept into her voice. 'I'm in the mood for a little vicarious romance.'

'I'm sorry to disappoint you, but there isn't anyone particular.' The decision not to tell her about Sebastian was made in a moment, before I had a chance to reflect. Dimpsie was the most broad-minded mother in the world but suddenly I couldn't bear even the thought of him. 'I don't really have time for men at the moment.' I yawned extravagantly. 'I'm shattered. I must go to bed. I'll see Tom at breakfast.' I saw the disappointment in her eyes. 'But before I go up you must tell me about Kate.'

Dimpsie's face brightened. She poured us both more coffee and popped a piece of halva into her mouth. 'Well, darling, it's really *rather* fascinating . . . I went to see her just before Christmas. You remember Dougall always made us take our shoes off in the porch? Well, now you have to put on plastic things like bath hats over your feet . . .'

8

I was anxious to look my best for dinner at Shottestone Manor. Luckily I had brought my best dress with me. Like many of my clothes it was a cast-off from Wardrobe. It came originally from a production of *Ondine*, Ashton's ballet about a water nymph. Now, unless you looked closely, you couldn't see the bad tear under the arm which I had spent hours mending, because the dress was made from several layers of chiffon in different shades of aquamarine and jade with a hem cut into long strips to shimmer like water. It had a high waist bound with silver braid which ran up over the narrow straps. Unfortunately the plaster cast, already quite grubby round the edges, and the black sock I wore over it to cover my bare toes seriously impaired the glamour lent me by the dress. While waiting for inspiration to effect some improvement, I wrapped a blanket round my naked shoulders and sat on my bedroom window seat to admire the view across the valley.

The hillside opposite was steep and thickly wooded. At this time of year the façade of Shottestone Manor could clearly be seen among the branches, though the distance was too great for its inhabitants to be more than moving dots. Like Dumbola Lodge it was built of grey stone but it had an altogether superior air. Two projecting wings made it an impressive size, a third storey with steep gables gave it an imposing height, and a pillared portico added gracefulness.

Isobel's bedroom had been on the top floor. As children we had sometimes signalled to each other by arrangement. You could just make out an energetically waved pillowcase as a fleck of white. Isobel had got into hot water when one had blown out of her hand and into the trees below, never to be seen again. For a brief period we had sent messages with torches using Morse code. I had swotted up all the dots and dashes, hoping to impress Rafe with my prowess. I dreamed that he might send me messages of love flashing in beams of light above the tree-tops, but of course it never happened. My exchanges with Isobel were laborious because she did not have the same incentive to learn the alphabet, so there were long intervals between letters while she looked them up. Also, having spent the day together there wasn't much to say.

Rafe's bedroom had been on the first floor. Once I had borrowed my father's telescope and trained it on Rafe's window for hours, hoping for a glimpse of my idol. I had been rewarded when he had leaned on the sill for a whole five minutes wearing an unbuttoned shirt and smoking a cigarette. I drank in the sight of his godlike head and manly chest, my heart thumping with excitement while the barrel of the telescope became damp from my perspiring fingers.

Evelyn's bedroom was on the floor below and took up three windows above the portico. Isobel had told me her parents slept in separate rooms. Even as a small child I had perceived that Kingsley worshipped Evelyn whereas my father barely tolerated my mother, yet they slept in the same bed and even shared bath water. At the time this had puzzled me.

A knock interrupted these reminiscences. Dimpsie came in.

'Just wanted to see how you were getting on. Hello, Siegfried poppet.' Siggy, who had been lying with every appearance of content on the rug beside my bed, dashed into the wardrobe as though in terror. I did not believe this for a moment.

Fear was an emotion unknown to Siggy, but he liked to be interesting.

I stood up, threw off the blanket and twirled, or rather, stomped in a circle, so she could see how I looked.

'Fabulous, darling! I *love* that dress! The sock does detract rather . . .'

'Perhaps bare toes would be better. But my nails are still growing out their bruises.'

Dancers feet are always ugly, with bunions, calluses, crooked toes, peeling bloody skin and discoloured nails.

'I'll paint them for you.' Dimpsie went away and reappeared a minute later with a box of acrylic paints. She sat on the carpet and worked away with dedication. On four nails she drew glittering stripes of gold and silver. On my big toe she managed a just recognizable Mona Lisa.

'You *are* clever!' I examined my foot approvingly.

'What a pity Tom's had to go out again. Poor Vanessa Trumball is worried about her blood pressure. You look so stunning. He'd be proud of you.'

My mother liked to maintain the fiction that my father entertained paternal feelings towards his daughters. He and I had met at breakfast that morning, not a good time for either of us. I was still tired after the journey and had slept badly. My bed was a converted paddle steamer from a derelict merry-go-round that Dimpsie had discovered long ago in a salvage yard. She had bought a little wooden bus for Kate and had converted them into beds by replacing the seats with boards and mattresses. She had painted them in bright colours and decorated our rooms to match. I had blue waves below the dado, sky and seagulls above. Kate had hedges and houses and Belisha beacons on her walls. These unusual sleeping quarters had been the envy of all our friends, but now the boat was too short and the high wooden sides delivered agonizing blows to my knees whenever I turned over. The plaster cast made things worse. A further cause of discomfort had been the turbulence caused by the gaseous vegetables. I had gone down to breakfast feeling tense and exhausted.

My father had looked up from the newspaper he was reading. 'Hello, Marigold. To what do we owe this unlooked-for condescension? If it's money I'm sorry to tell you that there's none to spare.'

I felt a violent return of all the old feelings.

'Don't be silly, Tom,' Dimpsie said before I could reply. 'I told you she'd broken her foot.'

My father glanced down at my leg. His hair, the exact colour of mine, was grizzled at the temples. Mine was straight as a pencil but his was curly and stood up in a shock above his white face, which now had a faint blush across the cheekbones where veins had broken. His once dramatic red and whiteness was merging to a generalized pink. His eyes, sharp with intelligence, looked at me through rimless hexagonally framed spectacles. 'What sort of fracture is it?'

'Comminuted.'

'I suppose you continued to walk on it after you broke it?'

'I didn't know I had. Broken it, I mean.'

He snorted and returned his eye to the page.

'What are you going to do today, darling?' Dimpsie had plopped two poached eggs on top of the wholemeal brick on my plate. 'Perhaps you ought to have a nap this afternoon so as to be sparkling for dinner with Evelyn. You can ring me when you're ready to come home. I shan't mind waiting up. I've some paperwork to do for the craft shop.'

'Aren't you coming?'

'Oh no. Evelyn said I'd find her guests too stuffy and conventional. She said they bore her to tears but she feels she has a duty to entertain the county and, besides, Kingsley likes them. She's always so unselfish.'

'Rubbish!' My father folded his paper neatly as he spoke, matching the edges precisely. 'The county could get on perfectly well without being patronized by Evelyn. What she means is, you aren't smart enough. Evelyn's a snob, but in this case I can hardly blame her. A fat, middle-aged hippy clinging to her Bohemian past, babbling about astrology and runes . . . you look and sound ridiculous.'

Though I ought to have known better, I was unable to suppress my indignation. 'How *can* you be so unkind—'

'Of course we all know what a kind daughter *you* are.' My father stood up, brushing toast crumbs from his trousers. 'When did you last visit? Was it at Christmas when your mother went down with flu? Oh, no, you were too busy. When was it? Let me see . . . perhaps two years ago when your grandmother was dying and your mother had to drive fifty miles each way to the hospital to see her? And of course the funeral wasn't sufficiently important to stop you going to New York—'

'I admit I'm a selfish beast. But that's no reason why *you* should be so nasty—'

'Please!' Dimpsie clasped a slotted spoon to her bosom and looked agitated. 'Don't let's quarrel on Marigold's first morning home. Love and peace, that's what matters.'

'I'm going to make a couple of house calls.' Tom went to the back door, took his scarf from a peg and wound it round his neck, smoothing the ends across his chest before putting on his overcoat. 'Surgery's at ten. Don't be late.'

'Oh!' Dimpsie looked anxious. 'But I made an appointment for Mrs Giddy at half-past nine. And Mr Honeybun at a quarter to. Yesterday you said you were starting at nine thirty—'

'They can wait.' Tom checked his appearance in the mirror, pulling back his lips to examine his teeth. I knew that women found my father peculiarly attractive, though he was not handsome, not to my eyes anyway. Perhaps it was his unassailable confidence they liked. 'There's nothing wrong with that ghastly woman that a little less gin won't cure. As for Honeybun, he's a ridiculous creature, puffed up with self-importance. And last week he refused to increase my overdraft. It'll serve him right to have to kick his heels in the waiting room and be coughed over by the pestilence-ridden until I'm ready to see him.' He grinned at his own reflection and went out, allowing the door to bang behind him.

I looked at Dimpsie. 'I'm sorry. I ought to have come home more. I ought to have been more help to you.'

'Nonsense, darling. You've got your own life. Your father likes to tease. He's devoted to all of us, really.'

I frowned, finding this impossible to believe.

'Tell you what, ' Dimpsie's face brightened. 'Let's have some hot chocolate. That was always your favourite, wasn't it?' I nodded to please her, though in fact I was already feeling full from the eggs and toast. 'And I know! Let's see how this evening's going to turn out.' From the shelf by the Aga she fetched a book and three two-pence pieces. 'We'll cast the *I Ching*.'

'Made it!' breathed Dimpsie.

It was our third attempt to get up the hill. The lights of Shottestone Manor glittered on the thick ice resulting from the falling temperature. Someone opened the passenger door.

'Marigold! You're an angel to come!' I recognized Isobel's voice, though in the darkness I had only an impression of a pale face and an arm half inside the car. 'Hello, Dimpsie. Sweet of you to bring her. I'll get someone to drive her home.'

'Oh, it's all right. I don't mind turning out—'

'Don't argue. I'm freezing to death.' She laughed, a sound I hadn't heard for years. But it was so familiar that my skin tingled faintly with the pleasure of recognition. 'I'm practically naked to the waist. Buck up, Marigold, or I'll shatter into a thousand pieces.'

'You go in. I can't hurry because of my leg.'

But Isobel insisted on helping me. By the time we had reached the hall door she was shuddering with cold, though I had hobbled as quickly as the cast allowed and had nearly fallen over twice.

'For God's sake, don't break the other one. Not before you've had dinner, anyway. I asked for Charlotte Malakoff for pud, specially for you. It always used to be your favourite.'

'You didn't? Not really? But how truly kind! Fancy you remembering that.'

'It *was* thoughtful of me, wasn't it! Now stop a minute and stand under the light and let me look at you.'

The hall was still the brilliant shade of Chinese Emperor yellow I had always admired. Isobel and I paused beneath the brass lantern and stared at each other. I was quite as curious as she. Isobel was taller than me by four inches and her frame was much bigger than mine. She was not fat but curvy, with a pronounced bosom I envied. Her movements were sinuous, so the overall impression was one of litheness, like a well-fed cat. Her thick fair hair was bobbed at her shoulders and framed a long Grecian nose, delicately arched brows and slanting grey eyes. It was a lovely face. She used to complain that her lips were too thin and her chin too small. As her face was rarely still, these defects, if they existed, were insignificant. This particular evening she was looking tremendously chic in a strapless dress of dark green moiré. Round her neck was a string of green stones cut into large cubes and linked by gold threads. I felt suddenly conscious that my dress was second-hand and mended, my pearls fake and my leg wrapped in plaster.

'You delicious little creature!' She seized my earlobe and pinched it hard. 'I've a good mind to send you straight home. Everyone's going to be looking at *you* instead of me.'

She took my crutches from me and rested them against the massive hall table. I got that tingling feeling again when I saw it. Once Isobel and I had pretended to feed jam tarts to the lions that propped up the marble top, and there had been a row as apparently the table was by someone important called William Sussex. Or was it William Kent? Apparently it had taken Evelyn two hours and a packet of cotton buds to remove the jam.

'Where did you get this *gorg*eous coat?' Isobel helped me out of it. The hall was chilly despite a log fire. It had never been possible to heat Shottestone Manor adequately. I tried not to shiver too obviously.

'I borrowed it from a friend. You're looking wonderful.'

'Oh, this old thing. It does for Mummy's dreary dinners. But really, Marigold, it's too annoying. How dare you make your old friends feel shabby by dropping down among us, wearing something that makes you look a spirit briefly visiting earth? Honestly, is that a fair return for my unselfishness about the pudding? You know I hate black cherries.'

'Do you really think it will do? It's only an old thing from Wardrobe. I had to steep the bits under the arms in Omo to get the sweat stains out.'

This was true. But I heard the old placatory tone in my voice.

'It's perfect. Come into the drawing room and meet the others.' She lowered her voice as she handed back the crutches. 'Did Dimpsie tell you about Rafe?'

I nodded.

'He's been so good. You'd hardly know he's been through unimaginable hell. He was completely deaf for a while but thank God his hearing's come back. Don't mention wars or people dying if you can help it. He's as brave as a lion but anyone would be knocked off their perch by something like that.'

'Of course.'

'As for Daddy, just smile and pretend everything's fine. Oh Lord, it doesn't sound as if it's going to be much fun, does it? And the others are such bores . . . Never mind, we'll be able to have a good talk while the men are sitting over their port. I've got masses to tell you. Come on.'

9

The other guests were standing close to the fire in the drawing room. Evelyn was conspicuous because of her formidable chic. Her hair, cut short, was silvery white and had been for years. Though she was nearly sixty her skin was hardly lined and her figure was excellent. On Evelyn's face, Isobel's features, the slanting eyes, the Grecian nose and the slightly receding chin, had sharpened and refined further with age. She reminded me of a beautiful hawk. She wore a full-length black-velvet-flocked chiffon dress, beautifully cut with a wide satin belt fastened with a diamante clasp. The drawing room, with its panelled walls painted several shades of grey, was the perfect background for her. I would have liked to be invisible for a few minutes so I could glide about uninterrupted and reacquaint myself with the furniture and objects in this most elegant of rooms.

'Marigold!' Evelyn advanced with outstretched arms. 'My poor wounded girl!' She enfolded me briefly in *Après L'Ondée*, the scent she had always worn. 'It's been too long, darling. I don't count that marvellous ballet. Such a crush and I was in a hurry. Too lovely, all those swans . . .' There had not been so much as a cygnet in *The Firebird* but I knew better than to contradict her. She ran her eye quickly over my dress. 'Hm.

Unusual. A good colour with your hair.' Sheltering me with her arm as within a palisade, she turned back to her guests. 'Everyone, this is Marigold Savage. I have known Marigold since she was a baby and I'm very proud of her. She is a prima ballerina.'

Most of the other guests looked blank but one man said, 'Not really! Well, this is exciting!' He stepped forward to shake my hand. He had pale wispy hair and a thin, lanky body. The only substantial thing about him was his enormous nose. 'Duncan Vardy. I'm something of a balletomane. Marigold Savage.' He wrinkled his nose as he thought, exposing a forest of nostril hair. 'I can't quite . . . which company are you with?'

'The Lenoir Ballet Company,' I said. 'And I'm not a prima ballerina, I'm afraid, just a principal dancer.'

'Jolly good.' He laughed uncertainly.

'Duncan is a writer,' said Evelyn. 'I'm reading his most fascinating book at the moment about . . .' she paused, hardly perceptibly, 'the Cosmic Visions of Volupsà.'

Evelyn liked to leaven the dough of hunting Tories with the yeast of artists and intellectuals.

'Voluspà,' corrected Duncan with an air of patience. He must have been used to people not quite grasping his subject. 'Are you interested in Old Norse, Miss Savage?'

'I'm sure I would be if I knew anything about it.'

Duncan's pale eyes gleamed. 'You have heard, I'm sure, of the Nornor.' He sucked his lower lip and looked at me expectantly.

'The gnaw-gnaw?'

'Yes, the Fates of Scandinavian myth. They spin the threads of man's destiny and when they decide that his end has come they cut the thread.' Duncan made a snipping movement with two fingers in illustration. They are usually represented as harbingers of suffering and misfortune. They tend the Yggdrasil.'

'Egg-drazzle?'

'Ig. *Ig*. It's an evergreen ash that connects heaven, earth and

92

hell. At its foot is a fountain of wonderful virtues. In the tree are an eagle, a squirrel and four stags. A dragon gnaws at its roots.'

'Really!' I tried to imagine it but there were too many components for a clear picture.

'Marigold.' A jolt ran through my nervous system as I felt a hand on my elbow. Rafe – my idol, my *prince lointain*, the top brick of my childhood chimney – stood beside me, holding a glass of champagne. 'Come and sit by the fire and rest that leg. You can talk to her later, Duncan.' He smiled down at me. 'Look, she's blue with cold.'

I smiled back. 'I hope not literally.'

Rafe was taller even than I remembered him, perhaps six foot three inches, and his shoulders were proportionately broad.

'Yes, your arms are the colour of forget-me-nots. It's perfectly charming.' He kept hold of my elbow and steered me over to the fireplace. Everyone was obliged to move out of the way because a person on crutches takes up a lot of room. 'Here we are.' He indicated a low stool before the fender, took the crutches from me and laid them on the rug before the hearth, thus securing the only two cubic metres of really warm air exclusively for us. I sat down gratefully. 'Move up a bit. I don't want to crush that pretty dress. Duncan's terribly disappointed. You'll have to be nice to him after dinner.'

'I'm sure he isn't.'

'Don't argue. A man knows these things. This is cosy, isn't it? Can't you feel envious eyes trained on our slowly thawing backs? You needn't thank me – you're just an excuse. I haven't been home long enough to acclimatize myself to steaming breath, frozen lavatories and ice on the breakfast milk.'

'I'm delighted to be of use to someone. Recently I've been nothing but a nuisance.'

I allowed myself to look full into his face. If he'd been an actor he would have got all the David Niven parts. He had fair hair and blue eyes but this softness was contradicted by the masculinity of the high forehead, straight nose and firm chin. Running from his temple to his jawbone was a thin red scar. This added a singularity to his appearance, which might otherwise have been too conventionally handsome to be truly magnetic. My tastes had become more exotic since we had last met. But I enjoyed looking at the Phoebus Apollo of my girlhood.

'A nuisance? I don't believe you ever could be.' Rafe smiled, making the scar crinkle attractively. A group of strangers finding themselves trapped in a lift or marooned on a desert island would have appointed him their leader without hesitation. 'Well, Miss Marigold Savage.' He smiled more broadly, showing strong white teeth, and a teasing light appeared in his eyes. He was more magnetic than I had first thought. 'Evelyn tells me you're becoming famous. I wonder if some day biographers will ask me about the carroty little thing I once knew who turned scarlet whenever she was spoken to.'

His voice was attractive too, light and good humoured. I imagined him, debonair in cricket flannels, acknowledging with a wave of his bat the cheers of the crowd as he made a century and won the match.

'How unfair!' I grinned to show I didn't mind being teased. 'By the time I was old enough to notice, you'd already gone through the stage of being gauche and gangling.'

How well he would look in the cockpit of a Spitfire, wiping the sweat from his eyes as he fired off round after round, single-handedly saving a phalanx of crippled bombers . . .

'Gauche, undoubtedly, but I deny that I was ever gangling. As a child I was short and fat. I didn't grow until I was about twelve. And I ate lots of tuck to compensate for having my head pushed down the lavatory every day at prep school.'

'You've made up for it since.'

'You, on the other hand, have scarcely begun.'

'Actually I'm quite big for a dancer.'

'The others must be leprechauns. How did you break your leg?'

'Foot. I landed too heavily. Nothing more than a stress fracture to begin with. But I went on dancing on it, that was the trouble.'

'No doubt you had a good reason for what seems to the uninitiated like idiocy?'

I told Rafe about Miko Lubikoff, explaining as briefly as I could why it was so important.

'Of course you want to be the best. I can understand that. When we're told as children that it's the taking part that counts, we all know that's bunkum.'

'Well, you have to be better than the others or you won't get the good roles. But, actually, what you really yearn to do above all else is to express something beyond just a beautiful line or speed or technique. You want to try to reach some sort of ideal of artistic perfection. You never can, of course, but you have to try.' Rafe was looking at me with a curious expression. I had the impression he wasn't really listening to me, which was just as well because what I had just said probably sounded horribly pretentious to someone not in the ballet world. 'What do *you* really yearn to do?'

'Me? I don't know that I've ever been ambitious, apart from silly ephemeral things like winning the boat race or beating the next chap at tennis. I've never had a great mission in life. I'm just a simple soldier. Or was. Now I suppose I'm a simple estate manager, a glorified farmer . . . Hello, Father.' Rafe stood up as his father approached. 'Like to sit here?'

Kingsley Preston had changed so much I hardly recognized him. I remembered him as a strong, upright man, wearing his years well. Now he stooped and his slack lower jaw meant that his mouth hung slightly open. The most disturbing change was his expression. Once sanguine and self-assured, this evening it was troubled. 'No, my boy. No, thank you.' His lips trembled as he spoke. 'I prefer to roam.'

'You remember Marigold, Father? Dr Savage's daughter,' Rafe added, seeing that Kingsley was looking vague.

'Savage. Yes. Consulted him last week about my prostate. Daughter, you say?' He glanced at me again as though baffled, then his expression cleared. 'I remember! Went off to be a singer. Yes, a sweet little thing. How are you?'

'Very well, thank you, sir. I'm sorry I can't get up very easily . . . my leg . . .'

He pressed his hand on my shoulder. 'Stay where you are, my dear. So you've been in the wars, eh? What happened?'

'I'm a dancer actually. I landed clumsily.'

'Really? That's too bad. Rotten luck. So the singing didn't work out, then? Never mind. I'd rather watch a pretty girl dance than hear her sing any day. Well, well, little Miss Savage.' He smiled, seeming genuinely pleased to see me. 'So you've come back to play with Isobel.'

I laughed, assuming this to be a joke, and Kingsley looked gratified. 'Sweet little thing. You must have another glass of champagne, my dear.' His eyes became glassy and he dropped his chin, muttering into his chest, 'I'd better go and pee. It takes some doing getting through dinner these days.' He shuffled away.

'He's changed, hasn't he?' said Rafe, turning his head to look anxiously after his father. 'But then . . . so have we all.'

'Isobel hasn't.'

'No. She's still the same. Just as . . . headstrong.'

I wondered what he meant but, before I could think of a tactful way of asking him, dinner was announced.

'Hello, Spendlove.' I gave my hand to the butler, who was waiting in the hall to direct guests to lavatories if they required them. He had been employed at Shottestone since before I was born.

'Miss Marigold! I heard you was coming. You're looking bonny. Apart from the leg, that is.'

'Thank you. How are you?'

'A bit of bother with me teeth and I don't see so well as I

did, but we must expect that.' His upper lids drooped heavily, bloodhound-like, obscuring most of his eyes; his nose was heavily veined. Evelyn had once forbidden him to drink any more whisky, but he had been so miserable, weeping over the breakfast table and into the silver polish, that she had been forced to withdraw the prohibition. 'Me feet are the trouble. The doctor says it's gout. If there's time you might think of popping down to the kitchen to have a word with Mrs Capstick.'

'Of course I will. I'd love to see her again. How is she?'

'Her stomick's playing up still but you don't hear her grumble. Better go in, Miss Marigold, or I'll get a ticking off for keeping you hanging about in the cold.'

I glanced up at the stairs, remembered coming down them in my first grown-up party dress, seeing Rafe standing by the front door kissing a girl called Olive Fincham, running upstairs again to cry, my whole evening spoiled.

The dining room looked just the same. It was dark red with lots of Georgian silver and mahogany. Isobel and I were sitting opposite each other, two places down from Evelyn.

'Would you say grace, Archdeacon?' said Evelyn.

The man on my left began an oration in Latin. His voice had a peculiar muffled boom, as though he kept it locked in a chamber inside his chest. The dining room had previously been hallowed ground, only ventured upon for Isobel's birthday parties. Mrs Capstick had made magical cakes. Had Rafe attended these occasions? I glanced up and found that he was looking at me. Next to him was a woman in mustard crepe with a crumpled corsage of pink silk roses. She saw me return his smile and looked affronted.

Grace over, I gave my attention to the man on my right. He had a pale rhubarb complexion, bulging dark eyes, a bald head and a prominent nose emerging from long stiff whiskers, the nearest thing I had ever seen to a prawn in evening dress. I saw from his place card that his name was Sir Ibbertson Darkly. He told me he had worked for the MOD (I had no idea what this was but he made it sound important) until his retirement. He was now an amateur historian (by implication rather brilliant). He told me about his career, his dead wife's saintliness, his children, his tastes in music, literature, painting and dogs. He was collecting material for the definitive book about Hadrian's Wall. Whenever I tried to say anything, he interrupted with more tales from the Darkly family chronicles.

'Gibbon,' I put in as he paused to swallow his last forkful of mushroom soufflé, 'says that we should not estimate the greatness of Rome solely by the rapidity and extent of its conquests. Do you agree?'

I knew this sentence by heart because it came at the beginning of Chapter Two and I must have read it at least four hundred times in an attempt to get to grips with the beastly thing. I must admit I was pleased with the way it came out trippingly on my tongue, as though I knew what I was talking about. The amateur historian turned to look at me, his prawn eyes wide with shock, as though I had said that I intended to lie naked on the table and make love with every man present.

'My dear young lady,' he began, 'how . . . what . . . Gibbon, you say . . . well, now . . . it may be so . . .' He stared into his empty ramekin and was silent.

For my first attempt at intelligent conversation, this was a disappointing result. Evelyn, who had been toying with her soufflé until the last guest finished, put down her fork and two girls in black and white uniforms, who must have been hired for the occasion, appeared like magic to whisk away our plates. I remembered the bell under the table near Evelyn's foot. Isobel had once hidden beneath the tablecloth during a lunch party and pressed it at random, occasioning much confusion until we gave ourselves away by laughing.

The next course was brought in. Mindful of the etiquette Evelyn had drummed into us as teenagers, I turned to the archdeacon. His card said, The Venerable James Cogan. He was a man of about fifty with a thick head of iron-grey hair. He was wearing clerical black and his shoulders were sprinkled with dandruff, which drifted down like snow whenever he shook his head for emphasis. I would have pitied this affliction had I not taken an immediate dislike to him. Having piled his plate with roast potatoes he ate quickly, almost gobbling as he told me about his unrivalled collection of incunabula. I had no idea what an incunabulum was but he never gave me a chance to ask. At last I tumbled to the fact that they were old books. I cheered up. Here was a perfect opportunity to display my newly acquired learning.

'Does *The Pilgrim's Progress* count as incunabula?' I managed to slip in as he shovelled down a grouse breast.

'Oh, *no*.' Another shower of dandruff. 'Bunyan wrote *The Pilgrim's Progress* in . . . ah-hem . . . 1700 so it is much too late—'

'Actually,' I interrupted with a swiftness born of certainty, 'the first part was written between 1667 and 1672.' Archdeacon Cogan seemed to flinch. Remembering that I had rushed the gate with the historian, I decided to take a chattier line, so as not to startle him with my unexpected erudition. 'I didn't quite understand what Bunyan meant when he said it was abominable to make religion a stalking horse. What is a stalking horse, exactly?'

The archdeacon dabbed his greasy lips with his napkin and bared his teeth in a smile that was so devoid of warmth it was like the opening of a tomb. 'It is . . . ah-hem . . . a device by which one may conceal one's true intention. By hiding behind his horse, a hunter may deceive his quarry.'

'Mm. I think Talkative's so much more interesting than Faithful, don't you?' The archdeacon looked dazed so I went on quickly. 'Faithful's rather a dreary, preachy sort of character.'

The archdeacon prodded at the skeleton of his grouse and frowned. 'It has been some years since I last read the work.'

'I didn't like the bit about the robin and the spider at all,' I continued. 'Everyone knows that robins don't have a sense of right and wrong and cheerfully eat anything they can get.'

He shot me a doubtful look, as though he suspected that I was completely off my head. The pudding was brought in so he gave his attention to Evelyn. Though it was my go for Sir Ibbertson Darkly, he went on talking to his other neighbour, so I concentrated instead on enjoying the Charlotte Malakoff. After the last delicious mouthful I found I was still between two backs, so I examined the portraits of Kingsley's ancestors and tried to look as though I was enjoying myself. Where had I gone wrong, I wondered? Usually I had so little to say on any subject other than ballet that I was reduced to inane interjections like 'really?' 'gosh!' and 'I'd never thought of *that*.' Could it be, I asked myself, that men liked to do all the talking themselves? Could it be that they were simply not interested in anyone else's opinions?

Evelyn's vigilant eye had seen that I was neglected.

'Marigold's career has been of the greatest interest to me,' she said to the table in general. 'It was my idea that she and Isobel should attend dancing classes. Marigold showed talent from the first. Isobel was also exceptionally graceful but she grew too tall.'

'I was crap, Mummy,' said her daughter. Evelyn closed her eyes briefly as though she felt the first pang of a headache. 'Really. I couldn't do a *tendu* to save my life.'

She sent me a look of smiling complicity across the table.

'Those are very pretty pearls, Marigold.' Evelyn seemed determined to shower me with approval.

'Thank you. I bought them in a junk shop for fifty pee—'

'Wearing them next to the skin,' Evelyn interrupted, 'is the only way to keep them glowing. The warmth, you know.'

'Apparently the same's true of ivory,' said Isobel. 'The only trouble is, when it gets warm it gives off a smell like semen. Rather embarrassing, mustn't it be, to find yourself stinking like a tart?'

A perceptible shudder ran round the table. Duncan laughed nervously, then, seeing Evelyn's face, broke off in mid-chuckle. Evelyn looked at Mustard Crepe and nodded, the signal for the women to depart.

Isobel took my elbow as I made my way slowly into the hall. 'You poor darling. Not only crippled but bored stiff. Such is the price paid by Mummy's darlings.'

'I'm really too impoverished and obscure to qualify,' I said, and instantly regretted it because it seemed so insulting to Evelyn.

'You're an artist and they're allowed to be poor. I can assure you Mummy definitely sees you as a trophy.' Isobel changed the subject. 'What are your plans?'

'I'm going to stay here until the cast comes off. Another five weeks. What about you?'

'Oh, I'm here for the duration. There are tremendous ructions afoot. I can't wait to tell you my news. You'll never believe it but I'm going to—'

'Isobel, come and take round the coffee cups.' There was a sharpness in Evelyn's tone as she swept past us on her way to the drawing room.

'I'll just go and say hello to Mrs Capstick.'

'All right. Don't be long. You must save me from the old cats.'

I limped in the direction of the kitchen. Mrs Capstick was sitting in her chair by the Aga, her legs stretched out, her work done. The two girls who were giggling over the washing up stared at me in surprise when I kissed her.

'How are you, my pet?' She smiled up at me. 'I knew you'd trouble yourself to come and say how do. You always was a dear girl. You're too thin. Don't they feed you properly?'

'Nobody cooks like you. Dinner was wonderful. Particularly the Charlotte Malakoff.'

'I had to hunt through my old books to find the recipe. Madam says it's too fattening but Miss Isobel begged her. All them layers of butter and cream and sugar . . . whip . . . whip . . . whip . . . my poor arm . . . excuse me, dear.' She took a swig from the dark brown bottle that stood on the warming plate of the Aga. 'It's my stomach as does play up so.'

Mrs Capstick's stomach was like Nelson's eye patch, a popular fiction. Everyone knew she had been addicted for years to Collis Browne's Mixture. Her lids drooped.

'It was so kind of you to make it for me.'

'Bless you, my love, I enjoyed doing it. You can have too much fruit salad . . . not like the old days when you children was little . . . plenty of good food . . . the sort Mr Preston likes . . . steak and kidney pudding and steamed treacle sponge. Now it's all consommé and grilled . . . chops . . .'

Her eyes closed. I would have tiptoed away but it was impossible in my condition. I clomped back to the drawing room. There was no sign of Isobel. I took up my former position on the stool by the fire and spent twenty minutes watching my goose pimples subside while pretending to listen with interest as Evelyn and the two older women discussed the inconveniences of living in large old houses, as though they might for a single moment contemplate living in anything else.

'Hello, Marigold.' Rafe and the other men had come into the drawing room. I was gratified to see that he made a beeline for me. 'What's it like to be back in the fold?'

He gave me his teasing smile again, which was magnetic enough to bring back a few goose pimples. I wondered which fold he meant – the inner circle blessed by Evelyn's approval or Northumberland generally? Or perhaps the bosom of my own family?

Before I could answer, Kingsley had wandered over. 'Hello, young lady. You look chilly. Rafe, put another log on the fire. We can't have Miss . . . er . . . Miss . . . feeling cold.'

'This is Marigold, Father. You remember. Dr Savage's daughter.'

'Savage.' Kingsley looked puzzled. Then his face brightened. 'Ah yes. Consulted him last week about my . . . my . . . that thing that begins with a P. Daughter. Yes, now I remember. Sweet little thing. Went off to be a singer. How are you, my dear?'

'Very well, thank you, sir.'

'Good, good. Delighted to see you.' He patted me quite hard on the head and wandered away again.

'Move up.' Rafe sat down beside me. 'You see how it is with my father. But he seems reasonably happy. Do you think anyone will notice if I take my shoes off and thaw out my feet? You won't mind, will you? Socks clean on this evening.'

'Of course I don't mind.'

He unlaced one speckless patent leather shoe and held his foot, clad in a black silk sock, before the blaze. The foot was large, as befitted a tall man, with straight toes. He had straight, strong fingers, too, with square, well-kept nails and no doubt a straight mind, open and honourable. It might have been all the wine I had drunk but the idea of a man who was chock-full of moral fibre and who would always get you out of a hole was fast growing on me. He was neither exotic nor a dancer, but he had a polished assurance that was headily romantic. The moment I thought this I told myself not to be a fool.

'Ah, Rafe. I've been wanting to talk to you.' Sir Ibbertson had come up behind us. He inserted his bulk between us and the fire. Rafe was obliged to stand up. He kicked his shoe under the stool.

'You've been in Northern Ireland, your mother tells me. What's the answer in the case of these wretched IRA hunger-strikers? The lowest form of emotional blackmail, not to put too fine a point on it!'

Rafe smiled politely. 'You'll have to forgive me, sir. It would be more than my life is worth to talk politics in Evelyn's drawing room. It's one of her cardinal rules.'

'What?' Sir Ibbertson looked round and saw that his hostess was busy handing the chocolates to the archdeacon. 'Oh, never mind that. She can't hear us. What's the government thinking of, letting these men make martyrs of themselves, that's what I want to know?'

Rafe stopped smiling. 'I suppose they don't have any choice in the matter.'

'Nonsense. They could get them into hospital and force-feed them.'

'I believe there's a law against that. Anyway, it really isn't something I'm qualified to give an opinion about.'

'But you spent time there. You know how those bog-trotters think.'

'The British army are the last people the Irish are going to confide in. It's a very difficult situation with a long, complicated history. Best left to politicians.' He turned to me. 'Can I get you some more coffee?'

The amateur historian seemed to be prompted by an imp of Satan. 'If we all took that attitude, we'd end up illiterate zanies. I consider it the duty of educated men to inform themselves on the subjects of the day and to have an opinion. What about our soldiers who've been blown up – murdered – in Northern Ireland?'

I heard a faint rattling. Rafe's hand – the one that held the coffee cup – was trembling. He put up the other hand to still it. 'Unless you've lived there for several years – I don't mean as a soldier but among the people – your opinion isn't worth having.'

All this time I had been trying to think of a way to stop Sir Ibbertson from goading Rafe. Now, seeing that Rafe's face was ashen and his eyes were glistening, I said, 'We took *La Sylphide* to Dublin once. Such a lovely city . . . all those beautiful eighteenth-century houses . . . I wish you'd tell me more about Hadrian's Wall.'

Sir Ibbertson, red in the face now and more like a boiled prawn than ever, ignored me and addressed Rafe in an offended tone. 'I'm sorry, but I don't agree with you—'

'Fine!' Rafe almost shouted, and I saw that Evelyn's guests were looking in our direction.

At that moment Isobel rushed between us and put her arm

104

through Rafe's. 'Silence, please!' she called. 'I have an important announcement to make.' She laughed, rather uneasily I thought. 'You're all extraordinarily privileged to be the first to know. Mummy, Daddy, Everyone! . . . I'm engaged to be married.'

10

'That was a dreadful evening.'

Rafe drove slowly, carefully, using the gears to brake on the steep bits. I sneaked a glance at his profile and saw he was smiling. From the back seat came excited barks. Rafe's dog, Buster, having been shut up in the boot room all evening was thrilled to be allowed to accompany us on our midnight journey.

'Not for me. I enjoyed seeing you all again. And the food was lovely. Except I feel so guilty that you've had to turn out so late and in this awful weather.'

Snow was blowing into the windscreen, making it impossible to see more than a few feet ahead.

'Shut up, Buster! I told you. It's a pleasure. I like driving. I like driving with you.'

'Thank you.' I held my breath as we came to the hairpin bend but Rafe took us safely round it. 'I can't think why Dimpsie hasn't answered the telephone,' I said for the thousandth time.

At a quarter to twelve, when Spendlove was staggering into the hall under a weight of coats and the other guests were delivering polite speeches of appreciation and gratitude, I had refused all offers of lifts, explaining that my mother was waiting up with the express intention of acting as chauffeur. I had dialled our number several times and let it ring what seemed like ages.

Evelyn and Kingsley went to bed, leaving Isobel, Rafe and me in the drawing room. There was plenty to talk about and the time went swiftly enough between fruitless telephone calls, but I was uncomfortably aware that they must be longing for me to go. At last, when Isobel yawned with a sort of groaning sound, I capitulated and Rafe went to bring his car round from the stableyard to the front door.

'Oh, Isobel.' I had put my arms round her neck and hugged her. 'It's been so lovely to see you again and I hope – I'm *sure* you're going to be wonderfully happy.'

'Of course I shall. Goodnight, darling. Promise you'll come and meet Conrad as soon as he arrives?'

'The minute I'm asked.'

'It was a memorable evening, wasn't it?' I said to Rafe as we reached the bottom of the valley and started to climb the other side. 'We shall none of us forget it.'

Evelyn, of course, had been the person most affected by Isobel's bombshell. When Isobel had announced her engagement I had looked immediately at Evelyn's face and seen it blanche. Several seconds of silence followed Isobel's announcement, before the archdeacon said, 'Well, well, Isobel. You have . . . ah-hem . . . surprised us.'

'Certainly,' said Mustard Crepe, who I had by then identified as the archdeacon's wife. 'Evelyn, my dear, how inscrutable you've been.' This was generous, as it was obvious that Evelyn had been as surprised as the rest of us. 'May we ask, who is the fortunate young man?'

I have never met anyone who did smiling rage as well as Evelyn. Her diamonds were flashing on her chest as she breathed fast. 'I assure you, Fanny, I am as much in the dark as any of you. I suppose it must be Harry Cunningham . . . a charming boy, devoted to Isobel . . . Kingsley and Harry's father were at school together—'

'Quite wrong, Mummy.' Isobel's face was lit by excitement. 'His name is Conrad Lerner.'

'Conrad . . . Lerner.' Evelyn mouthed the syllables as though she was eating bitter almonds.

'Will someone explain what's going on?' Kingsley asked plaintively.

'Isobel is telling us about the young man to whom she has become engaged.' The archdeacon's wife took charge of the situation as smoothly as though this was a meeting of the Mother's Union which threatened to get out of hand. Her tone was emphatic, almost severe. 'We are all delighted, naturally, but there seems to be some mystery.'

'No mystery at all,' said Isobel. 'Conrad's just the sort of man any girl might want to marry. He's very clever and very nice and very, very rich.'

'Conrad.' Kingsley wrinkled his face in perplexity. 'Conrad.' He looked helpless. 'Do I know him?'

'No, Daddy. I met him in London three months ago. At a party. We spent a brilliant week together. We had the most enormous fun. Then he went back to Germany. We kept in touch, of course. A few days ago he rang up, asking me to marry him. I said yes. So now you know all about it.' She looked triumphant but I saw that she was tense, anticipating attack from all sides.

'But Isobel,' Evelyn's voice had more than a tinge of anger to it now. 'Who exactly is this man? Who are his family? What is he doing in Germany if he has engaged himself to you?'

'Goodness! So many questions!' Isobel walked over to the drinks tray and poured herself a large brandy. 'He's in Germany because that's where he lives when he isn't in London or New York. He *is* German, you see. As to his family, I don't believe he has any.'

'But Isobel, my dear.' The Archdeacon's wife had taken over again seeing that Evelyn was having difficulty in ordering her thoughts. 'Was that quite wise? To engage yourself to man without family, of whom you and your parents know nothing?'

'Of course he must have *some* family,' put in Sir Ibbertson. 'Everyone has, be they never so humble.'

108

'What I meant was, they're all dead. His grandparents and all the rest of that generation died in concentration camps. And his mother and father were killed in a plane crash when he was eight. He was brought up by his uncle Charles who was the only relation he had left. He died last year so Conrad truly hasn't any family. Sad, isn't it?' Isobel did not look in the least sorry, only defiant.

Evelyn closed her eyes.

'Very sad,' said a girl who had been standing on the outskirts of the group. Her hair was cropped into a short back and sides, like a schoolboy's, and she wore an unbecoming brown dress with a halter neck that emphasized the squareness of her shoulders. All I knew of her so far was that her name was Bunty Lumbe. 'He must be a very interesting person.'

I liked her for this attempt to lighten the encircling gloom of disapproval, but Isobel rounded on her.

'Interesting? I hate that sort of morbid curiosity that finds people interesting just because they've had awful things happen to them.'

Bunty looked alarmed. 'I didn't mean . . . all I meant was . . . I don't think I've ever met a German.'

'Never been able to take to them, you know, not since the last shemozzle.' Kingsley had been something, a major perhaps or a colonel, in the last war. 'Lost a lot of damned fine men. But I suppose the same's true for them.'

'Conrad is a Jew, Daddy.' Isobel's tone was one of exaggerated patience. 'His people were on the side you were fighting for.'

'Does he speak English?' asked the archdeacon.

'A smattering. I shall learn Yiddish. *Oy, oy! Nach a mool!*' She grinned.

The archdeacon and his wife exchanged glances of absolute horror and everyone else looked grave, as though Isobel had said she was going to have to live in a ghetto and eat rats.

'What am I thinking of?' Evelyn roused herself as if from a

109

trance. She assumed an air of grim resolution. 'Ring for Spendlove someone. We must have some champagne. A toast to Isobel and –' she gritted her teeth – 'Conrad.'

'I do admire your mother,' I said to Rafe as we approached the bottom of our drive. 'Don't slow down for the bend if you can help it. If there's ice you have to take it at a run or you can't get all the way up the drive.' I shut my eyes and held on to the door handle in case we went over the edge into the river. I had read somewhere recently that, contrary to received opinion, you must get out as fast as you can and not wait for the car to fill with water. Would my cast weigh me down like divers' leaded boots? Don't scream . . . go on talking . . . pretend it's all right . . . pretend you aren't going to die . . . 'It must have been a tremendous shock for her – not having met this man – having it sprung on her in front of all those people.' I felt the wheels spinning, imagined us sliding sideways down . . . down . . . 'I expect they'll like him very much,' I heard my voice rise to a squeak, '. . . once they get to know him.'

'It's all right. Just a little skid. We're quite safe. And it seems to have silenced Buster.'

Buster had his paws on the back of my seat and was panting down my neck. The warmth of his breath was comforting.

'Of course you don't mean that,' Rafe continued. 'About my parents liking Conrad. Xenophobia is canon law at Shottestone. I begged her to wait until we'd all met him before agreeing to marry him, but you know how impulsive she is. She said she was the one who was going to live with him and it didn't matter what the rest of us thought. Which is nonsense, of course. One can hardly avoid seeing a great deal of one's in-laws.'

It seemed Rafe was the only person Isobel had discussed her engagement with. This did not surprise me. She had always set great store by her brother's opinion. Worshipping at the same altar ought to have brought us closer together as children, but I think in those days she had resented me as a coreligionist in case I drew Rafe's attention away from her. Not that I ever did.

'It will be nice for Isobel to have a lot of money.'

'You shock me, Marigold! What a mercenary pair you are!'

After everyone else had gone home, Isobel had dwelt for some time on the considerable riches of her betrothed.

I hastened to explain myself. 'I didn't mean it was the most important thing. I'd marry a shepherd with nothing but a dog and a crook and a hut on the moors if I loved him. But as I haven't met Conrad, I don't yet know what else there is to like about him.'

'Here we are.' Rafe pulled up outside Dumbola Lodge. 'Love is a state of madness. If money comes into it I doubt if there's much passion.'

I wondered if Rafe was speaking from experience. He was thirty-two. Naturally there must have been attachments. I felt something wet and hot in my ear. It was a long tongue.

Rafe turned to reprove Buster. 'Bad boy! Down, sir.'

'I don't mind.'

'He mustn't be allowed to lick people's faces. What bothers me,' he went on, 'is that this fellow means nothing more than an escape route to Isobel. It's hardly a sound basis for marriage.'

I was flattered that he should take me so thoroughly into his confidence. During all those years that he had been a fixed star in my imagination, he could only have thought of me as a silly little girl. If he had thought of me at all. 'What's she escaping from?'

Rafe was silent for a time. 'From home . . .' He spoke with an air of reluctance as though the words were being forced out of him. 'From Evelyn . . .'

'But surely that wouldn't need something so drastic as marriage? She could go back to London. She had a job, didn't she?'

'Yes. But she wasn't happy.' He turned off the engine. 'I don't know why I'm boring you with my family's concerns when you ought to be tucked up in bed. Come on, I'll help you in. And perhaps we'd better clear up the mystery of the telephone that didn't ring in the night-time.'

111

'There's only one in the house, in my father's study. He sleeps there when he's on call. The ring's always switched to low so you can't hear it from anywhere else except the drawing room if both the doors are open.'

'That's very considerate of him.' Rafe got out of the car and leaned into the back for my crutches. Buster gave me a farewell lick.

The truth was, this arrangement was entirely in my father's own interest. Even when he was not on duty, patients tended to ring him in the small hours of the morning to say that they had felt a slight twinge on bending over to pick the milk bottle from the doorstep that morning and might it be a heart attack? Or the cough which they had had for several weeks might be cancer and ought they to have an emergency chest X-ray? It was perfectly reasonable not to want to be dragged from sleep in order to prescribe aspirin for someone with thumb-ache, but the telephone had always been the cause of much vexation in our household. When my father was at home he guarded the privacy of his study with ferocity, as though it contained a treasure chest and he was the dog with eyes as big as mill-wheels, so we could only use the telephone when he was out.

We tiptoed into the hall. At least Rafe did, and I swung my leg and crutches with careful deliberation. A soft light shone through the open drawing room. We went in. A table lamp illumined the sorry scene. My mother was stretched out on the sofa, her neck crumpled against one arm of it, her bare feet projecting over the other. A glass and a bottle stood on the table beside her. Her eyes were closed and she was breathing slowly and heavily.

'I'd better wake her,' I said. 'She'll get terrible cramp with her head at that angle.' I shook her gently, then quite roughly, but she pushed away my hand and muttered something incomprehensible. 'I'm afraid she's had a very tiring day. I'd better put some blankets over her. She'll be cold when the fire goes out.'

112

'Tell me where they're kept. I'll fetch them.'

I gave him directions to the airing cupboard. While Rafe was upstairs I tried to move Dimpsie on to her side in case she was sick and choked on her own vomit, as I'd heard people sometimes did. But she was too heavy. When Rafe returned he had a go, but she lashed out at him with her fists so we tucked the bedclothes round her, turned out the light and crept back into the hall.

In the gloom I could see not much more than the whites of his eyes.

'Thank you so much for bringing me home.'

'I told you, I liked doing it. Come and see us again soon.' He paused and smiled, his teeth shining in the dim light. 'Give my love to Dimpsie,' he said eventually. 'I'm very fond of her, you know. A sympathetic soul.'

'Thank you. I will. Good night.'

I offered him my cheek. He gripped my shoulder in a friendly, man-to-man sort of way and left.

'Of course Conrad isn't a bit the sort of person Mummy wants me to marry,' said Isobel.

Two days had passed since the dinner party. We were in the morning room at Shottestone but it was afternoon. The morning room was charming, with walls of green silk, curtains patterned with honeysuckle and plenty of books. A large desk where Evelyn did her accounts and telephoning stood in the window, and in front of it was the sofa on which Isobel and I were sprawling. On our plates were crumbs of Mrs Capstick's orange cake, just as good as I had remembered it.

'You mean because he isn't English?'

'He isn't English, he hasn't a title, he doesn't know any of the people we know and he isn't even a Christian.'

'Your father hasn't got a title.'

'No. But then Mummy's father made his money in cotton mills That had to be lived down. An untitled landowner was quite good enough for her.' I remembered Dimpsie telling me years ago that Evelyn had confessed to her father being in trade and had sworn her to secrecy. I had wondered at the time what the fuss was about. I could see nothing wrong with being a daughter of the loom. Now I was older and wiser I understood that to Evelyn it was a shameful blot. 'She thinks because I've gentle blood in me I ought to aim higher. She's got Lord Dunderave's son in her sights.'

'How do you know?'

'She's been dropping his name – it's Ronald, can you believe it? – into the conversation whenever possible. Apparently he can play polo, waltz, carve, help a woman on with her coat, open champagne without spilling it and he changes his underpants daily. Also he's a bruising rider to hounds, a brilliant shot and the salmon he catches are so enormous they have to be brought home by Carter Patterson.'

'Really?' I envisaged a salmon as big as a whale, quivering with harpoons.

'No, you clot! But that's the gist of it. What she really means is he's a bit thick and never opens a book but he's a guaranteed, true-blue, copper-bottomed member of the English upper classes. He's just got back from Cirencester – he's been doing a course in land management to equip him to run the ancestral acres – so she's going to ask him to dinner. Meanwhile she's been lushing up to Lord Dunderave like mad. She had him to dinner yesterday. He's a pig of a man. Bad-tempered. And he was rude to Daddy when he repeated himself.'

'Honestly, Isobel, I think you're awfully hard on your mother. She's always been angelically kind to me and it can only have been out of genuine good-heartedness. I've never been able to give her anything in return.'

'When we were children it suited her to have someone around for me to play with. It saved her the trouble of finding things for me to do.'

'Yes, but she took the trouble to be sweet and generous to

me when she needn't have bothered. Now you don't need entertaining and she's just as warm and hospitable.'

I had met Evelyn in the hall that afternoon as she was on
her way to a meeting of charitable people busy raising funds
for impoverished war widows. She had looked stylish as usual,
a fur coat over her tweed suit and shining crocodile shoes. She
had stopped to ask me about my foot, my mother, my diet and
my prospects, and she had pressed me to come to Shottestone
whenever I wished. I only had to ring and Spendlove would
come with the car.

'She wants to get you on her side over the business of Conrad.
She thinks you might be a good influence on me. She sees you
as serious and hard-working and brainy.'

'No!'

'Oh, yes. She told me after that horrible dinner party the
other night that she was very impressed by the way you've
turned out. Apparently the archdeacon said you were decora-
tive but a little too intellectual for his tastes. He thinks young
ladies should be compliant and not argumentative. Mummy
knows the man's a first-class idiot, so she was rather pleased
by his not quite approving of you.'

'I'm afraid it's a con.' I explained about the reading list for
intelligent conversation and that I had so far only managed to
read a fraction of each of the two books at the head of it.

'Thank God for that. I was worried that you'd turned into
a prig. Have a cigarette.'

She picked up a packet of *Disque Bleu* and offered them to
me. I was about to refuse, mindful of my lungs, but I was afraid
of seeming priggish so I took one. Isobel lit it with a lighter
shaped like a silver pistol.

'You needn't hold it as though it was a stick of dynamite. It
won't blow up in your face.'

I took a puff. My body went into revolt. Even my toes and
fingertips got pins and needles.

'Tell me,' I blurted out between coughs, 'about Conrad.'

'Hm. Where shall I begin? Can I trust you, Mother's nark?'

'If you're going to be beastly . . . I shall . . . go home.' This had been my refrain when we were children.

'I *was* a beast. And I still am. I'm sorry, you're an angel.' Isobel put her hand – soft, with nails painted dark-red – on mine and looked solemn. 'Don't take any notice of me. Being at home does terrible things to my character. Say you forgive me?'

'Oh, I know all about that mock penitence.' I smiled and turned my hand up so that hers rested in my palm. 'You're trying to lure me into trusting you so that you can trip me up later. Tell me about Conrad. What does he look like?'

'Well,' Isobel appeared to be thinking, 'you couldn't say he was exactly good looking. Unless you have a taste for short, bald men with large stomachs.'

'Does anyone?'

'Some people might. And he has a very large hooked nose. His feet are very broad and long. It was almost the first thing I noticed about him, that he had very big feet. But though the packaging isn't beautiful, he has the most engaging personality and that's far more important, isn't it?' I agreed that it was, feeling impressed by Isobel's maturity. 'And of course he can afford the most elegant clothes, so you don't notice so much. He's one of those people who's always the centre of attention. He has a joke for every occasion. A fantastic memory. I can never tell jokes, can you?' I shook my head. 'Well, Conrad remembers entire stories *and* the punch-line. Honestly, he's a hoot!'

I tried to look captivated by her description. No doubt it was due to a reprehensible lack of humour on my part, but I was not particularly fond of jokes. I always found it a strain to try to rig my face into pleased anticipation before producing the mandatory laughter at the end. 'How can you tell if they're funny if he tells them in Yiddish?'

'Oh, yes. Well, he speaks French. And German, of course.

And I've got O levels in both. He's a great tease, too, tying people's shoelaces together when they're asleep and putting salt into the sugar caster, that sort of thing. He's got a disarmingly childish streak but he's really terribly clever.'

'Where does all the money come from?'

'I'm not sure. Property I think. And Conrad's made masses himself. He owns a lot of casinos.'

'Does Evelyn know that?'

'No, and she won't like it at all, though it's a more honest way to make a living than exploiting the poor like Lord Dunderave. He owns half of Paddington, apparently. Poor people are shoved ten to a room in his nasty tenements while Lord D creams off all the profits. I can't see what's so admirable about that.'

'I quite agree,' I said. 'But casinos do sound a little . . .' I paused, wondering how to put it. I took another puff of my cigarette and felt a strange giddy sensation, not unpleasant.

Isobel withdrew her hand from mine. 'Vulgar, you mean.'

'Oh, not that *I* think that. But your parents might . . . undoubtedly will. Do you think you could persuade Conrad, without hurting his feelings, not to mention the casinos?'

'I'm not ashamed of Conrad.' Isobel looked rather angry and I accused myself of tactlessness.

'Absolutely not. He sounds . . . remarkable. Such a jokey character when you consider how tragic his childhood was.'

'I can't live my life according to my mother's rules.'

'Certainly not.'

'One of the good things about money is that when you've got a lot of it you can do as you like.' Isobel threw herself back on the sofa and smiled with satisfaction.

I had a healthy respect for money myself, never having had any, but I wondered if Isobel wasn't relying too much on the happiness she imagined it would bring her. Altogether I began to fear for her future.

'Don't look so solemn, you little Jeremiah!' Isobel stubbed out her cigarette. 'Let's go and see Kate. He's in the conservatory.'

I put out my cigarette thankfully, for the room was beginning to spin and my mood seemed to dip and soar alarmingly. Isobel walked on ahead with that swaying sexy walk she had had from her early teens, while I stumped along behind. The conservatory looked west towards the head of the valley. On any day of the year it was filled with light; in warm weather it became steaming and sultry because the gardeners watered the plants several times a day. Years ago, during a rare heat wave, Isobel had dared me to see how long we could withstand the furnace-like temperature, lying on the burning encaustic tiles with the sun scorching our faces through the glass. I had given in quite soon, emerging scarlet and sizzling, but Isobel had stuck it out. She had been discovered by one of the gardeners in a dead faint. She was put to bed and my father sent for and there had been another row.

Now the conservatory was dazzling because of the snow. Rafe was standing with his back to us, looking out at the hillside, an easel in front of him, a paintbrush between his fingers. Isobel crept up behind him and put her hands over his eyes. He gave a shout, spun round, hit out and caught the side of her face with his hand. She staggered and fell. It all happened in a second and then he was on his knees beside her.

'Darling, I'm so sorry!' Tenderly he pulled her into the circle of his arm and examined her face, then stroked her head. 'I was miles away and you startled me. Did I hurt you?'

'I'm all right. It was my fault. I shouldn't have crept up on you. It was stupid of me.'

Rafe helped her up. 'Hello, ' he said to me, but his attention was given to Isobel.

'Lucky it wasn't Marigold.' Isobel laughed. 'Imagine the clatter of flying crutches and cracking of plaster and the crunching of bones.'

'I'm ashamed of myself, overreacting like that.' Rafe's voice was soft, his hands gentle as he smoothed his sister's hair. 'Are you sure you're okay?'

'I'm absolutely fine. Don't fuss. How's the painting going?'

'I was so absorbed trying to capture those shadows . . . there, beneath that line of trees –' he looked out towards the landscape and tapped his own painting with the end of his brush – 'that I was in another world.'

'Dancing feels like that quite often,' I said. 'The walls of the rehearsal room simply disappear. And on the stage during a performance you completely forget about the audience. It's a terrific jolt when you come back to reality.'

'Yes. Forgetting oneself is the best thing about painting for me.' I saw the incident with Isobel had jarred his nerves. His eyes were very bright in contrast with cheeks that were pale, unless it was the reflection of the snow.

I looked at the snowscape on the easel, a watercolour of greys and purples and blues, very bold, almost abstract. 'It's very good.'

'Thanks. I'm sadly out of practice.'

'But it's really lovely. It's caught the beauty of the countryside but it makes you think of other things too . . . sadness, resignation . . . that figure on the road . . . it's about the indifference of the hills, isn't it? The puniness of all our efforts.'

'You can see that?' He stared at me for a moment as if I had surprised him, then studied the painting again. 'That's what I was thinking of all the time I was doing it.'

Isobel folded her arms and looked stern. 'If you two are going to drivel on like Jean-Paul Sartre and Simone de Beauvoir with an attack of existential *angst*, I'm going away to wax my bikini line.'

I saw that for some reason she was put out.

'I must go home,' I said.

'Honestly, it wasn't a hint,' I said a quarter of an hour later to Rafe as I struggled into the car. No one had answered the telephone at Dumbola Lodge.

'I'd had enough of being indoors anyway.' He took my crutches and slung them in the back, then got into the driver's seat.

'And really it's too kind of you to give me this.' I looked at the watercolour, still a little damp, that rested on my knee.

'You saw what I meant to paint. That doesn't often happen. You must be a girl of rare sensibility.' The teasing tone was back. He started the engine. 'How's your sister? Kate, isn't it?' he said as we swooshed down the hill through a fresh fall of snow. 'Do you know, I haven't seen her since she was a tot.'

'She's married, did you know?'

'I have to confess that if Evelyn told me I'd forgotten. She hardly ever came to Shottestone, did she? Why was that?'

'She and Isobel didn't get on. Kate was a year older and rather . . . well, bossy, to be truthful.'

'And Isobel is nothing if not rebellious. I expect she tried to tyrannize and Kate wouldn't have it. Whereas you were angelically long-suffering, so she tells me.'

I laughed. 'I don't know . . . Kate always took my father's side in everything so she thought any friend of Dimpsie's – the Prestons, in other words – were the enemy. Our family was – is – sadly divided.' I paused, thinking. 'But what's even sadder, it's not very rewarding to be on my father's side. He doesn't need associates, you see.'

'Families can be hell, can't they?'

'Mm.' I closed my eyes as we came to the precipitous drop. Rafe was easy to talk to. He didn't bully, he didn't show off. It was restful being with him. Then I saw Isobel falling backwards, her arms outstretched, heard again the smack as she hit the floor of the conservatory. As I left, there had been the beginnings of a bruise on her cheek. Of course it had been an accident and no one could have been sorrier. 'I think I always envied Isobel her family. Though naturally I love Dimpsie dearly.'

'Of course you do. So what's Kate's husband like?'

'He's a surgeon, specializing in the pancreas. Kate went into nursing, hoping to please my father. She met Dougall in the operating theatre. Perhaps he looks attractive in a green hat and mask. Kate says he's brilliant but it's hard to tell because he isn't interested in anything but people's insides. And he's fussy about hygiene. They have covers for everything. They're whisked away to be washed the minute you even look at them. Soon they'll have covers for the covers.' Rafe laughed, a happy, relaxed sort of laugh. I felt encouraged by this response to my little essay in cattiness. 'Everything you eat with or drink out of goes into a tank to be sterilized. Last time I was there I watched her wash the vacuum cleaner nozzle in Dettol, then hoover out the toaster. We all know he's potty, of course, but no one likes to say so. Dimpsie is frightened of Dougall – he can be quite cutting – and she feels sorry for Kate. My father despises them both.'

'Poor Kate. It sounds awful. But I suppose everyone's lives look like torture if you get close to them.'

I wanted to protest that mine didn't, but we were approaching the tricky turn. I shut my eyes again until we had rolled to a standstill by the front door. Rafe got out and came round to open my door.

'I shan't come in. Dimpsie'll be busy getting supper. Give her my love.'

'All right.' He helped me out of the car, put me on the crutches and guided me to the door. 'Thank you so much for bringing me home.'

This time I did not extend my cheek. He gave my arm a squeeze and got back into the car. I waved as he drove off. His manner was friendly and unconstrained, almost brotherly. Probably I should conclude that he was not attracted to me. Was it just wounded vanity that made me feel for a moment quite disappointed?

I found Dimpsie in the kitchen – from where it was impossible to hear the telephone ring – pounding chickpeas to a slurry.

'Sorry, darling. I forgot you were going to call. I decided to make some houmous to go with the parsnip pudding.'

My father came in, threw himself into the armchair by the Aga, and picked up the newspaper without looking at either of us. 'When's supper?'

121

'About half an hour.'

'Make it twenty minutes, would you? I'm going out and I shan't be back until late.'

I had heard him come home the night before, long after the household had gone to bed. Presumably Mrs Trumball was getting a thorough medical overhaul. Though I had never met the woman, I hated her.

'Busy day?' Dimpsie asked brightly.

'When am I not busy? The antenatal clinic is hardly a picnic. Fat, ugly women, who haven't the intelligence to use contraception, determined to add yet more repellent half-wits to the population.'

'I'm afraid it's a busy surgery tomorrow,' said Dimpsie apologetically, though it could hardly be her fault. 'Have you thought any more about advertising for a receptionist? Of course I'm delighted to help out, but I'm beginning to worry about the craft shop. I've had a letter from the accountant. He wants to come and do an audit but everything's in such a muddle—'

My father turned a page. 'If you think that flogging a collection of tasteless artefacts to ignorant tourists is more important than the effective practice of medicine, you must be even more stupid than I had previously thought.'

'Please,' I said, feeling myself grow hot, 'don't.'

'Don't what?' My father looked at me for the first time that evening and I sensed that behind the cold, still features there was hidden a smile of pleasure.

'Don't bully her.'

'You have an inflated idea of your own importance. You stay away for years at a time, then the moment you come home you presume to interfere between your mother and me.'

My heart began to pound. 'One of the reasons I don't come home is because I hate seeing you being so . . . so horrible to Dimpsie.'

'Really?' His tone was sarcastic. His eyes behind the rimless lenses were keen with enjoyment. He cracked the joints of his long white fingers, as though preparing to pluck out an inflamed appendix. I knew he had once operated on that very kitchen table and saved a boy's life when bad weather had prevented even a helicopter from reaching the village. 'Let me put that intermittently troubled conscience at rest. Dimpsie, do you have any complaints about the way I treat you?'

'Oh no, Tom!' My mother paused in the process of chopping parsnips to send him a placatory glance. 'Of course not. You see, darling,' she looked at me, 'when people have been married as long as we have, we don't need to observe ordinary courtesies. Besides, all that sort of thing's rather conventional, isn't it, really? Our relationship is different.'

I recalled with acute pain the image of my mother stretched out on the sofa with the empty bottle beside her. But if the princess doesn't want to be rescued, it is absolutely no good bolting on armour and taking up one's sword. There was a ghastly familiarity about the argument. We had had something like it each time I came home. And always my father, with my mother's collaboration, won.

'If you really give a damn about your mother,' my father looked down at his newspaper, 'you might think of standing in for her at the surgery. It doesn't require a university degree or even a superior intelligence to answer the telephone and make appointments.'

'All right.' I knew it was game, set and match to him. 'I will.'

11

It may not have needed a degree, but conducting an orderly surgery was much more complicated than I could have imagined.

Dimpsie took me the next morning to the house in the high street where my father had his practice. We arrived half an hour before the first appointment so I could find out where everything was. There was already a queue of four people waiting outside. I could hear the telephone ringing inside as Dimpsie tried each key in turn of a large bunch. When she found it, the rush to get inside almost knocked me off my crutches.

'This is the appointments book,' Dimpsie explained as I seated myself behind the desk. 'Ten minutes each. Emergencies to be fitted into cancellations or at the end.'

'How do I know if it's an emergency?'

'Well . . .' My mother made eyes at me and lowered her voice. She had her back to the four early birds who had already taken their seats and were picking over the pile of tattered magazines on the table as though they were desirable worms. 'You've got to use your judgement. If it's someone very young or very old, better be on the safe side and fit them in anyway. Otherwise ask a few questions. Use a little psychology.'

'I don't think I know any.'

'Here's where you make the list of house calls.' She indicated a pad already covered with incomprehensible messages in her own flamboyant writing with its Greek 'e's and circles over the 'i's instead of dots. 'Remember Mondays, Wednesdays and Fridays are hospital afternoons. Dr Chatterji takes surgery on those evenings.'

'Dr Chatterji?'

'Dr Nichols retired last year. Poor fellow, none of the patients would see him. They insisted on waiting until Tom was free.' Dimpsie sounded gratified by this mark of confidence in my father's proficiency, but actually Dr Nichols had been blind, deaf and on two sticks when I had last met him four years ago. 'They won't see Dr Chatterji either. It's very embarrassing.'

'Is he blind, deaf and lame too?'

'No, he's young and healthy. It's a communication problem. And I have to admit people round here are absurdly prejudiced against anyone . . . you know, different. He's Indian. Poor chap, he finds the English winter awfully trying. The patients complain that they can't understand anything he says and they're convinced he's going to prescribe snake juice instead of antibiotics. But no one else wanted to come all the way up here so your father had to take him.' Dimpsie looked harassed. 'See if you can persuade some of them to see Dr Chatterji. I'm afraid he must feel awfully rejected.'

'I'll do what I can.'

'Anyway, this cabinet has the medical records. You have to find the relevant folders and put them on Tom's desk before each surgery begins. They're alphabetical. More or less.'

Less proved to be the case. We hunted through every drawer for Mrs Wagstaffe's notes, she being the first patient, and found them among the Bs. Mrs Copthorne's were in the S's and Mr Darwin's were in the downstairs lavatory.

'Sorry,' said Dimpsie, returning with them in her hand. 'I remember now I was sorting the notes yesterday afternoon, trying to get ahead, and then I dashed to the loo.'

The telephone had been ringing nonstop while we hunted,

and already I was feeling hot and flustered. Dimpsie picked up the receiver. 'Surgery,' she said crisply, then, 'Oh hello, Brenda. How are you? I was meaning to ring you. Must be telepathy . . . how are the peg-bags getting on? We ought to have, say half a dozen . . . oh, I think the patchwork . . . they seem to be the most popular.'

Brenda replied at length and wittily, judging by Dimpsie's peals of laughter, while I slowly built up a pile of folders. I imagined small children, who had accidentally run shards of glass into their necks, bleeding to death while the peg-bag question was resolved. Old ladies with heart attacks lying beside the telephone, their lives ebbing away, just able to tap in the doctor's number with a feeble forefinger only to hear the engaged signal. Just as I discovered the file for the last patient on the list, which had slipped down behind the cabinet, my father came in.

'I've been trying to ring in for ten minutes,' he said angrily.

I handed him the heap of folders while Dimpsie, looking guilty, put the receiver back on its rest. Immediately it shrilled with what seemed to me bloodcurdling urgency.

'Deal with that,' he snapped at me, 'then ring the nurse on duty and tell her to go to this address.' He put a slip of paper down in front of me. 'It's an oh-two. I've put in a morphine pump, tell her. She'll see what else needs to be done.' He picked up the armful of files. 'Coffee on my desk in five minutes with the first patient.'

He went into his consulting room.

'I think the nurses' roster is in this drawer.' Dimpsie burrowed, making a terrible mess.

'Could this be it?' I pointed to a torn scrap of paper lying by the telephone entitled *Duty Nurse Tel Nos*. 'It says,' I tried to make sense of the several crossings out, '*Tuesday – Rita Bunker*.'

I rang Nurse Bunker, explained that I was the new receptionist and that Dr Savage had asked me to give her a message.

She was evidently still eating breakfast. There was a terrific

126

crunching on the line that sounded like toast. 'He didn't say he'd got a new girl. Just as well, though. Between you and me, dear, you couldn't find a kinder heart than Mrs Savage's but she's not much of an organizer to say the least and she has to quench her thirst a bit too often if you know what I mean—'

'This is Dr Savage's daughter speaking,' I said hastily.

'Ooh! Sorry if I've spoken out of turn. You should have said.'

'Yes, I know. Never mind.'

'What's the message then?'

'You're to go to a Mrs Hatch, 15, Melton Lane. It's a case with a number – oh-two, I think.'

Nurse Bunker laughed. 'That's it, dear. O-T-W-O. Doctor's code. It means "On The Way Out". The poor old thing isn't going to be with us much longer. I'd better get over there. Ta ta, dear.'

'Ta ta,' I said without thinking and got a surprised look from my mother.

The telephone rang the minute I put it down.

''Tis wor Jack,' said a female voice. 'He's got the skittors like Niagara Falls. And there's blood pouring out of his ears. He's very bad.'

I was alarmed by this description. 'Perhaps you ought to take him straight to hospital.'

'He don't hold with hospitals, pet. He wouldna gan if he was at death's door. Which he may well be.'

'In that case I'd better put you down for a house call. Could I have the patient's full name, please?'

'Cyril John Chandler,' said the voice. I wrote it down on the appropriate list. 'But Doctor needn't trouble himself to come out. If he'll just sign a sickie, Jack'll fetch it up from the surgery this afternoon.'

'But won't he be too ill? Surely he ought to be seen before then?'

Dimpsie glanced at my note, then took the receiver from me. 'Is that Mrs Chandler? I'm afraid Dr Savage won't give Mr Chandler another sick note unless he comes to the surgery for

127

a thorough check-up.' She put the receiver down. 'Jack Chandler hasn't done a day's work for months. They're always trying it on.'

'How am I to know these things?'

'You'll get the hang of it.'

Dimpsie left soon after that to go to the craft shop which was further down the high street. I limped into the kitchen to make my father a cup of coffee as instructed. I was thirsty myself from a combination of nervousness and the radiant heater above the reception desk, which beat down on the top of my head until I thought my scalp might burst into flames. A bottle labelled 'lemonade' in Dimpsie's writing stood on the draining board. I made three separate journeys between the kitchen and the desk with the glass, the bottle and the coffee. Mrs Wagstaffe, seeing that I was encumbered by my leg, obligingly took the mug in with her.

The telephone rang constantly. I found I was entirely lacking in psychological insight. Every caller wanting an emergency appointment described their symptoms so colourfully that I soon felt sick, imagining streams of vomit, blood-laced evacuations, pus-filled carbuncles and gangrenous limbs. I searched in vain for a means of turning off the fire that continued to sear my brains. I gulped down the lemonade. It had a slightly bitter taste, no doubt produced by the lemon pips which swam about among shreds of pith. Patients not only came to see my father but to make appointments with Nurse Bunker and Nurse Keppel for vaccinations, ear syringing, blood tests and verruca removal. A good many of them recognized me as Doctor Savage's daughter and wanted a thorough debriefing about my career, my boyfriends, my salary, my health, and my opinion of the north of England as opposed to the south. I quickly learned that any tentative suggestion that there was anything to be said for living in the south, such as less rain or a greater variety of shops, gave grave offence. Meanwhile the telephone screamed incessantly.

A man so thickly muffled in coats and scarves that I could

only see a pair of sad brown eyes beneath his bobble cap muttered something indistinguishable and disappeared into the other consulting room. I gathered this was Dr Chatterji. I remembered my mission to get him some patients.

'You've broke your leg, I see,' said Mrs Niddercombe, after she had explained in unnecessary detail about her troubled waterworks. 'All that nasty concrete in London. It's surprising it's only the one. Most likely you'll have a limp. My sister's eldest boy broke his leg two years ago. Now all the dogs bark at him. Dogs don't like handicapped people, do they? They sense they aren't like the rest of us.'

'Would you excuse me while I answer the telephone? Hello. Surgery. Is it an emergency? We're very busy this morning. How old is the patient? Four months? *Green* stools? Good *heavens!* Oh, no, I'm sure it's nothing to worry about – yes, all right. Bring him in at twelve.' I put down the receiver.

'Are you okay, dear?' Mrs Niddercombe asked solicitously. 'You're looking a bit green yourself.'

I did not feel at all well. The room was going round and I was having difficulty focusing my eyes. 'I feel . . . giddy . . . and a bit sick—'

'Sick!' said Mrs Niddercombe. 'There's nothing you can tell me about *that!* Every pregnancy I've been sick as a gissie! Couldn't *look* at a cream cake. Them ones with butter cream and chocolate icing with a glassy cherry on top used to be me favourite, but whenever I was expecting just one look int' baker's shop window and I'd feel me gorge rise . . . where are you going?'

I hobbled as fast as I could towards the cloakroom.

'I'll answer this phone, shall I?' she called after me. 'Surgery. No, Doctor's too busy to see anyone,' I heard her say as I leaned over the lavatory. 'Well, I can't help that. Give him a dose of castor oil or some senna pods . . .' was the last thing that was audible above the sound of my own retching.

Afterwards I felt marginally better. I finished the lemonade, pressed a Kleenex to my perspiring brow and addressed myself to the task of removing something unpleasantly sticky from the pencil which made writing in the appointments book unnecessarily difficult. It looked horribly like a body secretion. I was relieved to discover later a lidless pot of glue in the drawer from which I had taken the pencil.

'Hello,' said a cool voice as I tried to scrape the stuff from my fingers. Standing in front of the desk was a woman wearing a coat of what I thought might be mink. Concealing her hair was a cone-shaped hat of dark brown suede trimmed with matching fur. Her eyes were hidden by sunglasses and her mouth by scarlet lipstick. The waiting room had gone deathly quiet as everyone stared at this modish apparition. Amid the anoraks, cycling capes and woolly hats, she looked like a peacock among crows. 'You *have* got yourself into a state. Why don't you answer that telephone before we all go crazy?'

It was Nurse Bunker with a message for Doctor to say that 02 was now 4B and would he pop down later and do the DC.

'When you've finished,' said the cool voice as I scribbled all this down, 'I'd like to see a doctor.'

'Is it urgent?' I asked.

'That's none of your business.'

'Name, please.' I swivelled round to the cabinet.

'Marcia Dane.'

Between C and E were nothing but L's. 'Address, please.'

'The Old Rectory. But you won't find me in your files. I've only just moved in. I was rather hoping that I'd be able to register with the local quack if he's at all house-trained. It'd be a bore to have to go all the way to Carlisle.'

The waiting room pullulated with interest.

'I'll take your details.' I wished I could focus my eyes on her face. Whenever I tried the room seemed to buck and rear in an alarming way. 'Miss or Mrs?'

'Divorced. So let's settle for Mizz. I like ambiguity.' She laughed, a long peal that descended the scale.

'I'll ask Dr Chatterji if he's got room on his list and let you know. Telephone number, please?'

'The dhoolie-wallah? No thanks. I hear Dr Savage is competent. But I need to meet him first to see if I like him. After all, I might have to take off my clothes in front of him. One doesn't want just *any*one exploring one's secret places.'

A current of excited whispering ran round the waiting room.

I stared up at the black lenses that seemed slowly to revolve. 'If you'll wait until the end of – hic – surgery, I'll ask if he'll see you before he rows on his grounds.'

The buzzer sounded like an angry bee trapped by a window pane.

'Don't bother. I'll go in now.'

Before the next patient could straighten his arthritic joints she had undulated into Tom's consulting room and closed the door behind her. I closed my eyes and waited for the explosion. The waiting room seemed to hold its breath. Even the telephone ceased to shrill trilly. Or was it trill shrilly?

'Marigold? Marigold!' I sat up with a start.

My father was leaning over the desk shaking my arm. 'What's the matter with you?'

'Nothing . . . just the heat . . . if only I could turn off the fire.'

'I think she's drunk.' Marcia Dane's scarlet lips were stretched wide with amusement.

My father picked up my glass and took an experimental sip of the pips and pith that lay in the bottom. 'Mm. Lemonade. Heavily laced with vodka. Where did you get it?'

'I found it in the kitchen.' I stared miserably at a pile of glue-bound paperclips, feeling sick again. Wherever I looked, those red lips hovered in the middle of my vision.

To my surprise, my father began to laugh. His eyes crinkled, his mouth opened, his face was convulsed with amusement. For the first time I understood why women found him attractive. With us, at home, he was always cold and sarcastic. But when he was in a good humour, he had a vitality that was alluring.

Marcia Dane tapped on the desk with a long red fingernail to attract my attention. 'Make me one of your little folders, darling. I've decided to sign on.'

My father took me home after surgery without waiting for Dimpsie.

'I'm awfully sorry,' I said. 'I never drink spirits so I didn't recognize the taste. I suppose it'll be the talk of the village.'

'Oh, for a while.' He shrugged. 'Let them. Little minds.'

We drove the rest of the way in silence apart from the noise of the engine as the gearbox coped with the hills, the squish of tyres on the slushy snow and the sound of my father humming. Despite my abysmal failure as a receptionist, he seemed in an excellent mood. He took the dangerous turn with precision and pulled up beside the front door. 'Go to bed.' He handed me a bottle of pills. 'Take two with water. They might help the hangover.'

'Thank you. I'm awfully sorry,' I said again as I leaned into the back to get out my crutches.

'I may not be in for supper. Tell your mother to leave something in the bottom oven.'

He put the car into reverse to turn round. I just had time to draw back my plastered foot before it was crushed by the back wheels.

12

The next morning I arrived at the surgery a full hour before the first appointment. With the aid of a crutch I directed the bowl of the heater to reflect its fire into the centre of the waiting room. I sent Dimpsie off to the craft shop to do her accounting, made myself some tea and settled down to sorting the medical notes into alphabetical order. After a good night's sleep my head had ceased to pound and the whites of my eyes were clear. Filing is easy mechanical work and I quite enjoyed it. By the time the telephone woke up I had already worked my way down to the third drawer.

'Surgery,' I said briskly.

'Hello, Marigold,' said a man's voice, 'you do sound efficient. It's Rafe.'

Surprise sent a shot of adrenalin to my heart.

'How did you know I'd be here?' I may have sounded a little defensive.

'I rang your house just now and got Tom. Why? Is it supposed to be a secret?'

'No. It's just that yesterday . . .' the door opened to admit the first patient of the day. I dropped my voice. 'I can't talk now. I'll ring you later.'

'Why don't I pick you up from the surgery and take you out

133

to lunch? Nothing grand. I know a nice little pub not far from here. One o'clock be all right?'

I saw him running athletically from the back of the Centre Court to pulverize a lob shot, driving it into the ground and winning game, set and match for England.

'That would be lovely,' I said primly.

He rang off just as Dr Chatterji arrived. He was wearing a red ski mask and a Chinese Army hat with the flaps tied under his chin.

'Good morning, Dr Chatterji. Lovely day, isn't it?' I said brightly.

A pair of reproachful brown eyes blinked several times before he went into his consulting room to take up his lonely vigil.

Excitement was dashing through every vein in my body. I was going to have lunch with the man with whom I had been in love practically all my life – well, anyway, for long periods, if not actually continuously. It was true that I had hardly given Rafe a thought in recent years, but only because it had never occurred to me that I had the remotest chance of seeing him again.

'Excuse *me*.' A woman wearing a tweed glengarry addressed me in a tone of belligerence. '*If* I might have your attention, I'd like the next available appointment. If it's not too much trouble for you.'

I dragged my thoughts from an inspiring picture of Rafe in a peaked cap, duffel coat and white polo-necked jersey, with binoculars slung round his neck, on the conning tower of a submarine, the surrounding sea pockmarked with exploding shells. 'Is it an emergency?'

'I cut myself on a rusty tin two days ago. Probably it's tetanus. I can feel my jaw seizing up as we speak and pain shooting up my arm.'

Before I could stop her she had pulled off a bandage to reveal a purple finger and a blackened nail oozing something yellow.

I shaded my eyes with my hand. 'Dr Chatterji can see you straightaway.'

'No, thanks. I want to see Dr Savage.'

'Dr Savage has already got five patients lined up.'

'I'll wait.'

She took her septic finger to join the other patients. I heard them whispering, then one of them said, 'Do you think it runs in families?'

'Booze, is it?' said Glengarry. 'I thought she was a bit –' she tapped her temple – 'you know, a natural.'

'Poor Doctor Savage,' said another. 'It's no wonder he . . .' She cupped her hand over her mouth so I couldn't hear the rest.

'How're the walking wounded today?' asked Rafe as the car climbed an almost vertical road.

Buster was leaning his chin on my shoulder, sighing from time to time as birds flew into his sight. He had a grey coat of stiff fur like wire wool, floppy ears, a square head, a heavy silver moustache and a soppy expression that betokened love for all humans in his golden eyes. Rafe said he was a Wirehaired Pointing Griffon.

'Do you mean the patients or me?'

'You, of course.'

'Disgustingly cheerful, actually.' I felt safe enough with Rafe driving to take in the wonderful views of banks of snow curling down to the road like giant breaking waves, their perimeters sparkling like foam where the sun melted them. 'Considering.'

'Considering what?'

'What a sheltered life I've led and how thoroughly unappetizing the human body is when it goes wrong.'

'It's good of you to help your father out.'

'Not really. I'm used to working hard and I've been horribly bored. It'll give Dimpsie a chance to get the craft-shop accounts in order. And to be frank . . .' I hesitated for a moment, then, remembering that Rafe had confided in me about his family, I rushed on '. . . I know Tom resents my reappearance under the paternal roof. I'm a drain on scant resources. Also he thinks I'm selfish and self-centred. So I thought I'd show willing. It's mostly filing and answering the telephone . . . easy compared with trying to perfect a *fouetté à l'arabesque* when your feet hurt like hell and you've already been dancing for six hours. It's just that I've lived in what I suppose is an artificial world devoted to the pursuit of beauty for so long that I've become squeamish.'

'Are you longing to get back it? To the artificial world?'

'It seems real when I'm in it. I don't know anything else, you see. And when the dancing goes well it's electrifying, like flying. You're free and at the same time totally in control. It's a extraordinarily wonderful sensation. Yes, I suppose is the answer to your question.'

'Lucky you. I shouldn't think many people feel like that about their work.'

'Perhaps not. But of course it's been at a price. There hasn't been time to think about other things. Like how lovely this is.' We had reached the high ground now, moorland without trees or hedges, the vast curves of rock, their featureless simplicity accentuated by the unbroken snow. 'Isn't it marvellous! Not a house, not a fence, not a telegraph pole. Even the road's hidden beneath the slush. We might be in prehistoric times. I wouldn't be surprised if we came across a man in wolf-skins carrying a mammoth tusk over his shoulder . . . Oh, look! Can you see in that little dip? There's someone putting wood on a fire. And there's a child helping him. They look quite ragged. Perhaps we *have* slipped back into another time.'

'They're probably burning the evidence of their last raid.'

'You don't mean – *reivers?*'

Buster woofed gently into my ear in response to his master's laugh.

'You *are* a romantic! No, they're tinkers. I expect they're getting rid of things they've stolen that are too incriminating. The locals are up in arms because the rate of petty theft has shot up since the tinkers came and the police are too afraid to go to the campsite and confront them. There it is.'

136

He pointed to the next valley where a row of caravans strag-gled beside a thin belt of trees – not the round-topped, brightly painted wagons of children's picture books, but modern trailers. Instead of piebald horses there were cars, untidily parked. A woman came out to peg washing on a line. It blew into her face and she stepped back to wipe her cheek on her sleeve, then crossed her arms to hug her shoulders against the cold.

'In the old days,' said Rafe, 'they were known as "muggers".'

'Because of the stealing?'

'Because they sold pottery mugs to make a living.'

We rounded a bend and the valley dropped out of sight. I saw a delightful little thatched and whitewashed inn nestling in the fold of a hill.

'That's the pub.'

'It looks lovely!'

It was lovely. Inside everything was made of wood, even the ceiling, but it was a marvellous silvery colour and not gloomy. Rafe said it was oak and part of the original sixteenth-century building. There was no one there but us so we had the table nearest the fire. On either side of it were high-backed settles which were awkward to get into because of my leg, but once inside I felt as though I was in the cabin of a man-o'-war – not that I'd ever been in one, of course, but I had seen the *Hornblower* film with Gregory Peck – because the slightest movement was accompanied by the creaking of ancient timbers. When I said this to Rafe he seemed amused.

'I hoped you'd like it. When I was away I often thought of this place. I used to come here with Isobel when we were both at a loose end. The menu's a bit limited. White wine all right to drink?'

'Wonderful.'

Drinking in the middle of the day was a hitherto unknown indulgence. We ordered steak and chips. The steak was the kind you needed your teeth sharpened into points to deal with, but the chips were excellent, really thin and dripping with fat. The

137

tomato was pale pink and hard but I ate Rafe's as well. Buster, who had been lying across our feet with his head resting on my cast, made short work of the bits of steak that were too tough to cut.

'I thought because of your size – your extreme slenderness – you wouldn't eat anything,' he said, transferring a lettuce leaf and the last few chips from his plate on to mine.

I was so moved by the idea that he had actually thought about me enough to wonder what I might eat that I felt a rush of affection, perhaps alcohol-induced, that made me say, 'This is such heaven being in this lovely place on such a beautiful day with . . .' I almost said 'you' but pulled myself back from the brink in time to say '. . . with an old friend.'

Rafe appeared not to notice this effusion of feeling. 'Sit, Buster. Quiet, sir!' He looked sternly in the dog's melting eyes. 'I'm having a bit of trouble training him. He doesn't seem as biddable as a labrador or a spaniel. The people I got him from assured me the breed was intelligent and quick to learn. Anyway, it's too late to think of taking him back.'

'Oh, no! He's such a darling! I wish I could have a dog. But it wouldn't be fair. I'm out all day.'

'Mm. I suppose there're several men in London, pining for your return? Not that I've any right to ask. But as you say,' he smiled charmingly, 'I'm an old friend.'

'Oh,' I tried to sound casual, 'there isn't anyone particular.' Was he just making conversation or did the question betoken a special interest? 'Dancers are notoriously . . .' I had been going to say promiscuous, but then it occurred to me that our careless sexual manners might not find favour outside artistic circles '. . . they don't have much time for passionate emotional involvements.'

Then I remembered that I was – possibly – engaged to Sebastian. Since arriving in Northumberland I hardly thought about him at all, and when I did I was unable to persuade myself to take him at all seriously. He had become a creature of fantasy, a von Rothbart or a Kashchei: sinister, malign, but contained within a world of fantasy, as insubstantial as the plywood of Giselle's cottage.

I asked Rafe how he was enjoying running the Shottestone estate. Apparently there was a problem with the agent, who had fallen into slipshod ways. Two farms were running at a loss and some of the houses and cottages were in a poor state of repair. Rafe didn't mention Kingsley, but the omission was like a jagged hole cut out of the picture. He outlined his plans for putting things right. The logs burned themselves into heaps of glowing ash. We had another glass of wine. There was no afternoon rehearsal looming, no impending performance, no criticism to fear, no Sebastian to dread. I had told Rafe that I was eager to return to London, but for the time being I was perfectly content.

'Do you want a pudding?'

I did but I shook my head. I could feel that my waistband was tighter.

'Isobel was hoping you'd come up to the house for tea. She's been shopping in Newcastle all day but she'll be back by four. I expect she wants to show you what she's bought.'

'That'd be lovely.'

'What shall we do meanwhile? I'd like to show you the old pele tower at Waterbury. I've always been fond of the place, though it's almost a ruin now. But it's a little way back from the road. I don't know if you could get there on crutches.'

'If you don't mind me being slow, I'd like to see it.' As we walked to the car, Rafe hovered solicitously at my side in case I should slip on the ice. It was a new experience to be taken care of. 'Lucky Isobel,' I said. 'I suppose money's no object now she's marrying a bloated capitalist.'

The remark was intended to be flippant but Rafe's tone was serious when he said, 'Is it important to you to marry money? Couldn't you be happy on a moderate income?'

'Of course I could. I've never had even an adequate one. Actually, I enjoy making something out of nothing and finding things in junk shops. I don't suppose I'd like being rich at all. I only said that because . . . because . . .' I paused, not wanting to finish what I'd been going to say.

'Because it seems to mean so much to Isobel,' he finished for me. He helped me into the car and stowed the crutches.

'I'm sure she wouldn't marry him if she didn't like him.'

Rafe started up the car. 'I hope you're right.'

'Well, she doesn't seem to mind at all that he's rather ugly. That's a good sign. Most people – I must admit, including me – put far too much emphasis on looks, which is every bit as superficial as liking money.'

'Is Conrad Lerner ugly?' Rafe sounded surprised.

'She didn't say *quite* that. I just assumed that if he was short, fat, bald and with a big nose and enormous feet that he wasn't exactly Cary Grant. But then Cary Grant's appeal wasn't only looks, was it? Conrad's probably extremely charming. And Isobel says he's very clever. That's attractive.'

'I'm sure he is,' said Rafe with a suggestion of savagery. Then he added, more calmly, 'Let's hope he's charming, anyway, because we're bound to have to see a good deal of him.'

There was a silence during which I admired the scenery. I had always known that the place where I had been born and brought up was beautiful because everyone said so, but I had never properly appreciated it before. The sky was the most glorious heathery blue near the horizon and, further up, where it merged with layers of cloud, it was a pearly grey shot through with white streaks like brushstrokes. This reminded me of Rafe's watercolour, which I had pinned to my bedroom wall where I could look at it as I lay in bed.

'I showed Dimpsie the painting you gave me. She thought it was terrifically accomplished. She used to paint, too. She spent two years at the Slade, you know.'

'I didn't know. Or if I did I'd forgotten.'

'She actually won a scholarship and had dreams of going to Paris and throwing herself at Picasso's feet, but getting pregnant with Kate put paid to that. It's a shame she's ended up surrounded by corn dollies, knitted tea cosies, pressed flower cards and mirrors decorated with barbola work.'

'What's barbola work?'

'I don't know but Dimpsie says it's hideous. She only takes it not to upset the woman who does it. Is there anything sadder than talent wasted?'

'Perhaps not having any, like me.' He didn't sound sad but, on the contrary, amused. I definitely had the feeling he was secretly laughing at me, but I didn't mind. I was glad I could cheer him up. 'Look, there it is. The pele tower.'

Fortunately for my leg, the square tower of rugged stone with a crenellated parapet and arrow-slits for windows was only a stone's throw from the road.

'It looks so ancient. When was it built?'

'Most pele towers were put up in the sixteenth century, though the Scots and the English went on fighting long after the Union. Killing and cattle-thieving was part of their culture. They enjoyed it too much to give it up.'

'I can't think why men like fighting so much.'

'It's an overrated pastime,' he agreed dryly.

I felt I had wandered into forbidden territory and was glad of the distraction created by the difficulty of getting me out of the car. The path to the tower inclined steeply with an unbroken covering of snow, so I needed all my breath to get there safely. Buster was thrilled to be allowed to run about and had to be discouraged from barking at every bird, gorse bush and stone, and from darting between my legs. Rafe told him off severely. Buster looked abashed for several seconds before launching himself at my shoulder bag, which was swinging from my neck in an enticing manner.

The pele tower was fairly dark inside. I was disappointed to find that the room contained nothing but a pile of logs, but Rafe stood rapt, as though he saw ghosts laughing, quarrelling, calling for food and weapons in preparation for a raid, kissing

141

women and children goodbye in the knowledge that they might not meet again in this world. He turned slowly, as though wishing to take in every detail, though the walls were bare of decoration, the floor was trampled mud and, apart from something that looked like a coffin in one corner and a flight of rough stone steps in another, there was nothing to see. I waited patiently, only moving when I felt my crutches sink into the mud.

He came to my rescue in time to prevent me toppling over. 'Come here where it's a bit dryer. See that water trough?' He pointed to the coffin. 'They used to bring the horses and cattle in here to keep them safe from the Scots. And look at these grooves in the buttress. That's where they used to sharpen their swords.'

I put my fingers into the indentations, imagining the sound of the blade being whetted on the stone and savage minds filled with bloodlust. But there must have been passages of love in this grim building, too. Or perhaps only lechery and child-begetting.

'It's a pity you can't get upstairs,' said Rafe. 'Someone repaired the floorboards in the nineteenth century and put glass in the windows, but the fireplace is original. There's some carving, flowers and birds – crude but strangely touching. A little poetry amid the blood-letting. Would you mind if I went up just for a moment?'

'Of course not. I'm quite happy.'

Rafe ran up the steps, Buster following, and disappeared into the room above. Rafe's interest in history was another virtue. Not only athletic and manly, but intellectual and artistic as well. I heard his feet on the floorboards as he paced back and forth for what felt like several minutes.

'You're shivering,' he said when he came down. 'I've been selfish keeping you standing here.'

He tugged my crutches from the mud and we went out into the light.

'Hang on a minute. I've got caught on a bramble.' I tried to

142

unhook myself from the thorny stem that twisted round the door.

'It's a white rose.' Rafe bent down to release the hem of Bobbie's beautiful coat. 'It flowers all summer long and smells of almonds—'

He was interrupted by an explosion that sent all the birds flapping into the sky. I screamed and Rafe threw himself to the ground. I would have done the same had I been able to. Someone had fired a shot at us. On the hill opposite I saw the tiny figure of a ragged-looking man, like a pencil scribble on white paper. The brilliance of the snow made my eyes run. When I blinked away the tears he had disappeared.

13

'Are you hurt?' I leaned precariously over Rafe's prostrate body. 'Oh God – say something, *please!*'

Rafe was lying face down with his hands clasped over his head. 'I'm . . . all . . . right.' He disengaged his fingers, rolled himself over on to his back and sat up. 'All right, good boy. That'll do.' Buster stopped barking and tried to lick his face.

'That was a gun, wasn't it?' I asked. 'Are you *sure* you're not hurt?'

Rafe dropped his head on to his knees. I always had difficulty with trembling legs and cramping feet before a performance, but Rafe's entire body was shaking. He tried to make his hands into fists but tensing them seemed to make it worse.

I had always considered him so much older, stronger and wiser that the idea that I might be able to comfort him seemed presumptuous. But sympathy overruled caution. I let my crutches fall and dropped down beside him. Tentatively I put my arms around him.

'It doesn't matter,' I said, not certain what I meant. 'Never mind. It doesn't matter.'

After a while the shuddering began to subside and he raised his head. 'Sorry. It's just a physical response . . . I can't . . . I can't—'

'I know. I know about the tank.'

He sighed and lifted up his arm to put it round my shoulder. We sat for another minute leaning our bodies against each other, not saying anything. Buster managed to insinuate his head between us, looking up into his master's face with perplexed eyes. The melting snow seeped through my skirt and tights into my knickers. It was agonizingly cold but I endured it willingly.

Then Rafe turned to look at me. 'I ought to have thought of you. But I'm afraid I was in a blue funk.'

I shook my head and smiled. I could see lots of different shades of blue in the irises of his eyes, like the stripey bits in glass paperweights. 'I thought of me first, too. It was all over too quickly for bravery to come into it. But why did he shoot at us? *If* he did. It might have been a mistake.'

'I'm sure it was. Probably a poacher trying to hit a rabbit. You're shivering again. Just a minute.' He stood up. 'I'll come behind you. It won't be dignified,' he tucked his hands into my armpits, 'but it'll be less likely to hurt your leg.' He lifted me up easily. 'What a featherweight you are.'

'I'm not as light as I was. Specially after that lovely lunch.'

He gave me the crutches. 'Let's get you back to the car.'

By the time I was safely installed, Rafe's hands were more or less steady. As we drove back to Shottestone Manor I felt the light-headedness which, with me anyway, always follows extreme emotion, like the brief freedom from anxiety that follows a performance before you begin to worry about how well you've danced.

I did most of the talking. Rafe asked me about Diaghilev and the influence of Russian ballet. I practically gave him a lecture on the subject. I was eager to erase the incident at the pele tower from both our minds.

'Oh, look!' I interrupted myself in the middle of telling him about Nijinsky who had put Pavlova's nose seriously out of joint. I pointed to a house built on a crag high above the valley. It was taller than it was wide and had several round turrets

145

with extinguisher caps. 'It's Sleeping Beauty's castle! That's what Dimpsie, Kate and I called it, anyway. We went there for a picnic once. It was such a romantic place! But it wasn't visible from the road in those days.'

'Some of the larger trees halfway down the valley were blown down in a bad storm a few years ago. They were all planted by the chap who built the house in the 1860s, so they were all getting a bit ancient. I've forgotten his name. An eccentric poet. A recluse. It's called Hindleep, after the hill it stands on, because long ago it was colonized by deer.'

'It had the most wonderful atmosphere, I remember, even though it poured with rain and Kate fell into some stinging nettles and I cut my hand on a piece of broken glass. I've still got the scar.' I glanced down at my wrist bone on which a jagged line was just traceable. 'Though it was ruined, it still seemed alive, like a haughty old woman with a magnificent past. Look how the clouds seem to be hanging on the pinnacles. You can just imagine a king and queen with tarnished crowns slumbering on thrones thick with dust and cooks asleep with their heads on the kitchen table beside bowls of dried-up cake batter and rotten candied cherries. And a princess lying on a bed veiled with cobwebs.'

'You make it sound romantic. I must admit that until now I've always thought of it as a Victorian monstrosity.' Rafe spoke with the contempt of one born and bred in an acknowledged Jacobean masterpiece. 'I believe it's completely derelict now. The parish council asked for tenders from salvage firms to have it pulled down or blown up, but it was much too expensive.'

'I'm glad!'

Rafe laughed. 'I don't think you'll find it has much atmosphere these days. They had to put up a lot of fences and barbed wire to stop people getting in. A few years ago someone killed themselves by jumping off the bridge that leads to the house. It's a sheer drop of several hundred feet.'

'I remember.'

'Come to think of it, that's how the poet died, isn't it? The original owner, I mean. The poor chap threw himself off because his poems weren't selling.'

'I never knew that.'

As we drove back to Shottestone I pictured the old house sleeping on through storms and sunshine, high on its frowning cliff. I imagined it hedged about by wire and fences, through which brambles and weeds and trees would have grown, as in the story. Because of the rain, Dimpsie, Kate and I had picnicked in the room that had huge windows on one side looking down on the lake. We had laid out our picnic on the only piece of furniture left, a long table with faces carved on the legs. Dimpsie had put cobwebs on my cut wrist, which was an old remedy for wounds. My father had been annoyed because a lot of dirt had got in with the cobwebs, but it had healed without any problems.

'Here we are.' Rafe turned off the engine. 'I expect there'll be tea in the morning room.'

'Thank you so much for a wonderful—' I started to say.

'Marigold.' He put his hand on my arm. 'You're remarkably kind and decent and generous. You mustn't let us Prestons take advantage of you.'

'What do you mean? It seems to me the boot's on the other foot. You've given me so much hospitality and I can't repay it. I've always loved coming to Shottestone.'

'Have you? That's good.' He got out and came round to help me out.

'Hello, you two!' Isobel came running down the stairs into the hall. 'You've been ages.' She kissed me. 'What do you think?' She twirled round to display the dress she was wearing. It was sleeveless, of a soft heathery-blue crêpe de Chine with a wide chiffon collar in the same shade. 'It's the best Newcastle can do. Do you like it?'

'I'm not sure about the colour,' said Rafe. 'It makes you look a little washed out.'

'I think it's beautiful,' I said truthfully.

'Oh, men never know anything,' said Isobel. 'I'll bring down all the stuff I've bought to show you, Marigold. But you,' she tugged at Rafe's collar, 'must listen and learn.'

'Thank you, Isobel darling, for including me in this important symposium, but I should only be in the way. Anyway, I've got a bit of a head.'

She looked at him properly for the first time. 'What's the matter? What's happened?'

To me Rafe looked wholly restored to his calm, quizzical self but she, of course, knew him much better.

'Nothing. Don't worry. I'm going up to my room for a while. I don't want any tea.' He walked off without another word, taking the stairs two at a time with Buster galloping at his heels.

Isobel's anxious eyes followed him. 'What's happened to upset him?' she asked me as soon as he was out of earshot.

'We went to look at a pele tower.'

'The one at Waterbury?'

'Yes. When we came out someone took a shot at us. Oh, by mistake,' I added, seeing Isobel's expression of dismay. 'I'm certain it was an accident and probably the bullet didn't come anywhere near, but it sounded very loud because everywhere was so peaceful. I nearly hopped out of my skin. Rafe thinks it was just a poacher . . .'

Isobel had turned away and was already running up the stairs after her brother. I was not offended. Isobel was the person most able to comfort him. I went in to the morning room.

'Marigold! How lovely!' Evelyn had been sitting on the sofa in front of a good fire, with her eyes closed. If she had been asleep she sprang awake remarkably quickly. She took away my crutches and helped me out of my coat. Balfour and Gladstone, the latest in a long line of Preston spaniels named after British prime ministers, came over to be petted, then returned to the hearth. 'Darling, you must be cold. Come and sit next to me. Have a sandwich. Mrs Capstick has her shortcomings but her sandwiches are second to none. Just like everything else, there's

148

a right way and a wrong way. You must have very thin bread, soft cheese not butter, and lots of cucumber with a scrap of tarragon vinegar, salt and pepper. How do you like your tea? No milk and no sugar, isn't that right? Wouldn't it be a good idea to put that leg of yours up on the stool?'

It felt pleasantly familiar to have Evelyn fussing over me. I had never resented it as Isobel did, probably because she was not my mother. Also she was right, as usual. My leg had begun to ache as it always did by this time of day and it was much more comfortable in a horizontal position. And the sandwiches were delicious. I complimented her on the tea's refreshing smoky flavour.

'It's lapsang souchong. I have it sent from London. Now where did Rafe take you? He tried to be mysterious about it but of course I knew at once when he said he was taking a friend out to lunch that it had to be you.'

'Did you? How?'

'I knew it must be a girl because he polished his shoes and put on a clean shirt. And it wasn't Bunty because I'd just spoken to her on the telephone less than an hour before and she would have told me. Poor darling, he's been away so much he doesn't know any other girls round here. And we all know how susceptible Rafe is to pretty, intelligent young women. Which is just as it should be before a man settles down.' She put her soft hand with its manicured nails over my collection of bitten ones and leaned a little towards me.

When Evelyn put on a particular face, lowering her chin and looking up into one's eyes with unblinking concentration, it meant she was telling one something for one's own good. Or sometimes hers. Her eyes, despite the tiny lines that had appeared beneath them and a slight sparsity of lashes, were still brilliantly blue, like Rafe's, with the same dark ring round the rim of the iris. Her skin was perfectly made up, very pale in contrast to the dark red mouth.

So what was she actually saying? That Rafe had a reputation

as a Lothario? I remembered Bunty from the dinner party. Sweet-natured but plain might sum her up if one were disposed to be uncharitable. Which I suddenly found I was. Evelyn wanted me to know that Rafe and Bunty were in the habit of lunching together. Wasn't it rather odd then, that as far as I could remember he had not addressed more than half a dozen words to her during the whole of that evening?

Evelyn continued to look up at me. 'I'm delighted that Rafe and Bunty have so much in common,' she said. 'Horses, shooting, fishing, all that sort of thing. She's a nice girl and it's obvious she simply adores him.'

Now I began to catch Evelyn's drift. I was being warned off.

'Of course you and I rather despise those things as philistine.' Evelyn smiled conspiratorially. 'You're a great artist, Marigold. I'm very proud of you. And I, in my own small way, with my garden and . . .' her eyes roved round the room before they fell on the cushion that had remained in her work basket in a half-completed state for several years until my mother finished it for her '. . . my petit-point, have artistic leanings. But Rafe will inherit this house and the estate and he needs a wife who can share his interests and entertain his sporting friends.' Evelyn seemed to have conveniently forgotten that her own lack of proficiency with fishing rod and fowling piece had not disqualified her from being a suitable chatelaine of Shottestone. 'Not that I imagine he's in love with her. But proximity will do great things. Friendship can develop into something closer. Of course Bunty is not a beauty, but gradually a man finds that the face that expresses sweetness and affection may be quite as charming as ravishing eyes and a pretty nose.' Evelyn gave my hand a little stroke. 'Love isn't always a hot-blooded thing, darling, is it? Sometimes the best relationships have their roots in mutual respect and companionship.'

The high-minded tone of Evelyn's conversation – reminiscent of our school chaplain's sermons – was new to me. But when she wanted something she was prepared to use whatever tools

150

lay to hand. Kindly but firmly, she wished me to understand that, though she approved of me as a person, the local doctor's daughter was not good enough for her only son.

I owed Evelyn much. I was sure that, had she not used her considerable powers of persuasion – even going to the lengths of a cosy little supper à deux – my father would not have agreed to pay for me to go to Brackenbury House. But fond of her and grateful though I was, I immediately determined to consider only Rafe's interest – and, of course, my own.

I decided to find out a little more. 'I did like Bunty so much.'

'Yes, such a reliable, level-headed girl. Never missish or winsome which is so irritating.' That told me that Evelyn thought Bunty unfeminine. 'And a fearless rider to hounds, apparently. The only child of dear friends of mine. John and Caroline Lumbe of Lumbe Hall. Such a pity! Two thousand acres and no sons to inherit.'

I imagined Rafe and Bunty cantering across the moors, her splendid horsemanship earning his unbounded admiration. I saw them dismounting at the pele tower, Rafe fastening the reins of both horses to the stout stems of the white rose . . . plucking a flower and presenting it to her . . . Bunty tossing back her hair (in my fantasy it was long enough to be wind-tousled). I imagined him picking her up and carrying her inside . . . the stairs were a slight difficulty being steep, and Bunty being on the brawny side, but in this fantasy he had the strength of ten. Upstairs was a bed left by the Borderers, a little mildewed but miraculously sound . . . I imagined him throwing her roughly on to it . . . ripping her shirt from her shoulders . . . No, it was hopeless. Bunty was as wholesome and as exciting as rice pudding and just not the sort of girl men lusted after. He might lust after the two thousand acres, though.

'Not missish at all,' I said innocently.

'But not entirely unfeminine.' Evelyn's voice sharpened and Balfour lifted his golden eyes to her face. 'With more becoming clothes and a better haircut I think she could be quite pretty.'

'Oh, yes.'

Evelyn frowned. 'I wonder if I might give her a hint or two. Her mother has no idea – looks like the wrath of God – though she is one of my best friends.'

'I should think Bunty would be eternally grateful if you suggested ways in which she could improve her appearance.'

Oh, Marigold, I admonished myself, how wicked and devious you are.

'Mm.' Evelyn stopped looking forceful and looked reflective instead. There was nothing she liked better than transforming dull houses or gardens or people into something aesthetically pleasing. She put her head on one side and looked at me, the beady expression replaced by an approving smile. 'What a good little thing you are, Marigold. Really, you've turned out to be so steady and sensible. I shall ask Bunty to tea tomorrow. We'll have it upstairs in my sitting room so we can be sure of not being interrupted.'

Probably Bunty would not realize how great was the honour about to be done her. Not even Kingsley was allowed in Evelyn's sitting room. Years ago, at Isobel's instigation, we had trespassed on the sacred ground while her mother was out and had spent an uncomfortable hour perched on pale blue Louis Quinze chairs reading Evelyn's diaries, which was the naughtiest thing Isobel could think of doing. The entries were cryptic and not very interesting, except when they referred to us – and even then they were mostly memos to do something about Isobel's posture or to speak to Dimpsie about my habit of chewing my hair which was not only bad for my health but repulsive.

Isobel had hoped to discover evidence of an illicit and passionate relationship so she could blackmail her mother into allowing her to wear make-up and letting her leave school early. But somehow, little though I knew about these things, I had been sure that Evelyn would not look at a man other than her husband. Instinctively I understood that sexiness had no place in Evelyn's character. For one thing, she mistrusted strong emotions. And gardening was the only activity she thought it worth getting untidy for. She was impatient of things that had no obvious results, that did not contribute to the perfect world she had constructed, in which everything was beautiful and where she reigned supreme. I guessed that she would put up with sex in order to procreate and to keep Kingsley happy, as long as he was quick about it, but while he gasped and groaned her mind would be busy choosing colour schemes for the new bit of garden or planning who and what to have for dinner when the lord lieutenant came.

'I don't think brown is Bunty's colour,' I said demurely. 'Perhaps black would suit her better.'

'Yes, and it would slim down that bottom. Black or navy. Though we want to emphasize her youthfulness.' I reckoned Bunty was thirty if a day. Evelyn looked thoughtful while straightening the magazines on the stool that had got a little crooked. 'I wonder about red. Or coral?'

'Mm . . . do you think? With that complexion?'

'Her colour *is* a little high. Green powder might do something.'

'I expect it's all that galloping about in cold winds and standing up to her waist in rivers for long periods.'

'Yes, yes, all that must stop at *once*.' The shared interests seemed to have been summarily discarded from the list of attractions. 'I shall give her a pot of Elizabeth Arden's Eight Hour Cream tomorrow.' I wondered if Bunty would take this present in good part. 'At least the riding must be responsible for her posture, which is excellent,' Evelyn continued. 'And you, Marigold, walk like a queen these days. It's wonderful what a little dancing can do. Though I've noticed you turn your feet out in a way that reminds one slightly of a fish standing on its tail. But better that than the languid slouch Isobel affects. After all I've said on the subject.' Evelyn sighed. 'Sometimes I think Isobel deliberately tries to wound me. This engagement.' She gave a little shudder. 'Sometimes I think it must be a cruel joke. What sort of man engages himself to a young girl of good family and then makes no effort whatsoever to make himself known

153

to them? He hasn't written to her. I know that because I've instructed Spendlove to let me know at once if a letter with a German stamp arrives. And he's supposed to pick up the telephone as soon as it rings. He keeps a list for me to see but there hasn't been anyone called –' she sucked in her breath sharply as though the very name was an affront – 'Conrad Lerner. He can't be very much in earnest if he's content to stay away for weeks without making contact, can he?'

'It does sound a little cool,' I said obligingly. At that moment I heard the telephone ring in the hall. It rang twice then stopped, presumably because dear old Spendlove had picked up the kitchen extension.

'And Isobel herself is on edge all the time. I've caught her hanging around the back door waiting for the postman. She's strung up. Irritable. Hardly the behaviour of a girl whose dreams have all come true.'

'Perhaps they've quarrelled.'

Evelyn said in a voice fervent with hope. 'Do you think they may have? Of course Isobel tells me nothing. But she's so fond of you.'

I felt guilty. Evelyn saw me as a confidante and perhaps Isobel did too. I must be careful not to betray either of them. 'She seems very fond of him. She says he's very clever.'

'I hope to God she hasn't already been to bed with him.' Evelyn made a *moue* of distaste. 'These days, if one can believe what people say, girls think no more of sleeping with a man than of buying a new pair of shoes. Less perhaps.'

'I don't know. We haven't discussed it.'

Evelyn gave me a searching look. 'I hope *you've* had the sense to refrain from tumbling into bed with every Tom, Dick and Harry who flourishes an engagement ring and pretends to be desperately in love.'

'Well . . .' I did not like to say that it had never occurred to me to demand even this degree of commitment. 'Of course in artistic circles people are inclined to be, ah . . . impulsive—'

154

'Tush! Artistic! What rubbish!' Evelyn stood up to reposition the ornaments on the chimneypiece that were not arranged to her satisfaction. The high-minded tone was distinctly absent now and she appeared to have forgotten our alliance as fellow practitioners of the creative arts. 'All men are sexually obsessed. And they only despise you for giving them what they want.'

I could offer no evidence to the contrary. But I could not bring myself to throw in the sponge without a fight. 'But perhaps women . . . some women anyway . . . feel the same. These days, with the pill, sex doesn't have to be taken quite so seriously. Dancers are under great pressure with each performance to achieve perfection. It's quite natural that they use lovemaking as a means of letting off steam—'

'Oh, Marigold!' I saw in the glass above the fireplace that Evelyn was frowning. 'What a silly girl you are! No!' She held up an admonitory forefinger. 'You needn't tell me about impulses and pressures and so forth. It's quite clear you've been allowing some man to take advantage of you. I hope it's only one.' She sat down beside me and took my hand. 'Now, darling, you're not to think I'm angry with you, because I understand how difficult it's been. You've been thrown upon the world with no advice or protection and it's no wonder if you've made a few mistakes.' I felt grateful for this dispensation until I remembered that in my own eyes I had done nothing wrong, particularly. 'We *all* make mistakes.' Evelyn poured us both another cup of tea and continued in a quieter, confidential tone. 'I did myself. He was Canadian . . . a student, working his way round the world. I met him at a lunch party.' Her eyes softened and her voice took on a different timbre, lighter, younger, almost fluting. 'His name was Rex Campion. I was your age. Twenty-two. He sent me flowers afterwards. White roses. They were so lovely.' Evelyn looked down and spread her hands, as though the flowers lay on her lap. 'Then he telephoned to ask if we could meet. We had tea in a hotel in Chipping Campden. He made me laugh so much.'

Now I thought about it, I realized I had seldom heard Evelyn laugh.

'We had lunch the next day. Suddenly neither of us could eat anything. We'd fallen hopelessly in love. His parents weren't well off. He had no expectations. But we were both young and foolish and we thought we could live on love. My father had other ideas.' I remembered the mill-owning parent Isobel had told me about, and imagined him standing with a thumb through his braces and a cigar in his other hand before a gigantic, humming factory. 'Rex begged me to give myself to him,' Evelyn went on. 'I wanted to make him happy. My father sent for Rex and told him that in England it was considered bad form for poor men to pursue girls who had money. He was insulting. I was waiting outside and I overheard it all. Poor Rex. He was almost crying when he came out. I told him I'd run away with him but he said I mustn't quarrel with my parents and that he'd write. I waited with, oh! so much *longing*, for a letter.' I saw Evelyn as a girl, her hair Isobel's colour, dressed in tennis clothes perhaps, with a short pleated skirt and long brown legs, saw her running down the stairs to intercept the postman. 'I waited and waited . . . But I never heard from him again.'

I felt tremendously flattered to be confided in. I wondered how many other people knew the story of Rex Campion.

'How awfully sad, Evelyn. I suppose he was too proud to write after what your father had said.'

She smiled rather coldly. 'He got what he wanted too easily so he didn't value it.'

'I'm sure it wasn't that—'

Evelyn shook her head. 'Anyway, soon after that I met Kingsley and I forgot all about Rex. Now, darling.' She handed me the plate of sandwiches. 'Tell me all about *your* young man. Is he very good looking?'

I intended to give her only the vaguest sketch but, due to a feeling that one ought to return a confidence for one received, and moral weakness under the pressure of relentless questioning,

Evelyn managed to coax more or less the whole story of Sebastian out of me.

'I must say, Marigold, I'm shocked that you should think of paying for career advancement with your body. Because,' she held up a forefinger as I opened my mouth to protest, 'that is exactly what you have been doing. You don't seem at all in love with this man and, if what you say is true, he isn't in love with you. I'm sorry to say it sounds . . . well, sordid is the word that comes to mind, exchanging sexual favours for profit.'

The sweet, flute-like note had gone from her voice. I was about to reply with some indignation that marrying people for land (I was thinking of the two thousand acres) and social position (Kingsley) seemed to me equally sordid, yet it was done every day of the week and looked upon as only common sense. But just then Isobel came in.

'What are you two talking about? You look as though you're plotting something.'

'We were talking about Bunty, darling.'

I was impressed by Evelyn's single-mindedness, for I had quite forgotten the original purport of our conversation.

'I was telling Marigold how glad I am that your brother seems so fond of her.' Evelyn smiled indulgently at Isobel. 'Another new dress? A charming colour.'

Isobel looked down as though she had forgotten she was still wearing the pale lilac dress. 'What? Oh yes, I bought it this morning. Of course Rafe isn't going to marry that stupid old Bunty. She looks exactly like a Shire horse. She ought to have a cart to pull about.'

Evelyn stopped looking indulgent.

'It really is a lovely dress,' I said quickly.

'You can have it,' said Isobel. 'I've gone off it. It'd suit you much better, anyway. I'm going to London tomorrow to buy some decent things. Newcastle's just too provincial for words. I'll be back on Monday.'

I could see that something had happened to excite Isobel.

There were red spots on her cheeks and she fidgeted with the scarf fringe as though nervous.

'Is that really necessary?' Evelyn looked annoyed. 'Ronald Dunderave's coming to dinner on Saturday and I particularly wanted you to help me entertain him.'

'Ask Marigold instead. He'll like her much better. As long as you don't get too intellectual, darling,' she smiled at me. 'Ronald has the brain of a woodlouse. Better still, Mummy, put him off until I get back. Then we can have a lovely big party to celebrate.'

'What is there to celebrate?' asked Evelyn sharply.

Isobel took a deep breath and announced with an air of nonchalance that failed to conceal her elation. 'That was Conrad on the telephone. He's in England. And on Tuesday he's coming here.'

14

Tuesday, the day of Evelyn's party, came at last. Time had dragged a little. Isobel had been in London and Dimpsie had been preoccupied by the craft-shop accounts. Rafe had not telephoned. I had managed to keep myself more or less busy. During Saturday morning surgery, which was emergencies only, I had finished off the filing. I had sorted the contents of the drawers and got rid of the glue. I had tidied the mountain of ragged *Woman's Realm* and *Knitting Weekly* and thrown away the ones without covers and with more than half their contents missing. They were so ancient that all the crosswords had been filled in and the quizzes disfigured by rows of ticks. I started to do one myself entitled 'How Good at Housework Are You?' Do you sweep under the beds a) once a week b) once a month c) once a year d) never. Everyone had mendaciously ticked a). If I were being truthful I would have had to answer d) to every question so the interest quickly palled.

I hobbled down to the craft shop to find Dimpsie fastening baby clothes on to a piece of pegboard.

'Hand me those drawing pins, would you, darling? I can't get these bootees to stick on.'

The bootees were knitted in emerald and puce wool. 'Aren't they rather strange colours? Don't people usually dress babies in pink or pale blue?'

159

'Oh, I know. Mrs Gribbling makes them. She unpicks her husband's old jerseys – he's been dead for years so he doesn't mind – and they're all the most awful colours. The last lot were khaki and rust. Quite hideous. And she knits day and night so I've boxes full.'

'Does she ever sell any?'

'Never. From time to time, to save her feelings, I pretend someone's bought something and give her a tenner.'

'You'll never make a business woman.' I bent down to kiss her. 'But I'm glad.'

'I'm not. I'd simply love to make some money.'

'What would you do with it?'

'I'd buy a nice old house and do it up for artists to come and live in rent free so they could concentrate on their work without worldly distractions. And I'd send tractors to Africa, clothes to Indian earthquake victims, that sort of thing.'

I looked sadly at the contents of the craft shop, at the crocheted shawls, the felt egg cosies, the dolls with crinoline skirts designed to disguise spare rolls of lav paper, the macramé plant hammocks, the donkey made of fur fabric with buttons for eyes. None of this seemed the raw material from which international philanthropy might spring.

'Let me do that.' I took the bootees from Dimpsie. 'You go and do some more accounting, then we'll go to the Singing Swan and have lunch.'

'That *would* be nice.' Dimpsie raised wistful eyes to mine. 'You can't think what a treat it is for me to have you home. Of course I couldn't be sorrier about your leg, but I do feel grateful to have this little time together. We've always got on so well, darling, haven't we?'

'Yes . . . always.' I don't believe she intended to pierce my heart with sorrow and guilt.

It was more difficult to fill the hours of Sunday. Dimpsie sat at the kitchen table, her head spinning with figures that refused to add up. As I was bad at arithmetic myself, I couldn't help, so I wrote to Bobbie, thanking her for her help and bringing her up to date with family news. Then I wrote a longer letter to Lizzie, mostly about Evelyn, Isobel and Rafe. In the early years of our friendship she had listened sympathetically while I raved for hours about his masculine beauty, devastating sophistication and sporting prowess. I described working at the surgery, hoping to amuse, and touched briefly on the sad state of my parents' marriage.

I didn't mention Dimpsie's drinking, though it had become part of our daily lives. She took secret little nips throughout the day. By about seven o'clock she was slurring her words and dropping things and weeping. Usually I succeeded in persuading her to go to bed before she lost consciousness. My father came home after hospital or evening surgery to change his clothes before driving off without saying where he was going and returning long after midnight. He seemed invigorated by this new regime. While he crackled with energy, Dimpsie spent more and more time in bed and looked puffy-eyed and grey. None of this would have made edifying reading for Lizzie.

Having finished my letter, I decided to tackle another book on my self-improvement list. I thought I would save *On the Origin of Species* and Gombrich's *The Story of Art* for later. A snowbound afternoon suggested the easier option of a novel. I found my second-hand copy of *Ulysses* by James Joyce and took it into my boat bed with a sense of reprieve from intellectual labour. It seemed a good idea to begin with the preface, so I could be sure I was getting every nuance intended by the author. After a paragraph or two under the tutelage of Professor Zubloch-Weizman my head was spinning with sentences as intricately woven as the macramé plant hammocks. What was neologistic wordplay, I wondered? What an exegesis? A somatic scheme? When it came to inspissated obscurities, I drifted into a gentle doze. I was woken by Dimpsie tapping on my door.

'Sweetheart, are you terribly busy? I'm at the end of my tether. I've added the same column six times and got a different answer each time. *Raiders of the Lost Ark* is on at the fleapit. I read a review saying it was enjoyable hokum and I thought it might be just what we both needed.'

Joyfully I snapped *Ulysses* shut.

On Monday evening I had received a telephone call from Isobel.

'Of *course* you're coming tomorrow. You've *got* to. Conrad's definitely going to be there and Mummy's asked half the county. I must have *some*one on my side.'

'Won't Conrad be on your side?'

'Oh yes, but he'll be fenced around by jackals and vultures, not knowing anyone and being foreign. I don't see how he *can* come to my defence. He'll be too busy looking after himself.'

'What are you worried about exactly?'

'You know what Mummy's friends are like. They disapprove of anyone who differs by a millimetre from them. You've got to talk the same, know the same people, live in the same sort of houses, grow the same sort of flowers in your garden . . . Mummy once dropped some poor woman after she found her garden was full of red-hot pokers. When I'm married to Conrad I shall tell the gardener to plant wall-to-wall red-hot pokers, just for the joy of seeing Mummy's face when she comes to visit.'

I was impressed by Isobel's idea of beginning married life. I could not imagine having a gardener, much less having the temerity to tell him what to do. 'Rafe'll be on your side, won't he?'

'Yes and no. He's worried that I haven't spent enough time with Conrad to be sure I'll be happy living with him.'

'Perhaps a week isn't very long—' I began.

'Don't you start. I can tell about people straightaway. We clicked immediately. I've never met a man I felt so positive about.'

I was reassured when I remembered Conrad's shortness, baldness, tubbiness and his enormous nose and feet. It was obviously the attraction of like minds and not some passing sexual infatuation.

'Come early so we can have a calming drink before the others show up. Conrad's plane isn't due into Newcastle until seven so he can't be here until eight-thirty at the earliest. Mummy's already briefed Mrs Capstick to keep things simmering.'

When I presented myself, early as bidden, it seemed that other things were simmering besides the food.

'Hello, darling!' Isobel shrieked down the stairs as Spendlove let me into the hall. 'I'll be down in a minute. I'm having trouble with my hair. It's chosen this evening to be a perfect pig. Spendlove, give Miss Marigold a drink, will you?' She disappeared before I could assure her that her hair looked lovely.

Spendlove took me into the drawing room, poured me a glass of champagne, then scuttled off to see to things in the dining room. I was happy to rest on my crutches and admire the drawing room, which I rarely had the privilege of seeing empty of people. The paintings were mostly Italian landscapes, romantic but at the same time distinguished. The sofas were a sort of grassy-green damask trimmed with dark red fringes. In alcoves each side of the fireplace were shelves of wonderful porcelain. Evelyn's collection of tortoiseshell objets de vertu were prettily arranged on a satinwood table. In just the right places were vases of hyacinths, snowdrops and anemones. I heard quick footsteps in the hall and then Evelyn, looking glamorous in dark blue taffeta, came in.

'Marigold!' She kissed me. 'That pretty dress again. Sorry I wasn't down.'

'Don't worry about me, please.'

'Well, if you don't mind I'll just go and check the table. Darling, could I detail you to keep an eye on Kingsley? If he starts talking about the war, create a diversion. Scream, faint, throw a tantrum, anything! Honestly, it's too bad of Isobel to inflict this ghastly man on us.' I realized she meant Conrad Lerner and not Kingsley. 'She's left it until this morning to tell me that he has a skin disease that means he can't shake hands! I've rung the other guests to warn them but someone's bound to forget. If he can't touch people's hands, how on earth are they going to . . . still, perhaps it's as well if they don't have any children . . . Oh!' she clutched her head, 'I feel as though I'm going quite mad. There's the bell! It'll be the archdeacon. He's always the first to arrive, hoping to get the lion's share of the canapés. His wife can't come, luckily, because she's even more idiotic than he is and we've far too many women . . . not that I'm not thrilled to see you, darling . . .' Evelyn rushed away. I had never seen her so discomposed.

'Good evening, Miss Savage.' The archdeacon's tone as he came into the drawing room was funereal. 'It behoves us all to put our hand to the plough tonight. Poor Mrs Preston. It is wonderful how she bears up under the strain. Children do not understand how great is their power to strike at their parents' hearts!'

'I'm looking forward to meeting Conrad,' I said coldly, planting myself on the stool and placing my crutches so he could not stand on the hearth rug. I noticed, having been primed by Evelyn, that the archdeacon downed his glass of champagne with a single gulp and took a handful of anchovy palmiers that nearly emptied the bowl. 'Isobel says he's clever and amusing. I'm afraid he'll find us all dreadful bores.'

The archdeacon looked offended. 'Perhaps – though I doubt it – in *cleverness* there may be found some compensation for a sickly constitution.'

'I wouldn't say a skin disease makes him sickly, exactly.'

'I refer to the unfortunate man's hydrophobia.' I must have looked startled, for the archdeacon recovered his usual infuriating complacency. 'Isobel telephoned me this afternoon to ask for my help in managing a delicate situation. Apparently

Mr Lerner was once bitten by a rabid dog and, though the marvels of modern medicine saved his life, he has been unable to throw off all the side-effects of the condition. The merest mention of water is enough to induce a state of nervous excitement.' The archdeacon scooped the remaining palmiers from the bowl and munched them up, looking well pleased with his role of trusted family counsellor. It was clear to me by now that Isobel had been amusing herself at his – and our – expense. I looked forward to an interesting party.

As the other guests arrived, the archdeacon whispered a few words to each one. I was cruelly amused to see the look of strain that appeared on their faces in consequence. I easily identified Lord Dunderave, a fat man with a bad-tempered expression who demanded single malt whisky instead of champagne. Ronald, a pale young man with crinkly gingerish hair and prominent front teeth hovered at his father's elbow.

Isobel appeared on the threshold. She looked seductive in a dress of sealing-wax red. It was made of the flimsiest material and was cut so low that the archdeacon's nostrils went white as he looked at her and glances of wonderment flew about between the other guests. Ignoring those who tried to attract her attention, Isobel came to sit by me on the stool.

'Brilliant dress,' I said.

'Amazing, isn't it? Practically like being starkers. I thought I'd remind Conrad what a sexpot I am.'

The archdeacon, who was hovering nearby, pressed his lips into a thin line of remonstrance.

'Sorry I couldn't get down earlier. My hair was being absolutely bloody impossible.'

She had fastened it to one side with a diamond clip. She looked marvellously vampish and ten years older. Perhaps this was in deference to the advanced years of her betrothed. Outwardly she was poised but I could hear tension in her voice. She drank her glass of champagne quickly, talking between sips. 'Mummy's extremely put out. She told me to invite Conrad to

165

stay here but he sent a telegram to say he always travels with his factotum so they've taken rooms at a hotel in Carlisle. She thinks people will think it odd that we aren't putting him up. Well, so they may but who cares? Oh, look!' She waved. 'There's Rafe.'

I had seen him the minute he came in. His tall figure and noble brow were the more striking because the other men were all, except for poor Ronald, on the downward path physically, with pouched eyes, rolls of neck and swollen stomachs.

'Good Lord, Isobel!' Rafe examined his sister's dress with something like alarm on his face. 'Are you the cabaret?'

'Don't you like it? It was very expensive.'

'I'm sure it was. I don't dislike it,' he added as Isobel's eyes grew stormy. 'It's just not how I think of you, that's all. Hello, Marigold.' He stooped to kiss me politely on both cheeks. 'You're looking lovely as always.'

During the days that had passed since our last meeting, I had debated whether I should ring him to thank him for the lunch, but then I worried that the sound of my voice might reawaken the memory of what happened at the pele tower and destroy a precarious equilibrium. The most exquisite tact was called for.

'Thank you. How's the painting going?'

'The light's not been too good the last couple of days. Too much cloud. Have you recovered from being shot at? It's not every girl who can boast of having been the target of a crazy gypsy. Like Lorna Doone.'

'I've never read *Lorna Doone*.' I was relieved that he was smiling as though recalling a most diverting incident. 'In fact I've hardly read any novels. But I've just started *Ulysses* by James Joyce. It's on my list of improving books. So far I'm completely befogged but I'm hoping light will dawn.'

Rafe laughed. 'You continue to surprise me, Marigold.'

I was gratified by what had to be a compliment. After all, no one wants to be *un*surprising.

But Isobel said, 'Don't be patronizing, darling. Marigold's zeal for self-improvement is sweet and absolutely typical.'

I had the feeling, but perhaps I was imagining it, that I had been subtly put in my place.

'Where's the nabob?' asked Rafe. 'Everyone's longing to see the poor man. The archdeacon's eaten all the cheese straws and my stomach's grumbling like thunder.'

'Poor?' repeated Isobel, frowning.

'Meeting a whole room of people and not being able to shake hands with them? Awkward to say the least.' Rafe gave his sister a searching look which she fielded with a charming smile. 'Besides, I'm sorry for any man whose value lies in his chequebook.'

'That's not true. He's exceptionally interesting and nice.' Before he could reply she laid her hand gently on her brother's arm and her habitual expression of defiance softened. 'Please, darling, don't make up your mind to dislike him. You know how I feel. What we agreed.'

Rafe put his hand on hers. 'The truth is, I'm envious, of course. Goldmines seem to be the least of what you girls expect.'

I was disconcerted by the enquiring look he gave me.

'Oh, Marigold isn't acquisitive in the least,' Isobel laughed. 'Unless she's changed a great deal in the last five or six years.'

They exchanged glances that to me were unfathomable. Could it be that Rafe's interest in me was more than fraternal? He was friendly and attentive but nothing more. Perhaps the casual promiscuity of the ballet company had impaired my ability to decode messages from other men.

Evelyn came up to us, allowing her smile to slip for a moment. 'Isobel, where is this *wretch*ed man of yours? I've already had Capstick reheat the soup twice.'

'*I* don't know. Perhaps the plane was late. Perhaps he's changed his mind and isn't coming . . .' The agitation in Isobel's voice made me wonder if she was as sure about Conrad as she claimed to be. 'We could tell everyone the flight was cancelled.

Or he's got the date wrong and is coming next week . . . Marigold,' Isobel grabbed my arm, 'come and give me a hand with my zip. I can feel it inching its way down. In a minute all will be revealed.'

Obediently I followed her through the crowd into the hall, accidentally stabbing quite a few shins and feet with my crutches. 'What's the matter with it?'

'What's the matter with what?' Isobel shook her head impatiently.

'Your zip.'

'Nothing. I just had to get away from Mummy's endless questioning. She's gone on and on today about Conrad until my head's throbbing. If she was in uniform she'd be arrested for contravening the Geneva Convention. I had to get away from all those ghouls staring at me, speculating about whether I've been jilted or invented the whole thing. Probably Conrad's got more sense than to— There's the bell! It must be him! It *must* be!'

She held my arm tightly, digging in her fingernails until I murmured in protest, while Spendlove went to open the door. A shower of snow blew in, followed by two figures wrapped in overcoats, bringing with them a gust of cold air that made me shiver.

'Conrad!' Isobel rushed at one of the men and threw her arms round his neck. 'You're a *darling* to come! Thank you! *Thank* you!'

He kissed her cheek. 'It was not so very much after all. Merely a dash over narrow, twisting, vertical tracks made for mountain goats through snow so thickly falling that we might have been travelling through walls of ice. But it was a matter of course that we should risk our necks for the pleasure of seeing you, my dear Isobel.'

I had already guessed that some, if not all, of Isobel's descriptions of her lover were invented to tease, but now I actually had Conrad Lerner before my eyes it would be no exaggeration to

168

say that I was thunderstruck. That I recognized him at once was no great feat of memory, since only a week before we had spent an hour together as fellow passengers in the same railway carriage. It was the man with the astrakhan collar.

15

Evelyn came into the hall. After everything Isobel had said about her future husband, Evelyn must have been surprised to find herself looking up into Conrad's face instead of down on to his shining pate. Not only was he of a respectable height, with a full head of ink-black hair, but his nose, long and curving downwards slightly at the tip, had an aristocratic refinement that few Englishmen could boast. When Spendlove had helped Conrad out of his coat, it could be seen that his figure was slender and his feet in perfect proportion.

'How do you do? I am Isobel's mother.' Evelyn held out her hand, remembered the skin disease and withdrew it just as Conrad put out his. A dash of pink appeared on her white cheek. 'This appalling weather . . . such an awful journey from Newcastle . . . I hear they are thinking of closing the airport . . .' She drew breath and a steelier look came into her eye. 'Isobel has told us something about you but – naturally we were surprised to learn that our daughter had engaged herself to a virtual stranger without consulting the wishes of her family.'

Conrad looked at Isobel. It was, I thought, a questioning look.

'Perhaps,' Evelyn continued, still with that small patch of pink on her cheekbone, 'these things are managed differently in

Germany . . . I'm assured by my children that I'm hopelessly out of date . . . Apparently it is now common practice to marry someone one barely knows, without considering the feelings of anyone else.'

Conrad had turned his attention from Isobel to look gravely at her mother as she disburdened herself of this little speech, which I suspected she had rehearsed, hoping to pierce the *amour-propre* of the hated interloper. Faced with those black, un-wavering eyes, she had been unable to deliver it as smoothly as she had intended.

'Isobel tells me you are an industrialist – *un homme d'af-faires – molto occupato* . . . I suppose we must be grateful you have interrupted your busy schedule to come and see us. Oh dear!' Evelyn put her hands together and said almost pleadingly, 'Can you understand a word I'm saying?'

Conrad closed his eyes slowly and opened them again as though clearing his brain. 'I comprehend you perfectly, Mrs Preston. Forgive me, I am bewildered—'

'Of course you are,' Isobel interrupted. 'I expect you've got jet lag. Anyway, Mummy, he's here *now* – that's what matters. Hello, Fritz.' Isobel shook the hand of the man who stood beside Conrad. He had pale golden hair that hung in curls round his pink and white face. He smiled shyly and two dimples appeared in his fat cheeks. He looked like one of those painted cherubs that flutter about the vaulted ceilings in Italian churches – only with clothes on, of course. 'I hope you like being in the wild wastes of Northumberland. No, of course you don't. No one could. But it's good for you to take your nose out of a book. Mummy, this is Fritz Wolter. He's a scholar and terribly serious and Conrad never goes anywhere without him. Fritz, this is my mother.'

'How do you do?' Fritz bent over her hand, kissing the air a centimetre above it.

Isobel seized Conrad's arm. 'Come and meet Marigold. My very best friend from years and years ago. She's a brilliant dancer

171

only she's broken her foot so for the moment she's only hopping along – very gracefully.' Isobel made a face at me that Conrad could not see. 'And she's a tremendous bluestocking.'

'We've already met,' I said.

'I think not,' said Conrad, 'I should have remembered it.'

I understood why Evelyn's usual *sang froid* had deserted her. It was not easy to maintain one's composure beneath the stare of sharp, treacle-black eyes like reflecting glass, revealing nothing of the thoughts of their owner. I felt confused and foolish. Had I dreamed it? Or were there two men of distinctive appearance and identical coats at large in Northumberland? 'But the train—'

'It is encouraging to meet with so youthful a *savante*.' A slight pressure from his hand before he released mine told me I had not been mistaken. I understood that I was to say nothing more about our meeting. But why had he been travelling on a train in England when Isobel believed him to be in Germany?

'Oh, Marigold's *years* older than she looks,' said Isobel. 'She has to be like a strand of gossamer so that she can be twirled about above people's heads.'

Conrad's face remained impassive. 'An exacting stipulation.' Though his accent was noticeably foreign, his command of the English language was better than that of many of its native speakers.

'Come along,' Evelyn sounded rattled. 'Everyone's starving. We'll get the introductions over with as fast as we can.'

If Conrad was unnerved to find himself the object of frankly curious stares, he hid it well. At least half the guests instinctively offered their hands only to snatch them back when they remembered the skin contagion. I watched this little pantomime with amusement. After two or three such incidents, Conrad kept his hands clasped behind his back and responded to introductions by drawing himself up and bowing from the neck, which looked dignified and rather glamorous.

'Well?' said Rafe in my ear. 'Not quite what we were led to expect. Isobel is a minx. No sign of a squint as far as I can see. And I'd hardly call those jug-handle ears.'

'Is that what she told you? No, I'd say he was remarkably handsome.'

'He seems to have the usual complement of features. What's remarkable about him?'

'Those eyes, most of all. You can't tell what he's thinking. But you can be sure he is.'

'Is what?'

'Thinking something.'

'So I should hope, unless the man's a moron.'

'Whatever he is, it's a relief to know that if Isobel does marry him she won't be condemned to go to bed with a tiny Mr Punch whose feet rip holes in the sheets whenever he turns over.'

Rafe laughed and tugged at a strand of my hair in a brotherly way. 'He's a gentleman anyway, which is more than I'd hoped for.'

I looked again at Conrad, who was listening to Lady Pruefroy, a big woman in brown velvet with a bossy manner who tapped his chest with her finger as she talked, like a woodpecker hammering at the bark of a tree. 'How can you tell?'

'I don't know. Something about his manner, his self-confidence perhaps . . . It's impossible to describe but it's unmistakable.'

'Not to me. Would you say all the men in this room are gentlemen?'

Rafe's eyes wandered round the room, examining the little groups of conversing guests.

'Yes,' said Rafe. 'Not Spendlove, of course.'

'Is the archdeacon a gentleman? He's awfully greedy. I've just seen him eat the last two vol-au-vents.'

'Nonetheless, he is a gentleman.'

'His eyes are cold and mean. And he was catty about Isobel.'

'Gentlemen are sometimes greedy and catty. It's more a question of style than of virtue.'

173

'Actually I like Spendlove better than anyone. Except you. And Kingsley, of course.'

'That's because you're a wild young bohemian, Lorna Doone.' Rafe stared at me in a way that was not quite brotherly. 'And very fetching, too.'

I suspected, but could not be absolutely certain, that he was flirting with me. Before I could think of a suitably wild reply, dinner was announced.

The moment we sat down a maid came in with a jug of water. Isobel, who was sitting next to the archdeacon, played her part very prettily, tapping his arm to draw his attention to the fact that his glass had been filled with the baleful substance. His face became consternated, he sprang up and whispered something in the girl's ear. She looked surprised but left the room, taking the water jug with her. Isobel pointed to the archdeacon's glass. Manfully he picked it up and drank off the whole tumbler without pause, only panting a little when he put it down.

I turned to Ronald on my right. 'I feel sorry for the soldiers in the Falklands.' I had read a long and rather boring news-paper article about the Falklands War over lunch, with the self-less intention of entertaining my neighbours at dinner. 'Apparently the weather's awful. Mr Galtieri shouldn't have put up his flag in South Georgia, but I don't think we should have colonized the islands in the first place.'

'Eh?' Ronald wrinkled his nose. 'Good thing, the war. Teach those dagos what to expect when they trespass on British territory.'

'But whose land was it before we claimed it in 1833?'

Ronald looked at me with something like distaste. 'Haven't the foggiest.'

'Apparently a lot of the Argentinian bombs are no good and don't go off, which is lucky for us.' Ronald was noisily sucking up soup and didn't seem to have heard. 'I can hardly believe,' I went on, 'that the whole thing started because of a whale slaughterhouse that employed Argentinians instead of English people. It seems too silly for words.'

Ronald gobbled down a piece of Melba toast.

'Actually,' I was provoked by Ronald's lacklustre response, 'I think all war is stupid and wicked whichever side you're on.'

He paused mid-suck to look at me in a startled way. 'Steady on. This is damned good soup. What is it?'

I picked up one of the menus written in Evelyn's elegant hand. '*Potage de Crevettes*. That's shrimps, isn't it?'

'Haven't the foggiest.' Ronald buttered another piece of toast.

The Falklands had proved a damp squid – or was it squib? – conversationally. 'Do you know what inspissated means?'

'Eh?' He blinked his sandy lashes and stuck out the end of his tongue. 'Haven't the foggiest.' There was a pause. 'Nasty blizzard,' he announced when he'd got down his toast.

'I agree it makes getting about difficult, but it's so beautiful. This morning there was an icicle a foot long hanging from the eaves above my bedroom window. It's supposed to be the perfect murder weapon. But not terribly convenient. What are the chances of the murderer, the victim and the icicle all being in the same place at once?'

Ronald looked at me as though he doubted my sanity. 'M'father's in a bate on account of the weather.'

'Is he?' I leaned forward so I could see Lord Dunderave, who was sitting on Evelyn's right. He was slumped sideways with one arm on the table, his hand curled round a whisky glass. His lower lip was thrust out and his forehead was crumpled over his eyes. He looked about as furious as anyone could look without actually shouting and banging their fists. 'Why?'

''Cause he can't hunt, of course,' explained Ronald. 'That's all m'father likes doing. Last season he killed twenty-four foxes and two horses. Bung me another bit of toast, would you?'

I removed the silver bread basket from beneath the archdeacon's outstretched fingers.

'You mean he *shot* the horses?' I knew little of country

pursuits, but I had an idea that horse shooting was not *comme il faut,* as Evelyn would say. However Lord Dunderave looked so horrible I was prepared to believe anything of him.

'Oh no. Rode one into a ditch and the brute broke its neck. And the other into a plough some fool had left the other side of a hedge. I'm not that keen on hunting myself.'

I felt thoroughly disgusted. 'I should think not!'

'It's expensive. M'father's tight with my allowance. If I got married he'd have to stump up.' Ronald looked across the table at Isobel, who was sitting between Conrad and the archdeacon. 'I like shooting better than hunting. Does Isobel go out with the guns, d'you know?'

'I've no idea.'

'A girl can be useful. Picking up, holding the cartridges, that sort of thing. These days some of 'em actually shoot but I don't like to see that. A girl ought to stay behind the line. I read in s'morning's paper some of 'em even want to be vicars. Perish the thought! Vicars in knickers, the headline was,' Ronald snorted with amusement. 'Damn good, eh? Vicars in – ha-ha – knickers.'

Ronald lifted his upper lip and whickered like a horse. Evelyn sent me an approving glance. The soup was taken away and replaced by slices of very rare beef with braised celery and roast potatoes. I glanced timidly at my right-hand neighbour, Conrad's man of business. I remembered that his name was Fritz. He was staring at the silver candlestick in front of him, his pink and white forehead wrinkled in thought.

'Is this your first visit to Northumberland?' I began.

'No.' He turned his eyes slowly to meet mine. They were large with curly eyelashes. He made a noise like *tsk* and looked quite alarmed. 'That is, I desire to say – yes. Forgif me. My English is not good.'

'It has an interesting history. For a long time it was a battle-ground between England and Scotland and they fought each other and stole each other's cattle and Hadrian built a wall.'

'Ah yes, I haf much about it read. Zo I do not English vell speak I can it read.'

I decided to give up the intellectual pose. 'In that case you know much more about it than I do. We hardly did any history at school, only the Tudors and Stuarts about four hundred times. I'm a complete ignoramus really.'

'Vat? You haf the English history of sixteen and seventeen centuries studied *four* hundred times? You must be most wise. And what is ignoramus? This word I do not know.'

'Oh, it just means someone who doesn't know anything. I expect it's slang.'

'Ah, *das ist sehr gut*.' He brought out from his trousers pocket a notepad and a pencil. 'Please, gracious miss, to spell it for me. I am most interesting in ze dialects of Englant.'

I spelt it for him and he solemnly wrote it down. 'And it means *Unwissende*? I am sure zat zis is not true of you.' His mouth curled into a smile, dimpling his plump cheeks attractively. 'May I ask it zat you me tell of ze English kings zat you haf so much studied? I like wery much King Charles II. A most witty and laughable man. I haf read soon ago about the Treaty of Breda vich as you vill know ended ze Second Dutch War. Vat zink you of zis policy?'

I laughed. 'Honestly, Fritz, I can't tell you anything. I'm a dancer. Ballet. That's all I know about.'

'Ho! *Das Ballett?* I love ze ballet. And you it dance? *Wunderbar!* Please, tell me about you.'

So I did, and Fritz listened and questioned and looked fascinated and for once I was a genuine social success, but only because Fritz was the most stimulating audience. I remembered just in time that I was supposed to be encouraging him to talk as well.

'Do you know what "inspissated" means?'

'I am sorry not. Vat is ze situation you find it, gracious miss?'

'Do call me Marigold. It's in the preface to a famous book called *Ulysses* by James Joyce. Inspissated obscurities.'

177

'I know ze book, of course. But I haf it read only in German, I regret. It is remarkable for – excuse me, Conrad.' Conrad broke off a conversation with Isobel to look at him enquiringly. 'Marigold and I talk of James Joyce. How you say in English *der Bewußtseinsstrom?*'

'Stream of consciousness,' said Conrad.

'Ah yes.' Fritz scribbled this on a page in his notebook. 'And vat means inspissated obscurities?'

Conrad drew his black brows together in thought. 'In general inspissated means something that thickens. By process of evaporation, for example. Like salt crystals. In the context of James Joyce I take it to mean that the complexities and riddles of the novel pile up one upon another.'

The guests at our end of the table looked both alarmed and disgusted by the highbrow tone of our conversation, but Evelyn sanctioned it with a smile of approval. I was sorry that Rafe was sitting too far away to witness my triumph. The archdeacon was holding forth to Lady Pruefoy and did not see Isobel point to his water glass. Obediently the maid brought back the jug and filled it. Isobel tapped his arm. Bravely he gulped it down. Perhaps it would do his dandruff some good.

'I say,' Ronald paused in the rapid consumption of his chestnut ice, 'that fellow of Isobel's.' He cast an unfriendly glance across the table at Conrad. 'Can't believe she really likes him. He's a Jew, isn't he? D'you think if the weather improves Isobel might like a day out next week picking up?'

'I'm absolutely certain she'd hate it.'

I disliked Ronald too much to talk to him. I stole a look at Rafe who had Bunty as his neighbour. He said something to her which made her eyes light up with pleasure. I felt a pang of something suspiciously like jealousy shoot through the melange of soup, beef and ice in my stomach. Could it be . . . was I actually in love with him? My eyes wandered to Isobel and Conrad. He was listening as she talked earnestly. It was not difficult to see what had persuaded Isobel to agree to his proposal. By comparison with the other men at the table, Conrad was as a pomegranate among potatoes. You cannot sustain large peasant populations with pomegranates, but Conrad's mysterious and exotic air made the others seem stodgy and colourless.

And the mystery was more than a combination of foreign looks and an enigmatic gaze. What had he been doing on that train from Newcastle to Carlisle? Why had he kept his presence in the neighbourhood a secret from Isobel? I smiled as I thought of the surprise it must have given him to find a witness to his deceit turning up in the heart of the citadel he was set to conquer.

The savoury, *cornes de jambon*, was brought in, little cornucopias of golden pastry filled with finely chopped ham in a pale green sauce. I saw Evelyn beckon to the maid, point to her own and then Conrad's water glass. Conrad sipped the water as calmly as though it were mother's milk. The archdeacon was talking over Lady Pruefoy's head to her other neighbour and did not notice. Heartlessly Isobel instructed the girl to fill his glass.

'Well?' demanded Lady Pruefoy of Evelyn as soon as we women – except Isobel, who had gone to the lavatory – were gathered in the drawing room. 'What d'you think of him? I must say he's not at all what I expected.'

'I have to admit,' Evelyn leaned over the tray to pour the coffee, 'I'm agreeably surprised. He knows a great deal about furniture. And porcelain. He seems intelligent. Though I dislike the idea of my daughter marrying someone whose background is so different from her own, at least he is not a blockhead.'

'He's so very black in his looks, though,' said Lady Pruefoy. 'Not his skin, I don't mean – that's so sallow as to be positively unhealthy; perhaps it's that nasty disease you rang to tell me of this morning – but his hair and eyes. You'd never guess he was European, would you? I suppose it's the –' she lowered her voice – 'Jewish blood. Dear Evelyn, I feel for you,. One hardly wants one's grandchildren to look like little gypsies.'

Lady Pruefoy had silver hair piled up into a cone, like a Norman helmet, only without the nose-piece, of course, and a snow-white moustache. Some small allowance had to be made for the nastiness of her remarks, for she had spent a dull evening sitting between the archdeacon and a man who had lectured her about Common Market agricultural policies until her chin had sunk on to her brown velvet bosom and her eyes had rolled upwards.

Evelyn frowned. 'Dark, yes, but handsome. And he has good teeth and bones.'

'Teeth can be corrected. But one can do nothing about bad blood.'

Evelyn smiled. 'Fortunately Isobel will move in international circles where racism is considered extremely provincial.'

I looked with interest at Lady Pruefoy to see how she was taking that. She inflated an already large bosom to say, 'I wonder how a delicately nurtured girl like Isobel will like the society of greasy Greek shipping magnates and Sicilian mafioso.'

'Mafiosi,' said Evelyn, mimicking astonishment rather well. 'But I forgot, dear Poppy, you have never learned Italian.'

Isobel returned just then, so that conversation was halted.

'Evelyn's so cosmopolitan.' Bunty perched next to me on the sofa, her dress caught up on her large knees, exposing enormous feet in black suede court shoes that had seen better days. 'I do so admire her.'

'So do I,' I said truthfully.

'And Kingsley is such a sweet old man and Isobel is so . . . so original.' Bunty's already pink face darkened a shade and her eyes became dewy. 'Rafe is . . . perfectly charming.'

'Isn't he?'

'I know you and he are just like brother and sister. Evelyn's told me how you came every day to play with her children and I do envy you.' Bunty's slightly bulging eyes grew wistful. 'Being an only child the hols were awfully lonely. My pony, Raffles, was my best friend.'

'Lucky you to have a pony!' I gushed.

'Yes. He was lovely – a bay with a blaze and white socks – but my relationship with Raffles wasn't much of a preparation for adult life.' She laughed self-deprecatingly. There was something attractive about this gangling girl that had nothing to do with looks. Probably it was her honesty. 'Often I find it quite difficult to talk to men. Usually I'm looking down on the tops of their heads, which doesn't help. But Rafe's so tall . . . and he's so good at putting one at ease.' She leaned a little closer and I saw the edge of a woollen vest above the neck of her dress. 'We used to meet at tennis parties and sometimes he came to Lumbe Hall to shoot. You won't tell him, will you?' Bunty's eyes were softly appealing. 'I used to call him Prince Charming. Only to Raffles, of course. I'd shut my eyes and pretend I was waltzing with him in a beautiful dress . . . me wearing the dress, I mean . . . oh, it was all too silly. Promise you won't tell?'

'I promise.'

'Oh, here they are.' Bunty stood up as Rafe, with his arm through Kingsley's, led the men into the drawing room. 'Will you excuse me, Marigold? I promised Evelyn I'd help take round the cups.'

I watched her as she went to the tray. Several inches of yellowish petticoat hung down beneath the hem of her dress. Evelyn saw it too and frowned, instantly changing the frown for a smile of encouragement as Bunty looked up. Spendlove came in with a decanter of brandy and a soda-water siphon. The archdeacon tried to make him take it away, but Evelyn gave him an angry look and summoned it back. I felt almost sorry for the archdeacon. He did not seem to have had a moment's relaxation all evening.

'Hello,' said a voice at my elbow. It was Kingsley. One of his shirt studs had popped, revealing a diamond-shaped section of chest, sparsely whiskered. 'I don't believe we've met.' He plumped himself down on the sofa beside me. 'Phew! It's a relief to take the weight off my feet. I'm not as young as I was and these late nights don't suit me.' He put his face close to mine. His sagging lower eyelids and trembling lips were sad to see. An old soldier whose battles were all fought now, save the last and most fearful battle of all. 'But not past it, you know. I can still do it.' He contorted his face into a satyric leer. 'Oh, yes. The brave lad still stands to attention.' He took hold of my hand and tried to guide it towards his crotch. 'Out in Egypt it was hot – by gum, the beggars and the dirt and the flies made you sick to your stomach, but those dusky little girls were so beautiful, it gives me an ache in my belly to think of them. Your hair's the colour of flames. I'd like to dive naked into them.'

'There you are, Father.' Rafe was leaning over us from behind the sofa. 'Lord Dunderave wants to know if you'd like to take a rod in Scotland this August.'

'Good God, no!' Kingsley looked horrified. 'Can't stand the man. Tell him no, my boy.'

'That won't do, Father,' Rafe's voice was firm. 'You must tell him yourself.'

'Can't think why Evelyn's always inviting him,' Kingsley protested as his son helped him up. 'He's bad-tempered and a rotten shot.' Grumbling he walked off.

'I'm so sorry,' Rafe said as he drove me home an hour later. 'Sexual disinhibition is a classic symptom of dementia, according to the specialist. Buster, be quiet! This morning I caught him trying to goose Mrs Capstick. She's very loyal and said she quite understood that the master wasn't himself. I hope you aren't too shocked.'

'Not at all. He's never been anything but very kind to me.'

'Bless you for that. If it gets any worse I suppose we'll have to keep him within bounds somehow. Shut up, Buster! But you don't want to hear all my family problems. I hope you didn't have too bad a time with Ronald at dinner. He's a bit of an ass.'

'I expect he thought I was completely deranged.'

Buster was yelping directly into my right ear, making my head swim. I slipped my arm between the front seats and groped around in the back to stroke him. I found his paw. The minute I took hold of it he stopped barking so I hung on.

'You and Fritz were getting on like a house on fire.'

'He's a darling. I did think Conrad was rather exciting, didn't you?'

'Exciting? That wouldn't be the adjective I'd choose. After you women left the table he hardly said a word. I suppose to be fair, none of us had much to say. Dunderave and Crimple-Pratt started a row about the Common Market which set Father off about the Germans so I had to pretend we'd run out of port.'

We both laughed. The post mortems in the car going home were almost the most enjoyable parts of Shottestone dinners.

'I could see you were having great success with Bunty.'

'We were talking about horses.'

'She looked as though she was enjoying herself.'

'I hope so. But I wouldn't want her to get the wrong idea. Don't think me conceited – the thing is, Marigold, you're so sweet and easy to talk to and I mustn't abuse that – but my mother's been trying to throw us, Bunty and me, together with marriage in mind. Did you ever hear anything so ridiculous? Of course it's impossible.'

'Is it? Actually I think she's unusually honest and nice.'

'Do you? Well . . . yes, I suppose she is. But what man marries for niceness? She has as much sex appeal as dear old Nanny Sparkles.' Nanny Sparkles had looked after two generations of Preston children and now lay beneath the snow in Gaythwaite churchyard. 'I simply couldn't go through with it.'

I was puzzled by the despondency of his tone. 'Do many men marry to please their parents these days?'

'No,' he said slowly. 'No, I suppose not.'

'Evelyn would want you to be happy.'

'Yes. But she's convinced she knows better than I do what would make me happy.' The fierceness with which he said this surprised me. 'Bunty'll inherit a large estate. And Evelyn would be able to keep her under her thumb. She'd never be a threat to my mother's supremacy.'

183

'To be fair,' I said, 'I expect all mothers want their children to marry the sort of people who'll fit in easily with their own circle. All mothers except mine, that is. Dimpsie would adore it if I married a flamenco dancer or the ringmaster of a travelling circus. That's because she doesn't have a social position to maintain. And she's a romantic.'

'I hope you won't.'

'Probably not. It would be so difficult to juggle careers – and I hate animals being kept in cages and made to perform.'

'If you were married, would it be absolutely necessary for you to go on dancing?'

'Oh yes. I'm horribly ambitious, you know.'

'Is it quite impossible that you might ever love someone enough to give it up so you could be with them? I don't know much about ballet but I suppose it involves hours of practice and world tours and so on. If – I admit it's unlikely – your fancy happened to light on some poor fool who was obliged to live in the remoter regions of . . . let's say, for argument's sake, Northumberland, where his family had lived for generations – let's imagine that because he's the only son he feels it's his duty to carry on the tradition – in those most improbable circumstances, might you contemplate sacrificing your career in order to rusticate in the wilderness with him?'

I grew hot suddenly and my heart drummed so violently that my ears squeaked. Rafe's choice of words was light-hearted but his voice was serious. The porch light of Dumbola Lodge appeared up ahead and at the same moment the wheels started to spin on the icebound drive. I felt us slide backwards, felt the car tumble down, down, down into the black foaming waters below . . . we stopped. I opened my eyes and took my gloved fist, the one not holding Buster's paw, out of my mouth. We had pulled up beside the front door.

'Sorry, did that frighten you? I had to let the car roll back a bit to get the tyres to grip.'

I hoped I had not actually screamed. Before I could begin to

184

repair my dignity, the front door opened to reveal my father, muffled in overcoat and scarf, standing in a segment of light. He inched his way over the frozen ground and came to peer into the car.

'Oh, it's you.' He opened the door. 'I was expecting someone else. Hello, Rafe. Hurry up, Marigold. It's bloody perishing out here.' He took hold of my arm.

'Hello, sir. How are you?'

'Fine. Don't bother to get out. I'll get the crutches.'

I only had time to express the briefest of thanks before I was bundled indoors. Two minutes later I heard the sound of another car. I looked out of the drawing-room window. Something large like a Range Rover skidded to a halt. My father got in. The interior light came on for a few seconds, long enough to show me the sharp, rather exaggerated features of Marcia Dane.

16

'So he's gone away for ten days.' Evelyn's tone was exasperated. 'And I don't believe Isobel has any idea where. Germany, Timbuktu, the North Pole. Isobel and Rafe have gone to Edinburgh to visit friends. Her idea. I think she didn't want to seem to be hanging forlornly about waiting for her fiancé to drop in when he felt like it. It's very strange behaviour for a newly engaged man. When I agreed to marry Kingsley he sent me flowers every single day and wanted to take me out to dinner every evening. He almost wept if I said I was busy. And what about the ring? He hasn't given her so much as a rhinestone.'

We were in the sitting room at home. It was a measure of Evelyn's unease that she had driven over to see Dimpsie instead of summoning her to Shottestone. I knew she found the decoration at Dumbola Lodge unsettling. She had waited until my mother's back was turned before flipping over the sofa cushion to see if the other side was cleaner. So Rafe was in Edinburgh. I need not hang about the hall, listening for the telephone. After our last conversation, which I had mulled over endlessly whenever I had leisure, I had expected that he would ring.

'Perhaps Conrad's gone to get her one,' I suggested. I had offered to leave Evelyn and Dimpsie to a tête-à-tête, but Evelyn had said she would value my opinion. 'Perhaps at this moment he's deep in a mine in South Africa watching eagerly as men stripped to the waist with sweat running like water down their backs are carefully chipping an enormous sparkling diamond from the bare rock by the light of flaming torches.'

'Sometimes, Marigold, I think you allow your imagination too free a rein,' said Evelyn reprovingly. 'For one thing, if Conrad wanted to buy diamonds he could go to a shop in Bond Street. And for another, diamonds in their natural state look like lumps of cloudy glass. It's the cutting that makes them sparkle.'

'How disappointing! I always imagined them shining in the darkness like fragments of ice. Shall I get a knife?'

Evelyn had brought us one of Mrs Capstick's delicious seed cakes. A cynic might think this mere self-interest, ensuring something to eat that had been cooked in a clean kitchen, but she had also brought us some rose-pink rhubarb forced under big pots in her garden and some tobacco brown eggs from her hens, from which she could not expect any personal benefit. Generosity was one of her most attractive qualities.

'I'll go.' Dimpsie stood up. 'It takes you so long with your poor leg.'

Evelyn's eyes rested briefly on the string sculpture from the craft shop, which hung on the wall above the bookcase. She averted her eyes from the carving of an African warrior with spear and protruding navel and fixed them on me.

'Your mother's not looking well. Her complexion's grey and her eyes are bloodshot. Is she drinking again?'

I knew I could trust Evelyn. 'I'm afraid so. At least a bottle of wine a night. And I keep finding glasses of what looks like water hidden behind vases and things. Only it smells like gin.'

Evelyn made a sound like *hrrr*. 'I hoped your being here might help. The thing is, it's a ghastly situation for her. I don't know how much you know – I don't want to upset you, darling—'

'If you mean, do I know that my father has other women, yes, I do.'

'Oh, Marigold!' Evelyn looked at me with compassion. 'How horrid for you!'

'I suppose I've always known but I didn't want to think about it. Now I can't avoid seeing what's going on. Vanessa Trumball came to the surgery today.'

'Beastly woman!' Evelyn put her cup on its saucer quite violently. 'Mrs Capstick tells me – not that I allow the servants to gossip, of course, but apparently it's all over the town – that her husband left her because of her relationship with your father. The Trumball woman clearly has no idea how to conduct herself. All men stray but if they're discreet it hardly matters. No, the problem is that your poor mother minds so much. Well, sooner or later Mrs Trumball will find that life beyond the pale has its disadvantages. I hear the Red Cross have voted her off the committee. Not that that's altogether a misfortune. If I have to go to one more grisly coffee morning and drink Nescafé and eat buns like cement I shall commit adultery myself.' She smiled to show she wasn't serious and leaned forward to place her hand on my knee. 'Never mind, darling. Vanessa Trumball will live to regret her unscrupulous behaviour. From all I hear, your father is incapable of being faithful even to his paramours.'

'Actually, I think she's regretting it already. This morning I could see she'd been crying and her hair was standing up at the back as though she hadn't brushed it since getting out of bed. She's been ringing the surgery at least five times a day all week. My father told me on no account to put her through. I tried to stop her going into the consulting room but she dashed in while he had Mrs Wiggins on the examination couch with her skirt round her waist.'

'You don't mean—?' Evelyn looked shocked.

'Oh no, not Mrs Wiggins. She must be at least a hundred and ten. She's got a prolapsed womb. There was quite a scene and Tom took hold of her shoulders – Vanessa Trumball's, I mean – and marched her out through the waiting room and pushed her into the street. He told her if she didn't leave him

188

alone he'd get an injunction to prevent her coming to the surgery. The other patients were utterly thrilled, watching all this with eyes out on stalks like a row of snails.'

'So he's finished with her? Well, that's something to be thankful for. Perhaps your poor mother will feel a little happier.'

'I don't think so. Not long after Vanessa Trumball had been thrown out on her ear, Marcia Dane rang.'

'Marcia Dane? The woman who's just moved into the Old Rectory? All teeth and eyes? I met her at the Harvey-Somerton's lunch the other day. She smiled like a crocodile at every man in the room and smoked between courses.'

'That's her.'

'Perhaps she's got gynaecological problems too?'

I shook my head. 'Tom told me to take her off his list yesterday. Nurse Bunker and Nurse Keppel were there and they started tittering and winking at each other, only they daren't say anything in front of me. Of course he'd be struck off for having an affair with one of his patients.'

'I see.' Evelyn looked worried and I knew what she was thinking. Marcia Dane was an altogether different proposition from Vanessa Trumball. Marcia Dane had striking looks, money and pizzazz. It was not easy to imagine her being chucked out onto the pavement.

'Well, we must hope *she* gets bored with *him*. What a nuisance men are . . . we were just saying, Dimpsie,' she added quickly as my mother, looking flushed and smelling strongly of alcohol, returned with the knife for the cake, 'what a bother men are. However, before he left, Mr Lerner did condescend to accept an invitation to lunch next week. Marigold, you'll come and make up the numbers, won't you? I've asked Dame Gloria Beauwhistle, the composer. I haven't met her myself but she's bound to inject a little fizz. She had such a success last year with that opera – what was it called? Something medieval. *The Knight of the Holy* something . . . an odd name . . . something to do with kitchens.'

189

'*The Holy Colander?*' I suggested.

Evelyn did not have a sense of humour. 'No, no, that's not it.' She pressed her fingers to her temples. '*The Knight of the Burning Pestle*. I didn't see it myself – I don't care much for anything later than the First Viennese School – but it had wonderful reviews. Her family have lived in Northumberland for generations and she's just bought back her ancestral home in the village of Coldthorpe. I received a charming letter of acceptance from Dame Gloria and I've asked Sybil Hinchingbrook as well. People seem to think quite a lot of Sybil's flower paintings. To me they seem perfectly insipid but possibly I'm missing something.' It was apparent that she did not really believe this. 'She's bringing her brother, Basil. He's a very successful publisher. Sybil says he's been staying with her for two weeks, recovering from a particularly exhausting book fair. After two weeks of Sybil's conversation he must be nearly dead with ennui. I wonder,' she added musingly, 'if he might do for Isobel. Sybil did mention that he wasn't married.'

'What about Ronald?' I asked

'Oh, he won't do at *all*,' Evelyn said impatiently, as though I was making a preposterous suggestion. 'He's far too stupid and besides his father is such an un*pleas*ant man. He complained that the beef we had at dinner the other night was overcooked. It was as rare as it could possibly be without actually oozing blood.'

'Is Basil good looking?' I asked.

'I've never set eyes on the man. Why?'

'I was just wondering what he might offer that would make Isobel prefer him to Conrad.'

'For a start he's English. They'd have a common culture.'

'I'm not sure that Conrad's differentness isn't a major part of his attraction.'

'You mean dissimilarity, darling. Differentness is extremely ugly . . . I'm surprised with all this reading you do . . . however, I see your point.' She frowned. 'Then we must hope that his casual attitude towards her – neglect would not be an exaggeration – may be enough to wean her from such vitiated tastes.'

'Marigold liked Conrad,' Dimpsie put in. She was sipping tea thirstily and had a job to find the saucer when she wanted to put down her cup.

'Marigold is young and impressionable,' said Evelyn tartly. 'Mr Lerner talks well and knows how to make himself agreeable.'

I remembered that Evelyn had softened towards him after that dinner and had as good as defended him to Lady Pruetoy.

'Surely that's very much in his favour?' protested Dimpsie. 'You make it sound as though he's an impostor.'

'Perhaps he is. I know nothing about him. That's the trouble. Who are his parents? His grandparents? No,' she sat up straighter and smoothed the wrinkles from her dove-coloured cashmere cardigan in a decisive gesture, 'he may be well educated and *sortable,* which I admit is a relief after everything Isobel told me, but he is in every other way unsuitable. Marriage is not about falling in love with a handsome face and a beguiling manner. It requires a sound footing, a strong sense of commitment, the same values, a common purpose. Sexual attraction is of minimal importance.'

'I don't agree,' said Dimpsie. 'Anyway you could have all those things – commitment and values and whatnot – *and* he could be handsome and interesting into the bargain. And you might want to go to bed with him.'

Evelyn grimaced. 'Isn't that asking for the moon? One must be practical, above all, when it comes to marriage. It lasts for such a very long time.'

'It seems to me,' Dimpsie's speech was slurred, 'that you're judging others by your own experience. Just because *you* didn't fancy Kingsley doesn't mean that sex isn't important.' No doubt drink was responsible for this unusually blunt speaking. 'I married Tom because I thought he was the most desirable creature I'd ever set eyes on.'

There was a pause. I could see that Evelyn was struggling to

191

swallow the little sting in Dimpsie's accusation. And there was so much Evelyn might legitimately say in refutation. Dimpsie's disastrous marriage was a perfect illustration of the folly of marrying for love. Resentment warred with good nature and good nature won. 'Well, darling, we must each follow our own inclinations. What on earth is *that?*'

She had spotted something lying on the desk that was round and flesh-coloured with what looked like a raspberry stuck on top.

'It's a paperweight,' explained Dimpsie, 'shaped like a breast. It's been in the shop for several years but no one's shown the least interest in buying it so I've brought it home. I think it's rather witty, actually.'

'Do you?' Evelyn looked at it again. A dribble of red paint from the nipple had run into the pink part, which was beginning to flake. Her eyebrows went up. 'How extra*ord*inary.'

My father did not come home that night and was half an hour late for surgery the next day. Despite murmurs of unrest in the waiting room he hummed as he took off his coat, flexed his arms above his head and came over to the desk to look at the list of appointments. He seemed perfectly unconscious of my presence, as though occupying another, far happier planet. I thought of my mother that morning, uncharacteristically silent as she had driven me into the town. After I'd got out, when she thought I wasn't looking, she had leaned her head on the steering wheel. I had never hated him so much.

The patients whizzed in and out. Tom was evidently in a decisive mood. By half-past eleven only Mrs Mansard was left in the waiting room and I began to look forward to an early lunch with Dimpsie at the Singing Swan. As I started to put away the files, I wondered if it might be possible over beans on toast to breach the silence on the subject of my father's love affairs. Sex affairs would be a better description, I thought angrily. I heard the front door bang and the next moment the waiting room was taken up by a giant of a man accompanied by a young woman.

'Where's t'e doctor?' he demanded, bringing an enormous fist down on the appointments book. 'We must see him right away. Me girl's in trouble.'

I was about to ask if it was an emergency when she let out a low groan rising to a scream like a factory siren and sank to the floor. I picked up the telephone to ask my father to come quickly but he must have heard her yell for he was kneeling beside her before I had time to press the intercom button.

'Marigold, ring for an ambulance,' he said after a cursory glance.

He and the giant lifted the girl between them and carried her into the consulting room.

Emergency services said they would send a helicopter as the road from Carlisle was blocked with drifting snow. Tom appeared in his shirtsleeves in the doorway. 'You'd better come in, Marigold. I may need help.'

I hopped in, wondering what use I could possibly be to anyone in my hobbled state. The girl was lying on the examination couch, her knees apart, grimacing and screeching.

'How long's she been in labour?' Tom asked the giant, who was pacing the floor and clutching his head.

'Two days, near enough.'

'All right. You go outside and wait.' Tom pushed him towards the door. He tried to resist but my father said more urgently, 'You're just in my way. I need room if I'm going to be able to help her. Look, I can't promise anything. You ought to have brought her in long before this.'

Then the poor man went away without another word.

'Marigold, in the cupboard – a metal box marked Obstetrics.'

I found it and took it over, averting my gaze from the sufferer not only because I am extremely squeamish but also to save her embarrassment. But she was probably past caring about modesty. Two days! I had seen plenty of films in which women made granny knots in the bed rails and pleaded to be put permanently out of their misery. I covered my face with my hands as Tom burrowed between the girl's legs.

'Ah-ha,' he said, 'fully dilated.' The girl yelled loud enough to damage our eardrums. Not that I blamed her one little bit. I was close to yelling myself. 'Breach,' he muttered. 'I'll try and turn it. Marigold, come here and hold her hand.'

Tentatively I patted the girl's shoulder. She seized my hand and appeared to derive comfort from sobbing into my sleeve. I was only too willing to take her into my arms. For one thing it prevented either of us from seeing what was going on at the other end. Also, I would have run naked to Carlisle and back, with both legs in plaster casts, if it would have brought her relief. God knows what Tom was doing. The girl gave several shattering shrieks.

'I can't turn it. Where's that fucking ambulance? What's your name?'

'Nan. A-h-h-h-h!'

'All right, Nan. Don't push if you can help it. I'm going to do an episiotomy. Stay where you are, Marigold. I'll pop in an anaesthetic.'

I could not have moved if I had wanted to. Surprisingly for such a small girl, Nan had a grip like Mr Universe. Tom went over to the cupboard. I caught a glimpse of a large syringe. I dislike injections of any kind but there are some parts of the human anatomy that ought never to have needles stuck in them. I made a vow never to have sex again.

'I'm putting it in now. You won't feel much.'

Nan and I were clutching each other as though going down for the last time, our heads pressed together, sweat and tears transferring themselves from her cheek to mine. She uttered a prolonged shrill squeal like an officer being piped aboard, then went limp.

'I think it's worked,' I said to Tom. 'She's gone to sleep. Thank heavens!'

'Don't be a fool! I've only given her a local. She's fainted. Just as well. I'll be as quick as I can.'

I glanced round to see him brandishing a wicked-looking blade. 'You're not going to cut the baby out!' I cried in horror.

'If I don't the mother may die. And the baby most assuredly will. Now come here and open that pack of dressings. There's going to be plenty of blood. Shine that anglepoise directly on to the perineum.'

I did as I was told, getting an involuntary glimpse of frightening anatomical details.

'Hold that leg . . . she's coming round. For Christ's sake, hold her still!'

He brandished an instrument like a giant pair of nutcrackers. I clutched Nan tightly in my arms; for a few dreadful seconds Tom and I seemed to be engaged in a tug-of-war, with her body as the rope. He cursed descriptively and told her to push for all she was worth. Nan bawled and all was confusion and horror as flecks of blood flew onto my sleeve. Then he shouted, 'All right! It's coming! One last push!' and the next moment a high-pitched cry rose above our cursing and screaming, the wail of an infant dragged forcibly into the world. The moment I heard it, a rush of entirely unexpected emotion made me weep uncontrollably.

'I'm going to cut the cord. Find something to wrap it in – something reasonably clean.'

I held out a towel. Tom placed something with waving limbs, streaked with blood and white sticky stuff, into my arms. It stopped crying, knitted up its tiny forehead and opened its eyes. I looked into blue-grey spheres like black pearls. They flickered about a little and then fixed for a moment on my face and widened as though astonished. I saw a question in them. If the baby had been able to speak it might have asked 'Who are you? Who am I? What is life?'

'Hello, you darling little thing,' I crooned, broken-voiced with love. It was the first time I had held a baby. It was so real, so warm, such an individual presence, and yet a moment ago it had not existed. It had been alive, of course, but out of sight inside Nan. I smiled as it stared solemnly back at me and flourished a tiny fist. Then, remembering with sorrow that this was not *my* baby, I laid it reverently on Nan's chest. She stopped screaming and looked with amazement at the tiny monkey face gazing up at hers.

'Blimey!' she said, expressing my own feelings exactly. We exchanged glances of wonder. The baby remained calm, looking at its mother's face. It parted its violet-pink lips. 'Blimey!' said Nan again.

'You'll have to push again,' said my father. 'We want the placenta out.'

There was a brief bad moment, then I saw something out of the corner of my eye that was dark red and glistening, which Tom put into a plastic box. 'That'll have to go to the hospital with you so they can be certain it's all come out. Now,' he had returned to the business end, 'I'm going to put in a couple of stitches. Can you feel that?'

'Ye-ho-o-w!' cried Nan.

'Nan, dear.' I bent over her. 'What are you going to call your baby?'

'Oh-oh-oh!' she wept. 'I don't know. It hurts like buggery!'

'She's so pretty. What about a lovely flower name like Lily? Or Primrose? Um . . .' I struggled to remember the names of the flowers in the bouquets that were presented during curtain calls. 'Mimosa perhaps? Or Carnation?'

My father gave a shout of laughter. 'You can't call a child after a tin of milk. Besides, it's a boy.'

'No! Is it? Oh well, not a flower then. Except there was a boy called Narcissus. What's your surname?'

'It's . . . ow-aarh! . . . O'Shaunessy.'

'Narcissus O'Shaunessy. Too many s's. Hopeless if you had a lisp.'

'All right. That'll do for the moment,' said my father standing up. 'They can tidy her up at the hospital.'

'Well done!' I squeezed Nan's hand gently. 'You were so brave. I'd have made *much* more fuss.'

She wiped away tears with the back of her hand. 'It did bloody hurt.'

'I can't bear to even think about it. I'm hopeless when it comes to pain.'

'Yeah?' She gave me a wan smile. 'Well, I'm never goin' through *that* again, anyways,' she said with angry emphasis.

'I've heard women say – my mother included – that you forget all about the pain once the baby's been born.'

'I bloody shan't! I'm not goin' te let another man lay his fuckin' hand on me for the rest of me natural.'

'Wise words,' said my father, who was standing at the sink washing his hands and arms. 'But I doubt if you'll remember them.' He dried himself with a paper towel then went to the door and opened it. 'You can come in now, Mr O'Shaunessy. You've got a healthy son. A good eight pounds, I'd say, at a guess.'

The giant came in. Though he was the instigator of so much suffering, I felt sorry for him. His eyes were red as though he had been weeping.

'*Grand*son, you mean.' He strode over to where Nan lay. 'This's my daughter. And if I ever catch the bastard who got her into this state . . .' He stopped and appeared to be suffering some sort of internal conflict. Then he lifted his arm to point a finger at the ceiling. 'Vengeance is Mine, saith the Lord. I will repay.' His beard waggled fiercely, like Charlton Heston's in *The Ten Commandments*. It was an impressive sight.

'Oh, Dad!' Nan looked annoyed. 'Don't go on so. It was my fault as much as his.'

The giant shook his head. 'Yer only a little kid. A slip of a motherless girl.' He appealed to my father, in mingled sorrow and anger. 'Sixteen, she is. Fifteen when t'at bogger had his way wit' her. A gent.' His tone became sarcastic. 'Looks down on folk like us, I'll be bound, but 'twasn't beneat' him te take advantage of a child who doesn't know t'e ways of t'e world.'

Even I, who am so hopeless at accents, had gathered by this time that he was an Irishman. He said gorl for girl and loike instead of like.

'Shut it, Dad.' Nan turned her head away as if unbearably weary. Another tear slid down her cheek. 'I hate men. I thought he'd take me away from that bloody caravan, but he didn't want to know once I was up the duff.'

'Never mind, darling.' The giant laid a huge hand on her shoulder and dropped his voice to a soft growl. 'Daddy'll take care of ye. And I'll look after t'e little laddie too.' He pressed a sausage-sized finger against the infant's cheek. 'A fine boy. He can't help who his father was. I'll make it op to him for being a poor wee bastard. We'll call him Paddy after me brother.'

'Uncle Paddy was a drunk and a thief,' said Nan fiercely. 'He's my babby and *I'm* choosing his name.'

They had no time to argue the point, for at that moment two paramedics arrived. She was placed on a stretcher and carried away.

'T'ank you, Doctor.' Mr O'Shaunessy wrung my father's hand. 'You saved me daughter's life and the lad's and I'm grateful—'

'No need for gratitude.' Tom drew back his hand and massaged it tenderly. 'It's what I'm here for.'

'Gosh!' I sank into a chair as soon as we were alone and pressed my hand to my forehead. 'What an experience! I feel as though I've been taken apart and remade from scratch.'

'You've obviously been leading a very sheltered life.' Tom was putting all the instruments he had used into the sink. 'Ring Bunker, will you? This lot will have to be sterilized. Damn! I've got blood on my trousers and I'm going out to lunch.' He took a cloth and began to scrub at his knee.

I was dismayed. 'Not the Singing Swan?'

'Good God, no! I'm going to the Castle in Carlisle.'

'Isn't that terribly expensive?'

'Yes. And it's extremely good. Don't worry,' he added,

grinning at me over his shoulder as he went out, 'I'm not paying.'

I did not need to ask who was.

'It brought it home to me,' I said to Dimpsie twenty minutes later, 'how different his life is from ours. I was so frightened that Nan might die. That the baby might die. I was horrified by the pain and messiness. It seemed so . . . primitive. Barbarous, even. He was marvellously cool, despite everything depending on him. I have to say I admired him tremendously for the way he dealt with it. If the responsibility had been mine, I think I'd have gone to pieces.'

'Not if you'd had his training and experience.' Dimpsie waved an anaemic-looking chip speckled with burnt fat on her fork. 'But I know what you mean. All the time he's dealing with the sharp end of life while you're standing on tiptoe in sequins and tulle and I'm cleaning the bath.'

Because I loved her I did not say that these days unless I cleaned it the bath remained dirty. My father seemed to be getting his baths as well as other things elsewhere. 'It was such a darling baby,' I said. 'So tiny and soft and delicate, but you felt a presence. When I looked into his eyes I felt there was a proper person looking back at me.'

'I'm sure that's true.' Dimpsie prodded at a bit of fried black pudding. She'd ordered a glass of beer with her lunch and I was certain it wasn't the first drink of the day. 'When you were put into my arms I knew immediately you were nothing like Kate.' She sighed. 'You said the girl was brought in by her father. So where's the baby's father?'

'He's done a bunk. It's such a shame. Nan's father said he was a gentleman.'

'Obviously not in the strict sense of the word. I suppose he meant middle-class.'

'Being a gentleman has more to do with style than virtue.' I repeated Rafe's lesson.

199

'It's disgraceful, anyway. Are you sure they were tinkers?'

'Nan mentioned a caravan she was keen to escape from.'

'Why don't we go and visit them?' Dimpsie suddenly looked brighter. 'We could take them some of the less hideous baby clothes from the shop.'

'Mightn't they think we were patronizing them?'

'We could just take one or two little things at first and test the water.'

'Perhaps they don't like people who aren't tinkers visiting them.'

'Well, then we can go away, can't we?'

I remembered times during my childhood when Dimpsie had tried to befriend what one might call social outcasts. Two occasions stood out particularly clearly in my memory. There had been the old man who lived in the shepherd's hut on the top of the moor. It had been Christmas Eve and Dimpsie's soft heart had been touched as she thought of him all alone when all about were surrounded by their loved ones and, in the case of Tom's spiteful old mother and his crabby Aunt Bernice, not-so-loved ones. As it was miles from the nearest road, we had walked a long way carrying heavy bags of plum puddings, mince pies and crackers. The three of us had carolled *The First No-well* outside his front door. A window had opened above our heads and we were told to put a sock in it and bugger off. My mother had attempted to woo him with kind words but he had chucked an iron at us which had hit Kate on the head and drawn blood.

Then there was the woman who had been ostracized by the townsfolk because it was rumoured she was a Satanist. She had invited us in for a cup of herbal tea before taking off her clothes and dancing in a pentagram. Kate and I had refused to undress but my mother was always game for anything. She had hopped about in the buff while Circe – probably not her real name – had chanted something incomprehensible.

'Come on you two stick-in-the-muds,' my mother had called

200

gaily, her breasts and stomach bobbing and wobbling like frightened animals trapped in sacks. 'This is fun!'

She had changed her tune when Circe produced a live cockerel and a chopper. Kate and I had screamed and run away as fast as our legs could carry us. Dimpsie, naked beneath her coat, had caught us up on the road to Dumbola Lodge, carrying the cockerel under one arm. The RSPCA man was called and soon afterwards Circe moved away. We gave the cockerel to Evelyn and it fathered a long line of handsome, pure white progeny.

'Oh, all right,' I said reluctantly.

Dimpsie looked pleased for a moment, then grew thoughtful. She traced the pattern of the tablecloth with the end of her knife. 'Does your father seem in good spirits?'

'Much as usual.' I could not bring myself to tell her that he was disgustingly cheerful.

'Oh.' She looked through the window at a passing car. 'Do you know where he is now?'

'No.' Another lie.

'Did he say when he'd be home?'

I shook my head. All my recent admiration for my father's handling of the crisis had been replaced by angry contempt.

17

'Hello, Marigold. You're looking particularly gorgeous.'

It was the day of Evelyn's lunch party and Rafe had come to fetch me. As soon as I heard the car, I swung myself into the porch and shut the front door behind me. I was reluctant that anyone should see the state of the house. Some things, like washing floors and carrying laundry upstairs, are next to impossible with crutches. Dimpsie had been in bed for several days with a rampaging headache. Sometimes she came down in her dressing gown to replenish her flask of tea. I knew it contained mostly gin, but I didn't like to object. She was desperately unhappy and I had no idea how to help her.

Before Dimpsie had taken to her bed, she had met Brenda of the peg bags in the chemist's. Brenda had made a point of telling her about Marcia Dane's arrival in Gaythwaite, describing her, in a voice full of meaning, as good-looking, rich and a positive man-eater. She had not actually mentioned Tom's name, but Dimpsie had understood. She had returned without the toothpaste and aspirins and I found her in tears by the hat stand. We had had a soul-baring talk and she admitted she had always known that my father's relationship with Vanessa Trumball had gone beyond the knees. Often during the twenty-four years of their marriage he had come home late without explanation, but this was the first time he had taken to staying away all night.

'Why don't you have it out with him?' I had asked indignantly. 'Why should he get away with behaving so badly?'

'What good would it do? It would only make him cross and me upset. This affair with Marcia whatever-her-name-is will peter out like all the others. I'm his wife and the only woman he's had any deep, lasting relationship with. The others are just amusements.' Her chin wobbled when she tried to smile.

'But he's making you so miserable!'

'Well, darling, I'm pretty much used to it. It's just that this affair's come so close on the heels of the last one and my defences are down.'

In fact they were completely destroyed. Her eyes were permanently swollen and pink with drinking and weeping. Perhaps it was not to be wondered at that, by the time of the lunch party, Tom had ceased to come home at all except to collect clean shirts. I washed and ironed them myself to save Dimpsie from harsh words.

I had spent a long time deciding what to wear to Evelyn's lunch, so I was pleased to be paid a compliment. Bearing in mind the temperature of the dining room at Shottestone, I had settled for an aquamarine velvet jacket trimmed with white fur, one of the costumes for the corps de ballet of *Les Patineurs*. Beneath the jacket I wore a pale pink satin dress from *Liebeslieder Walzer*. As usual my feet had been a problem. I had solved it by wearing a silver boot from *Les Patineurs* on my good leg and painting the cast and the exposed part of my other foot with silver metallic paint from the model shop.

'How was Edinburgh?'

'It *was* full of dresses and shoes and bags. Now its stores are much depleted. Isobel was inexhaustible. There can't be a shop we didn't visit or a square inch of pavement we didn't cover several times.' He guided me to the passenger seat and paused before closing the door to look in at me. 'Are you addicted to shopping?'

'I've never had the chance.'

'I can't understand what women see in it. I like clothes that are old. Familiar. I don't like change.' He walked round and got into the car. 'I suppose all men are the same,' he said as we accelerated away.

'Not the ones I know.'

Carefully he negotiated the turning at the bottom of our drive. 'But I daresay your experience isn't extensive. How old are you? If that's not an impertinent question.'

'I'm twenty-two.'

'You don't look it. Had many boyfriends? No, that *is* impertinent. Let me rephrase. Have you ever been in love? It's all right to ask that, I hope, considering how long we've known each other?'

'Quite all right. Anyway, I haven't got any secrets. In the ballet world everyone discusses their love life in shocking detail.' Then I remembered Sebastian and thought that I should not like Rafe to know quite everything. 'Not that we always tell the truth, of course.'

'I suppose it's *de rigueur* for artistic people to kick over the traces.'

I wondered about this. I had never been conscious of trying to rebel. I had been too busy dancing to worry about the conventions. By this time we had reached the market square in Gaythwaite.

'Isn't the Singing Swan the prettiest little place you ever saw with that lovely stone roof and those lattice windows?' I said as we drove past it. 'It's such a pity Mrs Peevis can't cook for toffee nuts. If there was somewhere decent for tourists to eat, they'd come in droves and then buy things from Dimpsie's shop.'

'You didn't answer my question. About having been in love.'

Had I been in love with Sebastian? Quite a few of the girls were, in a romanticizing, masochistic sort of way because he was diabolically attractive, mean and powerful. And they all wanted to sleep with him because of the chance of promotion. Had I been just a little in love that first time?

I had been running to get to a class and had literally bumped into him in the corridor. He had scowled, then the expression in his eyes had changed from anger to surprise. I had been in the company for nearly four years but he seemed to see me for the first time. He had asked me where I was going.

'Madame's eleven o'clock,' I panted.

Sebastian had looked at his watch. 'You're one minute late.'

'I know.'

I had started to edge away but he gripped my shoulder. 'Come into my office.'

'Oh, but Mr Lenoir, Madame's casting *Lac!*' *Lac* was what we all called *Swan Lake*. 'I'm in with a chance of being one of the cygnets—'

'Never mind that.'

'Couldn't I come back after class?'

'No.' He opened the door and propelled me inside.

'But if I'm any later she won't give it to me. And I want it so *bad*ly.'

Sebastian locked the door, his expression now one of anticipation, like a hungry man who has made his choice from the menu and knows that nothing now remains but to avail himself of a knife and fork. Without a word he had pulled down my leotard so he could feel my breasts. 'Get your clothes off.'

When he ran his hand over my naked bottom I had definitely felt a violent surge of excitement. But I was wondering what my reward might be for allowing myself to be spread over his desk and taken from behind without so much as a five-minute warm up. Ten minutes later I had entered Madame's class. Her flinty little eyes had screwed up with rage but Sebastian, walking in behind me, had cut short her scolding. He had taken a chair, folded his long legs, lit a cigarette and signalled to Madame to begin. The class had proceeded at a terrific pace and we had all danced ourselves into states of exhaustion. Every time I looked in the mirror I could see him watching me. My extensions had always been one of my strong points, and I practically kicked the lights out that day. At the end of class he and Madame went into a huddle by the piano, and when the cast list went up I was down for the Act III Spanish pas de deux. I absolutely knew it had been worth it, but remembering those cynical intimacies while driving through the cold, clean air of Northumberland in the company of Rafe, a knight *sans peur et sans reproche* if ever there was one, I felt a revulsion that was laced quite painfully with self-disgust.

Now we were on the road that climbed steeply to the gates of Shottestone Manor. The hills were particularly beautiful that morning. The sky was like grey silk, appliquéd with pompoms of cloud.

'No,' I said, 'I've never been in love.'

A silence greeted this admission. I glanced at Rafe. He was staring ahead at the road but there was a slight smile at the corner of his mouth. He began to hum the 'Song of the Toreador' from *Carmen*.

An enormous car was parked to one side of the front door as we drove up.

'That'll be Conrad's. Germans are always punctual, so we're told,' said Rafe, as though aggrieved.

'Really? But in his favour you ought to remember that Conrad was dreadfully late last time.'

'So he was. The paragon has his imperfections. That's a comfort.'

'Don't you like him?'

'I think he's arrogant. I suppose having all that money gives you a pretty good idea of yourself.' He came round to open the passenger door. 'Don't take any notice of me,' he smiled. 'As I said before, I expect I'm envious.'

By comparison with me Rafe was as rich as . . . whoever that rich man was, but of course wealth is relative. No doubt I was

206

rich by comparison with a Vietnamese boat person. Conrad's car certainly was elegant. Its bodywork was two tones of blue and there was a large B with a pair of wings on the back.

'You needn't envy anyone. I think Shottestone is the most beautiful house in the world.'

He put his hand on my arm to detain me. 'Do you?' His eyes were two shades of blue, like the car.

'I've always loved it.'

'Then I won't be jealous any more. What good angel made you break your foot and brought you home, I wonder?'

As I walked into the hall, I experienced one of those painful moments of cold rationality, rare for me, that made my stomach turn over. I asked myself what the hell I thought I was doing flirting with Rafe. When my foot was better I was going back to London to dance. Why did I not say so at once? It was ignoble curiosity, perhaps, or worse, vanity. Rafe's mental state was precarious and if there was the least chance that he was seriously contemplating a love affair with me it would be the act of a louse to mislead him. Or could it be that I felt more for him than an ancient schoolgirl crush? He had turned his back to me to fling his coat over one of the hall chairs. It was a strong back with broad shoulders, but was it a back for which I could sacrifice everything I had slaved, starved, prayed, beggared and prostituted myself for?

'Shall I take that charming little jacket?' He was facing me now, his eyes admiring.

The top of my dress was low-cut with tiny straps and quite unsuitable for the middle of the day. 'No, thanks. I'll keep it on.'

In the drawing room, Conrad and Fritz were standing with Evelyn in a stiff little group, drinking champagne.

'Marigold, *dar*ling!' She came over to kiss me. 'You know Conrad and Fritz, of course.'

The two men bowed. I would have curtseyed but my leg made that impossible. Instead I gave them my radiant Giselle smile, hoping to make up for Evelyn's frost. 'Hello, Fritz. Hello Conrad.'

A line appeared between Evelyn's brows. I understood it to mean that I must not ally myself with Lucifer and the servant of Lucifer. They were bundled up in thick tweed jackets with woollen jerseys beneath, a sign that the chill at Shottestone had been noted. But on this occasion Evelyn had gone to great trouble to boost the temperature. The grate was stacked with blazing logs and fan heaters had been placed discreetly about the room. I perceived that Evelyn felt embattled and was anxious that Conrad should not hold her housekeeping in contempt.

'Hello, little girl.' Kingsley approached from the window where he had been standing gazing out at the view across the valley. 'How nice that you've come to play. I'm Isobel's daddy. Would you like to see my model soldier? You can hold it if you'd like—'

'Kingsley!' snapped Evelyn. 'Go and tell Mrs Capstick fifteen minutes at least. There are three more still to come.' As Kingsley shuffled away, Evelyn looked at her watch. 'Great artists are allowed to break all the usual rules of social intercourse, but I can't imagine what Sibyl's excuse will be.'

'I don't see why artists of any stature should be allowed to inconvenience the rest of us.' Rafe handed me a glass. 'As they probably have much more fun than us ordinary mortals, I think they ought to make amends.'

'But surely, darling, geniuses inhabit another plane. They don't in*tend* to be troublesome. Time doesn't exist when you are selecting from the two hundred thousand words of the English language exactly the right adjective. Or capturing a mood with a flick of the brush.' Evelyn mimed the action on an imaginary canvas. 'You may have heard of Dame Gloria Beauwhistle.' She looked at Conrad, who bowed again, which could have meant anything. 'She is a composer of international reputation.'

'Two hundred thousand vords, you say?' Fritz took from his pocket the notebook and pencil. 'Do you include vords vich are spelling the same but haf not the same meanings?' He pointed to a table lamp. '"Light", for example. And "light" that means not heafy. It is counting one vord or two?'

Evelyn looked distracted. 'Two. I think.' I knew how she felt. Entertaining is murderous to the intellect. Whenever I had people to supper, my brain went into orbit the moment the guests arrived. I was incapable even of boiling a potato.

'And vat of dialect vords?' Fritz continued. 'I am thinking to write a little study of Northumberland language for a literary vork to vich I send zings time to time. I haf been reading *Brockett's Glossary of North Country Vords vith their Etymology and Affinity to other languages*. Most curious and interesting. I regret my English is so bad. "What fettle?" means "how are you?". "Gey snell comin' doon the brae" means "Most cold coming down the hill". And vat means "carrying coals to Newcastle"?' Fritz looked at Evelyn with an air of expectation.

Conrad, the interloper, came to her rescue. 'It is, as one says in German, *Eulen nach Athen trage* – to carry owls to Athens. An idiom meaning a useless effort. The owl was a sacred bird in Ancient Greece.'

'I was most disappointed in Athens,' said Evelyn. 'The acropolis was full of tourists.'

'In Greece the equivalent idiom is "carrying vampires to Santorini",' said Conrad. 'The island of Santorini was believed to be the birthplace of those malign creatures.'

I liked the way he spoke English. He chose his words with precision, and none of them ran into each other as ours did. 'Do you mean vampire bats?' I asked.

Conrad looked at me with an expression that was chilling. 'No, Miss Savage. I mean the kind that change into human form when the sun dips below the horizon in order to bite your neck and drink your blood and which can only be killed by a stake hammered through the heart.'

His black eyes widened slightly and seemed to pierce as effectively as any stake. I felt he was penetrating my mind and seeing into my thoughts. If so, he must have been disappointed, for they immediately struck tents and decamped. I pulled myself together and asked, 'Do you believe there really are such things?'

'Don't be absurd, darling,' said Evelyn. 'Conrad is teasing us.'

'Oh, but am I? If there can be a lump of rock and iron populated by humans, elephants and ants speeding through dark matter and dark energy in an ever-expanding universe, I see no particular difficulty with believing in vampires.'

It was a good answer, but for the purposes of polite conversation rather stumping. I would have liked to ask how anyone could tell that the universe was expanding, but Spendlove came in to announce Mrs Hinchingbrook and Mr Shinn.

'Sybil, *darling!*' Evelyn went to embrace a tall woman clad in flowing draperies in misty greens and browns. She had longish grey hair, also flowing, and a pale face with small features set close together.

'Evelyn! So kind of you to include us in your little party. Basil is just changing out of his driving shoes. I'm sorry we're a bit late but I *had* to finish a painting for my exhibition. I do hope you'll come. It's at the Old Mill in Hexham. Hardly the most exciting of venues, but it's one up on that ghastly little craft shop in Gaythwaite—'

'You must meet my other guests.'

Evelyn marched Sybil up to Conrad and Fritz. I missed the introductions because Basil Shinn came into the drawing room just then. I saw at once that he would not 'do' for Isobel. He had a curious high-stepping gait which drew attention immediately to his elegant brown and white co-respondent shoes. He was thin like his sister, but where she flowed he was angular. As befitted a man of books, his dress was carefully negligent and his white hair had been rinsed to an interesting shade of purple. Nature had saved him the trouble of dying his nose which was purple also.

'A party!' Basil clapped his hands, which looked a little blue.

'Such heaven! How sweet of you to invite me! Sybil and I were getting just the teeniest bit fatigued with each other.'

Basil shook my hand without the smallest sign of interest, but appeared galvanized by Fritz and at once asked him where he had got his de*lici*ous accent. Rafe was drawn into a painting conversation with Sybil and Evelyn darted out to check that Spendlove had remembered to build up the dining-room fire. That left Conrad and me.

'What's dark matter?' I asked.

He looked at me with a question in his eyes. His hair was thick, black and shining and beautifully cut, coming into points just in front of his ears. 'You are really interested?'

'I'm not just being polite, if that's what you mean.'

'Well, please stop me if you find the explanation dull. You must first understand that objects in the universe can be seen with a telescope because they emit light waves.' His skin was a marvellous shade of pale gold. 'Or, in the case of a radio telescope, radio waves. Or their existence can be inferred by the effect they have on observable phenomena.' His lower eyelids were full and curved, as though chiselled from marble by Michelangelo. 'But there is a significant amount of matter, perhaps as much as ninety per cent, in the universe that we are unable to observe. This we call "dark".'

I remembered that he had been reading the *New Scientist* on the train. I had a faint idea what he was talking about while his lips were actually moving – his upper lip was finely shaped, the lower was full and defined by a tuft of black hair beneath it which was separate from a short fringe of neatly trimmed beard on his jaw – but the difficulty was to keep hold of the information long enough to absorb it. He had marvellous cheekbones.

'What do you mean by matter, exactly?'

Conrad must have realized then that he was talking to an idiot, but he did not allow this to register on his face or in his voice. 'Matter is anything that takes up space. Atoms, molecules. You are matter.'

'I'm afraid I'm awfully ignorant,' I confessed humbly.

Conrad shrugged. 'No one knows everything. Remember the first law of thermodynamics. Matter can neither be created nor destroyed.'

'. . . neither created nor destroyed,' I repeated.

He pushed back his cuff, held out his hand and spread his fingers, then turned it over so I could see there was nothing in it. Then he made a fist and opened his fingers in one rapid movement, like the opening and closing of a fan, to reveal a salted almond. 'Matter,' he repeated, 'can neither be created –' he folded up his fist again then showed me his empty palm – 'nor destroyed. But it can be changed –' again the fan-like dexterity – 'from a gas to a liquid or from a liquid to a solid. Or in this case . . .' He showed me a stuffed olive.

It was astonishing. I had watched most carefully and neither the nut nor the olive could have been hidden between his fingers or up his sleeve. 'How did you do that?'

Conrad shrugged. 'The art of prestidigitation is the first thing any amateur magician learns.'

He opened his mouth and threw in both the almond and the olive.

'Do you *really* believe in vampires?'

'No.' Then his cold, rather severe face broke into a charming smile and his black eyes lit with amusement.

'Dame Gloria Beauwhistle,' announced Spendlove.

'A thousand apologies, Mrs Preston.' Dame Gloria came into the room at a run. 'I wish I had as many excuses for being late but the truth is I overslept. I do my best work after midnight and my desk faces an east window, so the pleasure of staying up to see the dawn is one I can rarely resist.' She did not look like the sensitive aesthete Evelyn had led us to expect. She was a big woman dressed in a brown boiler suit, the sort of thing men wear in inspection pits in garages. I guessed her age was somewhere between sixty and seventy. She shook Evelyn's hand energetically. 'I woke at half-past twelve, threw myself into my car and came straight here.' It was evident that she had not stopped to brush her hair. It was cut short and stuck up in browny-grey tufts like a newly hatched bird's. 'Luckily Butterbank – that's the name of my little cottage – is on a hill so I can always get the car to start. I just give it a push and then run like stink and . . . Conrad! But how extraordinary, I thought you'd gone back to Germany.' Dame Gloria strode towards him in her large brown boots, her arms held wide. 'What joy!' They embraced each other. 'This is a marvellous surprise!' she said to Evelyn. 'Why, only the other day Conrad was at Butter—'

'Yes,' Conrad interrupted her, 'I did go to Germany. But as you see I have returned.'

If Evelyn was put out to discover that her chief lion was apparently the best of chums with her arch enemy, she hid it admirably. 'What a coincidence! I'd no idea you had friends in Northumberland.'

Dame Gloria whacked him on the back making him cough. 'Oh, Conrad and I go back a long way, don't we?'

He smiled. 'We certainly do.'

'We met at Heidelberg when I was visiting professor of music. Conrad was a student then. All the girls had crushes on him.' She poked him in the chest. 'Remember the one who used to sleep in the corridor outside your room and bite the legs of the other girls? With yellow plaits and enormous tits.' Dame Gloria chortled. 'You certainly made the most of your educational opportunities.'

'Conrad is engaged to marry my daughter.' Evelyn's smile was a little wintery.

'Conrad? Engaged?' Dame Gloria looked at him, astonished. 'But you never said anything . . . that is, ah-ha—' She looked confused as Conrad gave a slight shake of his head. 'I wish you all the best, naturally . . . engaged!' Her eye went round the room, paused for a moment on Sybil, then travelled on to me. 'And is this the young lady?' Dame Gloria bounced on her toes and swung her arms out from her sides. 'Do introduce me.'

'My daughter hasn't come down yet,' said Evelyn. 'This is Marigold Savage, a friend of the family. Marigold is a ballerina.'

I was not actually entitled to be called a ballerina, as this means not just any female dancer but an exceptional one, usually the leading dancer of a company. But it was not the moment to clear up this common misunderstanding.

Dame Gloria's grasp made my bones crack. 'Hello, dear. I don't know as much about ballet as I should, considering Stravinsky's my hero. *The Firebird, Petrushka* and *The Rite of Spring* are works of genius as everyone knows, but there are others, *Apollon Musagète* for example, *Les Noces* and *Agon*—'

Evelyn moved her firmly onward. A sprinkling of erudition had its place at her lunch parties, but it should not be so cumbrous as to exclude the uninitiated. 'As you know Conrad, I presume you also know Fritz?'

'Fritz, dear old thing, how are you? How's the dissertation on the similes of Catullus going?'

Fritz smiled shyly and submitted to having his shoulders clapped and his ears pulled. Before Dame Gloria could be introduced to Sybil and Basil, Isobel made her entrance. Her dress, of black and gold stripes, was eye-catching. It was sleeveless, with a puffball skirt that came down to the tops of gleaming patent-leather boots. Her hair was fastened into a tight chignon, with a black feather tucked into the topknot like a squaw's headdress.

'Here you are at last, darling.' Evelyn's tone was disapproving. She had strict ideas on what was convenable for lunch in the country and they did not include feathers, shiny gold or false eyelashes. 'You must go without a drink. Our guests must be faint with hunger.'

I thought Isobel's appearance was wonderfully dramatic, but

I saw by two little white dints above his eyebrows that Rafe also seemed to dislike it. Perhaps he thought she ought not to court Conrad's approval so plainly. As for Conrad himself, he looked as inscrutable as Providence.

Lunch was a success, largely thanks to Dame Gloria – Golly, as she insisted we call her – who ignored all the rules and entertained the whole table with stories of people she had met and things she had seen. She told us about her grandfather who had been a milkman. Her happiest memories were of accompanying him on his rounds with horse and cart. Golly had round brown eyes and round nostrils in a broad, upturned nose. In fact she reminded me of a cow. I don't mean this disrespectfully as I have always liked cows. Her real name, she explained, was Gloria Toot, but her agent had been afraid that Toot's First Clarinet Concerto would excite ridicule.

Golly described picnicking during the saffron season in Kashmir on a sea of purple crocuses with not a fingerbreadth between them, of seeing a bearded lady being shot out of a cannon in Romania, of meeting Sophia Loren in a cloakroom at Bologna railway station. Basil, perhaps feeling that he was being outshone, told an amusing little story about diving into the sea to rescue a pretty young lady's dog and being struck by cramp after only a few yards. He had been rescued and given mouth-to-mouth resuscitation by a burly fisherman. When he came to, he found the pretty young lady kneeling by his side in tears while the dog ran heartlessly up and down the strand barking at gulls. Evelyn was in for a big disappointment if she believed that there was a chance that Isobel might transfer her love from Conrad to Basil. I was quite certain that the kisses of the burly fisherman were more to his taste than the tears of the pretty young lady.

Golly was a hearty eater. She cut everything that was placed before her into bite-sized pieces, then shovelled it down with a spoon. She addressed Spendlove as 'old boy' and leaned back in her chair to ask his opinion on the subject being discussed. Mindful of Evelyn's sharp eye upon him, he replied each time, 'I really couldn't say, Madam,' but I got the impression he rather liked being consulted by a dame of the British Empire.

After Golly had finished the last of the rhubarb tart, she leaned back in her chair, patted her stomach and gave several deep whooping belches like a ship steaming through the English Channel on a foggy day. Sybil and Basil exchanged shocked glances. Rafe confined his reaction to a lifted eyebrow. Conrad was looking at Isobel who was giggling. Evelyn affected deafness and summoned the cheese.

The only impediment to thorough enjoyment of a fascinating lunch was that, thanks to the blazing fire and two fan heaters, the temperature of the dining room was tropical. I saw Conrad and Fritz pulling at their shirt collars. By the pudding course I could bear it no longer and took off my fur-lined velvet jacket. I caught Evelyn's eye. She looked surprised to see me at the lunch table with naked shoulders and a bodice embroidered with silver thread and liberally scattered with sequins. When Golly dipped her napkin into the water jug and mopped her forehead with it, Evelyn gave Spendlove orders to remove the heaters.

'I must say, Mrs Preston, you're a first-class cook!' Golly threw herself back in her chair and undid the middle button of her boiler suit. 'That was top-hole! Well, Conrad,' she grinned across the table at him, exposing food-encrusted fangs, 'I'm looking for a subject for my new opera. What do you say to a little jaunt somewhere to spark off a few ideas? China, perhaps? Or the Azores?'

'I have no plans to leave Northumberland at present,' said Conrad. 'Yesterday I bought a house here. And I think it will take much of my time.'

'Conrad!' Isobel looked excited. 'You didn't tell me!'

Evelyn's curiosity overrode her intention to be distant and unfriendly. 'Surely you haven't bought Shawcross Hall? Really,

Conrad, I think you should reconsider, the proportions are very bad—'

'No,' Conrad interrupted her, 'I have not bought Shawcross Hall. But I doubt if you will think better of my choice. I have bought Hindleep House.'

'You're kidding! You *can't* have! It's madness!' said Golly, Isobel and Rafe respectively.

'It is true. I have.' Conrad folded his arms and looked down his nose at us. It was difficult to see the libidinous student in the aloof autocrat of today. 'And I think it will suit me admirably.'

As soon as I opened the front door I heard sobbing. I waved goodbye to Rafe, then hopped upstairs as fast as my leg permitted. Dimpsie was lying on the bathroom floor, weeping and clutching her hand from which blood dripped. The bath mat was a crimson puddle, and for a dreadful moment I thought she must be haemorrhaging, until I realized it was red wine.

'I'm sorry,' she moaned, 'I tripped on the rug.'

'Let me look.' Luckily the cut was shallow. I cleaned it, found a plaster in the bathroom cabinet and picked up pieces of broken glass from the floor. 'Dimpsie,' I said, when she was sitting on the bathroom stool, more or less dry-eyed, 'you can't go on like this. Supposing you'd cut an artery. No man is worth killing yourself for.'

Dimpsie's eyes welled again. 'I heard someone drive up so I went to the window . . . a sports car . . . the roof was down. Tom got out to fetch something . . . she sat in the passenger seat, smoking. Then she looked up. I bobbed down but I think she saw me. She's frighteningly glamorous . . . sexy . . .'

'She reminds me of Cruella de Vil.'

'You've seen her?'

'She's been into the surgery.'

Dimpsie screwed up her face with pain. 'Vanessa Trumball was just a plaything. I knew he'd get bored with her. This woman is different . . .'

'You've got to stand up to him. Even if he wasn't seeing other women, you oughtn't to put up with being sneered at and trampled on.' Fine words, I thought, coming from Sebastian's doxy. But I pressed on. 'It isn't doing you any good. If you carry on drinking like this you'll pickle your liver and be really ill. And it isn't doing him any good either. It's corrupting him, making him think he can get away with anything. Okay, that's not your responsibility, but—'

'It is, though,' interrupted Dimpsie. 'I can't separate my good from his. I've known Tom since I was eighteen. He's the only man I've ever loved. If I try to imagine life without him there's nothing but howling darkness.'

'Where's your courage?' I asked in rallying tones. 'Where's your determination not to be beaten?'

Dimpsie shook her head. 'Without Tom I'm nothing.'

'Rubbish! You've got brains and talent and a generous spirit and a sense of humour – most of the time – and you've got Kate and me.'

'Kate doesn't care about me. She's only interested in acquiring coasters to match her place mats. And you, darling Marigold, my pride and joy, you inhabit another world where I'm nothing but a fond memory. Don't think I'm blaming you,' she added as I felt myself blush with guilt. 'I *want* you to be a success every bit as much as you can possibly want it. I revel in your achievements. Honestly. But as soon as the plaster cast's off your leg you'll be – quite rightly – going back to London. And the last thing I want is to be a weight on your conscience.'

I wrestled with myself like that bloke with the serpents – I had seen the famous statue in the Vatican Museum when we were dancing *Romeo and Juliet* at the Teatro Dell'Opera di Roma – and for a while it felt as though I had as little chance of winning. But at last I got the words out. 'I'm not going back to London until I'm sure that you've stopped drinking and you've got yourself back on your feet. With or without Tom.'

'Angel, it's sweet of you to be so concerned but I couldn't accept such a sacrifice—'

'I've made up my mind. You haven't any choice. I refuse to go until you're better.' I looked at her swollen eyelids and shiny pink nose and said in a softer voice, 'So what's it to be, old thing? A permanent hangover or my name up in lights?'

18

I so badly wanted my mother to conquer depression and the bottle that, even if it meant being hit on the head by an iron, I was prepared to pay the price. Unwilling to trust the springs of the ancient Mini to the deeply rutted track, we walked across the field towards the caravans, carrying the best the craft shop could offer in plastic bags. Dimpsie forged ahead, fired with the zeal of doing good.

During the past week we had been to the cinema in Hexham and to Carlisle for a shopping trip. We had visited the oriental stall on the market to stock up on incense and kohl as part of her rehabilitation. Though she had pretended to enjoy herself, her eyes had remained lacklustre and her mouth retained its downward droop. My father, when he came to pick up letters or clothes, was colder than Murmansk, where I had once danced the Sugar Plum Fairy in a vest with chilblains. My feet, not the vest. Dimpsie must have craved the numbing solace of alcohol, but such was her determination not to blight my career that she had abstained heroically. She had not had a drink since our conversation six days before and already her skin was a better colour and her hands were steadier. I had volunteered to accompany her to see the new baby and had been rewarded with the first genuine smile since Brenda had told her of the man-eating insatiability of Marcia Dane.

The nearest caravan was called 'The Pathfinder' by its manufacturers. Its pathfinding days were over. It stood on logs instead of wheels, and a section of one side had been replaced by corrugated iron.

'If yore from the Social ye can bugger off before Ah set the dogs on ye,' said the woman who had poked a bedraggled head out of the door to see why they were barking. Three of them were tethered by shamefully short pieces of rope to the wheels. 'And if yore from the animal crooltly place, Ah know my rights—'

'No,' said Dimpsie, 'I just wanted to ask you—'

'If it's about them lawn mowers we don't know nothing about them. And if yore from the Jehovah's Witnesses ye can shove yer blooming *Watchtower* up yer blooming—'

'It's about the baby.'

A scared look came into the woman's face. 'Yo look here! Lawn mowers is one thin' but babbies we *don't* deal in. Ah divvent care what anyone's telt ye, it's a filfy lie—'

'What's up?' A fat man, who looked as though the tip of his nose had been stapled to his upper lip, emerged from the caravan. The dogs immediately stopped barking and lay down with cowed whines. 'What d'yer want?'

'Ow, Jem,' said the woman, her voice softening in appeal. 'They think we've took a babby!' She started to whimper, 'It's always the same when owt goes missing and—'

'Shut it!' He pushed her roughly inside the caravan and slammed the door. 'Now then.' He took out a frightening-looking knife with a long thin blade and began to clean his nails with it. 'Ye canna coom here making accusations.'

'I didn't mean to accuse anyone of anything.' Dimpsie looked alarmed as the man threw the knife into the air as though tossing a coin. He caught it between dirty hands with scabbed knuckles and his eyes narrowed to wicked gleams. 'My husband delivered a baby,' Dimpsie rattled on nervously, 'I thought the mother might live here . . . her father said—'

'Now listen, yo!' The man's face became even uglier with

menace. 'Ah know nowt about any babby. Ah niver laid hands on that little draggle-tail. An' anyone that tells ye different is a liar, see?'

'What my mother means,' I attempted to clarify the situation, 'is that we'd like to see the baby and we've brought it – him – some presents.'

His hand tightened on the handle of the knife, its blade pointing towards my heart. I imagined turning to run, the crutches slipping on the slush of snow and mud, my leg weighing like lead as I tried to escape. I felt the cold burn of steel in my back, the world turning all to white as I began to faint from loss of blood, saw my mother's anxious face as she bent over me before my vision dimmed for ever . . .

'Aal reet. Turn out they bags. Let's see what ye have.'

'They're only things for the baby,' I protested, but Dimpsie was already fumbling inside the plastic.

She brought out a wool bonnet knitted in a repulsive mixture of beige and teal, followed by a matinee jacket in puce and olive. The man cleared his throat and spat with disgust. One really couldn't blame him.

'Let's look in that bag.' He pointed to the one Dimpsie had put down.

She disinterred a crocheted cot blanket and a pottery bowl with LAD written on it. Or it might have been DAD, the glaze had run badly. I was made to remove the bag that hung round my neck and show him a stuffed giraffe made from hideous brown chenille and a painting of a kitten. Or it might have been a pig.

'Yah!' The man was contemptuous. Undeniably our offerings looked pitiful laid out against a background of grubby snow. 'Ye can piss off an take yer trash wi' ye. An if anyone else tries te lay that kid at me door,' he ran his finger down the edge of the blade, 'ye can tell them Ah'll gi' them a facelift fer free. It wez that gobshite that came here sniffing after her like a dog after a bitch on heat. With a heighty-toity voice an fancy claes.

222

It wez him, aal reet.' He threw back his head to laugh, exposing a lack of dentistry and a filthy neck. 'Cuckoo O'Shaunessy's got his deserts. Ha, ha, ha! He thinks he's bloody God Aalmighty but his daughter's nowt but a whore.'

'Which is his caravan?' asked Dimpsie.

'O'er yon brae.' He pointed towards a group of trees, tiresomely distant. 'Now sod off!' He went back into the caravan and slammed the door.

We set off doggedly towards the horizon. The giraffe and the kitten pig painting banged against my chest and the crutches dug into my ribs. By the time we reached the trees, our shoulders and spirits were bowed with weariness.

'That must be it.' I indicated with my nose a small caravan parked in the shelter of some pines. 'It's an awfully long way to run if they attack us. Cuckoo isn't a very encouraging name, is it? He seemed reasonably sane in the surgery, but perhaps he has bouts of madness at the full moon. Don't you think we might go home and try again another day?'

'We've come so far. I think we should go on.'

This caravan was called 'The Intrepid'. A dog barked from inside as we approached.

'That's an encouraging sign,' said Dimpsie. 'I've a good mind to ring the RSPCA when we get home about that other man keeping his dogs tied up outside in weather like this—' She broke off as the door was opened by a man I recognized as Nan's father. He seemed to have grown in the last week.

'Well?' His hair was grey and long, fastened back in a ponytail, and his eyes were fiery. His cheeks were scored with deep creases, and a long scar ran from his nose to his chin and halfway round his neck, as though someone had tried to hack off his head. Even his ears were ravaged and puckered.

Dimpsie shrank back as he scowled at her. 'Mr O'Shaunessy?'

'T'at's me.' He glared ferociously. The scars seemed to turn red and ugly. 'Who's asking?'

'How do you do? I'm Dimpsie Savage and this is my daughter,

Marigold. I hope you don't mind – we'll go away at once if we're intruding – we brought a few things for the baby . . . My husband delivered him—'

'You,' he stabbed in my direction a finger the size of those miniature Swiss rolls that come wrapped in silver and red foil, which I've always rather liked. 'I remember ye now. At least I remember t'e leg. Yore the doctor's girl.' He nodded and allowed his eyebrows to part company. Dimpsie and I let out our breaths which we had been holding in preparation to making a dash for it. 'Ye'd better come in.'

He jumped down, making the earth shake – or perhaps that was my imagination – and waved us ceremoniously up the steps. As I was anxious not to provoke a frenzy of murderous fury, I propped the crutches against the side of the caravan and hobbled obediently in. A delicious warmth hit my frozen face. A gas heater was belting out kilowatts, and in front of it a wooden clotheshorse was hung with nappies folded into neat rectangles. With the smell of clean laundry was mingled an appetizing aroma of baking, which reminded me of the inadequacy of that day's lunch. My father had stopped giving Dimpsie housekeeping money and the craft shop was in arrears with the rent. The cinema tickets, the incense and the kohl had used up a large part of my savings, so we had been living on tins of stuff from the larder. We had got down to the impulse buys, things like chestnut purée and stuffed olives, delicious but not in combination. Fortunately each week Evelyn sent a dozen eggs from her own hens, but there is a limit to how many unaccompanied eggs you can eat.

A black and white dog came over to me, wagging his tail, then lifted a paw in greeting. I shook it and he allowed me to stroke his head. Normally when within reach of a friendly animal, I pursue the acquaintanceship single-mindedly, but on this occasion I was distracted by the caravan's remarkable interior decoration. On every available inch of wall space hung an elaborately carved, brightly painted cuckoo clock.

'These are wonderful!' Dimpsie said admiringly. 'What superb workmanship! Just look at those squirrels. They look quite real. And I love this one with the cat and the St Bernard.'

'Ye'd care to see it working perhaps.' Mr O'Shaunessy seemed to be thawing a little in the warmth of her approval. He set the hands of the clock to twelve and tapped the pendulum into motion.

Not only did a tiny robin on a spring burst out through the doors at the top with each cuckoo, but the cat jumped up and down beneath it and the dog went in and out of his kennel.

'It's magnificent!' Dimpsie was sincere in her appreciation. For her the excellence of the craftsmanship outweighed any ideas about cuckoo clocks being kitsch. I'm ashamed to confess that my enthusiasm was dampened by the certainty of the disapproval of my chief taste arbiters, Evelyn and Sebastian. When the company had been touring southern Germany, Sebastian became so sensitive to the sight of cuckoo clocks that someone would be sent ahead of him into any restaurant or Bierkeller to request their removal before he could be induced to dine there. This of course gave great offence, but that may have been his purpose. The flavour of the *Schwarzwälder kirschtorte*, sharply alcoholic and quite different from sickly English versions, came back to me as my insides gnawed with emptiness.

Dimpsie pointed to a workbench on which lay chisels and hammers among curls of wood shavings and said in a voice of awe, 'You don't mean to say you've made all these marvellous clocks yourself?'

Mr O'Shaunessy looked sternly at her, as though suspecting her of false flattery but Dimpsie's mild brown eyes as she looked up at him from beneath her crinkled fringe were without guile.

'Aye. T'is is t'e latest.' He set it going. A pair of wooden figures came out from a little doorway and travelled along a semicircular gallery followed by two more couples, rotating to the 'Merry Widow' waltz.

225

I was preparing to launch into fulsome praise, when the door opened and in came Nan, muffled up in white fake-fur coat with black spots on it, like a large, damp Dalmatian.

'Whatever are *you* doin' here?' She looked surprised but moderately pleased.

'Hello, Nan. How are you?' I gave her my Princess Aurora birthday smile, judging that the radiant Giselle might be a bit much at such close quarters. 'This is my mother.' I indicated Dimpsie over my shoulder. 'She's mad about babies and wanted to see yours. I hope you don't mind.'

'Help yerselves.' Nan shrugged and pointed to a large wooden box, which we had been too engrossed by the clocks to notice.

'O-o-h!' cried my mother and rushed over to peer in.

Mr O'Shaunessy joined Dimpsie beside the box, dwarfing her to the size of a child. 'What d'ye say, Missus? Isn't me grandson a champion?'

'He's absolutely bea-utiful!' The tremor of genuine emotion in her voice was evidently not lost on the proud grandfather, for his harsh features broke into a smile. 'What's his name?'

'Harrison Ford. Did ye ever see t'e like fre hair? An he's the appetite of a blacksmit'.'

'Look at his darling eyelashes.' Dimpsie straightened up to look at Nan. 'He's gorgeous. You must be so proud.'

'Can't say I am,' Nan replied rather grumpily. 'He's got the lungs of a blacksmith an' all. Wah, wah wah! in the middle o' the night.'

'Oh dear, yes,' Dimpsie said sympathetically, 'I remember how tiring it was constantly having to get up. But it gets better.'

'As te that,' said Nan, 'Dad gets up te him, not me. But however much I stuff me ears wi' cotton wool, I can hear him greetin'.'

'What about a cup of tea, ladies?' said Mr O'Shaunessy.

'That would be heaven – ee-ow!' I ducked and put up my hands to protect myself as something gripped the top of my head. I felt feathers.

''Tis only Petula,' said Mr O'Shaunessy. Something sharp

226

tapped my scalp. 'Now don't peck, Pet,' he commanded. 'I t'ink tis the colour of yer hair. She isn't sure what ye are.'

He came over to lift the bird from my head. Petula was a magpie, with iridescent black and white feathers and a bright yellow beak.

'I found her injured. She couldn't fly. Magpies are said te be vermin but t'ey're canny birds. T'ey can't help but do what t'ey were made for. Pet's better now, but I reckon she stays cos she's fond of me. Who's a bonny lass, then?' he crooned, stroking the bird's throat.

'Pet's a bonny lass,' replied the magpie. Her voice sounded croaky, as though coming through an ancient loudspeaker.

'How clever!' Dimpsie came over to see. 'What else can she say?'

'What does Pet like for tea?' her master asked.

'Pet likes cake,' croaked Petula.

'T'en Pet shall have some. Sit down, ladies, and I'll put t'e kettle on.'

Petula hopped onto the table to be admired while we squeezed onto the banquettes that surrounded it on three sides. Nan scowled at the bird and opened the magazine lying in front of her.

'Bloody nuisance! Always poopin' everywhere.'

'I think she's beautiful.' Dimpsie stroked her long black tail and Petula pecked her hand hard.

'Nasty spiteful thing!' said Nan.

Dimpsie smiled, rubbing the place which had turned red. 'I expect she thought I was taking liberties.'

Petula hopped on to Nan's magazine, deposited a white blob on the face of Princess Michael of Kent and then flew up to the top of the cupboard.

'Dad! That damn bird's done it again!' Nan wailed.

Mr O'Shaunessy zoomed over with a hanky and scrubbed the princess's face clean. Then he covered the table with a clean cloth which, though unironed, was as white as the snow outside and put on it blue and white striped mugs and plates with a matching sugar bowl and milk jug. He set a brown teapot in front of Dimpsie and indicated with a nod of his head that she should pour. I was so hungry I could not take my eyes from whatever was beneath the checked tea towel. He lifted it to reveal a Singin' Hinny, which is a speciality of Northumberland, a cross between a cake and a large flat scone filled with currants. He cut it into four pieces, split each one and buttered it. I shut my eyes to savour fully the taste of childhood, sweet and rich and satisfying.

'This is perfection.' I opened my eyes to smile at Mr O'Shaunessy.

He gave me a doubtful look. 'Ye don't disdain our simple food t'en?'

'Certainly not.' I felt rather indignant at the imputation that I was a snob. But I reminded myself that people who live unconventionally must often be in receipt of slights and snubs. 'It's one of my favourite things.'

Nan looked up. 'My favourite thing's smoked salmon. I've only ate it once. I suppose ye eat it all the time.'

'No, I don't. I can't afford it.'

'Ye canna be poor. Yer fatha's a doctor.'

'Yes, but I support myself. Anyway, my father isn't interested in food. He'd be furious if we spent his money on things like smoked salmon.'

'If I had any money, I'd eat smoked salmon every day. I'd never look at another Singin' Hinny. Daft name, anyways.'

She returned to flicking through the magazine while eating the despised Hinny, her little finger extended to express disgust. Mr O'Shaunessy looked annoyed but said nothing. The warmth of the heater condensed on the windows in silvery trickles. The cosy cheerfulness of the caravan ought to have put anyone in a good mood, yet it was clear that father and daughter were not happy. I wondered what had happened to Mrs O'Shaunessy. Above the sink was a plate-rack that held two plates and two glasses. A Tilley lamp shed light on a tidily folded pile of blankets and two pillows. Presumably each night the banquettes became beds. I tried to imagine myself living in such proximity with my father, sleeping, dressing and undressing in the same room and shivered inwardly at the thought.

'Are your clocks for sale, Mr O'Shaunessy?' asked Dimpsie.

'Aye. Twice a year a man comes from t'e USA and takes t'em all away.'

'I suppose you wouldn't think of trying to sell them locally? I have a craft shop in the village.' She pulled a face. 'I'm afraid most of the things are pretty awful. But if I could get people to supply me with nicer things it might do better in the summer when the tourists come.'

'The Americans send me the innards, the clock mechanism, see. I'd have to pay for the parts.'

'Well, couldn't you do that? Or better still, let me. We could try just one to begin with.' Dimpsie looked eager.

Mr O'Shaunessy stuck out his lower lip, debating inwardly. 'Well, Mrs Savage, I don't know—'

'Oh, do call me Dimpsie. It's a nickname – so silly, isn't it, but it's what my father called me because I was a fat little baby covered with dimples.' Mr O'Shaunessy looked taken aback. I could see my mother was going on too fast for him, but that was her way when she liked people. She wanted to know everything about them immediately and to tell them everything about herself. She clasped her fingers together. 'And may I call you Cuckoo?'

Mr O'Shaunessy looked affronted. 'I know t'at's what t'e bastards call me behind me back.' He clenched his fist, a scarred gorilla's paw. 'I'd like to see t'e man who'd dare say it to me face!'

Dimpsie looked dismayed. 'I do beg your pardon, Mr O'Shaunessy.' She put her small hand on his arm where it was immediately lost among thick black whiskers. 'It was stupid of me.'

Seeing contrition in every feature of her gentle face, Mr

O'Shaunessy relented. 'I was baptized John. But me friends call me Jode.'

'Jode!' My mother beamed, relieved to be forgiven. 'So suitable. A very manly name.'

Mr O'Shaunessy – Jode, as he was from that moment on – squared his shoulders and looked gratified.

'That's settled then,' she said. 'You'll write and ask them?'

He seemed to shrink a fraction. 'I can't read nor write. Nan deals wit' letters and t'at.'

'Oh . . . well . . .' Dimpsie looked uneasy. There seemed to be so many opportunities for giving offence. 'Why don't I save Nan the trouble and send the letter myself? What do you say, Nan?'

She had been deep in an article about the best way to store fur coats. When the matter was explained to her, she shrugged characteristically and said, 'Okay.'

'I'll do it tomorrow.' Dimpsie lifted her mug of tea. 'May this be the beginning of a fruitful partnership. A pity we haven't anything stronger to celebrate with.'

'Dad don't approve of drink,' said Nan, not looking up.

'Oh, no, of course not. Neither do I, actually.' She caught my eye and blushed.

Jode exposed teeth like anti-tank bollards. 'What say we have a singsong instead? Not'ing like a hymn for lifting t'e spirits.'

Dimpsie and I exchanged glances of alarm. Neither of us could sing a note.

'Grow up, Dad!' Nan growled. 'Who wants te yawl their lungs out on a pissin' awful day in a van in the middle of a clarty field? Anyway, you'll wake the babby.'

Jode frowned momentarily, then rubbed his face with his hand to restore an expression of good humour. 'Have another bit of cake, Nan. Maybe it'll sweeten yer temper.'

'It'll take more'n a bit of cake to do that!' Nan flashed out.

'You'll forgive her kittle humour.' Jode turned to Dimpsie. 'She's been disappointed in love and there's no pain so sore.'

'Dad! Give over talking about me as if I woren't here!' Nan's

230

eyes filled. 'I hate men and I don't want owt more to do wi' them.'

Casting about for a diversion, Dimpsie remembered the things we had brought with us. After a cursory glance Nan showed little interest, but Jode exclaimed politely over each article as though we had opened a casket of precious jewels, which made their awfulness more embarrassing. While he was admiring the kitten-pig, the involuntary beneficiary of the craft-shop cast-offs began to cry. Tenderly Jode lifted the infant from the box and brought him over to the table. He offered the bundle of waving arms and legs to Nan, but she turned to stare out of the window.

'May I?' Dimpsie held out her arms. Her expression as he laid the baby in them made me feel that every step of the way had been well worth it.

Little Harrison Ford's face was salmon-coloured with emotion. His mouth was wide open, showing pale pink gums and a uvula that trembled proportionally with the volume of his crying. Jode gave the feeding bottle to Dimpsie with the air of one bestowing the freedom of Newcastle on its most illustrious citizen. My ears rang in the sudden silence as the baby stopped howling and sucked urgently, opening and closing its tiny fists, its entire body tense with concentration. Jode watched dotingly as the child consumed the bottle's contents, while Nan read an article about shopping in the Brompton Road, which could only serve to embitter. The baby lay still for a few moments, at peace with the world. Then his face turned from salmon to crimson. Even his eyes seemed to redden.

'He's filling his nappy. Regular as clockwork,' said the happy grandfather. 'Give him te me.'

He took him to the other end of the caravan, which was not far. Nan held her little upturned nose while the changing was going on. I tried to breathe through my mouth. Dimpsie looked as delighted as though her nostrils were assailed by the sweet gums of Araby. She and Jode were under a spell woven by Nature to ensure the upbringing of at least some of her progeny.

231

I glanced out of the window at the darkening sky.

'We must go,' I said to Dimpsie.

'Oh dear, yes.' She stood up. 'Goodbye, Nan. Thank you so much for letting me see your lovely baby.'

Nan put her finger on a word to keep her place and looked up. 'Seeya.' Her head went down again, her mind absorbed by what was described in the headline as a raw silk pants suit.

Jode would not hear of us setting off alone and he was not a man to be argued with. He insisted not only on seeing us to the car but also on carrying me, as in his view I was looking all in. I put my arms round his neck and clung to him like the child on the back of St Christopher. He set out with seven-league strides across the moor, beneath a white whirling sky, while Dimpsie, her face hidden by the hood of her red duffle coat, ran behind carrying my crutches like an attendant dwarf. From time to time he shook his head to dash the flakes from his eyes, and strands of wet hair and particles of ice would fly into my face.

'Well,' said Dimpsie as we drove away, narrowly missing an oncoming milk float. 'That was a fascinating experience.' I was delighted to hear a note of buoyancy in her voice. 'What an adorable baby! And such an interesting man! Poor little Nan, such a pretty girl but she seems rather lost. We must see what we can do to help her.'

I made no reply. I was watching in the wing mirror as the milk float twirled like Odile on a patch of sheet ice and slid gracefully to a standstill in the hedge.

19

'I wish you girls would stop screeching.' Rafe slowed to climb an almost vertical hairpin bend. 'It's not like you to be nervous, Isobel.'

'Fear's contagious.' Isobel was sitting next to him. 'Every time Marigold screams I feel sure there must be something to worry about.'

'Sorry.' I was sharing the back seat with Buster so I could put up my leg. 'I really can't help it.'

'Close your eyes,' suggested Isobel.

'They are closed.'

'At least Buster isn't barking. Usually I have to put my fingers in my ears to stop myself going completely crazy.'

'All he needs is a little firmness and consistency.' Rafe sounded satisfied.

I didn't have the heart to tell him the reason Buster wasn't barking was because I was holding his paw. I only had to relax my grasp slightly for him to make the little growling sound that was preparatory to a good howl.

'Whoever built this road was impatient to get to the top,' said Isobel. 'I'd have been inclined to make it more gradual. Think of the poor horses having to drag carriages up here.'

'And from what I can remember it gets worse,' said Rafe. 'It doesn't help to have a fresh layer of snow over last night's ice.

The surface is like glass. Even the snow chains aren't gripping properly.'

I don't believe he meant to torture me. Other people's neuroses are baffling if you do not happen to share them.

'I suppose there's so little traffic they don't bother to send the gritting lorries up,' Rafe continued. 'Or the road-menders, come to that. The verges are so broken down it must be dangerous at the best of times.'

'This is probably a pimple compared with the mountains of Bavaria,' said Isobel dreamily. 'Anyway, I expect Conrad'll have a new road made and fences put up.' These days all her waking moments seemed to be spent in contemplation of Conrad's fabulous wealth and how they were going to spend it.

'Ah, yes,' said Rafe, 'I remember this. It used to be as far as you could get. Those gates have always been chained and padlocked.'

I risked a peek through spread fingers. A fence looped with barbed wire straggled down to the aforementioned gates, which stood open. The track was darkened by trees. Rafe put the headlights on and proceeded with extreme caution. Overhanging branches scraped the roof and sides of the car with teeth-jarring squeals.

'There!' Isobel pointed ahead. 'I saw a light through the trees.'

'It's a godforsaken spot to have chosen!' said Rafe a little crossly, perhaps thinking of his paintwork. 'I hope there'll be some form of heating.'

'Darling, you're beginning to sound like an old, old man,' Isobel reproved him.

'I'm beginning to feel like one. Could it have something to do with the extravagant whimsicality by which I'm surrounded? What was *that* scream about, Marigold? We're going about three miles per hour.'

'Sorry. I was afraid you were going to run over that rabbit.'

'I thought at least you'd seen an army of Berserkers coming through the forest waving axes with bloodcurdling ferocity.'

'You see, you too are capable of extravagant whimsicality.' Isobel tugged her brother's ear lobe affectionately.

'I must put up a sign. It is an offence to molest the driver.'

'I never met a man yet who disliked being molested.'

This sort of friendly bickering was what I chiefly remembered about Rafe's and Isobel's relationship. There was never any teasing in my family. Dimpsie was too easily hurt and my father and Kate instantly rushed from the defensive to the violently offensive. I suppose we were none of us confident of being loved.

'Bloody hell!' Rafe jammed on the brakes. We slid to a stop where the trees ended and the ground fell away. On a rocky promontory in front of us stood Hindleep House, its fairytale turrets, buttresses and pinnacles wreathed in mist that was purplish in the fading light. Spanning the gap of perhaps two hundred yards between us and the house was a narrow bridge. The floor of the valley was a terrifying distance below. 'Did you ever see anything like it? Look at the drop! No wonder the sale went through so quickly. Whoever owned it must have been delirious with joy that someone was insane enough to want to buy it.'

'I think it's thrilling.' Isobel sounded a little annoyed. 'And very romantic.'

'I can see why Conrad wanted it,' I said. 'It's a bit like a smaller version of that castle belonging to Mad King Ludwig. We were taken to see it when we were dancing *Symphonic Variations* in Munich. I can't remember what the castle was called but it's near a lake called Schwansee, which means Swan Lake. He built it to stage Wagner's music because he was nuts about him.'

'I've always thought insanity was a necessary qualification for liking Wagner's music,' said Rafe. 'All that emotional wallowing. Give me Mozart any day.'

'I'm beginning to resent this harping on madness,' said Isobel. 'Conrad's just about the sanest person I've ever met.'

235

'Well, of course you know him so much better than I do,' said Rafe. 'Two and a half weeks, is it now, that you've actually spent in his company?'

Isobel snorted huffily and did not deign to reply.

Rafe said, 'I wonder if it's safe?'

The bridge looked far from well, with potholes in what had once been a metalled surface and gaps in the stone balustrade.

'Perhaps we ought to leave the car here,' I suggested, 'and just tiptoe across one by one.'

'Don't be a baby,' said Isobel, 'of course it's safe. Conrad's expecting us. You don't think he'd let his future wife tumble miles to her death from a wonky bridge?'

'Certainly not,' said Rafe. 'Not on such a short acquaintance, anyway.'

Isobel giggled and put her arm behind his neck to pull his other ear in retaliation.

'Ow! Don't be so rough! I need to be in good shape to drive us safely over this collection of crumbling stones and rusty girders.'

'They must have taken the Bentley across and that's a much heavier car than this one.'

'It may have been heavy enough to weaken the bridge fatally.'

'Don't tease poor Marigold. Can't you see she's really frightened?'

'How can I see her when she's sitting behind me? Now, Marigold, you choose. Shall I dash across on the principle that it's better to skate fast over thin ice, or shall I crawl so as not to create shock waves like a marching army?'

'Let's assume the ice is the only thing holding it together,' said Isobel. 'I vote we go as fast as we can.'

'Oh, please!' My arteries seemed to jam at this idea. 'I'd much rather we crawled.'

'All right. Here goes.'

Rafe put the car into gear and we moved slowly forward. Though I had tried to enter into the joke, I really was terrified,

236

and one glimpse of the tiny pinpoints of light from Gaythwaite fathoms below made my head spin and my muscles contract painfully. I shut my eyes again. If I was going to trust any man with my life it would be Rafe. And it would be a merciful death, a sensation like going down fast in a lift and leaving one's stomach behind, perhaps oblivion before one hit the ground—

'Good God!' said Isobel's voice. 'Look at those statues!'

'Don't clutch my arm when I'm driving to the inch.'

'But did you ever see anything so creepy? Looming up in the dusk like the reproachful ghosts of suicides. They're sending shivers down my back.'

'Darling, you're exaggerating as usual. But I admit they do look rather sinister.'

I felt the car slow and I *had* to open my eyes to see what they were talking about. A slightly larger-than-life-sized figure of a woman stood on the parapet. Her stone face frowned down at us, her cheeks and robes blackened by the rain and storms of a hundred years. In one hand she held what might have been a spear. The still-falling snow and the failing light made it difficult to be certain.

'She looks fiendishly bad-tempered,' said Rafe.

'She looks positively sunny by comparison with this one,' said Isobel a few seconds later.

About fifteen yards further on, on the other side of the bridge, was the statue of a woman dressed in tattered robes, holding one hand to her mouth as though she was eating something. I thought I saw a snake coiled round her body. Even allowing for the depredations of weather, her face had a savage look of pain that was disturbing.

'She's horrible,' said Isobel, 'drive on quickly.'

Every fifteen yards there was another statue.

'I shall ask Conrad to get rid of them. I think they're beastly,' said Isobel as we neared the other end of the bridge.

'Well, I don't know . . . they're magnificent in their way . . . but they must weigh a ton apiece so it might be wiser . . . thank

237

God! Dry land.' We drove beneath a turreted archway into a courtyard. '*Phew!* I don't mind admitting that was pretty nerve-racking . . .' He started to laugh.

Parked in the middle of the courtyard was an enormous pantechnicon. Its reversing lights came on as it started to shunt to and fro to turn round, a manoeuvre made more difficult by the Bentley parked in one corner. Rafe pulled over to let him go by. The driver grinned at us and gave the thumbs-up sign as he set off across the bridge at a spanking pace.

'We'd better agree to keep quiet over the funk we were in,' suggested Rafe. 'Especially Marigold.' His voice was affectionately teasing and I felt better at once.

'Isn't this heavenly?' said Isobel.

It *was* heavenly. Though I knew, because Rafe had told me, that the castle had been built in the last quarter of the nineteenth century, it had a glorious air of medieval mystery about it. All the doors around the courtyard were pointed at the top, including the most important-looking pair at the head of a flight of stone steps. Everything was a little crooked and dilapidated, just as though it had endured five hundred years of weather and wars and the inconstancy of the human heart. It was the distillation of romance.

'Let's go in!' cried Isobel. 'I must see inside!'

The steps were steep and slippery, and more than ever I felt the frustration of my crippled state.

'You'll manage better without these.' Rafe took my crutches and propped them against the wall, then put his arm round my waist and half carried me up.

The door at the top was lit by a pair of hurricane lamps hanging on iron hoops obviously intended for something far grander, like blazing torches. He looked down at me and smiled. 'Light as a feather.' The flames cast dramatic flickering shadows on his face, deepening the creases each side of his mouth. I had that feeling again, and very delightful it was, that being with him made me feel terrifically happy and safe.

'Do help!' said Isobel impatiently as she struggled to turn the huge iron ring.

'Should we knock?' I asked.

'Don't be an idiot. When I marry Conrad this'll be home, sweet home. One of them anyway.'

Rafe grappled with the handle and the door opened with a spectral groan.

'My God! It's like the House of Usher,' exclaimed Isobel.

'Nothing that a spot of WD forty won't cure.' Rafe had evidently appointed himself the voice of reason. 'Good Lord!' he murmured less certainly as we entered a room panelled and carved to within an inch of its life. Some of the wood was rotten and leant out at an angle, exposing the stone behind. What light remained had to penetrate lace-like veils of dust-choked webs that draped the cracked and missing panes of glass. Despite the freezing wind that whistled through the gaps, there was a powerful smell of damp and decay.

Unexpectedly, strains of music came through a doorway ahead of us. I recognized *Parsifal*. One of my first roles as a member of the corps de ballet had been as a flower maiden in Act Two. Considering we had just been talking about Wagner, the co-incidence seemed remarkable, but Rafe said afterwards when I mentioned this that anyone with the vaguest knowledge of German Romanticism would have made the connection.

The open door led us into the room that Dimpsie, Kate and I had picnicked in all those years ago. Now it was blurred by candlelight. When I saw Conrad standing with his back to the stone fireplace in which several tree trunks were emitting flames and sparks like fireworks, I could not help thinking of Klingsor, the sorcerer in *Parsifal* who lives in the Magic Castle. The plot of *Parsifal*, as I remembered it, was a cross between a children's bedtime story and a depressing morality play about lust. But as our production had been set in modern Communist China – the flower maidens had worn denim caps and black pigtails and our faces had been painted sunflower yellow – probably the opera had not been given a fair chance. Sebastian, a devoted Wagnerian, had been withering in his condemnation of the director's arrogance, but we needed the money.

Conrad kissed Isobel on both cheeks and shook hands with Rafe and me. He looked thoroughly relaxed, even pleased with himself. Had I been in his shoes I should have been tearing out my hair. Bits of plaster hung from the walls, exposing bare lathes, and the ceiling was black and bulging with damp. More plaster had been swept into heaps on the floor. One wall was composed of stone pillars and glass doors, the panes all broken, of course. But the view . . . I had forgotten the view, and when I saw it again all my reservations about the wisdom of buying Hindleep House vanished as quickly as smoke in a stiff breeze.

The nearest slopes were spiked with fir trees dusted with snow. Dun and amethyst-coloured clouds loured above them, marbling the surface of a lake that curved into a letter S. Beyond the lake rose hills that were blue in the hesitant light. Despite the icy streams of air that made my eyes water until tears ran down my cheeks, I could have gazed for hours.

'Do look what Conrad's just had delivered,' called Isobel. 'Isn't it *won*derfully impractical?'

She was sitting on the stool of a grand piano. This, the long table I remembered from my last visit, and two deckchairs were the only furniture.

'Let's hope it doesn't disappear through the floor.' Rafe kicked with his toe at a rotten section of floorboard.

'Don't be such a killjoy,' said Isobel. 'Look, it's standing on a sheet of steel. If *it* goes down, the entire floor'll go with it.'

'*That's* all right then.'

'Don't take any notice, Conrad. I adore it all. Let's have a tour at *once*.'

'I am waiting for Golly. Then we shall all look together.' Isobel began to protest, but Conrad shook his head. 'It will be all the better for a little anticipation.'

Usually any kind of opposition made her defiant, but now

she put her arm affectionately through his and leaned her head against his shoulder in an uncharacteristically kittenish way. I had always greatly admired Isobel's rebelliousness. Dancers have to submit to being told what to do and how to do it every second of our professional lives, and the habit of obedience becomes ingrained. Conrad made no response to this gesture of affection, but remained with his hands in his pockets, as immovable as one of his own statues; nor did he look down at her until she wrinkled her nose and drew away from him.

'You smell like a cross between a bonfire and a tar lorry.'

'This chimney was choked with twigs and leaves but, as the flume is wide, it was a simple matter to tie several bamboos together and push them out.'

'Flue, you mean. A flume is a stream for moving logs about.'

Conrad frowned. 'I meant flume. When it snowed the chimney was a conduit for water.'

I saw that Conrad did not like to be corrected. His English was so nearly perfect and his accent was lovely. He pronounced 'th' like a soft 'd' – 'dis' 'dat' and 'dem' – and said 'seemple metter' instead of 'simple matter'. His voice was not harsh like Nazi generals in films. On the contrary it was . . . mellifluous might be the word. Though he had recently been up a chimney, he wore a beautiful dark green coat and a heather-coloured jersey with grey corduroy trousers. On one finger was a ring with a black stone. By comparison with Rafe, who wore jeans and an old brown jacket, there was something of the dandy about Conrad. That, combined with his exotic dark looks, made me think of Kurt Weill's *Seven Deadly Sins,* in which I had danced the role of Pride. I had been much taken at the time with the glamorous decadence of the Weimar Republic.

'Vat fettle, honoured ladies and gentlemen.' Fritz came in with an ice bucket containing a bottle and several glasses. 'Excuse you me please for make you all to wait.'

'What have you been doing?' Isobel asked. 'You look as though you've spent the day down a pit.'

241

Fritz's delicate pink and whiteness was marred by black smudges. 'Excuse you me, please. Vat is pit? Oh, yes. The mines. I haf try to make the oven burn. He has bird nests in his pipe. There is a dog outside who very much barks,' said Fritz as he poured the champagne. 'Is it permitted him to bring in?'

'I'm afraid that's Buster.' Rafe looked vexed. 'He's still a young dog and his manners aren't all they should be.'

'Then let us set him a good example and invite him into the warm,' said Conrad.

Buster raced round the room, jumped into one of the deckchairs, leaped onto the table and yapped ear-splittingly at the fire before hurling himself at my knees.

'Honestly, it's perfectly all right,' I said as Rafe helped me tenderly to my feet. 'I bet if I jumped off that balcony my leg would be preserved whole, even if the rest of me was dashed to pieces.'

Rafe spoke sternly to Buster and directed him to 'lie down, sir!' Buster licked his pointing finger lovingly and raced round the room again in an excess of enthusiasm. While Rafe was concentrating on helping me out of my coat and settling me in one of the deckchairs with my foot raised on the stone hearth, I saw Conrad bend down and drop something discreetly beside Buster. It worked like a charm. Buster crouched down and began to push it round the floor with his nose until he and it had disappeared under the table, where he remained quietly for the next half-hour.

'Do tell us about the man who built this house,' I said to Conrad. 'Is it true that he killed himself?'

'Quite true. Orson Ratcliffe's diary, or a copy of it, is in the Gaythwaite library. Apparently, each year he had many printed and issued them to friends. Also his poems. He left a letter giving his reasons. It seems he was a man driven to communicate his feelings.' Conrad's expression was perfectly grave but there was in his eye, somewhere deep in its dark centre, a hint of what might have been amusement.

'So why *did* he do it?'

'He saw that inferior poets were exalted above him and he no longer wished to live in an insensible world.'

'Poor man. Were you playing *Parsifal* because this house reminds you of that castle in Bavaria?'

Conrad looked at me with something like surprise. I expect he thought me too much of a bird brain to recognize the music of the Master. 'Bavaria has many castles. But no doubt you mean Neuschwanstein. You are perfectly right. I happened to look up and there it was, this house with its towers springing up out of the forest and the lake below, and at once I was reminded of Bavaria. How does it happen that you know of it?'

'Oh, we did a tour of Germany and we danced three nights in Munich. They took us to see the castle, but it was so jammed with tourists you couldn't see anything below six feet. We were squeezed through the rooms like toothpaste through a tube. Luckily the ceilings and walls were wonderful. Did you buy this place because you were homesick?'

'Homesick? No. I have never experienced that. I like to move about. I bought this house because it amuses me. It is a failing of mine that I am quickly bored.'

Evidently being married to Conrad was not going to be restful. Fortunately Isobel, too, was easily bored, so they were well matched.

'Tell us about the statues on the bridge.' Isobel looked up from the keyboard. 'I think they're vile. I hope you're going to get rid of them.'

'On the right as you approach the house are the Virtues.' Conrad counted them off on his fingers. 'Faith, Prudence, Justice, Strength . . . who else? . . . yes, Harmony and Hope. On the left are the Vices. They are Falsehood, Sloth, Pride, Lechery, Gluttony and Envy.'

'I think they're all unpleasant and intimidating.' Isobel played a loud chord to express the strength of her feelings. 'A lot of stone bullies. Fancy being preached at by a bridge. Perhaps a garden centre would buy them. Or a museum. I expect they're worth something. Not that that would matter to you, of course.'

'Even if I wished to sell them, which I do not, they are listed along with the house.'

'Oh well, as far as that goes, our house is listed Grade One and we aren't supposed to put up even a compost bin without permission, but they never come to check. If you got rid of them at once—'

'I have no intention to get rid of them.'

Isobel looked at him, her mouth sulky, her eyes fierce, an expression I knew well and always gave in to. Conrad merely held her gaze, his face and body perfectly relaxed. It was going to be a tempestuous relationship. But Isobel would not have liked a man she could order about. After a while she lowered her eyes and smiled. 'All right, Conrad. Whatever you want.' She left the piano and came to stand next to him, holding out her glass to be filled. 'I expect I'll get used to them.'

Perhaps she thought it wise to give in gracefully to the man she loved. Or she had remembered that she was already deeply in his debt. Whatever it was, she had her reward at once.

Conrad waved his hand over her glass and a second later something sparkled in the bottom of it. Isobel gave a cry of excitement.

'Diamonds! Earrings! Oh! They're exquisite!' She fished them out and held the delicate teardrop-shaped clusters up to her ears. 'Where's a mirror? I must see!'

'There is no such thing here. You will have to wait.' He smiled at her impatience.

She kissed him. 'I adore them! How did they appear in my glass. I saw! You didn't even touch it! Are you a magician?'

'It was a simple conjuring trick.'

'When did you learn it?'

'I spent long periods in a mental institution when I was young. To while away the time I taught myself *Taschenspielerei* or, what do you say?, legerdemain. Sleight of hand?'

244

If it was a shock for me it must have been doubly so for her. Isobel laughed as though she didn't believe him. I caught Rafe's eye. He smiled rather grimly.

'Yoo-hoo! Conrad!' It was Dame Gloria Beauwhistle.

'In here, Golly.'

'My dear boy! You never fail to astonish me. Whatcha folks . . .' She acknowledged our presence with a wave. 'When you said house, I thought you meant a nice safe farmstead or a dignified presbytery. My poor old motor nearly gave up on those bends.' Golly sported a leather blouson over the boiler suit she had worn to Evelyn's lunch. On her head was a leather helmet, shaped like a baby's bonnet, which made her face more moon-like than ever. 'And that bridge! I've shed little bits of exhaust pipe in every pothole.' She looked about her, then sucked in her breath in a whoop and rushed to the windows. 'Now I understand!' She threw out her arms. 'Worth every pound of the garage bill. Dear old thing, this is Valhalla!'

'I thank God there are not five hundred and forty doors,' said Conrad. 'It is quite draughty enough.'

I should have liked to ask him about the five hundred and forty doors, but Golly saw the piano and rushed over to it.

'A Steinway! Of course, nothing but the best for you, you lucky dog! There's still nothing to touch them.' She ran her fingers up and down the keys. 'This is a fine instrument. Did you know they were auctioning Johannes Spiegel's last week? I went all the way down to London to bid for it, but some damned hustler bought it out of hand before the sale . . .' She struck her forehead with the heel of her hand. 'No, don't tell me! This is *it,* isn't it?'

Conrad shrugged. 'If you tell me not to tell you, what can I say?'

Fritz had gone away and returned with an extra glass and a plate of apple cakes covered with icing sugar. I had eaten such things on our trip to Bavaria. They are a trap for the greedy and unwary. If you draw breath while eating them, the sugar flies into your throat and you cannot speak or even breathe for several minutes.

'Hello, Fritz, old bean,' said Golly with a wave.

'Vat fettle, Golly.'

'Ah's champion,' she replied promptly.

Fritz put down the plate on the hearthstone and took out his notebook. 'Old bean,' he muttered to himself. 'Ah's champion.'

'Now can we have a tour of the house?' said Isobel like an impatient child.

From the beginning it had struck me as odd that Conrad had bought Hindleep House without confiding in his wife-to-be. When we were children, Isobel had always been sensitive to any suggestion that she was not the most important person to be considered. Perhaps she was so wildly in love with Conrad that she was prepared to suffer his high-handed ways with sweet-tempered passivity. Or possibly this house was merely an interim amusement and not intended to be the place where they would live as man and wife. All these ideas wandered through my brain as I watched him covertly for manifestations of lunacy. He must have been in the asylum a long time to have become so good at conjuring.

'This reminds me of the Chamber of Horrors at Madame Tussaud's,' said Isobel when we were standing in the basement kitchen, reached by a stone spiral staircase leading from the hall. It was fairly dark with a vaulted ceiling supported by sturdy pillars. Over the fireplace was a roasting spit with chains and spikes and an iron cage, presumably for the joints of meat.

'Perhaps it was a torture chamber,' suggested Golly, her mouth rimmed with an icing-sugar moustache to rival Lady Pruefoy's. 'How else could they have got through a wet Sunday afternoon with no entertainment but books of sermons and whist for penny points? I expect they liked nothing better than to lure a few shepherds and nymphs off the hillside and subject them to a little racking of limbs and screwing of thumbs.'

Leading from the kitchen were smaller rooms, with hooks for hanging game and marble slabs for storing food and a large barrel on a stand which Rafe said was for making butter.

'What are you going to do with this basement?' Golly brushed away a web that hung like a lace cap over her forehead. 'I can't see Mrs Lerner rustling up the Sunday joint somewhere so gloomy and inconvenient.'

'I can't cook anyway,' said Isobel in a decided tone. 'I suppose one of the village women will come in.'

Conrad gave the butter-barrel handle an experimental turn and was rewarded with a shower of dust and plaster on his shoes. 'That is not my intention.'

Isobel smiled. 'You're going to get a cook from London? That'll be much better. Or Paris. That'd be better still.'

Conrad peered into the funnel of a circular object that Rafe said was for sharpening knives. A giant spider ran out, making him jump back. 'No. Fritz is a good cook and he enjoys to do it.'

'But you'll get people in to clean and wait at table?' Isobel persisted.

'Who will come so far? And it would complicate what is to be a simple bucolic existence.' He spun round to look at me. 'Ludwig the Second had a table which sank on a mechanism through the floor to the kitchen, where it was recharged with dishes so he need not be waited on. He hated passionately to be stared at, particularly when eating. At state dinners he insisted that a barrier of flowers be arranged in front of him. He made the musicians play so loudly that there could be no conversation, and glared at the guests from between the leaves.'

'Scopophobic, poor old fruitcake,' said Golly. 'Or perhaps just cunning. I can't stand pomp and circumstance myself.'

'No one knows the real condition of his mind,' said Conrad. 'His wish was to be an enigma – to himself as well as to others. From a boy he lost himself in dreams and fantasies of being Lohengrin, the swan-knight. His servants had orders to let him

247

sleep all day and to wake him at midnight so that he could ride in his gilded sleigh by moonlight over his beloved mountains.'

'At least he wasn't dull,' said Isobel.

'Certainly he was not that. One of his desires was to travel in a flying car drawn by mechanical peacocks and powered by hot-air balloons across the Alpsee, but in those days there was not the technology to do it.'

Golly shook her head. 'Shakespeare has a speech about the madness of kings but I can't remember in which play. It must be an occupational hazard. Being kowtowed to is very bad for people.'

'It is the Bastard's speech in *King John*—'

'The girls must be getting cold,' Rafe interrupted, as though tired of providing an audience for a flow of information from Conrad. 'Let's move on.'

I wished we could tear ourselves away from the topic of madness.

My leg was a thorough nuisance on the tour. Rafe assisted me back up to the hall but I made him go on with the others while I recovered my breath.

Fritz was alone in the drawing room, sitting in one of the deckchairs, with a sprinkling of sugar decorating his flower-embroidered waistcoat, his eyes closed, listening to Wagner. The fire blazed high, and the music swelled to a climax in glorious sympathy with the ultramarine of the darkening sky, which was lit by a single unwinking star beyond the great windows. It was so like a stage set that, for the hundredth time that day, as every day since the accident, I wondered whether I would ever dance again.

Fritz opened his eyes and sprang up. 'Dear Marigold! Vat is the matter? Hurts your bone?'

'Oh . . . no. The spiral staircase took it out of me, that's all. Are there many more rooms on this floor?'

'Permit me. I show you. Zis,' he conducted me through a door leading off from the drawing room, 'vas, ve sink, vonce

248

a library.' Bookshelves covered with dust bore out this idea. 'Here ve shall do our vorks. It holds no welcome at present but I have faith.'

It was fortunate that this room also had a large fireplace, for it looked towards the hillside and was as dark and as cold as the bottom of a lake.

'Now this,' he led the way to another much smaller room, 'vill be a plunge pool. Ceramics all over and vith a big –' with his fingers he imitated something trickling down on his head – 'die Dusche . . . what do you say . . . douche? Conrad is most fond of taking seaweed baths.'

'Really?' To my ears, unaccustomed as they were to luxury – not only my ears, of course – the seaweed had a dangerously Ludwigian ring to it.

'Ve Bavarians have a strong pleasure in therapeutic walue of bathing. Our bath towns are most numerous.'

These three rooms made up the whole of the ground floor, since the house was only a castle in miniature. The stairs to the upper floors were too narrow and steep for crutches. Fritz and I returned to the fireside and shared the last Apfelküchen, while he gave me an interesting account of German confectionery, a subject evidently close to his heart, until the others came down.

'Four bedrooms and a bathroom of sorts,' said Isobel in answer to my question. 'Polythene tacked over the windows and plastic canisters of water.'

'Naturally, after so long unused, the system does not work,' said Conrad. 'It pours rust only.'

'I'm sure Mummy won't mind if you come over to Shottestone for a hot bath every day.'

'Thank you,' said Conrad, 'but I enjoy prevailing over difficulties and I believe in the benefits of cold-water bathing.'

'Poor boy!' Golly tapped his head. 'Wandering in his wits! I'm all for the simple life and I hate pretension above all else –' she broke wind noisily and quite unselfconsciously, as though to emphasize the point – 'but no water, no electricity, no telephone . . . For one of the world's richest men to choose to live in a ruin, surely this is taking eccentricity to the point of masochism?'

I was inclined just then to agree with Golly that the entire enterprise was the product of a seriously disordered brain, but later, as we sat by the fire in candlelight, watching the last ray of light die out of the sky and a panorama of moon and stars take its place, I had to admit that the project offered thrilling possibilities. When Conrad drew the stool up to the piano and began to play Chopin nocturnes so beautifully that they made me shiver, I was quite prepared to concede that the whole scheme was the cleverest thing ever thought of.

'How *good* Buster's been all evening.' Isobel bent to look under the table.

Rafe looked gratified. 'Dogs are pack animals. It's a matter of teaching them who's boss.'

'How revolting!' said Isobel. 'He's sleeping with his chin on a dead mouse!'

I looked at Conrad. He happened to catch my eye. To my surprise he bared his teeth and growled low like a dog. Then his black eyes filled with mischief. I was sorry to remember that he was undoubtedly deceitful and probably insane as well.

20

'Keep still.'

The nurse approached the frayed and filthy edge of the plaster with a small whizzing circular saw. I imagined flesh and blood, mine, splattering the walls of the outpatients' ward of Carlisle hospital. I had dreamed almost every night of being able to walk and run and dance again, free of the hated cast. Now that the moment had come, my heart was beating so hard I was quite worried about pulling through the experience.

'Steady.' The nurse frowned and stuck her tongue into the corner of her mouth. 'I don't like this job. I'm always afraid me hand's goin' ter slip. It's that hot wi' the radiators going full blast.'

She paused to wipe her forehead with the back of her arm. My own palms were moist and my skin prickled. I closed my eyes and thought of the view from Hindleep as the saw buzzed again like a furious bee.

A cracking sound made me open them quickly.

'Here we are.'

She was peeling away the plaster. There was my leg, incarcerated for six weeks, white, thin and feeble-looking, covered with a fine ginger down like a gooseberry.

The nurse examined the scar, a purple line. 'It seems to have healed up nicely.'

Feeling sick with fright, I flexed toes that hardly seemed to belong to me. But oh joy! I could point them! I stood up and put my feet in the turned-out position. Carefully I lowered myself into a plié, then rose and extended my leg in a trembly *battement tendu*. The arch of my foot would have disgraced a ten year old, but I would work, work, work to get back its flexibility. Tentatively I lifted my foot above my head. My thigh muscles hurt like hell, but feeling pain again after weeks of numb immobility was exquisite pleasure.

'Crikey!' The nurse was impressed. 'However did you do that?'

'I've been doing it every day since I was ten,' I explained. 'That way you retrain groups of muscles and ligaments. It isn't possible otherwise. I'm a dancer.'

'Really? Like Ruby Slipper and the Slipperettes?'

'No. Ballet.'

Her enthusiasm waned. 'Fancy.'

I took the sock and shoe I had brought with me from my bag and put them on. 'Thank you so much.' I picked up my coat. 'Goodbye.'

'You can't go till the doctor's seen you. He'll want to X-ray it and then you'll have to make an appointment to see a physio . . . You'll need your crutches until you get used to it . . .'

But I was walking away from her, concentrating on not limping, on distributing my weight equally between my feet, teaching myself to trust my newly restored leg. Had the crutches belonged to me I would have taken them to the nearest bridge and hurled the hateful things into the River Eden. As they belonged to the NHS, I left them propped against the wall in outpatients.

'Darling!' Dimpsie was walking down the corridor towards me. I had left her parking the car as we were, inevitably, a little late for my appointment. 'Sorry I wasn't there for the disrobing. I ran into someone I knew – literally, I'm afraid. Luckily he's one of your father's patients. He said he'd tell the insurance people he backed into a wall. As he was being so kind, I had to ask about his hernia . . . how is it?'

'I feel like a slave who's had her fetters taken off. I'm *free!*' I threw my arms around her, attracting the curious glances of those trudging up and down the corridor. 'I've got rid of that foul bloody cast and I shall never be unhappy again. Look!' I did an experimental, very poor pirouette in slow motion. 'Seriously,' I said later as we were driving home after a celebratory sausage and chips, ambrosia after an exclusive diet of eggs, 'I do think it might be going to be all right if I absolutely devote every waking hour to exercising it. A couple of months ought to do it.'

'Oh, darling, really? I'm so thrilled!' In her excitement, Dimpsie wandered into the path of a car transporter. The driver could not have been attending, because he had to slam on his brakes. Together with his burden of cars, he did a loop round the traffic lights. I looked over my shoulder to see a van collide with the transporter's tail. 'I was so afraid you'd be leaving the minute you got the cast off. And I wasn't going to say anything but I can tell you now: I was simply dreading you going. Two more months! That's absolutely wonderful!'

I had serious misgivings when I heard this. How to tell her that I intended to spend those two months in London attending classes? Having seen an old lady on a bicycle career into the crashed van, I turned my eyes to the front and wrestled with my conscience. Most immediately, ought I to tell Dimpsie of the mayhem she had left behind her? Her only crime had been to swerve into the wrong lane. If the driver of the transporter had been concentrating, nothing would have happened. But Dimpsie, I knew, would insist on going back and shouldering the blame. What good could that possibly do the old lady or anyone else? We were on the ring road now and leaving the scene of destruction behind. My anxiety about the old lady took the edge off my exultation at becoming a biped once more. I decided to ring the police station anonymously when we got home to find out if anyone had been injured.

But as we went in through the front door, the telephone

started to trill and, as things turned out, it was several hours later before I thought about the old lady again.

'Marigold? It's Rafe. How did it go at the hospital?'

'Very well. How sweet of you to remember.'

'Of course I knew how important it must be for you.'

I felt a rush of gratitude. 'It is rather. How are you?'

'At something of a loose end. Evelyn's taken my father to Newcastle and Isobel's gone to London with Conrad. I've been painting all day and it won't go right. Would you be angelic and come and cheer me up? Mrs Capstick's made an orange cake.'

'That does sound tempting. Hang on a second, would you?'

'Yes, of course, do go,' said Dimpsie when I consulted her. 'I must ring some of my weavers and whittlers to see if they've survived the winter.'

'I'll be back in time for supper.'

'Don't worry if you get a better offer. It'll only be scrambled eggs again.' Dimpsie's face folded into familiar lines of anxiety. I had had to pay the electricity bill with the last of my savings. I intended to send the gas bill to my father, but I had no idea what we would do if he didn't pay it. Also, the washing machine had broken down halfway through a cycle and was still full of soapy water. And we would soon become egg-bound. I had to think of a plan of action, but what?

I picked up the telephone again. 'I've got some shopping to do. I'll meet you in the Market Square in an hour.'

The walk down to the town was a time of purest happiness. For the first time for months I was able to enjoy the luxury of stepping briskly out – fairly briskly – in solitude, listening to the birds, admiring the trees, the clouds and patches of livid green grass that were beginning to appear through the snow. It was as though blinkers had been removed from my eyes and muffs from my ears now I no longer had to concentrate on the crutches and not falling over or banging my leg. It was offi-cially spring and, though the temperature was chilly, a silvery shimmer behind a grey cloud curtain revealed the whereabouts of the sun. I snuffed up the smell of cold earth and last autumn's decaying leaves, intoxicating after the stuffiness of houses and cars. A man cycled past without giving me a second glance. I was no longer an object of interest and pity, separated from the rudely healthy by plaster and crutches.

Rafe's car was already parked in the square, though I had arrived ten minutes early. He jumped out and came to meet me.

'My goodness, what a transformation! You look marvellous without your props!' Did I imagine it, or was his customary kiss more lingering, less of a peck? 'But you haven't walked all the way? Surely that's overdoing it for the first day?'

'Dancing's all about overdoing it. You have to push yourself until you've reached the end of your physical and mental tether and then you have to do it all again but much better.'

'Good Lord! Can it be worth it?'

'It is to me.'

'Well, you're the most interesting girl I've ever met. Now what about that shopping?'

'I've got to call at Miniver's. They save the vegetables that aren't fresh enough to sell for my rabbit.'

'You've got a pet rabbit?' Rafe laughed and squeezed my arm. 'How utterly charming and like you!' He opened the passenger door for me. 'Get into the car and I'll go to Miniver's for you. No, I insist.'

Being told I looked marvellous and was interesting and charming was irresistible. I slid into the seat to be greeted exuberantly by Buster. My leg muscles throbbed and tingled with the unaccustomed strain of walking. Rafe returned after a few minutes with two carrier bags which he put on the back seat before getting in behind the wheel.

'She'd only got some yellow-looking cabbage leaves and some green potatoes put by. Surely rabbits don't eat potatoes?'

'Not unless starving.' Pride prevented me from explaining that the potatoes were for Dimpsie and me.

255

'That's what I thought, so I got him some nice fresh carrots and cabbages and apples and things.'

'That was so kind. I must give you the money—'

'Don't be silly. It hardly amounted to anything. Besides, this is a celebration, isn't it? What's your rabbit called?'

'Siegfried. Siggy for short.'

'I like that.' He started the car and pulled away from the kerb. I thought it was sweet of him to be interested. But he was the kindest, most agreeable man I had ever known.

'Another unexpected thing about you,' Rafe continued, 'although you're so ethereal and elf-like and look as though you ought to spend all day in a hammock of cobwebs sipping nectar, you've got a definite way with animals. Buster's been a hell-fiend all afternoon, barking at every bird and leaf. The moment he sees you he's as good as gold.'

'It's simple really. I just hold his paw.'

'What?' For a moment I thought he was going to be angry with me for undermining all his careful training. To my relief he burst into laughter and laughed all the way to the outskirts of the town. He seemed to be in a marvellously good mood.

'You really are *quite* unlike other girls.'

'If you knew any other dancers, you'd find we were all boringly the same. Same hopes and fears. Same grumbles.'

'No, but truthfully I've never met a woman before who *really* wanted to do or be anything. Except of course to be told they were desirable to men.'

'Isn't that the message Nature intends men to pick up?' I said. 'Actually, I think most women want far more than that. We want success and recognition if we can get it.'

'Really?' Rafe changed down smoothly to take the road that led up to Shottestone. He had a splendid jaw line that would have looked good on the side of an Etruscan vase. 'Then it's very good of you all not to let on so we poor blokes don't get rattled. It's fortunate they aren't all as beautiful as you or we'd be completely emasculated.'

256

I could not prevent a feeling of gratification on hearing this, though I told myself that Rafe was just being polite.

Spendlove was taking the tea tray into the morning room as we arrived.

'How are you, Miss Marigold? It's good to see you back on your old form. Mrs Capstick'll be pleased when I tell her. You'll be spinning about again as good as new, I shouldn't wonder.'

'I hope so. Please give Mrs Capstick my love and thank her for the cake.'

Spendlove winked. 'It always was your favourite, I remember.'

Rafe threw another log on the fire. 'Thank you, Spendlove. We shan't be wanting you again until drinks.'

Spendlove winked again at me and withdrew.

'He's such a dear.' I looked hungrily at the cake.

'Mm. He seems to have developed an annoying habit of winking all the time. How do you like your tea?'

'Very weak, no milk or sugar, please.' I looked around appreciatively. 'Such a lovely room. Evelyn has the most wonderful taste. Thank goodness, now my plaster's off I'll be able to do more at home. I'm afraid everywhere's got into a bit of a state.'

'Really?' Rafe looked as though he was paying me polite attention while thinking of something else, and I couldn't blame him. We had fallen into an easy sort of intimacy in the last few weeks, but that didn't mean that he would be interested in the boring minutiae of my life.

'Did the painting go better after we spoke on the phone?'

'What? Oh, no. I gave it up for today. I had other things on my mind. Marigold . . .'

'Yes?' I had just raised a piece of cake to my lips, but I hesitated to take a bite because a tone of portent had entered his voice.

'Marigold.' He came to sit next to me on the sofa. 'All these weeks I've been wanting to say something but I decided, in the circumstances, it would be . . . ill-judged.'

'Oh? What was it?' I could no longer resist and took a large

257

bite. It was superb, sweet and tart at the same time, moist with ground almonds and syrupy on top. I took a second bite. Rafe was looking at me with a serious expression, as though troubled, so I swallowed it quickly. 'Is it about Isobel and Conrad?' I resisted the temptation to lick my lips, which would have looked greedy. 'I wish I knew what to think. One minute he seems eminently sane and the next—'

'I wasn't thinking about them. Occasionally my thoughts stray from fraternal cares, you know.'

'Of course. But you get ten out of ten for being a good brother in my book.' My eyes veered to the cake but I brought them back and trained them on his, while pressing my lips together in an attempt to rid them of their sticky coating.

'Surely you can guess what I'm trying to tell you?'

I shook my head dumbly.

Rafe leaned forward to look directly into my eyes. 'You adorable creature. Don't you know I'm in love with you?'

He bent forward swiftly and pressed his mouth to mine. I was taken completely by surprise. After so many meetings during which he had conducted himself with the probity of a newly appointed curate, I had more or less accepted that anything of a romantic nature between us was not to be. Naturally I hid my astonishment and kissed him back.

'Oh, how delicious your kisses are,' he said when he had taken his lips away. 'Darling, you'll never know how much I've wanted to do that.'

'Well . . . why didn't you?'

He smiled. 'I was afraid of arousing desires that perforce had to be denied. I mean my own, of course. While there was no possibility of taking them to any sort of satisfactory conclusion, I didn't dare to risk it.'

'What do you mean, no possibility?'

'Your leg, sweetheart.' He touched my newly peeled left leg and smiled. 'You can't have forgotten already.'

'No . . . only . . . I see, of course.'

I remembered how uncomfortable it had been making love with Sebastian with one leg in a cast and was grateful to Rafe for his gentlemanly forbearance.

'Oh, darling, I'm going on much too fast and I don't want to frighten you, but you might be able to imagine a little of my frustration.'

My predominant emotion was not fear but confusion. He had behaved so little like a man in love. Or in lust either. He held both my hands between his. I was conscious that mine were extremely sticky.

'Dearest Marigold,' he continued, 'do you trust me?'

'Of course,' I said at once. 'More than anyone I know.'

He lifted my fingers to kiss them. A little blob of orange syrup adhered to his upper lip. 'Oh, darling, I don't deserve you. But I want . . . I want so badly . . . Sweetheart, will you come upstairs with me?' He kissed my brow, presumably returning the syrup to my hair. 'To my room?'

Well, he wasn't wasting any time now he had begun. I debated internally, fast. It could not be said that I felt any violent physical desire to go to bed with him. The truth was that, in my previous lovemakings, it had all been over before I had a chance to get anything more than mildly interested. I was practically certain I had never had an orgasm. If I had not been constantly anxious about my balletic performances, I might have had time and energy to worry that my response to sex was so lukewarm. Perhaps tepid would be more accurate. But Rafe wanted to. And he was the stuff of dreams. Besides, if I said no he would be disappointed and angry.

'All right,' I said. Then, feeling this sounded a little cool, 'I've never been in your room before.'

He laughed. 'It's not a particularly exciting place. But I don't think we're going to worry about that. Not for the next couple of hours, anyway.' He stood up, still holding one of my hands. 'Come on, darling.'

A couple of hours! Gosh! No one in the company, wherein

259

lay all my sexual experience, had ever taken more than twenty minutes, start to finish. I allowed my eyes to stray discreetly to the clock on Evelyn's chimneypiece. That would take us up to six o'clock, which would leave plenty of time to get back and make sure that Dimpsie had something to eat. These days she tended not to bother unless I insisted, and she was losing weight alarmingly fast.

We had to tiptoe up the stairs because of Spendlove, and it was bliss to be able to, though the results of the afternoon's walk were beginning to make themselves felt with a steady ache in my calf muscle. I did a rapid inventory of my underwear and remembered with annoyance that I was wearing a pair of my father's old socks as all my tights were stuck in the broken washing machine. Luckily I had had a bath that morning. I knew where Rafe's room was, of course, and occasionally during the period of my youthful infatuation I had peeked round the door to refresh my spirits with a glimpse of the beloved one's cricket bat and rugby boots, but Isobel had once told me that he used to lay booby traps to keep her out so I had never dared to venture in.

'Here we are, darling.'

Rafe locked the door behind us. At last, after so many years of wistful daydreaming, I found myself within the tabernacle, the sanctum sanctorum, the holy of holies. It was disappointingly austere. The planes made from plastic kits that once dangled from the ceiling had been banished, along with the cricket bats and Rolling Stones posters. The walls were papered with grey and white stripes and the windows were hung with dark red linen curtains. It was smart and masculine.

A plain brass bedstead stood in the middle of the room, with two electric fires directed at it, every bar ablaze. I considered myself to be the least demanding of women when it came to the vocabulary of wooing. Dancers are perpetually in a hungry, exhausted and highly strung condition, and romance is saved for the tulle and sequins of the stage. But those fires suggested a presumption that grated I acknowledged at once that this was silly of me. The room would have been arctic without the heaters and it had been considerate of Rafe to install them. Anyway, with my record of sexual opportunism, I had not a leg to stand on.

I became aware that I was being observed. Rafe stood with his hands on his hips, smiling. Almost the tallest man I knew, he seemed to have grown a couple of inches since we were downstairs. I felt a quiver of something – I hoped it was lust but it might have been apprehension. He went over to the bed and sat down, patting the space beside him.

'Come here, sweetheart.'

I did as I was told.

'Now.' He put one arm round me and with his other hand stroked my cheek, and then let his hand run down my neck to my breast. 'Don't be afraid, my darling. We'll go as slowly as you like.'

'Thank you,' I said, hoping that it would not be *too* slow as I had to get back.

'Don't thank me, darling. It's I who should be thanking you.'

He pulled my jersey off over my head and we exchanged a fervent kiss. I put my hands up behind me to unhook my bra but he said, 'Not yet. Just leave it to me. I know this is your first time and I want it to be just what you've always dreamed of.'

I heard these words with such an unpleasant sense of shock that the blood rushed to my face. Rafe observed it.

'You're feeling shy. I understand. Just a minute.' He lifted my legs up onto the bed so that I was lying with my head on the pillow. 'Relax. There's absolutely nothing to worry about.' He went to the window and drew the curtains, throwing the room into semi-darkness. 'There. That's better isn't it?'

'Much,' I said to the head-shaped shadow that loomed over me. As he climbed on to the bed beside me accompanied by a violent creaking of springs, I was thinking furiously. What on earth had given him the impression that I was a virgin? Then I

261

remembered that he had asked me quite recently after we had become reacquainted if I had ever been in love. I had said no. Being a respectable, properly brought-up man used to respectable, properly brought-up girls, he must have assumed that I would only give my body where my heart had gone before. It behoved me to disillusion him as soon as I could. But he had his tongue in my mouth and was kissing me – rather expertly too, quite firmly and without dribbling.

'Rafe,' I said the moment he removed it, 'I'd hate you to get the wrong idea—'

'Don't worry, my sweet,' he interrupted. 'I know just what you're thinking. Of course I'm not going to respect you less for letting me make love to you. I just feel so *proud* that I'm the first one. You can't imagine how precious this moment is to me. I feel like a king. Oooh, what a lucky, lucky man I am!'

He folded me in his arms and held me so tightly that I had no breath to speak. Perhaps it would be better not to disillusion him until afterwards if it was as important as all that.

'Of course, there have been women in my life,' he continued. 'You mustn't mind. Men are different from women. They can love a woman physically without getting emotionally involved. Besides, I'm thirty-one. You wouldn't expect me to have remained celibate.'

'Of course not.'

'And that experience means I'm better equipped to give you pleasure.'

'Oh yes. I assure you I don't mind at all.'

'You're an extraordinary girl, Marigold. So innocent, and yet in some ways so wise.'

I blushed harder and was thankful for obscurity. Rafe unzipped my skirt and pulled it down so that I was naked but for my bra and pants and those terribly unsexy socks which I hoped he wouldn't notice in the dark. He started to stroke and kiss my body. His hands and mouth were light and it was soothing and delightful. When I attempted to stroke him back,

262

he murmured, 'No, wait. I don't want to get too excited and rush you. Just relax and think how much I love you.'

So I lay back feeling warm and comfortable, listening to the twitter of birds outside and the springs that squeaked with the slightest movement like a family of vociferous mice. He continued to caress my stomach and thighs and then undid my bra and kissed my breasts very gently. What with the darkness and the heat given off by the fires and the long walk after three months without exercise and the sedative effect of being stroked all over, my thoughts began to ramble. I tried to drag them back to Rafe's hitherto unsuspected passion for me, but the squeaks of the springs reminded me of the visit to Bavaria when Lizzie and I had taken a rowing boat on to the Alpsee and everywhere had been absolutely peaceful and still with barely a ripple on the water or a sound except for the noises oars make in rowlocks, a rhythmical creaky noise. ERRK, errk, ERRK, errk. The mountains had been majestic with their hoary peaks and green skirts . . . I seemed to be floating on my back on the surface of the lake, surrounded by swans, dipping their heads and shaking their graceful necks. The king of the swans – the one wearing the tiny gold crown – began to nibble my breasts with his hard wet beak and it was not entirely pleasant. I tried to splash with my hands and feet to get away and then woke with a cry of pain as my foot touched the brass bedpost, which was red-hot from the blazing electric fires . . .

'Ow-how!'

'Marigold! My angel!'

Rafe tore off my knickers and before I could galvanize myself into enthusiastic action, everything was over much more quickly than he had originally proposed. Afterwards I lay in his arms, so steeped in guilt that I hated myself. Listening to his thundering heart, feeling the pressure of his hand caressing my elbow, registering a kiss on my parting, I told myself I was the meanest woman in the world. For the first time in my life I had been made love to by someone who had unselfishly devoted himself

263

to my pleasure instead of greedily snatching his own and I had rewarded him by falling asleep. I put my arm across his broad chest and pressed myself against him, vowing silently to make it up to him at the next opportunity. Sebastian had taught me one or two little tricks that, according to him, could bring a man to the edge of swooning with pleasure. And of course dancers have splendid musculatures and can if necessary perform extraordinary contortions . . .

'Darling,' I whispered, 'thank you for being so kind and considerate . . .'

To my surprise he put his hand over my mouth. 'Don't. Don't say another word. I'm not kind. Or considerate. I'm the most despicable . . .' He groaned and broke off.

I pushed away his hand. 'Rafe?' I sat up and leaned over him, wishing that I could see his face properly. 'Why do you say that? It isn't true.'

He laughed bitterly. 'You don't know the half of it.'

'I don't need to know. Unless it would make you feel better to tell me.' When he didn't reply I went on, 'But if you can't undo whatever it is, what's the point of making yourself miserable? I expect you're exaggerating your guilt because you're still recovering from shock. Isobel told me you risked your own life to save someone else's. You ought to concentrate on that.' Then when he remained silent I added, 'We all do things we're ashamed of.'

'I can't believe you've ever done anything to be ashamed of.'

'Oh yes I have. And I've no intention of telling you what. Not yet anyway.'

'Well, then.' He put up his hand to touch my face. 'We'll agree to put the past behind us, shall we?'

'Let's.'

He pulled my head down, rolled me on to my back and kissed my mouth with a fierceness that seemed to border on desperation. His teeth pressed into my lower lip and really hurt. 'Marigold,' he murmured, 'Marigold, Marigold, Marigold.'

'Are you committing my name to memory?'

He did not reply immediately and I regretted the little joke, for he was clearly not in the mood for levity. Just as I was beginning to wonder how I might tactfully suggest that we got dressed, he sighed heavily and said, 'I promise, my darling, I'll do everything in my power to try to make you happy and that you shall never suffer because I . . . through any behaviour of mine.' I was about to tell him that no such promise was needed when he said words that made my heart do a *grand jeté*. 'Marigold darling, you're my salvation. Do you realize that? With you by my side I know I can kick these appalling fits of depression and become a rational man again. I don't deserve you but I'm going to try to.' His voice became eager. 'I think we ought to get married as soon as possible. The expense of a huge wedding would be unfair to your father. And a terrible strain for Dimpsie. Why don't we slip off to a register office and tell everyone about it afterwards?'

For a moment I felt as though my veins had been injected with air. The most desirable man I had ever known, the demigod whom I had worshipped from childhood, who could have had any girl in the county merely by snapping his fingers, was asking me to marry him. I felt as though I might float up to the ceiling, except that his body was pinning me to the bed. It seemed like an impossible dream. Just a minute – I tasted blood on my lips – it *was* an impossible dream. 'Rafe . . . let's not go too fast. There are . . . obstacles.'

'You mean my mother.'

I was not thinking of Evelyn, though she counted as a very large one. 'Yes,' I said quickly. 'She wouldn't like it one bit. The daughter of the local GP isn't good enough for her son. She said so, though not in so many words.'

'You mean you've talked about it? You told her you were in love with me? I'm so flattered. I really had no idea.'

'Not quite. She was leaping to conclusions because you and I seemed to be getting on so well.'

'Don't worry, my sweet. You can safely leave my mother to me. I don't want you to have a care in the world ever again. Of course I can't put things right between your parents. But you'll always be able to lean on me. I want to be your source of strength and comfort.'

How tempting this sounded. No one had even offered to put me into a taxi or pick up my dry cleaning before, let alone be my source of strength and comfort.

'I want to protect you. You're so tiny and fragile. Quite, quite beautiful and . . . damn! That was the front door! They must be back from Newcastle already. Quick! Get your clothes on!'

He sprang out of bed and flung back the curtains.

I grabbed my skirt and zipped myself up. 'Rafe, we've got to talk—'

'Shh!' He put his finger to his lips. 'Wait till they've left the hall and then go downstairs and get in the car. If anyone sees you, pretend you've been to the lavatory. I'll come down in a minute with a book I'll say you were asking about. Wait a minute.' He flung me a comb. 'You'd better tidy your hair.'

I made the best of myself as instructed and went out to the head of the stairs. I heard Evelyn say, 'There you are, Spendlove. Some tea, please. And bring Mr Preston's pills . . .' her voice trailed away.

I crept downstairs and out to the car. The temperature was falling fast with the onset of dusk. I sat and shivered for five minutes until Rafe joined me.

'Sorry. I met my father in the hall. He was convinced he was at his club and that I was Lord Bledsoe. Poor old chap, it's so sad to see him in that state.' He started the engine and set off down the drive. 'Never mind, darling. Now I've got you,' he rested his hand on my knee, 'I feel as though I could never be very depressed about anything ever again. Do you know, I haven't felt as happy as this for years. Not since our crew won the boat race by half a length, in fact. *If you were the only girl in the world*,' he smiled as he sang, '*and I was the only boy . . .*'

266

'Rafe. Darling. Naturally I love you more than anyone in the world . . .'

He smiled more broadly. 'So I should hope.'

'But I do just wonder if it's a good idea to think about getting married actually straight away . . .'

'Why shouldn't we? If you're worrying about Dimpsie, don't. As a son-in-law I'd be in a much better position to help her. I'm very fond of her.'

'Yes. I know.'

'As for Evelyn, I've told you not to give it another thought. Once she sees my mind's made up, she won't stand in my way. How can she? I'm thirty-one years old and already running the estate. I know she can be difficult, but she's devoted to her children.'

'Yes.'

I told myself that for once I must not be a silly little coward. I must make it clear to Rafe that I was on the point of leaving for London to resume my career and that I could not marry him this year or next. Perhaps never. I opened my mouth to do this, but instead out came a yell as Rafe jammed on the brakes to avoid a moped without rear lights and we went into a skid.

'Are you all right, darling?' he asked as he brought the car to a halt several yards further on. He had kept his head and saved us going over the edge of the hillside and down into the river. 'Sorry, but I must go and make sure that idiot's all right. Shan't be a jiff.' He got out of the car and disappeared into the gloom. Before my circulation had returned to its usual speed, he was back. 'That was Jack Banks, son of our builder. He's all right, thank the Lord. Just a bit shocked. And frightened that I might report him. I said I wouldn't, provided he promised to get his rear light fixed in the morning. I'll ring him tomorrow to make sure he has.'

Rafe was a model of responsible, adult behaviour. I thought of the old lady and was filled with shame. So much so that I couldn't say another word until we pulled up outside our house.

'Goodbye, my darling.' He leaned over to kiss me. 'Sweet dreams. I know I shan't be able to sleep for happiness, but I shall think of you and I shan't mind a bit.'

'Come in for a minute, will you? I want to talk to you.'

'Couldn't it wait? Naturally I want nothing more than to talk to you – apart from making love to you, that is – but I ought to get back and see to my father.' When I looked at him pleadingly he said, 'All right, dearest girl. Your slightest wish is my command.' He turned off the engine, then sprang out to come round and open my door. 'Do you know, it's wicked of me, but I rather miss having to fetch those crutches. You were so deliciously dependent.'

I found my latchkey and let us in. Glancing up at the long-case clock I saw the moon-face, its mouth drooping between fat pale cheeks, disconsolate in the dim light of the hall lantern. The radio was on in the kitchen. Someone was singing, '*I don't know why there's no sun up in the sky, Stormy Weather*' with melancholy pertinence.

'Let's go into the sitting room,' I said.

Rafe followed me in. Dimpsie was lying on the sofa as though asleep, the neck of a wine bottle in her relaxed grasp. She opened her eyes as I leaned over her and said, 'Go to hell!' Then she was horribly sick.

21

'Anyone'd think it was a royal command,' grumbled Dimpsie as we set out the next morning to drive across the valley to Shottestone. 'I'm not tidy enough for an audience. And did it have to be so early? My head is agony.'

The truculence in her tone was explained by the residual alcohol in her bloodstream. When sober, nothing that Evelyn could demand of her was too much trouble. Once, when Mrs Capstick had burned her hand, Dimpsie had stayed up practically all night, poaching salmon and setting it in aspic and piping meringue baskets under Mrs Capstick's direction. When Evelyn had complained that the aspic was too soft, the cucumbers too thickly sliced and the baskets too crooked, Dimpsie had taken the criticism without a murmur and had eagerly put on an apron to help serve the guests at the party to which she had not been invited.

'Poor you,' I said with less sympathy than usual. I was busy steeling myself to face the ordeal ahead. I was certain that the summons, issued to Dimpsie via the telephone while we were breakfasting without enjoyment on a boiled egg apiece, had to do with Rafe and me.

'Oh, I know I've only myself to blame and I apologize more than I can say for making such an exhibition of myself in front

269

of Rafe. It was weak and it was selfish and I'm thoroughly ashamed.' I glanced sideways and saw that Dimpsie's eyes were filling with tears once more. 'Beastly *bloody* woman! I never thought I'd be wicked enough to wish anyone dead, but I'd really enjoy seeing her head on a spike.'

I did not need to be told that she was not talking about Evelyn. Over the boiled egg, I had pieced together disconnected sentences between bursts of crying, and gathered that barely five minutes after Rafe and I had driven off for an afternoon of decorous swiving, Dimpsie had answered the front door to find Marcia Dane practically driving the bell push through the wall with her forefinger. She had been swaddled in furs, according to Dimpsie, and wearing enough lipstick to paint Newcastle red twice over.

Marcia Dane had accused my mother of refusing to release my father from a marriage that was a hollow mockery. Furthermore, Marcia said she could afford to free Tom from the wearisome monotony of a GP's existence so he could pursue a medical career better suited to his talents. Unless Dimpsie was a monster of unimaginable selfishness, she would instantly grant Tom the divorce he had several times requested.

Dimpsie had replied that if he did ask her for a divorce she would agree to it, but so far he hadn't and she didn't believe he ever would. Marcia said that Tom had said Dimpsie was as exciting as cold porridge in bed but she was clearly a barefaced liar as well. Further hard words had been exchanged, which Dimpsie could not perfectly remember, but the upshot had been that she had threatened to call the police if Marcia did not leave the house forthwith. Marcia had complied and Dimpsie, standing forlorn in a dusty, dirty, empty house that had once been a cosy domestic nest containing an adored, if not adoring, husband and happy little children, had to choose between the noose and the bottle. At this point in the narrative I had said with genuine feeling that I was heartily thankful she had chosen the latter and Dimpsie had done some more weeping in my arms. Then the call from Evelyn had come. When I asked my mother what sort of language and tone Evelyn had used, she had only been able to come up with the adjective 'crisp'.

'I wonder what could be so important that she wants to see both of us?' mused Dimpsie.

I was too distracted to reply. By the morning post had come a letter from Lizzie. She had quarrelled with her grandmother, and she hoped I didn't mind but she had moved into my room in Maxwell Street while she looked for somewhere to live. Naturally she would leave the minute I returned but would pay the rent meanwhile. She told me about the US tour and brought me up to date on company gossip, which I found I had missed more than I knew. The last paragraph had worried me, though. *When I got back from the States, rumours were flying around that you and Sebastian were engaged! I was able to tell them that it was complete poppycock, because of course you'd have told me if there was the remotest possibility of anything so wildly preposterous. And the rumours have died down now anyway, because Sebastian's sleeping with a new girl who's just joined the LBC. Her name's Sylvia Starkey and she's quite pretty but her dancing's not a patch on yours. She says he makes her do horrible things – what, she wouldn't say. I bet he'll chuck her as soon as you come back, but I thought you ought to know how things stand so you can be on your guard against bitchy remarks from the other girls . . .*

Sylvia Starkey was welcome to Sebastian's sexual predations, I thought, as we drove through Gaythwaite.. But did that mean that he would no longer give me the principal roles? I was so worried about this possibility that I allowed my mother to ramble on without listening much to what she was saying.

'She was most insistent that you came too,' said Dimpsie as we turned into the drive that led to Shottestone. 'Perhaps she's having a drinks party and needs help with the canapés.'

I wondered whether to tell her about Rafe and me. All night, whether waking or dreaming, my brain had struggled to find the right words to explain why I could not marry him. Each time, the expression of pain and disappointment I imagined on his noble, dear – supremely noble, infinitely dear – face nearly killed me. At dawn I had cried hot tears of misery into Siggy's comforting flank. Evelyn might scorn my inferior pedigree all she liked. The angry speech she was no doubt preparing this very moment worried me hardly at all. Of course she would accuse me of ingratitude, duplicity and presumption, but I would be able to set her mind at rest on that score. However much she was hating me now, she could not hate me more than I did myself.

'I'm afraid it's going to be something rather unpleasant,' I said, feeling that perhaps I ought to prepare her. 'Yesterday Rafe and I . . . look out!'

There was a delay while Dimpsie apologized to the gardener whose wheelbarrow she had run into, then we were on our way up to the front door and there was no time for explanations. The strange noise coming from the front of the car turned out to be half a rake that had wedged itself under our bumper.

'Good morning, Mrs Savage.' Spendlove opened the car door on Dimpsie's side. 'A *very* good morning, isn't it? I might venture to say the best I've seen for a good many years. How are you, Miss Marigold?' He scampered round to my side. 'A happy day indeed.'

I smiled weakly.

'Madam is in the drawing room.' Spendlove winked hard at me. 'With Mr Preston and Mr Rafe.' He skipped across the hall, flung open the door and trumpeted our names as though we were persons of consequence.

'Marigold!' Evelyn came to greet me arms held wide. '*Dar*ling! We're so thrilled!' She enfolded me in her scented embrace. I wondered if fatigue and anxiety were making me hallucinate. 'Kingsley and I have always been so proud of you and now you are to be one of us.'

Rafe went to kiss Dimpsie. 'I hope you approve of me as

272

your son-in-law.' It was clear that he expected an answer in the affirmative, but this was reasonable. After all, I was the daughter of an impoverished philanderer and he was a member of one of the oldest families in the county and heir to a large estate.

Dimpsie looked at me. 'I don't understand.'

'You haven't told your mother?' Evelyn patted my cheek. Though her usual immaculate self, I noticed she had dark circles under her eyes as though she too had slept badly. 'Naughty girl. But perhaps you wanted to be sure that Kingsley and I approved before getting up Dimpsie's hopes? In which case that was very wise of you, my dear, and proof, if we needed any, that you have grown into a thoroughly sensible and intelligent young woman.'

'You mean you don't mind?' I had counted on Evelyn as my greatest, though unwitting, ally.

'Well, darling, though I must admit at first I *was* inclined . . . we had expected that Rafe would choose someone of his own—'

'Mother!' Rafe's voice was peremptory.

'Oh, surely we know each other well enough to be frank?' Evelyn took my hand and looked into my face almost pleadingly. 'Haven't I always treated you like my own daughter? But the mistress of Shottestone must have certain . . . qualities.' She made a jerking movement with her chin and neck like a snake attempting to swallow its victim whole. 'Which I'm certain you possess, my darling. You are an exceptionally graceful and lovely young woman, and not without erudition. And anything lacking, I can teach you myself,' she added, rather spoiling the compliment.

'This is all nonsense,' said Rafe almost roughly. 'Good heavens, this isn't Chatsworth. It's hardly more than a glorified farm. If Marigold doesn't mind the considerable inconveniences of living here – inadequate central heating and a fitful hot water supply just for starters - I shall think myself extremely fortunate.'

'You will inherit my collection of first-period Worcester,' Evelyn said, with some emotion.

'Oh . . . thank you.' I was desperately trying to remember

some of the sentences I had composed during the long reaches of the night which would make clear the absolute impossibility of combining marriage and my career. I was distracted by Dimpsie, who broke into violent sobbing.

'Marigold! You and Rafe! Oh, I can't . . . believe it! Just when I thought . . . I had nothing left to live for. Oh, this is too wonderful . . .'

Evelyn put her arms round my mother and guided her to a sofa. Kingsley flapped his arms and grimaced in alarm as Dimpsie howled like a baby.

'Your mother's been under enormous strain,' Rafe said in a low voice to me. 'This is all about your father really, isn't it?'

I nodded, grateful for his understanding. Honestly, the man was making it more impossible every minute. He was a saint, an angel, a pattern of perfection.

'Someone ring the bell for Spendlove,' said Evelyn when she had succeeded in stemming the flow of Dimpsie's tears. 'We must celebrate.'

He must have been hovering outside the door, for he appeared in seconds with the customary champagne. My stomach, queasy with exhaustion and distress, revolted at the sight of it. 'Mrs Capstick says she couldn't be more pleased, not if someone had given her ten thousand pounds,' whispered Spendlove as he handed me my glass. 'I left her in the kitchen with her apron at her eyes.'

'To Rafe and Marigold.' Evelyn lifted her glass, smiling bravely.

'To Rafe and Marigold,' echoed Dimpsie, her face shining with happiness.

'To Rafe and . . . ah,' Kingsley looked perplexed.

I seemed to be standing at a crossroads. In my imagination I looked one way, saw myself married to Rafe and living at Shottestone. I saw a boy who looked like Rafe, fair and straight-backed and clear-eyed, and a pale little girl with red hair and a tendency to let her powers of invention carry her away. I saw myself coming downstairs, having kissed them a tender goodnight, and going into the drawing room – perhaps a little shabbier now but more lovely than ever – for a glass of sherry before dinner. I saw Evelyn, older and rather frail but her wits still sharp, smile at me over her bulb catalogues as she planned the spring borders. I saw Rafe reading aloud to us something from the newspaper that had amused him. I saw him happy in all his occupations with farm and estate, his demons banished, tolerant of his wife's inability to make anything but a muddle of Red Cross committee meetings . . . the vision became a little blurred. But the scene changed and I saw myself walking across the valley to our old house where Dimpsie still lived, busy and cheerful, a much-loved mother and grandmother. I saw her before an easel in the drawing room which had been converted into a studio, painting with a passion. I saw her come to greet me, her face alight with inspiration.

I looked down another road. I saw myself standing in the wings beside Miko Lubikoff, waiting for my entrance. Fate had been kind to me. I had recovered my former strength, avoided further serious injury, and the critics had been on my side. I had worked and starved and suffered, narrowing my sights to the one great goal. I had had more than my share of luck and was invited all over the world to dance in the most coveted roles. For ten or perhaps fifteen years this life would be mine, before I grew too old and had to resign myself to teaching girls whose eyes were fastened on the same prize. But I so ardently desired that it should be mine, at least for a time! Then I saw in my mind's eye my mother, a wretched slattern, lying on the sofa in the dirty, echoing house, a bottle in one hand, a glass in the other. I saw Rafe racked by headaches, suffering the torment of rejection, perhaps in his dejection marrying some hard-faced, cold-hearted, socially ambitious debutante who did not love him.

I looked down the third road and saw myself dancing in the corps de ballet of third- or fourth-rate companies, in daily agony with my intractable foot, disappointed and bitter, all my dreams destroyed. Nights spent in cheap lodging houses, saving coins for the meter, boiling up sausage rings for sustenance, exchanging my body for more infrequent roles. I saw Dimpsie lying on the sofa with an empty bottle of pills in her hand and a note propped up on the chimneypiece . . .

'I'm so proud, darling.' Rafe kissed my brow tenderly.

I tried to smile. 'You're all very kind. I don't think I deserve it.'

I drank a little of the champagne, which tasted like poison, and winked back a tear. I drank a little more and vowed that not a soul in the world should ever guess that there had been sacrifice. What was more, I would teach myself that no sacrifice had been made until I had learned the lesson thoroughly by heart.

22

'You're being admirably restrained, darling.' Rafe slowed as we approached another stiff climb. 'But you're squeaking at every bend. It's rather sweet, like a nestling cheeping. I can stand a little more volume if it helps.'

We were on the road to Hindleep. Conrad and Isobel had returned from London that morning and had asked us to tea. We were to take Isobel back to Shottestone afterwards.

I was trying as hard as I knew how to distract myself from visions of annihilation. Most of the snow had disappeared in the last few days and the countryside was blindingly green, pulsating with unfurling buds and leaves, nest-building and egg-laying and all those spring-like things.

'Do you think Isobel will be pleased?' I asked. 'About us, I mean?'

'You asked me that before. Of course she'll be delighted. It was she who suggested it in the first place. Not that I hadn't thought of it for myself, of course,' he added quickly. 'What I meant was, Isobel was the first to put it into words.'

This was reassuring. When I wasn't worrying about Dimpsie, money, Siggy (who was showing signs of cabin fever) and measuring up to being Rafe's wife and eventually mistress of Shottestone, I worried that Isobel would resent me sharing the limelight with her as a newly-engaged-and-about-to-be-married person. I twisted the ring on my finger. It had belonged to Rafe's grandmother and, since her death, had been kept in the bank until he should select a bride. It was dazzlingly beautiful and the most – in fact the only – valuable present I had ever been given, but it was much too big. We were to take it to a jeweller's in Newcastle next week to have it made smaller; meanwhile Rafe said he liked to see me wearing it. To stop it sliding off, I wore an old ring of my own next to it. The little circle of peridots I had paid a pound for at a jumble sale looked ridiculous beside the enormous square-cut diamond, which constantly slid round into the palm of my hand.

'All the same,' said Rafe, 'I think I'd like to tell her myself, if you don't mind. When there aren't hordes of people around.'

'Oh yes. Whatever you want.' I fell silent for a while, musing. Then I said, 'It's none of my business, I know, but don't you think it's a bit odd that Isobel never stays with Conrad at Hindleep? Presumably Evelyn wouldn't mind as she doesn't object to them going off to London together.'

'Isobel may be pretty much a free spirit – in fact she's a little hooligan sometimes – but she knows better than to make tongues wag.'

'You mean she isn't going to spend the night with Conrad because of what people might say?' I could not keep the amazement out of my voice.

'Darling, you've forgotten what it's like in the country. Everyone knows everyone else's business, and what they don't know they make up.'

'I can well believe it, but I don't see why that should make one behave any differently.'

'Ah well, but you see being a member of an important family – I only mean important in this part of Northumberland, don't think I've got delusions of grandeur – one has an obligation to observe the conventions.'

'Oh.'

'People look up to us and in a sort of way, by example, you know, we set standards of behaviour.'

I knew instantly that I could never be a beacon of good conduct, even had I been going to marry the prince of Wales.

'That's why, darling, I'd like you to put in an appearance at church on Sunday. It'll look better if you've already been a few times before the banns are read.'

This was said in the lightest possible tone, to which only the most unreasonable person could object.

'But I've never *ever* been to a church service, not even as a child. Tom's a staunch atheist and he wouldn't let Dimpsie take us, though she sort of believes.'

'Never mind. The rector won't quibble about marrying you, however lately you've joined his flock. You'll be a brand snatched from the burning. Anyway, he's much too frightened of Evelyn. You were christened, I suppose.'

'No.'

'Oh. Well, I expect he'll insist on that.'

'But I'm not a practising Christian. I mean, I do believe in God and I pray quite often – mostly, I admit, when I want something – but I don't think I believe in vestments and wafers and prayer books and Sabbath observances. I thought we were going to be married in a register office.'

Rafe sighed. 'It's what we'd both have liked, I know. But Evelyn won't hear of it. She says it would look as though we were ashamed of you. Which,' he turned his head to look at me, 'we most emphatically are not.'

'Mind that tree!'

'Certainly I'll mind it. I've no intention of killing you, or myself either.' He sounded annoyed and I forgave him completely because it is infuriating to be nagged when you know you are doing something perfectly competently.

'Sorry. Once when we were on tour in Austria our coach hit a truck on a road a bit like this but higher. We skidded right to the edge. The door jammed so we couldn't get out until they'd

279

fetched someone to unjam it.' I felt myself growing hot and cold just talking about it. 'I was sitting right at the back and the coach was nearly on its side, leaning over the valley—'

'And you've been terrified of cars ever since. I wish you'd told me before.' Rafe put his hand comfortingly on my knee. I would have preferred him to keep both hands on the wheel, but naturally I did not say so. 'My poor darling! I'll drive extra slowly and carefully now I know. What a lot we have to learn about each other. Won't it be fun finding out?'

It occurred to me then that this – not knowing much about each other, I mean – was not only true but, these days, unusual. Though I had been acquainted with Rafe all my life, our relationship until these last six weeks had consisted of a few teasing remarks on his part and a corresponding number of blushes on mine. So why had we rushed into an engagement? There had been no contractual obligation to join two great estates or to prevent nations going to war. When Dimpsie and I had driven over to Shottestone at Evelyn's behest, it had seemed to my exhausted, troubled mind that I had to choose between marrying Rafe or returning to London. It had not occurred to me then to plead for a postponement of the decision.

But there could be no going back now. Anyway, I had no desire to. I was marrying the person I loved best in the world and I was rejoicing in the luxury of having all to myself a man – and such a man! – who considered my wishes and was anxious for my comfort. I continually marvelled at my good fortune and vowed to deserve it. 'Yes, won't it?'

'Oh, and while we're on the subject, Evelyn thinks we'd better have the reception at Shottestone. Your house, though delightful in every way, would be much too small. I shouldn't think Dimpsie'll mind, will she?'

'Not a bit. I expect she'll be relieved, if anything. But it won't be a very big wedding, will it?'

'Evelyn's basing her calculations on about three hundred and fifty guests.'

'*Three hundred and . . .*' Hearing the sudden anguish in my voice, Buster began to bark. 'Shush, Buster!' I tightened my grip on his paw. 'Rafe! I don't *know* three hundred people. At least not well enough to invite them to my wedding. There are sixty-five in the company, but they aren't all close friends. I don't suppose I know more than thirty people who wouldn't be surprised to be asked.'

'It's all right, darling.' Rafe spoke soothingly. 'Most of the guests will be friends of my parents, families we've always known. And our tenants, of course, but there won't be room for them in the church. They'll have to have the service relayed by loudspeakers to the village hall. You'll be able to ask all of your friends, naturally, and Dimpsie all hers, but the majority will be the county bigwigs. It'll be a terrible bore but they'll expect to come.'

'But my father won't be able to afford it.'

'No, my love, but there's no need for you to worry. It'll come out of the estate. It's very often done when the bride's family is not quite as well off as the groom's.'

I realized he was trying to slide over the subject to save my feelings which was sweet of him. 'You mean Kingsley's going to pay?'

'What does it matter who pays as long as we get married? You mustn't mind. No one will know except your parents and mine.'

'I don't have any false pride about it, if that's what you mean. I've always been too poor for that. But won't it cost a ridiculous amount of money? They'll all have to have something to eat and drink, I suppose.'

'Don't give it a thought. Evelyn'll see to everything. She'll consult Dimpsie, of course,' he added.

I could imagine how much consulting would take place. Dimpsie would have as much idea about how to organize a county wedding as about how to construct an atom bomb.

'Couldn't we do what you said and just go and get married

somewhere quiet and then tell everyone afterwards? It would save so much trouble and expense.'

'Yes, but I said that before I'd really thought about it. Having talked it over with my mother, I can see that it would look as though there was something hole-in-corner . . . as though there was something not quite . . . *comme il faut* about our marriage. I'm so proud of you, darling. I want the world to see you walk up the aisle looking staggeringly beautiful.'

'That's awfully nice of you. But actually I don't give a bugger about the world.'

'Of course you don't. Nor do I. But you care about your mother. And perhaps just a little about mine.'

This was irrefutable.

'Sweetheart.' Rafe squeezed my knee. 'If you're having second thoughts, now's the time to say. I can't pretend I'd be anything other than utterly heartbroken, because knowing you and loving you has given me back my courage . . . has made me feel hopeful . . . my old self again. I don't expect you to love me as much as I adore you, but I want you to be just as happy as I know I'm going to be.'

When he talked like this I felt I could happily allow myself to be hacked to pieces on his behalf. I put my hand on his. 'I do love you.'

'And you want to marry me?'

'Honestly, Rafe, I've said so, haven't I?'

'No regrets?'

'None.'

'If you can't be frank with me, then it would be the most awful mistake.'

'Of *course* I want to marry you.'

'That's all right then. I'd kiss you but I think I ought to concentrate. Here's the bridge. Don't worry. I'll take it carefully. You're quite safe, my darling.'

I shut my eyes and closed my fingers over the diamond, which had worked its way round into my palm again. It was natural that Rafe and Evelyn would want a proper party to celebrate this important *rite de passage*. For centuries there had been christenings and coming-of-age balls and birthday parties and wedding celebrations at Shottestone. It was what they were used to. So I must do the decent thing and go along with it.

'There! That wasn't too bad, was it?'

I opened my eyes. Only seven days had gone by since our first visit to Hindleep, but already great changes had taken place. The courtyard was filled with men and vans and piles of planks, pipes and stones. Two storeys of scaffolding had been erected against one wall and a third was in the process of going up.

'Good God!' said Rafe. 'It's wonderful what money can do. I've been waiting two months for Banks, our builder, to come and mend the stable guttering and . . .' He broke off with an exclamation of annoyance, 'There *is* Banks, dammit! After all the custom we've given him over the last thirty years, I'd have thought a little loyalty . . .'

He turned off the engine and got out of the car. Banks, when he saw him, looked sheepish and hurried away beneath an archway. I joined Rafe as he stood, frowning, with his arms folded, staring around him at the frantic activity. His frown grew more pronounced. 'Isn't that Dame Gloria's car?' He pointed to a yellow sports car with huge headlights.

'Yes, isn't it lovely! I'm glad she's here. I do like her, don't you?'

'Like is perhaps too strong. She's probably a genius but I'm not musical, I have to confess. And you must agree that her manners leave something to be desired.'

'Actually I rather admire her for not caring about appearances. Nothing matters to Golly but her work. She's such an honest person. I'd never dare to be so uninhibited.'

'I'm delighted to hear it,' he said dryly. 'I'm looking forward to spending the rest of my life in your company, but the idea of our conversations being drowned by a chorus of deafening eructations isn't appealing.'

I could tell Rafe was still cross about Banks, so I decided to give up defending Golly. 'Let's go in.'

The front door had been stripped of its flaking paint and repainted a dark mulberry colour, which looked marvellous with the grey stone walls. It had been fitted with a large iron knocker, a head of Medusa surrounded by writhing snakes. We made energetic use of it, but no one heard above the din of machinery and the clanking of scaffolding poles, so we pushed open the door and went inside.

Isobel was standing alone by the great windows, her arms folded and her expression brooding. As soon as she saw us she ran to fling her arms round Rafe's neck. 'I've been waiting and waiting for you. I've missed you so much . . . Marigold!' She kissed me. 'Hooray! You're no longer a cripple! We've been slaving from the moment we got back to arrange everything . . . I wanted you to see – isn't it extraordinary?'

She waved her arm expansively. The drawing-room walls had been cleaned and patched with new plaster. The fireplace wall, which had been in a relatively good condition, had been glazed a deep sapphire blue; a man in overalls stood with his back to us, carefully painting with a small brush a design that had been marked in chalk. I went over to take a closer look.

'That's lovely,' I said to the man. 'Did you draw it?'

'Nay, lass, I'm nowt but a decorator. Mr Lerner had a lad up from London to do it.' The pattern was of leaves and ferns and waving stems, covering the walls from the skirting to the ceiling. In between the foliage were birds and squirrels, and on the ground were pheasants, rabbits, foxes and mice. Above the branches was a flight of geese, or possibly swans. 'The cornice is to be picked out in gold leaf,' said the decorator. 'No expense spared.'

'It's so beautiful! You must be enjoying doing it.'

The decorator pursed his lips and squinted sideways at the squirrel he was painting in shades of russet and grey. 'It's what I'd call old-fashioned like, along wi' they cracketts. I'm a magnolia man mesel'.'

I inspected the despised 'cracketts' that stood one each side of the fire. They were long low divans, oriental in style and upholstered in crimson silk, with round, tasselled bolsters at the arms. Another, covered in green velvet, was positioned by the window so that one could lie gazing out at the stupendous view. The floor had been scrubbed and polished and overlaid with Persian carpets.

'What d'you think?' Isobel came to link her arm through mine. She wore an amber-coloured wool suit with a little jacket that fastened asymmetrically and a full skirt appliquéd with quilted satin zigzags. Her hair had been cut short in a spiky urchin style.

'It's ravishing.' I fingered her sleeve. The wool was as soft as rabbit's fur.

'Oh, this? It's Tonio Cellini, darling. It cost my entire year's dress allowance. Except Conrad paid, of course. But I meant the decorations.'

'It's enchanting. Now the inside of the house will fit the outside. Extravagantly fantastical.'

'You haven't seen anything yet. This pipe that they've had to put in to shore up the ceiling,' she pointed to a pillar perhaps half a metre in diameter in the middle of the room, 'is going to be made into an oak tree with gilded leaves and a silver trunk and warm air'll be directed through it to heat the room so there won't have to be any radiators. Rafe.' She beckoned to her brother who had been walking round, hands in his pockets, looking at the improvements. He came to join us. 'What do you think of it?'

'It's very . . . fanciful.'

'You mean you don't like it?'

'I didn't say that. It's just a bit more –' he described circles with his hands – 'elaborate than I'm used to. I like early Georgian.'

'*He* says he's a magnolia man,' I said in a low voice indicating the decorator. 'Does it mean men can only like one thing? How dull for them.' I smiled to show that I was teasing.

285

'I won't have my sex impugned by a slip of a girl,' replied Rafe. 'Be careful, Miss Savage, or I shall take my revenge.'

Isobel stared at me and then at him. She could not have failed to hear a note in his voice that was flirtatious and at the same time proprietorial.

'What do you think of my new look?' she asked with a hint of challenge.

Rafe inspected her then turned her round so he could see the back. 'Very smart. Highly fashionable, I'm sure. But you know I'm conservative in my tastes. I liked the old you better.'

'I'm still the old me inside. Nothing can change that.'

'Oh good, you've arrived.' Golly came in carrying a tray of tea things, followed by Conrad, who acknowledged our arrival with one of his graceful little bows. She was wearing her brown boiler suit as usual. 'Marigold! No crutches! And what a very nice leg it is! Every bit as nice as the other one.' She put the tray on a table and kissed me warmly, took a step towards Rafe as though she might kiss him, then thought better of it. 'Fritz is bringing the cake. I'm ravenous.' She threw herself onto one of the divans by the fire and seized the silver teapot. 'I haven't eaten since yesterday. The milk was off this morning and ants had got into the bread bin.'

'You should have a cook,' said Conrad.

'My dear boy, I only eat three times a day. What would they do for the rest of the time? Besides, I should feel fidgety having someone huffing over my shoulder.'

'Fritz does not huff. He makes himself useful in countless ways.'

'Fritz is an exception. You're a lucky dog. Good things come to you like flies to a stale bun. I suppose you wouldn't consider lending him to me? Just while I write my new opera?'

'Certainly not. I need him myself. I did not know you had begun it.'

'My opera, you mean? Oh, I've only just jotted down a few musical themes. I'm looking for a plot. Something fresh and timeless but with contemporary resonances. Not Shakespeare or Goethe or any of the big boys. They've all been done to death. I want something that seems charming and almost light-weight on the surface, but into which you can read all sorts of darker themes. A medieval fairy tale perhaps. What do you think of the *Morte d'Arthur*?'

'A terrible idea. We have all had a surfeit of Camelot.' He looked at me. 'Your leg is better?'

'Yes, thanks.'

'So you will return to London straightaway.' He sounded almost as though he was eager to see me go.

'Oh . . . well, no . . . there are plans . . . lots of decisions to be made.'

He narrowed his eyes slightly but did not question me further. Instead he turned to observe, with a slightly pained expression, Golly pouring the tea and dripping it over the tray. Conrad certainly looked as sane as anybody, I thought, as he took the teapot from her and finished filling the cups. He handed one to me. It was lovely, very fine pale yellow porcelain painted with birds. No, he did not look mad. His eyes did not start, his mouth did not foam and his hair was free from straws. His clothes were not disordered; on the contrary they were neat and stylish and he gave the impression of being quite frighteningly clever. But presumably madness comes in many guises.

Prompted by this idea, I asked Conrad what Ludwig the Second had looked like.

'He was extremely handsome as a young man but then he became gross. Also because he liked sweets and cakes his teeth fell out. Why do you ask?'

I tried to imagine Conrad fat and toothless. 'Oh, no particular reason . . . I suppose he wore beautiful clothes?'

'He had a preference for ermine and blue velvet. He was an effeminate man.'

I asked myself if Conrad might be gay. Two bachelors living in isolation on a hilltop strongly suggested the possibility. And he was so keen on interior decoration. His headlong pursuit of Isobel after such a brief acquaintance might be a desperate attempt to resist his natural inclinations. I was quite sure that Fritz preferred men to women, but Conrad was a dark horse.

'What happened to him in the end?'

'He withdrew from affairs of state and bankrupted himself decorating castles. Finally he was deposed on grounds of insanity and soon after he drowned in Lake Starnberg. It is generally believed that he committed suicide.'

'Oh dear.' I glanced towards the window where Rafe and Isobel were standing, talking earnestly. It was unlucky that there was a lake quite so close.

'You are interested in Ludwig.' Conrad gave me one of his penetrating stares.

'I can't help thinking of him when I'm in this house. It's very suitable for a magician.'

'I prefer the term illusionist. Ludwig was himself obsessed by illusion. He had a grotto made in the castle of Linderhof with an artificial lake and a waterfall and machinery that made waves. He dressed in the costume of Lohengrin and rode in a boat shaped like a cockleshell, drawn by a giant swan. The lights were programmed to change colour after ten minutes, ending with a rainbow. It was ingenious and technically advanced for the time, powered by twenty-four dynamos and heated by seven furnaces. Was it the vision of a genius or a lunatic, would you say?'

Conrad put his hands behind his back and I saw in the depths of his dark eyes the gleam that suggested he was amused. Suddenly I was very nearly certain that he knew why I was asking about Ludwig.

Fritz came in with the cake. He was accompanied by Buster who greeted us all with screams, as though he had not seen any of us for weeks. 'You permit I bring in the good little dog?' he asked Rafe. 'He vas loning in the car and he bark.'

'He won't learn if he's always given in to,' said Rafe crossly.

'But it was kind of you to fetch him,' he added more graciously. 'I just hope he won't make a nuisance of himself.'

'No nuisance. Ve like ze animals. Vat fettle, Marigold? How is your leg? Or I must say, vait you a minute,' he put down the cake, pulled his notebook from his pocket, riffled through it, then brought out with a little effort, 'Ha . . . is . . . yor . . . liggie?'

'Much better, thank you,' I replied. Fritz looked disappointed. 'Oh, I mean champion. You must remember I've spent most of my life in London. You already speak the local dialect better than I do.'

Fritz brightened. 'Let us take tea.' He consulted his notebook. 'Me troat's aaful gyezend.'

'Honestly, Fritz, I think you're making it up,' said Isobel. 'Now, Marigold, come and sit next to me.' She drew me down onto one of the divans. 'I want to hear all the latest gossip. Is it true what Mrs Capstick tells me about Tom and a femme fatale called Marcia Something?'

'Isobel!' said Rafe reprovingly. 'Have some sensitivity, for God's sake!'

'Oh dear,' she said with a laugh. 'Is it a sore subject?' Though I tried to look insouciant, she must have read something in my face for she said in a softer tone, 'Your father's very attractive to women. Can he help it if women fling themselves at his head? And personally,' she lowered her voice so that no one else could hear, 'I think an unfaithful husband's better than a dull one.'

Isobel had always defended my father. In some ways they were alike, particularly in their conviction that society's rules need not apply to them and that any attempt to call their behaviour to order was the result of the most tedious kind of egotism on the part of the moralizer. My father called it cant; Isobel called it eyewash. He had once commended Isobel for being sensual but not sentimental, which he said was a rare combination in a woman.

'Dimpsie ought to see that Tom's affairs are nothing to do with love,' continued Isobel. 'Of course he's going to make the most of any opportunity that comes his way. What man wouldn't? It's just a physical release, like going to the lav.'

'That'll do, Isobel.' Rafe looked annoyed.

Isobel smiled mischievously. 'I'm only repeating the lesson you taught me, that it needn't mean anything more than scratching an itch.'

The little hollows appeared above Rafe's eyebrows. 'I was trying to put you on guard against smooth-tongued philanderers, that's all. Might we find a more suitable topic for tea time?'

'*Pas devant les enfants*, you mean.' She pinched my arm. 'But Marigold isn't the innocent she appears.'

Perhaps it was just the pricking of my conscience, but I thought there was something questioning in the look Rafe gave me. I was thankful I hadn't said anything to Isobel about Sebastian. Her first loyalty would always be to Rafe. But the fact remained that I still hadn't found the right moment to enlighten him about my previous sexual experiences and this was both craven and dishonest. I sought a diversion.

'This is so pretty,' I said, referring to the decoration of the fireplace embrasure.

Bits and pieces from out-of-doors – what Evelyn would have called *objets trouvés* – had been arranged to add to the charm of the room. Each side of the fireplace, a six-foot pine bough had been upended in a bucket of sand. At the end of every branch was a candle. Makeshift shelves of planks and bricks were filled with books interspersed with pebbles, fir cones, nests, eggs and feathers. Presumably Fritz included nature study among his many interests. I could not imagine Conrad troubling himself about such things.

'I can't understand why everyone makes such fuss about sex,' said Golly. 'I once had a boyfriend and we tried it a few times. It was hell on the knees and I always got a sore throat afterwards.'

Isobel gave an explosive laugh, which she tried unsuccessfully to turn into a cough.

'You may laugh, my dear,' said Golly equably. 'It's different for a good-looking woman like you. Men want to make you happy. No man ever cared a damn for me. I was born with a plain face and I never learned the art of improving it. When I was a child, my mother said that if you looked at yourself in the mirror for more than ten seconds you'd see the devil grinning over your shoulder. Even now, though I know it's silly, I never take the risk. Sex seems to me a terrible waste of time – but I suppose millions of people can't be wrong.'

'Not everyone has your dedication, Golly,' said Conrad. 'For all those who never read a book or go to a concert or an art gallery, and we are informed that they are in the majority, there is plenty of time to waste.'

I could tell that this conversation was doing nothing to endear Golly to Rafe. His eyebrows were making more pronounced V-shapes.

'How do you make this wonderful cake?' I asked Fritz.

'You make a bottom viz flour and lemons and eggsies and *die Hefe* – vat is zat?'

'Yeast,' said Conrad.

'Yes, yeast and zen you add it a mix-up of wanilla and cream, zen you it smozzer viz butter and nots and honey. It is very good . . . no –' he held up a finger, pulled a piece of paper from his pocket and consulted it – 'it is purely belta, wey aye?'

'I've never heard anyone say that. Are you sure?' Fritz showed me his vocabulary list. It seemed to be a foreign language.

'I haf here,' Fritz searched in his other pocket and brought forth a small battered book, 'some folk fables of Northumberland. This helps me viz the language. They are most charming. I like this one called *The Ring and the Fish*. It is a love story. Shall I it to you read?'

It was a complicated tale about a handsome prince and a beautiful dumb peasant girl. They were madly in love but the king objected to the peasant girl as a daughter–in–law on the grounds of her class and disability and made her undergo a

291

series of trials in the company of blue-blooded loquacious princesses. After the peasant girl, aided by her superior intelligence and a magic singing cake, had thrashed her competitors, the king declared that any contestant who brought him his own diamond ring would become the prince's bride. Then he hurled the ring into the sea from the ramparts of his castle. The princesses went back to their kingdoms in terrible tempers and the peasant girl became a cook. She found the ring inside a giant cod, presented it to the king, the young couple married and lived happily ever after.

'I wish she'd been granted the power of speech at the end,' I said. 'It must have been a frustrating marriage having to communicate through a cake. And they were already down to the last few crumbs in her pocket by the wedding day.'

'The prince was unbelievably pathetic,' said Isobel. 'Why didn't he just elope with the girl of his dreams and save her all that misery?'

'Perhaps he had a care for his inheritance,' said Conrad.

'Oh, pooh! I despise that sort of caring.'

I had the impression that Isobel intended something particular by this remark, perhaps that Conrad ought to marry her at once. I had spent some time watching him while we were listening to the story. He had been sitting with one leg crossed over the other in the only chair, which had a high back, not unlike a throne. He reminded me of the painting of the sultan on the cover of my copy of *The Arabian Nights*. I remembered that the sultan, convinced of women's falsehood and inconstancy, had decreed that he would take each wife for one night only and have them strangled at daybreak. Conrad might be nearly as difficult to please. As he looked at Isobel, there was a suspicion of a smile curving his lips.

'But it might have been that the peasant girl was anticipating a crown and a dress spun from gold and the prince did not wish to disappoint her. Not all women are as unworldly as you, my dear Isobel.'

Isobel affected to laugh but I thought, by the way she with-drew from the conversation, that the thrust might have gone home.

'That's it!' Golly, who had remained pensive, one finger pressed against her brow, sat up. 'That's the story for my new opera. A tale of supernatural romance with supernatural elements and yet with universal themes. The triumph of the eternal veri-ties, truth, virtue . . . *The Ring and the Fish*. Or *The Fish and the Ring* . . . better.'

'You don't think the title confusingly like another quite famous operatic cycle?' suggested Conrad.

'Oh, yes. I hadn't thought of that. All right, I'll make up something. *The Cake and the Fish*.'

'That will never do. It will come to be known as *The Fishcake*. And does it not present a difficulty to have an opera in which the female lead is dumb?'

Golly frowned. 'Hm. I admit that is a slight . . . This needs thinking about.' For a moment her face was screwed up in thought, then her eye fell on me. 'I know! I'll write some truly ravishing music for the dumb heroine to dance to. It'll be an opera ballet with hints of the baroque and the rococo, in deli-cate homage to Rameau and the early eighteenth century. But at the same time it will be searingly, uncompromisingly modern and original. There will be a chorus *and* a corps de ballet, leaping about the stage in a menacing way with swords and things . . . yes, I like the idea of a sword dance.' She stood up and snapped her fingers, which woke Buster who had only just gone to sleep, lulled by bits of cake fed him surreptitiously by Fritz. 'Pencil! And paper. I must jot down a few ideas!'

'In the library,' said Conrad. 'You will find all you need on my desk. But please not to get my documents in a mess.'

Golly strode away, her eyes ablaze with inspiration.

'Buster, quiet! Lie down!' said Rafe. 'So that's genius. A great work created from an improbable nursery tale. In years to come we'll be able to tell people that we were present at its conception.' He spoke pleasantly but I suspected he thought it ridiculous.

'Remember what Goethe said,' said Conrad.

We all, Rafe included, looked blank.

'I translate roughly. In music the dignity of art finds supreme expression. There is no subject matter to be discounted.'

I was interested in this idea. 'You mean it doesn't matter how dull or silly something is, because music always ennobles it?'

'Exactly so.' Conrad stood up abruptly and went to the piano. I wondered if he was annoyed with Rafe for failing to appreciate his old friend. He began to play. The music began as something charming and pretty, then went into a minor key and became hauntingly sad, then finally thunderous and angry. I thought how marvellous for Isobel to be married to someone who played so wonderfully, but she wasn't listening. Instead she was telling Rafe about her trip to London. I overheard phrases such as 'ten floors up and its own lift' and 'a little cul-de-sac off Bond Street.'

Fritz offered me another slice of cake.

'No thank you, I'm full to bursting.' I pressed my hands to my stomach in demonstration.

'What the *hell* . . . ?' Isobel was staring at me, at my hands in particular, with an expression of bewilderment that changed rapidly to distress.

I saw that the diamond had twisted on my finger so that it faced outwards and flashed in the light from the fire.

The corners of her mouth stretched in a grimace of rage and she clenched her fists. She looked at Rafe. 'You . . . you've gone ahead . . . without telling me—'

'Isobel!' Rafe looked alarmed. 'Don't be an idiot . . . Buster, if you don't stop barking this minute I shall take you back to the car!'

'Have . . . you . . . asked . . . her . . . to marry you?' she demanded with terrific emphasis.

'Yes. I have.' Rafe's expression became stern. 'And, luckily for me, Marigold has said yes.'

294

'Of *course* she said yes.'

Her scorn wounded and angered me. It had been by no means a foregone conclusion that I would jump at her brother's offer of marriage. In fact, if I had consulted only my own interests . . . I felt a lump in my throat.

Fritz picked up the tray and moved quickly to the door. 'Not to be excited, good folks. I go to fetch drinks.'

'Isobel! Don't say another word!' Rafe said with tremendous warning in his voice.

She jumped up, her eyes filled with tears. 'You . . . you . . . *fool!*'

Then she fled, first towards the door that led to the hall, but Fritz and the tray were in her way. She dashed towards the library but remembered that it was occupied by Golly. She actually stamped her foot with temper before flinging open one of the doors that led on to the balcony and running out to stand by the parapet, her head bowed, her shoulders heaving.

'I'm so sorry, darling.' Rafe stood up and came over to press his hand on my shoulder. 'You mustn't mind . . . you know Isobel's rages . . . it'll be over in an instant. I'd better go and see—'

But it wasn't over in an instant. I watched them for what felt like an age through the glass – Rafe had closed the French windows behind him – as the two of them talked and gesticulated in dumbshow against the backdrop of hills and the rapidly darkening sky. I became aware that Conrad was playing something so familiar that for a moment or two it seemed like a tune tripping along in my head, just a background to my thoughts. Then I recognized Odile's pas de deux with the prince from the third act of *Swan Lake*. I looked at Conrad. He was looking straight back at me, his expression cold, even hostile. I felt utterly wretched.

Isobel and Rafe came in, her face woeful, his troubled. She rushed over to me at once and I stood up in case I needed to defend myself.

'I'm sorry.' Her expression was contrite. 'It was a shock. I hadn't expected it so soon.' Her mouth trembled like a child's. 'There isn't anyone I'd rather . . .' She drew her breath in suddenly like a sob. 'You'll be good to him, won't you?'

However trivial the cause of her pain might seem to me, it was real to her, and my anger began to dissolve.

'As good as I know how.' I smiled. 'We probably won't get married for ages, not till long after you. And your wedding's bound to be a much more magnificent affair. It'll eclipse ours by miles.'

'Oh, as to that . . .' She put her arm round my waist and gave me a squeeze. 'You're an angel to forgive me.'

'Telephone, Conrad.' Golly dashed out of the library, waving a notebook. 'Presto pronto. I must get hold of my librettist. There's not a moment to lose. I've sketched out the main themes but I mustn't run ahead too fast. He can be the most tiresomely uncooperative fellow but quite brilliant – where did you say the telephone was?'

'I didn't.' Conrad brought the phrase to an end, closed the lid and got up. 'There isn't one.'

'But my dear boy! You can't mean it?'

'They have to blast through rock to make channels for water pipes and telephone and electricity cables. It cannot be done in a moment.'

'Yes, I see that, but all the same . . . the inconvenience . . . Thank you, Conrad, for a delightful . . . I must find a telephone at once . . . Goodbye, darlings.' She kissed her fingers to each of us in turn and rushed out. Seconds later I heard through the open door the roar of an engine being revved and driven off at speed. Remembering the bridge, I shuddered inwardly.

'Drinks!' Fritz had brought in a tray of glasses. 'And the calming pills, Conrad, you remember you must them take because the good doctor says. *Verdammt!* There is wind in the house!' He went out to close the front door.

Isobel looked puzzled. 'I didn't know you took pills, Conrad?'

Conrad raised his eyebrows. 'Ah, well. We do not yet know everything there is to know about each other.' He took from his pocket a little red box, extracted a blue pill the size of a five-pence piece and swallowed it as easily as if it had been a crumb.

Isobel was looking at Rafe. He lifted his eyebrows fractionally. She gave the tiniest shrug of her shoulders.

I examined Conrad's face suspiciously. I was standing closer to him than the others. The pill had gone down without the slightest movement of his throat. Our eyes met. He must have read the question in mine, for in less time than it took me to draw breath he had swallowed the pillbox too. He uncurled his fingers and spread his palm flat afterwards to show that his hand was empty, so I knew it had been a trick.

'I think,' said Conrad, 'I would like some fresh air. And perhaps a little walk.'

He opened the French windows, walked out onto the balcony and jumped up onto the parapet.

'Conrad!' cried Isobel. 'Be careful!'

He stretched out his arms like a tightrope-walker and ran along the narrow ledge.

'He's mad!' exclaimed Rafe. 'It must be a three- or four-hundred-foot drop! He could be killed!'

'Someone get him in!' cried Isobel.

Fear made us impotent. We watched with half-stifled gasps and groans as he swayed forwards, backwards and forwards again. Someone – it might have been me – screamed on a rising note like a kettle coming up to the boil as Conrad flung up his hands, leaped high into the air and plummeted feet first into starlit space.

23

'It was a thoroughly childish and irresponsible thing to do,' said Rafe as the car wound down the mountainside. 'It could have had serious consequences.'

Isobel giggled. 'I think it was funny.'

'But you were distraught!'

'Yes, but only for a minute or so. Don't make such a fuss about it.' Isobel was in the passenger seat beside him. She leaned across to rest her hand on his shoulder. 'It hasn't done me any lasting harm.'

'Shock is bad for people. You might have fainted. Or even had a heart attack.'

'Don't be silly, darling. I'm twenty-three and fit as a fiddle. I admit the hairs stood up on my scalp and I did feel the most terrific desire to shriek, but it probably did wonders for my circulation.'

I wondered what it had done for mine. I was fairly certain I *had* screamed when Conrad had jumped off the balcony, but after that my muscles had turned to wood and I had been unable to move so much as an eyelash. Isobel had moaned and hidden her face against Rafe's chest within the circle of his comforting arms. Fritz had run out onto the balcony to look over the parapet, followed by Buster who had caught the general mood of agitation and was thrilled to be able to bark uncensored at the rising moon. I had no idea how long we stood motionless in a state of horrified disbelief before a voice behind us said, 'There is no reason to be distressed. I have, as you see, returned to you without injury.'

'Conrad!' Isobel had lifted her head from Rafe's jersey. Her face was white, her eyes glazed. 'What the . . . ? I don't understand . . .' She had taken a step towards him and staggered a little. Rafe had caught her arm. 'It's all right. *I'm* all right.' She had smiled tremulously. 'You *beast!* It was another trick, wasn't it? How did you do that? Don't tell me you grew wings and flew!'

Conrad lifted his eyebrows and bit his lip, as though forced to conceal a laugh. 'Well, unfortunately, that I am unable to do. I am truly sorry if I frightened you unpleasantly. I was unable to resist.'

'You scared us out of our wits!' Rafe did not try to disguise his anger. 'You might have had some thought for my sister—'

Isobel put up her hand to stop him. 'Never mind, darling. I'm perfectly all right. Don't make a scene.' She turned a bright face to her fiancé. 'Now, Conrad, it was bad of you but delightfully in character. I insist on knowing how you did it.'

'As always in cases of illusion, it is the simplicity of the solution that baffles the audience. On the floor beneath, leading from the kitchen, is a platform that has been cut from the mountainside. It is a mere three or four metres below the balcony and a little larger. I jumped down to it and then let myself in.' He spread his hands, his expression mock-serious. 'It was ridiculously easy but,' he laughed suddenly, 'the effect must have been dramatic.'

'How wicked you are!' Isobel linked her arm through his and smiled up into his face.

'It was insane!' Rafe was still furious. 'You might have missed in the dark. Or broken your leg!'

'Oh, no.' Conrad smiled. 'When I was a boy I ran away from

home and joined a circus. I admit it showed a sad lack of originality. I was only part of the troupe for eight weeks before my uncle found me, but during that time I learned to walk the tightrope and how to fall without hurting myself.'

'Shall I fetch more champagne?' Fritz had come in from the balcony and was smiling round at us. Clearly he had been in on the joke.

'Thank you. No.' Rafe could not bring himself to smile. 'We ought to be getting back. My mother is expecting us for dinner. Besides, I need a clear head for that road. Buster! Stop that at once!'

Buster had taken advantage of our inattention to finish off the cake. We had said our goodbyes in an atmosphere of awkwardness.

'You may be fit now,' said Rafe as he negotiated the steepest bend where the car seemed to stand almost on its nose, 'but what sort of state will you be in in a few years' time if he's going to make a habit of dangerous practical jokes?' When Isobel did not reply he went on, 'I still think it was a crazy thing to do. I'm not at all sure you ought to marry him. He needs to see a doctor.'

'Oh, nonsense!' Isobel said crossly. 'He just likes to make things exciting, that's all. Imagine if you've grown up being able to have whatever you wanted – and with complete freedom, most of the time. He saw more of the servants than his uncle.'

'Plenty of Englishmen were brought up like that. But it didn't make them madmen.'

'I don't know. What about all our famous aristocratic eccentrics? What about our grandfather, come to that? He always preferred cows to people. And he left his watch and chain to Ruddigore, his favourite bull.'

Rafe gave a short laugh. 'So he did. I'd forgotten that.'

'Besides, apparently Conrad *is* seeing a doctor. The pills, remember?'

'If that's supposed to be reassuring, I'm afraid it fails

completely. And, quite apart from these fits of what I'd call mania and you'd call making things exciting, Conrad doesn't seem to be particularly devoted. Perhaps it comes from always being able to get his own way. He's become solipsistic.'

'What does that mean?'

I had been wondering this myself. We had reached the bottom of the mountain and I was able to breathe freely again. I had been too frightened to speak and they seemed to have forgotten my existence.

'It means that you only believe in yourself, in your own experience, as being real. Of course we've no grounds for being certain that the universe is anything other than a figment of our imagination, but most of us assume that we're not the only person with thoughts and feelings.'

'I don't know,' said Isobel slowly. 'Actually I think he's extraordinarily decent.'

'Really? What's he said or done to make you say that?'

But Isobel remained silent.

'I rather like the idea that it's all in one's imagination,' I piped up from the back. 'Then you wouldn't need to feel guilty.'

'I thought you'd fallen asleep,' said Rafe. 'I can't believe you've ever done anything to feel guilty about.'

It was my turn to be silent. I shifted about to relieve the pressure from Buster's bony haunches. He was sitting on my knee, breathing honey and almonds into my face.

'You'll stay for dinner this evening?' Rafe said over his shoulder.

'Thanks, but I think I'd better get back.'

'What on earth have you got to get back for?' asked Isobel.

'I ought to get an early night. I start a new job tomorrow.'

'You mean you've given up working at the surgery?' asked Rafe. 'You didn't tell me.'

'I'm carrying on with that. But being the practice receptionist is just in return for being allowed to live at home.'

'You mean you aren't getting a salary?' Rafe sounded shocked. 'I don't want to criticize your father, but is that quite fair?'

'Perhaps not but there's nothing I can do about it. And we've got to eat. Evelyn's eggs have been a lifesaver, but Dimpsie and I'll be getting scurvy soon if we don't have some fruit and vegetables, so I've taken a job as a waitress at the Singing Swan starting tomorrow afternoon. Mrs Peevis is a nice old thing, and desperate for help as her hips are playing her up. She's on the list for replacements for both but there's a nine-month wait till she can have even one done. I'm going to get one pound fifty an hour and tea thrown in—'

'I had no idea you and Dimpsie were so hard up,' interrupted Rafe. 'I'm so sorry. I should have thought. We'll make you an allowance from the estate. There's no need for you to be a skivvy, Marigold. Why didn't you say?'

'Don't be an ass, Rafe,' said Isobel. 'You can't expect Marigold to say she'll marry you and in the next breath ask you for money. A girl has pride about such things. Conrad just sent me a chequebook without saying a word.'

'Oh, did he?' Rafe sounded intensely annoyed. 'Well, he's clearly more practised in such things.' He changed down as we turned into the drive of Dumbola Lodge and made the engine roar in sympathy with his feelings. 'Anyway, Marigold, I'll open a separate account for you tomorrow and you should be able to draw on it in three or four days' time. Until then—'

'That's enormously kind and generous of you.' I leaned forward in my eagerness and smelled the cologne he always wore that made me think of the only time we had been to bed together. 'But I don't in the least mind being a skivvy and I couldn't possibly accept your money until . . .' I wanted to say not until we were married, but I still felt awkward about making a bald statement of fact in front of Isobel. 'Not yet, anyway.'

'I insist.'

'And I insist on refusing. But thank you anyway.'

'Don't be silly. You're going to be my wife. Naturally I've an interest in seeing you don't starve.'

'Now I've got my leg back there's no possibility of my starving.

302

I've already told Mrs Peevis I'm taking the job. She was so relieved she almost cried. Last year the Singing Swan made a loss and if she can't bring it round this year she'll have to close down. She won't be able get another job at her age—'

'Yes, well, I'm sorry for her but there's no need for you to sacrifice yourself. That's what the welfare state is for.'

'It isn't a sacrifice. I'm looking forward to it. It's been horribly boring not doing anything.'

'I'm sorry you've been bored.' Rafe sounded slightly offended, though it could hardly have been his fault. 'If you like you can come round with me and visit the farmers. And we can go shopping in Newcastle whenever you want to. There's a reasonable play coming on soon, I'm told.'

'That would be lovely. But I need a challenge. It's what I've always been used to. Hard work. I hate being idle.'

'What Rafe really means,' Isobel sounded amused, 'is that he doesn't think it's seemly for the future Mrs Preston to be seen by her tenants and inferiors trundling about the local caff in a cap and apron.'

'I don't believe that's got anything to do with it. Has it, Rafe?'

Rafe thought for a moment before saying, 'I quite appreciate that it must sound snobbish and old-fashioned, particularly to someone who's led the sort of glamorous Bohemian life you have, but I *do* think it would be inappropriate for you to work as a waitress.'

Rafe drew up outside the house. I wondered what I ought to say. It made it ten times more difficult that what might turn out to be our first row had to be conducted before a third party. When I did speak I was unable to prevent a little note of rebellion from creeping into my voice. 'What am I expected to do with my time then? How must the future Mrs Preston conduct herself?'

'Like Mummy, of course,' said Isobel. 'You must arrange flowers and order meals and do good to those less fortunate. You must read the latest novels, naturally, and go to art exhibitions in

London, and the occasional opera and play, but you mustn't be boringly intellectual. You're allowed to soil your hands with gardening and dogs. And horses if you like them—'

'Isobel, stop it,' commanded Rafe. 'You're deliberately trying to make mischief. I'm perfectly aware that times have changed and that Marigold's an independent liberated woman and I thoroughly respect that. I take it for granted that she's going to want to do something else besides be my wife.'

My spirits rose dramatically on hearing this. 'Oh Rafe,' I leaned forward to put my hand on his shoulder, but found Isobel's already in situ, so I confined the expression of my gratitude to saying, 'I'm *so* glad you understand.'

'I'm not a Victorian patriarch. I don't want you to be sitting twiddling your thumbs until I come home. I know you'd be restless and . . . bored. There are plenty of things you could do. Join the board of one of the local theatres, for example. You'd enjoy raising funds to keep it going and giving parties for the actors and directors at Shottestone. Evelyn was talking the other day about having the amphitheatre restored. You could organize a little local culture. Open-air plays and operas – a mini Glyndebourne, even. And you might start a scheme to foster young acting or dancing talent. Scholarships and bursaries, that sort of thing. I imagine that would be very rewarding.'

The rush of hope evaporated. For one crazy moment I had thought he was going to say I could spend all week dancing in London and come back to Northumberland for weekends and breaks between tours. Raising funds for theatres, for other people to act and sing and dance in them! That would be like setting food just out of reach of a prisoner in chains.

Buster began to whine reproachfully as I removed him from my knee. 'I'd better go in.'

'I'll telephone you tomorrow.' I could hear tension in his voice. 'Give my love to Dimpsie.'

'And mine,' said Isobel.

I sprang out of the car. 'Bye.' I waved through the window

at them as Rafe was winding it down, and sprinted to the porch. Since we had been engaged we had always kissed each other goodbye, but the disagreeable feeling that a quarrel was brewing deterred me. I thought Rafe looked crestfallen as he drove away and my conscience pricked me unpleasantly. The moon-face of the longcase clock was on the wane. It looked depressed.

'Hello, sweetie-pie.' Dimpsie was in the kitchen, up a ladder with a paintbrush. 'Had a lovely time? I'm getting rid of the vegetable stencils. Evelyn said they looked like the scribblings of a psychopath. She used to do quite a bit of prison visiting. I've decided to paint stripes on the walls and ceiling, like a tent in the Arabian desert. Can't you picture it?'

She waved the brush.

'It's difficult when the kitchen's so cold.' I took a paper hanky from my sleeve and started to rub blobs of paint from the table and the floor. 'I think the Aga's gone out again.'

'Oh, no! Damn! And we're out of firelighters. I forgot to riddle the bloody thing. I was so busy painting I didn't notice.' She began to descend the ladder. 'I *am* sorry, poppet . . .'

'Never mind. You carry on. I'll light it.' While I was on my knees stuffing paper and candle ends and what turned out to be the last of the coal into the furnace part, I was turning over in my mind the conversation we had had in the car. Was I being selfish and inconsiderate? Ought I to do what Rafe wanted, despite disagreeing with his notion of what was suitable for a Preston-by-marriage?

'I've had the most interesting afternoon,' said Dimpsie. 'I went to see the O'Shaunessys. Nan wasn't there, only Jode and the baby. I took some more things from the shop which he seemed pleased with. I fed the baby and changed him while Jode made tea and he told me how worried he was that Nan takes no interest in the child. Then we chatted about this and that and I just happened to mention I was planning to start a new vegetable garden because the one we've got's in too much shade and nothing does well there. He said the ground near the caravan is too stony for vegetables so he's going to dig a new plot here and twice a week he'll pop over to look after it in return for being able to grow stuff for himself. Isn't that a great scheme?'

'Terrific!' I had no faith in Dimpsie's vegetable plots, since after the first few weeks everything became hopelessly overgrown and got clubfoot or whatever it is that carrots get. But I was delighted that her enthusiasm for projects had returned. 'I don't suppose we've got anything for supper?'

'Oh!' Dimpsie looked guilty. 'I meant to go and get something on credit from Armstrong's but I forgot.'

I toasted the last crusts of bread and we scraped out the marmite and marmalade jars and made cocoa with hot water and some powdered milk which refused to dissolve properly. Siggy had a rusty tin of corned beef which he seemed to relish. I didn't mind the short commons too much, having eaten a large slice of cake. And besides, I had put on weight since breaking my ankle and I was determined to get properly fit again, even though my dancing career was over.

'Just think, darling,' said Dimpsie, 'when you've married Rafe you'll have Mrs Capstick's gorgeous food every day.' She put down her piece of toast and looked at me solemnly. 'There isn't a minute that goes by without my thanking God for your marriage. You'll be *so* happy. And so shall I, having you always near by. I was *dreading* the loneliness. I can admit that now, can't I, without sounding like a selfish clinging mother? You and Rafe falling in love has given me the strength to face life again.'

I slept badly that night. When the sky began to pale I decided I would have to tell Mrs Peevis that I could not take the job after all. I dozed off again feeling relieved that a decision had been taken, only to be shaken awake what felt like seconds later by my mother.

'Rafe's on the telephone. He must have spent all night thinking about you. Isn't it romantic!'

306

I went slowly downstairs.

'Good morning, darling.' Rafe sounded in good spirits. 'You sound sleepy. Have I woken you?'

'What time is it?'

'Eight o'clock. Horribly early. But I've been going over and over our conversation last night. About you being a waitress at the Singing Swan. And I realized when I had time to think that my attitude must seem to you inexcusably reactionary and snobbish. I can't bear there to be any disagreement between us. Will you forgive me, darling? I think your determination to support yourself and Dimpsie is admirable. Take the job with my blessing.'

'Oh! Rafe!' I felt an overwhelming gratitude. 'I was dreading telling poor Mrs Peevis. She was so pleased when I said I'd do it. *Thank* you!'

'You needn't thank me, darling. You're the one that's going to have aching feet. I'm sorry to have disturbed your sleep. I just hated to think we were on bad terms.'

'I'm glad you did. I was unhappy about it too.'

'What about dinner this evening? We could go to the Castle in Carlisle.'

'That would be fun.'

'I love you, Marigold.'

'Oh, good. I love you, too.'

24

I heard the telephone trilling in its maidenly way as I let myself in through the front door.

'Hello, Marigold. I can't speak for long. I'm in the call box on the corner of Maxwell and I've only got three fifty-pee coins. How's the foot?'

'Lizzie! It's fantastic to hear you. A bit stiff still but it's heaven to have got rid of that bloody old cast.' I manoeuvred the telephone so I could sit down in my father's armchair. Siggy jumped on to my knee. Since my father had left, Siggy had been allowed the run of the house and had been marginally better tempered. 'What have you been doing?'

'We've started rehearsals for *The Prince of the Pagodas*.'

'Who's going to dance Belle Rose?'

'Sebastian's ex, Sylvia Starkey. She'll make a complete muff of it, if you ask me. She's technically competent, but has about as much sweet simplicity as Carabosse.'

Carabosse is the bad fairy in *The Sleeping Beauty*. I tried not to be glad that Lizzie thought Sylvia would be hopeless. This would be the lowest, meanest, vilest kind of dog-in-the-manger-ishness since I had no chance of dancing it myself. Nonetheless, I did feel an unpleasant little dart of envy.

'I honestly think Sebastian's losing his grip,' Lizzie continued.

'The trouble is, the Russian tour's been cancelled because of some diplomatic row, and both Freddy and Alex are off for at least six weeks with injuries. Have I told you about Mariana? Her knee operation revealed extensive osteoarthritis so her career's finished.'

'No! How terrible!' I was really sorry. 'She can't be much more than thirty.'

'Twenty-nine. Very bad luck, isn't it? And gossip has it that the man who was going to sponsor *The Prince of the Pagodas* dropped dead with a heart attack before he could sign on the dotted line. Certainly Sebastian's face is as black as thunder the whole time. I wouldn't be in Cynthia Kay's knickers for anything.'

'Who's Cynthia Kay?'

'Oh, haven't I told you about her? She's just joined the corps. Quite pretty and as hard as nails. Sebastian's screwing her but she's nowhere near good enough yet for any principal roles.'

I remembered what it was like to be in bed with Sebastian and felt sick. In this case envy didn't come into it. Nothing, not even the offer of star billing with the best company in the world, would have persuaded me to let him lay a finger on me again. I hated myself for having let him treat me with such contempt. 'Any news of Miko?'

A short pause. 'I don't suppose for a minute it's true, but I heard a rumour that he's talking to a Russian . . . Valentina something-or-other . . . who's just defected.'

'Oh.' I understood that it was all signed and sealed, but Lizzie was trying to break it to me gently. It could not possibly matter to me in my present circumstances, yet I felt a tremor of envy, which I tried at once to quell. 'What are *you* dancing?'

'Need you ask? Back row as usual and lucky to be there. I made a dog's breakfast mess of this morning's rehearsal.' Lizzie was exaggerating, of course. She was a pretty good dancer and to the untrained eye her performance would probably have looked ravishing, but we were talking about standards of perfection here. 'I don't even want to think about it,' Lizzie continued. 'Entertain me with your doings.'

'Well . . . last week I started a new job as waitress in the village café. I work from two until six. The customers are mostly polite and nice and leave good tips. Yesterday a man tucked a whole pound under a saucer. Sadly his wife saw him do it and filched it back. A substantial tea chez the Singing Swan was supposed to be one of the perks of the job, but now I know what state the kitchen's in I can't face a thing. I have to smuggle in apples to keep up my strength.'

'That bad?'

'The chip fat looks like molasses but doesn't smell as nice. Luckily the chips are always served with a slosh of glue-like gravy, so no one notices what an odd colour they are.'

'Chips and gravy? How peculiar.'

'It's a north-country thing. Mrs Peevis is a lamb but she hates cooking and she's in pain all the time from her hips. The only thing she enjoys is betting on horses. She has a nephew called Dale who drives into Hexham every morning so she can have her flutter on the gee-gees, as he calls it. She wins small amounts occasionally and that makes her happy. But I know for a fact that she bets ten pounds every day, so no wonder the café isn't doing well if she's regularly losing fifty pounds a week. How are you getting on at Maxwell Street?'

'Okay. Nancy and Sorel had a bawling match one night so Sorel's moved out and we've got a lumberjack in her room.'

'A lumberjack?'

'Officially he's a forester but I don't know the difference. Sylvia Starkey's looking for a new pad and Nancy and I thought we couldn't stand living with her so we didn't let on to the company and put an advertisement in the evening paper instead and Nils answered it. He's Swedish. He wanted somewhere to stay in London while he spends time with his girlfriend who's a chartered accountant in the city. He's very clean and tidy, awfully good natured and knows nothing whatsoever about dancing. The perfect flatmate. How're you getting on with Rafe? Is he still being cool and brotherly?'

'No-o-o . . .' I hesitated.

'You can't be so mean as not to tell me?'

'Well, we made love and . . . I'm going to marry him.'

A scream from the other end of the line. 'Marigold! You're joking!'

'I'm perfectly serious. Evelyn's giving a drinks party next week to celebrate our engagement.'

'It's just that in your letter you said Rafe hadn't so much as patted your cheek. Was it the sudden release of a torrent of passion that had been dammed up for years?'

'Not exactly. We just sort of suddenly realized . . . I have to confess it feels a bit unreal.'

'How deliciously romantic! Please, *please* ask me to the wedding!'

'I was hoping you'd be a bridesmaid.'

'Duckie, of *course* I will! Oh, I'm so excited! A good old-fashioned wedding! How many bridesmaids are you having altogether?'

'Four little ones plus you and Isobel.'

'Crikey! It does sound smart! Have you thought yet what our dresses'll be like?'

'Evelyn thinks palest blue duchess satin with garlands of green and white flowers.'

There was a brief pause. I imagined Lizzie leaning against the glass wall of the telephone box digesting this. 'She's going to be your mother-in-law so naturally she'll be interested. But you're not going to let her dictate your own wedding, surely?'

'Rafe's parents are paying for the whole thing – your dress, my dress, the flowers, the food, the champagne, every crumb of cake, every grain of rice. My parents haven't got a bean. Evelyn's planning the most beautiful, stylish wedding in the history of the world. I understand her. It's not just to show off or be competitive but because she's extremely discriminating and a perfectionist. And it *will* be brilliant.'

Another pause. I could picture Lizzie's frown as she wound

a ringlet round her finger. 'I can see how difficult it must be for you,' she said eventually. 'But surely Evelyn ought to consult you? It isn't just about money, is it?'

'She firmly believes she *is* consulting me. She asks me what I feel about this and that and before I can answer she tells me what I ought to have and why and she's probably right. She's got several yards of ivory *pointe de Venise* lace that she bought years ago for Isobel's wedding dress which she says would be perfect for me. How could I possibly turn it down without being churlish and ungrateful?'

'I don't like the sound of that. Not the lace – that'd be fabulous – but how does Isobel feel about it?'

'I admit I felt my blood drain when Evelyn said it. But apparently Isobel isn't going to be married in church because Conrad's a Jew. I'm so stupid that it had honestly never occurred to me.'

'Oh dear. *Now* I see. It's one great tangle of emotions – disappointment, compensation, gratitude, obligation – for ever and ever, Amen.'

'And you've got to remember I shall be living under Evelyn's roof for quite some time. So it won't do to begin on the wrong foot.'

'Marigold! It's a recipe for disaster!'

'Everything's complicated by the fact that the Dower House, which is the only other decent-sized house on the estate, has been let on a long lease. All the other houses are farmhouses and not sufficiently grand. Besides, the tenants have been living in them for generations. We couldn't possibly ask them to go.'

'Why don't you buy somewhere not on the estate?'

'Apparently people like the Prestons don't buy houses. I gather it's a rather vulgar thing to do.' Lizzie giggled and I found myself giggling too. 'I know it's silly, but that's the way they look at things.'

'Mm. I suppose that wraps it up really. But don't you feel just a little bit resentful?'

'I'm so conscious of having nothing to bring to the marriage – no blood, no acres, no dowry. Evelyn's being utterly sweet to me, saying that I'm just like a daughter to her and she knows I'll make Rafe happy and be a good wife. I just hope I will.'

'You're not having second thoughts?'

'No-o.'

'Marigold?' This was said sternly. When I didn't answer Lizzie said, 'Of course I know what it is. You love the man but you love dancing more.'

I felt a fierce pain just below my ribcage. 'Oh, Lizzie!'

'And you feel guilty for being ambitious. You're accusing yourself of being a cold-hearted bitch and you can't bring yourself to disappoint Rafe and his parents and your parents. So you're going to throw all that talent and years of training away to please other people.'

'Have a heart. What would you do in my shoes?'

'I'd ask him to wait a while. If he loves you . . . oh damn, there are the pips . . . we're about to be cut off . . . promise you'll write and tell me everything . . .'

'I will. Goodbye, darling Lizzie, and thank you so much for ringing . . .' A burring sound told me I was talking to the ether.

25

For the past week I had been rising at half-past six and slipping out of the house before breakfast. These days it was light by seven. The air was freezing at this hour; each frond of bracken was rimed with frost and last year's fallen leaves snapped under my feet like fine porcelain. But trees were greening and birds were nesting. My plan was to run a little further each day. Already my joints felt looser and my muscles stronger. I always took the path that began a few hundred yards from the end of our drive and wound up through woods to the foot of the great rock on which Hindleep was built.

As I jogged to a steady rhythm, Benjamin Britten's music for the second act of *The Prince of the Pagodas* ran through my mind and I tried to remember the sequence of steps for Belle Rose's pas de deux with the salamander. By the time I reached the place where the trees grew more closely together and the path disappeared, I was always breathless and dripping with sweat.

It was with a sensation largely of dismay therefore that on this particular morning I came panting into a small clearing where the canopy thinned to admit a faltering ray of sunlight and saw Conrad.

His surprise must have been even greater than mine. He at least was in the grounds of his own house.

'Hello,' he said, recovering first. 'What are you doing here?'

I put my hands on my hips and dropped my head forward to ease my breathing. Half a minute passed before I could speak. 'I'm trying . . . to get fit . . . again. What . . . about . . . you?'

'I was looking for a particular lichen. It is called *teloschistes flavicans*. Look.'

He pointed to a branch just above his head. I tried to stem with my sleeve the flow of perspiration that poured into my eyes, so I could see the tiny clusters of golden yellow tufts.

'It's . . . very pretty.'

'I think so.'

'Are those things in the . . . house yours, then . . . the feathers and stones, I mean. I thought they must . . . belong to Fritz.'

'Oh? Why did you think that?'

He gave me a look that seemed to appraise. I became conscious of the skimpiness of my leotard, the depressing grey colour of my pink crossover cardigan which I had washed by mistake with my black tights and the drops of sweat hanging from the end of my nose. He was wearing a red scarf tucked inside the coat with the astrakhan collar. His face was pale with cold and his hair and beard looked blacker by contrast. His eyes were like shiny pieces of jet. He took a handkerchief from his pocket and handed it to me. I pressed its soft white folds to my face. It smelt faintly of pencil boxes.

'I don't know. You seemed too . . . too . . . sophisticated.' I could hardly say too materialistic, though that would have been nearer the truth.

'You mean spoilt and worldly. You think I must drink only out of gold cups and dine on roast birds of paradise.'

'Oh no.' I shook my head and regretted it at once, because my nose began to stream. I was obliged to blow it on his hand-kerchief.

'That, if you will forgive me, is a lie. It is generally assumed that those who have money must necessarily be servants of mammon. In fact frequently the opposite is true. Those who

315

must be frugal and calculate the price of a piece of cheese are often unable to value things except in terms of dollars and shillings.' I acknowledged the truth of this. I had never had the opportunity to be extravagant, but since living at home my brain had become a calculating machine. I was unable to look at a rotten tomato without comparing its price with that of a blackened banana.

Conrad picked up a pine cone, examined it closely, then put it in his pocket. 'You have heard of Epicurus, the Greek philosopher?'

'Um . . . wasn't he awfully fussy about what he ate?'

'That Epicurus was a hedonist is a common misconception. On the contrary he advocated living simply, enjoying modest pleasures in order to find happiness in an imperfect world. He held that a garden, a handful of figs, a pot of cheese and a few friends are all that is needful for contentment. This seems to me intelligent.'

I visualized this charming scene and saw the snags immediately. 'I don't expect you do much shopping so you wouldn't know that figs are fiendishly expensive in England,' I said apologetically. 'Also the weather . . .'

Conrad gave me a sudden sharp look, whether because I had dared to disagree or because of my fruity sniffing I didn't know. He closed his eyes briefly, as though reordering his thoughts, then said, 'The hall is finished and the drawing room is halfway. Come and see.'

'I'd love to but I have to get back. I'm my father's receptionist. He's the village doctor and the surgery opens at nine.'

'Then come afterwards.'

'I work at the local café in the afternoons.'

'This evening then?'

'I'm meeting Rafe.'

My face, which had been cooling, grew hot again in case he thought I was being untruthful and making up excuses. Since our last visit, when Conrad had enlivened the occasion by jumping from the balcony, Isobel had asked us to Hindleep for drinks, tea and even supper, but Rafe had been determined in his refusal. I put this down to a combination of things; his annoyance at the abduction of his own workmen, the pervasive Bohemian atmosphere, and most potent of all, his disapproval of Conrad as his sister's lover.

'I see.' He did not press the invitation further but stared up at the ragged circle of sky that could be seen between the branches. 'What do you consider should be the springs for one's actions?' he asked, still looking up. 'What principles should operate in the process of decision-making?'

I hopped from one foot to the other. The sweat was growing cold on my body and the chilly air was making its temperature felt. 'Um . . . I don't know really.'

'You have some notion of the difference between right and wrong, I suppose?'

'Yes, but sometimes one chooses to do wrong all the same.'

'And why?'

I thought hard. 'Because it's easier. Because there's something you want so badly that you're prepared to lie and cheat and steal to get it.'

'So you are saying that one *ought* to be impelled by honesty. By truthfulness.'

'Yes, of course.'

'But you yourself do not always consult the truth?'

'I'm not the only one.' I began to feel indignant. 'Everyone fudges the truth.'

'Does that make it all right?'

'No. It makes it human.'

'Is it reasonable to disregard ethics when they are inconvenient?'

'No! I'm sure it's a mistake to pursue something whatever the cost to one's conscience.'

'Truth, then, must be our guide. We should aim in all situations always to stick to the truth and nothing but the truth as we may perceive it.'

'Certainly. That is . . . unless the truth might hurt someone else.'

'Ah.' He brought his gaze down from the treetops to look at me with that characteristic gaze that seemed to see into the smallest crevices of my mind but told me nothing of what he was thinking. 'You lie out of consideration then.'

'Doesn't everyone?'

'Tell me, Miss Marigold Savage, do you prefer that others deceive you out of the kindness of their hearts?'

'Well, I shouldn't like it if people blurted out horrible things about the shape of my nose or the rottenness of my jokes. But if it was something important, naturally I'd want them to be honest with me.'

For a while we continued to look at each other until I was forced to do more mopping and blowing. The dripping of my pores and nose placed me at a disadvantage during this catechism, as I felt it to be. Conrad's tone was neutral, but I felt there was something more behind his questioning than a mild desire for a little early morning philosophical argument.

He smiled suddenly. 'I saw a mountain hare this morning.' His eyes were softer now and a degree of friendliness permeated the biting air. Sudden changes of mood seemed to be characteristic. I was tempted to ask him about our meeting on the train, but on second thoughts decided this entente cordiale was too new and fragile to risk.

'Are they different from ordinary ones?'

'They have shorter ears and tails. But the chief difference is the whiteness of their coats in winter. Beautiful things.'

'I should like to see one.'

'Do you like flowers? Of course,' he added, not giving me a chance to reply. 'All women do.' He pushed up his sleeves and spread his fingers to show they were empty, brushed one hand over the other and held out a tiny posy.

I took them. The petals and leaves were wet with crystals of melting ice. 'Thank you. They're lovely.'

318

'You are familiar with the sweet violet, the primrose and the anemone. But you may not know this little white one. I have looked it up and its common name is spring snowflake. That is charming, is it not? Now you had better run off for that appointment with your father.'

My dignity had already been so compromised that I made no objection to being dismissed like a bad child. I tucked his handkerchief into my sleeve and turned to run back down the hill.

'Come another time earlier,' he called after me, 'and you may see the hare.'

'How pretty.' Dimpsie picked up the vase in which I had arranged the small posy and held it to her nose. 'Mmm. Delicious scent.'

We were enjoying fried mushrooms and tomatoes, the fruits of my labours at the Singing Swan.

'Conrad gave them to me.'

'Really? When?'

'About three-quarters of an hour ago. I happened to meet him in the woods.'

'How romantic! But as you're both engaged to someone else, of course it wasn't,' she added quickly.

'No. Actually, I rather think they were in the nature of a lesson.'

'A lesson. What about?'

'Oh – about roast birds of paradise.'

But when Dimpsie pressed me to explain, I said I had to rush or I'd be late.

26

'What do you think?' I came down the stairs at Dumbola Lodge and twirled about in the hall for my mother's inspection.

'You look terribly elegant. Rafe will love it.'

The dress was cream figured silk, with a piecrust frilled neck and a long row of tiny silk covered buttons down to the waist, in the style the princess of Wales had made so fashionable. It was quite unlike the things I usually wore, but I had chosen it with Evelyn's taste in mind.

'I hope so. I've never spent a hundred pounds on a dress before. Or on anything, come to that. I feel utterly decadent and I must say it's a heavenly sensation. You really don't think it was wrong to let him buy it for me?'

Of course this was a question to which there could be only one answer. Whatever she thought, Dimpsie would not have wanted to spoil my pleasure. I was reminded of my conversation with Conrad several days before. But surely we were all guilty of saying what we thought people would like to hear?

'Of course not! He's going to be your husband, for goodness' sake!'

Rafe had said, 'Really, darling, I insist. You must stop being so independent. Besides, some of my parents' friends are dreadfully old fashioned. They wouldn't be able to appreciate your splendidly individual clothes. I admire your flair immensely, but you'll probably feel more comfortable looking a little more . . . blending in. I don't mean I want you to dress like a batty old dowager. Just fractionally more . . . ordinary. You don't mind, do you? It's as much to please Evelyn as anyone.'

I had said that I did not mind. This was not absolutely true but I dismissed a slight feeling of pique as being petty and selfish. And when Rafe had driven me to the superior dress shop in Newcastle where his mother had an account and gone off to find himself a fishing rod with the injunction to buy whatever I pleased, I had thoroughly enjoyed the luxury of shopping without the usual restraints on my purse. We had met for tea afterwards at the Beauchamp Arms. As I entered the hotel sitting room, he had folded his newspaper and stood up to greet me.

'I've ordered China tea for you, darling, and chocolate cake. Is that all right? Come and sit near the fire.'

It was very pleasant. I had rejoiced that this good-looking, self-assured man, who gave the impression that he would be thoroughly at home anywhere from the Athenaeum to Crim Tartary, was mine. I had not allowed him to see my dress, wanting it to be a surprise. And there had been, I admit, a touch of pride that rebelled against the notion of needing his approval. He had said with a most charming smile that he did not doubt that I would make every man in the room deeply envious of him.

I pointed my toe so Dimpsie could admire my new black suede shoes with agonizingly high heels. It had been Dimpsie's idea that I should pawn our silver forks to buy them. I was confident I would be able to redeem them fairly soon with the money I was earning at the Singing Swan.

'Smashing!' she said.

I tried to flex my feet but my toes were crammed into tight bundles. Madame would have gone into spasms had she seen them but, as it was on the cards that I was going to give up dancing for good, what did it matter? Dimpsie was wearing a black velvet dress that was nearly bald at the elbows, but it made her skin look luminous and showed off the beauty of her large, kind eyes. 'I wish you'd let me pop the spoons as well, so you could have had something new. Not that you don't look jolly nice,' I added.

Jode O'Shaunessy came into the hall. He was so tall that he seemed to shrink any room he was in. He had been digging the new vegetable plot all afternoon and after dark had been in the garage sharpening the blades of the lawnmower and oiling the shears. Harrison Ford O'Shaunessy was fast asleep in his box in the kitchen.

'T'at's done now. She'll go a treat when t'e time comes te cut t'e grass . . . sure, but yor a fine-looking cailin!'

Despite the scars and the glare of his eyes beneath his cliff-like brow, Jode's face looked almost soft as he beamed shyly at my mother. Two of our kitchen chairs had already broken under him, but his hands when he fed and changed the baby were gentle. Not that he often got the chance in our house, because the tiniest snuffle from Harrison Ford drew Dimpsie to his box as though she were attached to it by taut elastic. As I saw Dimpsie blush and look self-conscious, an idea came to me which at first I dismissed as absurd. But when I reviewed it I thought, why not? It might be just what she needed.

'I'll be goin' then.' Jode bobbed his head, knocking it against the brass lantern that hung from the ceiling, making the light swing wildly. 'See ye tomorrow, Dimpsie.'

I became aware that the hall's atmosphere was filled with a pulsing excitement created by somersaulting pheromones. The face of the moon on the longcase clock seemed to take on a prurient smirk.

'If you're sure that's convenient.'

'Aye. Ten o'clock.'

'He's taking me to see this couple he knows who are weavers and use only vegetable dyes,' she explained after he'd gone with a crashing of the front door that made the house shake. 'I thought they sounded like possible candidates for the craft shop.

It's so kind of him to take the trouble. It's not as though there's anything in it for him.'

'Terribly kind. Will you fasten my necklace for me?' I leaned towards the hall mirror while Dimpsie fastened a little collar of diamonds and sapphires round my throat.

Evelyn had given them to me the day before. When I had protested that she had already given me far too much she said, 'Don't be silly, Marigold. These belong to the family not me. You'll have to hand them on to your son's wife in due course. Anyway, I prefer the pearls. Much more flattering for older skin.' She had turned to stare at herself in the morning room looking glass. 'I'm fifty-seven, but I think I could pass for fifty in a dim light, don't you?' Another question with only one answer.

'Fifty, if a day.'

Evelyn had frowned.

'Or forty-five really . . . thirty-nine? . . . You don't think Isobel will want the sapphires?'

Evelyn had given a chilly little laugh. 'Conrad will be able to buy her ten necklaces like these.'

I was sorry to observe an increasing coldness between Isobel and her mother. Perhaps this had something to do with the fact that Evelyn seemed daily to be investing more enthusiasm into Rafe's and my engagement.

Now Dimpsie kissed me. 'I'm so proud of you, darling. Oh dear! I can still smell chip fat.'

'Blast! I've shampooed my hair until I'm almost bald.'

Not possessing any scent myself, Dimpsie fetched hers, called El Souk. It was quite overpowering and made me think of the stuff you put down the lav, a disguising sort of smell, but it had to be an improvement on the chip pan. I dabbed it lavishly on every available centimetre of flesh. Then, while Dimpsie cleaned the earth from her fingernails, I combed the twigs from the back of her hair. When we were as lovely to behold as Nature and our wardrobes allowed, we got into her Mini and set off.

'I hope we aren't late,' I said as we looked for a space to park, the drive being lined with large and expensive motors.

Dimpsie scrunched into reverse. 'How far am I from the car behind? . . . oh, bugger! Never mind, that's what bumpers are for.'

We tottered up to the house, leaning forward on heels that felt like stilts, our carefully arranged hair standing up like sails in the stiff breeze. Spendlove helped me out of my . . . Bobbie's coat.

'Happy days, Miss Marigold,' he whispered and winked. This was a tiny comfort.

Evelyn came into the hall, looking striking in dark grey. The Preston pearls, three magnificent strands with an enormous side clasp of cabochon rubies and emeralds, were her only ornament. 'Marigold! *Darl*ing! There you are! And *dear* Dimpsie.' She embraced us both.

When we walked into the drawing room, the swell of well-bred voices subsided momentarily as guests craned their necks to examine the outsider who had crept past the favourites to steal the matrimonial jackpot from under their noses. It was a little like making one's first entrance. I drew myself up as tall as I could and assumed my Odile smile, brilliant but with a hint of something snaky in it, just in case there were those present who had come to find fault.

'You look lovely, darling.' Evelyn took my arm. 'Rafe was quite right to trust to your good taste.'

I did not like to be told quite so plainly that my appearance had been a matter for discussion between them.

'Marigold.' The archdeacon loomed up, looking flakier than ever, like a monument under snow. 'My felicitations. I think as an old friend I may claim the privilege.'

He saluted my cheek with cold lips. Two meetings, during both of which he had been peevish and ungracious, hardly constituted a friendship of any kind, but as Odile I was prepared to be false and hypocritical. When Lady Pruefoy pressed her white moustache to my face I did not flinch.

'I always knew how it would be,' she lied without a blush. 'I saw at once how taken with her he was,' she assured a woman at her elbow, who kissed both my ears, though as far as I knew we were complete strangers.

There was much more of this sort of thing. Bunty came to murmur congratulations. She dabbed vaguely at my face with a smiling mouth but her eyes said she was in pain. Rafe, on the other side of the room, was enduring congratulatory embraces with a magnificent suavity. He looked as Alexander must have done after he'd given the Persians what-for: relaxed, charming and unassailable. As soon as he saw me he came over. He pecked my cheek decorously but his eyes were admiring. 'Beautiful dress, darling. I knew you'd come up trumps.'

'Thank you.'

'Hello, Bunty.'

He gave her a perfunctory kiss. Bunty went red, except for the tip of her nose which remained white. I was sorry to be the inadvertent cause of her distress. She gave him a look blent of longing and sorrow and walked quickly away. Rafe made a face at me, as if to say that some people were rather hard going. It was clear to me that he had not the least idea of the love raging in Bunty's breast. 'This is pretty good hell, darling, but it can't last more than a couple of hours. You really are looking the tops.'

'Thank you,' I said again.

A superior-looking woman slid between us. 'How do you do?' She looked at me with implacable eyes. 'You must be Marigold. I'm Miranda Delaware. Hello, sweetie.' She kissed Rafe, leaving a lipstick mark on his chin. She presented me with her shoulder. 'Rafe, darling, I've got the Battersbys staying next weekend. They're bringing his sister. You remember Ingrid? Tall and blonde and terrifyingly intelligent. Don't pretend you don't.' She tapped his arm reprovingly and looked provocatively up at him through black spiky eyelashes. 'You danced with her all evening. Anyway, I'm a man short for Sunday lunch. Would you be an angel and come?' She glanced at me. 'You needn't worry, my dear. Ingrid's not the sort of woman men want to marry. Far too much competition for them, poor vain things. They always choose girls who'll worship them with doglike devotion. And then they wonder why they're bored.' She gave a laugh that was not so much silvery as pinchbeck.

'Actually, I think men find bitchy, competitive women fairly boring,' I said coldly

'Marigold, you haven't met the Stitchcourts yet.' Rafe took hold of my elbow and led me away, leaving Miranda Delaware, I hoped, with her composure a little ruffled. 'That was unnecessarily sharp, darling,' he said when we were out of earshot.

'I don't think it was. She meant me to understand that she thought I wasn't good enough for you.'

'No, no. She was just tactless, that's all.'

'Besides, it's rude to ask someone to lunch in front of someone else you haven't asked.'

'Yes, very. And I shan't accept. But it would have been better to ignore it.'

'Not for me it wouldn't. Why should she have all the fun?'

'All right, don't look so fierce. People are wondering what's the matter.' He smiled, whether for my benefit or to convince onlookers that we were not quarrelling I didn't know. 'Who'd have guessed you had such a temper, darling? I suppose it's your red hair.' He pinched my cheek. 'It's very sexy. I can't wait to get you on my own.'

I could not exactly put my finger on why his remark about the colour of my hair made me feel even crosser. Possibly because it seemed to suggest that I was being irrational. But I owed it to Rafe and Evelyn not to spoil the party, so I answered Mrs Stitchcourt's probing questions with smiling sweetness and listened to Mr Stitchcourt's description of a horse he owned two legs of and the races it had nearly won with an expression of pleased interest.

I was glad to see Duncan Vardy, the Old Norse expert,

approaching, his large teeth gleaming, his spotted tie twisted under his ear.

'Heigh-ho, Marigold! Splendid news about your engagement.'

'Thank you. How are the Nornor?'

He looked pleased that I'd remembered. 'The book's getting on quite nicely. I'm writing about Aegir, the Norse god of the sea. He lived on the floor of the ocean with his wife and nine daughters, the billow maidens. Naturally fire was impracticable, so his house was lit by heaps of gold.'

Duncan was a true enthusiast and I liked listening to him. I drank another glass of champagne and felt cheerful again. When Isobel came over to us, I kissed her and said she looked like a magical creature of the forest. Her elfin haircut and her clinging leopard-print dress, with one long sleeve and one bare shoulder that reminded me of Tarzan, prompted the remark.

'Really?' she said coolly. 'You look like a cross between Lady Di and a governess. Exactly what Mummy likes. How quickly you're learning your part.'

Before I could decide how to respond, Duncan said with a nervous titter, 'You both look *ravissantes*. I'll get you some more champagne.' He snatched my glass from my hand, though it was nowhere near empty, and scuttled off, the coward.

I decided to pretend unconcern. 'Where's Conrad?'

Isobel scowled. 'He sent Fritz with a message to say he might not be able to come. Apparently he's got an unexpected visitor. I told Fritz to tell him he *must* or I'd never forgive him and to bring the visitor if he couldn't get rid of him. Can you imagine how everyone'll be whispering behind their hands if he doesn't show up?'

'They might think – quite reasonably – he'd had to go back to Germany. Or London or somewhere.'

'That just shows how little you understand them.' Isobel's tone was scathing. 'I despise them all and they know it so they'll be delighted to see me humiliated.'

Isobel glared about her with an expression of detestation

before glancing towards the hall. Her profile, that of a vengeful goddess, melted swiftly into beaming satisfaction. 'There he is!'

I caught a glimpse of Conrad's dark head before Isobel, hurrying to meet him, blocked my view.

'Well, Marigold!' The archdeacon appeared at my elbow. 'You have been fortunate indeed to capture the heart of so estimable a young man.' He cracked a grisly smile. 'Privilege, of course, brings obligations. My advice to you,' the archdeacon lowered his chin to look up the more impressively from beneath thick, scurfy eyebrows, 'is to lay aside your books and apply yourself to the study of how best you may use your new privileges in the service of those less fortunately circumstanced.'

Conrad had entered the drawing room with Isobel. He turned to speak to the man beside him. When I saw who it was, everything seemed to dim and grow bright in waves. I wondered if I could be hallucinating.

'Humility,' droned the archdeacon, 'is a rare virtue. Knowledge puffeth up, as the Good Book says, but charity edifieth.'

With his inimical eyes and hooked nose, Sebastian Lenoir resembled a particularly bad-tempered bird of prey. He stared about him unsmiling until his gaze rested on me. He began to walk towards me with his customary panther-like lope, looking straight ahead, as though Evelyn's guests were so much litter beneath his feet.

Rafe was talking to Ronald Dunderave. I signalled desperation with every feature. My face must have been eloquent for he began to make his way to my side of the room. But Sebastian was there before him. Before I had an inkling of what he meant to do, Sebastian gripped me tightly, forcing me onto my toes, and kissed me long and hard on the lips. Everyone within eyeshot looked astonished by such behaviour at a country cocktail party. I was equally startled. He had never done such a thing before. In the old days he generally greeted me by pointing a finger towards a chair while he finished whatever he was doing.

'Good evening.' Rafe's expression and bearing were indicative of grave affront. 'I'm Rafe Preston. I don't think we've met.'

Sebastian took out his handkerchief and wiped my lipstick from his mouth. 'I'm Sebastian Lenoir. I apologize for gatecrashing, but I hope my connection with Marigold will excuse it.' Blank looks all round. Sebastian smiled like the splintering of a glaze of ice on a pond. 'Perhaps she hasn't told you that we are engaged to be married.'

27

At half-past seven the following morning I came panting into the clearing. Conrad was looking up through a pair of binoculars. He was wearing a brown velvet jacket with discreet black frogging round the buttons. Something about his appearance, his finely trimmed moustache and beard, his elegant profile like a Byzantine painting, made me think of the eponymous cad of *Eugene Onegin,* who callously rejects a young girl's passion for him. I had twice danced the role of Tatiana.

'Oh . . . thank goodness!' I said between gasps. 'Please, Conrad . . . you must help me. Where is he?'

Without removing the binoculars from his eyes, Conrad took a handkerchief from his pocket and handed it to me. This was the third time in six days that we had encountered one another by accident in the woods. Conrad was interested in a nest of pink-legged bustards and I enjoyed the dramatic scenic accompaniment to a really stiff climb that the hill below Hindleep House afforded.

'He has just brought back a mouse. Or a vole, perhaps.'

'*What?* Oh, I'm talking about Sebastian of course!'

'He is tearing it to small pieces for the young.' He lowered the binoculars to look at me and turned down the corners of his mouth. 'Not an attractive sight.' I wondered if it was the magnified view of dismemberment or my disreputable leotard and laddered tights that repelled him. 'As for Sebastian, he is asleep on a sofa beside the fire which I have refreshed this morning for his benefit.'

'But why is he here?' Conrad averted his gaze as I mopped the perspiration that ran in rivulets down my face and made my eyes sting. 'Do you have any idea how long he's staying?'

'He informed me last night that he was thinking of remaining in Northumberland for several days, perhaps even a week,'

I uttered a faint shriek. 'Oh God! This is terrible!' In my agony of mind I hopped from foot to foot. 'Will he stay at Hindleep?'

'I imagine that the sofa and our primitive bathroom will drive him to seek refuge in a hotel. I hope so. While I have respect for Sebastian, he is not one of my particular friends.'

'How do you know each other?'

'He was acquainted with my uncle Charles. Sebastian probably knows everyone who is responsible for distributing a charitable trust.'

'A charitable trust?' I echoed stupidly. 'What's that exactly?'

He took back his handkerchief, found a dry section and began to polish the lenses of his binoculars. 'My great-great-grandfather made a fortune building railways in the Balkans. Thanks to careful management, it has survived two world wars and innumerable smaller skirmishes, though frequently its trustees did not. I inherited, on the death of my uncle, the task of investing the capital and distributing the interest to artistic and educational projects as I think fit. Sebastian has more than once invited me to put money into the Lenoir Ballet Company.'

'But you never said! I had no idea you'd even *heard* of the company.'

'As I decline to sponsor not only the LBC but all ballet companies, I preferred to keep that knowledge to myself. People are apt to resent those who do not admit the paramount importance of their special cause. It is better to keep business and pleasure as separate as one can.'

'Why don't you give money to ballet? Don't you like it?'

331

'I do like it.' Conrad paused. 'But there are other areas of the arts that are not so well funded.'

'But really the LBC has the most awful struggle to keep going . . .' I realized I was about to become one of those persons Conrad had just complained of, convinced that my own particular passion was the most deserving of support. 'Well, of course it's none of my business who you give money to.'

'Whom, surely?'

'What?'

'The dative case. To *whom* I give money.'

'Oh, well . . . perhaps. Do you know, Conrad, I think you're the most puzzling man I ever met.'

He drew his eyebrows together but said nothing. You might have thought him effeminate with his clothes and his hair and his dandified air – except for his eyes. There was no feminine softness or sympathy in them. Always they were challenging, often with that spark of amusement that might even have been derision, as though he thought us all hypocrites, liars and idiots. And no matter how heated the emotional temperature, he remained serene, as though he felt himself to be beyond the fitfulness of fortune. He was secretive, even guarded . . . my mind was temporarily diverted from my anxiety about Sebastian to the question I had been burning to ask him since our first meeting.

'You still haven't told me what you were doing on that train. I haven't mentioned it to a soul. But why didn't you want anyone to know that you'd already been two weeks in Northumberland before coming to dinner at Shottestone that first time?'

'That was unfortunate. Not only the same train but the same carriage. The chances were a million – several millions – to one. It almost makes me inclined to believe in Duncan Vardy's Nornor: troublesome creatures meddling in our lives and rendering us all absurd. They are more famously known as *die Walküre* or the Valkyries – demi-goddesses with shockingly vindictive tempers.'

'Oh, yes, Wagner.' I was delighted to be able to display a

crumb of knowledge. When talking to Conrad I was often conscious of my appalling ignorance. I reflected, happily, that Rafe never made me feel my lack of education, which must be a good thing. 'But when Duncan was talking about them I imagined them as old black crones, not blonde maidens in helmets.'

'Teutonic myths are closely tied to those of Old Norse. The gods Wotan and Odin correspond. The differences are subtle.'

'I'm afraid I don't know anything about them.'

'The northern myths were attempts to make meaning of life. They were not revealed religions with divinely inspired scriptures, like the Bible, the Koran or the Jewish Torah. The gods themselves were mortal – destined to die in the last battle between good and evil at the end of the world, called Ragnarök. That is the same as Götterdämmerung in Teutonic myth. The gods not only observed the folly of men but also intervened to help them. Or to make things much, much worse.'

Conrad had resumed his observation of the nest while he was talking. He offered me the binoculars. 'Would you like to look?'

I wanted to hear more about the gods but it seemed the tutorial was over. I took the binoculars and looked up into an unintelligible blur of branches and sky.

'You adjust them by closing your right eye and turning this little wheel.'

His hand, thin with long fingers, so different from Rafe's broad strong ones, fidgeted with something just beyond the end of my nose. A dark shape, which was probably a nest and something that was either a baby bird or a pine cone came into focus. It occurred to me then that, with that little lecture about Norse mythology, he had neatly sidestepped the question of why he had been on the train. He intended to keep me in the dark and I knew him well enough now to be sure it would be futile to press the point. And there were more urgent matters.

'How did Sebastian find out where you lived?'

'An article in one of the financial papers mentioned my purchase of Hindleep. Yesterday Sebastian sent his card from

333

Alnwick to say that he would be obliged if I would see him. As he had gone to so much trouble, I sent Fritz down to the nearest telephone to call him and offer a bed for the night.'

I lowered the binoculars. 'Then he wasn't looking for me? Well, that's a comfort, anyway!'

'I would not be so sure of that. As soon as he arrived he mentioned your name. He appeared much gratified when I told him not only that I knew you but also that I was destined to see you that very evening. When I told him that the party was a celebration of your engagement to the son of the house, he seemed annoyed. But he kept his own counsel. Had I known he considered you to be engaged to *him* I should not have brought him to Shottestone. But how could I have guessed?' Conrad's expression was serious but I had the feeling he was observing my folly with godlike amusement.

I groaned. 'It was the most awful piece of bad luck.'

'Bad luck, you call it?' Conrad smiled broadly. 'Were we living in medieval times I should have said you were accursed. Indeed, though it has been a fixed principle of my life to espouse no religion, however tempting its promises and charming its wrappings, I think I must acknowledge the existence of the Nornor as a positive fact.'

'Beastly old things!' I said with feeling. 'It was one of the worst moments of my entire life.'

Conrad held out his hand for the binoculars. 'I am sorry.' He did not look sorry at all. 'But you have to admit there was a piquancy in the situation.'

'I'm glad you thought it was funny,' I began stiffly, but then honesty obliged me to add, 'but it was a good thing you did.'

When Sebastian had announced in a carrying voice in Evelyn's drawing room that I was engaged to be married to *him,* there had followed an appalled silence. I had looked from Sebastian's Mephistophelian grin to Isobel's shocked face and then to Rafe's incredulous one, and hoped to be struck dead on the spot. Lady Pruefoy, standing nearby, had screamed like a peacock. Wherever

I looked, I saw various degrees of disbelief, dismay and disgust on people's faces. Then Conrad's forehead had started to pucker, his eyebrows had lifted in the middle, he had pressed his lips together and made a snorting sound in his nose. Finally he had given way to outright laughter. This had been infectious, and other people had smiled and tittered, reassured to find it had all been a joke. Even Rafe had managed a twitch of his mouth, but I saw that he was fuming with rage. Only Sebastian remained perfectly calm. It was evidence of my former thraldom that when he looked at me and narrowed his eyes my stomach had hopped with fright.

Spendlove had brought a tray of drinks, providing a useful distraction. I had taken another glass but my hand shook so much I had been unable to get it safely to my lips. I heard mutterings and whisperings. 'Perhaps he's one of those new kissograms I've read about . . . a joke in questionable taste, *I* consider . . . I thought Germans weren't supposed to have a sense of humour . . .'

Sebastian had seemed indifferent to the sensation he had caused. 'How's your foot?'

'Better . . . getting stronger . . . Rafe,' I put my hand on his arm and tried to smile, though my lips were uncooperative, 'Sebastian is director of the Lenoir Ballet—'

'You'd better get back to classes straightaway,' Sebastian interrupted. 'You might manage the last few performances of Belle Rose in *The Prince of the Pagodas* if you get down to it and work every minute of the day.'

'What about Sylvia Starkey?'

The nostrils of Sebastian's blade-like nose became pinched. 'I suppose Lizzie's been gossiping.' He had given me a look of sharp displeasure. 'Sylvia's as light as a young bullock. I can hear her land from the back of the auditorium.'

'Look here, Sebastian.' Golly had pushed her way into our circle. Several new stains had been added to her boiler suit in the interval since we had last met, mostly dark blue, possibly ink, and a yellow streak that might have been egg. 'You're just the chap I want to see. Oh, hello, Marigold, old thing. How are you? Conrad, dear boy, what a pleasure it is to see you . . . Hello Rafe, lovely party . . . Sebastian, I want to talk to you.'

I was not surprised that Sebastian and Golly knew each other. Sebastian made it his business to know everyone of importance in the arts world.

'Hello, Golly.' Sebastian leaned forward to embrace her, spotted the stains and changed his mind.

Golly clutched his sleeve. 'When Conrad said you were coming I knew it was fate. I'm writing an opera ballet. If opera can be said to have a fault it's that it's too static. A lot of vast people standing about like monoliths, roaring their heads off. Well, my idea is to have masses of action and I've written two brilliant entr'actes for a corps de ballet.' Her face assumed an expression of Machiavellian cunning. 'Now, who would you recommend as choreographer?'

'A choreographer? Well, now –' Sebastian pretended to think – 'there's Hereward Boncasson . . . no, he's past it. His *Aux Anges* was almost step for step the same as his *Tourments de L'Enfer*. Noah Cantrip? He'd be all right if you can wait five years. Too much opium's made his mind costive, as well as his gut.' He ran his hand over the silver streak in his hair that gave his appearance such distinction. 'What about Abel Welsummer?'

Abel Welsummer was English Ballet's choreographer.

'Oh, I've already spoken to Miko. Their schedule is crammed full for the next two years. I couldn't possibly wait that long. I want to put it on this autumn. I've already arranged financial backing – can't you think of anyone else?'

'Of course there's Orlando Silverbridge.'

'Orlando?' Golly would never have made a career as an actor. Her inflection of surprise would have fooled no one. 'Oh yes. And he's *your* choreographer, isn't he? I've just had a marvellous idea. What about the Lenoir Ballet Company for the entr'actes?' I saw she meant to draw Sebastian into her web and bind him fast with silken threads, in the hope that the dazzling prospect of being involved in the creation of a new work by one of England's foremost composers would make him her cat's paw. Of course it would never work. If the LBC danced the entr'actes, Sebastian would see to it that he had the last word about everything to do with them, down to the colour of the sequins on the dresses of the back row of the corps. Golly's round eyes attempted ingenuousness. 'Orlando Silverbridge! That *is* an idea . . . I loved his *Nerve Endings* . . . but how's your schedule? I heard on the grapevine that your Russian tour had been cancelled.'

Sebastian looked even haughtier than was natural to him. 'We *might* be able, with some adjustments, to fit you in.'

Golly struck him a blow on the bicep that made him stagger. 'Good man!'

She and Sebastian had moved away, engrossed in conversation, the party and my existence forgotten. Rafe had drawn me into the window embrasure. 'What did that fellow mean by barging his way into this house and saying you were engaged to him?' he asked in a low voice. 'You'd better smile. People are looking.' He bared his teeth.

'Of course we aren't! You've got to believe me! Sebastian's a brute and a pig and I hate him! He's not happy with the girl who's dancing Belle Rose and he thinks I'd be better. So he'll say anything to get me to come back to London.'

'It seems a peculiar way to go about it. Are you telling me that there's nothing between you and that man?'

'Absolutely nothing! Since I left London he's had two other girlfriends.'

'So there was something? Not that I've any right to mind. What you did before we met is your own affair, of course. But I don't like being made a fool of in front of the entire county.'

'I really am most dreadfully sorry and I never loved him the least bit even when we were . . . going out together.'

Rafe's expression grew stormy despite his stretched lips. 'He

337

doesn't look to me the kind of man who'd be content with holding hands. Were you lovers? Keep smiling.'

I hesitated.

I had always intended to tell Rafe the truth but it had been impossible to find the right moment. Each day that passed seemed to make my confession more difficult. His pride was his tenderest part and naturally he would be annoyed to have been misled. And sometimes I thought my youth and supposed innocence were what he liked most about me.

'Well?'

I opened my mouth to deny it.

'Marigold!' Evelyn waved an imperious hand. 'Come and meet Lady Peckover.'

Rafe's godmother, a gorgon in moiré and diamonds, cross-questioned me about my parents and grandparents and my prospects of inheritance and seemed to think very little of any of them, but I was grateful for the reprieve. For the rest of the party I talked and nodded and smiled while trying to decide what to say to Rafe when the guests had gone. I might admit that I had been under pressure to consent to some sort of relationship with Sebastian, which would account for the sham engagement, without actually confessing that I had cold-bloodedly traded my body umpteen times for the sake of my ambition.

I was only a little less anxious about what I was going to say to Sebastian. I knew that once I had convinced him I was giving up dancing for good, I would matter less to him than the poor legless tramp who played the mouth organ outside Piccadilly tube station, but Sebastian was not a man to take disappointment well. If he suspected that Rafe was jealous he might hint all sorts of dreadful things about me just to pay me out. I dreaded to see disillusion in Rafe's candid blue eyes. By the end of the party I had decided one thing only. I was in a hole.

Fate – or the Nornor – had postponed the moment of truth. Just as people were starting to go, poor Kingsley had tripped over an umbrella and fallen, hurting his wrist. Rafe was deputed to take him to the hospital. The business was complicated by Kingsley thinking he was going to a regimental dinner and insisting that Spendlove fetch his medals. Rafe had driven away looking thoroughly unhappy. I had longed to comfort him.

Sebastian had been taken off by Conrad, but not before the former had kissed me and squeezed my earlobe so hard that I could not suppress a small scream.

At the time, though naturally sorry for Kingsley, I had been extremely thankful to have escaped my own personal Ragnarök, but I had woken that morning to the disagreeable realization that the evil hour had only been postponed.

'What am I going to do about Sebastian?' I asked Conrad with the kind of despair that does not hope for an answer.

Conrad withdrew his eyes from the nest and fixed them on me. '*Are* you going to marry him? Of the two suitors, I would advise Rafe as being most likely to grant his wife an easy moment or two in the ensuing years. Sebastian has a dangerous look in his eye. If he were a horse, I should take care not to find myself alone in the stable with him. But perhaps etiquette dictates, as with dinner engagements, that, having accepted the first, one ought to refuse the second, however superior its attractions.'

I could not expect him to sympathize. In my present predicament I must appear ridiculous.

'You wouldn't mock if you only knew. Of course I'm not going to marry Sebastian. I'd rather be torn to pieces by wild beasts. I've got to make him see he can't go around telling people we're engaged. I'm working this morning and this afternoon. It'll have to be during my lunch hour. Do you know where he'll be?'

'With me at the Castle in Carlisle. Golly is taking Sebastian to lunch and I – at a considerable sacrifice of my own pleasure and convenience – have agreed to go with them. I am to be the . . . *die Zugabe* . . . how do you say "makeweight", as in a boat?'

'Buoyancy bags, do you mean?'

Conrad frowned. 'Certainly not. I am to keep stable the negotiations. Golly is afraid of giving Sebastian too much power. The opera is her infant and she wishes to be in charge of its upbringing.'

'Damn, blast and bloody hell!' I said with considerable energy. 'Is it as bad as that?'

'Worse. I don't know you well enough to use the sort of language that might come anywhere near to expressing my true feelings.'

Conrad put the binoculars into their leather case and slung them round his neck before saying, 'We shall have returned to Hindleep by six o'clock. You could come and meet Sebastian then. I can arrange for you to be alone.'

'Thank you, that's so kind, but Rafe's picking me up at six. We're going out for dinner. He'll have been in Carlisle all day sitting on the bench.'

Conrad looked surprised. '*All* day? What makes this bench so peculiarly attractive?'

'I mean it's his day for being a magistrate. You know, like a judge.'

'Ah, *der Richterstand*. I understand.'

'I've got to be able to tell him that it's all finished between me and Sebastian . . . you see, Rafe doesn't know . . .' I felt myself blush. '. . . I didn't tell him that Sebastian and I . . . oh, it's such a mess.' I hugged myself and clapped my hands against my arms because the sweat was cooling on my skin and though it was sunny the air was still bitterly cold. 'Sebastian wanted to stop me joining English Ballet. He didn't ask me to marry him . . . he just assumed I'd be only too delighted.'

Conrad looked sceptical. 'He seems to have more than his fair share of audacity. Do you tell me that when he made this announcement he was no more to you than the man on the Clapham omnibus?'

I blushed harder. 'Well, we had been . . . I was his girlfriend . . . of course I went to bed with him . . . Sebastian runs the LBC like a dictatorship . . . what else could I do?'

340

'Ah.' Conrad lifted his eyebrows. 'Indeed. What else *could* you do?'

I was perfectly alive to the sarcasm in his voice, but my pride was already in the dust. 'Sebastian's incapable of loving anybody. He's hard and cold and cruel and the very idea of being married to him makes me feel horribly sick.'

'In that case,' to my relief Conrad smiled suddenly and looked perfectly human and friendly, 'if I were you I should send etiquette to the devil and favour the second engagement.'

'I know you're not taking any of this seriously. But when I tell Sebastian I'm giving up dancing to marry Rafe he's bound to want revenge. He might tell Rafe about our affair . . . you see I *had* to . . . I wanted to dance more than anything in the world . . . oh dear,' I shivered hard.

'I think I do see.' In the bright early light, Conrad's large eyes were blacker than coal or soot or ink or anything black is usually compared with. For a moment he looked thoughtful. Then he said, 'I want to show you something.'

'What?'

'Come and see.'

My curiosity grew as we walked in single file along a path that petered out in a tangled thicket. When Conrad dropped onto his hands and knees and began to crawl through the undergrowth I remembered that there were doubts about his sanity. The tunnel seemed to go on for a long time and I could see little but the soles of Conrad's shoes as he crawled ahead of me. My legs were bare except for my practice tights and the ground was covered with prickly twigs and pine needles. I was sure that Conrad was as sane as anyone – if anything, saner . . . it was probably I who was going mad, driven to lunacy by the impossibility of reconciling the needs of those I loved . . . I thought of Sebastian . . . and hated . . . My incoherent train of thought tailed off as I grew conscious of a sound not unlike London traffic in the rush hour. After another ten metres or so, the tunnel ended in a glittering arc and the volume increased to a roar like a jet engine's slipstream.

341

I scrambled into the light and found myself kneeling on a lip of rock. Ahead of me was a sheer drop to the valley floor. We were probably directly under Hindleep now, but it was hidden by a projection of land above. The sound of crashing water was close and I could see droplets flying outwards and flashing in the sun's rays. I heard Conrad's voice raised above the din.

'Come to your left. Be careful! The ground is slippery.'

I inched my way along a ledge less than a metre wide. When I was on my own two feet I had no fear of heights. I rounded a shoulder of rock and saw Conrad standing about five paces away. The water fell in a torrent so close to him that droplets sparkled on his coat.

'Quick!' he commanded. 'I am in danger of drowning!'

We sidled further along the narrowing ledge and entered a sort of cave behind the waterfall. The sun shone through the curtain of water, splitting it into the colours of the spectrum. From within two feet of the edge the cave was quite dry, with a floor of leaves and earth. I was surprised to see the remains of an iron bedstead in one corner.

'I read about this place in Ratcliffe's diary.' Conrad looked about him with an air of satisfaction. 'It took me some time to find it. Ratcliffe paid a local man to live here as a hermit. But people were so afraid of the precipitous approach that they refused to visit and the fun went out of it. Also in winter it must be damp and disagreeable.'

To the left of the waterfall, the mouth of the cavern widened, affording a view of natural terraces on the hills across the valley where sheep ambled, tearing up mouthfuls of grass.

'If this is paradise,' I said, 'then it more than lives up to reports.'

'Goethe said all beauty is a manifestation of natural laws that we would otherwise be unconscious of. What do you think?'

I found it flattering that Conrad always talked to me as though I might have ideas of my own worth listening to. Sebastian spoke to me as though I had the intelligence of a worm. Rafe treated me as someone delicately female who it was his privilege to humour and protect. Or should it be 'whom'?

'Well,' I said, plucking up courage, 'if beauty is really a manifestation of natural laws, then we all ought to admire the same things, shouldn't we? And we obviously don't.'

Conrad gave me one of his piercing looks until I felt my seriously underused brain had been cauterized in its darkest recesses.

'Lucky old hermit!' I said, feeling quite uncomfortable under such scrutiny.

'The post had its disadvantages. Ratcliffe insisted he learned his poetry by rote so that he could recite it to visitors. And he was not a very good poet. You are shivering.'

He took off his coat and handed it to me.

'Oh, but then *you*'ll be cold—'

'Put it on. I kept horses as a boy and I know that they must have rugs after exercise.'

I did as I was told. A moss-cushioned rock made a soft seat. We had to raise our voices to be heard above the cataract but otherwise I was as comfortable as in a drawing room. In my present circumstances I felt I could have been completely happy as the hermit, even taking the poetry into account.

Conrad remained standing, turning his back to me to stare out across the valley. For some time we were silent. This gave me time to wonder if I had been wise to take him so much into my confidence about Sebastian. He was Isobel's lover and would be bound to tell her my misdeeds. And she would tell Rafe. It would sound much worse from a third party . . .

'Why don't you try Rafe with the truth?' asked Conrad abruptly.

'I can't. He's so honourable. He wouldn't understand that one might want something so badly, a good thing, that you'd be prepared to do anything – perhaps nothing *wrong* exactly but not particularly edifying – to get it.'

'You don't think you may be exaggerating the high tone of his principles?' Conrad twitched his lips. 'He is but a man.'

'You're laughing at me again. I admit Rafe's always been my hero, ever since I was a girl.'

'And now you are an old lady you want to keep him on the pedestal, a plaster saint.'

'You think I'm an idiot.'

'No. I think you are romantic. You like to live in a fairy tale and Rafe is to rescue you from the evil enchanter. But who is your von Rothbart? Not Sebastian, surely? I do not believe he is evil. Merely an opportunist.'

'You don't know how sadistic he can be. I know that sounds melodramatic but you haven't seen the side of him he shows to the girls he . . . he's interested in.'

'He has never attempted to make love to me, certainly.'

'He would if he thought he could get something out of you by it.'

'In my experience, one's best protection against the manipulation of others is to be transparent in all one's dealings. Open and honest always, even if other people may dislike it.'

I had to admit Conrad practised what he preached. He was polite to Evelyn's friends but made no attempt to earn their good opinion. He had told the archdeacon that he distrusted all religions and never went to church. He had informed Lord Dunderave that, in his opinion, anyone who gave funds to a political party should be automatically excluded from receiving a peerage. And he was not gallant. The wife of Kingsley's agent, trying to flirt with him, had asked him to guess how old she was. He had said forty-five without a second's hesitation. As this was two years older than her actual age, or so she claimed, she had gone away looking cross. Perhaps it was this refusal to dissemble that had made me feel he could be trusted . . . that I might ask him to help me.

I thought about injecting some transparency into my dealings with the world. But if I had refused to make love with Sebastian he would have blighted my career. If I now told Rafe the truth about Sebastian he would be grieved, disappointed, perhaps disgusted. He would most probably end our engagement and withdraw into depression. I would have to go back to London and try to climb ballet's greasy pole again. Dimpsie would turn to drink. I would be fiancé-less, jobless, guilt-ridden and broke. Would my gleaming integrity be sufficient compensation? On the whole I thought not.

I sighed and looked down at my hands, filthy from crawling through the tunnel. 'I can't pretend to be anything other than cowardly and deceitful.'

'There is no need to put on sackcloth and ashes. You are not a hardened voluptuary. Merely someone who has spent so much of her life in a world of make-believe that she cannot always separate the dreams from the reality.'

'Can one live without caring what other people think?'

'One ought to try.'

'I don't know that I'm strong enough for that.'

'Then make yourself strong enough.'

'Is it just a matter of wanting?'

'Of course. Nothing determines your character but you yourself. Not fate, not inheritance, not circumstances. If you apply the self-discipline that enables you to be an accomplished dancer to your conduct, you will be strong.'

'But it isn't as straightforward as that. Rafe's been ill. Depressed. He had a dreadful experience in a tank in Northern Ireland—'

'Isobel told me about it.' Conrad took from his pocket a notebook and pencil and wrote something on the first page. 'I think I shall plant ferns here. Most will enjoy this damp shade. The *Athyrium felix-femina* group to begin with. She and her brother are devoted.'

'Oh, yes. She feels as strongly as I do that everything that can be done *must* be done to help him recover. I don't mean to sound conceited but he says I've helped him . . . perhaps he needs to believe that I'm better than I am. Wouldn't it be selfish of me to salve my own conscience at the expense of his happiness?'

'Hm. One can always put a favourable interpretation on one's

345

own doings. Also the *Polystichums* and the *Cyrtomiums*.' He was writing busily. 'I wonder about the *Woodwardia fimbriata?* I think I remember that it dislikes lime.'

I took off his coat and stood up. 'What time is it?'

He looked at his watch. 'A quarter after eight.'

'I'd better go. Surgery begins at nine.'

He continued to write. 'Can you get back to the path by yourself?'

'Yes.' I laid his coat on the mossy rock where I had been sitting. 'Thank you. I hope I haven't bored you with my problems . . .'

'Do not delay and make yourself late. Goodbye. *Dryopteris. Asplenium* . . .'

'Goodbye.' I smiled but he did not look up.

28

'God knows why I agreed to go,' Rafe grumbled as he turned the car onto the road that led up to Hindleep. The woods were mere shadows now, unfriendly; a nothing colour like deep water. 'I'm really too tired to be sociable. My fellow magistrates were determined to hang, draw and quarter every grandmother up for shoplifting.'

'You don't mean – not really?'

'Of course not. Sometimes, Marigold, I wonder if you live in the real world.'

'Sorry. That was stupid of me. I wasn't thinking properly . . . it's just that I get so tense on this bit of road . . .'

'Oh darling, I'm a *brute* to snap at you when you're so patient and sweet. Don't take any notice of me. I'm just cross. The traffic coming out of Carlisle was appalling and there was a hold-up on the A69. It took me an hour and a half to get home. And this rain hasn't helped.' During the afternoon dark clouds had destroyed the beautiful day and it had rained for the last two hours. 'The last thing I wanted was to get behind the wheel again. But it's sheer refreshment to see you.'

'Thank you.'

I hoped he would continue to feel the same way after we reached Hindleep. Arriving home at lunchtime, I had found a blue envelope lying on the mat, addressed to me in an elegant, upright script.

Come to supper this evening. We have the rudiments of a kitchen now and Fritz can work miracles. Rafe will be invited also. Sebastian will be there but there is no cause for alarm. Conrad.

Though I dreaded seeing Sebastian again, it had not occurred to me to refuse Conrad's invitation.

'I must have been crazy to accept,' said Rafe. 'No doubt it's catching. But Isobel said in her note that she'd never forgive me if I didn't show. She's been up there all afternoon and we're to bring her home.'

This made me even less enthusiastic about the evening's entertainment. I knew from some rather cool looks Isobel had given me at last night's party that I was out of favour.

'Goodness knows what she does at Hindleep,' Rafe continued. 'He doesn't consult her about the restorations as far as I know. He's impossibly autocratic. The last person I'd have thought she'd want to marry. I fear he's going to be the husband from hell.'

'Perhaps Isobel doesn't want to be involved with the decorating. Does she like that sort of thing?'

'Don't all women? Don't you?'

'Oh, yes, I love it. Even on a shoestring. I wish you'd seen my flat. Luckily there were always lots of theatrical props going begging. Our bathroom was absolutely horrible, no window and white tiles like a morgue, so I stuck pink, red and yellow taffeta flowers from the flower girl's stall in *Nocturne* all over the walls and painted the bath yellow. Then I took up the hideous lino and did the floor in pink and yellow stripes. It looked quite good in a bold, Matisse kind of way.'

'It sounds . . . extraordinary. I hope you'll like living at Shottestone.' I heard doubt in his voice.

'Of course I will. You know I've always loved being there.'

'I'm afraid it doesn't lend itself to flowers on walls and stripey floors.'

348

'You needn't worry. I shouldn't dream of changing a thing.'

'Don't be silly, darling.' I heard relief replace the doubt. 'Shottestone isn't a museum. Things will need replacing from time to time.'

'I shall certainly ask your permission first.'

'Perhaps that would be as well. Marigold?'

'Yes.'

'Is that fellow Lenoir going to be there this evening?'

'I think so.'

'I know I've no right – yet – to sound like a jealous husband but I didn't like the way he kissed you on the mouth like that. And the business about your engagement . . . Was it a joke, in very poor taste, or were you and he – Christ! Look out, you fool!'

Two headlights shone in our faces and there was a squeal of tyres as Rafe pulled hard to the left to avoid the lorry that came round the bend in the middle of the road. There was a grating sound as we scraped against the rock of the hillside.

'Bloody idiot! I've a good mind to go after him . . . except there isn't anywhere to turn round. *Damn!* That'll be another hundred pounds at the garage. *And* the inconvenience. Last time they lent me a three-wheeled van. I looked perfectly ridiculous turning up at the magistrates' court in it . . .' With increased wrath, 'What's so funny?'

'Sorry, it's hysteria . . . I was so frightened . . . I hope there isn't much damage.'

Rafe drove the rest of the way to Hindleep in a silence which I did not dare to break. I had prepared a speech that afternoon, in the intervals between taking greasy plates mounded with chips and red cabbage to depressed-looking customers. I had so phrased the speech that it was essentially truthful without, I hoped, making me sound like . . . what was Conrad's expression? A hardened voluptuary. But it was not easy to deliver it to an already hostile audience. When we drove into the court-yard I began in a rush, 'Rafe, I need to talk you. I've been an

349

awful fool though I never meant . . .' but he had already jumped out. I saw him by the light of the headlamps, which turned the rain to slanting gold threads, bending down to examine the wing, his face taut with annoyance.

Someone opened the door beside me. 'What fettle, Marigold? I have the umbrella. Come in quick before ze rain wettens you.'

Fritz and I ran up the steps into the house. The hall was looking marvellous now, the panelling restored, the windows repaired, an old Persian rug on the polished flags, a fire burning in the hearth. Something large stood in one corner beneath a tarpaulin

'Is it another piano?' I asked.

'Not a piano. I was at the moment of unrappening ven I hear you come. I shall undo so you haf a lovely surprise.'

He started to unfasten the buckles that held the tarpaulin in place. The object beneath ended in a long point like a prow.

'I know! It's a boat. For sailing on the lake!'

'Wrong!' Fritz laughed with pleasure. 'You vill never guess.'

He was right. I never would have. Fritz drew away the tarpaulin.

'A sleigh!' I stepped back to admire it properly. 'How perfectly beautiful!'

It was about ten feet long and made of a bright silver metal, perhaps polished steel. The prow, or whatever the front section was called, had been moulded into the head and neck of a swan.

'Conrad buy it from a sale in New York. But it is Russian. Wonderful, eh? Or I must say canny.'

'I don't know if that quite describes it.'

'I go to fetch him.'

While Fritz was looking for Conrad, I admired his most recent acquisition. Two glass lanterns, prettily ornamented with garlands of silver ivy leaves were projected on brackets each side of the swan's neck. The seat behind was deeply buttoned in blue velvet.

'Oh, it's divine!' Isobel had come into the hall. 'What a shame we have to ride about in dreary old cars.'

She was wearing a white wool dress with a red patent-leather belt, which emphasized her small waist and curvaceous bottom and red patent high-heeled shoes. Her wardrobe must be enormous by now since she never wore the same thing twice.

'Hello, Isobel. You look jolly nice.'

'Thanks.' She smiled but I was not altogether convinced. 'So do you. Original, I must say. Been at the dressing-up box again?'

'Yes, I have actually.' My knee-length skirt was made of white pleated organza with sleeves of the same stuff. Both were trimmed with crimson ribbons. The bodice was crimson too, decorated in curlicues of gold braid. 'Do you really like it? It's a costume from *Daphnis and Chloë*. It's coming apart at the seams which is why they got rid of it. But it's one of my favourites.'

'All you need is a tinsel crown and a fairy wand.'

'Good evening, Marigold.' Conrad had come to inspect the sleigh. He wore a black jacket, a pleated lawn shirt and a paisley bow tie. And trousers too, of course. You would never have mistaken Conrad for an Englishman, but no one could have accused him of ostentation. Perhaps discreetly prosperous would best describe his style. Rafe's everyday clothes were well worn without actually being in holes, usually green or brown. Actually, I rarely noticed what Rafe was wearing, but he always looked distinguished without making any concessions to fashion, which he probably thought vulgar.

I stroked the swan's neck. It was as cold as the snow it had once skimmed over. 'Has it really spent its youth dashing over frozen wastes somewhere utterly glamorous like the Urals?'

'I know nothing of its provenance,' Conrad said, 'except there is a label behind the seat which says "Made in Moscow". I bought it on an impulse. No one else seemed to want it.'

'Not many people would have anywhere to put it,' said Isobel. 'Can you see it cheek by jowl with a hostess trolley or a cocktail cabinet?'

'Are you going to buy a horse to pull it?' I asked Conrad.

He shook his head. 'A horse requires a stable and a groom and regular exercising. And we have no field to graze it.'

351

This was disappointing. I had imagined spanking along snowy lanes, buried to my ears in fur rugs, listening to the tinkling of harness bells and the swish of the runners on ice.

'You could use it as a toboggan to go down the hill,' suggested Isobel.

'I fear only as far as the first bend. There is no method of steering it.'

Rafe came in, his shoulders dark with rain, his golden curls flattened over his forehead.

'The wing *and* the door will have to be resprayed. It's the outside of enough.'

'What's the matter?' Isobel kissed him. 'You're looking terribly grumpy.'

'Some lunatic came down the hill much too fast and shoved me into the cliff, that's all. A bloody great juggernaut, careering round the bend as though it was the Monte Carlo rally.'

'That will be the lorry that delivered this.' Conrad indicated the sleigh. 'As he was careering on my instructions, you must let me pay for the damage.'

Rafe flushed. 'Thank you, but no.'

'Don't be silly, darling,' said Isobel. 'It'll be a fleabite to Conrad and you know you're always complaining about making ends meet.'

Rafe looked incensed but, before he could answer, Sebastian strolled into the hall. Though I had known he would be there, actually seeing him at Hindleep gave me a shock and I felt my hair stand on end – just the roots, fortunately.

'Hello, Marigold.' He kissed me politely on both cheeks, then he held out his hand to Rafe. 'That was a delightful party last night. Congratulations on your engagement. I'm sure you'll both be very happy. I hope you'll forgive my little joke. Marigold and I are old friends, as no doubt she's told you.'

I had forgotten that Sebastian could be charming when he chose. He had never bothered with me.

352

'Thank you,' Rafe muttered, not able to rid himself of his temper immediately.

Sebastian continued to smile pleasantly at him. 'This is such beautiful country. Conrad tells me your family have been here longer than anyone.'

'Well,' Rafe allowed Fritz to relieve him of his damp coat, 'I wouldn't quite say that. There may be one or two families who have the start on us. But the Prestons have lived at Shottestone since the fifteenth century.'

'Really? I envy you. It's a superb house.'

Rafe was obliged to make an effort to avoid appearing boorish. 'Are you staying long in Northumberland?'

'I have to be in Geneva tomorrow, unfortunately. The fifteenth century, you say? It must be fascinating to have such strong links with one's ancestors . . .'

While Sebastian and Rafe talked, the latter visibly unbending, I marvelled at Sebastian's diplomacy. I knew that scenery and pride of place meant less than nothing to him. He was indifferent to everything outside the world of ballet, yet he was plying Rafe with questions about his forebears as eagerly as a novice pursuivant of the College of Arms.

'Come along you two.' Isobel took hold of Rafe's arm with one hand and Sebastian's with the other and led them off to the drawing room. 'The champagne's beginning to boil.'

'What did you say to Sebastian to make him behave like that?' I asked Conrad. 'Are you a mind controller?'

'I used a little psychology.' Conrad looked rather pleased with himself which I felt he was entitled to do. 'On our way to the Castle I told Sebastian that his success with women had preceded him and that you had been desolated to learn that you had been supplanted in his heart. Naturally as we were speaking man to man I put it less delicately, but that was the substance.'

'I suppose you had a reason for rolling my pride in the dust?'

'Of course. In gaining the upper hand it is wise to have regard for the pride of one's adversary. Sebastian can tell himself and

353

others that you have become engaged to another man from pique. I applied my understanding of Sebastian's psyche further and warned him that Golly was extraordinarily devoted to you. Being a woman strong in her affections, she would take it ill if you were made unhappy. I advised him not to make difficulties for you if he wished to be successful in coming to terms with Golly over the opera. Sebastian wants this contract desperately and he will do anything to get it.'

'You don't mean to say it was as easy as that?'

'Things become easy only when you have perfectly understood them. I also suggested that he might turn the situation to his advantage by inviting Rafe to put some money into the company as a graceful farewell on your behalf.'

'But Rafe hasn't got any money. He doesn't make a secret of it, so it's all right for me to tell you.'

Conrad stood silent for a moment, as though considering. I liked the contrast between the pronounced cheekbones that gave his face an almost feminine beauty and the masculine nose like a Moghul prince's. 'The Prestons, while not possessed of a king's ransom, are most comfortably situated,' he said, just as I was wondering whether a turban would suit him. 'They own two thousand acres of good farmland, for one thing, and much real estate, besides an impressive portfolio of investments.' I must have looked astonished. 'You really did not know this?'

'How *could* I know? I shouldn't dream of asking Rafe. Naturally I didn't think they were starving, but he always seems so keen on economy.'

'The English upper classes, I have observed, like to make a display of poverty. They like their food simple, their pleasures rustic, their possessions old, preferably shabby. Luxury and newness are the province of the *nouveau riche*. Fortunately they generally make an exception in favour of their cellars.'

'How odd! I like wine but I'm quite happy drinking the stuff that comes in boxes from the Co-op.' Conrad made a face of horror that made me laugh. 'I'm so *grateful* to you for putting

354

things right with Sebastian. I was nearly dead with anxiety and now I feel sure I could do thirty-two perfect *fouettés* without thinking about it. That's what Odile has to do in the black act of *Swan Lake*,' I explained. 'Every dancer pretends to despise them as nothing more than acrobatics but even Margot Fonteyn used to dread them.'

'I see.' Conrad smiled suddenly. It really was a nice smile and made me feel that Rafe was wrong when he said Conrad would be the husband from hell. 'As for gratitude, the debt is small enough. I simply used my wits instead of panicking like a helpless chicken cornered by a fox.'

'It's all very well for you. You aren't so frightened of Sebastian that your insides turn to water when he looks at you.'

'How strange you girls are. No, I am not in the least afraid of him, nor need you be. You have made him a villain when he is merely an egotist.'

'I expect now he knows I'm not going to dance any more he doesn't give a damn about me anyway.'

'I had that impression, certainly.'

Perversely I felt depressed to hear this. Of course it was a relief that Sebastian had given up his spurious claim to my affections, but it also meant that there was now no one in the world to whom my dancing career mattered a jot. I heard a car roar into the courtyard. Its engine note rose to a scream, then was abruptly cut off.

'That will be Gólly,' said Conrad. 'She has promised to bring the rough working of the much bruited opera.'

Sebastian had taken Conrad's advice to heart. He hardly looked in my direction all evening.

29

The large room that looked over the valley had acquired a magical glitter from the installation of mirrors and candle sconces dripping with lustres. The painting of flowers and birds on the walls was three-quarters finished, and against one wall was a console table with a malachite top, like a slice of emerald. It reminded me of the ballroom scene in *Cinderella*. I would have liked to waltz round it with a besotted prince, but Rafe was not the sort of man to indulge in fantasy. He was often romantic but only in a grown-up way, with flowers and presents and compliments. At the moment disapproval was in the very slope of his shoulder and the tilt of his head. Or perhaps, I thought with sudden compunction, it was merely tiredness.

'Here I am, my dears.' Golly came into the drawing room looking as though she had been swimming in ink. Her teeth gleamed white in contrast. 'Fresh from the agony of composition. Hello, Marigold.' She kissed me enthusiastically. 'I've been staring at five lines all day until my eyes have crossed so many times I'm almost blind. But I can see *you,* you delicious little creature.' It was at once clear to me that Conrad had cautioned Golly about the need to appear devoted. She put her arm round my shoulder and gave me a squeeze, beaming into my face. I wondered if she wasn't overdoing it. She tweaked my sleeve. 'That looks picturesque. Who are you?'

'Chloë, of *Daphnis and Chloë*.'

'Ravel! Sublime music! But – dare I say it? – not as sublime as what you are about to hear.' She went to the piano and clapped her hands. 'Concentrate, everyone. You'll have to imagine the middle parts because I haven't quite finished it. And you must overlook the bum notes. I'm not a pianist. I can only strum along. But it'll give you a rough idea of the work. This is the moment when the king looks into his Book of Fate and reads that his son, a lusty lad of nine, will one day marry a humble peasant girl who's just been born in a shepherd's hut. Only I'm thinking of setting the whole opera in Japan. Think temples, kimonos, fans, cherry blossom . . .' Golly waved her hand in a gesture intended to sum up an entire culture, then launched herself at the keys like a tiger pouncing on a lamb. '*Catastrophe! Apocalypse!*' she raved in a nasal, wobbly contralto. '*The ruin of my king . . . DOM! Let eagles pluck out my EYES and wolves tea-ea-r out MY heart for I would rather die THAN see the shame THIS lowly wench brings on my HO-USE! . . .*'

The song did the opposite of what your ear expected. Just when you thought Golly's voice would drop to a low croon of grief it rose to a shriek and when you expected a blast of rage it lapsed into a dulcet whisper. If there were bum notes, none of us would have known. Except perhaps Conrad, who sat with his head back and his eyes closed, obviously on a higher plane than the rest of us. It was a long aria and I was amused to see Rafe's jaw become rigid and his nostrils pinched as he swallowed a yawn. Gradually his head twisted slightly in an attempt to read the book that lay open at an angle on the table in front of him.

After the first few bars, Isobel abandoned any pretence of attending. She talked in a low voice to Sebastian who was sitting beside her on one of the divans, his limbs composed with careful elegance. You could tell from the way he pointed his feet and held his hands, as though cupping a ball, that he had once been a dancer. He looked at Isobel's breasts quite hard while she was talking. I thought of foxes and chickens again. Isobel's hands moved restlessly, stroking her bare throat, smoothing her sleeves over her round white arms, tugging the hem of her dress over her knees as though she was not quite comfortable under such scrutiny. Sebastian's expression became raptorial.

Guiltily I tore my eyes away and returned my attention to Golly. Twentieth-century music is always interesting to dance to, but some of it was extremely demanding. Stockhausen's *Ziggurat* had been particularly challenging. Having to concentrate on the counting, which was fiendishly complicated, affects the artistry of one's performance. It was generally a relief to get back to composers like Stravinsky or Prokofiev who had recognizable tunes and beats. Incredibly *The Rite of Spring* had created such a furore at its first performance that Nijinsky had to shout counts and cues to the dancers because they couldn't hear the music above the hisses and boos from the audience. Now it seemed almost old hat. No doubt, one day, Golly's new work would make people think of a more elegant and tuneful past, much softened and romanticized by nostalgia. At present there seemed to be nothing for one's mind or ear to hold onto, just a violent thumping and screeching, not helped by Golly's frequent pauses during which she swore filthily and scribbled furiously on the score.

'Supper, *meine lieben!*' Fritz came in bearing a tray.

We waited politely with rumbling stomachs for another five minutes until Conrad went to the piano and told Golly to stop. When he put his hand on her shoulder she stared at him as though in a trance. It was evident that she had forgotten that we were there, even where she was or what time of day it was.

'Well?' she asked him eagerly. 'What do you think?'

'I think –' Conrad hesitated – 'it may be your masterpiece.'

I had no idea whether he was being transparent or tactful.

A table had been laid near the great window. The valley was

now invisible. Tonight there were no stars, only a yellow glow where clouds had doused the moon to a glimmer. I sat between Golly and Fritz. Isobel, sitting opposite, talked in a low voice exclusively to Sebastian. Rafe did his best to interrupt their tête-à-tête whenever he could. I guessed that, though he disapproved of Conrad as a brother-in-law, his strict sense of honour was affronted by Isobel's coquettish behaviour. Conrad, however, neither watched her nor seemed to avoid doing so. Sometimes he half-smiled to himself, as though contemplating some delightful secret. The food was superb. We began with *Zweibelkuchen,* which were little patties of puff pastry enclosing onions, bacon and cream with an extra zing which Fritz said was caraway seeds. These were followed by *Bayerischer Sauerbraten.*

'It is beef cooked a long time vith lemons and beer. In Bavaria we haf much beer. I like it but Conrad hate it. He is a snob.'

'Certainly I am,' said Conrad overhearing this, 'if by snobbish you really mean discriminating. Also I hate leather shorts, cuckoo clocks, schuhplattler, zithers and accordion playing. Yodelling I abominate.'

I was sorry to hear about the cuckoo clocks. Though it would have been a case of carrying vampires to Santorini, I had hoped to persuade Conrad to buy one of Jode's.

'I call that thoroughly unpatriotic,' said Golly. 'But I agree about the yodelling. Marigold, dear girl, let me help you to more of these wonderful *Kartoffelpuffer.*'

'No, thanks.' I looked regretfully at the golden potato pancakes. 'I'm trying to lose weight.' I no longer needed to be thin to dance, but my smallness and slenderness seemed to be an important part of my attraction for Rafe and he would no doubt be annoyed to find himself married to Bessie Bunter.

'But, dear old thing,' Golly patted my cheek, 'I never saw such a wonderful figure. Nice firm little breasts . . . tiny waist . . . long, long legs. Quite delicious!'

Rafe looked at Golly and drew his brows together.

'I am not unpatriotic,' Conrad said, also frowning at Golly.

'I admire in varying degrees Holbein, Dürer, Cranach, Richard Strauss, Bertold Brecht and of course Wagner – all Bavarians.'

'For myself I confess I dislike *Semmelknödel*,' said Fritz.

'What's that?' I asked.

'Zey are round shapes of old bread drowned in milk and afterwards boiled. They lie heavy on ze stomach. Less ewen than *Semmelknödel* I like *Drudenacht* vich is anozzer Bavarian folklore. People go about making loud noises to send avay the vitches on May Night but each year become the jokes vorse. Last time I was in Bavaria on *Drudenacht* I sat down unknowing that some people haf put the brain of a pig on my chair.'

'Oh, the poor pig!' I said.

'The pig feels nothing. But I vas going to dinner and I had no more pair of trouser. I was necessitated to vash them and sit all evening in vet clothes and I caught a bad *Schnupfen*—'

'Aha!' cried Golly. 'I shall have witches in my opera.' She was in that state of creative fervour when anything and nothing had meaning except in connection with the great work. 'Three witches will foretell the marriage between the heir and the peasant girl. It will be a hundred times more dramatic than a dreary old Book of Fate. A nod in the direction of *Macbeth*, you know.'

'It sounds more like straightforward plagiarism to me,' said Conrad. 'Do they have witches in Japan?'

'Of course,' Golly declared with tremendous conviction. 'The place is thick with them.' She grew thoughtful.

'Do you believe in the supernatural?' Conrad looked across the table at Rafe. I spotted a gleam in those usually opaque black eyes which alerted me. 'I do not speak of the major world religions,' he continued, 'merely of witchcraft, astrology, consulting with the dead . . . the occult?'

'I shall go to fetch the pudding.' Fritz smiled at me as he rose to gather plates. 'Boiley, as you Northumbrian peoples name it.'

I did not like to disillusion him. 'Do let me help.'

He pressed a plump hand upon my shoulder. 'Thanks but you must remain.'

360

Then I was sure that something surprising was planned.

'Do you call religion supernatural?' Rafe asked Conrad with a shade of disapproval in his voice.

'In all religions, adherents are required to believe a great many things that defy explanation by natural laws. God himself is a supernatural being and the idea that the Jews are his chosen people is as much wishful thinking as the Resurrection—'

'Wishful thinking, maybe, but not necessarily untrue,' Rafe interrupted.

I wondered what Rafe did believe. I had dutifully accompanied him to church and had quite enjoyed it, especially the singing. The Preston family pew was at the front beneath the pulpit. It was bigger than all the others, with higher sides and its own door, as though to keep out peasant smells and germs. In the side aisles were several handsome monuments to former Prestons, including a life-sized marble effigy of the first Sir Ralph Preston in chain mail lying on his tomb. The title had died out sometime in the eighteenth century. This must have annoyed Evelyn.

Rafe had read the lesson in a clear, authoritative voice and I had thought how handsome he looked doing it. Afterwards, as Evelyn, Rafe and I walked down the path to the lych gate, the other churchgoers broke off their conversations to murmur polite good mornings and doff their hats, tributes we acknowledged with smiles to left and right and little waves from Evelyn as though we were royalty. We had driven back to Shottestone for sherry and lunch. None of us had exchanged a word about anything remotely spiritual.

'Most of the occult, particularly things like table-turning and séances, seems to me actually dangerous,' said Rafe. 'Not that I think it's possible to invoke the devil, but some people are tremendously susceptible to suggestion.'

'Dangerous . . . yes, perhaps. Or sometimes merely foolish. I do not think the acolytes of the Order of the Golden Dawn or the Hermetic Kabbalah have done much harm. Less, anyway, than the followers of Judaism and Christianity.'

'That's undeniable. But I suppose one must believe in something.'

'Not ghosts, however?'

Rafe smiled and for a moment seemed to relax. 'Certainly not.'

'What if I were to tell you that this house is haunted and that Fritz and I have seen the spectre of Orson Ratcliffe?'

Rafe smiled. 'I should say – with respect – that you had allowed yourselves to be deceived. Or perhaps were running a temperature.'

'If you yourself saw something that could not be rationally explained, you would take a liver pill and resolve to go to bed earlier?'

'I should investigate the room thoroughly for draughts, flapping curtains, tricks of moonlight and shadows.'

'In Ratcliffe's diary, he writes that it was his fixed habit to take a turn on the balcony at half-past ten o'clock each night, whatever the weather. It now lacks,' Conrad consulted his watch, 'one minute to the half-hour.'

I became excited, wondering what was going to happen.

'He's a punctual ghost then?' Rafe's smile was derisive.

'Oh yes. After all, he now has nothing else to do but await the moment of his walk abroad.'

'Honestly, Conrad, I don't believe a word of this,' said Isobel, distracted from flirting with Sebastian for the first time that evening. '*I* never heard anyone say that Hindleep was haunted—'

'Look!' Golly seized my hand and held on so tightly it hurt.

On the balcony was a white-robed figure, wearing a large hat low over its face and holding a book up to its nose. What made us – that is, Isobel, Golly and me – shriek in unison and a shiver run over my whole body was the indubitable fact that the figure was as transparent as a moonbeam. You could look straight through it and see the balustrade behind it quite clearly. I stared in amazement as it drifted slowly from left to right before our awestruck gaze and then disappeared

362

as suddenly as though it had been snuffed out like a candle flame.

'Good God!' Rafe stood up. 'Isobel, you're hysterical.' He gripped her shoulder as she shrieked again. 'It's a trick. It must be. But what on earth? . . . I'm going out there to see how you did that.'

I felt a violent admiration for such bravery and a corresponding surge of love. Even Sebastian, who I had always assumed was immune to human feelings like doubt and fear, had become pale. I was frightened myself. I only hung onto reason by remembering the look on Conrad's face when he had begun to talk about Orson Ratcliffe. Also, I had always imagined ghosts to be frail, attenuated beings, but this one had a generous girth.

'Golly, my hand will be crushed to powder in a minute,' I said as a matter of urgency.

'Sorry, dear.' She let go. 'That made the hairs on my neck bristle and my sphincter contract. Hell when you've got piles.'

'I never saw anything so terrifying in all my life.' Isobel turned to Sebastian and leaned against him as though for protection.

He stood up, letting her overbalance sideways and began to walk round the room, picking up cushions and looking under chairs. 'There's a projector somewhere. There must be.' I noticed he kept a distance between himself and the window.

Rafe was trying to open the door that led onto the balcony.

'You will find it locked.' Something about the set of Conrad's mouth, an exaggerated gravity as he pretended to be indifferent to the universal excitement, banished my lingering fears.

'Aha!' said Rafe. 'I insist on being allowed to inspect the territory.'

'It would be a brief inspection only. Yesterday the workmen removed the floor of the balcony as it has been found to be unsafe.'

'Here, *meine lieben,* is ze boiley.' Fritz came in with the tray, his eyes slyly merry in their beds of flesh. 'Vat ve call *Äpfel in Weingelee.* Ze traditional boiley of Bavaria is *apfelstrudel* but

363

I have no courage to try in the kitchen still a little desiring. You must ze paste roll so fine zat you can read ze *Berliner Morgenpost* zrough it.'

I gave a cursory glance to the dish of pink translucent jelly in which were set whole peeled apples, their cores filled with dark red jam. 'It was you, Fritz, wasn't it, pretending to be Orson Ratcliffe?'

Fritz looked at Conrad.

'Oh, Conrad, tell me it was,' cried Isobel. 'I shall never get a wink of sleep again if you don't.'

'Don't be silly, Isobel,' Rafe said in an admonishing tone. 'It was a trick. A clever one, I'll admit.' Then he looked at Conrad. 'Was it kind to frighten the girls like that?'

'I don't think they will have come to harm. According to Aristotle, a person incapable of feeling fear would not be able to develop the virtue of courage. He recommends we make moral exercise as important as physical exercise. You are not upset, Marigold?'

'Oh no!' I shook my head. 'I wouldn't have missed it for anything. If I'd been on my own it would have been horrible. And if I hadn't been expecting it. But I knew you were going to do something, so though I *was* frightened it was thrilling more than anything. But you *must* tell us how you did it.'

'I'll never forgive you if you don't,' said Isobel with feeling.

'Very well.' Conrad poured himself another glass of wine and took a sip while we waited impatiently. 'It is an illusion so well-known that I feared that none of you would be taken in. It is called Pepper's ghost, named for an English showman in the reign of Queen Victoria. It is as simple as it is effective. You require a black background and a sheet of glass placed at forty-five degrees to the horizontal, which the audience cannot see as they sit in a more brightly lit area. At the outer edge of the terrace below I have put up one of the workmen's spotlights with a wide beam which runs off a small generator. When Fritz in suitable disguise – a bed sheet and his sun hat – walks below through the arc of the spotlight, his image is reflected onto the glass and the reflection is displaced so that you think you see it on the balcony itself. A fortuitous collection of circumstances – the large sheet of glass that had just been delivered for the new balcony window, the removal of the balcony floor, the starless night for a background – these ingredients conspired to make the attempt to stage it irresistible.'

'It was marvellous!' cried Golly. 'Properly cathartic. My adrenal glands have had a thorough spring clean. I wonder . . . supposing we made my three witches transparent, appearing and disappearing as if by magic! Think of it! It would be a sensation!'

Conrad again made that little shrug of his lips. 'It would be impractical. You would have to construct a special arena below and in front of the stage for the witches which would interfere with the orchestra. Also the plate glass will obscure the actors' voices so you must have microphones—'

'Oh, don't be such a wet blanket! What do you think, Sebastian?'

Sebastian rested his chin on his linked fingers while he considered it. 'It could be effective. But you'd have to make sure it was a large stage so it didn't interfere with the dancers.'

'I'd be prepared to cut down on the dancers,' mused Golly. 'A pas de quatre instead of a corps?'

Sebastian's nose became knife-like with displeasure.

After supper we regrouped round the fire with coffee, brandy and *Kastanienkugeln* – little balls made from chestnuts, almonds and chocolate, rolled in cocoa powder. I made up my mind to get up half an hour earlier to run them off.

To my surprise Isobel moved to sit next to me. 'I'm sorry I was a bitch,' she said in a low voice. 'About the fairy wand and the tinsel crown.'

She lit a cigarette and poured herself another brandy.

'That's all right. I didn't mind.' Which was nearly true. I was used to Isobel's moods. I reminded myself that I no longer had to keep my body in racehorse condition and tried a sip of brandy myself. It was like drinking fire. I imagined flames licking the rapidly blackening lining of my stomach. I picked up her cigarette lighter to examine it. It was green and enamelled with fish. 'This is charming.'

'Conrad gave it to me. It's sweet of you to be forgiving but you oughtn't to let me get away with it.'

'I don't like rows. And if I did protest you'd just get angrier and say something that'd hurt me more.'

Isobel made a face expressive of contrition. 'Marigold, I want to tell you something. I'm mean to you sometimes because I'm jealous.'

'Really? But what of?' I asked, astonished.

'Oh, let's just say, one of the things I envy is your ability to lose yourself in another world. I saw you dance once. It was *The Nutcracker* and you were the Sugar Plum fairy. You were glittering, immortal. I could see that while you were on the stage you were actually *in* that enchanted world.'

I allowed my mind to drift back into remembering the old life. 'Yes, that's how it was. It's a three-sided world but, because you can't see the audience until the house lights go up for the curtain calls, it's easy to pretend it's real. Even though the other dancers' faces are dripping with sweat and all that fake snow they blow about the stage is filthy by the end of a run – they sweep it up after each performance and use it again and you get showered with dust and hair and sequins and bits from other performances; I once had an apple core bounce off my arm – you do believe it's all really happening just for that moment. Or rather, that seems to be all there is. You forget about pain and poverty and trouble with the other girls and –' I looked across at Sebastian – 'whatever problems there are. I didn't know you'd seen me dance. Why didn't you come backstage?'

She shook her head. 'I meant to. But afterwards I went away feeling sick with envy because you had this great gift.' She drew in a lungful of smoke and closed her eyes. 'I'm always *me* and I can't escape myself. Things go round and round in my head, torturing me, and I can't get away from them except in sleep and even then I dream the same dreams . . .' She put her free hand up to her forehead and stroked it as though to ease a pain.

'Isobel!' I was moved from my usual slightly cynical attitude to Isobel's freaks to genuine concern. 'What's wrong?'

'Oh,' she stubbed out her cigarette and attempted to laugh, 'I can't have what I really want: the one thing that makes me forgetful of myself, that makes me better than I am. It isn't my fault. It isn't anyone's fault. You have it and sometimes I can't forgive you, that's all.'

Isobel seemed to have forgotten that I had given up dancing and self-forgetfulness to marry her brother. But it was not the moment to talk about me. 'Are you sure? What is it?' I was mystified. I assumed something must have happened during those years in London which had jolted Isobel out of her usual devil-may-care attitude. 'I'd do anything to help you if I only knew what.'

'All you can do for me is to remember that when I'm beastly to you it's because I'm jealous, and that I can't help it. You know me so well, better perhaps than anyone.' She looked at Rafe, who was sitting on the other side of the fire, flicking through the book he had tried to read before dinner. 'We were like sisters once, weren't we? We share the past. And we'll go on sharing it.'

I kissed her, surprised and touched. I had always believed Isobel to be unsentimental. I wondered if she was a little drunk. I was fairly sure I was.

I heard Conrad say, 'I'm sorry I'm not in a position to invest in *The Fishcake,* or whatever it is to be called. There has been a tornado in the Mid West and Lerner Charitable Foundation has underwritten many of the losses. We are liable for substantial sums and must draw in our horns.'

'My dear chap,' said Golly, her moon-like face wrinkling sympathetically, 'I'm very sorry to hear it.'

I looked at Isobel. She seemed not to have heard.

Rafe put aside the book. 'My O-level German isn't up to Schiller, I'm afraid. What are you girls talking about? You both look very serious.'

'We were talking about you, of course,' Isobel said teasingly, with one of her lightning changes of mood. 'That's what everyone secretly hopes, isn't it?'

Rafe lobbed a cushion at her which she caught and threw back.

'Leave that, you old *Hausfrau*,' called Golly to Fritz, who was spitting on his handkerchief and rubbing at marks on the dining table. 'Let's have some music.'

'Good idea.' Sebastian put down a marble figure of a naked woman, which he had been examining closely.

'Sing to us, dear boy,' said Golly to Fritz, 'and Conrad shall accompany you. Your guests clamour for it.'

'Yes, do,' we all said, except Rafe who confined his enthusiasm to a half smile.

Conrad went to the piano and began to play a series of descending scales. It took me several seconds to identify Schubert's *Winterreise*. Orlando Silverbridge had choreographed a not-very-successful ballet to an orchestrated version of it. Freddie had been the suicidal lover and Mariana the faithless girlfriend. I had danced the crow and Alex had been the hurdy-gurdy man. The critics had been enthusiastic. Even Didelot had given it lukewarm praise, but the piece had been too gloomy to appeal to audiences.

'Move up, Marigold,' whispered Golly. 'I want to sit next to you, you ducky little thing.' She squeezed her ample bottom onto the divan and put her arm round my shoulder. This, of course, was for Sebastian's benefit.

Fritz leaned against the piano and began to sing, in a wonderfully expressive light baritone, the song of farewell to his love which begins the cycle. Fritz's expression became anguished as he bemoaned his youthfulness and the bouncing health that kept him from the grave. I thought how good looking he was if one ignored the prevailing fashion for thinness. His hair was a rich butter yellow, his eyes sapphire blue, his alabaster skin tinted with pink like the jelly we had just eaten. From time to time, Conrad looked up as he played, gazing at us with unseeing eyes, evidently in another world, of racing clouds, swirling snow and frozen rivers. I thought of Isobel, of her longing to be able to forget herself. Now she was sitting very still, her eyes half-closed, her mouth drooping. She seemed to have abandoned her flirtation with Sebastian. It had failed in its purpose – to arouse Conrad's jealousy.

Through the window I saw that the clouds had thinned enough to let one or two stars shine through. They seemed to swirl as I gazed, or perhaps it was the brandy. I was moved by the music, the beauty of the room, affection for my companions, the extraordinary turn my life had taken . . . being loved by Rafe . . . Golly's arm felt heavy on my shoulder, a great weight bearing down on my spine . . .

'Conrad plays the piano marvellously, doesn't he?' said Isobel as we drove home.

'He certainly does,' said Rafe. 'I'm not in the least musical, but I found I was actually quite enjoying it, though I've no idea what it was all about. *Sturm und Drang,* I suppose.'

'You were full of *Sturm und Drang* when you arrived, weren't you? I thought you were going to burst into tears just because someone scratched this awful old banger. I don't know why you don't buy a new car.'

'It goes. My self-consequence doesn't require me to drive around in something flashy. I know you like swanning about in Conrad's Bentley.'

'Scrooge!'

'Show off!'

These insults were exchanged with good humour.

'What annoys me most is having to do without the car for a day while they fix it. And I admit my self-image isn't resilient enough to withstand the dirty-white three-wheeler they lent me last time. Not only did I have to go to court in it, but I was going to dinner with the Howell-Joneses afterwards.'

Isobel giggled. 'And they really *are* snobs.'

'What's more,' he began to chuckle, 'it had *Ramsbottom's to the Rescue* emblazoned on the side.'

Brother and sister howled with laughter all the way down the hill.

'Are you all right, Marigold?' asked Rafe as we drove into Gaythwaite to catch the pub before it closed because Isobel wanted more cigarettes. 'You and Buster have been so quiet I forgot you were there.'

'I'm fine.'

'You had a lot to put up with this evening. I hadn't twigged before that Dame Gloria is a lesbian. If she'd been a man, of course, I'd have intervened to protect you, but somehow I didn't feel I could . . . It explains her clothes and her manners, anyway.'

'What a prejudiced old thing you are sometimes,' said Isobel. 'I've met some extremely pretty and well-dressed lesbians. High femmes aren't they called? Did you know there's a hanky code among lesbians? A pink hanky worn on the left means you like to wear a dildo – or is it the other way . . . ? Look! Isn't that Tom?' It was indeed my father, walking fast, as he always did, along the dimly lit pavement. 'Shall we say hello?' Isobel began to wind down her window.

'No, don't!' I said.

Marcia Dane walked across the road in front of us. She waved to my father to attract his attention and he waved back.

'Put your foot down and run her over,' said Isobel with unexpected savagery. 'We'll go to court and say you couldn't help it.'

For a moment I quite hoped he would and was ashamed of myself immediately afterwards.

'Apart from not wanting to spend the rest of my life in prison after you'd made a muff of it on the witness stand, I can't see that it would do much good,' Rafe said somewhat grimly.

'Oh, I know what you mean. Tom's the most disgraceful

womanizer,' said Isobel as we drove on, leaving them both behind. 'But it doesn't mean anything. He's just amusing himself.'

'It's not very amusing for my mother,' I said more sharply than I'd intended.

Isobel turned round to stare at me, her eyeballs flashing as we passed beneath the street lamps. 'But he's always gone back to her, hasn't he? I think she's lucky. Think how awful to be stuck with someone who comes home every night without fail to his slippers and television. No uncertainty, no excitement, no agony of jealousy, no thrilling reconciliation.'

'What rubbish you talk sometimes,' said Rafe. 'Marigold?'

'Yes?'

'I've just had a good idea. You must learn to drive. It'll cure you of your car phobia. Anyway, you can't live in the country and not be able to get about.'

Suddenly the brandy felt like a pool of poison in my stomach.

'I'll teach you myself,' he continued. 'When we were in Northern Ireland I taught a fellow officer to drive who was so terrified every time we passed a civilian he had to keep winding down the window to be sick. He was used to the protection of being in a tank.'

A hand crept through the gap between the front seats and took hold of mine. 'Poor Marigold!' Isobel said. 'You haven't made it sound exactly enticing.'

'Nonsense! Once she gets the hang of it she'll love it.'

30

'When I said straight across at the next roundabout I didn't mean literally!' Rafe dropped his head into his hands. Buster, who was sitting on the back seat sucking one of my old gloves, began to bark when he heard emotion in his master's voice.

'Sorry.' I fought back tears of fright and humiliation.

'I meant you to go *round* the roundabout and continue in the same direction!' Rafe spoke slowly and angrily as though talking to a particularly obtuse and uncooperative child. 'Honestly, Marigold! Sometimes I wonder . . . I'd better take over and try and reverse us off the bloody thing.'

He got out of the car and came round to the driver's side. I was so nervous by this stage that, as I sprang out, I left a shoe lodged between the pedals and put my stockinged foot up to the ankle-bone in the wet earth that had recently been planted with pansies.

Rafe squeezed behind the wheel and moved back the seat. 'Get in,' he said with unlover-like terseness.

I squelched round to the other side. Rafe put the car into reverse gear and revved gently. Nothing happened. He swore and pressed the accelerator more violently. The roar of the engine made Buster yelp hysterically. The car lurched suddenly then stopped and seemed to sink. I looked over my shoulder. Clods of mud were slithering down the rear windscreen.

I could hardly blame Rafe for being impatient with me. Who could have imagined that driving a car was so difficult? Each time he told me to change gear I became panic-stricken and forgot to steer. We had already been in collision with the stone pier of a bridge and I had begged to be allowed to return home. This had occurred early on, just after we turned out of the drive of Dumbola Lodge and when Rafe still had his temper in check.

By the time we had reached the outskirts of Gaythwaite, I was shaking so much that my hands and feet were scarcely able to obey the confused demands I made of them. The dreadful sound the car made when I had put the car into reverse instead of fourth, like a thousand fingernails being scraped down hundreds of blackboards, made Buster howl and me scream. Going downhill I had mistaken the accelerator for the brake and we had rushed headlong towards the beck. By wrenching the steering wheel to the left and pulling on the handbrake, Rafe managed to stop us shooting over the edge. When the roundabout came in sight, what remained of my wits had deserted me altogether.

'I'll have to get out and push,' Rafe snarled. 'Be quiet, Buster, for God's sake! Change places again, Marigold, and, when I tell you, put it into gear and press down the accelerator *very* slowly.'

I tottered round again on legs that trembled and got back behind the wheel. A gang of boys, who had stopped by the side of the road to watch, broke into piercing wolf-whistles.

'Ready?' Rafe shouted, leaning forward with his hands on the bonnet. 'Now *concentrate*. Foot on the clutch . . . reverse gear . . . clutch up slowly . . . accelerate . . . what? . . . oh, for heaven's *sake!* the pedal on the *right* . . . e-e-ow!' As the car leaped forward he flung himself sideways and vanished from sight.

'And just what d'you think you're playing at?' A face appeared at the open window. Buster darted forward like a striking cobra, seized the peak of the cap surmounting the face and snatched it from his hand. 'Here! Give me that!' cried the policeman

373

indignantly. I risked a perfectly good hand trying to wrest the cap from Buster who was savaging it on the back seat in a paroxysm of excitement. 'That there cap is public property, Miss, and if you can't control that animal I'll have to ask you to accompany me . . . Mr Preston! Are you all right, sir?'

'Yes. Thank you, Robson.' Rafe stood up, breathing hard. 'Buster! *Drop,* sir!' Buster let go of the cap as though it had been red-hot and sank his head on his paws. It was the first time he had obeyed a command, but now was not the moment to be jubilant. I picked up the cap, and handed it, somewhat the worse for teeth-marks and saliva, back to its owner. 'Sorry about all this,' said Rafe. 'I'm afraid we've made rather a mess of the flowerbeds. Naturally, I'll pay for the damage. And for your cap, of course. It might be quicker if I have a word with the relevant people. No need for you to concern yourself. If you wouldn't mind just giving us a shove . . . ?'

The policeman frowned. 'I'm afraid I'll have to ask the young lady to step out of the car, sir.'

By the time I had been breathalysed and we had had our licences and insurance papers examined, an interested crowd had gathered. While PC Robson made copious notes on the incident, six of the fittest spectators lifted the car back onto the road. Rafe drove us back to Dumbola Lodge in a silence I dared not break for fear of bursting into tears. A battered Land Rover was parked outside the front door.

'Who's that?' asked Rafe.

'It's Jode O'Shaunessy. He comes to help Dimpsie in the garden.'

'The tinker?'

'Yes.'

'I don't want to see him. I had to turn him off our land last year for unblocking earths the hunt had stopped.'

'He's awfully fond of animals. Besides, it's a mean thing to do, blocking up their escape. It doesn't give the poor things any sort of chance at all.'

'Mean or not, there's a tradition among landowners that we support the suppression of vermin.'

'Why are foxes vermin?' All the pent-up emotion of the last hideous hour threatened to burst out and I could not prevent my voice from wobbling. 'Why aren't people vermin, for that matter? We do far more harm with our wars and pollution and tortures and horrors than a poor innocent fox that just tries to keep alive in the only way it knows how . . .' A tear trickled down my face.

'You don't know what you're talking about.' He turned the car round and started back down the drive. 'We'll go to Shottestone for tea.'

'I don't *want* any tea!'

'Well, I do! For heaven's sake, if anyone has a right to be annoyed . . .' He broke off.

All the way to Shottestone, I stared unseeingly at a landscape blurred by tears as I tried to compose a speech of freezing politeness that would sever our relationship for ever. I was angry and sad and indignant and apologetic all at once. I was furious with him but at the same time I was broken-hearted . . . Dimpsie and Evelyn would be so disappointed . . . perhaps even Rafe when he had cooled down . . . when I thought of all the plans that had been made for the wedding I felt sick with guilt . . . Madame Merle, a French woman of terrifying chic, had already made the calico toile for my wedding dress . . . but our marriage would be a disaster, we thought differently about everything that was important . . . I loved him despite everything . . .

As we turned into the drive of Shottestone Manor, I tried to compose myself for the soul-shattering speech. Dear house! How beautiful it looked, with its gables and mullioned windows of weathered stone framed by clipped yew hedges. But Shottestone was Evelyn's, and I could never be anything but an inadequate understudy.

I felt a little better when I saw the Bentley parked outside the front door. We would have to wait until Conrad and Fritz

375

had gone before opening hostilities. Perhaps, after all, tea would be a good thing to bolster our strengths before the parting of the ways. I leapt out before Rafe had time to open my door and dashed into the house ahead of him. I saw in the hall mirror a distraught face with staring eyes and untidy hair. I combed the latter through with my fingers and fumbled in my bag for a lipstick.

'Hello, you two.' Isobel came into the hall, carrying a teapot. 'You're in luck. Mrs Capstick's made a cherry cake. You'd better tell her two more cups.'

'Where's Spendlove?' asked Rafe.

'He's looking after Daddy. He thinks he's taking part in the Royal Tournament. He's got Spendlove assembling an imaginary gun carriage on the nursery sofa. Conrad and Fritz are here.'

'So I saw,' said Rafe. 'All right, I'll go and tell her.'

He stalked off in the direction of the kitchen.

'How did the driving go?' asked Isobel, then, without waiting for an answer, 'We went antiquing yesterday. Conrad's bought some wonderful bits of porcelain. Come and see.'

'Ought he? I mean, if he's lost all his money, should he be buying things?'

'Don't be silly. A few thousand here and there isn't going to make any difference.'

Accustomed all my life to counting pence, I was impressed by this prodigality.

Conrad and Fritz stood up as I came in. The morning room looked at its most welcoming with a good fire burning, vases of white and purple double tulips on the desk and a scrumptious-looking cake covered with pink icing on the tray. I kissed Fritz on both cheeks. I would have kissed Conrad but the stool and the tea things were between us so we shook hands instead. They had been in London for the last two weeks so there had been no meetings in the woods.

'Thank you so much for supper the other day,' I said. I had

376

written a note of thanks immediately after it but it had seemed an inadequate expression of my profound gratitude.

Conrad bowed and said solemnly, 'Thank you for your letter.'

'Yes,' said Isobel before I could reply, 'it was an interesting evening. But afterwards I thought how *odd* it was that you and Sebastian hardly spoke to each other.' Isobel's face was a mask of innocence. 'After all, you worked together for all those years. You must know each other pretty well. So I came to the conclusion that there was some smouldering tension between you and the only reason I could think of was that you must have been lovers when you were both in London. Am I right?'

If Conrad had not been standing there I should have denied this categorically, but I was reluctant to expose myself to him as a barefaced liar.

'You were going to show me what you bought yesterday,' I said, with what I knew at once to be an unsuccessful attempt to look and sound unruffled.

Isobel smiled as though satisfied. She allowed a speaking silence to fall before saying, 'Conrad, do show Marigold that basket.'

Conrad unwrapped one of the packages to reveal an exquisite porcelain basket about ten inches long, which stood on a flower-encrusted stand beneath a lid decorated with twigs and petals and leaves.

'Isn't it lovely?' Isobel took it from him and held it out so I could examine it in detail. Each join in the piercing was marked by a small flower.

'It's fabulous!' I enthused. 'Oh, the joy of *things* when people are so difficult.'

'I do agree,' said Isobel, 'but what made you say that? Have you and Rafe had a row?'

I blushed up to my forehead.

Rafe came in and put two cups on the tray. With a face like thunder he shook hands with the two men, then sat in the chair furthest from the fire and began to flick through the pages of

Country Life. A miasma of rage seemed to shimmer round him. Conrad and Fritz exchanged glances.

Isobel raised her eyebrows and smiled. 'I don't know what you've been doing this afternoon but it seems to have involved a good roll in the mud. Rafe, if Mummy sees you sitting on her silk cushions in those filthy trousers, you're for it. And Marigold, your foot's black! Have you been potholing?'

Rafe scowled. 'Actually I've been teaching Marigold how to drive. But it seems that *some* people are constitutionally unsuited to be in charge of anything mechanical.'

I caught Conrad's eye. He gave me his unwinking stare but then his forehead puckered and his eyebrows lifted in the middle. I shook my head discreetly. I was certain that if he laughed Rafe would be very angry indeed. Conrad went to the window, turning his back to the room to look out at the garden.

'But how did you get so muddy?' Isobel persisted. 'Did you stop for a picnic?'

'Marigold tried to drive over a roundabout.' Rafe's tone was clipped. 'And of course we got stuck and I had to get out and . . . Well, I'm glad you think it's so funny.' He glared angrily at Conrad's back as he let out a strangulated sound poorly disguised as a cough.

'Oh, darling!' Isobel giggled. 'You must admit . . . a round-about . . .'

'Vat is it?' demanded Fritz. 'Marigold drives ze car *on* ze roundabout? *Das Rondell?*' He gave a hoot of laughter, then put his hand over his mouth.

I looked apologetically at Rafe. To my relief the stern set of his features softened. He smiled reluctantly, then started to laugh himself. Once he'd begun, he laughed harder than anyone. I expect it was the release of nervous tension.

'Oh . . . oh . . . oh!' cried Rafe, crossing his arms to hold his sides with tears in his eyes, 'and who should happen to come up just as I was flat on the ground but Police Constable Robson who I'd ticked off the other day for muddling his evidence in court. It'll be all over the county in hours. I shall never live it down. And Buster . . . his cap . . . Oh dear! ha, ha, ha!'

I was not at all offended to be laughed at. In fact it was decidedly pleasant after having been the object of Rafe's angry contempt. The more everyone laughed, the more I enjoyed the joke. I began to feel I had done something quite clever and original.

'You all seem in remarkably good spirits.' Evelyn brought in a blast of cold air from the hall. She was wearing a well-cut suit of chartreuse bouclé and a mink scarf. I would never achieve such elegance even if I devoted my whole life to the attempt. 'If you'd had *my* afternoon, you wouldn't be laughing. Two hours at the municipal pool – they call it a leisure centre these days but it still smells of lavatories – watching a lot of unattractive children doing something perfectly ridiculous called synchronized swimming. It seems to consist of getting into a ring, sticking one leg in the air and sinking beneath the surface. If they did it once they did it a *hun*dred times. As entertainment it was only just preferable to having sand rubbed in one's eyes. Marigold darling, ring for Spendlove, will you? I should like some tea . . . o-o-o-oh!'

I had been standing between Evelyn and the stool. As I moved towards the bell pull she let out a sound between a groan and a gasp, expressive of inordinate desire.

'It *can't* be! A First Period Dr Wall Worcester chestnut basket! Oh, let me look at it!'

Evelyn shoved Fritz aside without apology and dropped into a half crouch before it, caressing the twigs and flowers with reverent fingers.

'Conrad bought it,' said Isobel, her eyes alight with malice. 'Apparently it's extremely rare. The dealer said he'd only ever seen one in a museum. But we could always ask him to look out for another like it. You never know your luck.'

Evelyn looked up at Conrad. 'Where did you find it?'

'In a shop in Kensington Church Street. He gives it the date Seventeen sixty-five. Beautiful, isn't it?'

'Bea-u-tiful! Bea-*uti*ful!' Her voice, usually clipped, was mellowed by love. 'It's the *love*liest thing I've *ever* seen.'

Conrad nodded as though approving her judgement. 'I should be pleased if you would accept it as an expression of gratitude for the entertainment Fritz and I have received at Shottestone Manor.'

Evelyn's face, usually so pale and immobile, became the colour of bricks and her mouth worked like an old woman mumbling biscuits sopped in tea. I had never seen her so moved. 'Me? You don't mean . . . oh, it's *too* generous of you but I couldn't *possi*bly . . . such a valuable piece . . .' She shook her head. 'Of course I can't accept it.'

'In Bavaria it is considered a terrible insult to refuse a gift.'

Conrad looked so serious that I was sure he was making this up.

'Oh, really? Well, in that case . . .' Waves of colour flooded Evelyn's face. 'It's *too* wonderful . . . no one's ever given me anything so marvellous in my entire life . . .' Tears stood in her eyes.

'What about the needle case I embroidered when I was eight?' said Isobel. 'The one with the pink rabbit on it. You said that was the nicest present you'd ever had.'

'Conrad, I don't know *how* to thank you.' Evelyn rose and advanced upon him. He bent his head so she could kiss his cheek. 'So extraordinarily kind . . .' She picked up the chestnut basket with infinite care and cradled it against her chest. 'The *pièce de résistance* of the collection . . . I wonder, perhaps the pier table . . . ?' She drifted from the room as though stepping on air.

'Conrad!' Isobel was half amused, half annoyed. 'Tell me the truth! Did you mean to give it to Mummy all along?'

Conrad smiled and shook his head, which I took to be a refusal to reveal the workings of his mind rather than a denial.

'Honestly, that's quite the most shocking case of bribery I've ever come across.' She linked her arm through his and looked up into his face. 'How cynical you are! Everyone has their price according to you.'

Conrad picked up the hand she had placed on his arm and caressed the wrist that was decorated by a bracelet of diamonds and emeralds. As I had never seen it before, I had no doubt it was a present from him. 'I do your mother the justice to be certain that, had I offered her the monetary equivalent of the chestnut basket, she would have flung the notes in my face. Beauty she could not resist, however.'

'It's extremely generous of you,' said Rafe, standing up and jingling the coins in his pockets, with evident discomfiture. 'I'm not sure my father will approve . . . the value of the thing so far exceeds any hospitality . . . and your connection with our family makes it unnecessary—'

'Don't be pompous, darling,' Isobel interrupted. 'Conrad gives away ten times the cost of that basket every day to people he's never even met. Besides, poor Daddy's too gaga to object. And if you think you'd ever be able to persuade Mummy to give it up now she's got her claws on it, you evidently don't know her. A crocodile defending its babies would be a baa-lamb by comparison if you tried to take it away now.'

'Talking of rabbits,' I had been following my own train of thought, 'I want to ask you a great favour, Conrad.'

'Were we talking of rabbits?' Rafe looked bemused.

'Isobel mentioned a needle case she'd made embroidered with one.'

'So she did.' Rafe came to stand next to me and put one arm round my shoulder. His eyes, the colour of a cloudless sky with that fascinating distinct outline to the irises, were so full of affection that all ideas of breaking off our engagement melted away like lumps of lard in Mrs Peevis's blackened frying pans. 'How interestingly your mind works, my darling. I'm sure no one else picked up that little arrow. Certainly not the person it was aimed at.' He gave me a little squeeze and said in a low voice, 'Forgive me for being a brute this afternoon?'

381

'If you'll forgive me for making such a muff of things.' How delightful was the calm after the storm. I felt a resurgence of . . . was it love or gratitude? Probably both. 'I *am* constitutionally incapable, I'm afraid. But perhaps I needn't go out much. And when I do I could take taxis.'

'Oh, no, darling. You'll find it'll come after a while.' He beamed at me, impervious to the message in my beseeching eyes. 'Now what about pouring the tea?'

I looked at Isobel.

'Go ahead,' she shrugged. 'I've practically flown the coop. You're the one who'll assume the mantle of chestnut-basket dusting, eventually. I'm awfully glad. I should hate the responsibility.'

'Oh, well . . . perhaps we ought to give it back to you and Conrad when . . . later on.'

Isobel laughed. 'You mean when Mummy's dead. I hope you won't find yourself anticipating that event too eagerly.'

'Isobel!' Rafe frowned at her.

'Why shouldn't I say what's true? Mummy's a fiend to live with and you know it. Marigold'll be bossed about from first light until her head hits the pillow. And you won't stand up for her, will you, my dearest dear?' She looked up at her brother, her expression challenging.

Uneasiness percolated through the room.

'Please, I should like a piece of cake,' said Fritz. 'Ve haf a hasty lunch had at a not good restaurant.'

'Oh what an excellent idea,' I said quickly. 'Isobel, are you going to cut it?'

When she continued to stare at Rafe without replying, I picked up the knife and proceeded to hack it about rather in my agitation. No one could say that being with Isobel was dull. I poured the tea and handed round cups.

'Marigold, you wished me to do something for you?' said Conrad.

'Oh, yes. You know the terrace below the drawing room that

382

leads off the kitchen – the one overgrown with grass. You said you didn't want to use chemicals to spray the weeds because of the birds, but you thought it looked untidy—'

'I know the one,' replied Conrad gravely.

'Well, my poor rabbit's been housebound for months ever since I got here and he badly needs fresh air. I bring him handfuls of grass every day but it isn't the same as tugging it up for himself. We've got a fox living at the bottom of the garden so it's no use making a pen or anything.'

'You've got a rabbit?' Isobel looked incredulous. 'But Marigold, what on earth for? I had some once, do you remember? A dead loss, really. They just sat in their hutch and moped and got diarrhoea periodically from eating too much lettuce. And they needed cleaning out about every five minutes.'

'Yes, I remember. The black one was called Fred and the white one was called Ginger. That puzzled me for ages but I didn't like to ask why. I thought they were adorable, so gentle and soft.'

'Adorable perhaps, but hopeless as pets. What can you do with a rabbit? You can't ride it or train it or take it for walks. We gave them away in the end. You cried for days when I told you Jebb had wrung their necks and Mrs Capstick had put them in a pie.'

The memory returned sharply though I had not thought of it for years – the pain of imagining those two much-loved little creatures struggling helplessly in the horny hands of Jebb, the Preston gardener in those days, a gruff-voiced tattooed ex-prisoner whom I had hated and feared . . . I felt tears well.

'For heaven's sake.' Isobel was inconveniently eagle-eyed as always. 'You're not going to cry *now*? I was teasing you, you fathead. Of *course* Mummy wouldn't have let Jebb wring their necks! She gave them to Mrs Capstick's niece.'

'I knew that.' It was a lie. I hadn't known. I felt a slight but welcome diminution of the burden of sadness I carried always with me on behalf of the vulnerable and mistreated, human and animal.

'Marigold's rabbit is not adorable in the least,' said Conrad. 'He is a limb of Satan who likes the sweet young flesh of infants—'

Our eyes met and I saw in them a flash of awareness that he had put his foot in it before he turned to look out at the garden again.

'How do you know?' Isobel stared at the back of his head.

'I've already bored Conrad with a description of Siggy's very bad habits,' I said.

I was confident that Conrad would guess I intended to save him from the necessity of lying as he was always so fussed about the need to be transparent and speak pure truths and so on. My soul was already deep-dyed in deceit so a little more tinkering with the facts wouldn't matter much.

'I'm so glad you like animals, darling,' said Rafe as we took Buster for a run in the garden after tea. 'It's another thing we have in common. I couldn't imagine life without dogs and horses.'

A soft mist was rising from the damp lawns and paths as the air grew moist with impending rain. Sweeping down to the elaborate stone fountain in the rose garden was a hedge of double pink hawthorn, the tiny flowers like iced gems, a kind of biscuit Isobel and I had once had a passion for but which Evelyn had disapproved of. She considered all cakes, biscuits and jams bought from a shop to be vulgar.

'I do like animals but I don't know much about them. I've always been too busy to have a cat or a dog.'

'Well, that's going to change now. You'll have plenty of time to look after them. When you aren't looking after our children, that is.' He took my hand and tucked it under his arm. 'I hope we'll have six, at least.'

'Six!' I expect I sounded as horrified as I felt. My response was automatic. Babies were nearly always bad news for dancers.

He said, with a little pique in his tone, 'You want children, surely?'

384

'Well, I suppose . . . eventually.'

'Darling.' He stopped, put one arm round me and lifted my chin so I had to look straight into his eyes. 'You're not having second thoughts, are you?'

Speak! I urged myself. Tell him you're fonder of him than of any man on earth but even that isn't enough. Tell him you want to dance. I looked into his face, saw his forehead pleated in perplexity, remembered his fragile self-confidence, Dimpsie's happiness, Evelyn's happiness.

'I thought perhaps *you* were. Having second thoughts,' was the best I could do, and hated myself for my weakness. 'I'm so stupid about so many things. I'll never be able to run the house as well as Evelyn does. The garden will go to pot, I'll offend all the local big cheeses, my flower arrangements will give rise to scandal and my dress sense will be the subject of letters to the *Northumbrian Gazette*. And I shall never learn to drive.'

'Oh, sweetheart, you make me feel so guilty! Tomorrow I'll book you some lessons with a qualified driving instructor. I'm thoroughly ashamed of myself for losing my temper. You're such a sweet forgiving soul that I'm inclined to take advantage of you. Oh darling,' he held me tighter until my nose was buried in his jersey, which smelt deliciously of *Roger et Gallet* and Buster. 'I don't deserve you, I know. If you did have second thoughts I'd have no grounds for complaint. I'm taking your marvellous youth and adorable innocence and spoiling it with a second-hand love—'

I fought my way out of the jersey. 'Second-hand? What do you mean?'

'Oh, ah! . . . what *do* I mean?' He gazed into the mid-distance over my head. 'I suppose, the fact is that you aren't my first love . . . and you ought to be—'

'Oh, never mind about that!' I said quickly, with a rush of guilt as I remembered that I still had not told him about Sebastian and all those others who had cynically availed themselves of my adorable innocence.

Experience had taught me that the hearts of men (Sebastian's excepted) were softened immediately after sex, so I had decided to undeceive Rafe the next time we were in bed together. But here circumstances had conspired against me, as they seemed only too ready to do. Rafe did not feel relaxed about making love at Shottestone, which I completely understood. Kingsley had taken to wandering all over the house at odd hours in order to make sure none of the rooms was missing. If any of the doors was locked he rattled the handle and bellowed in distress. He had already upset Mrs Capstick by getting into bed with her at two in the morning.

I don't think Dimpsie would have minded in the least if we had slept together at Dumbola Lodge, but neither my little boat bed nor Kate's bus would have accommodated Rafe's large frame. A few days ago he had booked a room for the night at the only decent hotel within twenty miles, to find that the receptionist was the wife of one of the tenant farmers. Our waitress, the daughter of Banks the builder, had practically curtsied when Rafe walked into the dining room. Rafe and I had had what was nearly a row over the soup and roast lamb. I had said I did not mind anyone knowing that we had slept together before getting married and that most people would assume we had anyway. Rafe said that it was important that the estate workers looked up to me. I had said I'd prefer them to like me. Rafe had said I was being childish and I had become indignant. The unpleasantness was not helped by having to pretend, each time the waitress brought the breadbasket or topped up our glasses, that we were having a lovely time.

I hate rows so I had given in before pudding and apologized. After dinner we had tried to find another hotel. Rafe, who was miles fussier than me, had rejected them all as being 'impossible', so we had ended up having what would pass for sex in anatomical terms in the back of the car. The experience had been cold and uncomfortable and thoroughly unromantic, good only for taking the edge from the frustration Rafe said he was feeling. It had not seemed the right moment to tell him that I had bartered my body for my career.

'I honestly don't mind about the women in your past,' I said, 'as long as they stay past. I don't think I'd like to share.'

'Coo-ee!' Isobel was standing on the terrace, calling down to us. 'Conrad, Fritz and I are going to the Castle for dinner. Want to come?'

'No, thanks,' Rafe shouted back. 'Marigold's had enough of cars for today. We'll have something here.'

'All right. Tootle-pip.' She blew a kiss and went indoors.

'With them it's a hectic round of gaiety,' he said, staring after her. 'It makes one wonder if they actually enjoy just being together.' He glanced down at me. 'I'm glad you're not the sort of girl who wants to go out every evening.' I smiled agreement, though in fact I had just been thinking that I would have liked to have gone to the Castle with them. 'You're looking cold. We must go in.' He fastened the buttons of my coat protectively and we began to walk back to the house. 'What were we talking about?'

'I can't remember.'

'I can. I was telling you that you're a wonderful girl and you make me the happiest of men.' He kissed me again and looked at me expectantly.

'Mm. You make me happy too.'

So there we were, our love affirmed, our troth replighted with renewed exchanges of confidence, yet not two hours ago I had decided that, whatever the cost to our mothers and to ourselves, I must break off our engagement. Life among sensible, properly grown-up people was utterly baffling, I decided. It was evident that I was unfit to dwell among them.

'Am I allowed to see what you're painting?' I asked as he held open the conservatory door.

'If you like.' He turned the easel round. 'Yet another view of the hills, I'm afraid. I've taken a leaf out of Monet's book and I'm doing a series of the same prospect to explore the effect

387

of light and shadow from dawn to dusk. This morning the sun was sending shafts through the clouds like beams of enlightenment from on high.'

I examined the watercolour. It was lovely but bleak: blues, greys, browns and shades of white. It struck me as odd that the brilliant fresh greens in which the countryside was clothed these days had made no appearance. Was this because Rafe's inner landscape was bleak? Was he telling the truth when he said I made him the happiest of men? Was I in fact not the only practised liar within our small circle?

31

'Hello. Lovely day, isn't it?' I said briskly, when Jode came into the kitchen the following morning.

I was not surprised to see him at Dumbola Lodge at this early hour. I had been kept awake long into the night by shrill cries and moans from Dimpsie and the occasional bass groan of ecstasy. Finally I had tied two pillows to my head with a scarf, but poor Siggy, whose grey velvet ears were of the upright variety, had been condemned to eavesdrop.

'Can I help you find anything?' I asked, seeing him looking around in a vague embarrassed way.

''Tis a bottle for Harrison Ford I'm after making. He's in bed with Dimpsie.' Then a slow purple tide rose from inside his shirt collar to his eyebrows.

'I'll put the kettle on. Can I make you some breakfast? Bacon and eggs?'

'Thank ye but I don't eat meat. 'Tis my intention not to cause pain to any living creature so long as I may live.' He looked severe.

'I do agree! But it's so hard to live in the way you know you ought,' I said, perhaps a little gushingly. 'I always find myself weakly giving in to temptation, don't you?'

'No. I can't say that I do.'

*   *   *

'He made this solemn vow while he was in prison,' explained Dimpsie. She, Harrison Ford and I were enjoying the warmth of the kitchen while, outside in the driving rain, Jode double-dug the last segment of the garden that had not already been subject to his excavations. Now and again, through the misted panes, I saw clumps of earth fly past as he prepared the brassica bed. He had explained the importance of crop rotation and I had hung onto his every word for fear that this scarred giant might take it into his head to beat it into me. There was about him an aura of violence that made me fearful for my mother.

'He was in prison?'

'He nearly strangled his wife's lover. Luckily when he saw the man's face turn blue he came to his senses and let go. Jode has terrifically high principles but he was goaded beyond bearing. Also in those days he drank. The boyfriend pressed charges and Jode spent eighteen months inside for assault. His wife put Nan into care and ran away to Spain with her lover. That was ten years ago. He left Ireland and came to live here. Since then he hasn't touched alcohol, tobacco or animal flesh, or raised his voice in anger.'

'He's a model of good behaviour. I feel the terrible burden of my wickedness in his presence.'

Dimpsie beamed. 'It's inspiring, isn't it? He's so hard-working and self-disciplined and responsible. And kind. Last night he insisted on washing up the supper things while I rested on the sofa in the sitting room because he thought I looked a little tired. After a bit I came and dried up because I was getting bored on my own. It was as I was reaching up to put away some plates and he took them from me that we kissed for the first time.' Twinkly stars appeared in Dimpsie's eyes as she recalled the scene. 'Then we couldn't stop and I dragged him upstairs to my room and into my bed.'

I began to get a little fearful at this point, for Dimpsie enjoyed talking about the details of sex more than I did. 'How lovely for you both. Look, Harrison Ford's falling asleep.' Dimpsie removed the rubber teat from the baby's milky lips and shifted her arm slightly so that his head could flop back against her shoulder. Tiny veins like navy silk threads straggled lids that drooped over eyes as blue as the sea on a summer's day. His head was covered with pale yellow down.

'He's such a darling,' Dimpsie said fondly.

'And very handsome.' This was true. Not every baby would look good dressed in woollen coat and leggings of a hideous shade of salmon trimmed with ox-blood red crochet.

'Jode is so gentle with him. He has the most wonderfully sensitive hands.' Dimpsie took a deep breath and let it out slowly as she looked reflective. 'When he touches you it's like being brushed by swansdown. Every nerve-ending comes alive. I can feel my skin rippling beneath his fingers. Every part of me sings with pleasure—'

'Oh, good.' I stood up. 'That's excellent. Perhaps I ought to wash up the breakfast things. "He that is filthy, let him be filthy still," as it says in the Bible, apparently. The rector quoted it in his sermon last week. I've no idea what he was talking about as my brain had pretty well shut down by then and I was wondering what we were going to have for lunch, but that little sentence struck my ear unkindly.'

'I never knew before what a sensuous organ the ear is.' Dimpsie's eyes became dewy. 'Your father has never once in twenty-five years of marriage licked my ears.'

'I'll just give Siggy these crusts. I don't like the way he's eyeing Harrison Ford's toes.'

'It just shows that fidelity isn't everything it's cracked up to be. I always believed Tom was a good lover because he told me he was. But actually it isn't true. I had simply no idea what I was missing.'

'Oh, you're such a fussy rabbit! All right, I'll put a little Marmite on them.'

'Do you realize last night was my first proper orgasm? I used to get excited with your father but he'd always had his before mine came to anything.'

'He doesn't seem to like Marmite this morning. I know, there's some fish-paste in the fridge.'

'I must have been a worm-hearted fool to put up with being treated so badly for all those years. All that misery, the loneliness, my self-confidence shrinking to non-existence . . . the *tort*ures of jealousy . . . Well, I've seen the light. Last night was the most wonderful experience I've ever had – apart from you children, of course but that's quite different – and I shall expect nothing less from now on. No more taps on the shoulder just as I'm drifting off to sleep, hauling up of nightdresses, plunging straight in without so much as a kiss, a few thrusts before dropping like a ton weight—'

'*No!*' I may have spoken rather sharply. I turned from the open fridge door with a jar of *Porter's Pilchard Pâté 'Paradise in a Pot'* in my hand to see Dimpsie's eyebrows raised in surprise. 'Absolutely not. That is . . . you mustn't swap one kind of slavery for another. Sex isn't everything.' I warmed to my theme as Dimpsie looked disbelieving. 'I really do believe it's rubbish that women need a man to be happy. Women need a proper job to do which gives them a sense of self-worth and achievement – the freedom to make mistakes and learn from them and do it better next time, whether it's being a ballerina or a fishmonger.' Absent-mindedly I stuck my finger in the jar and licked it, then shuddered. If this was Paradise in a Pot give me Purgatory in a Pitcher, Hell in a . . . I couldn't think of a vessel that began with H. Luckily I was not a slogan writer. 'Much more important than sex, there's thinking and experimenting and creating and achieving. We've got the vote and equality in the workplace and all that but still women are doing most of the housework and laundry and looking after the children. I do agree Jode is an exception, but the majority of men would rather live in a slum and let the children tumble up anyhow than take the trouble. I say to hell with men!'

392

'But darling,' Dimpsie looked troubled, 'have you forgotten you're engaged to be married to one?'

'Come in, petal.' Mrs Peevis eased her bulk into the old moquette-covered armchair which was propped on bricks so she could stir things on the stove without getting up. Her feet rested on a stack of the *Encyclopaedia Britannica*. A grease-caked saucepan shot out a jet of steam that filled the Singing Swan kitchen with the smell of mouldy hay. 'Yer late but it doosn't matter. There's ernly been one customer aal day.'

It was just after two o'clock, and I was still glowing from an extra hard work-out in the study. Usually I did my lunchtime exercises in the hall because there was a largeish mirror there but, as it was within earshot of the kitchen and Jode was lunching at Dumbola Lodge, accompanied by Harrison Ford, Petula the Magpie and Nell the sheepdog, I had moved to the study in case he and my mother should feel moved by the presence of so much animate nature to indulge in ear-licking or other biological urges. Also there was Siggy to be considered. He thought himself above such company and had made himself a nest in my father's chair and closed his marvellous marmalade eyes in disgust.

'Sorry.'

'Tha's the shop bell.' She put the frying pan over a flame. 'See if ye can persuade them te tek a bite o' blood puddin'. Aa've a half a ring tha'll be off by temorrow.'

I put on my apron and went into the café. A man, a woman and two children were on the point of going out again.

'Good afternoon,' I said cheerily, 'can I help you?'

'No, thank you,' said the woman coldly. 'We've decided not to stop . . .' She threw a contemptuous glance at the tables draped with plastic tablecloths that curled up at the edges like so many miniature pagodas, on which stood lamps with shades speckled like thrush eggs with fly droppings, and ginger-beer bottles in which bundles of dried flowers listed to port or starboard.

The man looked me up and down. 'Oh, I don't know, Maisie.' He walked back into the room and smiled at me with all his teeth. 'You were just saying how desperate you were for a cuppa.' He winked at me, turning away his head so that his wife could not see.

'Tea? Certainly. What would the children like?'

'Coca-Cola,' said the little boy promptly.

'You'll have milk,' said his mother sourly as she flipped with her scarf at the crumbs and smears of butter on her seat. She sat down, her nose wrinkled and nostrils flared. I wondered if she could smell the bleach Mrs Peevis was always pouring down the lav in a vain attempt to get the brown stains off the bowl.

'Could I tempt you to a little black pudding?'

'Black pudding?' echoed the woman in amazement.

'Likely it's a local kind of cake,' suggested the man. 'We're from the South,' he explained in a friendly way. 'It's our first visit up North.'

'Lovely scenery, isn't it?' I said conversationally.

'Not the only thing that's lovely,' he muttered with another covert wink. 'I'll try some black pudding if you recommend it.'

'With chips and red cabbage?' I smiled to conceal my embarrassment at this strange offering.

'E-uch!' said the woman. 'You're joking, I *do* hope.'

The man looked less than enthusiastic. 'Well . . . if you really think . . .'

'Don't be silly, Bert!' said his wife, handing me the ashtray to take away before wiping her fingers fastidiously on a paper handkerchief. 'You've only just had lunch. We'll have four scones –' she pronounced it to rhyme with thrones – 'with strawberry preserve. Children, go and wash your hands. Chips indeed! At twenty-five-past two in the afternoon.'

She looked at me with frank dislike. I walked gracefully into the kitchen then, as soon as the door swung shut behind me, I threw off my apron and put on my coat. 'Put the kettle on,' I said. 'I'm going to Belinda's Buns for scones.'

394

'No blood puddin'?' said Mrs Peevis in disappointed tones to my departing back. 'Looks like yer in luck, Jelly.' Jelly was Mrs Peevis's cat, a friendly tabby shaped like a zeppelin.

I zoomed down the street and over the road to the bakery and managed to buy the last four scones. Belinda herself was serving. Her generous figure had given rise to many quips in connection with the shop's name.

'These scones are stale,' said Maisie when I brought them breathlessly to the table.

'Made this morning,' I lied for the second time in half an hour, thought of Conrad, banished him from my mind. I was well aware that Belinda made batches of scones once a month, then froze and unfroze them at frequent intervals according to her wild calculations of demand, which had given them the texture of Harrison Ford's matinée coats.

'And this is jam, not preserve.'

'I didn't know there was a difference.' This rare moment of truth was immediately undone. 'It's homemade.' Actually the Singing Swan jam came from an enormous tin from which I had earlier fished out three dead flies and a quantity of Jelly's hairs. It had dyed the plastic spoon a sinister dark purple.

'Mum, we couldn't flush the toilet and there wasn't any paper,' said the little boy returning to the table. 'Someone's had diarrhoea in there. It stinks!'

'Oh dear, how horrible!' I said. 'I *am* sorry.'

Mrs Peevis was always complaining that her digestive system was giving trouble – what she called 'the skittors' – no doubt because she ate her own food. I had a terrible vision of ex-customers crouching in agony in lavatories throughout West Northumberland. Perhaps there were people lying in hospital wards taking tearful leave of their families . . . research scientists examining unheard-of bacteria under microscopes . . .

'We saw a big mouse,' said the little girl.

'Don't be a looby,' said the little boy, 'it was a rat.'

'That does it!' Maisie spat out her mouthful of scone and

stood up, glaring at her husband. 'You can stay and ogle that girl, who I dare say isn't a bit better than she should be, but me and the children are leaving. She looked at me. 'I'm reporting you to the environmental health inspector.'

'Sorry about that.' Bert grimaced apologetically and put two pound coins on the table. 'I thought the scones were A1.'

I allowed him to pat my bottom without protest because he had had so little return for his money.

Mrs Peevis's mouth drooped as I recounted the disaster. I spared her none of the details because I had a plan.

'If tha' bloomin' health man cooms round agin, Aa'm for it.' Her rust-coloured eyes filled with tears.

'Mrs Peevis,' I said. 'I think I may be able to help. But you must promise to do exactly as I say and not argue with me because we haven't much time. I'm quite sure that beastly woman will be as good as her word. She's the sort that's only happy when high on a cloud of righteous indignation.'

'On a what, pet?' Mrs Peevis looked confused.

'Never mind,' I said, and went to turn the notice on the door to CLOSED before beginning to outline my scheme.

Nan sat down at the Dumbola Lodge kitchen table and slumped wearily forward, her chin propped on one hand. There were dark circles under her lovely grey eyes and her hair hung in limp hanks. 'Who'da t'ought hairdressin'd be worse t'an school? Bossed about from mornin' till night, sweepin' floors, washin' basins, and now me skin's had an allorgic reaction to t'e perms and dyes. Look!' She displayed her hands that were covered with pink weals. ''Tis ever so sore.'

'Couldn't you wear gloves?' suggested Dimpsie. She was giving Harrison Ford his bottle. Nan had said she was that flaked out she'd rather not. Though she had not seen her baby for two days, she had given him only the briefest of glances before embarking on the tale of her own woes. I did not condemn her for this, nor, I'm sure, did Dimpsie. At sixteen

Nan was only a child herself and it was evident that her spirits were depressed.

'I'm allorgic to latex,' said Nan glumly. 'T'e woman who owns t'e salon, Miss Diane, she's as hard as nails. She was always tellin' me I'd have to smarten op. I'd like to see *her* look somet'in' on five pound a week and livin' in a caravan and all where t'ere ent nowhere to hang yor clothes.' Poor Nan did look rather untidy in a fake leopard-skin coat that had large bald patches. The heels of her boots were scuffed down to the white plastic. 'Someone told Miss Diane me dad was a tinker. T'at's why she didn't like me.'

'People are so full of ridiculous prejudices,' said Dimpsie kindly. 'I know how it hurts. I've often been looked down on because I don't dress and behave like the stereotypical doctor's wife.'

Nan looked surprised. 'But you talk posh and you live in a big house.'

'Not by some standards.' Dimpsie smiled. 'Anyway, you mustn't take it to heart, Nan. All that matters is that you should work hard and do unto others as you would be done by and be true to your gods. You must set your own goals and try to live up to them—'

'Is t'at real?' Nan interrupted, looking at my engagement ring.

'Yes.' I slipped the big square diamond from my finger and held it out to her to try on. 'Do you like it?'

'It's beautiful.' It looked sadly incongruous on her thin reddened hand. Her face grew yet more mournful. 'If Rhett woulda married me I'd've had a ring like it.'

'Rhett?'

'Harrison Ford's dad.'

'Surely that couldn't be his real name?'

'The only Rhett I've ever heard of is Rhett Butler from *Gone with the Wind*,' said Dimpsie.

'That's right,' said Nan. 'He called me Scarlett. Said it was

397

more romantic than Nan. But I think his name really is Rhett because I cried when I was telling him I thought I'd fallen for a baby and he gave me his hanky and there was an R sewn on one corner.'

'How many times did you meet him, dear?' asked Dimpsie in a gentle tone.

'I donnaw, six or seven times. The first time he took me to a pub for lunch. The other times he brought a bottle of bubbly wiv him.' She looked resentfully at Harrison Ford who was dropping asleep in Dimpsie's plump, freckled arms. ''Twasn't much, was it, for a lifetime of being stock wiv a baby?'

'He won't always be a baby,' I pointed out.

'Did he visit you at the caravan?' asked Dimpsie.

'Naw. We used to meet in the old pele tower on Waterbury hill. I was up there one day havin' a fag, Dad goes mad if he catches me smokin'. I like it up there. There's a white rose that grows round de door that's ever so pretty. Rhett came walkin' his dog. He said I looked like a queen in among the roses and we got talkin'. Then we kissed.' Nan giggled. Evidently it was a happy memory in a rather sad life. 'Upstairs in the tower there's a bed. Really romantic it is, wiv a wooden bit over the top and blue curtains hangin' down. Someone's swept it out and put sheets and all, a bit cobwebby but wit' real lace. Rhett said he thought one of the shepherds had a lass and he didn't see why we shouldn't make use of it.' She giggled again and her pretty little face became enchanting. 'He said it was a nest for lovers everywhere.'

The pele tower. Rafe had gone upstairs while I waited below, unable to follow because my leg was in plaster. I remembered the sound of his footsteps on the floorboards as he had walked up and down, up and down. Then we had gone outside and someone had taken a shot at us. Could that have been Jode? Not a shot to kill – that would have been inconsistent with his avowed pacifism, but perhaps to warn? It wasn't the first time a dreadful suspicion had sidled into my thoughts like an unwelcome visitor.

Before I had always firmly shown it the door, but while Nan was talking it crept back in and took up permanent residence.

'Here's your ring, Marigold.' Nan put it into my hand. 'When's the happy day?'

'Not till September. It seems silly really to wait that long. I mean, if one's going to do the thing one may as well do it at once. But there's a lot to organize.'

'And it shows people you aren't in a rush to marry because there's a babby on the way,' said Nan, with surprising worldly wisdom. 'I'll stand in the churchyard and watch you come out in all your finery and chock confetti, shall I?'

'I very much hope you and your father will be guests at the wedding,' said Dimpsie. I caught her eye and she looked, for her, quite stern, as though reading some protest in mine. Here she wronged me, for my objection to having Jode and Nan at my wedding had nothing to do with snobbery.

'Eh?' said Nan in amazement. 'Dad and me at a grand weddin'? But we don't have t'e clothes! And what would people say if t'ey found t'emselves kneelin' in chorch next to a tinker and a tinker's brat?'

'In the sight of God we are all equal,' said Dimpsie sententiously. 'Though of course even in church no one believes that for a moment, such is the beastliness of human nature. Marigold and I would be delighted if you'd both come, wouldn't we, darling?'

She looked at me and kicked my leg under the table.

'Of course,' I said. 'Nan, how would you like to be a waitress?'

32

'Good morning, Marigold.' Conrad was crouching with his back to me in the far corner of the hermit's cave. He was busy with a trowel and did not turn round.

'How did you know it was me?'

'How did you know it was *I,* surely?'

'Oh, all right. How *did* you know?'

'The footsteps were light, obviously female, and quick, obviously someone young. And you put down your toe first like a dancer.'

'Gosh! Really?' I was impressed by this display of Holmesian detection.

'Not really. I knew it was you because you are the only person besides myself who does not fear the terrible drop into the abyss. Fritz has tried it once but had to be blindfolded for the return journey. Golly and Isobel, when brought to the brink, have refused altogether.

'What a shame. And it's so lovely.' I sat on the mossy rock and breathed in the delicious damp, sparkling air. The sun transformed the droplets of water into brilliants. In front of me was a table, neatly constructed, with rustic poles for legs and planks of wood for a top.

'How did you manage to get this here?'

He glanced over his shoulder. 'I brought it in pieces and assembled it in situ of course.'

'You mean you made it yourself?'

'And why should I not be able to hit a nail with a hammer? You would have me not only dining on roast birds of paradise but fanned by eunuchs and bathed in unguents by women of the seraglio.' He stood up and turned round, arching his back to ease the muscles. 'Pour the coffee, will you? My hands, as you see, are dirty.' He displayed palms thick with cement.

On the table were two thermos flasks and two cups. I poured coffee from one flask and added hot milk from the other.

'What's in this basket?'

'Breakfast. Help yourself.'

I unfolded the napkin inside the basket. The round dimpled cakes, sprinkled with icing sugar, were still warm. I bit into one eagerly. It was like a doughnut, light and sweet with apricot jam in the middle.

'I wonder, do you think Fritz would give me the recipe? I'm planning a dietary revolution in Gaythwaite.'

As I ate the doughnut and drank the strong sweet coffee, I told Conrad about the Singing Swan. He had just returned from a week in Bavaria, so he knew nothing about the letter from the divisional environmental health officer that had flopped like an exhausted bird of ill omen onto Mrs Peevis's doormat several days after the visit of Maisie and Bert. Conrad gave my story his full attention and seemed to find Mrs Peevis and Dale and the customers amusing, which encouraged me to exaggerate the ghastliness of my experiences just a little. Conrad laughed as much as I could have wished.

'I expect you think I'm crazy to even think of trying to make a go of it.'

'Crazy?' He took up a cloth to wipe his hands and came to sit next to me at the table. 'No, I think you are bored.'

'Not at all! I'm fond of Mrs Peevis and she's so worried about money and her hips are bad and it seems a shame to miss a good opportunity. We're all to get a share of the profits if there are any. Dimpsie and I are practically beggars, you know. I can say that now because you aren't rich any more so you can't possibly think I'm asking you for money.'

Conrad gave me one of his speciality looks. Opaque, I think is the word. I found myself saying, with unwonted truthfulness, 'All right, I *am* bored. But only because I'm used to working hard and always having something to work *for*. Dancing was my life. I hardly even thought about anything else and of course I miss it. Naturally once I'm married to Rafe I shan't be bored at all. There'll be a thousand and one things to do. Evelyn's going to teach me how to run the house and how to garden. And there'll be committees and good causes galore. She took me to a WI meeting the other day. That's a sort of society of country women, supposed to promote tolerance and fellowship. Evelyn's the chairman of the Northumberland Federation and she does the rounds of the various branches. I could see at once that they all hate and fear her. Part of the evening's entertainment consists of a lecture, and this time it was about arboretums, given by a friend of Evelyn's. That's trees, you know.'

'Thank you, yes. It is the same word.'

'Is it really? Well, anyway, the man giving the talk was rather grand and he used a lot of Latin names and everyone yawned and fidgeted. Except Evelyn who was taking notes in a furious scribble. He said that every garden, however small, ought to have a plantation of oaks. Then we had tea and Evelyn made a sharp little speech to the effect that UHT milk and Mr Kipling's Viennese Whirls were not in the spirit of the founding ethos of the Women's Institute. There was a lot of muttering and dark looks and one woman, perhaps the organizer of the refreshments, went away in tears.'

'I can hardly believe she was allowed this autocracy.'

'Oh, I know *you've* never been frightened of her. And, of course, after giving her that chestnut basket you could spit in her eye and she'd go on adoring you. We're all getting sick of her singing your praises.'

Conrad looked satisfied, even a little smug. 'Go on about the society. Evelyn is a woman among millions.'

'Well, then the minutes were read – only it seemed like hours, they were so dull – and Evelyn judged the jars of marmalade. She told them she would send the recipe her own cook uses as the results were superior. After that, we departed to a chorus of barely restrained boos and hisses. Honestly you may laugh,' Conrad took full advantage of my invitation, 'but it was agony being so unpopular.'

'So,' he said when he had finished laughing, 'you expect that your energies will be fully absorbed by such entertainments? After the newness wears off you will be bored and annoyed and as out of place as a leopard in a basket by the fire. You must be very much in love to make this sacrifice.'

I looked away, out to the sky that was turning a delicious shade of blue as the sun rose higher. 'Yes, I am.'

Conrad made a clicking noise with his tongue to express impatience. 'The more I think of it, the more criminal it seems. To throw away rare talent and hard-won achievement for any cause, even for something worthwhile – to cure diseases or to relieve ignorance or poverty – I doubt the rightness of it. But merely to act a part according to an inflexible set of tribal rules that serve only to maintain the artificial barriers of a pernicious class system, that seems to me the height of stupidity.'

This plain-speaking stung.

'I love Rafe and I want to make him happy. Isn't it better to think more about other people's happiness than your own?'

'I do not say anything against you marrying Rafe, but why must you give up dancing? Cannot you combine the two things?'

'It's quite impossible. Besides, you don't know if I have *any* talent, let alone a rare one.'

'Sebastian said you had the capability to become first-rate.'

403

'Did he? Did he really?' I felt excited. Whatever his short-comings as a lover, I had the greatest respect for Sebastian's judgement in matters balletic. 'He never told me that.'

'He is not the kind of man to give bargaining power to his dancers, I imagine.'

'No.' The euphoria was fading fast. 'Anyway, it's too late. Come to that, Golly said you could have become a professional pianist.'

'Perhaps, yes. But I do not have the temperament. One must give up so much of one's life. Practice, practice, practice. And then travelling all the time at the wink and shout of concert engagements.'

'Beck and call, we say.'

Conrad looked annoyed and I realized that, though he considered it necessary to correct me, he did not like the favour returned. 'As I was saying, the necessity for a performing artist to dedicate himself to that one thing alone would not suit me. Besides, there are so many truly fine pianists who compete for the few seats on the platform. There is no need for another one.'

'But can you really be happy not making the attempt?'

'Really I can.' He looked me squarely in the face to convince me he was speaking the truth. We were so close that I could see the light from the mouth of the cave reflected in each lustrous eye as a tiny silver triangle. 'My intention is to write. A writer may live in the world; he may read, observe, reflect, experiment, without obstruction to his work. Everything is water to his mill. No, I remember, you say gristle.' He frowned. 'Peculiar though it sounds.' I remained tactfully silent. 'I have a collection of short stories that are to be published in Germany this autumn. Soon I shall begin a novel.'

'You *are* a dark horse. Why didn't you say? About the short stories, I mean.'

'A dark horse? That means?'

'You're always telling me I ought to be more truthful.'

'I have not lied. I *never* lie.'

404

'You fibbed to Sebastian about Golly liking me so much.'

'Not at all. She does like you.'

'But not as much as you made out. Now Rafe's convinced she's gay.'

'Of course she is.' I must have looked startled for he added, 'But you need not be alarmed. Golly has too much sense to expose herself to rejection and ridicule by pursuing a girl less than half her own age.'

'I really had no idea. All right, I admit you didn't exactly lie about the stories, you just kept quiet about them. But you said we all ought to be transparent. I think you're one of the least transparent people I ever met. I can't tell what you're thinking at all. With most people you can tell when they're cross or embarrassed or putting on a good face, however hard they try to hide it, but not you. That's what a dark horse is.'

He permitted himself a small smile and I saw that he was not displeased by the sobriquet.

'Tu, was ich dir sage, und nicht, was ich selber tue.'*

I liked hearing him speak German. His voice became deeper and softer and less inflected than when he spoke English. It reminded me how unlike we were in every way – in nationality, race, education and experience. These differences intensified for me the elusive and mysterious side of his character that were such an important part of his fascination.

'What does that mean?'

'You have jam on your cheek.'

He took a clean handkerchief from his coat pocket and gave it to me. I wiped my face quickly. I had quite a pile of hand-kerchiefs at home, waiting to be laundered.

'We have strayed from the point. Now I have swollen your head with praise, do you not reconsider the abandonment of your career?'

'But even if I danced day and night without stopping except

*Do what I say, not what I do.

405

to put on new pairs of pointe shoes, I might not succeed. You've no idea how difficult it is. So much depends on luck as well as hard work—'

'You might not succeed but you will have tried! It is offered to you to experience the sublime in realizing the near perfection of your art!' He raised his voice and lifted his finger in admonition and looked so like the statue of Prudence on the bridge that, had I dared, I might have giggled. 'And for *what* do you throw all this away? To sit by the hearth and contemplate the pride of your position, your possessions, your fading beauty, as you squander the rest of your life in idleness?' He made an obvious effort to control his irritation by pressing his lips together and scowling until he was able to assume an expression of smiling contempt. 'But no doubt there is an irrefutable argument to explain this seeming imbecility. Please unfold it. I should *so* like to be enlightened."

'Oh, Conrad, I hate it when you get sarcastic. I *much* prefer you angry. If you really want to know it's because Rafe needs me. Until recently so did my mother, but that seems to have sorted itself out. I know this is going to sound conceited but *he* says I encourage him to hope that he'll get over the awfulness of that business in Ireland. It was so horrible for him and he still gets headaches and nightmares. He told me that before I came back he had ideas of killing himself.' I looked at Conrad's face still twisted into an expression that somehow managed to combine polite attention and savagery. 'I sort of cheer him up,' I concluded lamely.

Conrad sighed and turned his head so that I saw his nose in splendid profile. You could have cut cheese with it. 'What a little fool you are!' he said quietly, almost as though he was speaking to one of the sheep.

'Well, dammit!' I said indignantly. 'I call that incredibly rude!'

'Yes.' His expression of pained superiority vanished as he laughed. 'So it is. I apologize.'

'Oh, that's all right. But surely you can see I'm morally obliged

406

not to be selfish.' I could not prevent a note of interrogation creeping into my voice. 'Aren't I?'

Conrad winced. 'Aren't I? I are? Am I not? is better. As for sacrificing yourself for his happiness, it is common knowledge that the debtor, after the first flush of gratitude, comes swiftly to resent the creditor. So it is with less mercenary obligations. Gifts should be reciprocal.'

'I know what you mean. But Rafe's giving me so much that really the boot's on the other foot.'

Conrad looked down at my running shoes. 'The boot?' He subjected me to a brief but stern gaze then spread his hands and twitched his lips as though there was no more to be said on that subject. 'Meanwhile, until you become a leader of polite society, you are going to be a cook.'

'I won't be cooking. I'm hopeless at it. Anyway, it's to be a tea shop. Just sandwiches and cakes. My mother's boyfriend's going to make them. He's an excellent cook. In fact, there isn't anything he can't do. Apart from reading and writing. He didn't go to school because his parents were travellers and they moved all the time, but I think he must be a clever man.'

'You approve her choice, then?'

'Dimpsie's happier than I ever remember her being. My father treated her so badly but in spite of everything she adored him. Why should anyone want to be badly treated, I wonder?'

'Psychologists would say it reinforces the conviction of worthlessness. But also that some women find it exciting to be subjugated sexually. Most women have rape fantasies, apparently.'

'No! Do they really? How odd! My fantasy would be that they'd offer me something nice to eat and a good night's sleep instead.'

Conrad looked down at his hands and reapplied the cloth to his fingernails. 'Is one permitted to ask about Sebastian Lenoir in this context?'

'You mean did I have a rape fantasy? Good God, no! I hated it. I told you before, I did it because I wanted to dance the best parts.' When Conrad didn't say anything but continued to scrub away at his cuticles, I said, 'Don't you believe me? Was it *so* shocking and immoral?'

'Not at all. I merely wished to be sure. Ambition is much healthier than a complex of inferiority. And what is morality when reduced to its essence but the avoidance of the infliction of pain on others? You gave Sebastian no pain.' He smiled. 'On the contrary. It was tenacious of you. And tenacity is perhaps the quality most valuable in life.'

'Do you really think so?'

'Don't you?'

'I don't know. I'd like to believe it. Then everyone would have a chance of success, regardless of brains or talent or luck.'

'Of course those things will have a bearing, but they can be nothing without perseverance.'

'In that case the Singing Swan ought to be a triumph.'

Tenacity and perseverance had certainly been much in evidence there. Jode was the spearhead of activity. In seven days he had whitewashed the walls of the restaurant, kitchen and lavatory and cleaned the ovens and gas rings until they dazzled. Dimpsie had worked hard, too, making new tablecloths out of a roll of green-and-white gingham she had found in the back room of the craft shop. I had scrubbed the furniture. Even Nan was keen to be a waitress now that Dimpsie had made her a pretty dress to wear by remodelling an old one of mine.

'I hope it will be. Have another cake.'

'I'd adore one but I'm trying to get back into peak condition.' I saw a mocking look in his eye that told me he was going to ask what for, so I said quickly, 'It's just because I feel better when I'm really fit. What are you doing with the trowel?'

'I am making places to hold earth to plant the ferns.'

'Aren't you going to get a gardener?'

'Are you offering yourself?'

'Oh, no! I don't know anything about it. But I wouldn't have thought you'd like to do that sort of thing, that's all. Nothing to do with birds of paradise. Just that I thought you were too intellectual.'

'There you are mistaken. The study of botany requires brain. I am interested in the propagation of ferns. They reproduce by spores instead of by seed. When the spore germinates it produces leaf-like structures called prothallii containing both male and female sexual organs . . .'

Conrad gave me a three-minute lecture on the life cycle of the hardy fern and I listened gratefully. Not that I expected to do much fern propagation in the near future, but I thought it was nice of him to bother.

'How interesting,' I said when he seemed to pause. 'And how do the ferns know this is what they're meant to do? What makes things want to reproduce themselves?'

'To put it simply, it is a genetic instruction. Every living cell contains genetic material – we call it DNA . . .'

I listened attentively but I had to admit that genetic encoding was probably one of those things, like the workings of the internal combustion engine, that would never stick in my brain however many times it was explained to me.

'. . . the difficulty comes when we try to ascertain how species evolve, given that it would be necessary for one complete breeding pair to take the step simultaneously.' Conrad looked hard at me. I assumed what I hoped was an expression not often called for on the stage, one of terrific mental acuity. 'However, that would be at the risk of boring you.'

'Oh, no! I'm not in the least bored.' This was true. I had been thoroughly enjoying the explanation. I liked being in the hermit's cell, listening to Conrad's voice while new words and concepts swirled in my brain like melting snowflakes.

'Besides enjoying to do things for myself,' Conrad concluded, 'I shall not employ a gardener because I find I am even poorer than I thought. It seems that Uncle Charles forgot to take account of the vagaries of the weather. Not only the tornado

409

in the Mid-West but the severe drought in Australia has affected our investments adversely.'

'I *am* sorry.'

Conrad waved his hands, dismissing my concern. 'Markets are bound to fluctuate, otherwise there would be no profits. If we are careful for the next year or so we shall see a recovery. For myself I enjoy some lean living now and then. There are disadvantages to being a rich man, you know.'

'I can't think of any. Except, I suppose people want to borrow money from you all the time.'

'There is that. But Uncle Charles taught me from the beginning to insist that every request, however small, is expressed in writing and submitted to the Trust's solicitor. That puts off a great many would-be borrowers. No, what is worse for the rich man is that one is obliged constantly to doubt oneself. A prince can never know if his pronouncements are wise or his sketches accomplished. People fawn over a rich man as they do over rank. Unless one is a great fool one must constantly ask oneself, "What do I amount to apart from my rank or my fortune?" It is of vital importance to discover and it is easier to do so when one faces the buffets of life as does the poor man. But Fritz will be desolated if we have to give up the Bentley.'

And his desolation will be nothing to Isobel's, I thought but naturally did not say. 'You won't have to sell Hindleep?' The idea struck me as extremely disagreeable.

'Not yet. But I have ordered the builders to cease work. And I have cancelled the installation of the telephone.'

'I suppose that's inconvenient, but I think it's part of Hindleep's charm that it's cut off from the world. How lucky that you've finished the kitchen and the bathrooms and there's hot water and electricity. You'll be quite comfortable, anyway.'

'It is, as you say, lucky.' Conrad shot me a quick glance then gave his attention to cleaning the mortar from the trowel. 'What are you reading now?' I had told Conrad some time ago about my programme of self-education and he was inclined

410

to be critical of the hundred books on the list as being too dry for the autodidact, as he called me. I hoped it was not something insulting.

'I only got as far as page two hundred and fifty with *Ulysses*. Yesterday I began *The Faerie Queene* by Edmund Spenser. I think I might get on better with that. What do you think "pricking on the plain" means? Why are you laughing? Is it something obscene?'

'No, no. It means riding, spurring his horse. But I laugh because that is the first line of the first canto and it is such a very long poem. Poor Marigold, it is as though you are a kitten trying to bring down a gazelle.' I was not offended by this patronizing comment. There was no point in getting huffy with Conrad because he so obviously meant his criticisms for one's own good. Besides, I acknowledged that the simile was apt. 'Why do you not read something that you could enjoy easily, like a modern novel?'

'I've so much catching up to do, that's the trouble. Intellectually, I mean.'

'Intellectual powers would seem to be superfluous for intimidating other women, which according to you will be your role as the future Mrs Preston.'

'It isn't for them. It's for me.' I put my elbow on the table and leaned my chin on my hand. 'What on earth am I going to think about while I'm judging jams?' Then I remembered that, not many minutes ago, I had stubbornly rejected the suggestion that my new life might have elements of tedium.

The moment the words were out of my mouth Conrad seized on them as I had known he would. 'And yet you persist in saying that you make this sacrifice willingly and happily. Were I Rafe, I should be seriously worried that I might not be able to atone.'

'That would be awful. But I really don't think Rafe's going to feel burdened by a millstone of gratitude because he has no idea what I'm giving up to marry him. He isn't at all interested in ballet.'

'In this case, don't you think there may be grounds for incompatibility?'

The church clock struck half past the hour. I sprang up. 'I must go. Thank you so much for the coffee and the heavenly doughnuts.'

Conrad murmured, as if talking to himself, '*Was hat es, daß es so hoch aufspringt, mein Hertz?*'*

'What did you say?'

'I say you must hurry or you will be late.'

*'What is there about her that makes my heart leap so?' GOETHE

33

'Anyone would think you *wanted* that ruffian to seduce your mother,' said Rafe in a tone that was almost angry as we sped towards Carlisle to see a performance of *Separate Tables* by Terence Rattigan. 'By getting them both involved in that squalid little café you're practically throwing them into each other's arms.'

'It's much less squalid now,' I said pacifically. 'Honestly, it looks quite inviting. We've taken down the neon sign that said EATS AND TREATS and Jode's painted a beautiful new one. He's very artistic in a neat sort of way. Being interested in the visual arts is something he and Dimpsie have got in common and it's so nice for her.'

I did not say that the other thing Jode and Dimpsie had in common was a consuming appetite for sex at all hours and in all places. When duties to the café, the craft shop and Harrison Ford permitted, they took themselves off to any nook or cranny that offered and bolted themselves in, to emerge later with red faces and tousled hair. No one could have objected to this. They were discreet about their departures and refrained from public displays of affection. Apart from the occasional strangled moan they were as quiet as mice.

'And that nephew of Mrs Peevis's is a bad lot,' Rafe continued

413

as though he hadn't heard me. 'He's been up before the bench for receiving electrical goods. It was a first offence so he got off with a fine, but I thought he was a nasty piece of work.'

I couldn't disagree with him. Dale had an ingratiating manner, but the bold lechery in his eyes made me dislike being alone with him in the kitchen. He spent much more time with 'Auntie Edna' these days, dropping in at the Singing Swan at all hours to persuade her to increase the size of her flutters on the gee-gees, now the place was in a fair way to becoming a tidy little earner. If you disregarded his greasy hair, which he was always combing over the teacups, and a nose covered with blackheads, Dale had the looks of a second-rate film star in a third-rate gangster movie. He spread a roguish smirk over his oily countenance whenever he spoke to Nan, who responded with sniffs, flounces and tart remarks to show him she could not be taken in by men's wiles. But her large grey eyes followed him everywhere and it must have been as obvious to him as it was to me that she was far from indifferent.

'I don't like him but I can't help him being Mrs Peevis's nephew.'

'Why won't you let me make you an allowance?' Rafe put his foot on the accelerator and I closed my eyes to shut out the headlights of cars and lorries that rushed pell-mell towards us. 'I must confess I find your refusal hurtful.'

'Do you? I'm so sorry. I had no intention of hurting you. It's the very last thing I want to do.'

'Can't you see that it seems like a rejection? As though you can't bear to be under any kind of obligation to me. People who love each other ought to exchange sympathy and counsel and every sort of good fortune, spiritual and material, without even thinking about it. A marriage is a repository for the common good of the two people involved. I *want* to look after you, to give you everything I have in the world. And I hope you want to look after me. Because if not—'

'Oh Rafe. Of *course* I do.' I put my hand on his knee to

reassure him. 'Really, you shouldn't see it as a rejection. It's just that I'm so conscious of how much you've already given me, you and Evelyn, and I seem to have so little to give in return.'

'I wish I could make you see that what you give me is far above pounds, shillings and pence. Beauty, tenderness, companionship, someone to love wholly and openly and honestly . . . I can look the world in the face as long as I have you beside me. Let me take care of you now, as I mean to do for the rest of our lives.'

I always found Rafe's rare moments of demonstrativeness tremendously touching. 'Of course I will if that's what you really want.'

'Thank you, darling.' He took his hand from the wheel to clasp mine. I bit my tongue to stop myself yelling at him to put both hands on the steering wheel. 'I'll get on to Armstrong in the morning.' Armstrong was his bank manager. 'To be frank I'm hugely relieved. I've hated the idea of you skivvying at that ghastly place with those awful people. Working at the surgery's a different matter. The family connection makes that perfectly respectable. But if I'm allowed to express a preference, I'd like you to tell your father to find someone else as soon as possible.'

I had not perfectly understood that an agreement to give up work was a constituent part of accepting the allowance. Actually, there was much to be said in favour of resigning from my job at the surgery. My relationship with my father had deteriorated to the point where we spoke only when we absolutely had to, not always managing to prevent some exchanges of the hissing and spitting kind. Though the patients and Nurses Bunker and Keppel seemed to find our spats exciting, it was probably not good for the efficiency of the place.

Working at the Singing Swan, however, was fun. I was going to miss the challenges and the sense of achievement, even if it came from something as mundane as defrosting the freezer. The bottom six inches of ices and snowfrutes had thawed so often they had formed multicoloured layers like the geological cross section of the Continental crust in my school atlas. But Rafe could not object to me visiting my mother at the Singing Swan, so long as I abstained from menial tasks unbecoming to the future mistress of Shottestone. He was not buying me outright for his sole use. Immediately I was ashamed of this rebellious thought, which seemed petty and ungrateful.

'All right, I'll tell him. But I'll have to stay until they find another receptionist.'

'Of course.'

Rafe squeezed my hand, then let it go. Keeping my eyes closed, I began to breathe more easily now I could imagine those strong brown fingers firmly on the wheel at ten to two as Mr Lugg, my driving instructor, had demonstrated a few hours earlier. I heard Rafe humming as he often did when he was pleased about something.

'*Some talk of Alexander an-nd some of He-er-cu-u-les,*' he sang.

I was sorry to have given him pain, and for a while I felt quite cheered by the idea of marriage as an investment of good things from which we both could draw strength and inspiration. Then I started wondering again about my own contribution to this nuptial fund. Beauty? Though others raved about the colour of my hair I didn't particularly like it, and I always thought myself too small and thin to be beautiful . . . but anyway, whatever pretension I might have to good looks, they could not last. Tenderness and companionship: I hoped I would be adequate to the task. It occurred to me that so far all I had put into the conjugal pool was a willingness to give things up.

'*Of Hector and Lysander an-nd such great m-en a-s these.*'

Satisfaction radiated from him. He had got what he wanted. The Prestons almost invariably triumphed. They practised a kind of tyranny through benevolence that left the tyrannized feeling grateful, even as they bent their necks beneath the yoke . . . I accused myself of disloyalty and reminded myself how much I owed them. Only a few days ago Evelyn had given me a set of

416

garden tools for my own use. They had wooden handles and shining stainless-steel blades and prongs. Evelyn said they were the very best sort and would last me all my life. She had cut short my thanks with, 'If it isn't raining on Saturday we'll get going on the tulip border. You can be here by ten, can't you, darling? Don't worry, I'll tell you exactly what to do . . .'

'How did the driving lesson go?'

'Oh,' I felt a stab of guilt because Rafe was paying for my lessons, 'not awfully well, I'm afraid. I ran into the back of a caravan. Luckily no one was injured. And Mr Lugg says the driving school's insurance will pay for the new bumper. After that Mr Lugg said he didn't think I'd be much cop, as he put it, after the shock, so he drove me home. It wasn't a very good beginning.'

'Poor sweet.' Rafe patted my knee kindly. 'All that matters is that you weren't hurt.' Here were the dividends from that investment of mutual sympathy. 'Caravans provoke dangerous driving – either they're ridiculously slow or so fast they get blown over.'

'This one was parked. I don't think I'm ever going to be much cop. I simply can't persuade myself not to shut my eyes whenever I see something alarming. Perhaps I might learn to ride a bicycle, or even better a tricycle—'

'Don't be silly, darling. You don't want to be a figure of fun. You'll conquer your fear with a little practice, I promise you.'

I was thankful he was not annoyed. In fact he was the soul of sweet reasonableness for the rest of the evening. Until we got home, that is.

In the theatre he took my – Bobbie's – coat to the cloakroom, bought me a programme and steered me to my seat with a firm grip on my arm. Perhaps he thought I might miss my footing and somersault over the edge of the grand tier into the stalls below. When the lights went down for the first act I felt a terrible pang of regret that I was not on stage myself, but soon managed to lose myself in the drama which was about the

417

loneliness of the human condition. In the interval we went to the crush bar which was appropriately packed. Somehow Rafe managed to procure champagne and an ice for me while everyone else was complaining about the queues; he found a table near an open window so we were cooled by a refreshing breeze. Gracefully he acknowledged the greetings of people he knew, which seemed to be almost everybody. I encountered speculative glances wherever I looked and knew myself to be an object of curiosity. I shook hands and thanked for compliments, laughed at witticisms and accepted invitations. It was a relief to be ushered back to my seat by Rafe before he departed for the lavatory.

I entertained myself in his absence by looking at the audience. I recognized Lady Pruefoy's helmet of white hair in the box to the right of the proscenium arch. In the left-hand box I was surprised to see Conrad and Fritz, with Isobel sitting between them. Fritz was looking down into the empty orchestra pit and Conrad was reading his programme. Isobel put her hand on Conrad's arm and whispered something in his ear. He replied briefly and resumed his reading. Isobel gave a petulant shake of her shoulders and slumped in her chair, pouting. I saw that she was unhappy and that Conrad was the cause.

I wondered what could be wrong. Conrad was not unkind to her, in public anyway. He was not assiduous with his attentions like Rafe, but neither was he neglectful. He was a good host, providing food, wine, music, warmth, comfort, even breakfast, all of a high order. He did these things with a detached, almost negligent air, but he noticed if your cup was empty or you were cold or in need of a handkerchief. He could be critical, and sometimes harsh, but surely Isobel was a match for him? When he was in a certain mood those black eyes teased maliciously. They seemed to ask to be amused, at your expense if necessary, but Isobel would hate a compliant husband. On the other hand she was used to being petted. In the old days she had always had a string of suitors who submitted humbly to her caprices and hung on her every word. Conrad never showed the least inclination to do this. Sometimes he was cool to the point of indifference. Usually he was unromantically cheerful.

Isobel's expression grew sulkier. Conrad closed his programme, folded his arms and ran his eyes over the auditorium in a bored sort of way. With his extraordinary physical beauty he made the rest of the men in the audience look colourless and uninteresting. I hoped he would notice me but he seemed to look everywhere but in my direction . . . suddenly I knew with absolute certainty that Conrad and Isobel must be prevented from marrying. They would not make each other happy.

The strength of this conviction made my heart race and a most uncomfortable sick feeling gripped my internal organs, as though I had eaten something that disagreed with me. Rafe was the only person who had any influence with Isobel. I must make him see as a matter of urgency that their engagement was a mistake. Just as he came back to his seat, the lights went down and the curtain rose. Throughout the second act, though I registered the comedy and the poignancy of the play, the disturbing undercurrent of anxiety remained. We stayed in our seats for the next interval as I was incapable of eating or drinking another mouthful.

'Isobel and Conrad and Fritz are here.' I pointed to the box.

'Oh yes. Isobel said they were getting tickets. She asked if we wanted to join them but a box only holds four and as Conrad insists on taking Fritz everywhere . . . anyway, I'd much rather just be with you, darling.'

I was touched by the warm look that accompanied this remark. Rafe was an angel and I ought to be ready to give up anything and everything to make him happy.

'Besides,' he went on to say, rather spoiling it, 'it would have meant having supper at the Castle and there might have been awkwardness about who was picking up the tab. It's an expensive place, but on the other hand I've no wish to be Conrad's

419

pensioner.' While he was talking, Rafe acknowledged waves and salutations from other members of the audience.

'I suppose everyone's here because there isn't really much to do in the evening in the country,' I suggested. 'Apart from dinner parties and you can't have those very often for fear of getting fed up with the same old people. Perhaps we ought to join a spiritualist society or a Zen poetry group so we could get to know a different sort.'

Rafe assumed the expression he reserved for my more absurd remarks, one eyebrow raised and the other drawn down, nostrils arched. 'I hope you're not suggesting an evening spent in my company would be so dull you'd rather spend it with a bunch of crackpots speaking in tongues and wearing hand-knitted underclothes? Surely you've had enough of the Bohemian way of life? From what I saw of Sebastian Lenoir he didn't look like the sort of man who would make a girl happy for very long. Charming, of course, but I'd have said an absolute bastard.'

He looked at me very directly then, without smiling, and I read in his eyes a question.

I dropped my eyes under his gaze and fidgeted with the battered red plush on the arm of my seat. 'Rafe, I'm worried about Isobel. I'm not sure she's going to be happy married to Conrad.'

Rafe glanced across the auditorium. Isobel, prompted by that uncanny sense that tells you when you are being stared at, looked in our direction, waved and then pointed us out to Conrad and Fritz. Fritz smiled and Conrad lifted a hand in acknowledgement. Isobel said something to Fritz and laughed. Suddenly she seemed to be enjoying herself. Conrad tore a sheet of paper from his programme and began to fold it into smaller pieces.

'She looks all right to me,' Rafe said with brotherly uncondern. 'Anyway, she wouldn't take kindly to interference. There's the archdeacon.' He pointed along the row. 'I wonder what he makes of this play? I never met anyone so convinced of being perpetually in the right. Human nature must be a mystery to him.'

420

Something white flew from Conrad and Isobel's box in a wide arc over the auditorium. It came to rest on the padded top of the balcony only three seats away from where we were sitting. I leaned forward and saw a man brush it to the floor with his elbow, without noticing it.

'Isn't that your father?' Rafe was looking down into the stalls so he did not see the paper dart. 'Third row from the front. No one else, apart from you, could have hair that colour.'

Though I could not see Tom's face, I recognized not only the flaming head but also his ears and the set of his shoulders. Marcia Dane was sitting next to him. As we watched she put her arm round his neck and leaned towards him. He lifted his shoulder and leaned a little away from her. A slight movement but it spoke volumes.

Rafe took my hand discreetly in his. 'It looks as though Miss Dane's rule is nearly over, darling. I know how angry you are with him but, if your father's return is going to make Dimpsie rejoice, I think you ought to put a good face on it and pretend to rejoice too, for her sake. Perhaps next week we'd better ask him to Shottestone for drinks. I know you won't enjoy it but it'll reassure him that he's going to be welcomed back into the fold.'

I squeezed his hand. 'I honestly think it's probably too late for both of them, but it's nice of you to care.'

'Of course I care. Even if you weren't so important to me, I've always been fond of Dimpsie. She's eccentric, of course, but so obviously on the side of the angels.'

I reproached myself for having accused him in my heart of caring too much about appearances. 'I'm not sure I deserve you,' I said solemnly.

'What nonsense . . . sssh! The curtain's about to go up.'

34

'Wasn't it odd seeing Ronald Dunderave and Bunty together?' I said as we drove back afterwards. 'What a hopeless mismatch!'

We had run into them in the foyer as we were leaving the theatre. As soon as Bunty saw Rafe, her entire face and neck had reddened, but she had made a gallant effort to talk about the play. Then she had asked me about my leg and, with a yet deeper blush that made her eyes glitter, how the wedding plans were going. Ronald had tried to persuade Rafe to join a club of which he, Ronald, was secretary, called the Oenophiles.

'I'm pretty busy at the moment,' said Rafe.

Ronald looked at me for the first time. 'Oh, yes, of course.' He wrinkled his upper lip showing rabbity teeth. Only Siggy's were miles more attractive. He muttered something to Rafe in an undertone. I heard, '. . . Mustn't let it take you over entirely, old man . . . like good wine . . . pleasures of the flesh . . . occasional abstinence, you know?'

The accompanying grin, as he ran the side of his hand along his parting to smooth his pale, crinkly hair, was annoying. I felt nothing but the purest sympathy for Bunty as she said goodbye with a brave smile that quivered at the corners of her mouth.

'I'd have thought it quite a good match,' said Rafe. 'Neither's a candidate for Mensa and she's got enough money to keep the Dunderave property from falling down for another generation or two, besides adding her own property to the pile.'

'She's so sweet-natured,' I protested, 'and he's quite horrible. She deserves much better.'

'She isn't pretty, she dresses like a governess, and her only accomplishments are riding to hounds and delivering pups. Ronald's about as high as she ought to look.'

I felt for Bunty when I heard this cold appraisal. 'Doesn't goodness, kindness of heart, sincerity, that sort of thing . . . count for anything?'

'You can't make a decent marriage out of a warm bath of sentiment.'

I liked Rafe least when he was in one of his realistic moods. Doubts about my own qualifications for marriage, never far away, resurfaced. 'I don't see why Bunty's so much to be despised. I'm incapable of even getting onto a horse and I don't give much for the pups' chances. Most self-respecting governesses would turn up their noses at my clothes and I haven't even got any money to make up. Only an overdraft of five hundred pounds.'

'I'll tell Armstrong to get rid of your overdraft. No, it's all right, don't fuss,' as I started to protest, 'there's no point in you paying interest on it. And you can stop fishing for compliments. You know quite well you're an extremely beautiful girl. No man in his senses would require anything more. And particularly tonight in that charming dress. Is it new?'

'I've worn it once before.' Actually it was the cream silk dress I had bought with his money for our engagement party, but I wasn't offended. I knew all men, unless they were gay, were hopeless about remembering one's clothes.

'Well, I'd very much like to take it off you. Damn! We ought to have stayed the night at the Majestic. Why didn't I think of it?'

'When we tried it before you said you couldn't stand pokey

windowless bathrooms made out of corners of bedrooms. Or butter in packets at breakfast . . .'

'I remember. It was appalling. All right then, let's slip up to my room. My mother's out somewhere.'

'Ought we to? Evelyn wouldn't like it . . . and there's your father . . .'

'I'm thirty-two and I don't need my mother's approval. Besides, she'll never know. As for my father, we've started sedating him at night. I don't like to do it, but it's the only way any of us can get any sleep. Don't you want me to make love to you?'

'Oh, yes, of course I do.'

The hall at Shottestone was peaceful, the lights turned low. It smelt deliciously of beeswax polish and flowers. On the table beside a bowl of white freesias was a tray laid with glasses, a decanter of brandy, a soda siphon and a plate of tiny sand-wiches. Rafe went to get Buster from the kitchen while I took the tray into the morning room where the fire was still smoul-dering behind a guard. Buster greeted me as though he had been marooned for several years on a desert island with only a coconut for company. Rafe stirred the embers into flames and poured us both a drink. I sipped mine dutifully. I did not like brandy but I hoped it might get me in the mood.

Sex with Rafe was quite different from my previous carnal assignments. Past lovers had been intent on their own satisfac-tion and I could have been a warmed corpse without lessening what pleasure they got out of it, but Rafe required full partici-pation. He was talkative, asking me what I liked and where I liked it and I had to keep my mind alert to prevent any slip-up that might indicate prior hands-on experience. This was not conducive to 'letting myself go', which was what Rafe was always telling me to do. He was a very managing lover. Once he reached the peak of excitement he fairly barked out instructions. You could tell he must have been an excellent officer. Luckily I had once been taken to see a pornographic film in Paris when we were dancing at the *Opéra Garnier*. I had taken note of the

424

actress's tortuous writhings and shrieks as she enjoyed wave upon wave of stratospheric orgasms, so I felt reasonably confident about my performance.

'Darling, put that sandwich down and come and sit next to me.'

The sandwich was potted shrimp and watercress and perfectly delicious, but obediently I laid it aside and went to sit beside him on the sofa. 'God, I want you!' he murmured, pulling me towards him and kissing each eye and then my nose. We kissed for some time and I tried, not entirely successfully, to forget my half-eaten sandwich. Probably I would be able to cram it in on my way upstairs . . .

'Darling!' Rafe was attempting to undo the tiny silk-covered buttons that ran from my neck to my waist. 'How frustrating these are—'

'No, no! Those are just for decoration. There's a zip at the back. But Evelyn might come in.'

'All right. I must just kiss those gorgeous warm little breasts and then we'll go up and *drown* ourselves in lust.'

He had just pulled the zip far enough down to insert a hand through the gap and undo my bra when the door opened and in came Kingsley.

'Hello, hello, hel*lo!*' he said with a return of his bluff manner that had been notably absent during these last weeks.

'Christ!' said Rafe.

Kingsley was wearing one of Evelyn's dressing gowns – I assumed it was hers because it was pale pink satin with lace ruffles – and on his head was one of those old-fashioned bathing caps covered with rubber flowers.

'So sorry to keep you waiting.' He strode over to me, hand extended. 'How do you do? I'm Kingsley Preston. And you must be Miss Julie Andrews. I can't tell you how much I've enjoyed your work. *My Fair Lady*, what a show!'

'Thank you.' It was inexpressibly painful to see Kingsley like this. I knew it must be much worse for Rafe and I tried desperately to think of something to say that might show him that I felt for both of them in this awful situation.

'Father.' Rafe stood up and grasped his arm. 'You're not well. You must go back to bed.'

'Nonsense, my boy. Never felt better, never felt better! Besides, Miss Andrews has come all this way just to see me.' He put his hands on his hips and stood, legs apart, smiling at me. The dressing gown fell slightly open to reveal a wrinkled yellowish stomach and something purplish below, from which I averted my eyes. 'But you're smaller than I expected. And not as hairy. I don't know why you English girls have to strip every hair from your body. Underarm hair, dark and springy and smelling a little of sweat, that's what *I* like. Those Egyptian women, great forest of black hair all the way down to their knees some of 'em—'

'Kingsley!' Evelyn stood in the doorway, stripping off her gloves. She looked thoroughly self-possessed. 'You're making an exhibition of yourself.'

At the sound of her voice, Kingsley straightened his back and gave her a fairly snappy salute which made the rubber flowers on his hat wobble. 'Preston, Major, Northumberland Fusiliers.'

Evelyn went to the fireplace and pulled the bell rope. 'You must go to bed at once.'

'Bed? But I'm having fun! I request to be set at liberty on parole according to the terms of the Geneva Convention.'

'You're not in the army now. You're at home. Go upstairs and I'll send Spendlove up to put you to bed.'

'Home?' Kingsley looked around him. 'Am I?' His face fell into the lines of troubled bewilderment that had become habitual with him. 'Then who are you? And where's Nanny Sparkles?'

'Nanny Sparkles would be cross if she knew you were refusing to go to bed.'

'Oh, all right. I suppose I'd better then.' He gave me a faltering smile, then shuffled slowly out of the room.

'Go and see to him, would you?' Evelyn said to Rafe. 'Give

426

him another dose of Somnolenza. And find out what's happened to that old fool Spendlove. So sorry you had to see that, darling,' Evelyn said to me when Rafe had gone. 'Poor Kingsley. So tragic . . .' She gave me a brittle smile that failed to transmit to her eyes. 'We must all be very, very patient and try to remember the man he was.'

'Of course,' I said. 'I don't mind for me at all. Only for him.'

'There's a sweet girl. It's such a comfort that you're a member of the family now.' She took off her coat and flung it over the arm of a chair. 'I confess, darling, it wasn't what I'd planned, but when I realized Rafe's mind was quite made up . . . We've always understood each other, Marigold, haven't we? You know I've always thought of you as my own daughter, practically.'

'You've always been tremendously kind to me and I'm very grateful.'

'That's all right then. Pour me a large drink, will you? I'm fagged. Such a dull party.'

I did as I was told, keeping my unzipped back turned away from her, hoping she wouldn't notice the odd shape the unhooked bra gave my frontage. But it seemed her preoccupying emotion that night was irritation. She lit a cigarette and sipped the brandy and soda while describing her hostess's house, newly acquired and just decorated. 'Everything gilded like Versailles . . . one needed dark glasses and an aspirin . . . really Margot ought to know better. Her first husband was a drunken bore with a taste for little boys, but he had a marvellous collection of Paul de Lamarie . . .' and so on until she had picked the evening to pieces and got herself into a better mood.

'Evelyn . . .' I plucked up the courage to interrupt an account of Margot's simply horrible bathroom, 'I wonder if Isobel and Conrad are quite right for each other?'

Evelyn stared at me, jolted out of the pleasant feeling of expansion that a really good session of unfettered bitchy truth-telling can give one. 'What do you mean? I've been thinking recently that, despite everything, he's probably the perfect choice

427

for her. Of course a synagogue takes some swallowing, but I'm willing to count my blessings and, as your dear mother doesn't mind me butting in with *your* wedding—'

'Yes, but Evelyn, I'm talking about *after* the wedding. Do they really love each other, do you think?'

'Conrad's a man of taste and education. And he's extremely good looking. And rich. Most women have to put up with much less. He's self-assured without being egocentric and he doesn't put up with any nonsense from her. If I weren't her mother and absolutely devoted to her, I should say Isobel was selfish and destructive.' For a moment Evelyn's expression hardened and I saw she was pretty angry with her daughter. 'No, I admit at first I disapproved of Conrad, but now I know him I think Isobel's extraordinarily lucky.' I tried not to think that the chestnut basket was responsible for this change of heart. 'What has she said to make you think she's having second thoughts?'

'Oh, nothing. It's just that when they're together they don't seem very—'

'I've put him to bed.' Rafe came in, looking weary. 'Spendlove was fast asleep on the stool in Father's bathroom. He's too old to look after him. We're going to have to get a nurse.'

'Oh, Lord!' Evelyn turned down the corners of her mouth. 'It's so difficult to find staff to live in who aren't perfect nuisances. These days they have peculiar ideas about being treated as one of the family. I detest the way the lower classes get into a tizz about the tiniest thing . . . *no* self control . . . but you're right, of course. We'll have to have someone.' Evelyn sipped her brandy, looking thoughtful. 'I'll get on to it tomorrow after lunch and before the rural council meeting. Harriet Buchanan mentioned a new agency she'd heard of where they vet the people extremely carefully . . . I'll call her in the morning. She can sleep in Kingsley's dressing room.'

Rafe pretended to look surprised. 'Lady Buchanan?'

Evelyn smiled at him. 'The nurse, darling, as you know quite well.' She put on her brisk face and seemed to recover her aplomb. Often, I thought, she hovered perilously close to boredom, and any turn of events that demanded lots of tele-phoning and decision-making cheered her up. 'Now I think of it, perhaps you'd better take my place on the council.' To my dismay I found she was looking at me. 'They're agonizingly dull but pretty capable, and it'll be a good way for you to dip a toe into committee work. You'll find it's quite different from charity committees where the other members are of similar social standing. Or think they are.'

'Don't you have to be elected on to the rural district council?' asked Rafe.

'Yes. But I'll see to that.'

He looked amused but I was horrified by the idea of finding myself in a group of madly efficient people who had had Evelyn's daughter-in-law undemocratically foisted upon them; moreover a daughter-in-law who knew absolutely nothing about districts or ruralities.

'I'd better take you home,' Rafe said to me.

'Goodnight, Evelyn.' Leaning down to kiss her, I felt my dress begin to slide from my shoulders, so I had to bend my knees in a sort of curtsey, then walk backwards to the door as though she were royalty. But she seemed not to find this odd.

'Don't forget, sweet girl,' she blew me a kiss, 'tomorrow, ten o'clock sharp. Your first gardening lesson. You'll love it once you know what you're doing. It's the most marvellous *therapy*. Whatever my mood, by the time I've weeded or pruned for an hour or two I'm at peace with the world.'

I hoped I would love it. The sum of my gardening experi-ence to date was growing cress on bits of flannel when I was a child. The end result had not been particularly attractive.

'Any chance Dimpsie will be in bed, asleep?' Rafe asked as he turned into the drive of Dumbola Lodge.

'Oh, yes, I should think so. In bed anyway. But perhaps not asleep.'

'Would she mind, do you think, if we slipped up to your room?

429

I'm desperate to finish what we started. We could be terribly discreet.'

'She wouldn't mind at all but my bed isn't really—'

'Don't tell me he's gardening at a quarter past midnight!' Jode's Land Rover, parked by the front door, had appeared in our headlights. 'He's got a cheek! I suppose he thinks your mother's fair game. I loathe men who prey on helpless women.'

'Dimpsie likes him. He really is a nice man—'

'A *nice* man!' Rafe almost shouted. 'Marigold, sometimes I think you deliberately say ridiculous things just to be exotic.'

This was so annoying that I forgot he must not be upset. 'I'd rather be ridiculous than pompous and prejudiced!'

'Forgive me,' his voice became icy as he attempted to control it, 'but I think I know rather better than you what sort of man he is. He's been in prison for half killing someone.'

'I know. It was his wife's lover.'

'As though that excuses it! If everyone behaved like that, the population of this country would be halved in a matter of days.'

'Yes, but Jode *didn't* kill him. He stopped when he realized what he was doing and he hasn't taken a drop since.'

'Hasn't taken a drop? Really, Marigold! You're even talking like an Irish tinker. He's leading you and your mother – who's every bit as harebrained as you are – up the garden path. He's been before the bench twice in the last year.'

'Oh.' I had a sinking feeling, hearing this. 'What for?'

'Behaviour likely to cause a breach of the peace. He's a hunt saboteur.'

'Oh!' I said again, this time with relief. 'Well, you might not approve of that, but Dimpsie certainly does and surely that's all that matters?'

Rafe's voice trembled with rage and I felt the hand that was on my arm begin to shake. 'Do you mean to say you see nothing wrong in your own mother having a sexual relationship with an ex-jailbird who has a record of violence and civil disobedience and no visible means of support? A man who has to sign his name with a cross, who lives in a filthy trailer with a herd of gypsies who spend their time stealing and cheating and fornicating!'

'You don't know anything about him! His trailer isn't filthy – in fact he's much fussier and cleaner than we are, and he's hard-working and brilliant with his hands. And he looks after his grandson beautifully!'

'Really, Marigold! I suppose his grandson's another repro-bate with light fingers and a taste for his social superiors.'

I had got into a lower-class sort of tizz, which Evelyn would have disapproved of, but I couldn't help it. 'Don't keep saying "Really Marigold!" as though I'm a naughty little girl who's behaving badly! He isn't a reprobate! He's a darling little baby.' Here my voice started to break as fury and sorrow welled up within. 'And Jode feeds him and changes his nappy, and washes his clothes and gets up to him in the night, because his daughter's too young to look after him and the baby's father didn't bother to stay around because he's what she calls a gentleman and too good for her – but I think it was cruel and cowardly and mean . . . !' I stopped, afraid I was going to cry.

'What's the girl's name?' asked Rafe, some of the heat going out of his voice.

I couldn't see his face clearly because the porch lantern was flickering. 'Nan. But he called her Scarlett.'

Rafe was silent for a moment. Then he said, 'How old is it? The baby?'

'About two months.'

I could hear him breathing heavily and I saw him tighten the hand that rested on the steering wheel to stop it shaking.

'Oh, fuck!' he said at last. 'And double fuck!'

I knew why he was upset. But the confirmation of my suspi-cions, which I had so dreaded, brought unexpected consolation. It was quite obvious that until this moment Rafe had had no inkling of Harrison Ford's existence. He had not been guilty of dastardly behaviour, of refusing to help Nan and abandoning a helpless baby to an inhospitable world. There might be some tarnishing to the sheen of my *beau idéal* – I needed time to think about that – but his light had not been altogether put out.

'I'm sorry,' he said eventually, taking his hand from my arm. 'Forgive my appalling language. And I shouldn't have been angry with you. I apologize, darling.'

'Never mind. I was angry too.'

He rubbed one hand over his face. 'I won't come in now. I couldn't face meeting that man . . . though if what you say is true he's evidently not quite as bad as I thought . . . but all the same Dimpsie shouldn't . . . well, anyway, I'm suddenly awfully tired. Let's call it a day and I'll ring you in the morning.'

I opened the car door and started to get out. 'Don't bother. I'll be at Shottestone by ten. My gardening lesson, remember?'

I must have sounded rather bleak because he leaned across and caught hold of my coat. 'Sweetheart, I'm ashamed of myself. It's my wretched nerves. I can't seem to control my temper. Can't you forgive a poor old crock?' He hesitated. 'I do love you so.'

'I was just as much to blame.'

'Kiss me then.' I leaned back in and kissed his cheek. He caught my hair and kissed my lips before I pulled away. 'Say you love me, Marigold.'

But did I? How could anyone know whether they loved anyone else?

'Marigold?' He was looking up at me. The interior light was on and showed me his face clearly. It was anxious, pleading. 'I shan't sleep if you don't forgive me. When things look black and I wonder whether I'm going crazy, your love is the only thing that seems to matter. I spent eight weeks in the psychiatric unit and all they did was give me drugs and talk to me in a half-baked way about minds healing. One chap wanted to blame my attacks of nerves on a distant relationship with my father. The padre thought a programme of Bible study might do the trick. No one wanted to admit that the horror of seeing one's friends dying around one was an experience that couldn't be tidied away under a Freudian heading. But you've given me hope. Your love reassures me that, when I look up from the bottom of this deep dark well I'm in, I can see stars at the top. Won't you be merciful to the penitent? Say you love me.'

'I love you,' I replied, a few weak tears falling, which because my face was in shadow he didn't see.

In the hall, which these days, thanks to Jode, smelt strongly of Ajax and Mr Sheen, I looked at the face of the clock. The moon was nearly full, only a sliver concealed by the brass clouds. Its face looked disillusioned, the smile weary. I tried to imagine Rafe and Nan together at the pele tower. He had met her when he was horribly depressed and she had been pretty, innocent, admiring and, perhaps most persuasive of all, willing. I thought I could understand it. I could certainly forgive it.

He was guilty of seducing a schoolgirl and giving rise to false hopes, but nothing worse. This was perhaps bad enough, but probably he had not realized that to Nan the encounters had meant more than casual sex. The important thing was that he had not known she was expecting a baby. She thought she had told him but he must have misunderstood. In fact, the only aspect of the entanglement I could not find excuses for was his adoption of horribly corny pseudonyms, which just showed how superficial I was.

But what was to be done now? For one moment, seeing myself at the centre of the drama and getting some bittersweet satisfaction from the consciousness of my own nobility, I considered renouncing my claim in favour of Nan's but immediately gave up that idea. A marriage between Nan and Rafe was out of the question. They had not a single thought in common. And Evelyn would probably kill herself.

Siggy hopped downstairs towards me. I picked him up, pressed my mouth against the soft fur between his beautiful ears and stroked his bony paws. 'Dear Siggy. Shall we run away and leave everyone to sort things out for themselves? Would you like to go back to London?' Siggy wriggled in protest. He was happy

433

now that Fritz fetched him two or three times a week to run around the terrace at Hindleep, nibbling grass in his metier as a live lawnmower. I put him down and he scampered under the hall table.

I opened my bag and took out a piece of folded paper. As we were filing out along the front row of the grand tier I had pretended I had lost an earring and held everyone up while I searched under the seats for it. Another lie, but this one was partly Conrad's fault. The paper was ingeniously folded into the shape of a bird with a long tail which, like the wings, was torn into pretty feathery shreds. A bird of paradise. Perhaps he had learned how to do this during his stay in the lunatic asylum. I glanced up at the clock. Half past twelve. I must get to bed. I noticed that the moon face had assumed a hypocritical smile.

I heard a key turn in the front door lock. A cold wind gusted through the hall. The hexagonal lenses of my father's spectacles winked in the light from the lantern. He took off his coat and flung it on the hall chair. 'Where's your mother?'

'She's in bed.' My heart beat fast though, given my father's appalling behaviour, there was no reason why Dimpsie should not at this moment be lying in the arms of another man.

'Run up and tell her I'm here. I'd like something to eat.'

My alarm turned to indignation. 'You've got a cheek! After leaving us to practically starve so you could run after that hateful woman, how *dare* you walk in and demand food at this hour as if nothing had happened? It's after midnight!'

'Dimpsie won't mind.' Tom smiled. 'She'll be glad to see me. You can tell her I've come home.'

35

'I was afraid they were going to fight each other.' I took a sip of coffee and a bite of something called *Zwetschgen Kuchen*, a sponge cake marbled with the purple juice of delicious little blue plums.

'Is it considered polite in England to eat and drink in the same mouthful?' asked Conrad, quite mildly for him. He was busy with his trowel making places to plant more ferns. 'If they had come to blows, who do you think would have won?'

'My father's quite fit and wiry, but Jode's practically a giant. His head is knitted together with scars. And his eyes have a sort of scorched look as though he's witnessed all the sins of the world.'

'I wish I had been there to see the meeting.'

'You'd have thought it was funny, of course.'

'I dare say. There is little more ridiculous than the passions provoked by jealousy. And one's consciousness of appearing absurd only adds to the anguish.'

'Have you ever been jealous?'

'When I was eighteen, I fell violently in love with a beautiful actress. For three months we had an affair and then she threw me aside for another man. She said I was too young. I was hurt in my pride so badly that I followed one night as she walked

435

on the arm of her new lover and I punched him and knocked out a tooth. The most terrible thing was that I could not prevent myself from weeping in front of him. That humiliation was worse to bear than my disappointed love.'

I was touched by the idea of a youthful, vulnerable Conrad. 'How old was she?'

'Forty-eight. Have you ever been jealous yourself?'

'Never.'

'Then you know nothing of love. In that state of madness when the beloved looks up to heaven and smiles, one is jealous of the man in the moon.'

'Have you forgotten I'm engaged to be married?'

'*I* had not forgotten.'

'Nor had I. I love Rafe. He just doesn't happen to have given me cause for jealousy, that's all.'

'Not so far as you know.'

'Conrad! If you're trying to make trouble I think it's very wicked of you! And anyway,' I attempted to sound dignified, 'as it happens, I do know all about it.'

'Oh, you do?' Conrad turned to look at me, his eyebrows lifted enquiringly.

'Yes, and I quite forgive him. There can't be many men who wouldn't have taken advantage of a pretty young girl who was willing to go to bed with him. It's very bad but that's the way men are. Rafe had no idea about the baby until yesterday. And he broke it off with Nan before I came back to Northumberland so I've no reason to be jealous.'

'None at all, I should say.' Conrad dabbed at the cement then stood back to admire his workmanship. 'Who is Nan?'

'You mean you didn't know? But I thought . . . I assumed Isobel had told you. Oh, damn! Rafe will be furious with me. You must forget everything I said.'

Conrad shrugged. 'I can hardly do that but I can be silent. Isobel has told me nothing about Rafe's sexual pleasuring. Perhaps *she* does not know.'

436

I sighed. 'They've always told each other everything. As it happens, Nan is Jode's daughter, which does make it rather awkward, but so far he and Rafe have managed to avoid each other.'

Conrad paused in his handiwork and said in a reflective manner, almost as though talking to himself, 'Rafe has had an affair with a *Zigeunerin? Nun wohl! Ich glaube es nicht.*' He took up a chisel and attacked the rock face. 'So there is a Preston by-blow in the neighbourhood. Neither the first nor the last, I am certain.'

'I wish you wouldn't call him that. It sounds so cold and he's the sweetest baby.'

Conrad looked unrepentant. 'You like babies.'

'Of course. Doesn't everyone. Not for me though . . . I mean, I hadn't thought of having any. Dancing and babies don't mix.'

'You perhaps could adopt Nan's baby. And any other little babies that Rafe has fathered along the way.'

'You really are trying to make mischief. I *would* adopt him if I thought I had the smallest chance of prising him away from Dimpsie and Jode.'

'Ah, yes, Jode. You were going to tell me about your father and the lover.'

'Well, Jode came downstairs, his grey hair loose and his tame magpie sitting on one shoulder, like Samson on his way to pull down a temple.'

'Perhaps Elijah and the ravens?'

'Who's telling this story? Anyway, luckily Jode's pledged to non-violence and if my father had ideas of hitting him he sensibly gave them up. But what struck me as odd was that I could see my father really minded finding himself supplanted. I mean, after all those years of tossing my mother aside like an old glove—'

Conrad made a sound like tst! 'A cliché. And a particularly tired one.'

'All right, not appreciating her in the least bit. I mean what's sauce for the goose—' Conrad held up a cement-smeared hand in protest. 'Okay, but you'd think he'd be pleased not to have to feel so guilty about his own behaviour, wouldn't you? He called Jode a thieving beggar and a pox-ridden tramp among other things. Jode simply folded his arms and stared down at him with reproachful eyes. After a while my father ran out of insults, so he turned his attention back to Dimpsie. He said couldn't she see what a fool she was making of herself? Dimpsie said, "Why should I care about making a fool of myself when you've done it for me so successfully all these years?" Rather neat, I thought. Then she asked me if I'd take some of her clothes and Jode's that were in the washing machine to the Singing Swan in the morning. I hadn't properly realized until then that I was going to have to be alone in the house with my father. I didn't at all like the idea because we've never got on but I'd have felt awfully *de trop* in the caravan so I said I would. They went into the kitchen and my father swore and kicked the hall table a couple of times. Then I saw he was thinking about kicking me.'

'He was?' Conrad stopped plastering and gave me his full attention. 'What a maverick is your father!' He sounded quite admiring.

'Oh, yes, but to be fair he's not often violent. Though I remember when I was little he whipped my legs so hard with his stethoscope I had red marks for two days.'

'What had you done to deserve this beating?'

'I set his armchair alight while he was asleep in it. I put a match to the fringe. He didn't wake up until it was burning quite well.'

I was pleased to see that I had managed to shock Conrad. 'You hated him so much?'

'I did it because Isobel said I must. It was the first of a long list of tasks I had to accomplish that lasted nearly all one summer holidays. Very much like the *Faerie Queene* now I come to think of it. Isobel said she'd got a puppy locked in a secret cupboard and if I didn't do exactly what she told me she wouldn't feed it or give it any water. Of course I couldn't take the risk that she really had.'

'That was ingenious of her. What else did she make you do?'

'The worse thing was spending ten minutes submerged in the lily pond breathing through two drinking straws. That was horrible because I couldn't really get enough air and whenever I put my head up she hit it with the rake. Also the bottom was thick mud and seemed to be full of wriggling things, or perhaps that was my imagination.'

Conrad laughed. 'It seems that it was Isobel who had the imagination.'

'Oh, she was inventive, all right. It was only when Spendlove caught me gulping down Mrs Capstick's opium-laced Collis-Browne tincture – I was supposed to drink a whole bottle – that she was found out. My father was called and there was such a fuss that Isobel got scared and confessed.'

'What were your punishments?'

'Isobel wasn't allowed to go to see *Peter Pan* in London, which was hard because she'd been looking forward to seeing him fly around the stage more than anything. My punishment was that I didn't enjoy it nearly so much without her. Evelyn was very kind and took me round the house and showed me the insides of all the cupboards to reassure me that there wasn't a puppy.'

Conrad could hardly speak for laughing. 'Did you ever exact revenge?'

'Never. Not because I was too good natured, but because I've always been afraid a deliberately nasty action would backfire on me.'

Conrad continued to look amused and I guessed he was thinking what a bold-spirited girl Isobel had been. 'So . . . did your father kick you?'

'Not quite. Dimpsie came back into the hall with the baby followed by Jode staggering beneath the mountains of equipment a small baby needs to sustain life, and with Nell – that's his sheepdog and she's adorable – at his heels. My father said, "Ha! A gipsy bastard! So this sordid little affair has been going on longer than I thought." Though he only said that to be spiteful because he must have guessed this was the baby he'd delivered a couple of months ago.

'"He *is* a gipsy bastard," said my mother, "but unfortunately not mine. I forgive you, Tom. Goodbye." Then they sailed out through the front door, barefoot, locks flowing, Dimpsie in her nightdress and Jode in one of her kaftans because all his clothes were still wet, heads held high with ecstatic faces like Israelites departing for the Promised Land . . . oh, sorry . . .'

Conrad smiled. 'You need not worry. For me neither the term Israelite nor Jew is problematic.'

'Oh no, of *course* not . . . Anyway, they drove off, leaving me to bear the brunt of my father's rage. We've already had a blazing row. Siggy ran out from under the hall table to see what all the noise was about and my father tried to stamp on him. He said he thought he was a rat but no one could really mistake my beautiful Siggy for one. He said if I didn't get rid of him by tonight he'd put down poison and he will too. So I'm at my wits' end.' I looked at Conrad hopefully.

Conrad correctly interpreted my look. 'Very well. He can stay here. But I take no responsibility for him should he fall from the parapet or be eaten. I saw a marsh harrier yesterday.' I could tell by the way Conrad's eyes flashed that this had excited him.

'Really? How absolutely *thrilling!*' When Conrad continued to stuff cement into cracks without troubling to enlighten me I asked, 'What is it?'

'It is a large bird of prey that particularly enjoys rabbits.'

'Oh, how impossibly difficult life is! I wish I had the courage to run away.'

Conrad lifted an eyebrow. 'Is it so bad? Surely he will not kick you in cold blood?'

'I hope not.'

'Why don't you go to live at Shottestone Manor? You are very much a favourite with Evelyn, I have observed.'

I shook my head. 'I don't think that would be a good idea . . .' I had been going to say that these days I found it rather a strain being there when I realized Conrad, who was always quick to ferret out unwelcome inferences from everything I said, would immediately ask me why. I couldn't tell him that when I was with Rafe I seemed always to be treading on eggshells. Besides, he would have grumbled about the cliché.

'At least I can go for runs during the day. But it's so hard to know what to do with yourself in the country if you don't have a job.'

'You do not mean to say you have been dismissed from the café?'

I explained about my promise to Rafe to give up my two insufficiently glamorous jobs.

'I have something that will help to pass the hours.' Conrad picked up a book which had been lying on the table next to the thermos flasks. I had already seen that it was called *The Adventures of Nicholas Nickleby* and that the author was Charles Dickens. 'Dickens was a moralist as you are but he writes with passion. You will like it better than Joyce or Bunyan.'

'Am I a moralist?'

'In your own slightly confused way, yes.'

A shifting of cloud cast a soft beam on the hand that held the book towards me. His hand was narrow palmed with long fingers and well-shaped nails, not brown or pink or freckled like English hands but a subtle shade between ivory and gold. The sound of the waterfall became very loud, as though its volume had mysteriously trebled. I looked up and saw reflected in his black eyes segments of light that trembled as it pierced the wall of water.

I took the book. 'Anyway, no one can accuse you of flattery.' I frowned to hide an obscure feeling of pleasure.

441

'*Ich höre wohl der Genien Gelächter; Doch trennet mich von jeglichem Besinnen Sonettenwut und Raserei der Liebe,*'* said Conrad softly.

'What does that mean?'

'It means . . .' He paused and turned his head to gaze at the sheep on the far hillside who were trotting busily about, baaing bossily to their black-legged lambs. 'It means you must learn German if you wish to consider yourself well-educated. French and Italian, too, of course.'

'Can *you* speak all those languages?'

'Naturally. If I tell you I speak seven you will accuse me of boasting.' He lowered his eyes in an assumption of modesty that entirely failed to convince as he added, 'But I am not perfectly fluent in Mandarin. Here is a bookmark for you.' He held out a long feather of brilliant blue, edged with flecks of vivid red.

'It's beautiful. Thank you so much.' I ran my fingers gently along the delicate, clinging vanes. 'Does it belong to a marsh harrier?'

'No, you little ignorant. I visited the zoo when I was in Berlin. It is a tail feather from a scarlet macaw. I thought of you when I picked it up.'

'Of me?' I felt immensely flattered to know that I had figured in his thoughts while he was away. 'Did you really?' I put it carefully inside the book. 'I shall treasure it and keep it always.'

'Yes.' He assumed an expression of severity. 'On the perch was this magnificent creature, born to fly over mountains and through forests and when I put in my hand to pick the feather from the floor of the cage – it was spacious and had an artificial rock to represent the mountains and a branch for

*'I hear the genie's laughter at my fate; / Yet do I find all power of thinking fled / In sonnet-rage and love's fierce ecstasy.' GOETHE, Sonnet XI *Nemesis*, tr E A Bowring, 1853

the forest but it was a cage, nonetheless – then I thought of you.'

'Gosh, Conrad! You really know how to cut a girl down to size.'

The scowl was replaced by a smile. 'Yes, I have learned a thing or two since I knocked out that tooth. Now you must run along or you will be late for your gardening lesson.'

36

'Really, Marigold, it's *easy* to tell wild forget-me-nots from cultivated ones.' Evelyn snatched up two, to me identical, seedlings.
'Now look! The wild forget-me-not leaf is smaller and paler
and hairier. It's quite obvious!'

I examined them carefully. 'Small. Pale. Hairy,' I murmured,
thinking involuntarily of Kingsley.

'What did you say?' asked Evelyn a little snappily. Not five
minutes before I had trodden by mistake on an emerging lily
and it had taken a visible effort of will on Evelyn's part to
prevent an outburst of anger. 'Now, Marigold, weed that section
there to the left of the seat. And remember to give each proper
forget-me-not a minimum of nine inches of bare earth – w*hat*
do you think you're doing?' She darted over to inspect the
contents of the barrow being wheeled along the path by a young
man. 'My *Paeonia mlokosewichii!*' She held up a drooping
collection of leaves. 'Good heavens, how *could* you be so stupid!
If you haven't killed it you'll have set it back *years!*'

Evelyn was president of a charity concerned with the rehabilitation of ex-prisoners. She employed those with gardening
experience at a pittance, then sacked them in a rage when they
failed to measure up to her exacting horticultural standards.
The young man stared into the middle distance while Evelyn

lectured him. From time to time he ran his hand over his crew-cut, as though enjoying the sensuous smoothness of its pile, while he waited for her to finish. I felt sorry for him being dressed down with no possibility of retaliation, but he seemed indifferent. The world had judged him and found him wanting in all potentiality and the feeling was clearly mutual.

As soon as Evelyn had stalked off in a rage to replant what he had dug up, I gave the young man my Aurora birthday smile to show I believed in new beginnings and putting the past behind one. 'Lovely morning, isn't it?' I said. 'It's so nice to be outside in the fresh air after being indoors so much.' Then I blushed, afraid he might think this was a reference to his having been in prison. 'All winter, I mean. My name's Marigold. What's yours?'

He stared at me without returning my smile. Then he said, 'It's Crisp.'

'Yes.' I looked about at the shimmering greens of young leaves and the sharp blue sky. 'Crisp is *exac*tly the right word.'

'Crisp's me name.'

'Oh, oh, I see.'

'Gi's a bit o' the other leik while the aad blethorskite's oot the way,' said Crisp when Evelyn was out of earshot. 'Tho' she's bonny enyuf. Aa'd fettle her, givvin haf the chance.' By which I understood him to mean that, though Evelyn was an old windbag, he considered her attractive and wouldn't mind giving her a good seeing-to. He put out his tongue and waggled the tip suggestively, then bent down and took hold of me by my waist.

'Let go of me!'

'What a gan-on aboot a wee fuddle—'

He let go as Buster jumped on top of me, knocking me to the ground. Pinning me down with his front paws he gave my face a vigorous licking.

I picked myself up in time to see Crisp aiming a kick at Buster, whose usually equable temper was inflamed to wrath by this treatment. He seized the leg of the young man's jeans.

'Here, boy!'

In response to Isobel's voice, Buster let go of the denimed leg and ran to greet her.

'Good boy!' She bent down to pat him. 'Did the nasty man kick you then?'

'He's bit me!' complained Crisp, showing us an area of torn ankle from which blood dripped.

'You deserved it.' Isobel's voice was contemptuous. 'Go up to the house and they'll give you a plaster.'

Crisp sloped off, cowed. Isobel's assumption that man and dog would continue to defer to her as they had since the day she was born seemed to get much better results than my attempts to be ingratiating. I was certain he would never have dared to waggle his tongue at her.

'Hello, darling.' Isobel kissed my cheek before I had time to warn her about Buster's spit. The white rose pinned to her lapel smelt deliciously of almonds. 'So Mummy's got you slaving away in the mud, you poor idiot.' She looked dashing in a tweed hacking jacket and pale yellow jodhpurs. 'Rafe and I've had the most marvellous ride. Once it stopped raining it was the most perfect day. We galloped for miles.' Her short hair stood up in spikes and her cheeks were becomingly flushed by the exercise. 'Rafe said to tell you he'll see you at lunch,' Isobel continued. 'He's had to go and see someone. O blissful day! It makes me realize why I like being in the country. Yesterday I was tramping the pavements of Bond Street inhaling BO and petrol fumes.'

'I didn't know you'd been to London.'

'I went down for a couple of days to see if I could find something decent to wear. Conrad told me not to buy anything expensive, but I found this marvellous dress by Oscar de la Renta, strapless with a ruched taffeta skirt like a cream puff.' She giggled. 'Of course it cost an arm and a leg but I simply *had* to have it.' This must account for her manifest good humour.

'Where did you stay?'

She giggled again. 'At the Ritz, of course. When a girl's got

446

used to the good things of life, it isn't easy to give them up . . . Oh, Lord! Here comes Mummy on the warpath. I'm going to hide in the Bear Hut. Bye!'

She patted my arm in the friendliest fashion before running away in the direction of what Evelyn called the Wilderness and which I should have been inclined to call an overgrown field. On the edge of the Wilderness, beneath a circle of trees, was a thatched rustic building where a Victorian Preston had once kept a bear. It was charming outside but I had disliked its inside ever since Isobel shut me in there when we were children. She had used her skipping rope to tie the door handle to the foot-scraper and had run off howling with laughter. I had sat on the sofa for quite a while, eyeing a spider of extraordinary dimensions and getting sadder and sadder about the lonely bear being shut up in such a small dark place when it ought to have been romping on the steppes with others of its kind, until it occurred to me to try to escape through a broken window. I had made a dramatic entrance during tea in the drawing room, dripping blood, tears and cobwebs onto the Aubusson. I had told Evelyn the door had jammed. In gratitude Isobel had given me the skipping rope, a superior model to my own, with ball bearings in the handles. I had considered this a fair trade for half an hour of fear and sorrow and a few cuts.

Evelyn returned. I could see why Crisp admired her. Her gardening coat of lovat green with suede revers had an indefinable chic about it. She was *bien maquillé* as usual and wore a fetching little gardening hat. 'Didn't I see Isobel a few minutes ago? I could do with an extra pair of hands.' Without giving me time to answer she gave me a box of what looked like liquorice sticks. 'You can plant these *Cosmos atrosanguineus* where you've just weeded. By the time they come out – they're the most lovely velvety garnet colour – the alchemilla will be in flower. Plant associations are important. Dark red and lime green are so good together . . . in fact I think I'll put in some green zinnias here and lime-green nicotiana as well. Now I think

447

of it, we won't have any blue here at all. White forget-me-nots would be much prettier. Mind out, darling, and I'll just get rid of those.' Obediently I went to stand on the path while Evelyn seized a hoe and advanced with eyes agleam on the little seedlings I had carefully weeded round, disposing of them with ruthless thrusts of the blade.

'Telephone, Madam.' Spendlove's slippered feet had crept upon us unnoticed.

'If it's that ghastly little man from the planning department, he'll have to call back—'

'I don't think so, Madam. The gentleman had a foreign accent. American.'

Evelyn clicked her tongue with annoyance. 'All right. I'll come. Though I do think it's inconsiderate of people to ring when I'm in the garden. Tell him I shall be a few minutes.'

'Hello, Spendlove,' I said, smiling. 'Isn't it a lovely day?'

'Good morning, Madam.' Spendlove stared at the space six inches above my head, his face frozen into immobility.

This was so unlike the friendly Spendlove I had known all my life that I was nonplussed. 'What's the matter?' I asked. 'Are you feeling all right?'

'Perfectly well, Madam, thank you.' Without looking at me, Spendlove turned and started to hobble back to the house.

'What have I done to offend him?' I asked Evelyn in consternation.

'Nothing, darling, but I overheard Rafe ticking him off this morning about being too familiar. Apparently he winks at you all the time. I hadn't noticed it myself, but I agree that what was acceptable when you were a child is quite unsuitable now you are a member of the family. He's a feeble-witted old man and you mustn't encourage him to be impertinent. The same with tradesmen. It's awkward for you because everyone knows you as the doctor's daughter, so they'll be only to ready to encroach if you let them.' Glancing up and seeing my face, she added, 'I'm not asking you to go about being arrogant and high-handed – that would be vulgar and horrid. You've just got to be a little distant, that's all.'

'I see.' While she hoed I was silent for a while, thinking. The idea that I should crush the presumption of other people with my cool superiority was as unfeasible as it was hateful. 'Evelyn,' I said eventually, 'if two people were going to be married and one of them decided that they weren't very well suited after all, don't you agree it would be better if she said so, even though their families would be dreadfully disappointed and lots of wedding plans had been made and money spent. Even if it meant that the other one who wasn't very well – mentally, I mean – might get awfully depressed? I mean, it wouldn't exactly help him to find that he'd married someone who was completely wrong for him, would it?'

'Mm, perhaps some black opium poppies . . .' Evelyn put her head on one side and half-closed her eyes, envisaging. 'Rafe did tell me Conrad had been in some sort of sanatorium – some *crise de nerfs*, or perhaps he was tubercular, that's far more likely. Anyway, he seems perfectly sane to me and I think it's rather narrow-minded to hold this sort of thing against people. Two years ago Harriet Buchanan's brother tried to throw himself over his own battlements, but after electric shock treatment he wrote a very successful book about royal hunting lodges, and last month he was asked to lunch with the queen mother. Of course, Isobel doesn't confide in *me*, but at breakfast this morning she was more cheerful than I've seen her in ages. It's sweet of you to be concerned, Marigold, but you must just accept that, while you know a great deal about ballet – and no one's prouder of you than I am, my sweet girl – you don't know much about life.'

This was undoubtedly true. I experienced a painful confusion of ideas, as though my brain was being scrambled with a fork, like eggs.

'Evelyn, I'm not talking about Conrad and Isobel—'

'I suppose I'd better answer the telephone. You can dig out those celandines. Be careful. If you leave even one of those

449

beastly little bulbils on their roots there'll be a million in the same place next year.' She walked off towards the house.

When Evelyn returned some twenty minutes later, I could tell at once that something had happened to disturb her. She inveighed against the stupidity of gardeners, a familiar theme, but her heart did not seem to be in it. For some time she weeded and planted in silence, and when I asked her a question she didn't hear me. The gong sounded for lunch. Evelyn straightened up.

'When I think how much there is to do with only those two simpletons to help me – and you too of course, my pet – I can feel a migraine coming on.' But her eyes were dreamy and the customary snap was absent from her voice. 'Oh, well, it makes the tortures of old age, immobility and senility seem actually quite attractive.'

So much for the therapeutic effect of gardening, I reflected, as we hastened indoors to dig the dirt from our fingernails.

37

As we crossed the hall on our way to the dining room, Rafe came out of the library with Kingsley. He had a firm grip on his father's elbow, as though to restrain him from making a dash for the stairs or the front door. Kingsley looked at me with troubled eyes when I said hello.

'How d'you do?' he said with an attempt at his old manner. 'So delighted to see you. Have you come straight from Paris? How is the dear old place? I remember the most wonderful costume ball at the Hotel Chambertin just before the war. I went as Lord Nelson. It was damned difficult to eat lobster single-handed. I suppose Nelson had that Hamilton woman to cut things up for him. She was a hot little piece by all accounts, big breasts and red hair . . .'

'All right, Father, come and sit down.' Rafe steered Kingsley to his chair at the head of the table. 'Hello, darling.' He kissed me affectionately. 'Had a lovely morning in the garden?'

As he smiled down at me, his blue eyes tender, a stray beam of sunlight etching more deeply those attractive lines each side of his mouth, I felt a physical pain at the idea of hurting him. 'I don't think I was much help.'

'I know what Evelyn's like when she gets the scent of earth in her nostrils,' he murmured, putting his arm round my waist.

'I bet those poor ex-prisoners'll feel more kindly towards their gaolers the next time they go inside.'

Evelyn had taken her seat at the other end of the table. She rattled a silver peppermill to check that it was full, moved her glass half a centimetre to the right, shook out her starched napkin and placed it across her knee, but all the time her gaze was unfocused as though her mind was elsewhere. 'Rafe dearest.' She pressed her finger and thumb between her eyebrows for two seconds, as though to bring her errant thoughts back into line, then set the breadbasket in motion. 'Could you find time to give me a hand in the greenhouse? I'm surrounded by idiots and there are trays and *trays* of seedlings needing to be pricked out. You used to love doing it when you were a little boy.'

'You aren't calling my wife-to-be an idiot, I hope?' He sent me a look of good-humoured complicity.

I looked down at my plate, on which was an elegantly composed salad of melon, cucumber and baby tomatoes. When Rafe was in a good mood he was practically irresistible. And I so hated quarrelling. What woman in her right mind would not willingly make every sacrifice necessary to marry this handsome, charming, eligible man?

'He also loved peeing out of his bedroom window on to your friends' cars,' put in Isobel. 'But I dare say that excitement's worn off a bit now.'

'Did you?' Evelyn looked disgusted. 'How dreadful boys are. I'd be delighted if Marigold could spend more time with me, but she's so busy with her jobs at the surgery and that peculiar little café Dimpsie's so keen on.' She glanced at me, contracting the corners of her mouth into the beginnings of a smile. 'And who is that odd-looking man with the grey ponytail I saw your mother walking down the high street with the other day? Is she going through another Beatnik phase? Last time it had a deplorable effect on her vocabulary. Much though I admire Dimpsie's refusal to bow to the conventions, I object to being called "man".'

452

We all laughed and Evelyn looked pleased. She was rarely playful, being too busy making her life beautiful and combating the incorrigible slackness of her fellow men.

'His name's Jode,' I said, 'and I agree he looks alarming but he's really very nice.' She would know it all sooner or later, and it was better for Evelyn to hear the unvarnished truth from me rather than an embroidered version from someone else. 'He makes cuckoo clocks and has a caravan on the moor and Dimpsie's gone to live with him.'

The smile was wiped from Evelyn's face. 'You don't mean . . . a tinker?'

'Of course it's just a whim,' said Rafe. 'You know Dimpsie. She likes lame dogs and outcasts. And the good news is that Marigold's giving up both the café and the surgery.'

'Really? How sensible, darling. I shall make another appointment at once with Madame Merle. She rang yesterday to say she's cut out the lace and wants a fitting. And we must decide what to do about the veil. You're such a shrimp that mine swamps you.'

'I don't think Marigold likes being called a shrimp,' said Isobel, laughing.

If I looked resentful, it had nothing to do with hurt pride and everything to do with the feeling that I was being rushed to my doom.

'We must think of lots of things for you to do,' said Evelyn. 'We can't have you getting bored. Besides the gardening and the rural council, I think you had better do some voluntary work. And some bridge classes would be a good idea. You'll find it a great standby in the winter when the men are either shooting or hunting. But don't play with the archdeacon if you can help it. He never pays.'

'What an attractive little programme.' Isobel did not trouble to keep the sarcasm from her voice. 'Give her a silver-blonde wig, Mummy, and she'll be able to stand in for you at a moment's notice.'

Evelyn frowned at her daughter and gave the tiniest nod in the direction of Spendlove's back. He was arranging the main course on the hotplate that stood on the side table so we could serve ourselves. When the Prestons were *en famille,* which of course these days included me, Evelyn liked mealtimes to be informal. This meant that Spendlove sat on a hard little chair in the hall while we ate, instead of standing to attention near the door.

'We mustn't forget,' said Rafe as soon as Spendlove had left the room, 'that Marigold's been used to a very different kind of life. I think it would be unfair to plunge her into too much public service straightaway.' I sent him a look of purest gratitude, quite forgetting for a moment that he was the chief agent of my suffering. 'I've got my own plans for her.' He stood up and went to the sideboard. 'Oh, good, veal goulash. And braised leeks. Shall I give you some, Mother?'

She had fallen again into a brown study and had visibly to shake herself out of it. 'Thank you, darling. Not too much rice.'

'What are you talking about?' Isobel sounded annoyed. 'What are your plans for Marigold?'

'She's going to learn to ride.'

'Oh, but I couldn't!' I felt dismayed. 'I should hate it.' As a child I had been allowed to ride Isobel's pony, Mistletoe, and had got on quite well until Isobel had whacked him hard on the rump. He had tried to jump a hedge and I had fallen off and broken my collarbone. I had refused to mount him again. And once I began to dance seriously I avoided anything like riding, skating or skiing that might endanger my limbs. A dancer has enough injuries to contend with without risking more for recreation's sake.

'Nonsense!' Rafe shot me a reproving glance as he put Evelyn's plate in front of her. 'You're incredibly strong for your size and you've a good sense of balance. You'll love it once you get confident.' He returned to the sideboard. 'Plenty of goulash for you, darling?'

'Just rice and leeks, thank you,' I said pettishly. I never ate veal on compassionate grounds, and besides it was infuriating to be treated in this high-handed way.

He looked over his shoulder to say, with the air of one conferring a tremendous boon, 'I'll let you all in on a little secret. This morning I went to look at a nice quiet little pony. She'll be just right for Marigold. A dappled grey mare, fourteen hands. Pretty little thing and well schooled. The man who owns her is ringing me this afternoon to close the deal.'

I felt that everyone was looking at me to observe my rapturous reception of this unexpected and generous present. Isobel had had one of her violent changes of mood and was scowling at me as though hoping I'd be struck by lightning and fried to a heap of blackened crumbs. But it was not because of this that I felt both sad and angry. I should have liked a dear little pony to give apples and carrots to, so long as I did not have to ride her. But each caressing word and benevolent deed seemed like an attempt to bind me closer by ties that had more to do with dominance than love.

'It's . . . very kind of you.'

'See what you've done with your wonderful surprise,' said Isobel. 'Marigold's going to cry.'

'A horse, did you say?' Evelyn ceased to wool-gather. 'What a good idea, darling.' She smiled up at her son, then turned to me. 'I shall give you a jar of the night cream I use. It will protect your face against cold winds.'

'Don't feel burdened, sweetheart.' Rafe pressed my shoulder with one hand as with the other he put my plate before me. 'I can assure you my motives for buying you a pony are quite selfish. A beautiful woman always looks her best on horseback.'

I saw with intense annoyance that he had given me a mountain of goulash.

'How nice it will be for us,' said Isobel, 'to take you out on a leading rein.'

There was unmistakable irony in her voice. I wondered why

she seemed to dislike the idea of my learning to ride quite as much as I did. Surely she didn't imagine that I might outshine her as a horsewoman?

'We had better go to London, Marigold, to find shoes and some silk for the underskirt,' said Evelyn. 'We'll stay at Brown's. Shall we say Tuesday?'

'I have to give my father time to find a replacement.'

'Oh, very well. Let's say the week after next.'

'All right,' I said slowly, 'thank you.'

'I don't blame you for not being keen to be decked out in white like a sacrificial offering,' said Isobel. She leaned across the table and said in a low voice so that only Rafe and I could hear, 'And it isn't as though you're a virgin. I bet there've been plenty of others besides Rafe and that rather sinister Sebastian character.'

'Isobel!' Rafe's voice cracked like the whip that had beaten poor Mistletoe's rump.

'Isobel, I wish you wouldn't mutter,' said Evelyn. 'And you're slouching. You should follow Marigold's example. She carries herself so beautifully. Rafe darling, I think I'll have just a spoonful more of the leeks.'

As he stood up I happened to catch his eye. He gave me a look of such anger that I felt as though I had been slapped. The blare of a car horn outside and the entrance of Golly saved me from having to think of something to say. 'What ho, you lot!' She looked like an Ancient Briton decorated with woad. 'Sit down, you chaps.' This to Rafe and Kingsley who had risen with her entry. 'No ceremony. Waste of time. There you are, Marigold. I want to talk you. It's very important—'

Evelyn stood up and advanced, hand extended. 'Good afternoon, Dame Gloria. This is an unexpected pleasure. Do join us, won't you?'

'I suppose I may as well.' Golly threw her hat, gloves and goggles onto the beautiful Chinese Chippendale commode, then plumped down heavily next to Isobel.

Evelyn must have pressed the bell beneath the table before getting up, for Spendlove came in at once. 'Dame Gloria is joining us for lunch.'

'What is it?' asked Golly, leaning sideways to peer at her plate.

'Veal goulash.'

'Good-oh. Now, Marigold—'

'A glass of wine, Dame Gloria?' Evelyn interrupted. 'Or perhaps just water as you are driving?'

'Oh, wine, if you've got any. I always drive better when I'm tight. Not absolutely blotto, of course, just pleasantly oiled. It gives me the necessary confidence for things like four-wheel drifts. Now listen, Marigold—'

'Will you have rice, Madam? And leeks?' Spendlove had dashed back in with the necessary eating equipment and stood poised by the sideboard, panting heavily.

'Heavy on the rice. Light on the leeks. I know veg are good for constipation but I can't say I like them much.' Golly picked up her knife and fork and held them upright like spears until Spendlove had put her plate in front of her, then tackled her lunch with gusto. 'I say, this is good. Compliments to the cook.'

'You're too kind.' Evelyn's hauteur was quite wasted on Golly.

'Yes, smashing!' She looked up and down the table. 'Any mustard?'

'I shall ring for some.'

'Oh, don't bother that poor old thing. He looks as though he ought to be in a rest home. I'll go myself if you'll just tell me where the kitchen is.'

'That won't be necessary.'

Spendlove appeared once more and was sent away for the mustard. When he put it beside Golly's plate she seized his hand and beamed up into his face. 'Thanks. You're a trouper. Now go and put up those aching flippers. We can manage quite well by ourselves.' Golly looked across the table at me. 'Wait a minute while I shovel this down and then we'll talk.'

457

We all tried to look anywhere but at Golly as she suited her actions to her words, rather messily.

'That was very good.' Golly rubbed her stomach and belched. 'Now, my dear Marigold, this is my proposition. As usual we're trying out *The Fishcake* – it isn't really called that, just Conrad's joke, but I haven't been able to think of anything else – in the provinces first. Newcastle seems as good a place as any, given that I'm on the spot. I want you to take the part of Kayoko, the dumb heroine. If it goes down well in Newcastle, you'll dance it when we go on tour and then in London at the Royal Opera House next year. What do you say?'

For a moment I was too astonished to speak.

'Well, Marigold?' Golly held onto her plate as Spendlove tried to remove it. 'I'll have some more. No veg.'

Spendlove looked agonized. 'I regret, Madam, there is no more. An unpardonable oversight—'

'Oh, no, that's all right.' She gave up her plate. 'You didn't know I was coming. I'll have some pud instead. Come on, girl. You'd better say yes or I'll think you the most ungrateful creature this side of China. Or should I say Japan?'

I tried to think what the consequences of this offer might be. A new Beauwhistle work would command the attention of the world. It offered its principals international stardom. But I was far from the obvious choice.

'It's so kind of you to think of me, Golly. But I don't have a big enough profile—'

'I know. That's what I told myself. But because you were there when I thought it all up, I've always seen you in the part. I didn't realize that straightaway. I thought any old ballerina would do. But it's no good, when I think of Kayoko I see you and only you. So will you do it? It'll mean busting a gut. Several probably. We plan to start rehearsals in six weeks. Orlando Silverbridge is coming to stay at Butterbank so we can thrash out the choreography before then. Fritz is meeting his train this afternoon. We're definitely using the LBC for the corps so you'll be working with people you know.' Golly took up her pudding fork and slipped it down inside her collar to scratch between her shoulder blades. 'It's this damned psoriasis. I always get an attack when I'm staging an opera. Nerves, you know.'

Spendlove placed an apple dumpling before her.

'You'd be a fool not to grab this chance with both hands.' Golly poured a generous swoosh of cream over the golden pastry, collected the drips from the spout with a blue finger and licked it. She plunged her spoon into the steaming apple and brought out a fudge-like mixture of sultanas and sugar. 'It's a once in a lifetime opportunity. Oh, this is good! I must congratulate the creator of this magnum opus.'

'I know.' I registered a goatee of cream on Golly's chin before returning my eyes to my dumpling. 'But I haven't danced for nearly three months. It'll take me more than six weeks just to get back into shape. I'm afraid it isn't possible.'

'Of course it isn't,' said Rafe fiercely. 'I suppose I'm entitled to have an opinion?'

'Besides,' said Evelyn, 'there's the wedding. You'd be fagged to death dancing in every hole-in-corner theatre of England and be barely able to drag yourself up the aisle. The idea is ridiculous.'

'Oh no, dear,' Golly said thickly, displaying a mixture of half-masticated cream and sultanas. 'Nothing hole-in-corner about it. We're talking to the Met and La Scala.'

I felt frantic as conflicting ideas whirled in my head. If, as was likely, my dancing failed to reach the heights of sublimity worthy of such an artistically significant premiere, I would have let Golly down and the singers and the LBC and everyone else concerned with the production. Didelot would make mincemeat of me and my career would be as good as over. I felt sick as I imagined what my own disappointment would be. And I owed it to Rafe and Evelyn to take their wishes into account. The decision, probably the most important of my life, could not be taken on the spur of the moment. I needed at least twenty-four hours of cool reflection to reach a sensible verdict that would be fair to everyone, including myself.

'Well?' asked Golly.

'I'll do it.'

38

'Hang on to your hat!' screamed Golly above the snarl of the exhaust as the little yellow car shot away from the front door of Shottestone.

I wasn't wearing a hat, an oversight I soon regretted. Golly liked to drive with the windscreen folded down because the rush of air on her face made it more exciting. We flew down the drive with the needle quivering on forty. When we came to the road she applied the brakes with a sharp stamp of her foot, so I was almost cut in half by my seat belt, which was made of two pieces of rope knotted across my chest. I drew up my knees to keep my feet out of the several pints of water, presumably the morning's rain, which sloshed around in the passenger foot-well.

Behind us we left a slough of despond. When I had told Golly that I would dance the role of Kayoko, Golly had clapped her hands together and said, 'That's my girl!'

Evelyn had said in a voice like a glass shard, 'Marigold, I don't think you've given this matter proper thought. You already have a full programme of commitments.'

Rafe's face had been as white as the napkin he threw down. 'Marigold, come into the hall, would you, for a moment?' Then he had walked out

'You may as well go and dance since you're obviously too selfish to be any good to him,' Isobel had said. 'It'll serve you right if you break your sodding foot again.'

'Isobel! I will not have such language at the lunch table!'

'Oh, fuck off, Mummy! It's a piece of mahogany, not a delicately nurtured maiden.'

I went to join Rafe in the hall. He was pacing the stone flags, his hands clasped behind his back. He came up to put his face close to mine. 'What the hell do you mean by saying you'll take the part? I thought the whole point of you giving up those jobs was so we could spend more time together. You're completely irresponsible!'

The contempt in his eyes emboldened me to say, with an assumption of calm, 'That's not true. I gave them up because you thought my lowly employment reflected badly on you.'

'Naturally you'd rather believe that.' His tone was scornful. 'You twist everything to suit your own ideas.'

'Do I?' I was genuinely surprised. 'But then . . . doesn't everyone? Am I particularly dishonest?'

'Yes, dishonest is a good word for what you are! You slept with that shit Lenoir and you told Isobel, didn't you! But you couldn't own up to *me!* Yes! Dishonest and deceitful and . . .' He stopped. His mouth was working as though a string was tied to one corner and someone was jerking it rhythmically. 'God knows, I've asked little enough in return for being prepared to share my life with you.'

'I'm so sorry . . . I did sleep with Sebastian but I didn't tell Isobel I had. She was just guessing . . . unless Conrad told her . . .'

'*Conrad* knows you were Lenoir's mistress?' His face became suffused with blood. I was about to protest that mistress was too elevated a description, but realized this would hardly improve his opinion of me. 'You told my sister's fiancé about your sordid little affair? A man you've exchanged barely half a dozen sentences with?'

As though a torch had suddenly been turned on in the

labyrinthine obscurity that was my subconscious, I admitted to myself that I had been guilty of more than forgetfulness in failing to tell Rafe about the early morning conversations in the hermit's grotto. I had known that he, in common with most men, would dislike the idea of the girl he was engaged to marry breakfasting in highly romantic surroundings with someone else, particularly when that someone was handsome, clever and fascinating. Impossible to explain that my relationship with Conrad was based on nothing more than my liking to hear him talk and his pleasure in telling me how hopelessly ignorant and naïve I was. Who in this cynical, mistrustful world would have believed it?

'You told *him* but you let me go on in ignorance, you little—' Rafe pressed his lips together until his mouth turned white, either to suppress the jerking or to stifle a dreadful insult. 'You've made me look a complete fool! I shall never be able to forgive you!'

'I'm so sorry! I wanted to tell you about Sebastian, truly I did. But it was never the right moment and it seemed to matter so much to you! I didn't mind that *you'd* had affairs before we met.'

'It's quite different for a man.'

'How is it different?'

He snorted. 'Don't be disingenuous. You know perfectly well that a man can make love to a woman without it meaning anything to him at all. Whereas a woman is always emotionally involved—'

I started to feel angry myself. 'Frankly I don't think heartless, mindless bonking is very attractive in either sex. I'm ashamed of my affair with Sebastian because I hated him and I only wanted to get good parts, but I refuse to admit it was worse than you sleeping with girls you didn't care tuppence about, just because they were willing.'

'You don't know what you're talking about! You're heartless, ungrateful, vain, promiscuous . . . !'

Though I stood perfectly still as the insults broke over my

head like waves, I seemed in my mind to take a huge bound away from him. Despite my attachment to my juvenile dream of love and my abiding affection for his family, I understood that he and I were not the same kinds of people and that we could never be a help to one another. We could not protect each other from loneliness or fear nor add substantially to each other's happiness. We could not share worlds of ideas and imagination. Anger was replaced by remorse.

'Please . . . Rafe darling,' I said when he paused for breath, 'don't let's go on torturing each other. I'm sorry, so sorry . . . it would never have worked – our marriage – but I'll always be *so* fond of you—'

'What blood and thunder have we here!' Golly was pulling on her coat as she came into the hall. 'Tristan and Isolde on a wet day at an out-of-season funfair. Cheer up you two! Tragedy purges the emotions. Come along, Marigold. I'll take you up to Hindleep to see Orlando. Toodle-oo, Rafe. Splendid lunch.'

Timidly I put my hand on his arm but Rafe jerked away. He turned his back to me and leaned against the chimneypiece, staring into the fire.

Even as I was clambering into the little yellow car, I had misgivings.

'Hold tight for the humpbacked bridge,' yelled Golly above the rushing of the wind.

We took off from the top and sailed several feet through the air before landing with a teeth-jarring crash, which shot the water from the foot-well into my lap.

'Oh, Golly,' I cried, 'I'm a very nervous passenger. Do you think you could go a fraction slower?'

'Bloody ass!' Golly sounded her horn and shook her fist at the fish-and-chip van which was being driven at a sedate pace on its allotted side of the road. 'Don't worry, my dear, I'm in just that state of intoxication when driving becomes an art form. Watch this handbrake turn!'

We reached the bottom of the hill on which Hindleep was

built. I shut my eyes, feeling tears freeze on my cheeks, tears of grief and terror in equal proportion. As we screeched and squealed and roared our way up the precipitous road, I thought I was probably about to die and I found I had only one regret. I wanted to dance again, to hear a flood of music in my ears, spurring me to turn faster, leap higher, to become an indissoluble part of that exquisitely beautiful world of moonlight and death in which I was not myself but something much better, nearer to perfection, to the divine . . . There was a squeal from the brakes as we reached the bridge and I was almost garrotted by my seat belt. As we bounced over the potholes beneath the accusing eyes of the Virtues and the triumphant looks of the Vices, my past life flashed before my eyes: some of it glorious – the dancing bits, some of it reprehensible . . .

'Marigold. *Marigold!*'

It was Conrad's voice. I opened my eyes and unblocked my ears. His face and Golly's were side by side, looking down at me. We were in the courtyard at Hindleep.

'Thank the Lord,' said Golly. 'For a moment I thought I was going to have to find another Kayoko. I never saw anyone look so bloodless, almost corpse-like, did you, Conrad?'

'Certainly she is pale. But being driven by you, Golly, is enough to make the bravest person ashen.'

'Oh, rubbish! I'm a very careful driver. Is Orlando here?'

'He has this moment arrived.'

'I'm going to talk to him.' Golly departed for the front door.

Conrad leaned inside the car and switched off the engine. 'Come in and take the English panacea. Or you can have brandy.'

'Thank you.' I got out, grateful for his hand under my arm.

He gave me his handkerchief. I dried my stinging face, the effect of the wind on salty tears.

'I must send to the haberdasher's if you become a two-handkerchief-a-day girl.'

'Oh, I won't be. I was frightened, and Rafe and I have had a row. It's all over. The engagement, I mean.'

We walked towards the steps that led up to the front door. 'So you are distraught? Your heart is forever broken?'

'Well, if I'm truthful, a part of me feels relieved. I've been afraid for some time it wasn't going to be any good. In fact, even from the beginning I had doubts I refused to admit to myself. Why does one always make the same mistakes? I always think it'll be better to go along with things rather than make a stand and upset everyone, but afterwards I find myself in an even worse mess. Now I've badly hurt someone I'm terribly fond of. I *know* he'll be much happier with someone else, but I've wounded his pride and he'll never forgive me. Oh dear, and Evelyn was enjoying organizing the wedding and now she'll have to tell all her friends it's off. And Isobel's furious with me because I've hurt her beloved brother. Oh God, I feel terrible!' I pressed his handkerchief to my eyes again. 'I've known them all my life and always loved them really, even when relations were strained which they often were – but you can't love people without feeling angry with them sometimes, can you? Now I feel quite sick with shame and pity and . . . the most desperate guilty longing to escape.'

'That does sound uncomfortable, I must say.'

I paused on the top step and looked at Conrad to see if he was making fun of me. His black eyes were, as usual, difficult to read, but in general I thought the composition of his features might be intended to convey sympathy. Slowly he smiled and I was obscurely comforted, as though he possessed some mysterious power that could turn misfortune to good.

'You are not very old. It is an inalienable trouble of youth that one is carried helplessly along by a tide of action and reaction. Eventually, after some floundering, one gets the idea that it may be better to take charge of one's own boat and to pull for shore. At that moment is maturity. I remember very well the days when I was ruled entirely by my immediate passions – or worse, somebody else's.'

'I can't imagine that. You seem so . . . controlled isn't the right word . . . self-aware. And you're so reserved. I never know what you're thinking.'

'Do you not?' The smile remained but became a little more inscrutable, his eyes watchful.

'I do know you're often secretly laughing when you look most solemn. And you pretend to be irresponsible – like jumping off the balcony, and conceited sometimes, but perhaps that's put on too.' I had a sudden insight. 'Aha! I *see!* You're afraid of showing your feelings. That's the real reason you didn't want to be a concert pianist – nothing to do with not having the right temperament. It's because to play well – just like dancing – you have to show everything you feel inside with a sort of searing, soul-baring intimacy.'

'*Autsch!* That sounds agonizing. And when, you tautologous woman, does anyone feel *out*side? Your difficulty,' he let go of my arm to pull a strand of my hair across my face as though to shut me up, 'is that your imagination has been stimulated by fear. You need to be calmed by food and drink before you become frenzied.'

He stood aside to let me pass before him into the hall, his expression sardonic, but I was certain I had stumbled on the key to his character. This discovery went a little way to restoring my confidence, which had been badly bruised by my failure to make anything but a hideous mess – *un joli fouillis*, as Madame would have said – of all my relationships. Conrad had a marvellous talent for putting things into perspective. Though the quarrel with Rafe had left me sore and wretched, yet I found I was not entirely without hope for the future.

'Come on, Marigold.' Golly rushed into the hall, seized my arm and dragged me towards the drawing room. 'Let's get on with it.'

Orlando, who had been draped with sinuous elegance across one of the divans, got up to plant a light kiss on both my cheeks. Despite being racked by neuroses, narcotics and starvation diets, he was still beautiful in a weak light. His greenish-blonde hair, which hung like damp seaweed across his high knobbly fore-head, and his slanting green eyes gave him the appearance of a reasonably youthful merman. He must have been forty or forty-five, but still took classes daily and often taught them, so he was terrifically fit. His arms felt like runner beans, quite stringy with little bulges of muscle along their lengths. 'My darling,' he said in fluting tones, 'what an experience . . . that bridge . . . my vertigo . . . the journey . . . an overheated train . . . a small vomiting child: only the thought of seeing you kept me from turning back a hundred times.'

I was certain he hadn't given me a single thought the entire way, but I was used to his specious charm and actually quite liked it. Among the bullies, prima donnas, grabbers, braggers and sex maniacs of the ballet, Orlando's flowery, confidential manner made a refreshing change.

'*Ach,* Marigold!' Fritz was, as usual, carrying a tray. 'I haf for you some cake you vill like.'

'What fettle, Fritz?' I kissed his soft pink and white cheek. His eyes were almost violet in the gathering gloom as the rain clouds bloomed. Though there was a good fire burning, one of the huge windows that led onto the balcony was open and the air was rich with leafy smells from the forest below.

Fritz returned my kiss with plump ruby lips. 'Aah's champion.'

Orlando looked at the cake, which was loaf-shaped and striped brown and yellow, resembling a giant bumblebee. 'Usually sugar is death to my nervous system . . . I become insomniac and jittery . . . but perhaps I might risk—'

'You vill not suffer ills from my *Mohnstriezel.*' Fritz cut a slice and handed him a plate. 'It is yeast sponge vith poppy seed and almond nuts and lemon peels. Wery, wery healzy.'

'You're certainly an advertisement for your own cooking.' Orlando took a bite, then widened his eyes as though in ecstasy before running them appreciatively over Fritz. 'Mmmm. Marvellous!'

He made it clear that he included Fritz's curves, sheathed in a cream silk shirt, cravat and checked knee britches, in the compliment. Fritz's cheeks and forehead turned the colour of a damask rose. Excitement crackled between the two men. I was pleased by this turn of events. Orlando was inspired to do his best work when fired by love.

We drank tea with slices of lemon poured from a silver teapot shaped like a swan into cups enamelled in crimson and azure.

'If you've finished stuffing yourselves, we'll start.' Golly gulped down her tea. 'No thank you, Fritz.' She gave him a reproachful look as he offered her a slice of *Mohnstriezel*. 'Some of us have better things to do than indulge our coarser appetites.'

Unaware that she had lunched extensively at Shottestone within the last hour, Fritz looked a little hurt. Golly strode to the piano and placed several sheets of manuscript on the music stand, then pressed the button of a portable tape recorder. 'From Kayoko's first entrance, Conrad. Bar thirty-eight. Yuki, tenor, has been wandering about under the cherry trees singing of the mysterious visitation of a *tanuki*, in Japanese lore a racoon with magic, shape-shifting powers. The *tanuki* has prophesied a fateful meeting beneath the blossom, during which his heart will be possessed by an image of beauty.'

Conrad went to the piano. 'The racoon's heart?'

'Don't pretend to be dense. Yuki's, of course. You might give us the preceding twenty bars from where the key changes from six flats to seven sharps and the time to thirteen hemi-demi-semi quavers.'

Conrad grimaced. 'You have made it too easy.'

Orlando brushed crumbs from his fingers and went to stand in front of the open window, one hand on his hip, the other extended above his head, while he considered. 'Marigold, darling, we'll just walk through a few ideas. Begin by folding yourself up as small as you can, as if you were no bigger than the head of an opium poppy.'

Conrad crouched over the piano, his brows a black V of intense concentration, while his flashing fingers produced a violent cacophony of tinkling punctuated by crashes, as though a panic-stricken mouse were running up and down the keyboard and he was trying to hit it with a hammer.

I did my best to impersonate a tiny seed head, encumbered as I was by a flared woollen skirt and a thick jersey.

'Now, skim, skim, skim to centre stage, now *glissade, assemblé, bourrée* and *jeté* . . . let's try an adagio *enchaînement*, as though you're half this fellow's imagination, half a visitation from a spirit world . . .'

Orlando got more and more excited thinking up things for me to do, and Golly from time to time said, 'Yes!' 'Lovely!' 'Just right!' or 'Too expansive!' 'Too sexy!' 'Too European!' And several times they argued furiously, which gave Conrad and me a chance to rest.

'I want Kayoko to dance like a drifting petal, blown hither and thither by the wind!' cried Golly. 'Then as Yuki tries to take her in his arms she spins until her body is a blur, before melting into invisibility.'

'You don't want much,' said Orlando crossly. 'If she spins to a blur she'll probably have to be carted straight to hospital and I can't make her invisible. She could dodge behind a tree, perhaps. Besides, petals don't melt. They go brown and rot. You mean a snowflake.'

'I mean a petal.' Golly put on her stubborn look, lower lip thrust out, eyes glaring. 'And this one melts. There is nothing predictable about my opera—'

'If it comes to that, cherry blossom in Japan is about as trite as it gets!'

Conrad and I went to sit by the fire. We watched the rain pelting the terrace with bursting drops the size of marbles, while Golly and Orlando shouted and shook their fists in what Conrad said was an entertaining synergy between man and nature. Siggy, heavy with grass and cake crumbs, sat on my knee. I was not at all perturbed by the quarrelling, as that kind of thing went on all the time at the LBC. An artistic vision is nothing less

470

than a divine revelation to its conceiver and any attempt to tamper with its perfection is bound to be resented.

By suppertime we had sketched out the first dance sequence. Orlando was trembling with exhaustion, convinced he had a temperature and was possibly coming down with a chill. Conrad and I were in not much better condition. Though I had not danced 'full out', every centimetre of my body had been punished and was complaining about it. I kept a smile on my face and forbore to massage any part of me in case anyone should think I wasn't up to it. At least my left foot had responded to my instructions and hurt as much or as little as the right one. But that afternoon I had danced in bare feet. It might be different when I went up on *pointe*.

When Isobel, who was expected for supper, did not appear, I felt it necessary to apologize to Conrad.

'I'm afraid it's because she's angry with me. Or she doesn't want to leave Rafe on his own.'

'Do not worry. She had the choice whether to come or not. And she would not have liked to find us too fatigued to entertain her.'

Supper was restorative, a goose stuffed with apples and prunes followed by souffléd pancakes filled with jam and sprinkled with icing sugar. I exercised great restraint and only ate half mine. Golly lit a pipe and blew tarry smoke all over me, which was a helpful appetite suppressant. She had lost her voice with so much shouting, and Orlando said he was too enervated to talk, so it was a peaceful evening.

I left Siggy in his warm basket in the kitchen and put on my coat to be driven home by Fritz. I kissed Golly and Orlando goodnight, but when I approached Conrad he put up a warning hand.

'I am certain that being a sentimental Englishwoman you have been kissing that rabbit and I have no desire to contract a plague.'

'Surely not?' Orlando looked alarmed. 'Isn't that a mediaeval disease?'

471

'By no means. It no longer kills whole cities, but each year on average there are some two thousand cases reported. It can never be eradicated because the bacillus lives on healthy rodents and it is spread by ticks and fleas.'

Orlando covered his mouth with his mauve lace scarf and looked at Conrad with large, fearful eyes. 'What are the symptoms?'

Conrad smiled chillingly. 'Fevers, headaches, swollen glands.'

Orlando shuddered. 'Golly, take me home immediately, if you will be so good. I must go straight to bed with a hot-water bottle.'

'Don't own such a thing,' she croaked. 'Unhealthy to be too warm. Saps one's vitality. I like a good breeze through the house, don't believe in central heating.' Orlando's expression changed from alarmed to appalled. Golly grabbed his arm and hissed, 'Come on, you poor old stretcher case, let's get the wind in our hair.'

As I got into the passenger seat of the comfortable Bentley, I caught a glimpse of Orlando beside Golly in the little yellow car, his mouth open in a scream as they scorched out of the courtyard towards the bridge, her headlamps sweeping the dramatic façade of Hindleep like searchlights.

'A beautiful night,' said Fritz as we wound down the hill. 'Stars among ze clouds and ze moon trying to out itself.'

'Lovely,' I said, keeping my eyes tightly closed.

'You haf Orlando known long time?'

'For about five years, but never particularly well.'

'Ah. But vat a woyage it might be to discover his insides! He is a genius!'

All the way to Dumbola Lodge I did my best to answer Fritz's questions about Orlando. He dropped me at the door and drove away in a state of giddy infatuation. I let myself in quietly, hoping to slip upstairs, but the study door was open and a band of light fell across the hall. I started to tiptoe towards the stairs, leaping in fright as the longcase clock began to chime. A figure appeared in the doorway, the light behind him turning the tips of his red hair to fire and throwing his face into shadow.

'Where the hell have you been?'

39

'It's so kind of you to let me stay.'

Conrad, Fritz and I were having a leisurely breakfast of fried eggs, toast and coffee at Hindleep. I looked longingly at the homemade apricot jam, glistening copper-coloured hemispheres floating in amber syrup, but now I was a dancer again I had to eat like one. A brand-new Aga, installed during the time of plenty, took the chill from the morning mist that crept in through the open French windows. Siggy was hopping about on the terrace in the company of a pair of blackbirds who were eating the crumbs Fritz had thrown out for them.

Conrad poured himself another cup of coffee. 'Not especially kind.' He was holding a book in front of his face to indicate that he was not in the mood for conversation. It was dark green, much worn, and sticking out of the pages were pieces of paper covered with Conrad's writing. The title alone – *Treatise on the Emendation of the Intellect* by Benedict de Spinoza – was enough to crush me with a sense of my own ignorance. He looked at me over the top of it. 'We were hardly in a position to refuse.'

'You might have told me to go away. Or driven me to the nearest hotel.'

'As to the first, what sort of man refuses shelter to a young woman boltered with blood and mud and palpitating with fear,

474

who knocks on his door in the middle of the night? As to the second, we were in our dressing gowns and it would have been inconvenient, to say the least.'

Considering how exhausted Conrad must have been after his *tour de force* of piano playing, I thought he had been remarkably good humoured when I returned to Hindleep after midnight, unannounced and uninvited. I had certainly been a good deal upset. The friendly daytime wood of purling waters and leafy glades was altogether unlike its night-time persona of bogs, impenetrable thickets, screeches, howls and sinister black shapes. The rain had fallen in vicious spurts, brambles and thorn bushes had torn at my limbs and every step of the way I had imagined my father's hand hovering just inches from my shoulder, the knife blade and his spectacles flashing in dribbles of moonlight.

My appearance had been undeniably repulsive. In wiping raindrops from my eyes I had smeared blood from scratched hands over my forehead, cheeks and chin. Fritz and Conrad had taken it in turns to pump enough water from the spring so I could have a bath. There were no spare bedrooms in a habitable state, so I had slept in great comfort on one of the divans by the fire. It had been nearly two o'clock before any of us could close our eyes.

'Vat time your father go out so ve fetch ze closes and ze toozbrush?' asked Fritz.

'Let's wait until half-past nine to be sure.'

The idea of meeting my father again terrified me. When he had demanded to know where the hell I had been, I had answered with as much calm dignity as I could muster that I had spent the evening at Hindleep and was now going to bed. I had tried to walk past him, but he had beaten me to the foot of the stairs, gripping the banister knob with one hand and putting the other against the wall to bar my path.

'What sort of time do you call this?'

'I call it eleven o'clock.'

475

'Exactly. I've been home since six and I've had nothing to eat.'

'I didn't know you wanted me to make supper for you. I never have before.'

'Because your mother's always done it.' He smiled unpleasantly. 'Now she's romancing a syphilitic gypsy she hasn't time.'

'Couldn't you have had baked beans or something?'

He sighed as though weary, and dropped his hands to crack his fingers. 'I've spent a large part of today at the hospital trying to repair the sickly bodies of the brutish, the ignorant and the villainous. And though tomorrow's Sunday, I'm on call because Chatterji has had some sort of nervous breakdown. I can't get a locum until Wednesday, but that won't stop the lumpen-proletariat sticking foreign objects in their orifices and having lumpenproletariat babies. You, I can safely assume, have done nothing that might by the greatest stretch of imagination be called useful. Besides, there aren't any baked beans. I found half a loaf of stale bread, a piece of brick-hard cheese and a tin of palm hearts, whatever they may be.'

Dimpsie and I had eaten the larder bare but we had not managed to find a use for the latter.

'I didn't realize you expected me to be your housekeeper.'

'You live here, don't you? Surely even you, self-absorbed and narcissistic though you've always been, can appreciate that some contribution is due?'

I considered returning insult for insult. There were plenty that his recent behaviour merited, but I was as tired as I ever remembered being and my mind seemed to drop into bottom gear. The telephone began to ring.

'Answer it.' He jerked his thumb at the softly warbling instrument. 'Say I'm out on a call. Write down the name, number and any coherent symptoms.'

I picked up the receiver. 'Dr Savage's residence.'

'Who's that?' The voice was female, middle-class, crisp.

'This is Dr Savage's receptionist.'

'Oh yes – his daughter. I remember. I want to speak to him.'

'He's out on a call. If you'll give me your name and number I'll get him to—'

'This is Marcia Dane speaking. He's there, isn't he? Tell him he's got to speak to me.'

'Mar-cia D-ane,' I said slowly for my father's benefit, pretending I was writing it down. 'Is it an emergency?' I turned to look at him. He shook his head emphatically.

'Yes, it *is* a bloody emergency!' Marcia's voice became loud and angry. 'I want to speak to him *now!*'

'If you'd like to tell me what's wrong I could perhaps make you a priority—'

'What's wrong is that he's a cold-hearted *monster!* I've given him everything – *everything!* – and now he thinks he's going to walk away because he's bored. *Bored!* He's taken what he wanted and now he discards me like an old glove.' I could not help thinking of Conrad then. 'He's a shit of the first water!'

'In that case,' I said sweetly as she paused to draw breath, 'you must be two of a kind. I'll tell him the old glove rang, shall I?'

This was not at all nice of me, but she had made Dimpsie so unhappy. From the other end came a sound as though the receiver had bounced on its rest.

I gave Tom my most despising stare. 'I take it if Vanessa Trumball calls you don't want to speak to her either?'

He shrugged. 'I doubt if Vanessa's capable of making a phone call. And you needn't glare at me like that. She was unstable long before I had anything to do with her.'

'Then perhaps you ought to have left her alone.'

'Women are masochists. They find it exciting to be treated badly. It was what she wanted. After all, you've engaged yourself to that stuffed shirt who's going to put a collar and lead on you and try to turn you into his mother. How masochistic is that?'

I congratulated myself for recognizing that the introduction of Rafe to the conversation was a diversionary tactic. 'Do you always give people what they want? Your wife, for example?'

'What business is it of yours?'

'It's my business because I love her. Anything that wounds her, wounds me.'

I could hardly believe that for once I was managing to keep my emotions at a steady simmer rather than a rolling boil. Usually I lost my temper immediately and threw away the argument. It was annoying to be interrupted by another discreet trill from the telephone.

'Answer it. If it's Marcia again, just put the receiver down.'

'Hello? Dr Savage's residence.'

'Marigold!' I recognized the voice immediately. 'Where the hell have you been?'

'Hello, Isobel. I've been at Hindleep. We expected you.' I turned to look at Tom but he had gone.

'Well, I call that pretty damn cool! Rafe says you've broken off your engagement. He's miserable, poor darling. Absolutely wretched. And he's got one of his heads. Naturally you've been out enjoying yourself. I'm surprised you didn't throw a party.'

'But it was as much Rafe's decision as mine to break it off. In fact he was much angrier with me than I was with him. It's terribly upsetting for everyone, I do realize—'

'What a *fool* you are!'

'Look, it's late and I'm shattered. Can't we talk about it tomorrow?'

'I want to talk about it now.'

I sat down in my father's armchair and waited.

'Are you there? Marigold?'

'Yes. I'm here. What do you want to say?'

'You *know* Rafe's been ill . . . depressed. But you seem to think it's all just a game . . . don't you realize, you stupid girl, that you may be responsible for driving him over the edge?'

It was the third time that day that I had had to listen to harsh criticism of my intelligence and behaviour. But I stifled my resentment, reminding myself that she felt about Rafe as a mother hen feels about its only chick, and that this was one of her most likeable traits. Besides, though I had tried to dismiss them, my father's taunts had, as usual, burned themselves into my brain like a pokerwork motto. Why, disliking him as I did, should it matter what he thought of me? Probably it was something best left in the turbid deeps of my subconscious. But if I really was a self-centred narcissist, I no doubt deserved the reproaches that these days rained upon me from all sides.

'You didn't see him just after he left the hospital,' Isobel continued. 'When he first came home he couldn't eat . . . he had a permanent migraine. No one else knows this, but several times he actually cried.'

I understood from the quivering intensity in her voice that in Isobel's world men only cried when absolutely at the limit of endurance, as when standing in the dawn light before a firing squad and perhaps not even then. In my world men wept like babies because they had been given an unflattering wig to wear.

'If he gets into that state again I'll blame *you*. Everyone will blame you. They'll all hate you and I'll hate you more than anyone. You shouldn't have said you'd dance in Golly's ridiculous opera. You're supposed to be getting married, not prancing about on stage so people can say how clever you are.'

'That isn't why . . .' I stopped, knowing it was useless to try to explain why one might want to dance to someone who had never felt the least inclination. 'It isn't only the dancing. I'm terribly fond of Rafe but we aren't enough alike to be happy living together. This isn't our first row. We started disagreeing almost from the beginning only I so wanted to make it work . . . I've always thought he was so marvellous and I was flattered when he asked me and I wanted to help . . .'

'I don't believe that. I suppose it was the money. Or did you fancy being mistress of Shottestone?' Her voice became yet more sneering. 'Quite a step up for the local doctor's daughter, wasn't it?' I screwed up my eyes tightly and gritted my teeth to prevent myself from crying out in protest. 'But you're not prepared to give anything in exchange. You want to have your cake and eat it, you bloody selfish bitch! He's much too good for you!'

'Yes,' I felt tears of tiredness and mortification sting my eyes, 'I'm sure he is.'

'Is that all you can say? What about everything my family's done for you? Don't you think you owe Mummy something?'

A horrible smell of burning milk drifted into the study. My father had resorted to self-catering in his hour of need.

'I'll always be grateful to Evelyn, but that doesn't mean it would be right to marry Rafe. I don't fit his ideas of what a wife should be. He wants someone who can strike awe into the hearts of the lower orders and put the screws on bolshie committee members and shine all the other women down. I'm not up to it.'

'Mummy can teach you. And you bloody well *owe* it to her. You talk about being grateful, but it's time you knew exactly how fucking much she's done for you.'

'What d'you mean?'

Isobel laughed scornfully. 'I tried to make Tom tell you ages ago but he said he'd promised Mummy he wouldn't. Well, I promised too but I don't *care*. When Miss Fisher said you ought to go to Brackenbury House, your father said he'd no intention of bankrupting himself for the sake of an adolescent craze. Mummy tried every argument she could think of to get him to change his mind, but he wouldn't so she decided she'd pay for you to go. I overheard her arguing with Daddy about it, that's how I knew. He thought it was an unnecessary expense but it was her money, all those vulgar cotton mills. She said she couldn't bear to see talent go to waste and as far as she was concerned it was the same as giving money to orphans in Africa only much more likely to get a result. She made me swear that I'd never tell you because it would put you under such an obligation. Mummy's a silly snobbish cow most of the time, but she has her finer moments. And she's always loved you.' Isobel paused

480

as though expecting me to say something but I was dumbstruck. Isobel's voice buzzed in my ear like a furious wasp. 'Now you know, perhaps you'll feel differently about wrecking Rafe's happiness for the sake of your pathetic little ego.'

I registered the loathing patent in Isobel's voice but for once I was indifferent. Evelyn had paid for me to go to ballet school. I repeated the words to myself two or three times in an attempt to make proper sense of them. The burden of guilt I had carried because my parents had gone without quite modest comforts so that I might become a dancer rolled from my shoulders. Throughout my seven years of training I had been uncomfortably aware that my fees had been responsible for the inadequate food and heating, the ancient Hillman my father drove, the black moods when bills came, the lack of holidays, the fact that each year the already shabby house grew shabbier. And I could only guess how much my sister Kate had suffered, believing herself to be the less favoured child. It would not be an exaggeration to say that her envy had destroyed our relationship. I had accepted her hostility as my due. Now I felt liberated. But only for a moment.

'Marigold? Why don't you say something? Come on, you must have suspected!'

I had nothing to say. I had never for a moment had even an inkling of the truth. Evelyn was responsible for me being who and what I was, a dancer first and last – of that I was sure now – and she had done it out of simple generosity. There had been no calculation in it, no hope of repayment, just a desire to help me realize my ambition. Now, like Christian, I was compelled to take up my burden once more, but the load had shifted. It was some slight relief to know that the Prestons had not needed to make any material sacrifices to support my career. But one's parents are to a greater or lesser extent obliged to put their hands in their pockets for their children. Evelyn had chosen to do so out of the goodness of her heart and my debt therefore was doubled, quadrupled, tenfold – a hundredfold.

'Marigold! I know you're there. Say something, for God's sake!'

'Goodbye, Isobel.'

'No, wait a minute! I want to talk—'

I put down the telephone and went into the kitchen. Curls of smoke were rising from the toaster.

'Why didn't you tell me it was Evelyn who paid for me to go to ballet school?'

He was hacking at the cracked yellow lump of cheese with the bread knife and did not look up. 'She made me promise I wouldn't.' He appeared calm but I saw the muscles tighten around his mouth.

'You let me go on feeling guilty as hell, thinking you and Dimpsie and Kate were going without because of me.' He continued to hack, a model of unconcern. I struggled to contain my fury. He went to the utensil jar, selected the steak tenderizer that Dimpsie had bought years ago in one of her periodical fits of enthusiasm for cooking, and tried to hammer the knife through the cheese rind.

'I'm not responsible for your thoughts. As for feeling as guilty as hell, I doubt it.' For the first time he looked directly at me with eyes that were pinpoints of malice. 'Did you once think of giving it up? Did you even consider missing a performance to come home and see your mother, about whose welfare you say you're so anxious?'

'If you weren't paying for me, why was there never enough money for the boiler to be replaced or the roof to be repaired properly? Or a new car? What about Kate's riding lessons?'

'Now you mention her, Kate was not sufficiently on your tormented conscience to make it worth your attending her wedding, I remember.'

'We were in China! It was my first chance to dance Aurora. Besides, she wrote saying that it would be a waste of time to come back.'

'What a little hypocrite you are! As though you'd have dreamt

482

of doing so.' It was true I had not been altogether sorry that her letter had been a clear instruction to keep away. The return flight would have cost me two months' salary. 'You neglected your family because you had more interesting things to do.'

I felt the blood rush to my face. I could not deny it. Don't get sidetracked, I told myself, and above all don't give him the satisfaction of seeing how much he's hurting you. 'One of the reasons I didn't come home much was because I've always hated the way you've treated Dimpsie – going off with other women and breaking her heart each time in the most callous way, putting her down, destroying her self-confidence; you've always been absolutely foul to her and I couldn't bear to watch it.'

'So you left her to nurse her broken heart – if you must use clichés – alone. That *was* kind!'

'Well, I admit it wasn't very.' I was furious with myself for being unable to control my voice, which despite my best efforts was becoming strained and unnatural. 'I ought to have looked after her better. But you shouldn't have broken it in the first place. You've slept with every woman who caught your eye without a thought in the world for anything but your own sexual gratification.'

'Much you know about a man's feelings. I suppose you don't like it because Rafe's an indifferent lover.' For a moment I thought of telling him what Dimpsie had said about his own less than wonderful lovemaking but, even in my barely controllable rage, this seemed impossibly cruel. 'The Prestons think they've a duty to set an example to the nation. No one must be allowed to know their grubby little secrets. As though anyone cared! You're an also-ran. Did you know that?' He laughed, his eyes like slits behind his rimless spectacles. 'You'd be a fool to marry him.'

'What do you mean?'

'Can't tell you, I'm afraid. Patient confidentiality. But you'd better take my advice.'

I cursed myself for playing straight into my father's hands. I had to direct the conversation away from me back to him.

483

'You're the last person entitled to give advice to anyone. I shall do just as I choose.'

'Good. So shall I.' He returned his attention to the cheese. 'Oh bugger!' He had hit the knife so hard that the head of the meat tenderizer had flown off and knocked over a glass. The red wine it contained flowed across the table like blood.

'I absolutely hate you,' I said to my own astonishment, the words coming out of my mouth before I could stop them. Suddenly tears were gushing down my face. 'I hate you, I hate you, I *hate* you! I wish you were dead!'

My father's eyes glittered and he bared his teeth with bitter satisfaction. He had achieved his object. I was weeping, vulnerable, an emotional wreck, like all the women with whom he had anything to do. He had abandoned the cheese and advanced slowly towards me, knife in hand. I had turned and fled.

40

'One, two three – turn a little slower.' Orlando spun round himself to demonstrate. 'Elbows up, sharper . . . more abandoned . . . inside the demure little maid there's a sensual woman . . . four, five, six . . . prepare for a *brisé en avant* . . . right arm higher . . . watch that upstage leg . . . now astound your lover with an arabesque *penchée* . . . *perfect,* darling . . . you could drop a plumb line between your heels.' An arabesque *penchée* is when you stand on one leg holding the other above your head in the six o'clock position, like doing the splits vertically. '*Jeté élancé* to upper left . . . then *grand jeté développé en avant* . . .'

I made several low darting leaps across the floor of Conrad's drawing room, culminating in a great spring into the air, doing the splits horizontally this time.

'Let's have it again.' Orlando wound back the tape of Conrad's playing that Golly had recorded the day before. 'Turn your head to look back over your right shoulder . . . coquettish . . . juicy yet virginal . . .'

I did my best, though it was early in the day for that kind of thing. Also Siggy had whiled away the long hours of incarceration in my bedroom at Dumbola Lodge making my practice clothes into a cosy nest, so they were anything but virginal in appearance, being mostly holes. We worked until lunchtime when every muscle in my body felt like perished rubber. Orlando had choreographed several passages in which I had to imitate the way Japanese women traditionally walk, a modest pigeon-toed tripping quite the opposite of the conventional 'turned out' position that my hips had been forced into for more than a decade and they were feeling the strain. But I had been dancing on pointe all morning and my left foot felt fine.

'Wonderful, darling!' Orlando embraced me. 'I feel one or two teeny ideas are beginning to emerge from the creative fog. I hope that delicious smell is our lunch. My stomach's roaring like a grumpy old lion.'

'Didn't you have any breakfast?'

'My dear, I know I ought not to criticize my kind hostess, but *promise* you won't repeat. I requested my usual *petit repas* – warmed goat's milk with an egg white beaten into it and just a soupçon of nutmeg, but Golly drinks milk from tins and she doesn't possess a nutmeg. Can you *imagine* a household without a nutmeg?'

I easily could, having just moved out of one.

'I explained that one drop of cow's milk is enough to keep me in bed for a week unable to put a foot to the floor. She was most anxious to be helpful and together we perused the tin, but it was positively Sphinx-like in its refusal to divulge its contents.'

I could sympathize with Golly's anxiety about having an invalid Orlando on her hands. Using a chair back as a barre I did a few *grand battements en dehors,* to cool down.

'I didn't like to pursue the vexed question of the milk – no one can say that *one* is not the easiest, most considerate of guests, so instead I applied myself with a will to eat what was on offer. Cold toast the colour of underpants and a terrible black sausage-shaped thing, like a dinosaur's stool. It was all one could do not to scream. Only one's strict upbringing enabled one to get down two tiny bites of the prehistoric faeces.'

'It's called blood pudding. It's something of a national dish in the North.'

'*Blood* pudding?' Orlando paled, clutched his hands to his chest and closed his eyes.

'Vat fettle, Marigold, Orlando?' Fritz came in with a tray and began to lay the table. 'I haf a dish prepared called *Gefüllte Seezungenfilets*. It is fillets of sole stuffed viz lobster and mushrooms. Wery good. I serve it viz *Meerrettichkartoffeln* and *Schmorgurken*.'

In the process of folding the napkins into swans, he paused to steal a glance at Orlando who, as though unconscious of his audience, did three beautifully executed pirouettes *en dedans,* which caused his naked biceps to ripple and his powerful thigh muscles to pump. Fritz let the napkin fall from his fingers as he gazed open-mouthed. Despite the twenty-year age gap and Orlando's superior sophistication and experience, I thought it unlikely that Fritz would come to harm. Though an out-and-out sensualist, Orlando was not cynical. Also the strong light from the balcony made apparent the drawn yet crumpled look which smoking, sunbeds and dieting imparts to middle-aged faces. Fritz was young and beautiful, if fat, and the ball was rather in his court.

I lay on my back and put one leg over my head until I could touch my nose with my knee and the floor with my foot – the splits again, this time upside down.

'I wonder if Degas would have felt inspired to paint you.'

At the sound of Conrad's voice I sat up quickly. He had been in his office all morning, no doubt trying to salvage the wreck of his empire.

'He's always been my favourite painter.'

'Ah, yes, because he paints dancers. But he did not care for ballet particularly, only he wished to paint movement and pretty clothes. He painted many nudes also, but did not care much for women. He liked to paint them – his words – without their coquetry, as animals cleaning themselves. He was a misogynist. In his view women think in little packages; they are incapable of extrapolation.'

'In that case I don't like him nearly so much as I did.'

487

'When I hear a man claim that the feminine intellect is inferior to the masculine, then I know that he is afraid of women. Degas was a man of strong affections, generous in his evaluation of other artists he admired, a brilliant conversationalist. But he was sensitive and melancholic . . .'

Conrad put his hands in his pockets and strolled about the room while giving me a sketch of Degas' life and artistic theories. Some people, most perhaps, would have resented such a stream, almost a river, of information, but I was hungry for knowledge. While I listened I practised a few pirouettes *en dedans* myself, faster than Orlando's, using the half-painted squirrel with the red body and the chalk tail to 'spot'. This means whipping your head round faster than your body with each turn and focusing your eyes on a particular place, which prevents you getting dizzy. I wondered if the wall painting would ever be completed. The pale outlines of unfinished animals and birds were like ghostly creatures existing in another dimension. But probably Conrad would be bored by the project before he had made enough money to finish it.

'He became too blind to paint any more and this increased his eccentric behaviour . . . his irritability. He was lonely, yet he could not endure the stupidity of his fellow men.'

'Poor Degas.' I whipped my leg up into a *grand battement*. 'I'd sympathize except I know he'd have thought me as stupid as anyone. Are you ever lonely?'

Conrad folded his arms and looked towards the window. The sky, speedwell blue moments before, had turned ashen, and plump clouds were piling up like an elaborate pudding. 'I am not often alone.' He kept his back to me. 'But that is not what you are asking. You mean the feeling of isolation when in the company of those with whom one has no idea, no impulse, no enthusiasm in common. And the knowledge that others are quite indifferent to one's imaginative life. That is wounding because our amour-propre is so fragile and so easily we doubt the . . . the validity – can one say that? – of one's being.'

488

'I know. You start thinking you're the most boring, contemptible person in the world.' I saw that he was about to disagree. 'Well, *I* do anyway. Do you think that might be love? Wanting to understand another person completely, to see things through their eyes and feel what they're feeling?'

'It might be as much as one ought to hope for.'

'Dancers aren't very good at that sort of thing.' I sprang into an *échappé à la seconde*. 'Too self-involved. Dancing absorbs all the energy and thought and time that you ought to give to being in love with someone. You have to choose one or the other. I know that now.'

Rain began to dash itself against the window, blurring the greens and brown of the far side of the valley, as though we were seeing it through tears.

'Come to the table,' pleaded Fritz, 'the fish is colding.'

Golly burst into the room. She had been composing in the kitchen. 'I've decided you were right about the cherry blossom being trite – Madame Butterfly and all that – so I've decided to set *The Fishcake* in Alaska.'

'Alaska!' Orlando was indignant. 'But for the last three hours my entire *being* has been rooted in Hokusai and Miyagi, tea ceremonies, *yatsuhashis*, haikus, kotos and noodles—'

'Well, you'll just have to uproot it then. *My* being has spent all morning in ice-bound tundra, with howling winds, creeping glaciers, cracking floes, honking seals and screeching gulls. Alaska is a completely original setting. As far as I know no Westerner has written an opera about Eskimos.'

'I believe there's a sung version of Eskimo Nell,' said Orlando sulkily. 'Besides aren't you supposed to call them Inuit?'

'Not if we are talking about West Alaska.' Conrad took Golly's arm and led her to the table. 'They are ethnically different and prefer Eskimo to Inuit, and Yupik to either.'

'I meant West Alaska.' Golly looked triumphantly at Orlando. 'There's an Eskimo game called *Aratcheak* in which a piece of bone is hung up and the contestants have to do a standing jump

489

to kick it with both feet and land without falling over. My idea is that the shaman, who's the most important man in the Eskimo settlement, will use the game as a trial to find the most suitable bride for Ata, his son. Ilina – that's Marigold, the daughter of an outcast – wins the game. The two young people do a celebratory dance and fall in love. That's where the singing cake comes in, you remember the singing cake . . . ? What's this?' She poked a finger into the sauce that covered the sole stuffed with lobster, leaving a little swirl of blue ink. Fritz removed the dish from her reach and carefully spooned out the fingerprint. 'Naturally the angakok – that's Eskimo for shaman – is displeased—'

'Ang*akok*? Are you *sure* this isn't an operatic version of Eskimo Nell?' interrupted Orlando.

'Do shut up! – by this turn of events and sets another trial. Most unfair, of course, but that's the nature of fairy tales. There's an Eskimo jumping game called *Qijumik Akimitaijuk Itigaminak* in which the players have to jump as far as they can while holding their toes. Marigold – Ilina, that is – wins again. No acting will be needed for that. Most singers I know can't get anywhere near their toes or jump, let alone the two in combination. I say, this is excellent! I'll have some more.'

She dug her spoon into the delicious pink and whiteness of Fritz's masterpiece and slopped a bit on the tablecloth, which Fritz had ironed to the smoothness of glass. Usually the best-tempered of men, his face took on a brooding look and he disappeared in the direction of the kitchen.

'The angakok measures Ilina's winning jump with her hair ribbon, her prize possession, snips it in two and ties one half round the neck of a tethered reindeer about to be slaughtered for the pot. He releases the deer and gives it a whack, whereupon it gallops away into the freezing mists.'

'A small point perhaps,' said Conrad. 'Reindeer inhabit Eurasia. In Alaska you would find caribou.'

'Well anyway, it's a big shaggy thing with antlers. Who's

going to know the difference? The music will mimic the reindeer's . . . caribou's . . . bellow: E, E flat, G sharp, C . . .' She took out her pen, drew five lines on the tablecloth and scribbled the notes on the stave.

Conrad looked mildly displeased. 'Might I suggest a pencil for your composition?'

'I can't abide pencils. They always need sharpening and that wastes time. I wish you wouldn't interrupt.'

Conrad threw up his eyebrows and forbore to make further comment.

'The call of the reindeer . . . caribou . . . will be a leitmotif throughout the rest of the opera. It'll appear, subtly disguised, in the overture, and be repeated in the last dying chords. The angakok tells Ilina that if she can unite the two pieces of ribbon, he'll let her marry his son. The chances are of course nil as caribou,' she flashed a triumphant look at Conrad who was watching the rain clouds build, 'have vast territories. But after a year of tribulations, just to make things more difficult, the coming of spring breaks up the ice floe on which the little community is built and Alignak, the god of storms, creates an almighty whirlwind. I've been writing the music for that this morning and it's going to be the best thing I've ever done. Finally the beast is slaughtered for a feast – all right, it's a socking great coincidence, but no worse than when Jane Eyre runs away from Mr Rochester and happens to fetch up at the house of that St John bloke who turns out to be her distant cousin. Anyway, the reindeer's brought to the igloo where Ilina is working as a cook. Triumphantly she shows the ribbon to the shaman and he gives in and lets them marry. What do you think?' She looked around the table, her eyes bulging with excitement.

'I'm sorry the reindeer got eaten after all,' I said.

'I don't believe Eskimos have cooks,' said Orlando. 'How many things can you make with no vegetables? Come to that, how is she to make a cake? You have to have eggs and flour. Better have her working as a comfort girl. More balletic. And it ought to be a tent of skins. Igloos are winter houses which would make the sets very boring. Far too much white.'

'That's the whole point if only you'd bother to use your imagination.' Golly grew warm in defence of her brain-child. 'I see it absolutely in the dead of winter. Everything'll be shades of white, blue, grey and violet. Except the ribbon. That'll be red. Ilina'll tie up her hair with it, dance with it, wrap it round trees, etcetera, before it's cut, and then afterwards she'll knot the two pieces together and perform a dance of love consummated. Visualize this red ribbon flowing against the white, symbol of passion, life, menstrual blood and all that sort of thing.'

Orlando looked pained and put down his knife and fork. Fritz returned at that moment with a damp sponge. When he saw the music scrawled on the tablecloth, he withdrew to the balcony and walked up and down in the rain for several minutes.

'What do you think, Conrad?' asked Golly.

Conrad withdrew his eyes from the clouds 'You'll have to do something interesting with the lighting. For three months in winter the Alaskan landscape is lit only by the moon.'

'Really?' Golly sounded annoyed. 'You know you could hire yourself out as a continuity advisor. There *is* such a thing as poetic licence. All right, we'll have the aurora borealis. Shifting curtains of coloured light. Yes, that'll be gorgeous. We'll make a virtue out of a necessity.' She looked at Conrad, almost beseechingly. 'Don't you think it's got tremendous dramatic possibilities? It's got to be better than the plot of *Così fan Tutte*.'

'I can see that it gives you the chance to write some interesting music. But won't your librettist have something to say when you tell him the action has moved halfway round the world?'

Golly's expression became defiant. 'No one said art was easy. He'll have to square up to it like a man.'

'At least it'll have a cheerful ending,' said Orlando. 'The last opera I saw was *Peter Grimes*. Not one ray of hope or hint of redemption. I cried for a week afterwards.'

'Ah! Well, actually I've thought of a jolly good tune for a funeral march, so I think Ilina's going to have to pop her clogs at the altar.'

'The audience will be hysterical after so many changes of mood,' complained Orlando. 'Besides, at this rate it'll be ten hours long. My poor dancers' feet will be blancmange. You can't put things in just because you want to write the music for them.'

'Why can't you?' Golly glared at him. 'The music's the only thing that really matters. We can, if you like, make the dancing more of a sideline . . .'

'And what will you call it?' asked Conrad when Golly and Orlando had finished arguing. 'Rings and fishes seem to have gone quite out of the window.'

'Mm . . .' Golly flicked her upper row of false teeth in and out with the tip of her tongue as she thought. 'The title's always the hardest part. Let's make a list of possibilities. All suggestions welcome. What about *The Ice Maiden?*' She wrote it on the cloth.

'Zat I zink is charming,' said Fritz, perhaps with the idea of preserving the cloth from further harm.

'Too much like *Cinderella on Ice*,' said Orlando.

Golly shut her teeth together with a snap and glowered before saying, 'Oh, all right, yes perhaps . . . what about *The Alaskan Chronicle*? Shades of Hrolf and Beowulf.'

'Zat is wery nice,' said Fritz. 'It has dignity.'

'Sounds deadly dull to me,' objected Orlando. 'Who hasn't been bored half to death by Beowulf at school?'

'I haven't,' I said. 'I've never even heard of him.'

A three-cornered argument broke out, Orlando and Golly making suggestions which the other pooh-poohed roundly, while Fritz tried to keep the peace. Golly called Orlando a muscle-bound moron and he called her a pseudo *enfant terrible*.

'Oh, shut up, you pea-brained caperer!' yelled Golly. '*Snowdrift and Seal Blubber* has no resonance whatsoever. Let's keep it simple. *The Red Ribbon!* I like that.'

'Simple, certainly,' complained Orlando. 'It makes me think of the haberdashery department in John Lewis. What about *Twenty Things You Didn't Know About Eskimos?*'

'Why not call it *Ilina and the Scarlet Riband*?' suggested Conrad.

'First rate!' cried Golly. 'Easy and catchy with a dash of poetry.'

'Not bad,' said Orlando.

And so an important piece of history in the annals of twentieth-century opera was made.

41

'Oh, good, Evelyn's car's here,' I said as Fritz pulled up outside Shottestone's front door. 'I won't be more than half an hour.'

'As you like it, dear voman. I haf much shopping to do.'

Fritz drove away. I went round to the stable yard to make sure that Rafe's elderly Mercedes was not there, then I let myself into the house by the side door. Mrs Capstick was slumbering by the Aga, a dark brown bottle wedged between her thighs. She opened her eyes as I tiptoed past. Her pupils were like pinpricks.

'Hello, dear. Come to see Mr Rafe? That's nice.'

Before I could reply she had fallen asleep again. The drawing room and the conservatory were deserted. Kingsley and Spendlove were nodding in chairs beside the library fire, with Balfour and Gladstone at their feet. Balfour wagged his tail and Gladstone struggled up on stiff legs to greet me, but soon stumbled back to put his chin on Spendlove's slippers and add his snuffles to the chorus of laboured breathing.

I paused outside the door of the morning room. The house was peaceful, the silence broken only by the ticking of the clock at the foot of the stairs and the twittering of birds outside. The scent from the green throats of lilies on the hall table was strong enough to muddle one's senses. I took several deep breaths to fortify myself for the interview. Evelyn would be furious with me because of my quarrel with Rafe and no doubt would say blistering things, but I had to tell her how grateful I was for all she had done for me and how sorry I was at the same time.

I took a step inside the room. Evelyn was standing on the rug before the fire with her back to me. A strange man had his arms round her and they were kissing passionately.

Had the sun turned black and the sky the colour of blood, I could hardly have been more astonished. I must have let out a squawk of surprise because Evelyn sprang from his arms and whipped round to face me.

'Marigold *darl*ing! What a surprise . . . I didn't hear you come in . . .' She smoothed her hair and ran her fingers down the buttons of her shirt . . . 'I don't think you know . . . this is Rex Campion . . . an old friend.' I had heard the name before but I couldn't remember the context. 'Rex, this is Marigold, my daughter-in-law.' She laughed and attempted to regain her composure. 'To be.'

Rex and I shook hands. He was probably unaware that much of Evelyn's dark lipstick had been transferred to his mouth. It looked distinctly odd above such a rugged jaw. His teeth and the whites of his eyes dazzled against his tanned skin. His broad shoulders gave an initial impression of youthful vigour, which was contradicted by his cropped grey hair.

'Hi, Marigold – is it all right if I call you that? Rafe's a very lucky guy.'

As soon as I heard his accent I remembered the Canadian Evelyn had told me about when she had been warning me not to cast my lures at Rafe. That had been before Bunty's lack of dress sense put her out of the running. So this was the love of Evelyn's salad days.

'Thank you.' This was not the right moment to announce that the engagement was off.

'Evelyn says you're coming to live here. It's a beautiful house. I guess you're lucky too.'

His grey eyes were alert and friendly. I thought he looked trustworthy.

'Marigold will make an excellent chatelaine.' Evelyn seemed to purr. 'I shall be quite happy to hand over the reins to her.' She moderated this generous vote of confidence by adding, 'when she has had a little more experience.'

Rex laughed. 'Evelyn's afraid you'll get the linen closet in a mess and upset the head coachman. I felt the same when I handed over the ranch to my son. It took me a while to stop checking that he'd ordered the winter feed on time.'

'You're a cowboy?' I asked, keenly interested.

I pictured him in a Stetson and fringed chaps riding across a cactus-punctuated desert, pursued by dust devils and the bitter-sweet memory of his English love. But there was a son, so presumably there was a wife too or at least a mistress. He had not been inconsolable.

He laughed again. 'Not cows. Horses. The finest bloodlines in Saskatchewan. It started as a hobby and just grew. I'm a lawyer really. Or was. My wife died six months ago and it seemed a good time to take my head out of the money-making noose and see something of the world. I've been travelling ever since. Last week it was Budapest. Before that Leningrad.'

He grinned at me all the time he was talking. His face was crinkled, particularly about the eyes, as though he had spent the years since parting from Evelyn staring ruminatively into the sun.

'I loved Leningrad,' I said, 'and Budapest. Where will you go next?'

'That depends on Evelyn. I'm hoping to persuade her to come with me to Salzburg. All my life I've wanted to see Mozart's birthplace. We could stay at the Sheraton and take in concerts and the opera . . . visit the museums and enjoy the architecture . . . see those fountains at the Hellbrunn Palace. We could have a great time.'

I saw an expression of yearning cross Evelyn's sharp features.

Poor Kingsley's idea of heaven was a month in Scotland. Evelyn had once told me about their honeymoon. They had gone to stay with Kingsley's sister who lived in a vast Victorian mansion in the far north, where a sparse crop of trees grew at an acute angle because of the constant gales. The highlight had been a concert of *port-a-beul*, which is Gaelic for unaccompanied singing in imitation of bagpipes.

'But she seems to think everything will fall to pieces if she isn't here to hold it all together.' Rex gave Evelyn an affectionate pat on the arm to remove any sting of criticism.

'No man has the least idea what has to go on behind the scenes so that life can be comfortable,' said Evelyn. 'There's Kingsley for one thing . . .' She drew in her breath as she noticed the lipstick smear and tapped her own mouth to warn Rex.

He glanced in the mirror and took out his handkerchief to wipe away the evidence, chuckling to himself, not in the least abashed. 'Didn't you say you had a nurse arriving this evening?'

'Yes, but I can't just dash off, leaving her in sole charge. These girls are always complete dummies. One has to coax them along, show them how to get into a routine, how to deal with the permanent staff—'

'Hello, darling.'

It was an unpleasant shock to find Rafe standing right behind me. Before I could decide how I ought to react, he had kissed me on the lips. He had a delicious outdoor smell, as though he'd been rolling in wet bracken. Buster ran in and we greeted each other with wild yelping euphoria, which was the only sort of salutation Buster thought proper. I was grateful because it gave me time to gather my wits. It was certainly not Buster's fault that they refused to converge.

Rafe seemed to be brimming with good humour, unrecognizable as the man of wrath I had run away from the day before. 'Hello, Mother. Rex. Had a good lunch?'

Evelyn looked at Rex. 'The food was dire but we managed to enjoy ourselves.'

Rex returned the look and the air between them sizzled. 'It all seemed pretty damn perfect to me.'

Rafe lowered his eyes for a second and I perceived that he disliked Rex. Or was it Rex's effect on his mother? There was something almost girlish in the way she twirled on one foot to pick up a petal that had fallen from a vase of flowers. She held it to her nose, inhaling deeply with closed eyes as though intoxicated by its scent.

Rafe turned to face me squarely as if to shut out the sight. 'I'm so glad you're here. It's the perfect reward for an afternoon spent listening to Will Templeton's grievances. He seems to think the catalogue of disasters afflicting Bullbeck Farm is due to an envious god rather than his own mismanagement. You'll stay for dinner, of course?'

So craven is my nature that for a second or two I felt relieved to be forgiven. Then I remembered that under no circumstances must I be bullied or cajoled into resuming our engagement. I assumed what I hoped was an appropriate expression, cool without being cold, cordial but not enthusiastic.

'I'm sorry, I can't. Fritz is coming to fetch me up in about—' I looked at my watch – 'twenty minutes.'

Rafe tweaked my ear in a proprietary way before going to the tray to cut himself a slice of cake. 'I met Fritz just now in the newsagent's. He told me he'd arranged to pick you up. I said he needn't bother. I'll run you home later.'

I was dismayed and also not a little annoyed at this highhandedness. 'That's kind of you but I want to go to the telephone kiosk outside the Post Office to order some pointe shoes from Freed's—'

'You can ring from here. Have you had some of this cake? It's very good.'

'No . . .' I hesitated, then reminded myself that I did not need Rafe's approval of my domestic arrangements. 'Actually, I've had a row with my father so I'm staying at Hindleep for the time being.'

Rafe lifted the lid from the teapot to look inside, his brow fluted in a frown. 'This is stewed. I'll get another pot.' He tugged at the bell rope that had been prettily embroidered with flowers by a deceased female Preston, no doubt as a time filler while she waited for fresh instructions from her lord and master.

'Darling, did you say a row with your father?' Evelyn tore herself out of the little dream she had fallen into. 'How upsetting for you. He's the *most* impossible man and always has been. You mustn't reproach yourself. But Hindleep is so inconvenient – still in a half derelict state from what Isobel tells me, and no telephone. You must stay here.'

'Evelyn, could I talk to you? Alone?'

'Of course, my sweet. Is it about Tom and Dimpsie? I've met Jode, you know. Rex and I had a cup of coffee with them both in the Singing Swan – I must say you've transformed that ghastly place – this morning. That is, Dimpsie, Rex and I had coffee, but Jode had his own home-made teabag, full of dried bramble leaves apparently. He wasn't quite as bad as I'd expected – completely unsuitable of course but clearly he adores her.'

'I liked him,' said Rex. 'He's a kind of Thoreau type. Non-cooperation with evil and all that. The philosopher naturalist.'

Evelyn looked amused. 'He reminded me of the Pentecostal preacher who used to stand in front of the butter cross on market days and rave about hellfire and the sins of the flesh to embarrassed pensioners. But if Dimpsie doesn't mind, why should we?'

'I want to call in at the Singing Swan myself.' I looked nervously at Rafe who was flicking through the pages of the *Spectator* as though deaf to the conversation. 'Perhaps if I could just have a word with you, Evelyn – it needn't take long.'

'Hello, Marigold.' Isobel sauntered in and came over to kiss me on the cheek. 'How's the world's most famous ballerina?' The telephone call of the night before might never have taken place. 'Rafe and I have had a marvellous afternoon up on the moors. First it rained, then it sunned, then it rained again. Even my knickers got soaked. Now where did I put them?' She felt in her pocket and withdrew a scrap of black lace which she waved about. 'Hello, Reg. Sorry I wasn't down in time to see you at breakfast.'

'It's Rex, darling.' Evelyn's expression of maternal fondness had become strained.

'Oh. Sorry. Just hang these on the fireguard, would you?' She threw her knickers to Rex who fielded them expertly and draped them carefully before the fire as calmly as though airing a pair of cricket flannels. 'Did you have a lovely day?' Isobel continued. 'Is there any tea?'

'I'll go and see what's happened to it.' Rafe departed.

'We had a great time, thanks.' Rex smiled but I sensed he was wary of his hostess's daughter. I didn't blame him. She seemed charged by some invisible power, her eyes practically emitting sparks.

I concentrated on effecting an escape. 'Evelyn, could we . . . ?'

'Of course. We'll go and talk in the drawing room.'

Evelyn ushered me into the hall. 'Remember, Marigold, when married life and motherhood seem thankless, as they're sometimes bound to do, one's reward is to do the thing well. Your mother has decided to sever those ties, and frankly I think she has every right to do so. Tom has never appreciated her particular gifts. Naturally you're worried about her, but I don't think you need be. A sordid caravan on a desolate moor with a crazed evangelist for a companion may not be *our* idea of domestic bliss but – oh blast!' She broke off as a peal rang through the house. 'Where's that old fool got to?'

Spendlove, his slippers trodden down at the back, his eyes gummy with sleep, his white hair sticking up in a quiff, staggered out of the library and opened the door. Meanwhile the bell had been rung twice more by an impatient hand. 'Good . . . evening, Madam,' he gasped out between wheezes.

'Hello, dear.' A young woman wearing a blue nurse's uniform beneath a navy coat strode into the hall, shook Spendlove's hand

and then Evelyn's hand. 'You must be Mrs Preston. I'm Susan Strangward. I managed to catch an earlier train.'

Susan Strangward exuded confidence. She had shiny brown bobbed hair with a heavy fringe. Her figure was stout and neat, her legs muscular. Her voice was penetrating. The expression in her toffee-coloured eyes was direct and she would have won any staring contest hands down. She turned to look at Spendlove, whose trembling fingers were doing up his waistcoat buttons in the wrong holes.

'Is this the patient?'

'No, that's my husband. I mean, it is my husband who is the patient.' Evelyn seemed the tiniest bit put out by the woman's self-possession. 'This is Spendlove, our butler. You must be tired after your journey,' she added in a more commanding tone. 'That dreadful bus takes an hour to do a fifteen-mile journey.'

Susan did not bother to disguise her curious scrutiny of Evelyn's hair, clothes and shoes. 'So I discovered when I looked at the timetable. I took a taxi. I'll put it on expenses.' She examined her surroundings. 'Quite nice, isn't it? I like the yellow you've painted the walls. Some people might think it a bit gaudy, but a bright colour cheers everyone up, I always say.'

Evelyn, who had spent weeks matching the Chinese Emperor yellow with a piece of antique embroidery in her possession and who, anyway, considered any comment on her furnishings an impertinence, looked frosty. 'You'd better go up to your room, Susan. Spendlove will bring you some tea.'

'A cuppa and a sandwich would be just the biz, but I won't go up yet. I want you to tell me all about my patient, how long he's had dementia, whether he's incontinent, how well he's sleeping, what his morale's like . . . that sort of thing. And I prefer to be called Miss Strangward when I'm on duty. Is there somewhere where we can be private?'

Evelyn closed her eyes for the briefest moment. Then, perhaps thinking of Salzburg, she said coldly, 'We had better go into the drawing room.'

I watched Evelyn and Miss Strangward walk away. The expression of my undying gratitude had better wait until a more convenient time. After twelve years, another few hours would not matter.

'Ready, darling?' Rafe was beside me, jangling his car keys, the soul of amiability. 'Have you made that phone call? Then we can go to Hindleep and get your things.'

I telephoned Freed's and ordered thirty pairs of pointe shoes.

'It sounds like a foreign language,' said Rafe when I had finished. 'What does "vamps three and three-quarters long" mean? And extra paste at tips? And who is M maker?'

'Each pair is made to fit each dancer individually. We all have our favourite maker and they're known just by a letter. Everyone gets into a dreadful flap when their maker gets ill or retires—'

'I suppose it's a sort of sympathetic magic, is it?' Without waiting for an answer, he took his coat from the hall chair and Buster's lead from the umbrella stand. 'All right, let's go.'

'I want to call in at the Singing Swan.'

'Fine.'

'Jode will be there.'

'It'll be worse for him than for me.' He smiled more broadly. 'I'll buy him a cup of tea to show there are no hard feelings.'

Rafe seemed to be the spirit of cooperation made flesh.

'Honestly, Rafe, though it's enormously kind of Evelyn to offer to have me, I prefer for all sorts of reasons to stay at Hindleep. Working with Orlando, for one thing. I've only got six weeks before rehearsals begin. And for another,' I looked down at my feet, reluctant to meet his benevolent gaze, 'we've got to square up to the fact that we aren't going to get married. I know it's awkward having to tell everyone and Evelyn's already put so much effort into it and the lace has been cut up and everything but it's got to be done . . .'

'My poor darling,' Rafe took hold of my chin and lifted my face so I was obliged to look at him. 'I've made you miserable with my dreadful temper and I'm so sorry. I was utterly unreasonable yesterday.' He put his hands on my shoulders and pulled me close. 'Let me make it up to you. Surely after everything that's happened between us I deserve another chance?'

'But it isn't actually your temper that's the problem, is it?' I said earnestly while struggling to detach myself literally and romantically. 'The real problem is that we don't think enough alike to be happy together. I don't know why you wanted to marry me in the first place, and I can't understand now why you keep on with it.'

He laughed. 'Foolish girl! Look in the mirror and you'll see why.'

'You know perfectly well people don't get married because they like one another's faces.'

'I like your body too. In fact I adore it.'

'Oh, for heaven's sake! If I thought for one moment that you were as superficial as that I wouldn't waste another minute arguing with you. But you're pretending to be dumb. And you aren't even in love with me on that most trivial level.'

Rafe stopped smiling and looked grave. 'Is that what this is all about? You doubt that I find you desirable?'

'Yes! No! You're muddling me . . . Don't you see, it doesn't matter – there are too many things that we disagree about.'

'I admit I find your little pets and tantrums somewhat baffling, but all women have them and all men know that the best course is to lie low until the storm blows itself out.'

This was enraging. 'What about Nan's baby? That's one little storm that won't blow itself out.'

'Who is Nan and what's her baby got to do with anything?'

'Don't tell me you've forgotten that Nan is the mother of your child?'

'What *are* you talking about?' He looked perplexed for a moment, then his face cleared and he started to laugh. 'Do you mean the tinker's daughter?'

'It *isn't* funny! Poor little Harrison Ford is a darling and he deserves a father who's going to love him and look after him.'

'You're quite right,' he said soothingly, continuing to smile. 'Any child deserves that. Sweetheart, I don't know what absurd romantic fantasy has been going on in your pretty little head, but I can assure you the baby isn't mine.'

'You've already admitted it!'

'I certainly have not!' He was looking more and more amused. 'As far as I know I've never even met the unfortunate girl.'

'But when I told you about the baby, you asked me how old he was and you stopped being angry – don't you remember? You were very upset. That's why Jode shot at you when we were by the pele tower, isn't it?'

'Oh dear!' Rafe laughed heartily. 'All this time you've been accusing me in your mind of being some kind of heartless monster, exercising droit de seigneur and littering the countryside with bastards! I'm sorry, but I can't help finding it funny.' Seeing my face he stopped laughing. 'Darling, you're quite wrong. Just listen to me for a minute. Several months ago, Ronald Dunderave asked me to lend him some money. He'd got this girl pregnant and he was in a blue funk because she was under sixteen and he was afraid of being taken to court. Also, the girl's father was a gipsy with a violent temper who'd been in prison for GBH. I explained that I never lent money to friends on principle, but I'd give him what he needed. When you told me about the baby, I realized it had to be Ronald's. Perhaps the girl refused to have an abortion or Ronald didn't give her the chance. Whatever the truth of it, one of them kept my three hundred pounds for their own purposes which is dishonest. If I was upset it was because I was envisaging a pretty unpleasant scene, confronting him.'

'But if you aren't the father, why did Jode try to shoot you? At the pele tower, I mean.'

'It wasn't Jode.'

'How do you know?'

'Naturally I informed the police the next day about what had happened. You can't have hooligans going round taking pot shots

505

at people. They found a lot of televisions and microwaves in those old cart sheds behind the tower. One of the tinkers had been storing stolen goods there. He wanted to frighten us off, that's all. At this very minute he's being detained at Her Majesty's pleasure. Anyway, you know, darling,' Rafe patted my cheek, 'if the baby's two months old the evil deed must have taken place last July or August, and I didn't leave the army until the end of September.'

I grew hot with mortification. I had convinced myself of Rafe's guilt on the minimum of evidence, despite everything I knew of his character, which was truthful and honourable and practically stainless. 'Oh! Rafe! I'm so very sorry. I got it all hopelessly wrong. Why didn't you tell me about the stolen goods at the pele tower?'

'I'd made an ass of myself that day. I behaved like a pathetic coward. I didn't want to remind you.'

'Of *course* you weren't a coward . . .'

'It doesn't matter, darling.' He put his arms round me. 'I'm only surprised that if you believed me capable of such shoddy behaviour – getting a schoolgirl pregnant, then washing my hands of her – you consented to marry me. What a brute you must have thought me!'

'I suppose I thought, though it seemed wrong to me, don't men often do that kind of thing? I really only know dancers and I don't think they're typical—'

'I expect plenty do. But it encourages me to think that you could love me in spite of that. If there are any more skeletons in cupboards in your lively imagination, perhaps you'll let me know now so I can clear them out?'

'I'm so awfully sorry.'

'Let's kiss and make up.'

His face hovered close to mine. A door opened behind me.

'Sorry to interrupt anything sickly and inflaming,' said Isobel in her most sarcastic voice. 'Are you going up to Hindleep? If so you might give me a lift.'

* * *

We went first to the Singing Swan. Isobel elected to wait in the car but Rafe insisted on coming in with me. The customers all seemed to be enjoying themselves, and no wonder as it was probably the cleanest, jolliest café in the North of England. Several cuckoo clocks ticked on the sunflower yellow walls and Dimpsie had stencilled teapots, cupcakes and knickerbocker glories round them. Nan waved her notebook at me. Dimpsie was washing up in the kitchen.

'Hello, Dimpsie.' Rafe kissed her. 'My goodness, it's so bright in there you could get a retinal burn.'

Harrison Ford was in a laundry basket on the kitchen table. While Rafe and my mother talked, I picked him up. He seized a strand of my hair in his fist and tried to cram it into his mouth. His was a beauty that not even petrol-blue leggings and a turnip-coloured matinee jacket could dim. He had inherited Nan's large smoke-coloured eyes and there was no sign so far of Ronald's horrid complacent little chin.

'You make a charming picture, darling,' said Rafe. 'This is the little chap we were talking about earlier, I take it.' He gave me a meaningful look as he stroked Harrison Ford's cheek with a forefinger. 'Handsome little beggar!'

'He *is* gorgeous, isn't he? Do look at his little hands. They're so dimpled. And his *darling* little nose. And he's got particularly nice ears, so pink and perfect and they don't stick out . . . what's funny?'

'I diagnose a bad case of broodiness.' He gave me another expressive glance. 'But I think I know what to prescribe.'

Immediately I stopped doting and handed Harrison Ford to Dimpsie, who took her arms out of a sink of suds and sundae dishes to receive him.

'We'd better go,' I said, 'Isobel may be getting cold.'

'Goodbye, Dimpsie,' said Rafe. 'I congratulate you on disproving the proverb that you can't make a silk purse out of a sow's ear. You ought to get a dishwasher, though.'

'I know. But they're a hundred and fifty pounds. Jode and I

are investing all our money in shares in the Singing Swan, so we can eventually buy Mrs Peevis out. She wants to buy a house to share with Dale and Nan.'

Though it had been inevitable, I was very sorry indeed to hear that Nan had succumbed to Dale's overtures and that Mrs Peevis was about to be fleeced of her last shillings.

'What about the craft shop?'

'I'm putting it up for sale. And good riddance to it. I've rarely done more than break even all the years I've had it. And it was lonely sitting in there day after day selling one bookmark a week. This is much more fun.'

'I'd like to make a donation to the cause.' Rafe put his arm round Dimpsie's shoulder. 'I'll buy you a dishwasher.'

'Oh, no!' I said.

'It's angelically kind of you but I couldn't accept it,' said Dimpsie.

'Nonsense! You're my mother-in-law, or very soon will be, and if I want to give you a present I jolly well can. You don't want to offend me by refusing, surely?'

'No . . . well, in that case, if you really mean it . . .' Dimpsie kissed him. 'It's so generous of you! I'm so lucky to have such a wonderful son-in-law.'

'I've turned into the abominable snowman,' complained Isobel when we got back into the car. 'I thought you were never coming.'

'Sorry—' I broke off with a scream. Someone was bending down to look through the window. A white face was glaring at me through the glass. 'Drive off!' I shouted. I hung on to the inside handle with all my strength.

'But, darling, your father, shouldn't we—?'

'Drive!'

42

'Darling, this is all nonsense,' said Rafe.

The calm way in which he said this was proof of his determination to keep a brake on his temper. He had been so distracted by my screaming at him to drive away that he had pulled out from the kerb in front of a lorry. The lorry driver had retaliated by taking up a position about six inches from our bumper and following us through the town all the way to the foot of Hindleep Hill, continuously flashing his lights and beeping his horn. I could see by the tilt of Rafe's chin that the indignity of being thus made an exhibition of was searing his soul, but he refrained from uttering a syllable of reproach.

'He had the knife in his hand! If I hadn't run out of the house and hidden in the bushes he'd have probably killed me! He stood on the front doorstep for ages, yelling my name. Luckily it was pitch dark and the porch lamp is pretty feeble. Honestly, he meant to kill me!'

'Tom may be a cold-blooded philanderer, but he's not capable of killing anyone. You were upset, quite understandably, and your imagination carried you away.'

'If it was as easy as that to tell who's capable of murder and who isn't, we'd be able to lock them all up and then there wouldn't *be* any murders,' I said in a tone that was regrettably sulky.

'All right, darling, don't let's argue.'

'I think you're so unfair to Tom,' said Isobel quite crossly.

I did not reply. When we reached the courtyard, Isobel got out at once.

'Just a minute, darling.' Rafe put a restraining hand on my arm as I attempted to follow her. 'I must talk to you. I'm so unhappy, darling. I can't believe you don't care enough not to want to help me.'

'Of course I care but—'

'Marigold, you must believe me when I tell you that . . . that I want to marry you. I love you. I know I've been guilty of a lack of self-control. Perhaps you think I ought to be more of a man and pull myself together. You think I ought to have more backbone, stiffen my upper lip—'

'Oh, of course, I don't think that. I'd be a complete hypocrite if I took that thick-skinned, heartless sort of attitude. I'm more cowardly than anyone I know.'

'I wish I could believe you don't despise me.'

'I *don't* despise you.'

'Do you love me, just a little bit?'

'Yes.'

'More than a little bit?'

'Yes. But not enough to marry you.'

Though he screwed up his eyes he could not hide a look of pain. He said, very low, 'Is that final?'

'I'm afraid so.'

'Then . . . then it's all up with me.' To my horror he buried his face in his hands and dropped his head forward onto the steering wheel.

'Oh, Rafe, don't be upset! Please!' I leaned across to put my arm round him. 'You'll meet someone else. Of course you will. Someone much more suitable. I'm not nearly good enough. Women will be queuing up to marry you.' I stroked his hair.

510

'Besides, don't you think marriage is awfully overrated? I realize now I'm just not suited to it. I'm going to devote my life to dancing.'

I said this partly to reassure him that it was not a case of preferring someone else and partly because it was what I truly believed.

'I can't try to make myself pleasing to another woman,' he groaned. 'I can't . . . bring myself . . . to . . . do it!'

'Everyone feels like that when a relationship breaks up.' I knew this because I had so often extended a salt-soaked shoulder to members of the company. 'Everyone's convinced they'll never be able to fall in love again. But broken hearts can mend in the time it takes to exchange a look.' I regretted the unsophisticated nature of this speech, but love is difficult to talk about without sounding embarrassingly trite. 'I wanted it to work but dancing is my first love. The truth is, you can't just chuck away something you feel passionately about because it would be convenient. Can't you understand that?'

'Yes. I can understand it.' He was silent for a while, then he lifted his head and looked at me with an expression that was fierce. 'But it doesn't help. If you won't marry me then I'll . . . I'll . . . never mind.'

'What? What will you do?' Rafe assumed an expression of fainéant nobility but remained silent. 'You don't mean . . .' I clutched at his hand but he snatched it away, so I clung to his sleeve. 'Rafe, promise me you won't do anything silly.'

'Why should I promise you anything?' He continued to look at me as though I were a complete stranger to whom he had taken an unaccountable dislike. 'You won't help me.' He made it sound as though marrying him was the equivalent of lending him fifty pounds.

'I'll be your friend for ever and ever if that's any good. I'll . . . I'll . . . get you free tickets for anything I'm in and . . .'

It demonstrated with painful clarity how selfish a dancer's life was – had to be – that I couldn't think of anything else I

511

could do for him. I would be too busy and too far away to take his books back to the library or wash his socks. Besides, the Prestons bought all the books they wanted and they had a perfectly good washing machine.

He looked down at the steering wheel and sucked his upper lip, thinking. 'There is something you could do.' He gave a bitter laugh. 'If it's not asking too much.'

'Oh, just ask it!' I cried. At that moment, provided it didn't interfere with rehearsals and performances, I would have willingly made myself his slave.

'Will you agree not to tell anyone that you've broken off our engagement until I've had a chance to tell Evelyn it's all over?'

'Is that all? Of course!' I felt heady with relief. 'I quite agree she ought to be the first to be told.'

'Promise me then that you won't tell a soul.'

'All right, I promise. Cross my heart and hope to die. But I wouldn't have, anyway.'

I had the feeling I had got off lightly. I took a sneaky look at Rafe. There was an expression on his face that was best described as a steely smile, as though he was resolved to go through fire with as little wincing as possible. I was not reassured.

For the first time it occurred to me that Rafe might have some kind of mental affliction that had nothing to do with his experiences as a soldier. Might there be a streak of emotional instability in the Preston family? Kingsley was presumably suffering from some kind of dementia to do with old age, but there was also Kingsley's father, nuttier than Fritz's macaroons according to Rafe. Isobel's contradictory behaviour might be the result of a split personality. At what point could people be classified as mad? I thought about the people I knew well. Confusingly, they all had behavioural traits that seemed eccentric if not downright peculiar. I thought about me. Obsessive about dancing, neurotic about being in cars, possibly sexually

512

frigid, a ready liar, a coward, a compulsive people-pleaser. I was probably madder than anybody.

'You vill haf supper vith us?' Fritz asked Rafe genially as we stood on the balcony drinking a delicious flowery wine and eating *Zwiebelkuchen*, little onion tarts flavoured with bacon and caraway seeds. The late sun had banished the clouds, and we had a splendid view of the lake shining like crumpled tinfoil, while stealthy shadows of the hills crept over the treetops.

'Thank you,' said Rafe, 'but we've got an early start tomorrow. Isobel and I are going to stay with our uncle and aunt who live in Caithness. It takes the best part of a day to get up there.'

This was a surprise. 'How long will you be away?' I asked.

'About a week. Maybe two. I know it's very sudden, darling. We only decided this afternoon to make the trip.'

Conrad was leaning with folded arms on the parapet, looking at the view. Isobel put her hand on his shoulder. 'I hope you won't miss me too much.'

Conrad turned his head. 'I shall try to distract myself with work.' He appeared to take the news of her unexpected departure with tranquillity. But you could never tell what Conrad was thinking. He had been sitting on the balcony, reading, when we arrived, and had confined his greeting to a brief 'hello' before going downstairs to fetch a bottle of wine. He had hardly glanced in my direction during the hour or so we had been drinking and talking. Orlando had made up for this cool reception by squeezing me vigorously as though I were a bath sponge.

'We had a postcard from Aunt Billa this morning,' Rafe continued. 'Uncle George is convalescing from a stroke and she's in need of cheering up. We used to stay in their house on the edge of Loch Dubh when we were children. Rains without stopping, of course, but the scenery's unbeatable.' Rafe drained his glass and put it down. 'We'd better go.'

'Goodbye, Conrad, darling,' said Isobel.

He turned towards her and put his hands on her shoulders as she lifted her face to kiss him.

Rafe wrapped his arms round my waist. 'I'll jot down my uncle's telephone number on a postcard as soon as I get there. Goodbye, sweetheart. Don't bother to see us to the car.' He pulled me close and kissed me lingeringly on the mouth.

'You'll speak to Evelyn before you go?' I said as soon as I had regained control of my lips.

'Of course. Needless to say I shall miss you every minute.' He flicked his thumb and finger under my chin hard enough to hurt. 'Don't work too hard.'

Then they were gone.

I risked a glance at Conrad. His brows were contracted, his upper lip fractionally lifted and he was staring at me as though contemplating something thoroughly unpleasant. It must have looked to an outsider as though I had gone back on everything I had said yesterday about being relieved that the engagement was off, about knowing that it had been wrong from the beginning. I must appear weak and vacillating, incapable of knowing my own mind. Conrad held my gaze for a moment and then turned to resume his observation of the view. It was a snub . . . at least I felt it as such. I tried to shrug it off. What business was it of Conrad's what I did, I asked myself defiantly? I took comfort in the knowledge that as soon as Evelyn knew the truth I should be able to tell Conrad that he was mistaken.

During supper Orlando flirted extravagantly with each of us in turn. I guessed he wanted to make headway with Fritz without frightening him or making him feel conspicuous. *Kräutlsuppe*, a soup made from potatoes and chervil, was followed by *Lamperl*, lamb cooked with thyme and rosemary, accompanied by potato noodles and comfrey roots, boiled and dressed with oil and vinegar. Fritz was the only one of us to do justice to his cooking. Conrad's thoughts were evidently elsewhere and he appeared not to notice what was on his plate. Orlando and I were obliged to be abstemious. I felt unhappy. I had done Rafe a serious injustice in accusing him of being Nan's seducer and I had made him miserable when my intention had been to do good. It seemed I was not a very good judge of character – or of anything else. I only needed to make a mess of Golly's opera to prove finally to the world, and myself, that I was nothing but a liability.

Immediately after supper I went for a run to work off a few pounds of noodles. Orlando and Fritz were sitting on the balcony with coffee and *Baisers*, meringues flavoured with almonds and rosehips. Conrad had disappeared into his study. I would not be missed. I reminded myself as I ran that I had dedicated my life to dancing, and society therefore must come a poor second. I took the path down through the woods.

The soft evening light gave every tree and glade a mysterious beauty. Now and then my thudding feet startled birds into sudden flight. The simple pleasure of moving my body and stretching my limbs lifted my mood. The heady scent of hawthorn mingled with the pungent smell of wild garlic as my plimsolls crushed the aromatic leaves. I breathed steadily and slowly on the way down to the edge of the wood then, without pausing, turned and began the ascent. Naturally, running uphill was much more strenuous. By the time I emerged from the trees to the little plateau by the bridge, the sky had taken on an inky hue and I was breathing fast.

I started to walk across the bridge. My anxiety returned. Supposing Rafe became depressed? Despite the act he had put on in front of the others, he must believe that this time I meant what I said. I passed the statue of Justice with her blindfold and then Envy, gnawing her own heart and . . . fright made pandemonium of my circulation. Standing on the parapet between Avarice and Idleness, holding out her arms like an avenging angel, was a statue I had never seen before. Someone ran past me, pushing me aside roughly so that I fell onto one knee.

'For God's sake, Vanessa!' shouted my father. 'Stop playing

515

the fool!' Vanessa Trumball swayed backwards and forwards. 'I've had enough of your games!' he shouted. 'Get *down,* you bloody pain in the arse!'

I saw him lift his hand towards the teetering figure, saw her twist round and leap into the air. Then her body folded and she dropped headfirst into vacancy with a high-pitched wail of terror.

'Oh . . . *Christ!*' He leaned over the parapet to look down. '*Jesus!* Vanessa!' He sucked in his breath suddenly and then let out a series of gasps. It was the oddest noise. I realized that he was crying. Never in my life had I seen my father even mildly doubtful. Always he had been hard and certain and cynical. My one desire was to get away before he realized I had seen him exposed, suffering. While he leaned against the balustrade, weeping and cursing, I crept back towards the place where the bridge ended and the road began. When I heard footsteps approaching I flung myself to the ground behind a bush. He walked past me still talking to himself. '*Bitch! Bloody* fool! *Stupid* bitch!' over and over again. Then he shouted, 'Marigold! *Mari*gold! Where are you, for God's sake!' I hardly breathed until I heard a car door slam and the engine start up.

For some time after he had driven away I lay in the mud. I had a sensation of floating above myself, of being able to look down and see my body prone in the rain-filled tyre tracks left by turning vehicles. I suppose it was shock. At last the coldness of the wet ground returned me to my senses and I staggered up. My legs were stiff and heavy as though they were both encased in plaster. I stumbled across the bridge with my hands over my ears. This was foolish, I admit, because nothing could block out the memory of Vanessa's last despairing cry.

I ran into the courtyard and took the steps two at a time. I dreaded to find myself locked out, but the great iron ring turned under my hand.

'Where have you been?' Conrad stood back to let me in. 'I was on the point of going out to see what had become of you.'

He surveyed me critically. 'You seem to make a habit of impersonating *Die Schwarzen Buben*. In English *The Inky Boys*. It is a moral fable for children by Heinrich Hoffman. Three naughty little boys make fun of a blackamoor. Saint Nicholas is so angry with them that he dips them in his inkstand so they are as black as crows themselves.'

I caught sight of myself in the mirror. I was a figure of fun. I burst into tears.

'You must not be so sensitive,' said Conrad calmly, handing me his handkerchief.

'It was horrible . . . *horrible!*' I sobbed. 'I can't get it out of my mind. I think I'm going mad.'

'I perceive this is something worse than wounded vanity. You had better sit down and I will fetch you a drink.'

The drawing room was warm, candlelight glittered on the gold leaf, and Siggy lay sleeping next to an open book on one of the divans. I sat down facing the great windows. Orlando and Fritz were still talking on the balcony, their profiles gilded by a storm lantern. Moths drifted around them like sparks of fire. Conrad put a glass in my hand and sat down opposite me. He crossed one leg over the other and folded his hands. 'Well?'

'I've just seen . . . someone's thrown herself off the bridge . . .' I put my hands over my face in a futile attempt to shut the image out. 'I saw . . . it was . . . oh God! . . . terrifying!'

'Take some brandy. It will give you courage.'

I was afraid it would make me sick, but I had no strength to argue so I sipped obediently. 'She did it because of my father – at least . . . no . . . they'd been lovers but he'd ended it. He says she was mad. Do you think you have to be mad to . . . do that?'

'Finish that glass.'

'I don't think I should. I've got to dance tomorrow.'

'Drink it! I shall speak to Fritz.'

He went onto the balcony. I heard them talking in German. Fritz exclaimed in a distressed voice, then nodded and said

'*Jawohl!*' several times. He stood up. 'Please to come now,' he said to Orlando. 'I vill take you home.'

'Ta ta, Marigold.' Orlando took a second look at me. 'Is that a mud pack on your face? I find it's the only thing for my eczema. But it must be volcanic . . .'

Conrad took his arm and conducted him into the hall. The brandy had stopped me shivering but my body ached with tension. Siggy roused himself enough to climb onto my knee, which was comforting. I heard a murmur of voices before Conrad returned alone. 'I want you to tell me everything that happened.' He refilled my glass and poured one for himself.

'I don't know if I can bear to—'

'Everything.'

I was unable to prevent myself from weeping again as I described what had taken place, but the more I talked the easier it became. 'He tried to save her . . . honestly he did . . . that's what he does for a living. Save people. I don't know . . . perhaps I've been a bit unfair . . . I've always taken my mother's side, you see.'

'Isobel has told me he is a man misunderstood.'

'It's all very well for Isobel to stick up for him,' I said rather fiercely. 'I don't suppose he's ever chased her with a bread knife.'

'With a bread knife? Really?' Conrad filled my glass again which had become unaccountably empty. 'So prosaic an instrument.'

'I mustn't have another glass. I'm beginning to feel most peculiar.'

'Go on about your father.'

I did go on. In fact the whole sad story of our relationship came pouring out. I seemed unable to stop talking. The brandy tasted much less unpleasant now that my mouth and throat were numb. In fact I felt pretty numb all over. 'So you see,' I concluded, 'he *was* to blame and he wasn't . . . I hate him really . . . at least, most of the time I do . . . but now I feel sorry for him too . . . not as sorry as I feel for Vanessa, only

518

I didn't know her and knowing someone is everything really, isn't it?'

I dropped my head back to drain the last drops. When I sat up, Conrad had taken to swaying about and going in and out of focus.

'Certainly it is.' He filled my glass again.

'No more, thank you. What ought I to do? About –' I recalled her name with an effort – 'Vanessa.' Much to my surprise I hiccuped loudly. 'Sorry.'

'Nothing. Fritz has gone to the police. They will take care of everything. No doubt they will come here but you need not see them. You can say nothing that is useful.'

I blinked hard. The whole room seemed to be alight, the flames leaping up to the ceiling and then dwindling to pinpoints. 'It's so odd the way you keep coming very near and going very far away all the time.' I giggled and then put the handkerchief, now as black as the Inky Boys, over my mouth. 'What a ridiculous sound. Did I make that ridiculous sound?'

Conrad was smiling. 'It was not I.'

'Goodness! I thought I was laughing just then. But I'm never going to laugh again. I'm going to have to spend the rest of my life seeing her . . . hearing her . . .'

'I don't think so. It will do her no good and yourself harm. When my parents were killed, I thought I was bound to assume black garments and steep myself in woe for eternity. But the capacity for happiness that is in all of us renews itself so quickly it seems almost shocking.'

'Oh, Conrad. I'm so sorry. I'd quite forgotten . . . forgotten . . . I've forgotten what I'd forgotten . . .' As I struggled to remember, Siggy stirred in my lap, no doubt to remind me that I had stopped stroking him. 'Do look at Siggy. Don't you love it when he yawns and shows all his teeth?'

'It is a delightful sight.'

'He *is* a beautiful rabbit, isn't he? Don't you think he's the most beautiful rabbit in all the world?'

519

'Certainly. He looks perfectly charming.'

'And you look perfectly charming, too. Do I look cherfectly parming?' I was giggling hard now. It was undignified, which I deplored, but somehow I couldn't help it.

'Charming yes, but for perfection you need a cleaner face.'

'I do like you, Conrad. *So* much.'

'Thank you.'

'Do you like me?'

'Oh, very much.'

'Really? As much as I like you?'

'That I cannot answer, as I have no way of knowing your feelings.'

'I like you as much as . . . as anybody in all the world. Better. Much better. Actually, I'm crazy about you!'

'That is very nice for me.' Conrad stood up. 'Now I think you had better go to bed. Give me your glass and I will show you where Fritz has made your room.'

He seemed to tower above me. His face was so beautiful. He was like a god looking down from heaven. I tried to stand so I could put my arms round him, but my legs refused to obey my instructions.

'I can't get up. Do you think I've been paralysed?' I began to roar with laughter. Siggy moved away, annoyed. 'I'm never going to be able to dance again. Will you still like me if I can't dance?'

'It will make no difference. But you are not paralysed. Just drunk.'

'Oh, no.' I shook my head firmly. At least I thought I did but perhaps it was the room swinging from side to side. 'I never get drunk. It's bad for my body. Do you like my body?'

'I like it very much. Now you must go to bed.'

'And Siggy must come too. He always sleeps with me. Darling, *darling* Conrad, would you like to come as well? *Please* do. I love you so much. I want to lie in your arms and kiss your beautiful face.'

'That is a delightful idea but it must be for another time. Let go of your glass, Marigold . . . let go . . .'

I wanted to protest that another time might never come, but miraculously I grew a delicious pair of soft downy swan's wings and flapped slowly off over the lake and into oblivion.

43

A sadistic inquisitor was shining a brilliant light into my eyes. The sun beat through curtain-less windows filled with an unclouded delphinium sky. Something moved in the bed beside me. I put down my hand to find Siggy curled up beneath the bedclothes. He gave my questing hand a gentle nip to show I was disturbing him.

A piece of my life seemed to be missing. Only too quickly, like blows to the head, I remembered the bridge and Vanessa and my father. After that it was hazy. I had drunk a lot of brandy, which would explain why my temples were pounding and my tongue felt like a sun-bleached bone. Conrad and I had talked while I drank. I wished I could remember the conversation. I had no recollection of coming upstairs and getting into bed.

On the table beside my bed was a charming blue and gold enamelled clock. I admired it sleepily for some time before noticing that it said a quarter to nine. I flung back the bedclothes and sprang up. Orlando was arriving at nine to begin work. Apart from the bed and the table the room was bare of furniture, but in one corner was my old suitcase which I had collected from Dumbola Lodge the day before. The skirt I had worn the previous evening was folded neatly over it.

'And ze top of ze mornink to you,' said Fritz as I ran, dressed in leotard, tights and legwarmers, into the kitchen. He was looking particularly cheerful, I thought. He had washed his hair and it lay in damp golden kiss curls across his marmoreal brow.

'And to you,' I returned, 'but you've gone a bit off course. I'm not an expert in dialect but I'm practically certain that's Irish.'

'Is zat so?' Fritz looked disappointed and amended his notebook.

'I say, Fritz. You haven't got such a thing as an aspirin, have you? I've got one hell of a hangover and I've got to start dancing in a minute. My head's drumming like a restless native.'

'Oh, dear you!' he tutted. 'I haf exact zing for it. *Bismarkhering*. Vun moment. I fetch from store.'

The *Bismarkhering* turned out to be strips of salted vinegary fish. I ate them to please Fritz though they were the last thing I felt like.

'How feel you now?' he asked sympathetically.

'My mouth seems to have taken on all the characteristics of the desert we were taken to see when we were dancing in Chile. Apparently it's the driest place on earth, just lava flows and salt basins.'

'Ah, but you vill feel better in a vile. Haf tea. Trust Aunt Fritz.' He looked up, colouring beautifully like a poppy opening to the sun. 'Here is Orlando.'

Orlando ran gracefully down the stairs. He was wearing a sleeveless white unitard cut low enough in front to bare his nipples, which he had dusted with gold paint and drawn lipstick circles round, like the petals of a flower. The decoration was effective but I wondered if Fritz, for whose benefit this must have been intended, might not be a little alarmed by so much originality so early in the day. Fritz was shy and serious and intellectual and, I thought, probably inexperienced.

'My dears, I must have the smallest cup of coffee to get my creative juices flowing. Golly's house, though perfectly adapted for a milkman, is the temperature of a refrigerator. Also, my mattress has been carved from rock. By morning I had shivered myself into an identity crisis. I kept thinking I was a pat of butter, beaded with iced water, lying on a marble shelf.'

'Oh, zis is terrible!' said Fritz. 'Vy do you not say before?'

'Nanny taught us it was bad manners to criticize one's hostess.' Orlando looked virtuous. 'She was such a beast. My innocent little buttocks were frequently whipped raw.'

'Buttocks?' Fritz took out his notebook again. 'Zat is little pieces of butter? As in hillocks?'

'No, my dear.' Orlando put his hand on my bottom. 'This little seat of pleasure is buttocks.'

Camp innuendo was general currency among the gay members of the Company, so I was used to this sort of talk, but Fritz looked shocked. I hoped Orlando would see the wisdom of tempering his modus operandi. After he had fortified himself with coffee, we went up to the drawing room and Orlando taught class. Being the only student was forty times harder. There was not a centimetre of muscle he did not inspect or an angle of my body he did not criticize – but it was exactly what I needed.

Halfway through we were interrupted by the arrival of three large pieces of mirror, each six feet square, sanctioned by Conrad, ordered by Orlando and paid for by Golly. These were put in place on the section of wall that remained unpainted. When the workman left we continued the class but, now I could see myself, I was ten times as critical as Orlando. Dancers have a powerful love-hate relationship with their own image. Any perceived faults are galling and physical imperfections are a knife to the heart. But we are absorbed by and infatuated with our reflections. It is an extreme form of narcissism. By lunchtime we were tired and hot but the *Bismarkhering* had done its stuff and my head was clear. As the day remained unclouded, we ate on the balcony, a dish of pears, bacon and beans which was light yet restoring. Afterwards there were garnet-coloured cherries.

'This is so delightful,' sighed Orlando, leaning back in his chair and putting up his feet to rest on the parapet. He forgot for the moment to be flirtatious. 'I should like to stay here forever. Being so high up you feel cut off from the horrid world with its hordes of people who are quite indifferent to ballet and those fucking ignorant, insensitive reviewers. Do look at that patch of sunlight on the water, like a scattering of yellow diamonds. All I ask God for is beauty. Poverty, insult and betrayal I can bear, but I dread Butterbank.'

'Then it seems your prayers are answered.' Conrad walked onto the balcony. 'I have just returned from there. Golly has invited her librettist to stay. They have much work to do to change the setting for the opera from Japan to Alaska. As she has only one guest room, she asked me if I would offer you a bed. I said I would.'

While Orlando was expressing jubilant thanks, I examined my glass of iced tea with feigned interest. The moment I saw Conrad the conversation of the night before began to piece itself together in my mind. It grew more calamitous by the second. The brandy had acted as an emotional purgative. Not content with sobbing and heating my breast, I had poured out my life story and spread out my neuroses for his inspection like an unpalatable picnic. My face prickled with shame. There was worse. I had grown affectionate. Had I really said something about wanting him to come to bed with me? Feeling acutely miserable, I stared at a piece of boiled, sepia-coloured mint floating in my glass. How I wished it was deadly nightshade so I could gulp it down and put an end to my suffering.

'*Aber, Conrad, wir haben keine Betten*,' said Fritz in a low voice.

'*Er kann mein Bett haben. Ich gehe zurück nach Deutschland für ein paar Wochen.*'

'*Wirklich? Aber warum?*' Then remembering his manners, for they were both in general punctilious about not speaking German in front of us monoglots he said, 'Never mind. Ve talk later. Vill you eat zomezing?'

'I had lunch with Golly.' Conrad frowned. I could tell it had not been a good lunch.

'I shall the dishes vash.'

'And I shall help you.' Orlando leaped onto his toes from a nearly prone position, his muscles rippling in a fine demonstration of tensile strength. 'It's the very least I can do.'

Conrad took the chair Orlando had vacated, poured himself a glass of wine and took a sip, looking thoroughly at ease with himself and the world. He met my eye and smiled.

I grasped the nettle. 'I'm sorry about last night. I never normally drink so much. I must have bored and embarrassed you terribly. I've certainly embarrassed myself.'

'I intended that you should be drunk. You were traumatized by what you had seen. Now, after a good night's sleep, you feel better.'

Conrad spoke with an air of satisfaction. He could afford to be complacent. His behaviour had been as sober and dignified as an archbishop's on Good Friday, while I had made a complete idiot of myself. But he was right about one thing. Last night Vanessa's death had made life seem unbearably tragic and frightening. A long sleep and several hours of dancing had done much to remedy this. The image of her jumping from the bridge was deeply upsetting when it recurred, but I had to live with that. Now I felt more confident that I could. 'Yes. Thank you. I do.'

Conrad made a gesture with his hand as though to wave away my disquiet. 'Then that is all that matters.'

'Well, not quite. I can't exactly remember . . . but I think I said . . . I got carried away . . . you must think I'm a dreadful flirt.' I laughed uneasily. 'It was shocking of me to say . . . to suggest . . . whatever I did . . . of course I didn't mean it.'

Conrad smiled more broadly and helped himself to a cherry. I could see he was amused by my mortification and I thought it very mean of him. '*Hu!* These are insipid. I wonder what did Goethe mean when he said one should ask children and birds how cherries and strawberries taste? That one's palate dulls as one gets older, or that children and birds get the first picking?'

He was being tactful, changing the subject. I was as anxious as he to bury the whole ghastly incident but I had to be clear about one thing. 'You won't tell Isobel, will you?'

He laughed, displaying his excellent teeth. 'I shall have no opportunity. I leave today for Germany. I shall be away for some time.'

'Oh.' An extraordinarily disagreeable sensation, which I preferred not to analyse, made me speak more sharply than I might otherwise have done. 'You needn't think I'm in love with you or anything ridiculous like that.'

Conrad leaned across the table and, before I had any idea what he intended, took possession of my hand. 'Listen to me, Marigold, there is something I want very much to—'

He released my hand as Fritz came onto the balcony. 'Excuse me please. Two policemen vish to speak vith you.'

'All right. Keep them in the hall. I'll come.'

'You won't tell them anything about my father?' I whispered back, suddenly alarmed.

Conrad pulled a face of exasperation. '*Dummkopf!* What do you think?'

I was left to my own thoughts for five minutes, and very uncomfortable they were, until Orlando came up to resume work. For three hours we slaved nonstop. At five Golly arrived with the librettist, a small man with a bald pointed head, a large grey moustache and a fiery temper. His expression when he was not shouting with rage was lugubrious. His name was Joseph Stern, which seemed to suit him.

'Good afternoon,' he said when we were introduced. 'How are you to be made to look like an Eskimo I'd like to know? They're brown-skinned, dark-eyed and black-haired with flat faces.'

'Don't be such a grouch,' said Golly. 'It would have been just as hard to make her look Japanese. Anyway, it's practically a tradition in opera that all princesses of fabulous beauty should be played by fat middle-aged women with teeth like cowcatchers. And it'll be the designer's problem, not yours.'

'I need to be able to visualize the action to produce my best work,' Mr Stern complained. 'How are we to produce the effect of mutilated hands?'

'What's that?' said Orlando.

'It's the legend of Sedna, the goddess of the sea. During the storm her father throws her into the water to save himself, but she clings to the side so her father chops off her fingers with his hatchet. Dramatic, don't you think? I've been writing screams all morning.'

'Is it *too* much to ask,' Orlando spoke with heavy sarcasm, 'if at some point soon we might have a moratorium on last-minute alterations to the plot?'

A row broke out during which I went downstairs to help Fritz peel potatoes. That was the last time I had anything like a grasp of the story of *Ilina and the Scarlet Riband*, for there were so many more excisions and additions that I gave up attempting to follow it. It didn't matter. I knew who Ilina was and how she felt. Orlando and I resumed dancing, while Golly and Mr Stern fought it out. It was not until we sat down for supper that I discovered Conrad had left for Germany without saying goodbye.

Some days after Rafe's departure I received a postcard. *Darling, Good journey but have arrived to find chaos. George is pretty much bed-bound and Billa is arthritic means she can only walk with sticks so there's a lot to see to since the staff are either mad or drunk. Plus ça change . . . I miss you terribly, my sweet. Fondest love, Rafe. P.S. Could not speak to E. because she's gone to Austria with her old – in both senses of the word – boyfriend!*

A few days later I had a card from Isobel. *Darling Marigold, You would adore this place, so romantic and broken down.*

528

Buckets and rat-traps in every room. Thirty miles to the next house of any size, so no society but our own. Bliss. We exercise the horses every day. Fabulous scenery. George yells all day long for whisky. Billa says he has made her life hell with booze and beastliness(?!). Too Wuthering Heights. Love Isobel. P.S. The picture on the front of this makes me think of you. I turned the card over to see a photograph of a Highland calf covered in long red hair.

The next day I received a letter from my father. *Marigold. I've bought a partnership in a practice in Wimpole Street and I'm leaving this evening for London. Dumbola Lodge is on the market and Flagstaffe's, the estate agent, will handle everything. He needs your front door key ASAP. I've put the furniture into store. You can haggle over it with your mother and Kate. I don't want any reminders of twenty-five wasted years of bucolic boredom. As to what happened the other day, the less said the better. I shall come back for the inquest on the 24th. Fortunately, I know the coroner pretty well. I've given him the letter V.I. left me and he agrees it's clear evidence of an unsound mind. My new address and telephone number are below. Do NOT (underlined three times), pass these on to anyone. If Marcia Dane asks, say I've gone to the Outer Hebrides. Tom.*

No suggestion of meeting, no advice for my future, no message of love. I did not expect them, but still that chilly little note seemed to freeze another layer of ice over our relationship. I intended to throw it away as a gesture of independence, but instead it found its way into my album of press cuttings. The postcards I put in my bedside drawer.

By the end of one week, our days had settled into a pattern of work. Every morning Orlando and I took class for one hour, had a break for refreshments, then worked until lunchtime on *Ilina and the Scarlet Riband*. In the afternoon we did another hour of class then choreographed until tea time. There were some fiendishly difficult *enchaînements* and sometimes I despaired of being able to do them, but Orlando, so capricious and flighty in ordinary life, was a dedicated teacher and he stuck at it doggedly, never behaving worse than slightly unreasonably.

One of the most taxing sections was the game of *Atrakcheak*. I had to jump from a standing position to kick with both feet a piece of whalebone suspended above my head. I pleaded for a little run at it. What difference, I asked, could a couple of hops and a skip make to the audience who would know nothing of the rules of the game? Orlando informed me gravely that he was making a ballet not a gymnastic display, and that even one hop would ruin the beauty of the line. There was nothing beautiful about my falling flat on my back, I countered, displaying a fine collection of bruises, but Orlando was adamant.

An unexpected turn of events kept Rafe and Isobel in Scotland. Uncle George was found dead in bed one morning of a final stroke. Aunt Billa, after fifty years of revolt against the drunken tyranny of her spouse, was inconsolable. She refused to leave the haunts of her married life, so the old house must be sold and a suitable bungalow found. It would not be easy to find a buyer for a remote mansion with twenty bedrooms, one bathroom, and fireplaces that smoked so badly that all the windows had to be left permanently open so the occupants could breathe. Rafe needed to stay in Scotland to oversee the sale and Isobel was remaining to keep him company.

As the days and weeks went by, the five of us became more and more inward-looking as we concentrated on the making of the opera. Every evening after supper we read or listened to music, too exhausted to talk much. I was getting on famously with *Nicholas Nickleby* and longed to discuss it with Conrad. Every day I hoped for his return but he never came. I usually went to bed quite early and read until my eyelids felt heavy. I got into the habit of putting the feather he had given me carefully in my place before turning to the front page on which he had written *Conrad Wolfgang Lerner* in black ink. I would stare at it long enough to be able to see a ghost image in reverse, white on black, when I closed my eyes. Lying in the dark I tried to imagine what he might be doing, who he might be with and in what part of the world he might be.

Conrad was the only person who had thought it worthwhile to try to educate me. He was a kind and generous friend and several times he had come to my rescue. That was why I liked to go to sleep thinking of him. I knew that whether he married Isobel or not, his restlessness would soon take him away for good. I expected a letter to arrive any day, instructing Fritz to sell Hindleep and join him in Krakow or Kathmandu. Dancing was the most important thing in my life so I had no pressing need of friends. The growing feeling I had that the future might be a little grey, a little sad, a little hollow was nothing to be afraid of. That was the meaning of sacrificing oneself for one's art. When poor Smike died I went onto the balcony, pretending to admire the view while I had a thoroughly good howl.

With Fritz looking after us we did very well. Orlando and I struggled to keep off the pounds, not allowing ourselves cakes or puddings. Golly and Mr Stern began to get double chins, and his shirt buttons strained at their buttonholes. Luckily the boiler suit had built-in expansion.

'It's so kind of you to cook such lovely things,' I said to Fritz one morning during our coffee break. We were alone on the balcony. Golly and Mr Stern were drawing up new battle lines in the study. Orlando had taken the Bentley into Gaythwaite to ring up his shoemaker. The day was foggy but warm. 'I hope Conrad doesn't mind paying.'

'I send him bills to check. Really ve spend so little. You and Orlando,' he blushed as he said his name, 'eat like little flies and ve haf only ze simple food.'

'How is he?'

'Orlando?'

'Conrad.' I had seen letters in Conrad's handwriting, written in German of course, lying about the kitchen. I had glanced sneakily at one or two hoping vainly – in both senses of the word – to see my name. 'I expect he's awfully busy.'

531

'Yes, I zink zo. I hope Orlando vill manage ze bends. He has not drive ze car before.'

'Really he's much more capable than he likes to make out. All his neuroses . . . really he's as strong as a horse. I suppose Conrad has lots of friends in Germany?'

'Oh, many, many. But supposing he miss zem? He is so artistic zat he may be *distrait*.'

'Conrad?'

'Orlando.'

I perceived that our minds were travelling in different directions. 'Please don't worry. I've known Orlando a good few years and I have complete faith in him. You have to be really tough to survive in our world.'

'Tough, yes. The marvellous muscling. But he is so – how do you say it? – full of great promises.'

'Talented, you mean?'

'Yes! I am awed in his presence.' Fritz screwed up his eyes as the sun broke from the mist and bathed the balcony in strong light. 'It is difficult for me to haf confidence in love.'

I registered the note of enquiry, but I felt ill-qualified to give anyone advice about matters of the heart. 'The only thing I know for certain is that nothing that happens to you in life is *ever* anything like you imagine it's going to be, so there isn't much point in shivering in the wings. When you get your cue you'd better just get on and do it.'

I thought Fritz looked rather pleased.

The next day I found myself sitting in the same chair on the balcony, only this time it was late afternoon and I was alone with Orlando. The mist had cleared and it was hot. We had already towelled ourselves down so as not to present too revolting a sight, but still our brows glistened and our bodies steamed. Fritz had taken the tea things away to wash them up, refusing all offers of help. I heard a bellow from the study.

'This is a bit of all right,' said Orlando, abandoning his character of neurasthenic aesthete. When you work with someone as closely as we had done, all pretences seem irrelevant. We were now so intimate we might be sharing the same heart, muscles and skin. 'Wonderful place, scrumptious grub always on tap. Everything done for one, nothing to worry about but work. Reality's going to hit hard when we move to Newcastle. I shall have withdrawal symptoms going back to apples and yoghurt. Fritz is the most fabulous cook.'

'Isn't he?' I agreed. 'And a darling. It's extremely generous of Conrad to let us stay here.'

'Oh yes.' Orlando examined his own hands, lean and strong still but with veins like pale blue worms, and sighed. 'He is, as you say, a darling.'

'Quite.' A silence while we both brooded. 'You always feel when you're with Conrad,' I went on, 'that nothing could ever go too badly wrong. And that seems to have got into the house. I feel so safe here, which is odd really when you remember it's perched right on the edge of a cliff. Conrad's so clever that he always seems to be able to look round and through things. Though when you consider that he lost both his parents at such an early age and now he's lost most of his money, he's got as much right to be mixed up as anyone.'

'No, really? Both parents? I hope he wasn't fond of them.' Orlando interlaced his fingers and stretched out his arms in front of him. After a brief pause he said, 'So much of a darling in fact that, do you know, I feel absurdly afraid of spoiling things?'

He fixed me with a beady eye and I gave in gracefully. 'I think Fritz is ready for a little adventure.'

'Yes?' His expression became eager. 'Do you think he likes me? Just a little bit?'

'I'm sure of it.'

Orlando's face lit then clouded immediately. 'But whenever I try to show him I care about him, he seems to draw away. I get the feeling if I pursued it any further it would be like clomping over a field of virgin snow with muddy boots on. Or smashing a butterfly against a pane of glass.'

'Are you sure that's what you're showing him? That you actually care about him? From what I've observed he could be forgiven for thinking that you don't.'

'Oh, that's nonsense. Every day I demonstrate my feelings. If I hired a plane to write "Orlando loves Fritz" in the sky it couldn't be clearer.'

'That's what I mean. Fritz isn't a show-off like all of *us*. He's gentle and sensitive.'

'You think I ought to be more subtle?'

'Yes.'

'I'm making it too obvious that I want to powder his cheeks, do you mean?'

I frowned. 'Honestly, Orlando, don't you see how hopelessly crude your wooing is? If you love Fritz, you ought to tell him so. The cheek-powdering ought to be a result of that.'

'Love him? But of *course* I do. I *wor*ship his youth and beauty and his intelligence. He's a princeling, a saint, a sage. By comparison with him I know I'm an old ham. A show-off, as you say, soiled by pan stick and fake glitter and too much sex with all the wrong people. But what can I do but stay on the merry-go-round until I'm flung off? I don't know about anything much but dancing, and dancing's such a fickle beast she'll bugger off and leave me old and lonely and flabby . . .' Orlando's eyes swam. 'No one will love me because all my friends are just like me, selfish and ambitious and jealous and vain . . .'

A tear ran down his cheek. I would have put my arms around him but we were still so sweaty it would have been unpleasant for both of us.

'You're at the peak of your profession as a choreographer. You're handsome and virile and glamorous and Fritz is hugely attracted to you, I'm certain.' Orlando stopped crying. 'You know what?' I continued my homily. 'I think you ought to be truthful. Tell him how you love him and worship him but tell him you're sometimes afraid. How can he love you if you don't let him see the real you? All that other stuff you and the boys

534

get up to, that's just bravado, really, isn't it? Like peacocks spreading their tails. If you want to be really loved you have to take risks and let yourself be vulnerable to hurt.'

I don't know how I knew this. In fact I hadn't properly known it until that moment, but the minute I said it I was certain it was true.

'I think you may have something there, my child.' Orlando blew his nose on my towel. Knowing his mood to be fragile I did not protest. He slung his own towel round his neck and stood up. 'Anyway, Fritz deserves the best and somewhere inside me there *may* be something worth his while.' He put on his Eugene Onegin look – sorrow tempered by newly acquired wisdom – and went thoughtfully away.

He appeared for supper looking decorous in a plain shirt and jeans. He drank much less than usual and tamed his conversation. After supper we continued to sit with glasses of wine on the balcony, as the setting sun turned the sky to rose and the lake to pearl. Even Golly was silenced by the splendour of Nature, so we could hear the twilight song of a thrush from the hillside below the house. After that she became fidgety and she and Mr Stern drove away, leaving the three of us to admire the celestial streaks of salmon and indigo developing above our heads.

'What beauty!' sighed Orlando. 'I feel overawed.'

'Yes,' said Fritz. 'I too am owerowed by ze vonder of Nature. It remind me zo much of Bavaria. I feel a little *das Heimweh* . . . how do you say it? A vish for home. Zough I haf no more family zere. Only Conrad is zere to zink kindly of me.'

By a coincidence that was not at all extraordinary, given that we were living in his house, eating his food and sleeping in his beds, I happened to be thinking about Conrad myself just then. So he was in Bavaria. I imagined him wandering over snowy mountains picking edelweiss. Perhaps listening to the melodious tinkle of cow bells or the distant blast of an alpenhorn. I wondered if he was thinking of us. Probably not.

'Sometimes when we're touring I feel homesick for London just because it's familiar,' said Orlando. 'And yet there's no one there who really cares about me.'

'No?' Fritz turned his sweet plump face to look at him. 'But how can zat be?'

'Oh, I've been careless about relationships. I've put my art first. Now that I'm getting older and I'm neither so energetic nor so good-looking as I used to be, I wonder if I've made an awful mistake. Sometimes . . . I'm afraid I'm no longer lovable.'

There fell a long silence. Then Fritz said in a low tone, 'You haf not need to be afraid.'

'Oh, Fritz, my dear.' Orlando's voice throbbed with intensity. 'If I could only believe that!'

It was then that I slipped away, unnoticed, to bed.

44

I sat in the back of the Bentley clutching a carrier bag full of pointe shoes, my stomach queasy with fright. After six weeks at Hindleep, our remoteness from the modern world unpolluted by so much as a newspaper, Newcastle seemed unnaturally bright and busy. Golly had finished the score of *Ilina and the Scarlet Riband* and my solos had been refined down to the slightest inclinations of my head and the diameters of each circle made by my feet. Orlando and I had also worked on the choreography for the corps de ballet.

From this moment I was in receipt of a salary, so I had decided to rent a room in Newcastle to save myself three hours travelling each day. Also, though I doted on Fritz and Orlando, I was tired of playing gooseberry. They did their best not to make me feel excluded, but the atmosphere at Hindleep had become sultry with imperfectly suppressed desires interlaced with the euphoria of temporary satisfaction.

Newcastle is a hilly place. My digs were at the top of a long flight of steep steps called Leaping Dog Lane. Orlando said my room was too small even for a Pekinese. My landlady, more of a bulldog with bandy legs and a pugnacious chin, read me a list of prohibitions. No men, alcohol, smoking, drugs, food, pets, musical instruments, radios, record players or muddy shoes were allowed on the premises. The bath must be cleaned after use and no wet towels were to be placed on the bed. Between eleven at night and seven-thirty in the morning, the front door would be bolted, admitting neither ingress nor egress, and the lavatory must not be flushed during this period. I assured her I was ready to abide by the house rules and paid her a week's rent in advance.

Fritz drove us from Leaping Dog Lane to the rehearsal studio, a disused church near the theatre. Though the rehearsal was scheduled to start at ten, nothing seemed to be happening. This was quite normal for the first morning, but by the time the principal tenor, Giovanni Garacci, showed up I was practically fainting with nerves. Fortunately he had short muscular legs and large beefy arms so he would be able to manage the simple lifts Orlando had devised. Orlando tried to demonstrate them to Giovanni, but he wanted to warm up his voice and wandered off in mid-explanation. It soon became clear that the major flaw of an opera ballet, which perhaps explained why they had gone out of fashion, was the conflict of interests. The singers wanted to stand still and occasionally wave their hands about. If really necessary they would stomp woodenly to stage left or stage right. All that mattered was vocal perfection.

Trevor, the director, also seemed to think the ballet was subordinate to the singing. Giovanni complained that his dressing room was dark and full of dusty old bibles. Also there was no 'ot wartair'. He demanded a constant supply of iced pineapple juice or he could not answer for his 'tonzeels'. In the ballet world, Giovanni would have been given short shrift, but Trevor treated him like a royal lunatic whose most outrageous requests must be pandered to. We stood around for another half an hour, watching the stage hands sticking masking tape onto the floor to mark the lines and shapes of the stage and sets, while the pineapple juice, an ice dispenser and an electric kettle were sought. When Orlando asked for a changing room for the dancers, Trevor stared at him as though he had asked for a suite at the Savoy with river views. All this time more people were arriving – the other soloists, the conductor, the *répétiteur*, the stage manager, the chorus and the chorus master and the office staff. The din as everyone exercised their vocal chords was nearly unbearable. Finally Trevor returned and clapped his hands for silence.

'All right, ladies and gentlemen, thank you. Dame Gloria Beauwhistle will be arriving any minute to give you a little talk about her new work and then we'll begin at the beginning with Act One. So what we want is the chorus for the seal hunt, Giovanni, Luigi and Stefano, plus the lead dancer –' he glanced at his notes – 'Marilyn.'

'Marigold,' corrected Orlando.

'Oh, yes,' Trevor waved an arm. 'Everybody, this is Orlando Silverbridge, our distinguished choreographer. It's going to be very interesting for us to work with dancers for a change. I have complete faith in Dame Gloria's judgement. The dancing is there because it's an integral part of the work, not an entertaining interval.' Trevor gave an unmeaning smile. It was obvious he was repeating what he had been told and did not believe a word of it. 'Let's do all we can to persuade the audience of that.'

There was a bustle at the back of the hall as Golly arrived. She swept through the crowd, greeting those she knew with a kiss or a wave. 'What ho, you lot!' she called above the applause. 'Hope you're all full of vim. We're going to need it. You singers all know your parts by now, I hope. The dancers are going to have to start from scratch, but Orlando tells me they're a talented bunch and he assures me they'll bring it off. Where *are* the dancers, by the way?'

'Not here yet,' said Trevor. 'Their coach is caught in a jam on the A1.'

Everyone groaned, as though the dancers had deliberately chosen to be stationary in a hot bus amid smells of exhaust from surrounding traffic.

Golly caught sight of me. 'Never mind. We've got Marigold,

the lynchpin of our drama. Come here, dear, and let me introduce you.'

I made my way to the front, hearing mutterings of 'Marigold Who?' 'Is she Trevor's new mistress?' 'If that little girl's really the lynchpin we may as well give up now.'

'Now, everyone, listen.' Golly waved a paw for silence and got it. 'Marigold's dancing the dumb heroine.' Sniggers, but no one dared to laugh out loud. 'And you can take it from me that whatever may be the fate of *Ilina and the Scarlet Riband*, I guarantee that by the end of this first run, the name of Marigold Savage will be known the length and breadth of Europe.'

This was kind of Golly. People looked a little less disbelieving, which was a measure of the respect in which Golly's music was held. Of course she hadn't actually said whether I'd be known for triumphant success or humiliating failure . . .

'Now, just in case it's passed anyone by, let me outline the themes.'

Golly talked for ten minutes about cross-cultural analysis, mythology, folklore and spiritual verities, nothing of which was comprehensible to me. Then she told us to get on with it. She had one or two little ideas to incorporate in the score but she'd be back after lunch. Trevor took over, clearing the central space to begin blocking the first scene. This means teaching everyone how they are to move about the stage, where they're going to stand, fall, sit, lie, scream and die. The stage manager, who was called Bill, had a large clipboard on which he recorded each move.

The soloists were staged first. The pianist struck up the first chords and Giovanni and I entered from opposite sides. Our eyes met across what would be the Eskimo equivalent of a village square – a few igloos and a pot of simmering caribou hoofs. He sang the opening aria, telling of love at first sight. To save his voice, Giovanni marked the role, which means he sang softly and dropped an octave in the high bits. As there had been no opportunity to warm up, I did the balletic equivalent, walking

540

through my opening sequence. It was impossible, therefore, to tell how effective it was going to be, but by now I was thoroughly familiar with the music and had come to love it.

Quite quickly I forgot to be nervous and the morning sped by. Lunch was brought in, corned beef sandwiches and tea. In the afternoon the chorus was blocked for Scene One, the soloists waiting at the back of the hall in case they were needed. There is always a lot of hanging around at rehearsals, and old hands know to provide themselves with books or knitting or mending. In the scramble to get ready I had forgotten to bring anything with me to help pass the time. Orlando had not yet returned from lunch in the Bentley which was parked in a side street. He had pressed me to join them, but I was afraid of being a damper on the release of urges that had been bottled up for a whole morning. The singers smiled politely if I caught anyone's eye, but they seemed to be avoiding me. Perhaps because of Golly's championship, they didn't want to be seen to be sucking up. I sat a little apart, reading the *Newcastle Gazette*. Loneliness was inevitably a part of a dancer's life. As I had chosen to turn my back on marriage and companionship I had better not mind it.

I gave a little scream as a pair of arms stole round my neck.

'Hello, old darling!' Lizzie's dimpled face surrounded by blonde corkscrew curls grinned at me, enjoying my surprise.

'Lizzie! I'd no idea you were coming! Oh, how wonderful!' We kissed and hugged. It had been several months since we'd seen each other, the longest separation for twelve years. The other eleven members of the company who were to dance in *Ilina and the Scarlet Riband* had to be welcomed and kissed too. It was thrilling to see so many familiar faces. I noticed immediately that some invisible threshold had been crossed. As I had left the LBC I was no longer in direct competition with the other dancers, and my leading role in *Ilina* had exalted my status to potential international stardom. Deference was of course better than hostility, but I would have preferred

541

something cosier. I knew the score. One of Evelyn's oft-repeated precepts when we were children was that privileges always had to be paid for.

Also the unpopularity of the current principal dancer, Sylvia Starkey, worked in my favour. Apparently, when she had been briefly elevated to the position of Sebastian's mistress, she had become arrogant and boastful. In hindsight my ingratiating style redounded to my credit. Sylvia was in Bristol with Freddy, Alex, Dicky and the rest of the corps dancing *The Lilac Garden,* so everybody took advantage of her absence to be thoroughly catty about her.

Several hours of imprisonment in a coach on a motorway had made the dancers noisy and excitable. Trevor told us to go up into the gallery because we were distracting the singers. The gallery, which was to become the LBC's nesting place for the next two weeks, afforded seclusion combined with an excellent view of everything that was going on. It was rapidly strewn with shoes, legwarmers, wraps, bandages, aspirin ointment, antibiotic cream, sticking plasters, magazines, books, paper cups, hairbrushes, hairpins, make-up bags, sandwich crusts and bottles of diet Coke.

'I hope the dancing isn't going to be too difficult?' said Lizzie when we found a corner to ourselves.

'The only hard bit is the games. But you're not supposed to do them well anyway so I can win. You'll be fine.'

'Good. Because this'll be my last outing in the limelight. I only came to see you. I'm giving up ballet for good.'

'Lizzie! You can't!'

'I can and I have. I told Sebastian yesterday.'

'After all that hard work for all those years? Oh, Lizzie, how sad!'

'Not for me. Nor for anyone else really. When I told Sebastian he thanked me for saving him the distasteful task of booting me out. According to him, when I'm doing *fouettés* I look like a fat old woman running for a bus on a windy day.'

'Nonsense! And you aren't fat.' Though I had noticed she'd put on a few pounds. It really suited her. 'He only said that because he didn't want you to think he minded.'

'I know. But anyway, I don't care. I'm so happy, Marigold! I'm in love!'

'*No!* Who with?'

Conrad's voice in my imagination corrected this to 'with whom?' but I took no notice. One evening at Hindleep, Fritz had read aloud those parts of Conrad's letters that might be of interest to us, about the people he had met and the parties he had been to, the museums he had visited and the concerts he had attended. Conrad seemed to have become someone quite unfamiliar, part of a large and cosmopolitan circle of strangers. After three weeks in Germany he had flown directly to the United States. He had no plans to return to Hindleep. Obviously our friendship had been of little consequence for, though he always sent good wishes to everyone connected with the opera, he never mentioned me by name. Had it not been for the little posy of wild flowers I had pressed, the paper bird and the parrot's feather which I kept in my copy of *Nicholas Nickleby*, I might have imagined those conversations when we had talked so freely about what concerned us most. Or I had, anyway.

Dimples appeared on Lizzie's chin as well as her cheeks, a sign that she was much moved. 'You remember I told you about the lumberjack who took over Nancy's room at forty-four Maxwell Street?'

'The one with the city girlfriend?'

'Yes. Nils, that's his name, asked her up to the flat one evening to meet us, only Sorel had to go out at the last minute so we were a threesome. Fiona was rather superior and made snide comments about what she called the "outré" decorations, and she was rude about my cabbage curry. I admit my cooking isn't very good but Nils said it was absolutely delicious and food for the gods.'

I remembered the cabbage curry and concluded that Nils must already have been head over heels in love with Lizzie.

'So they had an almighty row which began in whispers when I was out of the room and ended in a shouting match halfway down the stairs. Nils came back full of apologies and I said I was sorry the food had been so awful and he said I was an angel to be so sweet about it and really he didn't think he could go on seeing Fiona because she was so mean and anyway he'd discovered that his fancy lay in quite another direction.' Lizzie put her head on one side so her curls bounced and I nodded to show I was fully abreast of their conversation. 'So what with one thing and another he ended up in my bed that night and he's been there ever since. I don't mean he's literally been in it ever since without getting out of it, but we always sleep in the same bed.'

'I understand. So you're giving up dancing to spend more time with him. I suppose there isn't much call for lumberjacks in England. Is he going to get another job?'

'Actually, his father owns a vast logging company in Sweden and Nils is learning the business to take it over eventually. He's going back to Sweden for good as soon as I finish here and I'm going with him. We're getting married in Stockholm in October.'

'Oh, dearest Lizzie! How marvellous!' I put my arms round her and held her in a long embrace until I could be certain that I had control of my face. 'I hope you'll always adore each other and have everything you've ever wanted.'

'We will.' I rejoiced at the note of certainty in her voice, even while I tried to crush an illogical feeling of being abandoned. 'So we'll soon be two old married ladies. Pity we can't have a joint wedding but we might be able to synchronize our first babies—'

'I'm not marrying Rafe.'

'What?'

'It's all off. Oh damn!' I felt the customary clutch of guilt whenever I thought of Rafe. 'I promised to keep it a secret until he's told his mother.'

To my great relief Rafe and Isobel were still in Scotland, disposing of their aunt's livestock and chattels and unravelling the complicated laws of Scottish land tenure. His letters were frequent and affectionate and sometimes it seemed he had forgotten we were no longer engaged. He always said how much he was missing me. The very idea of him made me feel anxious, as though I had in some way behaved badly despite my best efforts to be helpful. I had no way of knowing whether Evelyn knew that the wedding was off. She and Rex had spent only one night at Shottestone between returning from Austria and departing for Canada. I worried terribly whenever I thought of Madam Merle stitching away at the exquisite lace dress. The chances that Rafe would find another bride of my dimensions were slim.

I groaned. 'I've made a muff of things, as usual. You won't tell a soul will you?'

'No, of course not – but what a shame! I thought he was the love of your life. What's happened?'

'It wasn't his fault. But I don't *think* it was mine either. We aren't the same kind of people . . . and though we wanted to, we didn't really love each other. It was all a dream.'

'Marilyn,' called Trevor. 'Just come and walk through the next bit, would you, so I can see where the others are to stand?'

'Where's Sebastian?' I asked when I returned an hour later.

'He's gone to Bristol with the others. Poor Sylvia, he's so nasty about her *port de bras*. She gets shaking fits these days when he starts criticizing. She turned green when he said he was going with them. But her loss is Cynthia Kay's gain.'

'Cynthia Kay?'

'I told you about her. Can't dance for toffee nuts but Sebastian's screwing her anyway because nothing better offers. He gave her a tiny solo in *Pagodas* and she made a complete bungle of it, poor girl. I sat next to her on the coach. She says she's looking forward to being able to sit down comfortably after a few days without Sebastian's ministrations. That's her, over there.'

She pointed to a pretty girl standing by herself, looking listlessly through a magazine. I felt truly sorry for her.

'Anyway,' said Lizzie, 'never mind about Sebastian. Are you quite certain it's finished between you and Rafe? I was so looking forward to meeting the redoubtable Evelyn.'

But at that moment I was called for another walk-through. After rehearsals finished, Lizzie and I went out to supper with some of the other dancers so there was no chance to explain. But over the next few days, in moments snatched between classes and rehearsals, the story of my love affair with Rafe was told. At first Lizzie was inclined to think that in turning down a man who was kind, gracious, honourable, well connected, well heeled and resembled a Greek god, I was making a terrible mistake. But when I succeeded in convincing her that despite these allurements I was not in love with him, she agreed that I had no other option but to break it off.

'Besides,' she said solemnly, 'it would be a crime and a sin if you gave up dancing. I'd forgotten just how good you are.'

Orlando was keen that we should dance at full stretch to keep our bodies and techniques up to the mark. So, on the second day of rehearsals, when my first solo came up, I put everything I had into it. Not having danced before an audience for so long I felt extremely tense, but I pretended I was alone in the drawing room at Hindleep, dancing to the tape of Conrad's playing. I wasn't particularly pleased with my performance, but to my surprise it met with sustained applause and even a few cheers from the singers as well as the dancers. After that everyone, including Trevor, was much friendlier.

'Yes,' said Lizzie. 'You were right to finish with Rafe. You were born to dance. Men, love, marriage – those things go by the board when you've got that sort of talent. I'm so proud of you.'

I felt unreasonably depressed by this generous compliment.

'That's kind of you but . . . oh, Lizzie, so much of the success of the opera depends on my not making *un joli fouillis* of it . . . I've never felt so frightened in all my life.' Or lonely, I might have added, but didn't.

45

In the wings, Orlando and I embrace carefully so as not to smudge my make-up. Though he is not performing, he is quivering with tension and grey with terror. In the next two and a half hours, he says with a little moan, his reputation will be made or destroyed. My limbs seem to be set in plaster of Paris and my heart is beating so hard in my throat I feel as though I am being garrotted.

'I can't remember the first *enchaînement*,' I gasp.

'Nor can I. Wait a minute – *pas couru en avant, grand jeté croisé en avant* down to stage right . . .'

'Oh . . . yes . . . but what happens after Giovanni says I'm the girl of his dreams?'

Orlando bites his lip to stop it trembling. 'Haven't the foggiest. But you'll know when you come to it. Don't worry.' He stares at me with wild, tormented eyes. 'I have complete faith in you. Oh God! I think I'm going to be sick! Look out!'

We take a step back. The crew are rolling a huge magnet round the stage to pick up any nails or tacks that might have been left during last-minute adjustments to the sets.

'Is my hair all right?'

After the dress rehearsal Sebastian, who has been in Newcastle for the last week, coolly countermanding details of Trevor's direction and always, it must be admitted, improving the production, insisted I dispense with the thick black wig which had been specially made for me. He said it made him think of a clump of dead pampas grass. I'm to dance with my hair loose. I've fastened back the side pieces to stop it being sucked into Giovanni's airways when he's singing at full throttle.

'It looks perfect. *You* are perfect.' Orlando gives me a Svengali-like stare. 'You will dance like a dream. Remember, the worse the dress rehearsal, the better the performance.'

There had been panic when, two days ago, Lizzie discovered that her weight gain was due to pregnancy. She had wanted to carry on but Nils, who had come up to Newcastle to lend support, pleaded with her not to jeopardize the future of the third generation of logging magnates. He is a blond giant with a nice face and charming manners, but there has been no time to get to know him properly. A replacement for Lizzie has been flown up from London. Orlando has sacrificed two valuable hours to teach her the steps. Poor girl, in the dress rehearsal she and I collided when she did one too many *jetés battus*. Then the igloo I was supposed to crouch behind while overhearing Giovanni's passionate song of jealousy and betrayal before he stabs me with a narwhal tusk (the plot has undergone further changes) stuck on its way down from the flies, so instead of leaping out from behind it I had to weave my way through the corps and come in two beats late. Also, one of the singers fell backwards over a dog-sled, hurting his back and ruining his recitative.

'Iron coming in,' shouts the fireman.

I watch the heavy brown fire curtain being lowered. This is a safety precaution. It will be dropped again in the interval to muffle the sound of props and scenery being changed.

'Iron going out,' shouts the fireman as it is raised.

Orlando and I move forward onto the stage as the dry-ice machines for the blizzard sequences are brought into the wings and switched on. They make a distracting gurgling noise. The 'quarter' is announced over the Tannoy, which means the performance will begin in fifteen minutes. Now we can hear the audience coming in, a buzz of talk, a communicable anticipation. In the wings, members of the corps are dipping their feet into trays of rosin to give them a better grip. One of the prompt-side crew cuts his finger on the giant polar-bear sculpture and there is a frantic hunt for a sticking plaster. The stage manager rushes past, checking that the cue light boxes are all working. These signal with red and green lights when the crew are to move scenery. The follow-spot operator comes to consult with Orlando about picking up my moves. Trevor, looking white and not his usual ebullient self, joins them to countermand their decisions. They move away to debate a move in the third act. I feel terribly alone.

The 'five', meaning five minutes to curtain up, is announced over the loudspeakers. Squawks from the oboes, blasts from the horns and trumpets, scrapes from the strings as the orchestra tunes up. Suddenly the stage is flooded with brilliant artificial polar light. All this is familiar to me, yet I am possessed by a painful feeling of unreality. Two of the crew push on the gallows-like structure from which hangs the whale-bone that I must kick with both feet. My heart speeds to a gallop as I become certain that I cannot do it.

'Marigold, darling! Break a leg!' says one of the chorus, planting a kiss on my naked shoulder as he goes by. During the four weeks of putting the opera together, friendships have sprung up, crossing the divide between singers and dancers. Now we are partners with one aim only – that the performance should be a success.

'Beginners, please,' says a voice over the loudspeakers.

A current of excitement and fear runs through us all. Singers rub their throats and sip water, dancers stretch and bend. We exchange stricken glances, black-rimmed eyes staring out from masks of yellow make-up. The theatre manager comes to say that the audience is seated and waiting. I have a violent desire to burst into tears.

Orlando comes over to whisper, 'I've just heard! Didelot's here!' He squeezes my hand so hard I want to protest, but my lips are glued together with fright. 'You'll be wonderful, darling, he'll adore it.' He groans and totters away to collapse into the arms of Fritz who is standing in the wings.

Didelot! I cup my hands over my mouth to stop myself hyperventilating. This is monstrously unfair! Everyone knows he dislikes visiting the provinces. We all thought he'd wait until the production went to London, by which time it will be polished to a smooth shining gem, unrecognizable as the rough-hewn rock it is at present. I want to run from the stage, down to the stage door and out into the street all the way to the railway station and thence to Outer, or better still, Inner Mongolia. I look to Orlando for aid. He rolls his eyes in despair.

'House lights going down,' whispers Bill, the stage manager. I consider asking Bill to take me away from all this and live with me for ever in a hut in the middle of a dark, impenetrable wood. The orchestra noise fades. Giovanni comes running to put his arms round me. I can feel him palpitating with fright. We embrace each other passionately. On our performances the opera pretty nearly stands or falls. We communicate this with eyes that jerk with terror. I do not care that he is my height and ten times my weight, has hair sprouting from ears and nostrils and a nose like a banana. I love him. We love each other.

The audience breaks into applause. Bertram, the conductor has come in. There is a moment's silence. The overture begins. I have heard this music so often that I could hum even the xylophone parts. The celeste runs up the scale to evoke ice breaking. It is brilliant and sends shivers down my back. Over the ten weeks that I have been listening to this extraordinary music, I have moved from finding it a cacophonous screech to considering it a work of genius. As the bassoon plays the sonorous bellow of the reindeer, a lump comes into my throat because it is so beautiful.

'Stand by,' mouths the stage manager and pulls the lever that operates the curtain.

The spotlights show the audience an Eskimo village sparkling with icy whiteness beneath a sky dark with impending snow and populated with stuffed Tundra swans and white-fronted geese. It is exciting and new and the audience stirs in response. It isn't until you get on stage with an audience that a production starts to live. You can feel it, whether they like it, are bored and restless, apprehensive or loving it. I feel a surge of pleasure from them and my entire being catches fire in response. I see Giovanni open his mouth and hear exquisite sounds ripple from his throat. I realize that he is a genius. I hear the first violin play the Ilina motif – my cue. I lift my arms into high third position. Two light quick steps . . . I'm on the stage . . . a deep plié for the take off . . . *glissade precipitée* just clearing the floor . . . follow into *tombé effacé* . . . the arms *en bas,* brush back foot forward . . . and *leap!*

Two and a half hours later, Giovanni – Amaguq – thrusts the narwhal tusk between my chest and my arm and I fall gracefully forward to lie on the ground, half turned to the audience. He spills the scarlet riband from his sleeve with prestigious adroitness after much practice. Its dramatic reappearance symbolizes the flowing of Ilina's heart's blood. The music becomes so mournful that my chest tightens with emotion as well as shortness of breath. Something drips on my face. I look up to see tears making pink tracks down Amaguq's yellow cheeks. His huge chest shakes with genuine sobs. He is so deeply into his role that he only remembers at the last moment to stand back for the soul-shattering finale.

There is a tug on the harness that I have been wearing under my wedding dress for the whole of the last act – and very hot it is, too – which was hooked onto wires by a member of the crew while I waited for my last entrance, hidden behind an igloo. The music swells to a ravishing climax as I raise my right arm to the giant tangerine moon. Slowly I am lifted into the air to fly across the stage. I bend my right knee slightly and point my left leg out behind me. My white satin cloak falls away to reveal wings which I expand by pulling a concealed tab beneath my bust. The spirit of the persecuted outcast girl escapes to eternal life in a flying arabesque as a Tundra swan. It is a sublime moment. As I am pulled up into the flies, the curtains close to the last strains of Golly's masterpiece.

I am lowered swiftly into the wings. One of the crew is there to undo the wires. My dresser rubs my face and arms with a towel. While the igloos and other props are whisked away the chorus, who are to take the first bow, position themselves on the stage. A powder puff is dabbed over my forehead and cheeks. I hear the stage manager say 'Ready? Curtain up.' A roar of applause rushes from the auditorium like a great wind as the chorus steps forward and bows. Then the corps de ballet trips gracefully on to a rapturous reception and forms a line in front of the chorus. It is the turn of the soloists. First Sura, the girl in love with Amaguq, whom he spurns for Ilina's sake, then Amaguq's mother and the angakok; last Oogruq, the Iago figure, the jealous schemer.

It is our turn. Giovanni grips my hand and together we run onto the stage to stand in front of the others. Giovanni bends stiffly at the waist and I sink into a *révérence*, the formalized bow which all dancers make every day at the end of every class to show respect and gratitude to their teachers and pianists. Step, step, knees together, lift arms, lift head, deep plié, arms lowered to *demi seconde*, palms down, head slightly forward, drop chin and eyes. I hear the audience applaud, see the orchestra looking up, grinning. I remember to curtsey to them and acknowledge their contribution with a sweep of my arm. I see the smiling faces of the front row, Sebastian sitting in the middle looking, I think, pleased, but again the feeling of unreality has taken hold of me. Someone brings me a bouquet. I hear the clapping as though from a long distance away, as though there is a thick pane of glass between the audience and me. The conductor comes on, then Orlando, and finally there are shouts of 'Composer!' and Golly, looking splendid in a red velvet boiler suit appears. She has spent the evening walking by the river, trying to distract herself by thinking of her next opera. The curtains close and the crew rush to grip the handles that hold back sections of the curtains so we can take our solo and paired calls. When I go on alone a thundering noise breaks out as the audience stamp their feet and whistle and flowers are thrown onto the stage.

After so many hours, days, weeks, months of hope, despair, rages, tears and joy – the crest and the chasm of human experience – *Ilina and the Scarlet Riband* is no longer a thick bundle of manuscript music, notes on stage directions, painted flats, bolts of cloth, ideas in people's heads. It has been born. It lives.

46

'I don't like the look of that cloud.' Evelyn glared at it through the drawing-room window. 'I must be a complete fool to even contemplate giving a garden party in England.'

'If it makes you think more kindly of Canada, I'll be glad of a little rain,' said Rex, slipping an arm round her waist.

'Don't do that while I'm trying to make these delphiniums stand up . . . my darling,' Evelyn added to make up for her cross tone. 'I *do* like Canada. At least I think it's very beautiful but I'm just not sure about living so far from civilization.' Rex gave a shout of laughter. Evelyn frowned. 'What's funny about that? After last night, surely you can see how important it is to be within reach of people of culture and taste. *Dear* Marigold!' She sent me an approving look, though I was making rather a hash of arranging some roses in a bowl. 'Who'd have believed you'd grow up to be a world-famous ballerina!'

'Not yet,' I murmured.

The morning papers had contained three more or less favourable reviews. Golly's music had met with unreserved enthusiasm. The critics talked of 'mythic power', 'uncompromising modernity', 'transcendental melodies', and so on. One reviewer complained of the complexity of the plot, another of some ragged chorus work. Two queried whether the odd behaviour of one of the corps de ballet, who seemed to be frequently lost in the mist, was intentional. This was Lizzie's stand-in, of course. When leaping up to kick the whale bone she had done an accidental backward roly-poly, which made the audience hoot with laughter. After that, every time she made a mistake there was a ripple of appreciative amusement. One critic opined that she brought a welcome dimension of humour to what might otherwise have been a uniformly dark tale. They had all written kind things about me, which I had savoured and committed to memory. But only one person's opinion really counted.

In recent weeks Didelot had been here, there and everywhere. I had read his reviews from Tokyo, Stuttgart, New York and Shanghai with sympathetic anguish for the castigated clumsy turns, weak arabesques, facial contortions, uneven corps line. His few words of praise glowed like fireflies in the dark. Whenever I thought of the Monday edition of the *Sentinel* I felt a buzz of sick terror.

'You'll be as famous as Margot Fonteyn,' said Evelyn, who knew as much about ballet as I did about gardening. 'I'm quite sure of it.'

I smiled my thanks for her endorsement while accidentally knocking a few more petals off a beautiful rose called *Comte de Chambord*. When I had protested that I was hopeless at arranging flowers she had said, 'Nonsense! Even an idiot can arrange a mass of the same thing.'

Rex had laughed very much at that. He seemed to find everything she said wonderfully entertaining, which boded well for their future. Whenever she asked him what was so amusing, he said something like, 'You are, my darling. Not just funny but absolutely splendid.'

'Are you really thinking of going to live in Canada?' I asked.

'Yes,' said Rex

'No,' said Evelyn. 'I shall never leave poor Kingsley. I know he's behaving most unreasonably at the moment,' she went on as we remained tactfully silent. 'But if he *should* come to his senses, I should never forgive myself if I were not by his side.'

Only that morning, when Evelyn had gone into the library to give instructions to Miss Strangward about not allowing the dogs upstairs and certainly not letting them sleep in Kingsley's bed, Kingsley had screamed and hidden behind the sofa. He had bawled for Nanny Sparkle to come and save him from the wicked witch. I heard Miss Strangward tell Evelyn, not I thought without some satisfaction, that it would be better if she kept away.

Evelyn had come out of the library with a face of wrath but Rex had said, 'Darling, it's just that you represent everything precious that he's lost, poor man, and there's a part of his brain that doesn't like to be reminded of it.'

Evelyn had been a little mollified. Besides, she and Rex were patently so happy in each other's company that nothing upset her for long. They had flown home specially for the first night of *Ilina and the Scarlet Rihand*, and when they had come back-stage afterwards I had taken her on one side and told her I knew she was my benefactor and that it would be impossible for me adequately to express my undying gratitude.

'It was naughty of Isobel to tell you.' Evelyn had looked pleased. 'But, darling, I don't want thanks. I've had my reward in watching you tonight. You were wonderful.'

Evelyn had been infected by first-night excitement and told everyone who would listen that Golly and I were among her most intimate friends. Golly, like the kind-hearted old thing she was, had responded cordially to Evelyn's unprecedented enthusiasm. Sebastian, who was trailing a weary looking Cynthia Kay behind him, had greeted Evelyn with charming gallantry. Thrilled to find herself rubbing shoulders with artists who might well be in the vanguard of a new movement, Evelyn had invited the entire cast to Shottestone for a celebration garden party.

She was not the only loyal friend to attend the first night. I had felt a hand on my arm and turned to see a lovely face framed by softly waving fair hair.

'*Bobbie!* Oh, how marvellous! I'd no idea you were coming!' Bobbie, who was responsible for my coming home and to whom therefore I owed all the good things that had happened to me since returning to Northumberland, embraced me as closely as she could, given that her stomach was rounded by several months' pregnancy.

'I read about the opera in the *Irish Times,* so of course I had to come to see you. And you were *wonderful!* You reduced me to tears and I try so hard not to cry at the moment because it upsets Finn.'

'Is he here?'

Bobbie pointed to a tall man with greying hair and a square jaw who was hemmed into a crowd nearby. He looked in our direction and waved to us. We waved back.

'Bobbie! Your baby's going to be so handsome! He looks divine!'

'He is divine. I saw him brush away a tear at the end too. Darling, I'm so proud of you! I want to cry all over again with happiness. I was worried about you, you know. In your last letter you sounded just a little troubled. Is Rafe here?'

'That's him over there, talking to the conductor. But I'm not going to marry him.'

Bobbie clutched my arm. 'I'm so glad!' This was quite a different reaction from the one I had come to expect. 'No man who really loved you would want you to give up dancing for him. Remember that, if you meet someone else. It'll be a useful diagnostic aid.' She looked at her watch. 'Heavens! We must go. The plane for Dublin leaves in an hour. Promise you'll come and stay in November after we close Curraghcourt to the public? That's if you can stand babies. Constance, my sister-in-law, has a three-week-old daughter and I'll have had mine by then.'

'I adore babies. I'd love to come.'

'Excellent. You can meet Finn properly then.' She embraced me again. 'Bye, darling. I must just go and kiss Dimpsie and then we'll dash. Take good care of yourself.'

'Bobbie! What about your coat!' But it was too late. She was pushing her way through the crowd towards her husband. I saw him encircle her protectively with his arm and then Rafe blocked my view of them. He and Isobel had flown down from Scotland that afternoon, but such had been the euphoria as paper cups of champagne were passed around and everyone assured everyone else that they had surpassed themselves in virtuosity that he and I had barely exchanged a word. He had kissed me passionately on the mouth, but as all the men present including Sebastian (no doubt intending to make Cynthia Kay jealous) had done the same, and half the women too, I was not made unduly anxious by this. But when Rafe said, with an affectionate squeeze, that he was looking forward to getting me to himself at Shottestone that night I became worried.

'Don't be silly, Marigold.' Evelyn overheard my protestations. 'It's Sunday tomorrow; there's no performance and you can travel back in comfort with us.' She added sotto voce, 'And you will be able to help me get everything ready for the party.'

Of course I could refuse Evelyn nothing, though I had hoped to go to Hindleep with Orlando and Fritz. And Conrad, too of course, if he had been able to catch a plane from New York in time to see *Ilina and the Scarlet Riband*. I had looked for him in the fevered throng but there had been no sign of the elegant figure and the sharp black eyes. Orlando and Fritz had rushed off together the moment the curtain fell, so I could not ask them if Conrad had been there.

I had been driven away by Rafe in the family Daimler, with Evelyn in the front passenger seat and Isobel sitting in the back with me. The relief of the first night being over, combined with too much alcohol and the smooth motion of the big car as it swooshed round corners and down hills, made me irresistibly sleepy, and I dozed during the journey. I woke briefly when we stopped for Isobel to be sick . . . heard her say something about having eaten chicken in mayonnaise on the flight from Edinburgh . . . fell again into a dream in which I was trying to play *Akratcheak* but my shoes seemed to be nailed to the floor. I heard Isobel say, 'She's kicking the back of your seat but I think she's asleep' and Rafe say, 'Never mind, poor little thing, it doesn't matter. Don't wake her . . .' Then we were at Shottestone and Evelyn was helping me up the stairs.

'I'll sleep in my make-up,' I murmured.

'You will not. You'll get spots. And lipstick all over the pillowcases.'

I might have been a child again. The next thing I knew it was morning. Over breakfast no other subject of conversation seemed possible but the triumph of *Ilina and the Scarlet Riband* and the forthcoming party. In a moment of exhilaration, Evelyn had invited the orchestra, the stage crew and the theatre staff as well. We calculated there would be between ninety to a hundred people.

Rafe was in charge of drinks. Isobel's task was to deadhead the one hundred and fifty roses. Dimpsie was to help Mrs Capstick with the food. Evelyn railed against the ingratitude of her two daily helps, who had chosen to attend to their families rather than slave on the seventh day for an extra five pounds. The local butcher had been bribed with large sums to provide three baked hams. Rex had appointed himself chief vacuumer and, when everything was ready, attended to each fallen rose petal and crumb of dirt that had been trodden into the carpets by the helpers.

'Rex is so marvellously considerate,' Evelyn confided in me. 'Poor Kingsley never once considered how dust is got up. I'm sure he thought I had only to wave a wand and the house would be clean.' As she could not tell Rex how to turn the vacuum cleaner on, nor where any of the power points were, it seemed that Kingsley was not far off the mark.

'Evelyn's a phenomenon,' said Rex a little later. 'So bright, so elegant, so discriminating. I adore her way of looking at the world. Single-minded, even self-centred, you might say, but boy, does she deliver! And how much pleasure she gives us all!'

I could only agree.

Jode was to organize parking for those who had elected to drive themselves. Far from objecting to this lowly task, he seemed to enjoy pacing out the minimum space into which a car could fit, putting up tape barriers to keep them in line, raking the gravel drive to a perfect smoothness and pinning arrows to fences and gates to direct people into the field. For the other guests, Evelyn had organized buses. I had been appointed Evelyn's liaison officer and pencil carrier. I trotted after her all day long, marvelling at her energy. Rebukes for my dreaminess and inefficiency had continually to be bitten back as she remembered in time that I was her most successful creation to date.

By half-past seven every glass had been polished, every limp bloom beheaded, every nut devilled, every asparagus spear rolled in brown bread and every egg stuffed. On the kitchen table, besides the hams, were four large chicken millefeuille and several bowls of strawberries in Muscat syrup. Mrs Capstick's ankles had ballooned but she was triumphant.

We gathered in the drawing room in our best clothes, charged with the adrenalin that sustains a party-giver before the party becomes a reality. Consonant with our mood, the sky was very bright, almost yellow, and dark clouds outlined in gold hovered in the distance. It was hot and stuffy. Once I thought I heard a rumble of thunder. We exchanged opinions about the likelihood of rain for perhaps the fiftieth time, and again we agreed that if push came to shove everyone would just have to be asked indoors. Spendlove was sent to get out the drugget used on these occasions to protect the Aubusson from plebeian feet.

'What's the collective noun for guests?' asked Rafe, who seemed more cheerful than I had seen him for ages. We had been too busy for anything like a proper conversation, so his good humour had nothing to do with me. 'A gossip?'

'A thirst of guests,' suggested Rex.

'A gush of guests,' said Isobel, who was still pale. When I had taken her a mug of tea in the garden earlier, she had emerged

561

from the rose bushes, wiping her mouth with a handkerchief. 'A plague on all chickens everywhere,' she had said. 'Or was it the mayonnaise, I wonder?'

'A bus-full of guests,' I said, hearing the crunch of gravel. 'And here they come.'

Not only the guests but the rain came too, fortunately only in intermittent showers. This had no effect on the mood of the revellers, the rigours of their profession having inured them to much greater discomfort than a gentle wetting. They knocked back sparkling wine – champagne had been vetoed by Evelyn who said they would not be able to tell the difference – and devoured Mrs Capstick's delicious food as fast as Dimpsie, Spendlove and I brought them out. When it rained, they partied in the conservatory, the stables, the summerhouse, the swimming-pool changing room, the temple and the grotto. When the sun came out they danced to the music of a jazz band called the Heavenly Bodies, the best Evelyn had been able to find at such short notice. The Bodies were five pensioners with white hair and paunches but, according to those who knew about jazz, they swung. People were drunk on wine, success, the beauty of their surroundings, the scent of roses. As a celebration it was a smash-hit.

There was one blot on the gaiety. Evelyn had invited several of her own friends, including the archdeacon and his wife, and Lady Pruefoy. This mistake I attributed to her desire to show off as patron of the avant-garde. They took one look at the effervescent roisterers and retreated indoors to the drawing room to sip disapprovingly at the sparkling wine, which they knew at once was not champagne, and to talk in undertones about what poor dear Kingsley might have said could he have seen his wife flirting *in public* with a Canadian. After a time even the gossip ran out, and when I walked past the drawing room on my way to the kitchen I heard Lady Pruefoy say into a depressed silence, 'If this is what falling in love in one's riper years does to one's judgement, I thank heaven I am too old for that kind of thing.'

'Yes, indeed,' replied the archdeacon, with more truth than gallantry.

I reported the *froideur* within to Evelyn, who was sitting with Rex on the terrace in front of the summerhouse, talking to Sebastian and Cynthia Kay. Evelyn pulled a face and stood up, a little unsteadily. I was delighted to see that she had relaxed her rule of never more than two glasses. 'Perhaps I'd better go . . .'

'No!' Rex took her hand and drew her down again. 'The party's out here. If they want to bubble and stew indoors, let them. I mean to enjoy myself and I can't do that without you, my love.'

'But I should at least see if they have everything they want . . .'

'I'll go and ask them, if you like,' I said.

'That would be angelic, darling.' Evelyn turned to the others. 'Isn't Marigold an absolute *angel*?'

Clearly Rafe had still not told her that I was a traitor and a renegade.

'A poppet.' Rex winked at me.

'I have always found Marigold far from angelic.' Sebastian twirled the stem of his glass between his bony fingers. 'In fact, I would have said she is quite amoral. There is nothing too depraved or degraded that she would not do to further her ambition.' I expect my rage showed on my face. Sebastian was a brute, a sadist, a monster of cruelty and the worst tortures of hell were too good for him. 'But she is the best dancer we've had in the company and the two things may not be unconnected.' I modified my poor opinion of Sebastian somewhat. Did he mean he wanted to take me back? I reminded myself that I was now in a much stronger position to negotiate a contract and I was certainly going to exclude any hanky-panky in the director's office, or anywhere else, for that matter. 'By the way,' Sebastian smiled maliciously, 'Didelot is here. He wants to see you.'

'Didelot?' I yelled, and several people turned to look. '*Here?*'

'Didn't I just say so?'

'He wants to see me?'

'Apparently. He's gone back to the house.'

'Who is Didelot?' asked Evelyn.

I did not stay to hear Sebastian's reply. In a state of agitation I sped across the lawn. Didelot was strict about not fraternizing with anyone who had anything to do with ballet, particularly not dancers. I saw Orlando and Fritz in the distance, waltzing dreamily. They waved and beckoned but I shook my head and hurried on. All I could think of as I made my way through the frolicking guests was that perhaps Didelot had sent a searingly bad review of my performance to the *Sentinel* and then for some reason had been struck by remorse. Perhaps he wanted to explain to me in person just why he had effectively destroyed my career.

I ran into the hall. Someone was playing the piano. Chopin. Through the open door of the drawing room I saw a row of beatific smiles. The archdeacon, cradling a dish scattered with cocktail sticks and olive stones, was beating time inaccurately with his foot. Lady Pruefoy had rolled up her eyes to gaze at the ceiling in transports. I doubted if she had a tuneful bone in her body, but she knew she ought to like it. I could imagine her reporting the occasion. 'A consummate musician, my dear. Just a select circle of Evelyn's intimates. The riff-raff were entertained outside.'

I looked round the door. Across the polished mahogany of the Bechstein, Conrad looked up, saw me and smiled. My stomach did a hop-step-coupé. It had been two months and eighteen days since I had last seen him. I forgot entirely about Didelot and the ruin of my career.

'Hello, Marigold.' The sound of his voice did something volcanic to my insides. He continued to play the *Grande Valse*. 'How are you?'

I skipped to his side. 'Fine. Well, not fine all the time.

Sometimes I've prayed for a rapid and painless death. But *Ilina and the Scarlet Riband* was a huge success.'

'Indeed, it was masterly. A few rough edges, but they will be smoothed in time.'

'You were there? You saw it?'

He frowned. 'Don't speak so loudly. My audience is being appreciative.'

I loved the way he pronounced it, soft yet precise and hissing. His voice ought to be recorded for posterity. And he ought to be photographed from every angle and enlargements put in an album. It was unfair to have so much beauty wasted on a man. He was playing from memory. I thought it was very clever of him to do that and carry on a conversation at the same time.

'Why didn't you come backstage?' I whispered.

'I had an appointment that could not be put off. Then I went to bed. I had flown the night before from New York to London . . . then another flight to Newcastle in the afternoon . . . I was exhausted.'

'It *was* good of you to come. I wish I'd known you were there.'

He shot a glance at me. 'What difference would it have made?'

'Well, I would have liked it, that's all. Though you don't deserve the compliment. You never mentioned me in your letters or sent me any messages. I don't believe you gave me a thought.'

'I did think of you.'

'Really? Did you, honestly?'

A cough from the archdeacon made me look round. He had commandeered a tray of canapés and gave me a reproving stare as he chewed.

Conrad looked amused. 'How they all dislike you.'

'Do they? How mean of them!'

'Is not the feeling returned?'

'Mm, yes, I suppose it is. But they started it. And why particularly?'

'Oh, they dislike me just as much. Probably more.' He

pleased. 'I am a foreigner, a Jew *and* I am much richer than they are. It defies the natural order of things – as they would have it.'

I leaned on my elbow on the piano lid so that I could look into his face. '*I* don't dislike you.'

He shot me another glance in which I read satisfaction. I waited for him to say that he liked me too, which any polite person would have done, but instead he said, 'What was your own judgement of your performance last night?'

'Six out of ten. I slightly lost concentration in the second act adagio. My feet were good but one of my attitudes was a bit wobbly . . . oh!' I remembered with an unpleasant jolt. 'Have you seen a small balding man with curly grey hair and a black moustache? Quite insignificant looking?"

'Shhh!' hissed Miranda Delaware.

'No such person has been here.'

'Sebastian *said* he was here. I wonder if he was having me on, to pay me out for agreeing to marry Rafe instead of him?'

'Are you going to marry Rafe?'

'Don't be silly. You know I'm not.'

'You say not. But when I last saw you, you appeared to be on the most intimate terms.'

'I'm cast-iron positive I'm not going to marry him. And he knows it. I can't understand why he pretends to go on with it. He doesn't love me and I don't believe he ever did.'

'You don't realize why he wishes to marry you? But it is right under your nose.'

'I suppose you mean he desires my body.'

Conrad lifted his eyebrows but waited until he had got through a specially fast bit. Then, as he twiddled about on the black notes with his right hand, 'You accuse *me* of conceit.'

'That's unfair. Isn't it nearly always sex? Anyway, it's all I offer. He isn't interested in ballet in the least so it isn't trechat six. That's a sort of jump when you twizzle your

'I know what an entrechat is.'

'Oh, Conrad! You always know everything. It's very annoying.'

He did not react to this taunt but continued to move across the keyboard with great sweeps of triplets.

'Well,' I said, after he had pulled off a difficult few bars, 'if it isn't sex, what is it? I'm not exactly cut out to be mistress of the ancestral acres.'

Conrad seemed not to have heard me. He was engaged with a particularly expressive section. Eventually he asked, 'Who is it you are looking for?'

'Didelot. You won't have heard of him but you'll just have to believe me when I tell you he just happens to be the most important person in ballet right now, that's all!'

'*Shhh!*' said Miranda and Lady Pruefoy together.

'Surely not?'

'Truthfully. He's a critic and he sees everything and he can make mincemeat of one's career with a few sentences. His judgement is like the word of God and I'm terrified of him.'

Conrad played a series of emphatic chords which made the audience sit up straight and open their eyes. He looked me full in the face and said with an air of maddening imperturbability, 'I am Didelot.'

567

47

Of course Conrad was joking when he claimed to be Didelot. He had the strangest sense of humour.

'Oh yes,' I said. 'And I'm Ninette de Valois, but I'm travelling incognito at the moment so I'd rather you didn't tell anybody.'

He smiled. 'I have met Ninette de Valois. She is in her eighties. You are an impostor. Move out of the way.' I leaned back so he could play a twiddly bit with his right hand at the top end of the keyboard. 'But I *am* Didelot.'

'Sebastian pointed him out to me once. He doesn't look anything like you. He's a little grey man and his name is Karl Peters. Besides, you don't know anything about ballet.'

'I wonder if you will say that when you read my review tomorrow? Don't you know that Karl is German for Charles? My uncle Charles was Didelot for thirty-seven years. He took me to the ballet from the time I was eight years old and taught me what to look for in a *brisé*, how to judge a perfect *assemblé*, the essential qualities of a *pas de quatre*. When he died I was asked to assume his position as ballet critic of the *Sentinel* and to retain Didelot's anonymity.'

My brain seemed to have seized at the point when I imagined that Conrad had said he was Didelot. It was a fantastical notion. I must be dreaming, yet the floor on which I stood, the beam of sunlight that shot in through the window, the piano on which I put my hand to steady myself seemed quite real.

'You *are* joking. Aren't you?'

'I am perfectly serious. What was it I wrote about your Giselle? Something about your *épaulement* I liked particularly . . .'

'*An abandon in the* épaulement *which satisfactorily prefigured the descent into madness.*'

'Ah, yes. I must have been in an unusually mellow mood that evening. But I thought you were good. I said to myself, this girl has possibilities. She is not yet a great ballerina. But one day she may be. Your behaviour on the train undid a favourable first impression but, after all, your potential as a dancer was unrelated to your agreeableness as a fellow passenger.'

'But Conrad!' I paused. My thoughts refused to be knocked into any sort of shape. Could he *really* be the great Didelot – he of the penetrating eye, the incisive judgement, the remorseless pen?

He rounded his eyes and mouth, imitating my expression. 'You look very comical.'

'You . . . you *beast!*' I hissed. 'You liar! You cheat! You rat! You false . . . scheming . . . bamboozler . . .' I was unable to think of anything quite bad enough.

A sound like waves breaking on shingle as everyone shushed me.

'I deny it. I have never said I was not Didelot. You have never asked me.'

'But how could I . . . who could possibly have imagined . . . and all this time! . . . I thought we were friends! . . . how *wicked!*'

Conrad played the last few bars of the piece and acknowledged the burst of clapping with the briefest of nods before swivelling on his stool to face me.

'Uncle Charles took great pride in his impartiality. When, during his last illness, I undertook to replace him at the *Sentinel*,

I promised to be faithful to his precepts. Especially I would not have doings with the performers. During the time you were not dancing, my consorting with you was within the bounds of the agreement. Now, of course, I must either give up the job or I must give up *you*.'

'Mr Lerner!' effused Miranda Delaware. 'We are all in raptures over your marvellous playing. Could we trouble you for one more piece?'

Lady Pruefoy clasped her hands girlishly beneath her vast bosom. 'Oh, *would* you?'

'Hear, hear!' The archdeacon grinned widely, giving us a glimpse of the interior of the sepulchre.

'Very well.' Conrad turned back to the keyboard. 'My last piece shall be one of Schubert's greatest songs. It is called *Erlkönig* which is a poem by Goethe. It is a sinister tale about an evil spirit who steals away children. I translate roughly. A father and his little son are riding through a dark and dreary night. He asks his son why he hides his face in fear. Father, says the boy, don't you see the Erlking, with his crown and flowing robe? The father says it is nothing but a wisp of fog. The Erlking pursues them. The boy is afraid but the father insists it is the shaking of leaves. The Erlking promises to take the boy to a beautiful place where his daughters will rock him to sleep. If he will not come willingly, he will use force. Father! cries the boy. The Erlking is holding me fast! He has wounded me grievously! The father rides home in terror. He finds the child is motionless in his arms. Dead.'

Conrad began the introduction. After the silvery tunefulness of Chopin, Schubert's music was wild, disturbing stuff, full of menace. Lady Pruefoy brought her eyes down from the ceiling to stare fixedly at the floor in front of her, as though seeking comfort from the hearth rug. The archdeacon stopped chewing.

'*Wer reitet so spät durch Nacht und Wind?*' Conrad sang.

He had said he could not sing, but that was a lie. His voice was charming. But there would be no point in accusing him. I knew he would wriggle out of it by saying that I knew nothing about singing, which was true.

'*Willst, feiner Knabe, du mit mir gehn?*'*

Of course he was Didelot. The moment I admitted it was possible, it became probable and then certain. I repeated to myself things that Didelot had written and now I heard them all in Conrad's voice. He was so knowledgeable, so clever and sharp-witted. He was cosmopolitan and sophisticated and swam with the biggest fish in the arts world. Why should he not be a luminary of ballet as well?

A thousand questions flew around half-formed inside my brain. It was not to be expected that he would give up being Didelot. Our friendship, so valuable to me, so inessential to him, must founder. Outside the sky had become angry-looking. Clouds like great bronze pinions pressed against the tops of the trees. I felt a trickle of perspiration run down the back of my neck. Conrad's face was gilded by the stormy light.

'*Mein Sohn, mein Sohn ich seh es genau,*' he sang. '*Es scheinen die alten Weiden so grau. Ich liebe dich,*' he glanced up at me, '*mich reizt deine schöne Gestalt.*'**

I caught the look, felt it in the tenderest part of me, was practically annihilated by it. The little boy was killed by the Erlking. Though my wound was not fatal, I was afraid it would be permanent.

'*In seinen Armen das Kind war tot.*'†

Conrad played the last soul-searing chords, then closed the lid over the keyboard and stood up.

'Lovely! Perfectly lovely!' The archdeacon's wife ru

---

*   'Won't you come with me, fine lad?' GOETHE
**   'My son, my son, I can see clearly, / It is the old wil' so grey. / I love you, your fair form allures me.'
†   'In his arms the child was dead.' GOETHE

towards Conrad, a handkerchief held to her beady little eyes. 'You will think me absurdly susceptible, but you have moved me to tears.'

'I too am deeply moved,' said Lady Pruefoy, pushing her out of the way.

Miranda Delaware got out her lipstick, skilfully repainted her mouth and joined them at the piano. I found myself outside the circle.

Lizzie walked into the drawing room. 'I've been looking for you for ages. I've got to go with Nils to Stockholm tomorrow so I can be placed in the care of the best doctors and eat buckets of iron tablets. But I said I must be allowed to say goodbye to you properly. Nils is playing with the band. A dustbin lid and a gong stick. Not a musical sound, but he's enjoying himself. Don't you think he's gorgeous?'

'Gorgeous? Oh, Nils. Yes.'

Together Lizzie and I walked through the hall and out into the garden. The sky was overcast, yet the colours in the garden were vivid, particularly the humming blues and purples.

'It's most peculiar,' Lizzie tucked her hand through my arm, 'but somehow I find I don't mind being treated like a womb on legs. I always thought I was looking for a man who'd vanquish me with his masterful ways and Byronic good looks. Instead I'm trotting up the aisle with a mother hen. But I suppose that's love for you.'

She was my very best friend and I was tempted to tell her everything. 'Lizzie—'

'What?'

'Nothing. Let's walk down to the Bear's Hut.'

'⌐ there a bear in it?'

'⌐ any more. What does it feel like to be pregnant?'

'⌐ally, do you mean? Not particularly pleasant. Swollen, ⌐sts. The worst thing is being sick . . .'

'⌐lked my thoughts wheeled like a flock of star-
⌐nd contracting in an ever-changing pattern,

572

the individual parts evidently in some kind of communication, yet the whole seeming without an intelligible purpose.

'Not just in the morning either. I always used to be a good traveller, but now I only have to look at a car and whoosh!'

The entire flock of starlings dropped down to roost. Perhaps it wasn't food-poisoning that was making Isobel sick. Supposing, oh dear God!, supposing she was expecting Conrad's child? Suddenly my insides felt as though they were being grilled on a slowly turning spit.

'Oh damn!' Lizzie held out her hand to catch a large rain-drop. 'It's going to pelt. Where's that Bear's hideaway?'

'Through that gap in the hedge.'

We ran. Lizzie tripped on a paving stone but luckily I caught her before any harm could befall Nils Nilsson III.

'Where is it?' asked Lizzie. 'Oh, there. How pretty!'

I tugged at the door handle but it did not move. 'It must be swollen with damp.'

We stood beneath the deep eaves of the roof, as the rain streamed from the thatch, inches from our faces. Soon my dress, the one Rafe had given me, was splashed with dark patches.

'Damn!' said Lizzie. 'Our shoes will be ruined.' She was wearing pretty silver sandals. 'They were my first present from Nils.'

'Perhaps if we gave the door a gentle kick,' I suggested.

It was unyielding. I put my face close to the cobwebbed window and saw movement among the shadows. I rubbed a circle in the dusty surface of the glass. 'There's someone in there, lying on the sofa. I suppose they can't hear us because of the noise of the rain.'

Lizzie peered in, cupping her hands round her face to cut out the light. 'There are two of them and they seem to be tearing each other's clothes off. A romantic place for a tryst, isn't it! We ought not to look.'

She was right, of course, but I had glimpsed a face I recog nized.

'Isn't that Isobel Preston?' Lizzie, despite her better instincts, had remained with her nose pressed to the pane.

I felt guilty, but I could not tear my eyes from Isobel's rapt expression as she turned her head about in a frenzy of pleasure. Her dress was round her waist, one breast was bare. She put up her hand to caress the neck of the man who lifted her knees and thrust his body forward to get inside her. He began to move with convulsive jerks, as though in a desperate hurry to reach the climax of lovemaking.

'They're going at it hammer and tongs!' Lizzie whispered, trying to pull me away. 'Let's go, Marigold!'

I clung onto the sill. I had to see who the man was. I *had* to know. His head and body were in shadow but suddenly he turned his head, as though aware they were being watched. For a split second the world turned uniformly green and there was a strange roaring in my ears.

'No,' I said. 'No, *no!*' I jumped backwards, slipping on the wet stones in my haste. 'Quick! We must get away from here!'

'Wait for me!' called Lizzie when we were halfway back to the house. 'Don't forget I'm running for two.'

I slowed to a walk. We had reached the part of garden where I had received my first gardening lesson. That was when I had belonged to the charmed inner circle. I fervently wished I could return to those days when my naivety had protected me from seeing the dreadful truth.

'I don't know why seeing other people screwing is faintly unpleasant,' said Lizzie when she'd caught up. 'We all know everybody does it. I'm the living proof.'

'I've been such a fool! An absolute . . . bloody . . . idiot!'

'Why? What's the matter?'

The rain had slowed to a drip. I put my hands to my throbbing temples. 'It never occurred to me . . . how could it . . . ?'

'What do you mean? She's engaged, isn't she? Surely you didn't think they were just holding hands?'

'It wasn't him. It wasn't Conrad.'

'Blimey! So she's two-timing him before the ring's even on her finger? Call me old-fashioned but I'd say that's rather shabby.'

'Oh, Lizzie! I don't know! I begin to see . . . if ever there was love . . . oh, God! . . . what a mess!'

'If you're going to speak in riddles . . . Who was it if not the bloke she's engaged to?' She put her arm round me as I groaned. 'Are you all right?'

'I'm okay – no, I'm not, actually. I ought to have realized . . . My father, he tried to tell me—'

'Your father! Crikey! I can imagine how you must feel . . . how horribly embarrassing to catch one's parent in flagrante . . . and with one's own girl friend . . . sick-making, almost incestuous. You're right, it *is* a mess . . .'

A tall figure loomed. It was Nils. 'Lizzie! You should not be outside in this storm.' He gave me a reproachful look. 'You must come in now and rest. I shall fetch you a glass of milk.'

Lizzie submitted to being petted by a large hand. 'You are an old fusspot. I shall start to moo soon. All right, we're coming.'

'I'll stay out for a bit,' I said.

'You look perfectly tragic, darling. You've had a nasty surprise. Why not come in and have something to buck you up?'

'Honestly, I don't think I could face a crowd just at the moment. I'll be fine.'

Lizzie looked doubtful, but I reassured her and she allowed herself to be led away. I took off my shoes and, holding one in each hand, did what came instinctively to me when troubled. I ran past the Indian tent, past the rose garden, past the grotto and the fountain. I sprinted up to the house. The front door was open. I put my shoes, the black suede high-heeled ones I had bought with the silver fork money, inside for safe-keeping. No one saw me. The gravel of the turning circle was hell to run on and I was probably damaging my feet, but for once I didn't care.

I ran down the drive and turned left onto the road that led into Gaythwaite. The going was better on tarmac. I must have looked a sight, charging along in a silk dress with bare feet and my hair hanging loose. Several cars hooted as they overtook me. I pounded down the half-mile into the town. A group of men sitting outside a pub began whistling and shouting. One of them, holding a bottle, wove into my path, but I skipped round him.

'What's the hurry, pet?' he called. 'Yer old man after ye . . . ?'

I put on a spurt to get through the town, across the market square, past the surgery, the Singing Swan and the craft shop with its 'For Sale' sign in the window. I dashed past the mendacious sign outside Belinda's Buns which said 'Fresh Cream Cakes Daily'. Before long I was through the town, running uphill now, keeping the pace steady. Pad, pad, pad went my bare feet, and my mind kept in tune with them, relaxed, concentrating on sustaining the physical effort, empty of thought. Before me stretched the road, around me were trees and hills, their distinct shapes and colours starting to merge with the approach of nightfall. I was conscious of confusion and looming dismay, which would overtake me the moment I stopped, but for now anxiety was contained, dammed up, by the demands of running. I reached the end of the drive to Dumbola Lodge, now dignified by an estate agent's board. I had not thought of it as a haven for many years, but nonetheless I felt a pang of regret as I swept by.

A car came up behind me, slowed and tooted. I took no notice. The car crawled beside me for some way, two young men urging me to get in and have a bit of fun with them. When I continued to ignore the various inducements they offered – a tab, a gill, a ride in the shuggyboats, a trip to Newcassel – they became insulting. I ducked into the woods. It was dark under the trees. My feet suffered agonies from stones, thorns and nettles. Brambles tore my dress. A light far above my head, which must come from Hindleep, gave me encouragement. Perhaps ten minutes or quarter of an hour later I emerged onto the road and made for the bridge without pausing to catch my breath. The statues were transformed by obscurity into featureless columns of shadow, but I felt their censorious presence. I imagined stone hands reaching down to clutch at my hair and put all my energy into one last burst of speed.

The lanterns were lit in the courtyard, revealing the sleek outline of the Bentley. This was more than I had dared to hope for. I flew up the steps, wrenched open the front door, slammed it behind me and leaned against it, panting. A soft light came from the drawing room. I pushed my hair out of my eyes and went in. The windows were thrown wide, admitting a refreshing breeze from the lake which made the curtains stream like demented wraiths. Several candles burned beside the unlit hearth.

Conrad was sitting on the left-hand divan, an open book in one hand. The other caressed a pair of beautiful ears. They belonged to Siegfried, who was curled up on the crimson silk beside him. Conrad closed the book and yawned, then caught sight of me. An expression of something like satisfaction flitted across his face before he schooled it to resignation as he looked me up and down.

'I experience a strong sense of déjà vu,' he said, closing the book and standing up.

48

'Hello Conrad,' I panted. 'Hello, Siggy *darling*.'

'You look like Ashenputtel, with your dress in rags and your hair in disorder.' Conrad picked up the bottle of wine in front of him and filled the second glass that stood on the tray. He remained standing to strike a match and apply it to the kindling in the fireplace. 'Cinderella, as you call her. Sadly I have no turtle doves to bring you a golden gown and silver-embroidered slippers.'

I looked down at my beautiful dress. The hem was torn in several places and stained with mud.

'Come and sit here,' said Conrad, 'close to the fire.'

'I feel as though I've been brought to a rolling boil.'

'But you must remember the horses. Now wait. I shall be back directly.'

I did as I was told. Siggy stared up at me with marmalade eyes. His nose went into a spasm of twitching but he decided in my favour and climbed carefully into my lap. I stroked him and kissed the tips of his ears. I had missed him very much during my stay in Newcastle. Knowing how fastidious he was, I suppressed my panting as much as I could and tried not to drip.

Conrad returned with a bowl of steaming water, milky with disinfectant, and placed it on the floor beside me. 'Put in your ет.'

The water became an unpleasant muddy colour streaked with red, and the cuts stung like crazy. 'This is rather biblical,' I said.

'As my hair is too short to dry them, here is a towel.' He threw it on the divan beside me.

'It's so kind of you. Thank you.'

'Not at all. I have some respect for my carpets.'

I raised my glass. 'Were you expecting someone?'

'I was expecting you, *actually*, as you say.'

'No, do I really? How annoying of me. I must try not to. But were you really? What made you think I was coming here?'

'Oh . . . something I overheard. At the party.'

'What was it?'

'A boy who looked like Struwwelpeter and a girl with hair like springs were talking about you. She said she regretted having left you alone in the garden. Apparently you were much upset because you had seen Isobel and your father making love in a thatched cottage where they used to keep bears. When she saw that I was listening she drew him away. Naturally my curiosity was aroused so I went into the garden and down to the Bear Hut.'

'Oh, Conrad, I'm so sorry!'

'It was a pleasant walk. The rain had stopped.'

'Yes, but Isobel – did you see them?' I shivered, remembering the two lovers moving in the shadows. 'Lizzie didn't realize . . . She thought it was my father, and then I didn't want to tell her the truth. I don't know how to tell you, either, but if you knew them as well as I do you wouldn't be angry . . . People will say it's wicked but, oh, this is *so* hard . . .' The idea of giving him pain made me wretched.

'Don't be distressed, Marigold,' he said in a softer tone. 'I was sure the girl was mistaken. I went only to see if my surmise as to the identity of the two was correct. I have known for a long time that Isobel and Rafe were lovers.'

'Conrad! I don't believe you!' We stared at each other. His face was lit dramatically by the rising flames. 'I want to, desperately. But you always hate to be told anything.'

'Did I not tell you some time ago that the story of Siegmund and Sieglinde was something you should consider? If you were not a terribly badly educated girl, you would know that they were brother and sister who become lovers in *Die Walküre*.'

'You know I'm trying to improve my mind but it takes time – anyway, I'm so glad you know. I was afraid . . .'

'Afraid of what?'

'That you'd be terribly hurt. And that you might be angry with me because you're so proud and you'd be jealous of somebody making love to Isobel.'

'I? Proud? Jealous?' He drew himself up very straight and his eyes seemed to spark. 'Never!'

'I don't see either of those things as particularly sinful. You said yourself if you love someone you can't help it . . . but that's all beside the point. I had simply no idea and I still can't really believe it. It seems to stand everything on its head. Let me think a minute.' I tried to recall every detail of my relationship with Rafe and to weave this new strand into everything that had happened since my arrival in Northumberland. Eventually I looked up at Conrad, who stood with a glass in his hand contemplating me with an air of calm patience. 'You might have told me! I do think it was mean of you!'

'Have you not just said that you were reluctant to tell me? Why should not I also feel the unpleasantness of hurting you? I tried to suggest it to you, but two possibilities occurred to me. One: that you, the girl who loves to dwell in fantasy, might not wish to know the brutal truth. Two: you might know it, but you had decided to ignore it. Rafe was, after all, a matrimonial prize. All right, don't be angry,' he held up his hand as I began to protest, 'I know you now well enough to be certain that you would not compromise yourself either for money or social advantage. But what business was it of mine what you knew? I am ᵗ the bureau of information. I had no way to tell how things ᵗ between you and Rafe. First you were to marry him, then ᵗ not, then again you were.' He folded his arms and looked down at me in a considering sort of way. 'You do not appear to be broken-hearted.'

'Not for me. But I *am* broken-hearted for them. It seems utterly tragic. I've known Rafe and Isobel all my life. They always adored each other. But it honestly never occurred to me. I mean, Rafe is the last man you'd expect . . . he's always so bothered about what other people are thinking. That's why I know that they really, *really* do love each other and it isn't any good being angry with them.'

'Not the least good in the world. Besides, what is there to be angry about?'

'Well . . . Isobel . . . you're engaged to her!'

'No.'

'No?'

'I have never been engaged to marry Isobel.'

Siggy gave a squeak of protest because I was gripping his ears. I stroked them smooth and he rolled over so I could give attention to his stomach. 'I don't understand. We were all told . . . you were introduced to us as Isobel's fiancé . . . you bought this house . . .'

'Be quiet and I shall explain.' He poured us both another glass of wine. 'In December of last year I received from Isobel a letter asking me to marry her. I was surprised. And intrigued. One does not often receive proposals of marriage from beautiful, affluent young women of good family.'

'Never, I should think.'

Conrad smiled in a rather superior way. 'As to that, it is not so rare as you imply. She reminded me that we had spent an agreeable week together and thought that we would get on famously. That was her word. I remembered the week, much of it spent – no doubt you, who are so sensitive on the point, will think I am boasting – in a hotel bedroom. It had been delightful but I hardly knew her. You look at me with disapproval.' I straightened my face to bland neutrality at once. 'But have you never been guilty of making love where you did not love?'

581

'That was below the belt,' I said reproachfully.

He looked satisfied. 'As I said, I was intrigued. Golly had often invited me to stay with her at Butterbank, and here was the opportunity both to please her and to make enquiries into the Preston family. As luck would have it, all flights were cancelled because of the snow, and I met you on that slow and inconveniently crowded train. I recognized Giselle at once and I was concerned not to fall into any conversation. It was a blow to find you at Shottestone.'

'You certainly looked annoyed. I was quite frightened of you.'

He looked gratified. 'I had already discovered that the Preston family were not in debt. In fact they were in the most healthy circumstances financially.'

'How on earth did you find that out?'

'All such knowledge can be bought.'

'How shocking. Never mind. Go on.'

'I could detect no reason for Isobel's generous offer. No disgrace attached to the parents. Nor was there a clandestine relationship with a peripatetic shepherd or an escaped convict whose child I was expected to father as my own.'

'Oh, Conrad!' I laughed and began to feel less distraught. 'You're every bit as much of a dweller in fantasy as I am!'

He pointed a finger at me to shut me up. 'I replied to Isobel, saying that I would be delighted to improve our acquaintance, but I had no desire to engage myself to a comparative stranger. You can imagine that I was surprised to arrive at Shottestone and find myself almost a married man.'

'Crumbs! That was brave of Isobel!'

He looked mystified. '*Brösel?* That means . . . ? Never mind. As you know, I was introduced to her family and friends as her affianced and I was sufficiently taken aback that briefly my wits deserted me.' He looked expectant.

'I bet that doesn't often happen,' I said loyally.

'No. I was . . .' He paused and drew his jet-black brows together. I could tell he was running rapidly through the vocabulary of six or seven languages. '. . . nonplussed. I did not immediately deny the engagement because I was reluctant to be unchivalrous and humiliate her before her family and friends. Also I myself would have looked like a fool. Afterwards Isobel explained that she had been obliged to announce the engagement to draw attention from her brother who was recovering from melancholia. As an excuse it seemed to me disingenuous.'

'That was true – at least, as far as the timing was concerned. I was there.'

'Ah! Well, though I was sure that Isobel was not being perfectly truthful with me, there was a piquancy in the situation I could not resist. Isobel was as attractive as I had remembered her. Fritz and I explored the countryside and we saw this house. It reminded me of Ba—' he caught my eye and remembered in time that he was never homesick, 'I liked it. I decided to buy it. It seemed not impossible to me then that I might wish – if not to marry Isobel, at least to continue the affair for a time. She was an enthusiastic lover and she had an untamed spirit that was appealing. She asked me to cooperate with her scheme. Apparently her mother wished her to marry because she was anxious to have grandchildren at her knee. When I met Evelyn, this also I did not believe. But,' he smiled, 'I had nothing to risk. Isobel said she would not consider me bound by any agreement. If I could not reciprocate her passion for me, at least her mother would be satisfied for the time being.'

'I suppose that's just what every man hopes for. Opportunity and no commitment.' I looked at the contents of my glass and saw candlelight winking in its depths. 'You made love to her.'

He spread his hands. 'Of course. As you say, what man would object to a good-looking girl attempting to win his affection with all the powers at her disposal.'

'Oh, certainly,' I agreed coldly.

'Though, in fact, with a rapidity that surprised me, I began to feel that I was like a lapdog being fed honeyed sweetmeats, and there was an indignity in this that was putting off.'

'Off-putting.'

'Hm!' He looked disdainful. 'Perhaps.'

'Sorry. Do go on. I'm on tenterhooks.'

He looked sceptical. 'What is a tenterhook?'

'I've absolutely no idea, but if you don't get on and tell me everything I shall . . . do something desperate.'

'Well, then, don't interrupt. Now where was I . . . ? Ah, yes, for a while I considered the most likely explanation of the mystery was that Isobel had for me an overwhelming physical infatuation.'

'Oh Conrad, how *can* you?'

He looked amused. 'You are so easy to provoke. In fact I think that she chose me from among her plentiful suitors because she did like me.'

I tried but no doubt failed to look sceptical in my turn. Who, other than a madwoman with no eyes in her head, would not think Conrad the most . . . the most . . . I felt shivery again and took several gulps of wine.

'Have a good cough,' he said sympathetically. 'It never helps to bang on the back. I was talking of Isobel. For a woman it is a simple matter to pretend lust, but my lovemaking with Isobel, though energetic, seemed impersonal. We were physically attracted, nothing more. There was afterwards that ennui.'

'It's not that simple!' I said indignantly, remembering all the times I had pretended to like it.

'At least it is possible. You women are fortunate you cannot mistake when a man desires you.'

'Not so lucky as all that when you remember that most men will make love to anything warm with a pulse. And apparently there are some who aren't even that fussy.'

'Well, I *am* fussy, as you call it. Isobel consoled herself for my reluctance to take her to bed by spending my money. I did not object but, as it was already clear that I should never love her, to discourage her, I pretended to be a little mad.'

'You mean you haven't been in an insane asylum?'

'Oh, frequently. These last thirty years my aunt Friederike has been a permanent resident in a sanatorium near Mannheim. She is a charming woman, quite the most interesting of my relations, and I visit her regularly. She is fond of conjuring tricks, so as a boy I taught myself *Taschenspielerei* – legerdemain – to entertain her.'

'Thirty years! How sad! Is it quite impossible for her to lead a normal life?'

'Quite. She suffers from the delusion that she is Lola Montès.'

'Who?'

'Lola Montès was a courtesan, mistress of King Ludwig I of Bavaria, Franz Liszt and many others. She ended her days in a travelling circus. Aunt Friederike spends much of her time swinging from a trapeze to the strains of the Hungarian Rhapsodies.'

I had no way of telling if Conrad was serious, but there was an awkwardness in suggesting that the behaviour of his favourite aunt was so fantastic as to defy belief.

'I don't think Isobel thought you were mad any more than I did.'

'Or perhaps she did not care. My next ruse was to make a little more of a dip in the world stock markets than was perhaps necessary.'

'Aha! So you did tell a lie. You weren't in financial difficulties after all.'

'I said nothing but the truth. There was a cyclone in . . . I forget where it was . . . and some of our capital was temporarily embarrassed. I merely implied . . .' He waved his hand to convey the fluidity of words and meanings. 'My motive in publishing my new-found poverty was to give Isobel another chance to say she no longer wished to marry me. I am no different from other men in that I have a cowardly dislike to see a woman cry and to feel that I am the cause of her distress.'

'Sebastian enjoys it, I think.'

'Then he is unlike other men who would prefer to face a

tiger than a woman determined to create a scene. As it was, Isobel did not take the opportunity. Her insistence on holding to the counterfeit engagement was perplexing. Then I saw that there existed between Isobel and her brother an intense bond. I noticed the volatility of the relationship. They were so conscious of each other. They quarrelled like sweethearts. If he behaved towards you with affection and admiration she became furiously jealous. And he of me. After they had been together alone for any time she was elated and he was woebegone.'

This was true. I had dimly registered these things myself, though the real significance of these unpredictable moods had not occurred to me. I was capricious myself.

'It was clever of you to see what was really happening. I don't think it would have occurred to me in a million years.'

'You are not detached enough to be properly observant. You are so busy loving, pitying, admiring, sympathizing, hating, that your own feelings get in the way.' I was about to object to this description of my character, which made me sound like an excitable idiot, until he went on to say, 'But that is because you are a dancer. Too much cognition intercepts the expressiveness that must spring from deep within. Ballet is a language of emotion that you speak with your body and you must find a pure and individual voice that is not too self-conscious.'

I remembered then that I was talking to Didelot. All this time, from the moment I had looked through the window of the Bear Hut, I had thought only of Rafe and Isobel. I longed to ask him about the review of *Ilina and the Scarlet Riband*, but fear kept me silent.

'To tell it all, I myself was surprised to discover that they *act*ually had been lovers since Isobel was fifteen.'

He paused to enjoy my amazement.

'How do you know *that*?'

'She herself told me.'

'*No!*'

'When I was in New York I received from her a second letter.

586

In it she begged me, despite what she called an obvious cooling off on my part . . . off-cooling?' I shook my head. 'The English language is the most illogical in the world. Well, she begged me to hold to our engagement. She promised to be economical and to please me in every way she could. Unhappiness spoke through every line. I decided to end the charade. After the performance of *Ilina and the Scarlet Riband* I took her to the nearest hotel for a drink. Very bad it was too.'

'The performance?'

'The hotel. I saw at once Isobel was anxious. She tried to tell me that she was in love with me but I explained that I knew the truth, that she was in love with her brother and that there was no possibility of destroying this conviction of mine. I told her that I felt neither censure nor revulsion. When she saw I was serious she cried very much, poor girl. Luckily the hotel lounge was empty apart from one bored waiter, so she could make a clean chest of things.'

I was too gripped by the recital to correct him. 'Go on.'

'She told me that she could not remember a time when Rafe had not been her great love and that it was her fault that things had gone further. Though he adored her, he had been afraid to take the final step. She seduced him one day in the old building where they used to rest their horses and give them water.'

'I know, the pele tower.'

'Ah, yes? After that they made love there often and for a while they were guiltily happy.'

I remembered Rafe pacing up and down upstairs in the pele tower. How miserable he must have been, loving his sister so passionately, knowing that of all loves this was the most abominable and forbidden. Had he even then been teaching himself that, as soon as the cast was off my leg, he must try to love me? Poor Rafe. And poor Isobel.

'And then one day they took the risk of making love at Shottestone. Evelyn's meeting was cancelled and she returned

587

early, decided to check a faulty radiator or some such thing in Isobel's room and found them in bed together.'

I felt myself grow hot in sympathy as I imagined the horror of that moment. 'What happened?'

'Isobel did not go into detail but it was necessarily a painful scene. The short of it was that Rafe went into the army and Isobel was sent to school in Switzerland. For three years they did not meet and after that only briefly. They began to bring home boyfriends and girlfriends and Evelyn must have believed, as did Isobel herself, that the illicit passion belonged to the past. Isobel had decided that, though Rafe would always be her great love, for his sake she must give it up. All went on smoothly until Rafe was invalided from the army and came home. He was wretched. They resumed the affair. Isobel told me she felt that nothing else mattered but that he should be made better. And in that she was, I think, right.'

'I suppose so.'

'If you had spent much time in an institution for the insane you would not doubt it. Physical suffering is of course very bad, but the suffering of the mind, that is true torment. Though they made sure to be discreet, Evelyn became suspicious. She confronted them. Isobel denied it but Rafe was unable to lie. Evelyn was distraught. She even consulted your father, so worried was she about the effect on Rafe's health.'

'My father did try to warn me but I thought he was talking about Nan and Harrison Ford.'

Conrad looked bewildered. 'The film star? What has he to do with this?'

'Never mind. What did my father say when Evelyn consulted him?'

'He took the view apparently that they should be allowed to go on with it. Evelyn thought this preposterous. Her plan was that Isobel and Rafe should make suitable marriages as soon as possible, hoping that this would keep them apart and provide distraction so that the flame would eventually splutter out.'

'That's where you and I come in. Why did they agree, though?'

'Rafe was easier to persuade. He knew it was his duty to provide an heir. The idea of the Shottestone estate going to strangers after their deaths was to him, as to Evelyn, a disaster. Isobel did not care so much about it, but if Rafe married then she must too, or the situation would be intolerable. So she wrote to me. Naturally Evelyn had been thinking of an English milord and not a German Jew, but in the end she came to believe I was an acceptable husband for her daughter.'

'The chestnut basket had something to do with it,' I could not resist pointing out.

'True.'

In view of this handsome admission it behoved me to be honest. 'Actually, she thinks you're clever and fascinating and a strong character and –' I put down my glass – 'well, she likes you.' I had been on the point of saying that she liked him because he was wonderful to look at, but fortunately I remembered the horrifically embarrassing time after Vanessa's death when I had got drunk and made an idiot of myself.

'Whatever her opinion may be of me, Isobel was not the important one. Rafe disapproved of Evelyn's choice among the neighbourhood girls. Only you pleased him. You were of lowly status—'

'Hang on,' I interrupted. 'You make it sound as though I was born under a hedge.'

'Surely you do not care about such things?' Conrad looked surprised. 'And anyway, what could be more delightful than a hedge? I say only what Evelyn thought. But Rafe was obstinate and insisted that if he had to marry anyone, you were the only possible candidate. Apart from your lack of lineage you were in all other ways most suitable. Good bone structure, good teeth and supremely healthy. And because Evelyn loved you personally, she accepted it and quickly came to think it most suitable.'

I knew this to be true, so I forgave Evelyn for her willingness to condemn me to marriage with a man who was in love with someone else. And she could comfort herself with the hope that the sweets of domestic life would put an end to the inexplicable aberration of her son and daughter. Even Dimpsie, most unconventional of parents, would have been aghast to discover her children in an incestuous relationship. Evelyn, with her proud despotism and assumption of superiority, must have felt her world smashing about her ears.

'They meant to be true to us,' said Conrad. 'They abstained from lovemaking with each other while things seemed to be going according to plan. Not until you and Rafe quarrelled did they resume it.'

I remembered my gardening lesson. Isobel had seemed transformed, exultant, ablaze with happiness. In the buttonhole of her riding coat there had been a white rose that smelt of almonds.

'I did wonder why they were all so keen on marriage. But after my rackety life, almost everyone else's seems tidy and organized and ceremonial. Poor Evelyn.' The noise of a log falling as it burned in two startled me. 'What's going to happen? I love Rafe and Isobel. Though we aren't at all the same kind of people, I've known them all my life. Must they separate?'

'Oh, as to that,' Conrad bent to refill my glass but stopped at the halfway mark. I wondered if I appeared drunk. I felt as sober as I had ever been in my life. 'There is, as we say in Germany, no need to make an elephant out of a gnat. Isobel expressed a desire to throw herself from the bridge. I said there had already been far too much of that kind of thing and I should certainly sue the family for damage to the value of my property if she did.' He threw several more logs on the fire, making it spit and flare. 'There is a straightforward solution. Evelyn will go away with Rex. To Paris, perhaps, or Saskatchewan. It is quite likely that she will find more real happiness than she has ever known. Rafe and Isobel will continue to live at Shottestone. Though they loved each other right under our noses, neither you nor others suspected. Kingsley will stay in the house and be taken care of by Miss Strangward. She is not intelligent.

Provided they are discreet, I doubt if she will suspect an affair between the young master and the young mistress. As you so graphically said, it would not have occurred to you in a million years.'

'But Conrad . . . you mean they'll go on living together as lovers?'

'Why not? Incest is generally considered the last taboo, but there have always been societies that permitted it. In the New Kingdom of Ancient Egypt, in ancient Hawaii and Pre-Columbian Mixtec it was considered highly desirable for brothers and sisters to marry in order to hold together the riches of a dynasty. Between father and daughter or mother and son there is likely to be an element of what lawyers call undue coercion, but between adults of the same generation I see no objection. Who will be hurt by it?'

'Well, no one.' Now he had shown it in such a reasonable light, I saw it was not the disaster I had first thought. 'But supposing she gets pregnant?'

'As to that, it is no use to put a lid on the well once the infant has fallen in. Isobel made this last attempt to persuade me to marry her because she is expecting Rafe's child.'

I gasped. 'No! Oh dear, how awful!'

'You make a drama out of nothing. If there were a genetic disorder in the family of course it would be unfortunate, but as it is they are as likely as any other couple to produce a healthy child. There has been much exaggeration of the possibility of defects in order to deter the practice. Inbreeding is a reduction in genetic diversity, but animal breeders consistently use it to develop a trait that is thought desirable. In animals it is considered unwise to proceed beyond eight generations of sibling matings. Is it likely that there will be eight generations of incestuous Prestons? No. Rafe and Isobel's baby will grow up to mate with an Eskimo or some such different gene pool and no one will be any the wiser.'

I was impressed by Conrad's ability to see beyond accepted moral codes. 'Won't people wonder who the father is?'

'She will inform anyone who is interested that the child is mine. I shall make a gift of this house to the baby, which will confirm everyone in their thoughts that, though I behaved badly in inseminating Isobel without marrying her, at least I recognized a part of my financial responsibilities.'

'Conrad!' I tried to find the right words to praise his generosity. 'That's a magnificent thing to do—'

He turned away from me to walk to the window where he stood between the streaming curtains and gazed into the darkness. 'Isobel loves this house and she will take care of it for the sake of the baby.'

If Isobel did not, she must be the most ungrateful girl living, I reflected. I looked around the room at the wall paintings, the decorated columns, the great hearth, the graceful furniture, the balcony that gave one such a strong feeling of connection with Nature and felt the pain of separation. Hindleep had come to be the place I loved most in the world. Its character was by turns stimulating and soothing, like the best kind of friend. Here I had been able to be more myself than anywhere.

'Won't you miss Hindleep? I know I'm going to.'

'I expect so. But there are other houses. I had anyway planned to go away. I never stay in one place for long. In fact I leave for the airport in –' he looked at his watch – 'seven hours.'

He was going away again. My hopes, which had been encouraged to drift upwards by degrees during the course of our conversation, dropped as though they had been clapped in irons. They sank so fast and so deep that I felt quite ill, as though I had been injected with a deadly contagion, making my pulse feverish and my skin clammy. I remembered that he disliked scenes and women crying, so he would certainly not like it if I were sick. I forced myself to smile. It felt from inside like one of those grins Buster gave Rafe when he was being scolded. My lips were dry against my teeth and I was showing far too many of them. But I had spent my life in pursuit of feeling and I could not change myself on the spot into someone guarded and self controlled. Conrad looked at me and frowned. He, of course, was a past master of disguising what he was thinking.

'Will you be away long?'

'Perhaps.'

'Where are you going?' My voice broke on the 'going'. It quavered and came out very high. I took up the towel and began to dry my feet, shaking my hair over my face.

'To Copenhagen. The Royal Danish ballet are performing *Scheherazade* and I am to review it.'

Copenhagen! My geography was weak but I knew enough to know it was across seas and continents. One of each anyway. Time, the mean thing, was rushing by, and there was so little of it. I became aware that a great silence had fallen. I heard the shriek of a vixen far below the house.

'Come with me,' said Conrad. I looked up in time to see something like a tremor cross his face. The tremor, which was gone in an instant, was telling nonetheless. A gust of wind blew a breath of night into the room, redolent of the forest and the lake, and with it came courage.

'What about Wednesday's performance of *Ilina and the Scarlet Riband*?'

'I can bring you back by then.'

'I haven't got a ticket.'

'You will not need one. I'm travelling by private plane.'

'I thought you disliked needless extravagances.'

'This is not a jet staffed by thousands but a small twin-propeller Cessna, piloted by me.'

'You know how to fly?'

'I should not be taking off in –' he looked at his watch – 'six hours and fifty-five minutes' time if I didn't.'

'I'll come with you.'

'You trust me to fly you safely?'

I took a deep breath and pretended I was about to dance a difficult pas de deux. 'If you're going to die, I want to die with you.'

He stopped pacing. 'Marigold.' His eyes grew soft. In three strides he was by my side. He took my hands and drew me up so I was standing within the circle of his arm. We looked intently into each other's faces. So quickly had it been done, after all.

He traced the outline of my mouth with his finger. 'I ask myself why it is that it has been so difficult . . . so very difficult to attempt to make love to you. And I can come up with only one answer.' His cheekbones were miraculous. 'I believe even in that terrible train carriage I was in danger of feeling something that I wished to resist with all my might. You were disruptive of my peace in more ways than I cared to acknowledge. And then you were so frequently engaged to other men.'

'Well, you were engaged to . . . oh, no you weren't. But I wasn't to know that.'

His wonderful eyes were close to mine now. The curve of his lower lids was perhaps the most beautiful thing I had ever seen. He lifted one of my hands to kiss it. He took a handful of my hair and kissed that. Then he kissed my mouth. I put everything I had into that kiss. I wanted to show him that, if he would love me, I would devote everything to his happiness. There was nothing I would not do for him. I would give up dancing so he could go on being Didelot. He alone was joy, hope, comfort, solace, meat and drink to me. All this I put into that kiss.

'Marigold!' He rested his cheek against my temple. '*Mein Gott!* I do not mean to complain when I say it has been hard. I played the charade with Isobel because of you. Then I went away because I was afraid of revealing myself. I waited to hear that you had finally broken with Rafe but Fritz, though he kept me informed of laundry bills and grocery lists, could tell me nothing of that. I decided it was better to stay away so you could give your mind to dancing.'

'I'll willingly give it up for good if—'

'No! This will be the last time I am Didelot. Can you think, you ridiculous girl, that I would allow you to abandon it now?

Besides, I am about to put a great deal of money into the Lenoir Ballet Company. And it is because I believe they have a great dancer in the making.'

'Me?'

'Of course you.'

'Honestly?'

'Didelot never lies. Conrad occasionally – only for excellent reasons – but Didelot's whole purpose is to speak candidly without consideration for feelings, for reputation, for money or for advantage of any kind.'

I tried to think clearly what all this portended for me, but my brain was making a hash of it. 'Sebastian's terribly resistant to interference.'

'He agrees with me. He said as much when I talked to him after *Giselle*. He thought by marrying you it would be the cheapest way to keep you in the company.'

'Of course I knew he wasn't in love with me. And he never pretended he was.'

'That would give too much power to you. Besides, it is in Lenoir's character to enjoy giving pain rather than pleasure.'

It was certainly not in Conrad's character. I knew by now that he was extremely tender-hearted and just as strongly hated to let this be seen. An idea came to me then that ought to have occurred to me long ago.

'When he came here, did you suggest then that you might put money into the company? Was that why he agreed not to make trouble between Rafe and me? And all that stuff Golly told me about only being able to see me in the part of Ilina . . . it was you who persuaded her to give it to me, wasn't it?'

I tried to look at his face but he held me tightly to him so I couldn't.

'It would not have been possible had she not believed in my good opinion of your talent. However much I wanted to kiss you as I have done just now, I should not have risked humiliating either her or you.'

'It isn't possible that you can love me half as much as I love you.'

'You think not? Let me show you.'

'Conrad, what shall I do about clothes? Everything I've got that's halfway decent is at Shottestone.'

'It does not matter. We can buy things in Copenhagen. We can go to a theatrical costumier.'

'Don't you want me to wear proper clothes?'

'I like the way you dress. In fact I insist on making love to you dressed as a swan. You, that is, not me.'

I stopped in mid-laughter to groan. 'I've just remembered! My passport's in my luggage at Leaping Dog Lane. My land-lady always bolts the door and she won't be up until half-past seven. Oh, Conrad! I can't bear not to go with you!'

'*Ach!*' He looked despairing. 'What shall we do? I might try to bribe a customs official?'

'You mustn't do that! You'd be arrested! I know because Orlando tried once to slip a customs officer a ten-pound note so he'd let him bring in a temple jar full of human bones. He'd bought it from this man who was selling off his ancestors so he could buy a television. Sebastian had to get a terribly expensive lawyer in to prevent Orlando being carried off immediately to jail.'

'Well, it is a pity,' he kissed me gently, 'but it cannot be helped.'

'Couldn't you let someone else do the review of *Scheherazade*? I feel I shall die if you go away now!'

'I consider myself obliged. We must agree to kiss and part . . . but not for long. Two days only. Perhaps we can do more than kiss. There remain –' he looked at his watch again – 'six and three-quarter hours. Shall we make love?'

'Here? What about Fritz and Orlando?'

'They are spending the night at Shottestone.'

'But why?'

He kissed me quite roughly. 'I hoped they would be *de trop*.'

'Well, it's a change for the boot to be on the other . . . oh, all right, sorry, but sometimes clichés hit the nail on the . . . say things so exactly. But how did you get here?'

'I drove, of course.'

'I didn't know you could.'

'I can, perfectly well, but Fritz enjoys it so much.'

'Is there *anything* you can't do?'

'Let us see.' He kissed me again, much less gently, and I got a sick excited feeling like coming down a helter-skelter but a million times stronger.

'No,' I stopped him as he tried to undo the row of tiny silk-covered buttons. 'There's a zip at the back. But Conrad, I don't want to be a disappointment. I've had lovers, you know that, but I always had to think about something else, remembering steps or making a shopping list, to get through it without feeling sick.'

'I promise you will not feel unwell.'

'Yes, but—'

'Stop talking. Think only that I love you.'

'I can't believe you really do. Not as much as I—'

'Of course I do. Much more.'

'I love you so much, I—'

'Shh!'

I did shush and soon we lay naked on the divan, his golden body joined with my white one, with the wind blowing the curtains to the horizontal and all the sounds of the night, owls hooting and foxes barking and trees rustling like some sort of heavenly music and I tried to express my abiding love . . . and . . . quite quickly I stopped trying because it all happened without any effort at all on my part. Afterwards, as we lay breathless in each other's arms, my heart swelled with gratitude. Conrad was truly a magician. Only wizardry could be responsible for the extraordinary pleasure he had given me. I opened my eyes. Conrad was leaning on his elbow looking down at me.

'Well?'

'*Golly!* I could cry with happiness. Except I know you wouldn't like it if I did.'

'It would be one occasion when no man could possibly object. I enjoyed you very, very much. More even than I anticipated. Despite that rabbit who persistently tries to jump on me.'

'Oh, Siggy!' I turned my head as he came running out from beneath the table in response to his name. 'I'm afraid jealousy is his worst trait – what's he got in his mouth?'

Conrad stretched down his arm and pulled it from between Siggy's teeth. 'Gracious heaven!' He sounded astonished. 'Look! It is your passport!'

'Conrad! I don't believe it! It *can't* be! I know I left it in Leaping Dog Lane . . . how on *earth* did it get here . . .' He started to laugh. 'Conrad! You *devil!*'

I tried to hit him with it but he held my arm and continued to laugh.

'All the time you pretended . . . you *beast!* You thought I was a foregone conclusion!'

He kissed the inside of my elbow and my rage evaporated at once.

'I did not. But one must be expeditious in love as in other things. I was prepared to return the passport, if necessary, without your knowing. A foregone conclusion? No! Let us say I tried to see the future in *couleur de rose*. "Boldness has genius, power and magic in it." That's Goethe. Now I want to make love to you again. This time it will be even better. Last time I was a little nervous.'

'Really? It didn't show.'

He looked pleased. 'Well, of course these things are relative. But I must insist, this time you do not call me Golly.'

Clouds Among the Stars
Victoria Clayton

Harriet is the middle child of a celebrated theatrical family, all of whom continue to live a comfortable if eccentric existence in the patriarchal home. When her father is accused of murder – fracturing his rival's skull on stage – and kept in jail, the family are forced to find other means for supporting their way of life.

Harriet, struggling with a new job, her father's mistresses and an unlikely fairy godfather, begins a journey of personal education during which she learns that villains may smile and heroes be cunningly disguised.

'Social comedy is a difficult thing to do, but Clayton shows herself an adept practitioner.'   *The Times*

Witty and perceptive, with an outstanding cast of characters, wonderful scenes and outrageous theatrical behaviour, *Clouds Among the Stars* is a book to relish and re-read.

ISBN: 0-00-714255-2

The Tea Rose

Jennifer Donnelly

Fiona Finnegan, the spirited, ambitious daughter of an Irish dock worker, longs to break free from the squalid alleys of Whitechapel. But her dreams fall apart with the sudden death of her father and the disappearance of her childhood love.

Fiona flees to New York where she slowly builds a small grocery shop into a thriving tea house. But she cannot forget London. Convinced that her father was murdered, Fiona returns to the streets of her childhood, where she must attempt to bring his killers to justice and restore her family's good name.

From the bleak poverty and burgeoning businesses of London to the immigrant districts and glossy lifestyle of Fifth Avenue, from East End dock workers to New York socialites, *The Tea Rose* is a charming novel of family, fortune and tea.

'Most seductive…a splendid, heartwarming novel of plain, struggle, decency and triumph.'   FRANK McCOURT

'Vividly atmospheric and brilliantly told.'   SIMON WINCHESTER

ISBN 0 00 720800 6